D1440912

BETWIXT TWO *Hearts*

TRU | SWANSON | TRUMBO | TERRY | MONCADO | HAVIG

crossRoads
collection

Betwixt Two Hearts

Copyright Notice

BETWIXT TWO Hearts

TRU | SWANSON | TRUMBO | TERRY | MONCADO | HAVIG

crossRoads
collection

Published by
Olivia Kimbrell Press

Olivia Kimbrell Press™

Contents

Hopefully, this isn't your first visit to Crossroads, but if it is, let me welcome you and introduce how things work around here! If you've been here before, stay tuned to find out how we've switched things up a bit this time just for fun!

This collection of books is different from others you may have read. First of all, each book is a brand-new, stand-alone novel that, while it may be connected to the author's other series, is also a complete book. Each "Crossroads Collection" is stand-alone as well, and it doesn't matter which one you start with or if you read them in order or not. However, the individual set is intended for you to read the books in order. Though they are written by different authors with unique settings and plots, one book in the series ties them together as a whole. Part of the fun and surprise is seeing how the seemingly unrelated stories are linked together!

Usually, we design a Crossroads collection so that the last book in the set, my own, ties all of the stories together. From accidental deliveries, lost mail, and Christmas ornaments, we've enjoyed your visits to Crossroads and the unique stories we've shared.

This set is a little different from the previous collections. We thought it would be fun to reverse the order! Instead of the last book in the collection, my book tying everything together comes first and is the set-up for the rest of the books. Designed around the idea of a matchmaking website, called Betwixt Two Hearts, my story involves characters who set up the dates that occur in the other five books. Fun idea, right?

In all honesty, this was not a collection on my radar to organize. The "Crossroads Collections" originated with me, and while each author's book is her sole responsibility for content and editing, I'm the person in charge of everything from the idea, to the organization, to the publication. After organizing and writing for three other Crossroads sets, in addition to writing individual titles, I imagined taking a break and actually getting some sleep. However, with the popularity of the other sets, I was encouraged to release another one before Valentine's Day. In such situations, my prayer is always the same. If God wants me to write a book, I ask Him to give me a fantastic idea, and He never disappoints. In this case, I imagined a dating website that set up all of the other books in the set, and I knew I couldn't say no.

The problem was that we needed a short turnaround with authors who were able to produce a quality book very quickly. Two other wonderful Crossroads authors jumped on board, along with another author whom we saw in the first set. We then recruited two new, fabulous authors, and they said yes. I was excited and terrified. It never ceases to humble me when wonderful authors trust me and consent to jump in on one of my wild ideas. It's more than a little scary from my perspective. We now had six authors, one more than the other sets, and I had a very short time frame with which to write a page-turning book that connected five other books to mine in a seamless, captivating way while also communicating something of the truth of the Lord! Yeah, that's not an easy task, especially in my insanely busy, sleep-deprived world!

Thankfully, all of the authors were fabulous to work with. The overall collection idea and my plot itself required an extensive amount of detail so that none of us stepped on the others' toes. In the end, the connections from my book to theirs needed more time and effort than in any other set. With everyone using the same pretend website, we needed to be consistent on what Betwixt Two Hearts did and did not do. In essence, I designed a complete fake website, with details, procedures, and policies so that anyone who read wouldn't know that the site wasn't real. We even purchased the domain name for it to use as we so desire! The end result is a fantastic set of interconnected stories and a blueprint that someone could likely use to create a popular matchmaking website!

While the characters in each book connect with the same matchmaking website at some point, each author is entirely responsible for writing her own story in any way she wants. I, then, attempt to write around what they write, and we work together to make sure we get everything connected, down to shared characters, dates, time frames, and seemingly insignificant details. The result is a unique collection of books that share a common thread and offer beautiful stories filled with humor, tears, fun, surprises, and truth deeper than the superficial.

Now it is your turn to visit Crossroads once again. In *Betwixt Two Hearts*, Camden and Bailey set up a matchmaking website. When they can't agree on anything, they decide to hold a matchmaking competition with control of the website as the prize. In the books that follow, you'll see the results of their matches in both Cathe Swanson's Minnesota town full of heritage and family, and in a coffee shop that brews up friendship and love courtesy of Kari Trumbo. In the fourth book, an unexpected connection comes in the form of Alana Terry's surly detective, and in book number five, we once again get to have a royal tie in with Carol Moncado's world. The set concludes with Chautona Havig's book involving the ultimate bad dater, who we're all desperate to see get a second date!

I'm going to sign off and get some much-needed sleep while wishing you happy reading. My sincere hope is that you enjoy these books and come away with something valuable from them. The variety of styles and stories is fantastic, yet the thread that ties them together is an example of the beautiful way God can use our actions in the lives of others. Likewise, may our words be used in your life. Though you'll eventually reach the end and we go our separate ways, may you not forget that we met at a Crossroads.

Amanda Tru

Author of *Betwixt Two Hearts*

Introducing

As many authors do, I often run on a very tight schedule—little wiggle room for anything spontaneous. However, there are some people who, no matter what happens, I'll jump through hoops for. Okay, maybe it's more like crawl, and hope I don't fall flat on my face, but you get the picture.

So, when Amanda said, "I have an idea for another collection," I knew I was in. Period. The premise? Perfect for a book I've been dying to write for almost a year now.

Then came the kicker. "By December third? I want it ready for Valentine's Day." This was the end of September when I had one book to finish within two weeks and another to *write* and edit by the end of November.

I'd try. Seriously. It's Amanda, and when it's Amanda, you try. She said that we might have to push back to the tenth. *That* I knew I could do. So, I said it. "I'm in."

I'm pretty sure she knew I'd say that. Then everything that could happen to prevent me from finishing, did. Troubles with completing other projects, my eyes giving out the last week—everything. Still, I managed to finish only two days late. And she forgave me. It's who Amanda is. You'll find my book, *Random Acts of Shyness*, at the very end of this collection and what a journey you will go on before you get there!

In the previous three Crossroads Collections, Amanda's book has always been placed last—the book to tie up all the other storylines into a lovely bow. This time, however, our collection begins with Amanda's novel. What a way to begin!

In her book, you meet Camden and Bailey—business partners with different approaches to the same problem. She introduces you to all of our characters and, in perfect Amanda style, lays a foundation for a fabulous collection. I cannot wait for you to see what she's done. So, let me step aside and present to you, Amanda Tru and *Betwixt Two Hearts*.

CHAUTONA HAVIG
Author of *Random Acts of Shyness*

BETWIXT TWO *Hearts*

By

Amanda Tru

Published by

Walker Hammond

Publishers

Copyright Notice

Bailey stood on her tiptoes and tried to spot Camden Hutchins. Unfortunately, height was not a quality Bailey Whitmore could claim to own. Her fellow airline passengers effectively formed a wall between her and the glass doors leading out of the secure area of the airport, forcing Bailey to content herself with following the awkward, shifting line sifting through the doors to the lobby where friends, family, or in Bailey's case, a stranger she'd never met, waited to retrieve those safely deposited by the flight from Seattle.

What does Camden Hutchins look like? Bailey wondered, her brow furrowing in concern.

She really should have asked her friend, Elise, for a description of her cousin. She'd thought to ask about the important stuff and knew that Camden was basically a computer genius who had agreed to go into business with his cousin and Bailey. In retrospect, it seemed a little strange to have someone you'd never met as a business partner, but when Elise approached her about being a full partner in an online matchmaking site, Bailey jumped at the opportunity. It didn't matter that they wanted a short turnaround, that Bailey would need to relocate to the middle of nowhere for a few months, or that she needed to leave the day after Christmas. Bailey was following her dream, and the sooner she located computer genius Camden Hutchins, the sooner that dream could be fulfilled.

Finally stepping through the security doors, Bailey scanned the lobby area, looking for someone wearing a smile and holding a little poster bearing her name. People whirled around her like leaves scattering in an autumn breeze, but after turning a complete circle more than once, the crowd thinned out as travelers matched up with those awaiting their arrival. After standing center stage and making one more full turn, Bailey felt certain that she was missing her somebody.

No one held a sign or stepped forward to volunteer for the job. Bailey sorted through what she knew of her business partner, but only found frustration. She didn't even know his age. She knew he was Elise's cousin, so maybe that put him around thirty-ish. She also knew he was a computer geek, so drawing on stereotypes, did that mean she should be looking for someone with glasses and fashion issues?

December twenty-sixth at five-thirty. I know that's the arrival time I gave him. I guess I should have bothered him on Christmas yesterday for a reminder after all.

Her gaze played leapfrog, skipping over all the males in the vicinity and quickly dismissing each one. Too old. Too young. Too handsome. Too fancy. Too rustic. Too muscular. Too stylish.

Finally, her gaze lit on something different.

I guess he could be that kind of computer guy, she thought, studying the green Mohawk, multiple piercings, and ragged jeans that appeared so low they might meet the airport's carpet at any second.

Yet, he just didn't quite look like a Camden Hutchins.

Reluctantly dismissing him, Bailey's gaze hopped away to find the next candidate.

Her breath caught. *There he is!*

Dark hair parted carefully and combed neatly to the side. Shirt buttoned all the way up to meet the neck at the top and tucked in and anchored by a belt at the bottom. Black dress pants creased neatly to meet lily-white tennis shoes.

His eyes met her study. She saw him swallow nervously and push his glasses back up his nose.

Bailey confidently made a beeline to where the man huddled near a pillar.

"Hi, I'm Bailey Whitmore," she announced with a friendly smile. "Are you Camden Hutchins?"

The man's eyes grew as round as two full moons. He swallowed again, but this time he had so much difficulty that he gagged. His hand came up to his neck, and his fingers worked the collar as if trying to stretch just a few more centimeters out. "I... uh... I'm not sure... um..."

His face turned hot pink, and Bailey suddenly worried she'd inadvertently caused the poor man severe damage. Was he about to stop breathing and go into anaphylactic shock?

"Come on, Jeff, answer the woman!" A young woman with dark hair cut into a cute chin-length style bustled up impatiently.

"Jeff?" Bailey echoed. "So you aren't Camden Hutchins?"

"Hardly," the woman scoffed. "His name is Jeff Yates. I'm his sister, Kari. He's here to pick me up."

"I'm sorry," Bailey said, still looking at Jeff's red face with concern. "I didn't mean to upset him. I just thought he might be my ride, Camden Hutchins."

"It's not your fault that you're too pretty," Kari said easily.

"What?" Bailey asked in confusion, self-consciously raising her hand to tuck a strand of straight brunette hair behind her ear.

Kari sighed and rolled her eyes as if enduring some long-suffering trial. "Jeff becomes almost paralyzed if needing to speak to beautiful women. It's quite harmless and very hilarious. The fact that you approached him caught him completely off guard. If I hadn't shown up when I did, I'm sure Jeff would have forgotten his real name and agreed that he really was Camden Hutchins."

"That's not true," Jeff said, his voice thready. But the glare directed toward his sister was laced with steel.

"I'm happy to meet you, Jeff," Bailey said, extending her hand. "You, too, Kari."

"I'm sorry you caught me off-guard," Jeff said, beginning to recover. "I'm not used to having women like you ask me questions. Obviously, I don't handle shock well."

Bailey grinned, unashamedly flashing her dimples in his direction. "You shouldn't worry, Jeff. I think you're thoroughly charming. Any woman would enjoy talking to you, no matter how beautiful she may be."

Kari shook her head. "I've tried to tell him that. Jeff is a successful accountant with a huge heart. He's the sweet, dependable guy every girl is looking for. No matter what I say, he can't seem to manage to remember his own name when talking to a pretty woman."

With sudden inspiration, Bailey reached into her purse and pulled out a business card. She then extended it to Jeff and explained, "I'm actually setting up a new matchmaking site with two other business partners. The site will be live January first of next year. If you sign up within the first seventy-two hours of the launch, then you'll get a free match. I'd love for you to give it a try. We just may find you someone who will appreciate your unique qualities."

Jeff accepted the card but held it as if something dangerous might jump out and bite him.

"I'd love to find you a match as well, Kari!" Bailey said brightly, extending another card to Jeff's sister.

"Oh, I already have a boyfriend," Kari assured. However, she still accepted the card despite the disclaimer.

"We're an entirely different kind of site," Bailey explained. "We focus on matchmaking, not simply dating, and we're putting great effort into making the site safe and built on solid Christian values."

"Oh, so is it a Christian website?" Kari asked.

As if the website were completely ready and she'd done this for years and not just a few weeks, Bailey confidently explained, "You don't need to be a certain religion to join, but we are not interested in promoting a list of one date wonders. We want people to find a true love that ends in a successful marriage."

"Jeff, you should totally do this!" Kari said excitedly. "How else are you going to get married or even get a date?"

"I'll think about it," Jeff said noncommittally.

Figuring Kari would very likely take over her job of promoting the site to her brother, Bailey said a quick goodbye. "It was nice to meet you two. I need to see if I can find my ride with the correct name now."

With a wave and cry of, "Good luck!" Bailey went one direction, and the brother and sister headed for the escalator down to the airport exit.

They hadn't made it ten steps before Jeff turned and hurried back to Bailey. As out of breath as if he'd just run several miles, Jeff panted, "I don't want this to sound creepy, but do you need a ride somewhere? If that Camden guy isn't here to pick you up, I wouldn't want you to be stranded. But if you want to just wait, that's okay, too."

He's adorable! Bailey thought, touched that even though Jeff obviously felt awkward about it, he'd still stopped to make sure she was okay.

"Thank you for the offer," Bailey replied warmly. "Mr. Hutchins is probably just running late. I don't even know where I'd have you take me, so I think I'll just wait around here a little bit longer."

Jeff nodded and flashed her a hesitant smile before turning back to join his sister.

Once again, Bailey stood in the center of the large greeting area and turned a full circle. Only this time, there weren't really any candidates left. Impatiently, she tapped the toe of her designer heels in rhythm to the ticking clock on the wall. Clearly, her ride was not here to pick her up, and the possibility of him magically appearing seemed less and less likely.

Toe still tapping in sharp, little echoes against the tile, she stood in the empty corridor with one crucial question unanswered.

Where was Camden Hutchins?

His phone rang, and Camden immediately pushed the button to send it to voicemail yet again. He wished his mom would stop calling him. Constant phone calls made focusing on the task in front of him extremely challenging. Swimming in computer code took a lot of concentration, with important matters riding on his success. He couldn't make a mistake. Not that his mother understood that. For all she realized, he'd just moved back to his hometown and now worked at home, which apparently meant he was at her beck and call all hours of the day.

There it is, Camden thought, identifying the small piece of code he'd been looking for. *That's the problem. That's why it isn't working right.*

He fixed the problem quickly, sent out a few emails and just started tackling another issue when his phone rang again.

Camden sighed. She obviously wasn't going to stop.

He picked up the phone and answered, "Hi, Mom."

"Camden, do you know how many times I've tried to call you?" Lydia Hutchins asked, her tone clearly upset.

"Three or four?" Camden answered. "Sorry I couldn't talk, Mom. I've been working on something important."

"Ten, Camden! I've called you ten times!"

Camden winced. "I'm sorry, Mom," he said sincerely.

"Do you know what time it is?"

Camden sighed, wishing they could pass the twenty questions phase and get to the point of why she'd called in the first place. He knew that the rest of the world faded into the background when he focused on work. He also knew he lost track of time, obligations, and everything else. He didn't need his mom submitting evidence when he already knew he was guilty.

"No, Mom," he answered honestly. "I can't say that I have any idea what time it is."

"It's seven. On December twenty-sixth. Does that mean anything at all to you?"

Seven. December twenty-sixth, Camden mused. *That doesn't really sound familiar. Now five-thirty on December twenty-sixth, on the other hand. That sounds...*

Oh, no!

Camden jumped up, knocking his chair over in his haste. "The airport! I'm supposed to pick her up at the airport!"

"'Her' is Bailey Whitmore. And you *were* supposed to pick her up. At five-thirty."

"I'm leaving right now," Camden said, knocking things off his desk in an effort to find his wallet and keys. "Do you have her phone number? I can call and tell her I'll be there—"

"In an hour?" His mom's voice chided as if he were eight. "Camden, Brighton Falls is an hour away."

"I'll get there as fast as I can." Putting his mom on speaker, Camden grabbed a sweatshirt off the back of his couch and tugged on a pair of running shoes, not even bothering with socks.

"It's too late."

"What do you mean it's too late?" Camden fumed, wishing his mom would stop tap dancing around what she actually wanted to say.

Camden threw open the door of his apartment, ready to sprint down the stairs.

"Israel is picking Bailey Whitmore up at the airport right now. He'll bring her to our house."

The adrenaline abandoned Camden in a rush, and he stopped abruptly. Leaning his head back against the hallway wall for support, he closed his eyes in dismay. Not Israel. Anyone but his brother, Israel. Needing his older brother to clean up his mistakes was not going to come cheap, at least emotionally speaking.

Camden glanced at the time on his watch again, wishing for different numbers on the display. Unfortunately, he was already an hour and a half late from when he was supposed to pick up his new business partner. He no longer had a choice in the matter.

"Bailey called your cousin, Elise," Lydia explained brusquely. "When you didn't answer Elise's phone call, she called me and explained that Bailey was waiting for you at the Brighton Falls airport. I knew Israel was working late tonight in Brighton Falls, so I asked him to pick her up and bring her back to Crossroads. Then I called Bailey directly, apologized for you, and told her to expect Israel to pick her up shortly."

"I'm really sorry to put you in that position, Mom," Camden said with genuine remorse. "I was busy working on something important and lost track of time. But I'm sure you're quite familiar with that excuse by now. I'll come over and make my own apologies to Bailey."

Feeling like a total failure, Camden straightened from the wall and returned to his apartment. He shut the door behind him, closing the door on the possibility of actually retrieving Bailey and fixing his mistake.

"Fortunately, Elise is so sweet that she won't think ill of you," Lydia said, almost comfortingly. "But that's not exactly the first impression you want to make with a new business partner you've never met."

And the comfort just went out the window.

I never seem to outgrow the lectures, do I? Camden thought dejectedly.

"I'm not sure what more I can say, Mom," he admitted. "I'm sorry.

11

You're not telling me anything I don't already know. I'll try to make it up to Bailey somehow."

Lydia's tone softened, "I just don't want you to screw this up, Camden. Elise is depending on you, and this other woman is, too. You can't be off in your own little world anymore."

Why did I even think I could do this? She's right. I really am going to screw this up!

Unfortunately, though none of it had been his choice, Camden knew exactly how he'd landed here, and there was nothing he could do about it.

Finally convincing his mom to at least pause the lecture until he arrived at her house, Camden signed off with her and tossed his phone to the couch. Intending to turn off his computer, he reached down and righted his chair. Reaching over it, he then entered his password with the keyboard and caught another glimpse of the time when the screen woke up.

If Israel was picking Bailey up now, it would be at least fifty minutes before they arrived at Camden's parents' house. It was about a ten-minute drive to their house from Camden's current apartment. Realistically, that meant that he had at least thirty minutes before he needed to leave and meet them there.

The more he thought about it, the more he realized that he really didn't want to arrive too early and give his mom further opportunity to lecture with no one else around.

Camden promptly slid back into the chair and focused once again on the computer.

Thirty minutes, Camden promised himself. *I'll leave in thirty minutes.*

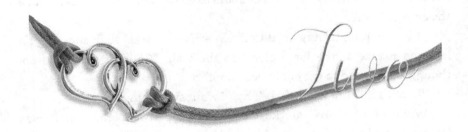

Two

"Bailey, can I get you another piece of apple pie?" Lydia asked eagerly.

"Goodness, no!" Bailey replied. "I am stuffed. I feel like I just had Christmas dinner all over again!"

What she didn't say was that this was actually the only Christmas dinner she'd had. While yesterday hadn't included a traditional meal, Lydia's leftovers this evening had more than made up for it.

Bailey watched wistfully as Lydia bustled around the kitchen cleaning up. How was it that Lydia Hutchins could be so warm and inviting, but graceful and sophisticated at the same time? She was a dainty woman, only about the same height as Bailey. Her hair, though likely helped by the aid of a bottle, shone glossy brunette in a cute, chin-length style. She hurried around the kitchen serving Bailey, her son Israel, and granddaughter, Chloe, whatever their hearts desired, but her movements weren't frenzied. Instead, there was an enviable grace about her that lent beauty to even the motions of cleaning off the counter with a rag.

What would it be like to call a woman like Lydia "mom" and belong to a family like this? The warm, homey atmosphere was one that Bailey had never experienced. Growing up being shuffled around between her divorced parents, Bailey had never felt like she belonged.

Israel Hutchins had picked her up at the airport and brought her straight to his parents' house where Lydia, having never met Bailey before, had welcomed her as if part of the family.

Strangely, Bailey felt almost as if she did belong.

Even the sound of little, three-year-old Chloe whining and pulling at her dad's collar with a ridiculous demand to go swimming didn't at all quell the envy of home.

"I was hoping to stay until Camden arrived," Israel said, shooting an irritated glance at the large clock on the wall. "Chloe is getting tired, though, so I'll need to get her in bed soon."

"I not tired!" Chloe howled. "I hot! I want swimming!"

While Israel glared at the clock and tried to explain that it was December and swimming outside wasn't an option, Lydia plopped another spoonful of ice cream onto her granddaughter's half-eaten piece of pie.

Chloe immediately stopped complaining, turning her attention back to her dessert. The little blonde girl was adorable, but there was an air of sadness about her that Bailey didn't quite understand. The fact that Israel's wife had not been mentioned and he'd talked about needing to get Chloe to bed made Bailey suspect that he was a single parent. Their small talk in the car had consisted of the weather, his work, and Chloe. Bailey's observations now only confirmed her suspicions that, for whatever reason, Chloe's mom was not in the picture. Furthermore, if Bailey could venture a guess, the fine lines on the father's face made her suspect he was more than a little bit over his head with such a task.

Though clueless as to what had caused the change in his daughter's attitude, Israel's forehead immediately relaxed with the reprieve from her demands, and he consented to another sliver of pie for himself.

The sound of the front door opening caused everyone to turn expectantly to see a tall man appear in the kitchen doorway.

"Uncle Cam!" Chloe squealed, leaving her ice cream and hopping off her chair to greet the newcomer with a hug.

Bailey startled, blinking as if she expected the man in front of her to disappear and be replaced by someone else. This man wasn't short, bespectacled, or awkward. In fact, in almost every way, he was the complete opposite of what Bailey expected.

"You're Camden?" Bailey sputtered. "Camden Hutchins?"

Holding the little girl in his arms, an amused grin lifted the corners of the man's mouth as he returned Bailey's gaze.

Bailey unashamedly examined him from the top of his sandy, brown, disheveled hair, past the gray-blue eyes and the strong jaw that hadn't seen a razor in several days, over the solid chest and strong muscled arms extending out of a short-sleeved athletic shirt, and finally ending past the khaki cargo shorts at the white socks and running shoes on his feet.

"Sure am," Camden replied smoothly.

Bailey swallowed. "Well, that's a relief," she covered. "Since you're dressed for June weather, of course I assumed that I'd somehow landed in the twilight zone and not December twenty-sixth in a town that probably didn't get above freezing today. I'm glad to know that you're actually Camden Hutchins and not an alien or anything."

"I don't know that I'd go that far," Israel inserted, his voice low. "Camden is definitely a different species. He dresses like that year-round. We aren't exactly sure where he came from."

Camden shot Israel a withering glance, apparently not appreciating the humor. Setting Chloe down carefully, he pointedly turned his back to his brother and addressed Bailey. "I'm really sorry I wasn't there to pick you up at the airport. I have no excuse, I just forgot, and I apologize. Hopefully, I can make it up to you someday."

"You'll have to get used to Camden, Bailey," Israel said, unperturbed by Camden's attitude. "'Dependable' is not his middle name."

Israel's remark earned him another icy, but silent, glare from Camden.

"You're later than I expected," Lydia chided quietly, reaching up to give her son a quick hug. "After I talked to you on the phone, I thought you'd be right over. I didn't expect you to arrive so much later than Israel and Bailey."

Camden smiled warmly at his mom and returned her hug. "I missed picking up Bailey on accident. I didn't come earlier on purpose. I was honestly trying to avoid a sequel on the lecture I had over the phone."

Lydia playfully swatted his arm. "Typical naughty boy."

"Thanks for waiting so I could see Chloe," Camden said, turning to his brother. "I haven't seen you much since I've been back, and yesterday was so busy, I didn't get to talk to you much or play nearly enough with my best girl." To emphasize his words, Camden tossed Chloe in the air a couple of inches and then caught her, much to her squealing delight.

Israel's eyes softened. "I'm sorry to hear about your job, Camden. I know Mom and Dad are happy to have you back in Crossroads, but that's a rough way to do it. Not all companies are laying off right now. Mine isn't."

Bailey looked at Israel with curiosity, trying to read him. Why did it seem that everything he said to Camden had a hidden meaning and teeth attached?

"Israel is right," Lydia said, squeezing Camden's arm in an affectionate gesture. "With your skills, I'm sure you won't have a problem getting a new job. Your new job will be much better than the old one. You just need to wait for exactly the right one."

"I don't think you need to worry about Camden," Israel assured. "He's picky. I'm very familiar with the fact that He won't take just any job." A calculating light dawned in Israel's gaze. "Unless your services were no longer needed for a reason other than company downsizing. If that's the case, you might be considerably less desirable for any job."

"Israel, don't be rude," Lydia chided, looking up from where she swept the hardwood kitchen floor with a broom. "Of course, it was company downsizing. Why else would they let someone with Camden's skills go?"

"Why exactly are you unemployed Camden?" Israel persisted. "I haven't yet heard the official story. I'm sure it's a good one. Were you laid off or fired?"

"I'm not unemployed," Camden clarified, obviously impatient with being the topic of his mom and brother's conversation.

Camden walked over and gently took the broom and dustpan from his mom, silently insisting on doing the work himself. "I'm building a website for the company I own with two others." With the broomstick in hand, Camden gestured to Bailey. "And here's one of them. Meet my business partner, Bailey Whitmore."

"So, you're serious?" Israel asked quietly as if he was uncomfortable with Bailey hearing his words. "I thought you were helping with this website as a favor for Elise. You're actually doing this as a job? Like a full-time one?"

Immediately offended, Bailey prepared to jump into the fray with both feet and explain precisely how serious a business venture it was, but

Camden replied before she quite got her feet under her.

"Sure," Camden shrugged, carrying the full dustpan to the trash. "It's a big project that requires full-time work. Why wouldn't I do it for a full-time job?"

Israel's eyebrows almost met his hairline, clearly appalled. "You running a dating website? Isn't that like a blind person trying to sell packs of multicolored crayons? Or someone who lives in the Sahara Desert selling snow boots? Or a vegetarian cooking up a platter of bacon? Or—"

"I get it, Israel," Camden said, putting his hand up to stop the flow of words. "Just because I don't have a full and stellar dating resume doesn't mean that I don't know how dating and love are supposed to work."

Bailey fought the desire to burst out in laughter that was both amused at Israel's words and suddenly nervous about her partner's qualifications. Camden looked good on the outside, but was he really an awkward misfit who wouldn't know the first thing about matchmaking?

"That's why Camden has Bailey and Elise," Lydia said brightly, calling from the sink where she washed the dishes from dinner. "Camden can handle all the technical stuff, and Bailey and Elise can handle the romance. If Camden chooses to take another job after the site is up and running, I'm sure he can. But I'm excited. I know whatever Camden chooses to do will be successful!"

"Spoken like a mother," Israel said under his breath.

Chloe impatiently grabbed Camden's arm and began pulling. "Come on, Uncle Cam. No talking. I play with you."

Israel stepped forward and scooped up the little girl in his arms. "No, Chloe, not tonight. We waited around for you to see Uncle Cam, but we'll come back to play with him another time—maybe when he's already here and we don't have to risk him showing up late."

Chloe promptly burst into tears and squirmed to get down.

"Don't cry, Chloe!" Camden soothed. "Are you coming to Grandma's house tomorrow?"

Chloe looked at her dad and then turned back to Camden, echoing his nod with her lip still pouty.

"Mom watched her today and will again tomorrow," Israel explained. "I have to work, and Chloe's regular daycare is closed for the holidays."

"Well, that's good news!" Camden said enthusiastically. "I'm coming to Grandma's tomorrow, too! We'll get to play!"

Bailey scowled. They had work to do. Play was not on the schedule, no matter how cute Chloe was. She just didn't want him to make her a promise he couldn't keep, but maybe that was typical Camden behavior. Her recent stint waiting at the airport didn't exactly provide evidence about his dependability.

Chloe brightened a little at Camden's words, but her bottom lip still didn't quite retract out of the pout.

"Wait a minute," Camden said slowly. "I have something that might help." He rummaged around in his pockets, finally extracting a small origami snowman. "I made this one for you. See, I even made the hat purple, your favorite color."

Chloe smiled and accepted the snowman happily. "Do you have a kitty, too?"

"Chloe, you need to say thank you for the snowman, not ask for something else," Israel chided gently.

Camden, however, returned to rummaging through his pockets. "As a matter of fact..." Camden pulled a closed fist out of his pocket and held it in front of Chloe. Then he slowly opened it to reveal a small origami kitty face. "Of course, I have a kitty. I know how much my Chloe likes them."

Hmmm... Bailey mused, studying Camden with curiosity. *A computer geek who folds origami for children. How interesting!*

With two animals clutched tightly in her hands, Chloe consented to goodbye hugs and kisses, and Israel quickly moved to escort her to the car.

"Israel," Camden called before his brother stepped out of the room.

Israel turned back around, his arms still full of little girl.

"Thank you for picking Bailey up for me," Camden said genuinely. "I appreciate it."

Israel nodded. "You're welcome. I'm your big brother. Cleaning up your mistakes seems to be what I do."

Camden winced. "Hopefully, I'll get to return the favor and help you out someday."

Israel shook his head. "Not likely. I seem to recall you passing on that years ago."

Camden froze, his face draining of expression.

Israel left, and it was several seconds before Camden seemed to rouse himself enough to fling out a, "Goodbye!" in response to Chloe's frantic calls.

Obviously, Camden and Israel shared some kind of baggage, but the discomfort exited with Israel, providing no further time for Bailey to wonder about the strange tension between the brothers.

"Sit down, Camden," Lydia instructed, practically pushing him into a chair at the kitchen table. "If you forgot to pick Bailey up, then I know it hasn't even occurred to you to eat. Let me make you a sandwich."

Camden didn't disagree, and Bailey doubted he would dare refuse Lydia anyway. Feeling suddenly awkward and not knowing what else to do, Bailey sat back down in the chair she had vacated when Camden first made his appearance.

Wanting to skip over the pleasantries and small talk and get down to business, Bailey opened her mouth to launch into describing her vision for their business.

"Did you have a good Christmas?" Camden asked, aborting her plans.

I guess we won't be skipping the small talk after all.

"Yes, I did," Bailey lied easily. Of course, she didn't feel the need to explain that she had spent yesterday packing instead of actually doing anything Christmassy. Her boyfriend had gone to his parents' house, but Bailey had cited her need to pack, refusing his anemic invitation to go with him. It wasn't as if she'd ever felt welcomed before at any of Dekker's family gatherings. It always felt like she was on the outside and that the Davidson family merely tolerated her.

In retrospect, Bailey realized she could have gone to either her mom or dad's house to celebrate, but they hadn't exactly volunteered an invitation. They probably assumed Bailey would be with Dekker, and it wouldn't occur to them that she may want to be with them. Bailey loved both her parents and their families, but they seemed very complete without her. Showing up for Christmas would once again feel too much like she was peering through the glass to watch them celebrate.

Nope. A bowl of soup and a fully-packed suitcase qualified as a "good Christmas" for Bailey, and she wasn't about to complain to Camden or anyone else about her decisions or dysfunctional family dynamics.

"What about you?" Bailey asked instead, resigning herself to the obligatory small talk. "Was your Christmas good?"

Camden nodded. "Yes, it was. Being home is nice. With my previous job, I haven't come home as often, so it felt good to have the freedom to do that this year. Not all of my siblings made it home, but it was nice to see those who did."

"How many siblings do you have?" Bailey asked curiously. "Elise told me a few things here and there, but she wasn't exactly a fount of information about her cousins. Then when we started working on the website idea, those type of details seemed less important."

"There are seven of us," Camden replied, smiling his thanks when his mom set a sandwich and a large piece of apple pie in front of him. Israel is the oldest. Then comes Dallas and me. After the boys are all the girls: Geneva, London, Sydney, and Brooke."

"Wow, and you're all named after cities or places?"

"Not quite," Camden clarified. "Brooke is just Brooke. London and Sydney are twins, and Brooke was our surprise. Dad chose her name. I think after six kids, he was done with place names and filled out the birth certificate for simply 'Brooke,' when my mom wasn't looking."

"She should have been Brooklyn," Lydia inserted cheerfully, approaching the table to deposit two large scoops of vanilla ice cream on Camden's pie.

"Mom still isn't completely at peace about it," Camden surmised, his eyes twinkling merrily. "What about your fami—"

"I'm glad you had a good Christmas," Bailey interrupted, wanting to take a sharp detour around discussing her family. "Hopefully we can buckle down and get a bunch of work done in the next few days. Elise said you'd been working on the website, but she was a bit vague on where you are at and what still needs to be done for the January first release."

Camden didn't seem bothered about the change in conversation. In between mouthfuls of pie, he replied. "I have things in a good position. Most of the framework for the website is in place, but there is still a lot of work to do in order to launch New Year's Day."

"Want to get some work done on it tonight?" Bailey asked eagerly. "I'm a night owl anyway. Maybe after I get checked into my hotel—"

"Where are you staying?" Lydia asked, coming back over and perching on one of the other chairs.

"I don't really have a reservation yet," Bailey confessed. "I wasn't sure if I'd need to stay in Brighton Falls or Crossroads. I saw on the drive that there only appears to be one hotel here in Crossroads, so I hope they still have vacancies. I figured I'd stay there a few days until I can find a place with a short lease. Elise thought I may need to stay one to three months until the website is running smoothly enough that I can return to Seattle. Then we can conduct everything remotely."

"There's no need for you to go to a hotel or even get a rental, Bailey," Lydia said quickly. "Why don't you stay here? We have plenty of room."

"That's very kind of you, Lydia, but I don't want to take advantage like that."

"Nonsense, I insist," Lydia said firmly as if the issue were already decided. "John and I have an empty house with rooms that aren't even used. You'd do us a favor by staying here!"

Bailey didn't quite follow the logic of how she would be doing them a favor, but staying with the Hutchins promised to reduce a great deal of stress. Though she'd never admit it to anyone, she didn't have a lot of money to spare right now. She'd quit her job at the library to pursue this business venture. Until the website started producing enough revenue to provide her with a paycheck, she would be living off of a limited nest egg. "Well, maybe I could stay for a few days. Just until I find something else."

Camden grimaced. "Unfortunately, you aren't going to find anything else. This is Crossroads. Rental properties are a very limited, hot commodity. You can talk to Brooke's fiancé, Dylan. He's into real estate. However, I'm pretty sure you're not going to find something at an affordable price or anything shorter than a year-long lease. Those kinds of rentals simply don't exist here."

"It doesn't need to be anything fancy," Bailey assured. "I figured I could always stay at the office if I couldn't find anything else. I'll probably spend most of my time there anyway, and I'm not afraid of roughing it."

"The office?" Camden echoed, swallowing his last bite of sandwich while his face clouded with confusion. "We don't have an office."

Bailey's heart leaped with alarm and then dropped to her feet. "What do you mean we don't have an office?"

"I mean we don't have one. I've looked a little, but I've been busy. Like I said, any rental space is hard to come by in Crossroads."

"You looked *a little*?" Bailey fumed. Too upset to stay seated, she stood and began pacing, trying to stay calm. "We're supposed to launch this website in six days. I've spent nearly all of my startup money on advertisements for the launch. Now you're telling me that we don't even have an office space to work in? You moved back after you got laid off, right? That was like six weeks ago. What exactly have you been doing?"

"Other things," Camden replied tersely, leaning back in his chair and folding his arms across his chest defensively. "Not looking for nonexistent office space."

Bailey pursed her lips. How was she supposed to make this business work if her business partner was a lazy, irresponsible, wanna-be computer genius who couldn't remember to feed himself or get an actual place to hang a shingle?

She'd decided to tell him exactly that when Lydia spoke up.

"Wait," she said, extending a calming hand to each of them as if she were standing in the middle of two fighters squaring off to do battle. "Camden, if you weren't able to find an office space, that was something you should have shared with your business partners."

"I did," Camden growled. "I told Elise. She said we could make do at my place until something came open. I already have all the necessary computer equipment."

"Elise didn't share that info with me," Bailey said irritably.

"She probably didn't think it would matter," Camden grumbled. "It's not like you can do anything about it."

Lydia sighed. "Camden, your apartment isn't big, and you'd likely need to hire a housekeeper before it would be suitable for any occupant other than you. Why don't you just use your dad's office here? He doesn't use it much anyway."

"Use what?" John Hutchins asked, coming into the kitchen.

"Use your office," Lydia supplied. "I just told Camden and Bailey that they should use your office for their business until they are established and able to find something else."

"Sure," John agreed. "I usually take my laptop upstairs if I do anything, or I just go to the office in Brighton Falls."

John turned to Camden, slapping him on the shoulder. "I hear you made a good first impression on your new business partner, son," he teased good-naturedly.

Camden groaned. "I suppose the whole family is already aware that I forgot to pick up Bailey at the airport."

John explained, "My meeting hadn't started yet when Bailey and Israel arrived, so I got to meet Bailey and hear the tale firsthand. I'm sure the rest of the family will hear about it eventually, but I don't think your mother has had a chance to call and tell everyone yet. However, I'm sure it will eventually make it to your uncle, Wayne, and beyond."

Camden shook his head and sighed dramatically, a slight smile playing about his lips, "Let me warn you, Bailey. In this family, you can never make a quiet mistake!"

John and Lydia laughed, and Bailey marveled at the good-natured teasing. It was something she'd never really experienced, and she wondered whether or not that close connection and humor was common in most families or unique to the Hutchins.

"Did your meeting go well?" Lydia asked John.

"Yes, it was fine," John replied, grabbing himself a plate for some food. "It wasn't really much of a meeting. Israel just wanted me to make contact with one of my old business associates. I paved the way for Israel to follow up with him tomorrow, but it was mostly just shooting the breeze with an old friend."

"Dad was a CEO of a large company in Brighton Falls," Camden explained to Bailey. "He's retired now, but Israel took over much of his work in the company. Dad is still on the board of directors and does a decent amount of traveling for consulting and schmoozing when needed."

"Fine," Bailey said, her tone still tight with stress. "If Mr. Hutchins is sure we won't be intruding by using his office, I don't see that we have a choice. Do you want to get started right now, Camden?"

"Oh, no! Not tonight!" Lydia protested, urging another piece of pie Camden's direction. "It's too late, and both of you are probably exhausted.

You'll get a much better result if you wait for a fresh start in the morning."

She's hoping we'll tolerate each other better after a good night's sleep, Bailey surmised, not needing too much effort to read between the lines. Unfortunately, after one conversation with her new business partner, she didn't know that the resulting stress would allow her a good night's sleep, nor could she promise to tolerate him better tomorrow or any other day in the future.

Camden didn't seem any happier about the situation than she did. With his jaw set, he ran a hand through his hair, lifting strands of hair to even wilder angles. "I'm going home. Thanks for the food, Mom. I'll see you tomorrow."

Bailey couldn't manage a response because everything felt like a lie. She couldn't manage a cheerful, "See you tomorrow," because that would conceal the fact that she was really irked with him. She couldn't say, "It was good to meet you," because it really wasn't. He was supposed to get things set up so she could come and put the finishing touches on the website before its release. He hadn't managed to secure them an actual business space or even pick her up from the airport at the designated time. How much more hadn't he done because he'd "been busy" being unemployed?

Bailey followed at a distance, watching as Camden went to the front door, ready to exit into the cold, December night in his T-shirt and shorts.

With muscles, rakish hair, a killer smile, and blue-gray eyes that would surely haunt her dreams, Camden wasn't at all who she'd expected. Shooting one last glare in his direction, it instantly collided with his returning glare, causing her to officially make up her mind. Kitty origami or not, Bailey did not like Camden Hutchins.

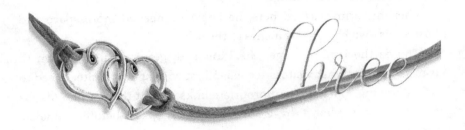

"Good morning," Bailey greeted Camden brightly as she entered the office the next morning.

"Hi," Camden replied shortly, not fooled by her cheerful attitude.

He knew she'd been mad at him last night, and it wasn't the kind of mad that is wiped clean overnight. At least, it wasn't for him.

On some level, he knew that all of his anger shouldn't be entirely directed at Bailey. Yesterday had involved a rough evening, at the end of a rough day, at the end of a rough few weeks, at the end of a rough few years. No one could aggravate him more than his older brother, Israel, and even though a large amount of his frustration last night belonged in that direction, directing it at Bailey became awfully convenient, especially when her attitude clearly communicated that she thought Camden incompetent and irresponsible.

"Pull up a chair," Camden instructed, ready to show her his work and prove her assumptions about him wrong. "I'll explain what I've done and where we are at with the website."

Bailey obediently scooted a chair up beside him and looked expectantly at the computer screen. However, Camden would have felt far more comfortable if she'd scooted not quite so close. While his dad's office was a good size, its dimensions made Bailey's proximity difficult. As much as she aggravated him, Camden couldn't deny that she was beautiful. The petite brunette possessed a firecracker personality, and her obvious distaste for him strangely made her even more alluring.

Same MO as always, Camden chided himself. *I find the impossible tasks to be the most appealing.*

When his arm brushed hers, he knew he needed more space and adjusted his own chair a few inches to the left.

"This is the landing page," he explained, getting quickly down to business. "This is what visitors see when first coming to the site. I need to finish attaching some of the appropriate links here at the bottom. Maybe you can review what I have for the 'About' page before I finalize everything."

"This looks really nice," Bailey admitted. "I like the logo and all of the graphics. Did we hire a graphic designer?"

Camden heard the hesitation in her voice and recognized it as worry about adding a graphic designer to their meager start-up budget.

"No, I did them myself," Camden replied simply.

He felt the sudden calculating look sent his direction, but he ignored it, enjoying that he'd obviously caught her off-guard. He knew that she'd assumed he was a computer geek with no room for artistic ability in his numbers-filled head.

"This is the button where clients can register," he continued, choosing to save his gloating for later. "As you know, our plan to launch the business is to do a promotion where anyone who signs up in the first seventy-two hours gets their first match free. When they click the button, it takes them to this form. We gather a few simple facts to register and then go immediately into the questionnaire. When they are done, they will be sent the top name on their list of matches. If they want more matches, they'll be charged our standard fee."

Camden leaned back in his chair and looked at Bailey, expecting her to be thoroughly impressed. The website looked good. He'd done a good job, and he knew it.

Does she scowl when impressed? Camden wondered, feeling a hint of trepidation at the decidedly sour expression on his business partner's face.

Camden waited, feeling the tension building so much that he almost expected his coffee cup on the desk beside him to start tremoring with anxiety.

"You've done it all!" Bailey burst out finally, throwing her hands up in emphasis. "You've made every single decision on your own, and everything is already a done deal. You want me to look over the 'About' page? That's it? We are business partners. My input matters just as much as yours. I think I deserve to be a little more than your copy editor."

"Are you serious?" Camden asked, taking a quick glance out the window to make sure the morning sun still rose in the east and he hadn't woken up in some weird alternate reality. "Just last night, you were upset because you didn't think I'd done enough work. Now, you're mad that I've done too much?"

"I didn't know that you'd done everything but find an office!" Seeming too upset to sit still, Bailey hopped off her chair, planted her hands on her narrow hips, and stared at him accusingly as if she played the part of a lawyer and he the criminal on trial.

"Exactly where do you want your input located?" Camden asked patiently. He didn't know if he could handle Bailey's dramatics, but maybe she would simmer down if he worked to appease her overreaction. "We haven't released, and nothing is set in stone. What do you want to change?"

"Everything." She folded her arms across her front, glaring at him stubbornly.

"Everything? Come on! You just said you liked the logo and graphics for the site." So much for remaining patient and trying to appease her.

"You're right. Let's change everything but the graphics." Her arms still crossed in front. Her eyes still glared.

Camden laughed a humorless chuckle and shook his head. "I'm sorry to be such a nag, but I'm going to need something a little more specific than that."

Bailey sighed. Her arms dropped, and she pointed accusingly at the computer screen. "It's a dating website just like the hundreds of others online. Why would anyone choose our site? We're not doing anything unique."

"Of course, we are!" Camden exclaimed, relieved to know the source of her concern. If she just listened to him, she would quickly realize it wasn't a concern at all. "You never gave me a chance to finish explaining everything about the site. I have already set up unprecedented security measures. Our site is the safest one out there by far."

With a few clicks, Camden landed on a different screen and began talking through the bulleted points describing the site security. "When someone signs up, we do automatic background checks. Though we don't give a detailed list that includes everything we do, clients grant permission for extensive background checks that include public records, information available on the internet, and records through law enforcement or government agencies, such as the police or FBI. Our checks are very thorough, more so than anyone will realize. We have the right to terminate an account for any reason, such as if something concerning comes back in any of the background checks. I also have security measures in place to weed out fake accounts. It takes a couple days to check the validity of an account to make sure there is an actual person attached to it. However, my programs run the check automatically, and if they can't verify its validity, the account is terminated at the same time I get a notice that it is a fraudulent account."

"That means clients are required to use their real names?" Bailey asked, nodding in approval and reluctantly leaning closer to better see the screen.

"Yes," Camden answered. "It very explicitly states that clients must use their real names and accurate profile pics. If these requirements aren't fulfilled, their information will eventually come back to me as fraudulent, and their accounts will be terminated."

Bailey straightened back up, finished with her examination. Unfortunately, her expression declared Camden's defense still inadequate. "I like the security, and I like that we can promote it as the safest site out there. However, there is nothing 'wow' about that. Normal people aren't going to understand the technical jargon enough for you to even explain how awesome and safe the site is. At the end of the day, all they are going to see is another dating website."

"Wait," Camden urged, holding up a hand to ward off any further protest. "I haven't finished explaining what makes the site unique. "You're awfully determined to find fault in whatever I do, aren't you?"

"No," Bailey said with a lift of her eyebrows. "You just seem to produce an abundance of faults for me to find."

Camden scowled, but turned to bring up another screen. "This is the page that explains our app."

"We have an app?" Bailey asked, not quite masking her interest.

"Yes," Camden said proudly. "It is part of our security measures, but it does much more. The site can be fully accessed from the app. The awesome thing about it is that it works with a device's location services. If a client wants to meet their date somewhere, he or she can also send a current location through the app. If clients go on a date, they activate the app, and it monitors their location. It also monitors the location of their date, making it easier to connect and also providing a safety net. Then it sends a push notification at different intervals in the date, checking in with options for the client to click whether he or she feels comfortable, uncomfortable, or in danger. Obviously, danger triggers an immediate call to law enforcement, but they can adjust their settings to choose if a certain number of 'uncomfortable' ratings triggers a text to a friend asking for a call to get them out of the date. It's kind of like having a chaperone who doesn't say anything. I'm still working on it, but those are the basics."

"You mean the app will arrange for a rescue call?" Bailey asked, unable to hide that she was more than a little impressed.

Camden smiled in satisfaction. "Yes, that's exactly what it will do if the user sets it up that way."

Unfortunately, before Camden could savor her approval, Bailey's gaze quickly lost the gleam of excitement and returned to what Camden saw as critical superiority.

"I admit, that's a pretty cool feature, Camden," she begrudgingly acknowledged. "It looks like you really know your technical stuff. However, again, it's not something that will grab attention. It's all so negative. If I make an ad that simply says, 'sign up for this app, and it will monitor your location in case we match you with a serial killer,' that just sounds a little creepy. If I say, 'the app can get you out of one of our really bad dates,' that's not much better."

"That wasn't quite what I was going for," Camden frowned. Admittedly, when she phrased things like that, it sounded terrible. *Why does she have to be so negative? If my app won't please her, then nothing will!*

Giving up, he scooted away from the desk and stood, lifting his hands behind his neck in a stretch and refusing to look at Bailey. She'd just twisted the knife a little too sharply, and in spite of himself, he felt more hurt than anger at her words. It didn't seem to matter what he said or did, she was determined to find fault and simply become more insulting the more he tried.

Bailey sighed, "I know that wasn't what you were going for, and I really do think it's a good feature. But I don't think it's *the* feature that defines the site."

While he'd always liked and respected his cousin, Elise, right now he couldn't figure out what had caused her to become mentally unstable enough to include Bailey Whitmore as a business partner.

"What is it that you want, Bailey?" Camden asked impatiently, turning to directly meet her gaze. Though she seemed to approve of his security measures and the app, she wasn't nearly as impressed as she should be. She didn't seem to realize the amount of work and genius behind the apparent simplicity. "I thought a dating website is exactly what we are supposed to be creating here. Do you want the website to sell hot dogs as well? Maybe offer some tax preparation on the side?"

Bailey glared, "No. Betwixt Two Hearts is *not* a dating website. It's a *matchmaking* website." She flung a hand out in a disgusted gesture that included the computer screen, the office, and Camden himself. "This is not what I envisioned at all."

Camden clenched his jaw, working to control his temper when she just insulted the entire website and all his work for the past month. "Are you just balking at the semantics?" Camden asked.

Though he chose to hope they were tripping on a verbal misunderstanding, his tone clearly said that he thought she was crazy. "Aren't dating websites and matchmaking websites the same thing?"

"No, not at all," Bailey replied, obviously offended by his tone, lack of knowledge, or both. "A dating website provides clients with lists of possible matches. The lists are usually computer generated and based on numbers. The client can then pick and choose who they want to contact from the list, and the website provides a social platform from which to do that. If they decide not to pursue a relationship, he or she can focus on one, or several of the other options. Dating websites are the buffet of the dating world."

"Ok, so how is a matchmaking site different?" Camden asked, raising an eyebrow skeptically.

"The difference is the human element," Bailey explained as if she were a scholarly professor and Camden the slow student. "A matchmaking website is personal. A professional matchmaker looks at survey answers, but she gives the final recommendation based on a personal opinion of who would make a good match. She may only recommend one match at a time, encouraging the clients to dedicate the time and necessary value, giving serious consideration to a thoughtful match. Ideally, I think the client should be required to either post a review of the actual date or give a reason for refusing it before the matchmaker sends an additional match. At least, that's what I envision for Betwixt Two Hearts. I haven't found another matchmaking site that is remotely similar. Personalized matches simply don't exist on the web."

Camden swallowed with difficulty, running a hand through his hair. How could he tell her that her dream was unachievable? "That sounds like a great ideal," he said cautiously, deliberately opening with something positive. "I've heard of professional matchmakers, but I don't understand how that scenario can work in an online format. It's not like a matchmaker could personally know all the internet clients, and the sheer volume of clients we hope to simultaneously handle makes automaticity necessary. There's no way one, or even several, matchmakers could comb through thousands of profiles and create personal matches for each one."

"I can do it." Bailey persisted. "I'm really good at reading between the lines of a profile to determine personality, and I intuitively know even what is not said. Plus, I won't be the only matchmaker. Elise will pull her load and probably some of mine. I think the hardest task will be handling the initial numbers with the launch and free promo, but if we get through those, then keeping caught up should be much easier."

She is insane. There is no way her fantasy could work in real life.

Though Camden didn't yet know Bailey well, he knew that using those exact words to explain his objections would not be received well. Instead, he needed to get her to see reason by approaching this from a different angle.

"What exactly are your qualifications as a matchmaker?" he asked casually instead. This time, it was his turn to fold his arms across his front and pin her with a direct gaze.

With a startled blink, Bailey's gaze faltered, and she suddenly showed a huge interest in the grain of wood on the hardwood floor.

I found her weak point!

Though he realized his words had found their target, he carefully maintained his casual, unemotional expression, looking at her expectantly.

"Obviously, I've worked with Elise," she said confidently, as if that decided the issue.

"Where exactly did you work with Elise?" Camden persisted.

"We worked at the same university library," Bailey stated, her confidence still intact even though she still couldn't look him in the eye. "After I inadvertently found out who she was and what she did, I helped her with matchmaking."

"Oh, so was this a special kind of library that also provided customers with matchmaking services?" Camden asked with an innocence that clearly communicated sarcasm.

Bailey offered only a withering smile, not bothering to dignify his question with a response.

Camden persisted, not willing to be put off. "Correct me if I'm wrong, but Elise isn't actually a professional matchmaker. She likes to set people up and is pretty good at making matches, whether or not the couple even realizes they've been set up. However, as far as I know, Elise hasn't actually ever made matches upon request by looking at a profile."

"Elise is gifted," Bailey said firmly. "She has an incredible intuition about people and can read them like no one I've ever met. Ever since I found out what she does, I've been trying to convince her to start a professional matchmaking company, and she's always said no, maintaining that if people paid her to do it, she wouldn't like it. She likes to look for opportunities to make matches. She doesn't like the thought of being required to find a match for someone."

Camden's forehead wrinkled in confusion. "What changed? Isn't that exactly what we're doing? People will pay us to find them a match. If Elise isn't okay with that, why are we even here?"

"What changed is that Elise got married," Bailey explained. "She wants to have more flexibility in her schedule to travel with her husband, and she wants to have the freedom to be able to start a family and not need to punch a clock at work. She doesn't want a brick and mortar matchmaking business, but when she floated the idea that maybe an online matchmaking site would be more agreeable, I jumped at the chance, and the rest is history."

"You quit your job for this?" Camden asked, suddenly putting two and two together.

"Yes, I did," she replied firmly and without apology. "That's how much I believe in it. Elise needed to be able to stay in Seattle with her husband and work remotely. She provided our entire start-up money, but she asked if I would contribute by coming out here to work with you and set things up while she acted more as the silent partner. Of course, I agreed. We need to make this website successful. Elise is depending on us to figure it out, and I'm not exactly flying with a safety net on this one."

Camden sighed. That certainly explained her attitude, at least to some degree. She was emotionally involved with living out her dream. That meant that no amount of reason would convince her to accept anything less than her fantasy. Unfortunately, Bailey had undoubtedly now added fear to her pre-existing emotional connection to the project. If the website failed, Bailey failed. She no longer had any other source of income, meaning her dream was now tied irreversibly to her security.

Camden didn't need a degree in psychology to recognize that as a dangerous combination. He needed to placate her expectations and find a way to incorporate just a bit of her dream and hope it enough to satisfy her.

Running his hand through his hair yet again, he resigned himself to the task and asked, "So if a dating website is a buffet, what is your idea of a matchmaking website?"

"A gourmet dinner prepared by a five-star chef."

Of course! Camden barely stopped himself from rolling his eyes.

"And I suppose you are that five-star chef." It wasn't a question. He already knew.

"Ideally," Bailey answered anyway.

That was it. He'd tried to be respectful and reasonable, but this now qualified as ridiculous. "I'm sorry, Bailey. I don't deal in the world of the ideal fantasy. I'm here in reality where you can very swiftly kill a website if you have someone with absolutely no experience handle potentially thousands of profiles and make personal matches for people she doesn't know. I've already okayed everything with Elise every step of the way, and she is completely on board with the scope and content of what I've done. I'm sorry, but you're going to need to find a more appropriate receptacle for your dream. Maybe opening a brick and mortar matchmaking business is more your speed."

Bailey's eyes narrowed. "You've okayed everything with Elise? I don't believe you! I have discussed all of my ideas with Elise, and she loves them! She already gave me her approval to move forward and instruct you to incorporate them."

"Instruct me?" Camden's incredulous look clearly communicated his disbelief. "Is that really what Elise said?"

"Well, she may not have used those exact words," Bailey back-peddled and her gaze flickered to the hardwood once again. "But she definitely approves and said we could move forward with them."

"We can't both be right. Maybe we should just give Elise a call and settle this right now," Camden said, wiggling his eyebrows and tossing out the challenge, fully expecting her to back down. He took out his phone and poised it expectantly.

"Fine with me," Bailey said, confidently folding her arms back in front of her.

"Good morning, you two!" Camden's mom greeted as she entered the office bearing two cups of coffee and a plate laden with two cinnamon rolls.

"Lydia, you don't need to wait on us!" Bailey protested, though the stress on her face immediately cleared with the entry of their visitor.

"Nonsense." Lydia handed the coffee to each of them and then set the cinnamon rolls next to the computer. "I thought you'd need some fuel to get your work done."

Bailey shot a glance at Camden, a calculating look lighting her eyes. "Well, we seem to have already hit a bit of a snag in the work department. Maybe you could—"

"No," Camden cut off flatly, setting the full coffee cup beside the empty one on his desk. At the rate things were going, he would need more than just those two cups to get him through the day. "Bailey, this is between you and me. We aren't asking Mom's opinion on our disagreement."

"Disagreement?" Lydia asked worriedly. "That sounds quite serious. Maybe I could—"

"No," Camden repeated firmly. "Thank you, but Bailey and I will figure it out."

This was exactly why he didn't want their office located at his parents' house. He'd managed to keep his mouth shut last night because they had no other options. He loved his parents, but he was fiercely independent. Their helpfulness could feel smothering at times.

Besides that, the fact that his business partner was currently living with his parents while they operated the business out of their home was difficult for his pride to manage. It felt too much like a grown man who lived in his parents' basement while holding his band rehearsals in their garage. Though he knew he didn't qualify as a failure in any sense, he also knew that on the surface, he'd just gotten laid off from his job and was now starting a business at his parents' house. Garage band or not, that didn't look so good, and he definitely didn't want his mother's assistance at all in their business matters.

"Alright then," Lydia said, not seeming bothered in the least by Camden's dismissal. "Enjoy your cinnamon rolls and get lots done. I'm planning on a light lunch of chef salad and homemade bread. I'll let you know when it's ready."

Bailey glared at him accusingly as soon as his mother left. "Is there a reason you didn't want her opinion?"

"Yes!" Camden said immediately. "Chances are, she would have sided with you!"

Bailey looked surprised yet triumphant.

"Not that you're right in the least bit," Camden hurried to clarify. "In my mother's mind, however, you're the guest, and I should adapt to accommodate you. Mom is unfailingly hospitable, and she has always expected her children to make the sacrifice for someone else, even if she doesn't take the time to understand the underlying issues. Mom isn't a part of this business, nor does she know the first thing about dating, matchmaking sites, or the internet in general."

"What are you waiting for then?" Bailey asked, indicating his phone laying on the desk by the keyboard. "If Elise is the only one with a valid opinion, give her a call."

Camden shook his head and snatched up a large bite of cinnamon roll. "Nope. I changed my mind. I'm not going to do that either," he said in between bites. "We are not two children who need my mom or Elise to solve our disagreement. If Elise really and truly liked both of our ideas, then she obviously intended for us to figure out a way to compromise and use both."

Bailey was silent, and Camden finished his cinnamon roll. After he licked the last, gooey drop from his fingers, he stood to his feet and stretched, completely ignoring the disgusted look Bailey wore as she mutely watched him eat.

Walking over to a shelf, he pulled out a piece of paper, scooted his chair over to an open space on the long desk, sat, and began folding.

He hadn't worked for three minutes before Bailey demanded, "What are you doing?"

"Folding origami," Camden replied, not bothering to look up from his task. "I thought that was obvious."

"Can you just not do that right now?" Bailey asked, her eyes narrowing and her voice going up in pitch with stress. "I can't focus with you doing that. We're supposed to figure this out, and you folding little origami animals isn't helping."

Wordlessly, Camden left the little cat half-finished and walked over to the open space in the middle of the office. He dropped to the floor, spread out, and quickly began pumping pushups.

"Arrgh!" Bailey cried. "That's worse! How am I supposed to think with you doing that? Are you purposely trying to aggravate me?"

"You think you're the only one who is trying to think?" Camden said, talking in between sets of ten pushups. "That's what I'm doing. You may focus by staring off into space, but I focus by doing something. If you won't let me fold paper, pushups are my only other option."

Bailey put her hands over her eyes, refusing to even look at him as he busted out another set.

Camden continued, determined to finish his set and also enjoying that he'd found a way to needle her. He didn't know why it bothered her so much, and he didn't know why he took such perverse pleasure in bothering her. But both were very much true.

"If you take your shirt off, I'm leaving," he heard Bailey mutter.

Breathing hard, Camden finished, stood up and grabbed his shirt as if intending to pull it over his head in one quick motion. "Is that a promise?"

Bailey groaned. "Do the origami. Please. Just no more pushups."

Camden laughed. "No worries. I'm done. I think I've figured it out."

"What?" Bailey asked, looking hopelessly confused.

Wow, the pushups really threw her off. I'll have to remember that!

"I think I have a solution to our problem," Camden explained, returning his chair to its position in front of the computer. "Why don't we offer two options to our clients? People who register can choose whether they want a match chosen through a scientific algorithm providing a high degree of compatibility or a match chosen by a personal matchmaker who is virtually a stranger."

Bailey smiled wanly. "You make that sound so appealing. We'll adjust the wording, of course, but that might be a good solution, at least while starting the business out."

"So how do you want to gather information when someone selects the personal matchmaker option? Do you still want them to do a survey, or are you planning to play eeny-meeny-miny-mo with selecting a match?"

"Show me your scientific survey," Bailey instructed leaning toward the computer. "I might be able to use the same survey answers to personalize the match. That would save time and make you happy, right?"

Camden brought up the list of survey questions, relieved that at least she seemed to be trying to compromise. If she consented to use the materials he'd already created, that would certainly make her ridiculous idea more attainable.

Camden moved aside to let Bailey scroll through all the questions, resisting the urge to scoot over and finish folding the origami cat. Camden had always needed to do something to focus or de-stress. As long as he could remember, he'd doodled in the margins of his school work. When he'd started focusing on computers, doodling was a more difficult option to carry with you. One day after college, he'd been in a particularly stressful meeting at work. Seeing a discarded sticky note on the desk, he'd picked it up and begun folding. From that moment on, origami had become somewhat of an obsession, but in a good way. Camden always tried to improve his skills with research and practice, and the more stress relief he needed, the more attention his origami habit demanded.

Now, with Bailey taking over at the computer, he needed something to occupy him, especially since he suspected this wouldn't end well. So far, Bailey hadn't approved of anything. She'd certainly given him no evidence to suggest this would be different.

The survey he'd developed was based on solid research, and he was proud of it. Though he'd never imagined himself the owner of a dating or matchmaking website, he firmly believed that Betwixt Two Hearts had the potential to be the highest quality, most successful matchmaking tool available, and it wouldn't be because of Bailey Whitmore's influence. Unfortunately, it would be in spite of it.

"This is quite the survey," Bailey muttered.

"Yes," Camden agreed. "I estimate it takes about forty-five minutes to an hour to complete, and we inform potential clients of that in the beginning. It is extensive, but not every question is weighted the same in the algorithm used to make the matches," he explained. "For example, religious preferences are weighted to a higher degree than similar educational backgrounds. I put a lot of research into looking at other websites and investigating the science of love to develop an algorithm that will predict a relationship's success with a high degree of accuracy."

"The 'science of love?'" Bailey echoed, her lips puckering up as if she'd bitten into a sour candy when she'd been expecting a sweet one. "How terribly romantic."

Camden scooted away from her and happily returned to folding his paper cat, ignoring her sarcasm and letting her finish scrolling. With that kind of attitude, Camden no longer felt remorse for indulging in something that potentially annoyed her.

He hadn't quite finished when Bailey's incredulous voice broke the silence. "Are these questions for real?"

Apparently, it was a rhetorical question. Camden hadn't managed to field a response before she spoke again, her tone reporting something so unbelievable, she found it humorous. "'What is your political party?' 'What is your view on abortion?' Seriously? What kind of questions are these?"

"Good ones!" Camden said firmly. "I did a lot of research. Scientifically, a couple has a higher rate of success if they share the same core values."

"But they are boring!" Bailey practically choked on her own words. "There's not even a smidge of romance in, 'What is your highest level of education?'"

"There are other more romantic questions," Camden protested, coming back to the computer and scrolling through the list. "See here? In this section, they need to choose if they are not skilled, somewhat skilled, or very skilled. The question is, 'How skilled are you at keeping the romance in a relationship?'"

Bailey laughed, a tinkling sound merrily ringing through the room. "That's your romantic question? That's the most unromantic way of reducing romance to a mere checkbox. Anyone could say, 'I'm very skilled at romance,' but there is no meaning attached. Really, what exactly does that mean?"

Camden sat back in his seat and glared. "Like I said, I did significant research and developed an excellent algorithm that can predict a couple's compatibility with a high degree of accuracy. Some of the questions might not be exciting enough to you, but the point of the site is to produce lasting relationships that result in marriage. These questions and my algorithm will do that. I'm not a matchmaker. I admit that. But neither are you."

"I've worked with Elise."

Camden nodded. "Right," he drew the word out sarcastically. "I remember. At the library. That means that you are no more qualified to know anything about matchmaking or a dating website than I am. And I'm the one who's done considerable research."

Bailey turned to face him directly, speaking earnestly and, for once, without ridicule. "You can't reduce romance to mere science and numbers, Camden. It doesn't work that way. The beautiful thing about love is the magic of it. Two people can be highly compatible and hate each other. Most people don't want to marry themselves."

"It's an algorithm," Camden defended stubbornly. "Sometimes it places a higher value of compatibility if people don't answer a question in the exact same way. For instance, it doesn't match an extreme introvert with another extreme introvert, nor does it match him or her with an extreme extrovert. Instead, the value is placed on someone who is closer to the middle on the introvert scale. Bailey, it is not a simple program. It is wonderfully complex."

"I have a boyfriend."

Camden shook his head in confusion, wondering what he'd just missed. "What? That qualifies you how?"

With her overbearing confidence firmly in place, Bailey held her head high, studying Camden while looking at him at a downward angle. "I have a successful relationship. Love is not predictable by science and numbers. Otherwise, someone smarter than you would have cracked the code thousands of years ago. Experience is the qualification you are missing. In your case, I don't think your relationship with your computer qualifies as a successful, long-term relationship. You cannot hope to predict something with which you have no experience."

This time, Camden was not offended. He was amused. She knew nothing about him but seemed to be searching to find his weakness. Romantic love didn't qualify as something he felt sensitive about, and from his observations of Bailey, he seriously doubted she was the love expert she claimed.

"How long have you been with your boyfriend?" he asked curiously.

"Two years," Bailey answered proudly. "We met at a fundraising event in Seattle and have been together ever since."

"Are you getting married?"

Bailey shifted uncomfortably in her seat. "Eventually, maybe. We're not in a rush. We're not the type of people who need marriage to define our relationship. We know how we feel and are committed to each other, not to a piece of paper that states that as a fact."

Camden snorted. "You're just pretending. You're no more qualified than I am, maybe less."

"Qualified in what? Matchmaking? I have made a successful match with Dekker."

"No, you haven't," Camden scoffed. "You're not married. You're not planning a future."

"And how does that disqualify me?" Bailey protested.

Camden smiled gently and stood to return to the origami cat awaiting a few more folds. "Love, Bailey. Love. How can you find love for others when you have no idea what love actually is?"

"And you think you do?"

Camden nodded thoughtfully. "Yes, I may not have experienced it yet, but at least I know what it looks like. From my perspective, you've only experienced a lie."

"You're wrong," Bailey said flatly, anger seething in the two words.

Camden shrugged. "Maybe. We'll set the website up so that people can choose either option. You can work to help people find your version of love. I'll give people their scientific results for their best matches and then pray that God blesses them with the real kind of love."

Bailey rolled her eyes dramatically. "How gallant of you and fortunate for them."

Camden grinned and wiggled his eyebrows. "Don't worry. You're not excluded from my gallantry. I'll pray for you as well."

"Pray for me what?" Bailey sputtered.

"True love, Bailey. I'll be praying for you to realize true love."

Four

"Bailey, are you even a Christian?"

Bailey gasped, too shocked to even know how to respond to Camden's question. After working with the man for the past six days, she should be accustomed to his rude, abrupt manner. It was the evening of New Year's Day, release day for their website, and they were caught in yet another argument. Yet again, Camden objected to the match she was trying to set up, claiming that the two clients didn't share the same faith and were therefore incompatible. However, disagreeing with her shouldn't excuse him for saying something so offensive.

"What kind of question is that?" she finally managed. "Of course, I'm a Christian."

Camden frowned, obviously not satisfied or willing to swivel his seat back around to his own computer. "It's just that you don't seem to value the typical Christian ideals," he explained. "When you tried to design your own survey, you weren't interested at all in including any questions about religion. Thankfully, we compromised and adapted my original survey to include the more romantic questions you wanted, but that wasn't your original preference. Plus...," Camden hesitated.

"Plus, what?" Bailey seethed, wanting him to just get it over with.

At his obvious hesitation, she leaned back in her chair, folded her arms across her front, and looked at him expectantly.

Camden finally sighed. "You live with your boyfriend, don't you? You've been with him for two years and have no desire to get married. That must be because you're already pretending to be married."

He said that as if it was a big deal. What was he—some old-fashioned, overly-religious fanatic? Didn't he realize that most couples nowadays lived together? It was the smart thing to do. Why would anyone want to make a marriage commitment before knowing if you could actually live with your partner?

However, instead of presenting him with numerous, solid arguments, Bailey opted for the bottom line. "I don't see how that is any of your business."

More bothersome than his obvious disapproval was the fact that he'd used the same words when he said she was pretending at love. He didn't know her and had no business acting as judge and jury over her life, and yet the word "pretending" had replayed through her mind frequently since he'd uttered it days ago. After his comment now, that incessant replay seemed louder in volume.

"This site promotes itself as being founded on Christian values with marriage as the goal," Camden said firmly, apparently completely unaware of the anger slowly coming to a hot simmer in Bailey. "You aren't required to be a Christian to join, but we do respect and value clients' religious preferences. You can't match someone who says they are a strong Christian with someone who claims no religious affiliation. Even if that is not your personal value, it is the site's value. You just can't do it."

"Give me a break!" Bailey said, throwing her arms up as she stood from her desk chair. "Did you even look at the rest of Craig's profile? Yes, Molly is a Christian and wants someone who shares her faith, but Craig runs a nonprofit and has received countless awards for community service. He is a kindhearted, great guy. They are a perfect match." Bailey pointed to her computer screen as if offering proof of her argument.

Camden shook his head. "None of that matters if they don't share the same core values—meaning faith. We must follow through with what Molly listed as most important. We would be just like all the other sites if we don't prioritize making matches that value what our clients value."

"Fine," Bailey said briskly, realizing she didn't have time to win this argument. "If clients rate it as highly important, I'll try to match people of similar faith."

Long lists of clients awaited her matchmaking skills, and if agreeing to his terms about religious preference allowed her to return to work, then it was worth it. From Camden's tone, she knew he wouldn't easily change his mind about this religion rule. However, that didn't mean she wouldn't be able to bend it on occasion when Camden's eagle eye wasn't looking.

However, she couldn't resist adding, "I just think you're being very narrow-minded about it. Not everyone's Christianity looks like yours."

Camden shut his eyes briefly, and Bailey couldn't tell if he was relieved she had acquiesced to his demands or offended by her words.

"I'm going to let that one slide for now," he said finally. "We literally have thousands of matches that we need to make in the next seventy-two hours. We don't have time for a theological debate."

"Elise is working as well," Bailey pointed out. "Last I checked, she'd gotten through fifty."

"That's a drop in the bucket when we're getting far more clients than fifty every hour," Camden grumbled. "I can't believe I agreed to let you do personal matches. So many clients are choosing that option. It'll be so much easier if you just review the results of the survey and approve the top match the algorithm recommends."

"I'm sure I'll do that for some of them," Bailey acknowledged, really trying to be agreeable. "But I'll also look at other clients in the area to check if there is a better one." She was the one trying to get along here, and all he could do was complain. Their site was pretty much going viral with the free promotion. Thousands of clients had already joined, and it hadn't been live for twenty-four hours yet. Instead of feeling excited and energized by their success, Camden looked for ways to criticize.

Seeming to prove her point, Camden groaned dramatically. "Fine, just please try to work quickly. Case in point, what are your plans for Molly?" he asked, referring back to the match that had started their argument. "As we already discussed, nonprofit guy is not an option because he isn't a Christian. Can you please just approve the top match generated by the algorithm?"

Bailey bit her lip, not wanting to continue the argument but desperate to make Camden understand the art behind matchmaking. "It's just so boring," she explained, looking at the profiles of both clients side by side. "The algorithm listed Molly's top match as Jason, but they are so very similar—too similar. If you won't let me match her with Craig, what about this guy right here? It looks like he's an hour away from where she lives. Did she give proximity preferences?"

"Yes, she selected within fifty miles."

"Yay! Marcus McDaniel is forty-nine miles away. Let's go with him. He's listed as a Christian, and his hobbies are more adventurous than hers. I think they'll be a good match."

"Fine," Camden agreed, though he obviously didn't want to. "His answers don't list his faith as important as she lists hers, but we'll go with it and mark it off the list. If Molly and Marcus don't work out, hopefully, she'll come back, and we can pair her with Jason, her top match from the algorithm."

When Bailey didn't respond or make a move to approve the new matches, Camden offered a long-suffering sigh and spoke again. "Bailey, you can't take this much time with every match."

"If you leave me alone and don't argue over every single one, things will go much more quickly."

"Fine," Camden said, once again, his tone in clear opposition to the curt "fine" he flung her way.

I really don't think he understands what the word "fine" means! Bailey thought sourly.

Turning his back on her, Camden focused on his computer. "I'll just continue sorting through the clients and sending you the ones who have potential matches. I've already set things up so that if a client does not have a qualified match in the area that is designated, they are sent an email after twenty-four hours. The email gives them options of continuing to wait or widening their search parameters. Since we are just getting started, we have a log of unmatchable profiles. Hopefully, we'll get many more clients who sign up in the next few days, and the problem will fix itself."

Not bothering to respond, Bailey focused on the profile in front of her, relieved that Camden had set up her own computer and workstation. They sat with their backs to each other on opposite sides of the office, which contributed to a much happier situation where they could work separately and not interact. Now, they just argued whenever forced to consult each other, as opposed to the nonstop arguing before.

Unfortunately, Camden had arranged so he could follow Bailey's progress live while doing his own tasks, ensuring that he had eyes in the back of his head. Even with him turned the other direction, Bailey never lost the feeling that his eyes always watched her, probably because they did.

His two huge monitors acted like all-seeing eyes. Every once in a while, he'd instant message her rather than speak across the few feet of space, and she actually preferred this. An instant message was easier to ignore, especially since they usually consisted of telling her what to do. Even now, though she worked steadily to approve matches, she also saw her to-do list increasing in a long trail behind where she currently worked as both the website and Camden added profiles and notes that required her attention.

"Here's one that you can approve really quick," Camden said while an instant message with a link to a profile popped up on her screen. "There is only one match within the twenty-five-mile radius he requested. Fortunately, the algorithm indicates they'd be a strong match. However, while she chose the algorithm match, he selected personal matchmaker. That means you just need to click your approval of the match on his profile, and they will be matched to each other. Then you'll be done and can move to the next on the list."

"I'll take a look," Bailey said distractedly. She could read the impatience in his voice. She was still working too slowly for his liking. Now he was trying to help speed things up, hoping she wouldn't notice what he was doing. She wished he would just back off. She didn't care if she worked all night. Getting these matches right was too important. Their success of the website depended on it!

Isn't it nice the way that he thinks I should drop what I'm working on to cater to what he wants me to do? As if I'm not busy at all!

Finishing the match in front of her, Bailey then opened the profile Camden had messaged. She looked over the results of Camden's algorithm and then went back to review specifics on the two profiles Camden intended to match and how each of the clients answered the survey questions.

"Having trouble?" Camden asked several minutes later, not quite managing to keep the annoyance out of his voice.

"I'm just not sure," Bailey hedged, feeling puzzled. "Something isn't right about this profile. Did you look at it?"

Camden stood from his desk and came to look over Bailey's shoulder and see what she was referring to. "I looked at it briefly. Do you think it's a fraudulent account?"

"No, it's not that. It's her." Bailey pointed to the picture of a pretty blonde-haired, blue-eyed woman on the screen. "Eleanor is twenty-seven and has a teaching degree. She taught for three years in Minneapolis and is now living in what appears to be the middle of nowhere and working at a company called Evergreen Services. That certainly doesn't sound like a school."

"It's not quite the middle of nowhere, Bailey," Camden pointed out, reaching over to bring the map window up on her screen. "Milaca is only about an hour from the Twin Cities. People change jobs all the time. Besides, maybe Evergreen Services provides educational services, and she's still a teacher. There is nothing strange about either one of those things."

Bailey gently swatted his hand away from her computer. He was far too close. "Maybe it's more of a feeling. There's more to Eleanor than the facts on this profile."

Bailey felt rather than saw Camden's eye roll. Camden liked facts and figures. Bailey doubted he'd ever had a gut instinct in his life.

"None of that changes the fact that there is only one candidate that fits David Reid's search radius," he insisted.

"That's another thing. Why is his search radius so small? If he bumped it to fifty miles, we could possibly consider other candidates in the Twin Cities. Eleanor's search radius is fifty miles. If his was the same, we could match them with different people."

Camden shrugged, "He obviously wants a local girl, and they are a strong match for each other. Why on earth would we match them with different people?"

He didn't get it, and she had no hope of explaining it to him. "Maybe I should email David and ask if it would be okay to bump his search radius up a bit. Then we'd have more candidates to work with."

"No, Bailey," Camden immediately objected. "Let it go. Eleanor Nielson is a strong match right in his town. The situation couldn't be more ideal. You don't need to make everything so complicated. Just click the little approve button and be done with it. See, the approve button is right here. Isn't it cute? I know you want to push it."

Bailey worried the hem of her black cardigan between her fingers, looking carefully at David Reid's profile. "Fine. I'll approve it. He's an engineer, and he's even a Christian. No wonder you approve. Eleanor lists herself as a Protestant Christian, and he says he's a conservative Christian and a seminary student. Is that close enough?"

"I certainly hope so," Camden said, a sliver of doubt creeping into his voice for the first time. "It isn't like we have other options to choose from with his search parameters."

"Unless we want to wait for more clients in the area or email him to widen his net," Bailey pointed out. "I'll go ahead and click your cute, little approve button. If it doesn't go well, though, I will email him and find each another match in the Twin Cities. She looks like she'd be better suited for the city anyway. I'm not quite sure she's the small-town girl he's looking for."

"Now who's being judgmental?" Camden asked. "Don't worry, I'll pray about it. David will find exactly who God intends him to find."

"Wait, you'll pray about it?" Bailey asked, looking at him sharply. "Is that really necessary?"

"Sure, why not? I always pray that God will use our site to help others to find who He designed for them to be with." Camden turned to his side of the room as if the matter were settled.

"Don't you think God has better things to do than concern Himself with a matchmaking website?" Bailey couldn't resist flinging back to him.

Camden paused and turned back around to answer seriously. "No, I don't. I believe God is very much interested in our daily lives and can even use things like a matchmaking website for His glory. He cares about Eleanor Nielson and David Reid. If His will is to bring them together, then I hope He uses us to do so."

Camden strode back to his computer, and Bailey wearily propped her head on her hand. With one little click of her mouse, she finally pushed the button to approve the match, but she didn't necessarily feel happy about it.

Unfortunately, she didn't know if her discomfort had more to do with the match or with Camden. Or maybe it had everything to do with the realization made uncomfortably clear in the past few minutes.

With Camden's "help," there was nothing easy about matchmaking.

It was going to be a very long night.

"Come on, Bailey. We've been working nonstop for the last seventy-two hours. Let's get out of here and take a break." Camden turned out the overhead light to the office while Bailey still sat glued to her computer screen.

This was a switch. Usually, Camden was the one who didn't know how to find a stopping place.

"Just let me finish this match," Bailey protested.

"It'll be here when we get back," Camden urged. "So will the hundreds of others. With the free promotion over, new sign-ups should slow down a bit, and we can finish getting caught up. I just checked in with Elise, and she's knocking out matches like a machine. We have time to take a break."

Despite his words, Bailey continued working in the dark while Camden leaned against the door jam.

"All done," Bailey sighed, finally shutting down her computer and standing to follow Camden.

Any impatient remark Camden could have launched died before it reached his lips. One glimpse of Bailey's face, and Camden felt bad for being impatient in the first place. Bailey was exhausted. They had both worked nonstop these last few days. However, Camden suspected that even after he finally called it quits for the night and went home, Bailey stayed up all hours working.

Their arguing finally settled down some, and Camden had backed off, letting Bailey handle the matchmaker matches on her own terms. She worked steadily, but at a much slower pace than Camden preferred. To her credit, she gave every single match she looked at her full attention. She gave her best every time, unwilling to ever simply mark one off the list for the sake of convenience. Though it drove him crazy from the business perspective, he admired the work ethic. In the end, Bailey did what she'd set out to do. She and Elise had played personal matchmaker to thousands of clients who signed up during the first few days of the site's debut. Bailey was as dedicated as she was stubborn. Strangely, those were the same qualities he admired and that drove him crazy on a daily basis.

"How about Mexican food?" Camden asked cheerfully, leading the way to his car parked out front of his parents' house.

"Okay," Bailey replied dully.

Camden looked at her sharply, concerned with her lackluster response.

Now he recognized his parents' absence tonight as a very good thing. They had gone to a theater production in Brighton Falls, which meant Lydia hadn't been around to prepare an unrequested evening meal, and Camden was glad. As much as he appreciated his mom's pampering, a meal in the house would not have worked well at all this evening. Bailey very much needed to get out of the house.

Camden couldn't get more than one-word answers out of Bailey the entire way to the restaurant. Fortunately, there was no wait, and their waitress showed them to a booth in a corner.

"Thank you, Marianna," Camden said after the young woman deposited baskets of chips and salsa at their table and took their drink order.

Marianna brightened at the use of her name, sending Camden a warm smile.

After a few minutes of munching on the chips, Bailey began to recover a little more color in her face. Marianna returned with their sodas, once again smiling at Camden and declaring she'd be right back to take their order.

"Who is she?" Bailey asked, frowning after Marianna left.

Camden shrugged, "Her name is Marianna Martinez. I don't know her well, but pretty much everyone knows everyone in Crossroads."

"Why doesn't she like me?" Bailey asked bluntly.

Camden scowled. "What do you mean? She doesn't even know you."

"Exactly, but both times she's been here, she's sent you smiles that would score a perfect ten on the flirting scale, and then she's thrown glares my direction."

"I'm sure you're being a little oversensitive. I think—"

"Here she comes," Bailey muttered. "And it looks like now we have an audience."

Out of the corner of his eye, Camden saw several lovely, little heads pop out from the doorway near the kitchen, their eyes glued to their table.

"Do you need any more bean dip or salsa?" Marianna asked brightly. Then, without skipping a beat, she said pointedly, "Mr. Camden, I don't think I've met your friend."

Camden blinked, surprised. Though he knew Marianna's name, it was only through his occasional stops at the restaurant. She was quite a bit younger than he was, and they didn't travel in the same social circles, if Camden could claim to belong to any social circles at all.

Nevertheless, he politely introduced, "Marianna, this is my business partner, Bailey Whitmore. Bailey, this is Marianna Martinez, the best waitress here at the restaurant."

"Your business partner?" Marianna echoed, the lines on her face immediately smoothing. "I have to say I'm relieved. You take a *mujer hermosa* to dinner too often, and you're likely to make every single woman in Crossroads cry. But a business meeting is different. What can I get you to eat?"

They both placed their orders, and Marianna hurried back to the kitchen.

"She probably needs to go make her report to the rest of the audience," Bailey remarked, watching her leave. "I didn't realize I was dining with the most eligible bachelor in town or that you had such a protective harem."

Camden burst out laughing at the idea. "I'm not, and I don't! I don't know what's gotten into Marianna. I've only ever seen her here at the restaurant. I've always been friendly, but nothing more."

"She likes you, so do the rest of the audience members. Haven't you seen all of the lovely waitresses sashay by here, sending you alluring smiles while offering me the evil eye?"

Camden looked at her blankly, clueless as to what she referred to. Maybe Bailey was suffering from working so hard. Couldn't hallucinations happen if someone was exhausted enough?

Bailey shook her head and laughed at him. "You're too naive to notice!" she accused. "Even though Marianna is relieved that I am your business partner, she still doesn't like me. Neither do the other waitresses. If you want, I can really set their minds at ease and make a general announcement that I have a boyfriend, so you're definitely still available."

Camden grimaced, glancing around the restaurant nervously. "I think you're overreacting. Marianna seemed friendly enough." Bailey was reading too much into it, but at the same time, he didn't want to do or say anything that may give Marianna or anyone else any encouragement to show interest in his personal life or lack thereof.

Bailey shook her head. "For a guy who owns a matchmaking website, you're clueless."

Fearing that Bailey's attitude could make the best food unpalatable, Camden immediately shot back. "For a woman who just successfully launched that same matchmaking website, you're in a sour mood."

Realizing how harsh he sounded, Camden softened his tone. "Bailey, you should feel really good about all we've accomplished this week. We have more clients than we could have ever anticipated. You've gotten through thousands of personal matches exactly as you wanted to. The feedback from users is all positive so far. Those are reasons to celebrate!"

Bailey smiled wanly. "I think I'll feel better after I get some sleep and after those first dates get reviewed. So far, everything is still a theory. When we know that clients are enjoying the matches we've created, then I can feel good about what we've accomplished."

Camden frowned slightly. Why did she have to put it that way? "I think it will be great to get good reviews, but I think it will be even more satisfying if the matches actually work. If clients develop strong relationships that result in marriage, then we know we're providing a valuable service."

"Isn't that kind of a self-defeating goal when you think about it?" Bailey pointed out. "If people find their soul mates, then they no longer pay for our services. We'll be succeeding ourselves out of business."

"If we aren't successful in our goal of creating marriages, then we'll soon be out of business anyway," Camden pointed out, idly swirling the ice around his cup and wishing he'd opted for coffee instead. "However, if we follow through in doing what we advertise, then the positive word-of-mouth should be more than sufficient to provide an ever-increasing supply of single clients."

Boring of chasing the ice around his soda with his straw, Camden unfolded his napkin carefully and began refolding it in precise lines that would soon transform the thin paper into a flower.

"When will we know if our free promo worked and clients are choosing to become members?" Bailey asked, in-between munching on tortilla chips.

"You want to know when we get paid," Camden translated, flashing a knowing smile up at her.

Bailey returned the smile and admitted, "My current nest egg does have a limited supply."

While meticulously making small, careful folds in the napkin, Camden explained, "Clients have full access to the site, the app, and all the features for forty-eight hours after they receive their first match. After that, they are locked out of everything unless they join as members for the monthly fee. When they join, they can then choose what plan they want. They can choose to receive a single match at a time from the algorithm or from the personal matchmaker. They can also opt to receive five or ten algorithm matches at a time, which they can then pick and choose from. With each option, they must give reasons or reviews before receiving additional matches."

Marianna arrived with their food. Admonishing that the plates were very hot, she placed them on the table and collected Camden's glass for a refill.

As soon as Marianna departed, Bailey asked, "All the Betwixt prices aren't the same for the different options, right? I think I remember you saying something about that."

Camden nodded. "The least expensive option is the single algorithm match. The next step up is the algorithm list of five matches, and then ten matches. The most expensive option is the personal matchmaker. With that taking the most man-hours, it makes the most sense for that to be our Cadillac experience, and hopefully, that pay structure will keep the workload for you and Elise down to a manageable level."

Abandoning his napkin origami for the moment, Camden picked up his fork to dig into his enchiladas.

Bailey had also ordered enchiladas. Before she popped a bite into her mouth, she asked. "What's to stop clients from simply taking their free match and running, or even paying for the batch of five names and then terminating their account?"

Camden ate a few bites before he answered, sure that at the rate Bailey was asking questions, his food would be cold before he had a break. "I'm sure we'll have some of that happen, but matches can only be contacted via the website. Contact information is hidden behind the site message system, and we strongly encourage clients not to reveal external contact info until they have corresponded and met a match in person. It's part of our safety features. If clients contact their free match within the first forty-eight hours and set up a date, that's fine, but if they don't obtain external contact info, then they will be unable to interact with that match when locked out of the website."

Bailey's eye brightened in understanding. "They'll need to pay the monthly fee to revisit the info and communicate with their match."

Camden nodded, "Exactly."

"Sometimes, Camden, you really are brilliant. Most times you're not. But sometimes..."

"I'll take that compliment," Camden grinned.

Marianna arrived with Camden's refill. By this time, Bailey's glass was close to empty as well, but after glancing Bailey's way, Marianna spun around and left.

Camden turned to try to catch her, but she was already gone. "I don't think she saw that you needed a refill."

"Oh, she saw," Bailey answered, amusement threading her voice. "I think she thought we were a little too friendly. At least that's what the glare she sent me clearly said."

"I'm sorry," Camden said, feeling bad. Maybe Bailey wasn't imagining things. Marianna had clearly left her unfilled glass on the table, and she was usually so conscientious about those things. "I'll get you a refill as soon as she comes by again."

They ate in silence for several minutes. Camden hadn't realized how hungry he was until two out of three of his enchiladas had disappeared.

Finally slowing down just a little, he looked up at Bailey, returning to talk of business.

"Did you get that match approved that I sent to you?" he asked. "It looked to be a quick one."

Bailey frowned. "No, not yet. I wanted to review it more before pressing that cute button you like so much."

Camden returned her frown. "Bailey, why is it that when two people show a high percentage of compatibility on the algorithm, you seem to have a problem with it? The better the results on the algorithm, the more you seem to want to find an alternative match. Do you resent the algorithm that much?"

Bailey ate a few more bites, obviously thinking before she replied. "It's not intentional," she said. "I don't consciously target those with a high percentage of compatibility, but it is possible that I do unconsciously seek to find a better match. It isn't you, nor is it your algorithm. From what I've seen, the algorithm is very effective and another example of your brilliance. However, I am a bit biased, and I know that."

Camden had expected an adamant denial but instead felt surprised at her thoughtful answer. "Why is that?" Camden asked, curious about her vague comments.

Bailey stopped eating and stared at her plate, scooting bites around in some unknown sorting pattern. "You have no idea how lucky you are, Camden. Your parents have been married forever and obviously still love and respect each other. My background isn't nearly so fortunate. My parents are divorced. They split when I was about three years old, and I don't really have any memories before that happened. The strange thing is that my parents are actually very similar in terms of values and personality. I'm sure your algorithm would have matched them with a high degree of compatibility."

Bailey set her fork down completely, and looked up at Camden, continuing her story. "I asked my mom about it once. She didn't disagree about them being very similar, explaining that they were high school sweethearts who did everything together. They liked the same things, even down to the same food and affinity for history. After they graduated, it seemed just a matter of course that they get married. After I was born, they both realized that, though they loved each other, it felt more like a friendship than romantic love. Even after their divorce, they remained on good terms and are still friends to this day. My mom said their relationship had always been based on friendship, but that friendship had never included a spark."

Camden looked at her with understanding and sympathy. "Thank you for telling me, Bailey. That certainly explains why you may have a natural aversion to an algorithm that pairs people together based on their similarities. Just so you know, that's not what my program does. As I explained before, different values are placed on different areas, and for some issues, more value is given if the two people are different."

Bailey nodded, speaking sincerely. "I have no doubt that you did a phenomenal job of designing it, Camden. Now that I know I have that bias, I will try to be aware of it and more objective about the matches that show a strong percentage. I admit that it is hard to see a ninety-seven percent match and not think that I'd better fix that to include some spark."

Camden smiled, appreciating her rare honesty. Unable to resist teasing her just a bit, he asked, "Isn't that spark part of the magic of romance that you can't really predict? I seem to recall someone saying something to that effect. Hey, did your parents ever find that spark and get remarried?"

"Oh, yes," Bailey nodded. "Multiple times." Laughing at her own joke, she explained. "My parents divorced when I was three. Both of them remarried before I entered kindergarten and had other children. Both of them got divorced again before I reached high school. They had on and off relationships and are now both remarried again."

The left side of Camden's mouth quirked up in humor. "Did you ever talk to your mom about that elusive spark again?"

"Oh, yes, I asked after her second divorce." Bailey looked like she was trying to hold in a smile but couldn't quite manage it. "She said it died."

Camden leaned his head back and laughed deep in his chest. "Which is worse, to have no spark or to have one that dies?"

Bailey's giggles were such that Camden could barely understand as she choked out, "I don't know!"

The bill came, and Camden paid it despite Bailey's protest. Still objecting even after Marianna returned with his card, Bailey intercepted the receipt to see how much she owed him. Though she glanced at the numbers, what caught her eye most was the name at the top of the paper.

"Wait a minute. Is this restaurant really called, 'La Bonita Sombrero'?" she asked.

"Yes, it is," Marianna responded, snatching the receipt from where Bailey had set it on the table and returning it to Camden.

Bailey's brow furrowed. "I'm not up on my Spanish, but isn't that a rather unusual name?"

"Quite," Camden agreed, looking to Marianna to see if she wanted to explain. After all, the restaurant belonged to her family.

Though she didn't look happy about the task, Marianna stated quite factually, "'Bonita' is a feminine adjective and should go with a feminine noun, but 'sombrero' is a masculine noun. Those two words aren't typically used together."

Marianna gathered the dirty plates and turned to leave.

"Marianna's parents are the restaurant's owners," Camden explained since Marianna obviously didn't intend to finish the task. "They disagreed on what the name should be, so they compromised. Since they are equal owners, they each chose a part of the name that represented them and combined it into one unique title."

At Camden's words, Marianna paused. When he finished, she added with a smile, "It doesn't follow the rules, but my parents have always done things their own way. 'La Bonita Sombrero' very much fits who they are."

"What a romantic story!" Bailey said warmly. Looking at Camden, she raised an eyebrow. "From the sound of it, I bet Mr. and Mrs. Martinez definitely have a spark!"

"I should say so!" Marianna answered, her words clipped. "But I think nine children qualifies them for a *gran fuego* more than any *pequiña chispa*!"

Bailey's eyes crinkled with amusement. Before she could question Marianna further, Camden laughed and stood.

"Thank you, Marianna. The food was delicious, as always. Please say 'hello' to your parents and sisters for me."

Marianna sniffed in distaste. "I'll tell my parents, but not Ana, Isobel, Daniella, or Natalia. They are already *las chicas tontas*. If I tell them you said 'hello,' they would surely assume a marriage proposal from you was

---

imminente. The younger ones should be safe, though."

Camden looked at Bailey and saw that her Spanish seemed adequate enough for her to understand Marianna was referring to her sisters as "silly girls."

"Marianna, are all of these other lovely waitresses your sisters?" Bailey asked, suddenly putting two and two together. "Do you have a brother hiding somewhere?"

"I wish!" Marianna laughed, finally seeming to warm up to Bailey. "My parents were blessed with nine daughters, and even the youngest helps out here at the restaurant."

"Mr. Martinez's 'sombrero' is the only masculine thing around here," Camden remarked dryly.

This sent both Marianna and Bailey into great fits of laughter. After saying their goodbyes, Marianna finally made her way back to the kitchen with the plates in her arms dangerously swaying back and forth to the rhythm of her giggles. Bailey still hadn't gained enough control to walk a straight line, so Camden gripped her elbow and guided her out. The cool air welcoming their exit from the restaurant calmed Bailey's merriment, though Camden didn't immediately release his touch on her arm.

"This is for you, Bailey," Camden said, handing her the napkin he'd folded in the restaurant. He shrugged. "I know you don't like origami, but I enjoyed having dinner with you. You can just throw it away if you want."

Bailey took the offered napkin. "It's a flower!" she said in amazement. "Almost like a poinsettia. Camden, it's beautiful! I never said I didn't like origami. I just didn't like it when I thought you were giving your attention to it rather than the problem we needed to solve."

She paused, her brown eyes sparkling as she looked up at him. "Thank you. I like it very much."

Camden nodded, feeling awkward at her thanks, but even more awkward at the thrill of pleasure her words caused.

Careful, he warned himself. *You certainly don't want to feel anything for her that could be construed as a spark, muy pequeña or otherwise.*

Bailey held the napkin flower in her cold hand, not sure what to do with it. She didn't want to put it in her purse because she couldn't stand the thought of it getting squished and crumpled in the close confinement. However, as delicate and pretty as it lay, poised on her hand, the January temperatures could quickly cause that hand to lose all feeling.

"I need to walk over to Brooke's store to pick up a gift for my mom's birthday," Camden said, not noticing Bailey's dilemma. "It's Israel's orders. Do you mind? If I take you home first, I think the store will close before I make it back."

"Brooke's shop is around here?" Bailey asked with interest, looking up and down the street. "I don't mind. I'd love to see it anyway."

Bailey had met some of Camden's other family members this past weekend. Though she still wasn't sure about Camden himself, she very much liked his family, especially his youngest sister, Brooke. She'd wanted to venture to downtown Crossroads and check out Brooke's shop, the Out of the Blue Bouquet, but she hadn't yet had time. Though the circumstances weren't ideal and she suspected frostbite to her cold fingers might be the price to pay, she knew she couldn't refuse.

"Yes, Brooke's shop is just a few doors down and across the street," Camden said, pointing in a vague direction.

That certainly didn't sound far. "Sure, let's go."

Camden led the way down the surprisingly busy sidewalks.

Bailey glanced at the time, seeing it was nearing nine o'clock. "Wow! I didn't realize Brooke kept such late hours with her shop." Maybe if she kept a conversation going, she wouldn't be so aware of her freezing hand.

"She doesn't usually, but this weekend Crossroads is hosting a special winter festival," Camden explained. "There will be a lot of events to draw in tourists. I was surprised that we got a table so quickly at the restaurant. I'm sure everything will be packed the rest of the weekend. That's why the streets are so busy this time of night. Everyone is arriving for the festival."

By the time Camden pushed open a door and set a merry little bell tinkling, Bailey's hand felt stiff, and she couldn't feel her fingers. They stepped inside to the warmth, and Bailey switched the napkin flower to her other hand and desperately tried to put the numb one in her coat pocket.

"Hi, Brooke!" Camden greeted his sister. "How is business tonight?"

"Good!" Brooke said, coming to greet them from behind a counter. "We've had lots of customers. This weekend should only get better."

"So, your shop is both a florist and a gift shop?" Bailey asked, looking around at the beautifully decorated shop filled with a kaleidoscope of treasures.

"Yes," Brooke said brightly. "It works well for us. We are the top florist in this area, and a tourist stop for visitors. All of our handcrafted wares do extremely well both in the store and online. Are you two here just to visit, or can I help you with something?"

Multiple customers milled around, and Bailey realized Brooke did not have the time to give a full tour that moment.

Camden also seemed to notice the other customers, and he hurried to explain, "Israel asked me to stop and pick up some kind of snowflake wreath for Mom's birthday. He said Mom saw it in the shop and liked it. He didn't think he'd have a chance to stop before we celebrate her birthday on Sunday, but he wanted to let Chloe wrap it for her."

"Oh, yes, I know what he's talking about," Brooke said, leading the way to a corner of the shop. "My friend, Emma Sheldon, made these beautiful snowflake wreaths. They've been so very popular that I think I only have one left."

Brooke carefully took down an exquisite wreath made from delicate snowflakes and handed it to Camden. "Here it is! Emma is making more of them, but I think it will be a few days before we are restocked."

"That is gorgeous!" Bailey gushed, reaching out to lightly feel one of the snowflakes. "Can you place one on hold for me, too? I love it."

"Sure!" Brooke said. "I need to start an order list anyway. I know you aren't the only person who will request one. I just wish I had more in stock going into this weekend."

Another customer stepped up to ask Brooke a question.

Before turning to lead the customer to a different display, she hurriedly addressed her brother. "Camden, Tylee can help you with that at the counter when you're ready. Bailey, I'll put your name at the top of the snowflake wreath order list for Emma."

Bailey turned around, wondering how much Camden would object if she looked around. She knew it would simply prolong the inevitable of going back outside in the cold, but the shop held so many things to see. On the other hand, maybe she should wait until after the website had some paying customers to do any shopping.

She reached out to touch a beautiful blown glass ornament hanging on a nearby Christmas tree. Bailey guessed the Christmas ornaments probably sold well all year long. Even though Christmas was passed, Bailey doubted Brooke had any intention of taking down all of the Christmas trees decoratively spread around the shop. Nor should she.

"Wasn't it right in this area?" a voice asked.

Camden scooted closer to Bailey to let the other two customers in for a better look.

"I thought so, but I don't see it right now. Oh, dear, I hope it isn't gone!" another voice said.

Bailey looked over to see a woman about her age holding the arm of a small, elderly woman with glasses.

"Oh, look! He has one!" the younger woman said, pointing to Camden. "Grandma, isn't that the one you liked? Sir, can you tell me where you got that snowflake wreath?"

Camden shifted back and forth, looking suddenly awkward. "Umm, well, I got it from right there, but I believe it is the last one."

"The owner did say that people could place an order for when she gets more in stock," Bailey added helpfully.

"Drat!" the younger woman's face fell with disappointment. "We are only here for the weekend. My grandma grew up here in Crossroads. With the winter festival, I thought it the perfect time to come with Grandma and have her tell me about when she was young. We saw the wreath earlier, and Grandma fell in love with it, but we didn't want to carry it while we finished looking around. I guess I should have bought it and had them hold it. It didn't occur to me that it might be the last one."

"It's okay, honey," the older woman said, patting her granddaughter's hand. "We'll find something else."

Despite her grandmother's words, the young woman looked close to tears.

"I believe the artist who made the wreath has other items in the shop as well," Bailey offered. "If you ask Brooke over there, I'm sure she'll be able to help you find something equally as nice."

"Thank you," the young woman murmured, turning to lead her grandma in Brooke's general direction.

"Are you ready to go?" Camden asked dully.

"Sure," Bailey replied. She didn't feel like browsing anymore anyway.

Camden led the way to the front counter, and Tylee rang up his purchase.

Out of the corner of her eye, Bailey saw the young woman and her grandma walking around some other displays, but they didn't seem overly interested in anything. She also hadn't noticed them seeking any direction from Brooke.

"Oh, Bailey, is that one of Camden's creations?" Brooke asked, passing by Bailey's outstretched palm. "Do you want me to box that up so your hand doesn't need to be the display pedestal for it?"

"Could you?" Bailey asked eagerly. "I know it's just a napkin, but I didn't want to crush it in my purse."

"No problem," Brooke said, gently taking the creation from Bailey's hand. "I know just what to do. I keep trying to convince Camden to turn some of his creations into Christmas ornaments or even frame them as artwork, but so far, I've struck out every time I've mentioned it."

Overhearing his sister's words, Camden frowned. "If a hobby becomes a business, it isn't a hobby anymore."

"Nonsense," Brooke disagreed. "It's still doing what you love. However, I understand. Computers are your first love. You don't want to commit to anything that might take you away from them, not even if it is your second love of origami."

"Not funny," Camden said shortly. "You go ahead and finish boxing that up for Bailey. I'll be right back."

Brooke carefully placed the napkin flower in a corsage case and padded it with tissue paper. Then she put it in a sack that could be easily carried on Bailey's wrist.

Curious as to where Camden had gone, Bailey turned around just in time to see him hand the elderly woman the freshly-boxed wreath. As if watching a pantomime, Bailey clearly read that both the older and younger woman objected, trying to return the wreath to Camden's arms. Camden refused, putting his hands up to avoid the package. Then he smiled and turned back to Bailey.

"Are you ready to go?" he asked Bailey, his empty hands finding the pockets of his jeans.

"Y-yes," Bailey stammered, too shocked to formulate coherent words.

Brooke gave Camden a goodbye hug, smiling as if she understood exactly what he had done. Then Bailey followed him out of the store with her own little sack riding on her wrist.

"Camden, what did you tell the woman and her grandma?" she finally managed halfway back to the car. "You just gave the wreath to them?"

Camden nodded. "I told them that they needed it more than I did and to enjoy it."

"But why?" Bailey asked, still aghast. "If you wanted to let them have it, why didn't you just give it to them before you paid for it? They should have reimbursed you."

Camden shot her a look of annoyance. "I didn't give it to them before because I didn't want them to pay for it. I wanted to pay and then bless them with it."

Bailey still felt completely mystified, and yet it seemed vitally important that she understand. She tugged at Camden's elbow, drawing him to a stop and forcing him to face her. "I don't understand. They had fully intended on paying for it. I don't get why you wanted to buy it for them."

Looking at her steadily, Camden explained, "Because I wanted to show them love. I wanted to do a random act of kindness for a stranger. I wanted to make their weekend memorable for both of them. I wanted to show them God's extravagant love by giving them something unexpected and doing it in an extravagant way. I wanted to be the reason for someone's joy tonight. I had the means and the ability to sacrifice for someone else, and wanted to do what God would want me to do."

Bailey's lips felt dry and cold, yet she insisted they vocalize her concerns. "But that wreath was for your mom's birthday! Didn't Israel tell you to get it for her? What are you going to tell him? You can't get another one by Sunday."

Camden shrugged and walked away a few paces, only to turn back around. "My mom will wholeheartedly agree with what I did. I'm sure knowing why she has to wait for her wreath will make it even more special. Israel is a different matter. He's never needed an excuse to be upset with me. I guess I'll help him out with an excuse this time."

Bailey just shook her head, mystified with what had just happened. She'd seen kindness before, but nothing like this. Camden didn't need to give that woman the wreath. In the long run, being without that wreath was far costlier to him than it was to her.

Maybe Bailey could help spin it to Israel to make Camden sound so very gallant for giving away the wreath. Maybe that would help smooth the waters a bit.

They continued walking, though this time, they were each so wrapped in thought, neither one of them hurried. Reaching a street corner across from where Camden's car waited in a lot, they stopped to watch a man working on some kind of ice sculpture. A bright spotlight illuminated the area as he worked chiseling details in a large block of ice. Bailey thought it was probably for the winter festival and had seen several others spaced along Crossroads' Main Street this evening. This sculpture was the only one currently in progress, though, and Bailey felt impressed by the artist's dedication in working so late.

"Why is it that Israel always seems angry with you?" Bailey found herself asking as they watched. She didn't know if it was appropriate to ask such a personal question, but she'd opened up earlier about her parents. Wasn't it Camden's turn? If she knew some of the background, maybe she could better help with the impending wreath issue.

At her question, Camden sighed, the sound loud in the still, cold air. His tone serious, he answered, "Bailey, I'm not sure I can condense a lifetime into a few paragraphs of explanation. I guess the short answer involves what happened after college. I studied computer engineering. By the time I graduated, Israel already held a high position in Dad's company and was well on his way to taking over. Israel expected me to join the company and take over all technology aspects. They made me a great offer and included a solid ladder for quickly taking over the title of Chief Technology Officer. I refused the offer. I admit I didn't give him any reasons, at least any that made any sense. My parents tried to be supportive, but they couldn't hide that I'd hurt them by my actions as well. It was the family company, and to them, I'm sure it seemed I'd rejected the family when I rejected the company. I took a job and at a company that, for all appearances, seemed a large step down from the family company. There are many more issues, but that one became the straw that broke the camel's back. My relationship with my older brother, and even my parents, has never been the same."

Bailey kept her eyes on the sculptor, not wanting to make Camden uncomfortable and cause him to clam back up. "Didn't they understand that you wanted to forge your own path?" Bailey asked with sympathy.

Camden shook his head. "They may have if I'd offered that as an explanation. But I didn't. Thanks for being understanding, Bailey, but the reality is that I didn't handle it well. I was young, and I guess that's my excuse. I didn't anticipate the hurt my actions caused. I hope I've gained a little wisdom along the way since then, but that doesn't help the irreparable damage I caused."

"It's not too late," Bailey said encouragingly, unable to resist turning to face him with an imploring gaze. "Have you and Israel ever talked about it? Maybe there's still room to make things right between you."

Camden shook his head. He didn't shy away from her gaze, and he didn't bother hiding the deep pain reflected in his eyes. "It's awfully hard to believe that when every little thing I do sets him off. I don't have any more explanation to offer him today than I did back then. Now, with everything that's happened with Marissa, there's no way I want to make mention of the past. Somehow, simply saying, 'I feel bad for the way you reacted to my decision,' doesn't seem like it would earn me any points."

"Is Marissa Israel's wife?" Bailey immediately asked. "I've wondered about what happened. Israel seems so sad, and I can see the sadness in Chloe as well. But I've been afraid to ask. What happened?"

Camden shook his head and turned back to watch the sculpture take shape. "I'm sorry, Bailey. They definitely have reason to be sad, but that's a question you'll need to ask Israel directly. It isn't my story to tell."

Bailey nodded in understanding, disappointed but somehow still admiring that he wouldn't tell her.

Camden smiled sadly, bumping her shoulder with his in an affectionate gesture. "It's okay, Bailey. I love my brother, but I guess every family has their own bit of dysfunction."

"Ha!" Bailey laughed shortly. "You have no idea how very fortunate you are. I'd take your brand of family dysfunction over mine any day!"

"I thought you said your parents remained friends after their divorce," Camden remembered.

"That didn't mean life was easy or drama-free!" The amusement left Bailey's voice, and her tone turned more serious. "Growing up, my time was split pretty equally with both of my parents, which they thought was the right and fair thing to do. As I mentioned before, both of them remarried and had more children. Because I was shuffled back and forth so much, I never really felt a part of either family. When I reached my teenage years, I realized I was the extra in each group. Neither family really needed me, and having me around often seemed to be an inconvenience, especially to my stepparents."

"You always felt like the outsider," Camden surmised.

"Yes," Bailey replied, glad that he seemed to understand. "Never feeling like you belong is a difficult thing to experience."

"Yes, it is," Camden agreed. "What about now that you're an adult? Have you finally found that belonging you craved when younger?"

Bailey held her silence, thinking as she focused on the sculpture. It was beginning to take shape, and she felt fairly certain that she could identify it as a gorgeous ice eagle with wings outstretched. No wonder the artist was working so late! The feathers likely took extreme detailing, and Bailey was tempted to move closer to look over his shoulder at the exquisite work.

"No, I can't say that I have," Bailey finally admitted quietly. "I'm sure it's just the residue from my childhood, but I've come to the conclusion that belonging is either extremely overrated, or else just a complete myth. Either way, it's not for me, and yet, I do fine without it."

Camden didn't say anything, and Bailey suddenly worried that she'd said too much. Guys didn't like it when girls got emotional or revealed personal thoughts, and she'd done both. He certainly hadn't pushed her into confiding. She'd just voluntarily spouted out her deepest struggle.

Bailey turned away from both Camden and the ice eagle, but before she could claim that she was cold and needed to get home, Camden's hand closed around her arm, and he gently turned her back around.

"Now it's my turn to say I'm sorry," he said softly, his eyes filled with compassion. "I know you say you're fine now, but I don't think not belonging becomes any easier for an adult versus a child. Adults are just better at hiding the hurt. We all want to belong, and when we don't, the hole in our hearts doesn't go away. I wish I could go back in time and make little Bailey know how valuable she is and how much she really does belong, even if she can't see it."

Bailey studied the strong lines of Camden's face, touched by his beautiful words. He was such an enigma to her. He was the type of man who forgot to pick up someone at the airport because he was too obsessed with his computer. He was the quirky guy who made origami kitties for his niece and was the highlight of her day. He was the confusing gentleman who paid for something just to give it away to someone who would never know the true, personal cost he paid.

Then she remembered the napkin flower tucked safely in her sack. It was such a beautiful piece of artistry from a man who, on the surface, saw life and love as a series of numbers to be interpreted with the right algorithm and an efficient computer program.

Somehow all of that was strangely appealing.

Then, when his blue eyes sparkled just like that...

"I have a boyfriend," Bailey said abruptly.

Camden startled, taking a step back from the hard edge of Bailey's voice.

For just a moment there, her brown eyes had softened, and Camden caught a glimpse of something so very alluring. She'd confided in him, and he'd hoped they might be making some progress in moving past all the anger and accusation their relationship had begun with. Then, with those razor-sharp words flung into the cold night, Bailey effectively slammed shut any door on a connection deeper than the next argument.

"Yes," Camden answered gruffly. "I'm very much aware that you have a boyfriend. It's what makes me off-limits for you. And you're not a Christian, which is what makes you off-limits for me. Neither of those means that we can't be friends, or at least treat each other with a decent amount of civility."

"What are you talking about?" Bailey protested. "Not that I'm not off-limits, but I already told you I'm a Christian. I really don't appreciate that you keep accusing me of something that isn't true. I'm a Christian. I believe in God. What more do you expect?"

"Bailey, I really don't mean to offend you," Camden said, putting both his palms up to face her. "I just think that you and I have different definitions of Christianity. What do you think it means to be a Christian? How did you become a Christian? What do you believe?"

Bailey rolled her eyes and looked like she'd rather do anything than answer his question. Finally, seeming to decide that she might as well stick it out, she responded, "Like I said, I believe in God. I even asked Jesus into my heart as a child. I believe Jesus died for my sins. I just don't believe the Bible should be taken as literally as some people seem to think. God and Jesus are about love. Love is the priority. In the Bible, they didn't have to deal with modern culture. We need to take the values that are in the Bible and apply that same love to how we handle things today."

None of this was a surprise to Camden. He'd suspected that Bailey felt this way, but hearing it from her lips felt a little daunting. He supposed he could simply back off and be content to finish watching the eagle emerge from the ice. However, he also felt that now was his chance. If he didn't take the opportunity now, he didn't know that he'd be given another one.

"You said you believe Jesus died for your sins," Camden said bravely. "What about the sins you are committing now?"

Bailey sighed. "I'm not as bad as some people, but I know I'm not perfect. I've made mistakes. I imagine Jesus died for those mistakes and all the things I did wrong."

"All of that is in the past tense. Do you not think you have anything to be forgiven for now?"

Bailey groaned, putting her fingers to her temples and rubbing as if she were getting a headache. "Just come out and say what you're trying to say, Camden."

Camden swallowed and forged onward. "You're living with your boyfriend. I believe that the Bible teaches that sexual relations outside of marriage are sinful."

Camden heard her sharp intake of breath at his blunt words.

"You think I'm not a Christian because I live with my boyfriend?" she asked incredulously.

Camden winced and hurried to explain. "No, that's not it at all, Bailey. Please understand. I'm not offering a commentary on the evils of couples living together before marriage, and I'm not judging the hearts and Christianity of those who do. My words are not to be painted in broad, general terms. I'm not talking about anyone else but you. You don't seem to prioritize God in any area of your life, and your actions are just symptoms of those priorities. Maybe I'm completely wrong about you, and if so, I apologize. But nothing about you tells me that you are wholeheartedly devoted to the God of the Bible. Please tell me differently. I'm certainly not perfect and manage to quite easily sin on a daily basis, but I do try to recognize sin for what it is. Even though it would be much more convenient to justify and label it differently, I try to go with God's opinion in such things and not mine, even if I don't particularly like His opinion."

Bailey turned swiftly and began walking, talking in staccato as Camden trailed along beside her. "Then you're definitely right, Camden. We don't share some of the same definitions. Like I said, I think the Bible needs to be interpreted through the lens of our modern culture. Marriage is a government institution. Dekker and I are in a loving and committed relationship. I believe that in God's view, we *are* married. We are not evil people. We are consenting adults and we aren't doing anything wrong. There is nothing inherently sinful about that."

Camden hurried around, getting in front of her so that he blocked her path, and she had to stop. Looking at her directly, unwavering in his conviction, he spoke, "A marriage is a legally binding contract, yes, but it is also a ceremony before God. You are making binding vows before God and sealing them with the legality of the government which you are under. It is an institution of value and not one to be taken lightly by saying that it doesn't really matter. Your lines drawing who God is are fuzzy. Mine are clear."

Bailey shook her head wearily and turned to go around him, her hand waving as if he were a pesky fly she was trying to dismiss entirely. "I guess we have a different view of just about everything then. Our views of love and marriage are different, and I don't believe I like your God much at all."

Bailey crossed the street to the parking lot while Camden remained at her elbow and persisted, "That's not really something you get to choose. God doesn't change with each person. If you aren't serving the one, true God, your version is just an idol. People don't get to choose who God is and what He looks like. God is."

Reaching the other side of the crosswalk, Bailey swung back around to face him, eyes blazing. "How do you know your idea of God is more accurate than mine? Maybe it doesn't even matter. We both believe in God. We both believe Jesus died on the cross. Isn't that enough?"

"No," Camden shook his head sadly, and his tone gentled. "You don't know God. He isn't in charge of your life. You know someone died, but you don't know who He is. God is personal. It matters to Him that you know who He is, serve Him, and let Him call the shots in your life. It matters that you love Him and want a relationship with Him that includes more than just viewing Him as the Santa Claus of Salvation."

Bailey looked at him with one skeptical eyebrow raised just a bit. "I think your view of God is a bit lower on the popularity scale than mine. I know lots of people who are Christians, but not many have such a narrow view as you."

"You're right," Camden admitted. "Our culture has heartily adopted a view of Christianity like yours, one that just takes what they like of God and leaves what they don't. Let me ask you something. If someone came up to you and said Elise Hutchins is a controlling busybody, would you agree with that?"

Bailey looked taken aback by his sudden change of subject. "Of course not! Elise is the sweetest person I know!"

This time, Camden led the way to the car. Casually, he shrugged. "What if this person told you that they'd met her. They know she makes matches for people without their consent. She meddles in people's lives. She's rude and pushy. She's also blonde and weighs over three hundred pounds."

Bailey laughed. "That's ridiculous! If someone said that, I'd tell them they obviously don't know Elise at all!"

"But they say they've met her," Camden insisted. "It's your word against theirs."

With the push of a button, Camden unlocked the car, but instead of opening the passenger side door for her, he turned to face her, leaning against the car and folding his arms across his chest.

"I'd ask them for proof," Bailey said, her tone conveying that she was rapidly tiring of this game and becoming annoyed. "I can at least show them a picture of what she really looks like."

"Wouldn't matter," Camden threw out, unrelenting. "They'd just say you're wrong. They'd met her and talked to her. They know her. Your perception of her wouldn't matter."

Standing upright, he stepped forward a little and pierced Bailey with an intense look. "Let me ask you this, Bailey. Does someone holding a different view of Elise change who she really is?"

"Of course not," Bailey scoffed. "Who cares what an idiot thinks? None of that changes the truth."

"Exactly," Camden said, his smile widening in triumph. "What you think of God doesn't change who He is. You might not even like everything about God. You might not like that He has very specific views on sin. That doesn't change Him at all. The challenge is to come to God on His terms. See your life the way He does, and then accept Him to both change you and transform your life with Him as the pilot. Bailey, you can't claim to be a follower of Christ if you don't know or accept who He is. That acceptance isn't simply an acknowledgment in your head to 'come into my heart.' That can definitely be part of it, but it can't be the whole story. To truly be a born-again Christian, one must allow God to come and take up residence, giving Him permission to change your heart. You cannot accept salvation without accepting the whole package. You don't get to pick and choose. 'Believe' is a verb. It is not a one-and-done-type thing. It is something you live every day of your life, believing that Jesus died for your sins of yesterday and the ones today, believing that God has the right to be boss of your life and that He is working to change you and accomplish His will, and believing that the same, exact faith that saved you is how God will help you finish the race and welcome you into eternity with Him."

Bailey fell silent for the stretch of several, long moments. Though she didn't raise her eyes to make contact, she finally asked, "Can we go home now?"

"Absolutely," Camden said, feeling awkward for the first time since the conversation started. He almost felt like he should apologize, but that was ridiculous. He didn't need to apologize for stating his beliefs, even if that made her feel awkward.

Bailey remained uncharacteristically quiet the entire way home while Camden relentlessly argued with himself, trying to talk himself out of the guilt and figure out what he should say to smooth the waters. He couldn't feel sorry for speaking the truth, but he probably didn't handle it well at all.

Back at his parents' house, Camden walked Bailey to the front door. "Bailey, I—"

"Camden, I appreciate and respect your views, but I think you're wrong," she said finally, her lips trembling. "The reason I think you're wrong has nothing to do with your reasoning or Bible scholarship. It's that I can't fathom the idea that you're right. If you are, then that means that a whole lot of people who think they're Christians really aren't. I can't believe God would do that."

"'Enter by the narrow gate. For the gate is wide and the way is easy that leads to destruction, and those who enter by it are many. For the gate is narrow and the way is hard that leads to life, and those who find it are few,'"

Camden quoted quietly. "That's Matthew 7:13-14. Sometimes God's ways don't seem quite fair when we look at them through our human eyes. That's where faith comes in. God is good, He loves us, and that never changes. Even if we can't understand the *why*, I believe we can know the Who."

"Goodnight, Camden," Bailey said simply, opening the door to the house.

"Goodnight, Bailey," Camden replied. "Please forgive me. I can't help but want you coming through the narrow gate with me."

Bailey didn't answer, shutting the door behind her. Fortunately, Camden knew that prayers could reach what his hands and words could not.

Lord, show Bailey the right gate.

Bailey paced the floor, mentally rehearsing what to say to Camden. She took deep breaths as she paced, trying to quell the anger boiling within, but today only added to the simmering fury from the other night. Though they both worked through the weekend on opposite sides of the office, they hadn't interacted much, allowing Bailey plenty of time to replay Camden's words about Christianity in her head over and over and providing ample fuel for them to fester.

By the time Monday morning rolled around, Bailey didn't need another excuse to be angry with Camden, but what she'd found upon logging onto the site had been enough to push her over the edge so that when the doorknob twisted, Bailey was fully prepared to unleash her wrath.

"Are you aware what you've done?" Bailey asked, her voice deceptively calm as Camden stepped into the room.

The pleasant, good-morning look on his face instantly died.

"Um... no. I guess I'm not. What did I do?"

"One of the dates set up by your precious algorithm completely flopped," Bailey informed him. "We just received the review, and it's terrible! I shouldn't need to tell you how important it is to get this right, especially at the beginning. Now we have dissatisfied customers. The date went so badly, I seriously doubt either of them will want to sign up for the service. Your stupid algorithm is going to kill the site before it even gets started. You should have listened to me in the first place. It was always a bad idea to let a computer make the matches without the human element. This proves it."

By the time Bailey finished speaking, she felt her face warm and her calm give way to dramatically deliver her words with the full emotion they deserved. She was angry, and Camden deserved the full force of that anger.

Camden reached back with one hand to rub his neck. "Can we redo this? Why don't I go out through the door, shut it, and come back in? That way, we can pretend this didn't happen, and you can try once again to explain to me the problem, this time without the insults."

"I'm not the one who set up a terrible date and put the website in jeopardy!" Bailey flung back, unwilling to allow even a tingle of remorse to creep into her fury.

Camden's lips tensed into a straight line. "Fine, show me the review, and I'll figure out what to do to fix it."

Camden logged onto his computer and let Bailey bring up the review.

Bailey watched as he read the review, swooping as soon as he finished. "See? I told you it was bad."

"Just give me a minute," Camden murmured clicking through a few screens. "Where is her review?"

"Well, she hasn't left one yet, but I'm sure it's coming. Obviously, the date was terrible."

"Not necessarily. Maybe from her perspective, it didn't go as badly as it did for him," Camden pointed out reasonably.

"How does that matter? If Drew Tanner starts talking to others about his horrible experience with Betwixt Two Hearts, then his dissatisfaction will spread like a virus, even without Kaylie's written review."

"Just let me check a few things before we pounce too hard on that panic button, Bailey," Camden murmured, continuing to click through windows on the screen.

With her arms crossed over her front, Bailey tapped her foot impatiently on the hardwood floor. Somehow, the staccato little beat relaxed her enough to wait. Though from the glares of annoyance Camden threw her way, he didn't find the sound nearly as comforting, and she didn't let any of his dirty looks cause her to miss a single step.

A couple of minutes later, he suddenly sat up straight. "Wait a minute. Hundreds of reviews have been posted, most of which were logged over the weekend. Bailey, did you even look at these other reviews? A lot of them are fabulous. A few of them are mediocre. Bailey, Drew Tanner's review of that one date is the only truly negative review in the lot!"

"Isn't that one more than enough?" Bailey retorted impatiently.

Camden made a few more clicks and then raised both arms triumphantly as if he'd just scored a touchdown. "Bailey, we have paying clients! Lots of them! Many of our clients seemed so happy with their free match that now they are paying for the site access!"

Bailey sighed dramatically, "Camden, that's great and all, but can you please focus on the problem at hand? We can celebrate later after this particular issue is addressed."

Camden turned to her, shaking his head. "Bailey, this isn't a problem. As much as I'd like us to be perfect, we are not immune to bad reviews. Of course, we will have them. It's to be expected. I just don't understand why you pick the one negative thing in a sea of positive."

"You screw up, and now you're lecturing me about how the cup really is half full?" Bailey asked, incredulous. "I don't think so! Own up to your mistake, Camden. It's time to make changes to the site before it's too late. We need to switch everything to the personal matchmaker option."

Camden looked at her like she was crazy. "Bailey, I never pretended that the algorithm could predict love with one-hundred percent accuracy. As you, yourself, have said, love requires a certain magical element that simply can't be predicted. I only ever say that the algorithm is highly accurate. The human element is one that no one, not even you, can control or predict. There are outliers on every bell curve. Just wait, the matches you made will have their own outliers as well. Looking at these numbers so far, the algorithm is performing much better than I anticipated!"

"Does that mean you aren't planning to do anything about these two clients and their bad date?" Bailey accused, placing her hands on her hips and glaring at him.

"No, not at all. Let me just click right here and right here... See? I anticipated bad date reviews when designing the site. If I simply click this little button here, then Drew will get an automated email apologizing that his experience didn't meet his expectations and offering a second match free of charge. When they respond to the email and accept the offer, then I'll send them a second name from his list."

"No," Bailey said sternly. "Move over. You are not going to send that man an automated email after his experience. I will send him a personal one myself. If he's getting a free match, then it will come from me, not the algorithm."

"Fine," Camden rolled his chair back and waved as if introducing the computer. "It's all yours. Find Drew his happily ever after."

Bailey sat down in Camden's chair and spent the next few minutes focusing on the profiles in front of her. She glanced through the algorithm-generated lists of matches and selected a few more profiles to view.

"This one is rather obvious," she finally declared, nodding at Drew's picture on the screen. Drew belongs with this woman right here."

Camden looked over her shoulder. "If you say so. Kaylie came back as a stronger match, but that obviously didn't work. We'll do it your way."

Bailey frowned. "The problem is that it looks like she is scheduled to receive our automated email saying there are no matches within her search radius. When Drew was matched with Kaylie, that took her out of the pool of candidates for other women, as per the free promo policies. I can't add him back in until I receive confirmation from him that he actually wants a new match."

"There isn't a whole lot you can do. Just send your personal email to Drew and hope that he responds quickly. If and when he does, contact the other woman and tell her a local match came open." Camden reached over her shoulder for the mouse. "I think I have an automated email for that exact situation. Let's see..."

Bailey swatted his hand away. "If I contact her, I'll do it personally. Not with one of your stupid emails."

"Fine, do it your way," Camden said, stepping away.

Bailey felt a twinge of guilt. She probably didn't need to use the word "stupid." She was so tired of Camden's computerized solutions that it was easy to be insulting, even when she didn't intend to.

Before Camden could change his mind and insist they handle things differently, Bailey typed out the email to Drew Tanner and pressed send.

Hopefully, he would get back to her soon, and she could work on setting up the other match.

"Now, what about Kaylie?" she asked, letting the cursor hover over the profile picture of the cute blonde. "Should I find another match for her as well?"

"No, let's wait on that," Camden said, returning to hover behind her shoulder. "She hasn't posted a review yet. When she does, she might change some of her parameters, which could potentially give us a few more options."

"Okay," Bailey agreed. She really wanted to just give Kaylie a call and talk to her directly, but she'd compromise with Camden on this one if only to show she wasn't as difficult to work with as Camden seemed to believe. "But I'll watch for the review to come in. As soon as it does, I'll contact her with the same offer of a personalized free match."

Camden hesitated. "Just so you know, Bailey, we can't do this for everyone who has a bad date. We can't please everyone, especially on the first try. The hope is that clients like our service enough that they want to try again, even if the first date didn't go as spectacular as they dreamed. I'm only willing to offer this single do-over because they are some of our first clients and because it seems like such a big deal to you. I don't intend to offer free matches as a general rule to future clients who post bad reviews."

So much for trying to be agreeable. She might as well throw caution to the wind and tell him what she really wanted.

"Knock it off, Camden," Bailey stood from the chair, glaring at him once again. "Stop pretending to be so gallant, like you're doing this for me. The reality is that you messed up. Even though you've managed a band-aid for this match, that doesn't change the fact that you have a larger problem. Your algorithm isn't as effective or meaningful as a human matchmaker. As you admitted, a computer can't predict love. This is my site, and I want it to be different. I need to have quality control over our product. Now that the free promo is over, I insist that we switch everything so that all matches are created by a personal matchmaker."

Camden's eye narrowed. With his voice calm but stern, he spoke. "Bailey, it's not just your site. It's my site, too. The algorithm works perfectly. Just look at all the positive date reviews. There is no problem. Like

I said in the beginning, providing a personal matchmaker for every match is unnecessary and unrealistic. And I refuse to do it."

"I know it won't be easy, but it's necessary," Bailey insisted, not dissuaded in the least. "We can't afford other reviews from bad matches, especially when I can choose a better match than the computer."

Camden ran both hands through his hair, his intense frustration obvious. "You sure have an awfully high opinion of yourself and your matchmaking abilities. A single date doesn't make one method a success and one a failure. I sincerely believe time will prove that the algorithm is a much better matchmaking tool than a woman sitting behind the screen playing eeny-meeny-miny-mo."

Bailey knew she should back off. In one part of her brain, she saw Camden and recognized his efforts to stay calm and treat her respectfully no matter what she threw at him. His control was slipping, and she knew she was to blame. However, she couldn't seem to stop herself. Something about him antagonized her, and she had the uncontrollable urge to locate his buttons and push them all simultaneously. Knowing that she was getting to him only gave her permission to needle him more.

"Ha!" she laughed mockingly, "Numbers spit out by a precious algorithm aren't romance. You know nothing about love. How can someone who has never experienced love or romance identify it for anyone else? You have no idea what you're looking for. That's like asking a blind man to paint a rainbow."

"I can be a better matchmaker than you any day," Camden retorted grimly.

Bailey just shook her head and answered in a singsong voice. "Your algorithm is no competition for a real matchmaker. Between romance and science, romance always wins."

"Is that a challenge?" Camden asked, cocking an eyebrow.

"I believe it is," Bailey answered confidently. "It isn't practical to wait until your algorithm does irreparable damage to our reputation and our site. I'm already tired of it. We need to settle this issue once and for all."

Bailey looked at him with sudden speculation, an idea slowly forming. "I know. How about we each set up three dates with our methods and see who is the most successful? Whoever loses agrees to let the winner decide how to structure the site using their method."

"A contest?" Camden's tone showed amusement and mild interest.

"Why not?" Bailey asked, liking the idea more and more as it formed in her mind. "We talked about wanting to figure out whose method works better. Why don't we make it official?"

Camden hesitated, and Bailey pounced.

"You seem so sure your algorithm works," she couldn't resist taunting. "Are you scared that you're wrong, and you'll lose?"

"Not at all," Camden flashed her a cockeyed grin. "Challenge accepted. Three dates, huh?"

A thrill shot through Bailey, quickly followed by a jolt of panic.

What have I done?

Despite her bravado, she didn't feel nearly as confident in her matchmaking abilities as she liked to pretend.

"Yes, three dates of your choosing," she confirmed, working to hide her true feelings. "You just need to choose the dates prior to the results. No cheating."

Camden dramatically rubbed his hands together in anticipation. "I guess we need to find our victims—er—beneficiaries."

Bailey ignored his confidence and sat down in her own chair to get to work. She hadn't anticipated Camden's eager response to the challenge, and it unnerved her.

Don't let it bother you, she coached herself. *It isn't really a question of if you'll win. It's just a matter of how long it will take Camden to lose!*

More than getting to set up the website her way or finding a couple their perfect match, she most anticipated proving Camden wrong.

"Camden, can I talk to you a minute?" Lydia asked, popping her head into the office.

Camden sighed. He didn't really have a minute to spare, but it just seemed wrong for a guy to refuse his mom's request to talk.

Shooting an uncertain glance at where Bailey worked at her own computer, he answered, "Sure. What's up?"

Hopefully, she didn't want to discuss anything personal. Maybe he should ask Bailey to leave. Nervously, he shot a glance to where Bailey worked at her desk across the no man's land of open hardwood floor.

Unfortunately, he already knew that asking her to leave would not be received well. But then, he couldn't say that Bailey received well anything he did.

"Do you want to talk in the kitchen or in here?" he asked finally.

"Oh, in here is fine," Lydia answered easily. "As long as our conversation doesn't disturb Bailey."

Bailey didn't look up from her computer, but offered, "It's no problem, Lydia. With you in here, that means Camden won't try to micromanage my every move. Trust me. Your voice is much more pleasant than his."

"You two aren't fighting again, are you?" Lydia asked sternly.

Suddenly, Camden felt very much like a little boy being scolded by his mom.

"I don't know that we're fighting 'again'," Camden hedged uncomfortably. "I think in order to fight again, you must first stop the previous fight. With Bailey, it's all just one big, long fight." He waved his arms in ever-increasing circles.

Lydia shook her head sadly, put her hands to her hips and looked disapprovingly at both Camden and Bailey. "I want to see each of you treating the other better. No excuse can justify days upon days of arguing."

Out of the corner of his eye, Camden chanced a glance at Bailey. Her sheepish expression and the fact that she couldn't meet Lydia's gaze confirmed that she also felt like a child caught misbehaving.

Camden swallowed with difficulty and bravely told his mom. "We're adults, Mom. We'll work things out."

Never mind they hadn't managed to work things out yet. Never mind they hadn't even spoken to each other since they'd agreed to a childish competition with control of the website as the prize. Never mind the tension in the office never dropped below DEFCON 1.

They *would* work it out. If for no other reason than his mother said so.

"What did you need to talk to me about, Mom?" Camden asked, hoping to shift the topic back to why she was here in the first place.

Lydia smiled easily, "I have a small favor to ask. Bailey, this actually includes you as well, now that I think about it."

Camden's eyes narrowed suspiciously. While normally, a "small favor" didn't sound alarming, one requested by his mom was potentially a different story. She'd usually just tell him what to do, politely, of course. Not following through was simply not an option. For example, before he left this evening, he could guarantee that his mom would pull him aside and instruct him to get along with Bailey. This asking for a favor was definitely cause for concern.

Bailey stood from her chair, eagerly giving her attention to Lydia. "How can we help?"

"My brother has a friend who signed up for your dating website. The poor man has a long history of being a very awkward dater, which is a shame because he's a lovely boy. Anyway, his sister, Selby, wants to help him out by finding him numerous dates in which to practice his skills, but she needs the list of dates, preferably prior to Heath receiving the list. Your Uncle Wayne passed your phone number along, Camden, and I think Selby is going to call and ask you directly. I just wanted you to know who she was so you'd be sure to grant her request."

Camden turned away and took his seat in front of his computer again. "I already spoke to her," he said matter-of-factly. "She called yesterday."

"She called, and you didn't tell me?" Bailey protested.

"What's to tell? I explained to Selby that I couldn't give her that information because it was against company policies. I told her 'no.'" Camden brought up his computer screen and began working again. In his mind, the issue was solved. He'd taken care of it, and they didn't need to be having this conversation at all.

"Camden Hutchins, you did what?" Lydia asked, steel in her voice. "That poor young lady was trying to help her brother, and you refused?"

Camden shut his eyes briefly, recognizing only too well his mother's tone. Sighing, he turned to face her directly. "I told her 'no,' Mom. I cannot share clients' information with a third party, no matter who he or she may be."

Lydia's eyes flashed incredulously. "Camden, this is entirely different than official company policies. Those are good to have for strangers, of course, but this is a family matter!"

Camden barely stifled a groan. He hated when his mom got like this. He really wished one of his siblings was around so he could tag them to deal with her and then take off running. "How exactly is it a family matter? I didn't think we were related to Selby and Heath."

"We aren't, but you are related to your Uncle Wayne," Lydia didn't miss a beat and explained as if Camden should have known all this without asking. "Wayne knows Reid, who knows Kelsey, who knows Selby. Of course, Selby heard that Betwixt Two Hearts is your company. Your uncle is so good about spreading family info like that. When Heath signed up, Selby got your info to contact you directly."

Camden rolled his eyes, which he really couldn't remember doing since his teenage years. However, in this case, it was entirely justifiable! "Mom, this is ridiculous. I can't break company policy. I just can't."

"I don't know," Bailey said, speaking up for the first time. "Doing a simple favor for a friend doesn't sound too bad. It isn't really breaking the rules, just bending them a little. Heath will still get the info from his list, as will anyone else who is matched with him. I don't see what the harm is or why it would matter if Selby received the info, too."

Lydia nodded eagerly, looking ready to disown Camden in favor of Bailey's immediate adoption. "What's the worst that's going to happen? If Heath is upset, he'll be upset with his sister, not you. Wayne will smooth any wrinkles if any come up. He's good at that sort of thing."

"No," Camden said firmly, tempted to stomp his foot for emphasis. "We simply cannot make an exception to the company policies. Selby understood when I explained things to her. I checked and found that Heath did register for the site. He created a very nice profile and paid for a single match generated by the algorithm. He hasn't yet been sent his info, but it should be going out this evening or tomorrow morning. I advised Selby to obtain any potential date names from her brother, not from me."

"A single date isn't enough," Bailey murmured as if doing mental math. "Five names would be better. Lydia, do you think five names are enough? Exactly how bad a dater is this guy?"

Lydia shook her head sadly. "I don't think even five is enough. From what Wayne describes, he needs lots and lots of practice. Smart, lovely boy, though. A strong Christian who loves God. He'll make a woman a wonderful husband."

Camden groaned. "How can he make someone a good husband if he has never earned a second date? That's another thing, are we really okay with setting multiple clients up with someone who is notoriously bad at dating? Bailey, just yesterday, you were complaining about a single bad date review. Now you want to purposely generate more of them by setting multiple women up on dates that are sure to fail?"

"Hmm," Bailey mused, seeming to completely ignore Camden. In fact, her eyes sparkled with excitement. "The more I think about it, the more this whole situation sounds like a great opportunity for our contest! Lydia thinks Selby needs more than just five names. What if I draft my own list of five names for Heath. That way, he'll have a list of five from the algorithm and five from a matchmaker. If he ends up with one of the ladies, then whoever recommended her is the winner!"

"What do you mean by 'end up with'?" Lydia asked hesitantly. "Finding him an actual girlfriend seems a little ambitious, especially since Selby just wants him to practice. What about if he just makes it to a second date with one of them? Could that work for your contest?"

"Oh, brother," Camden groaned, sinking into his chair and putting his hand to his head as a sudden headache exploded in his temple.

"Yes," Bailey said thoughtfully. "That should work. As long as there is a clear way of telling which list is the winner, then I think it would be perfect!"

Bailey's eyes suddenly flew wide. "I know! What if we put Eleanor from Milaca, Minnesota on Heath's list? Remember? She's a Christian. Her search radius wasn't big, but maybe Heath's is wide, and he could travel to her. Where does Heath live?"

"He's in Rockland," Lydia supplied. "But I think he'd need someone more local than Minnesota."

"That's too bad," Bailey said, sighing dramatically. "If only they were in the same area. I just have a feeling Eleanor and Heath would be perfect for each other!"

"No!" Camden vehemently protested, feeling like he was the only sane person in a mental institution. "No to Heath and Eleanor. And no to any other Machiavellian cupid plans in your head. We will not use this situation for our contest, nor will we break company policy for anyone or any reason!"

"This is a family matter, Camden," Lydia said with utmost seriousness. "You do anything in your power to help family. And this is very much within your power. With just a few little clicks, you can copy and paste Heath's list into an email to Selby and be done."

How am I losing this stupid argument? Camden thought, feeling he might see more success if he pounded his head against his computer screen.

Taking a deep breath, he spoke with a slow and exact tone as if talking to a disobedient child. "A family matter? Wayne, to Reid, to Kelsey, to Selby, to Heath? That's family?"

"Absolutely. Your uncle requested it. Your mother is asking you to do it as a favor to her. All to help a lovely boy. Camden, this is very much a family matter."

If she says, "lovely boy" one more time, I'm going to lose it!

Blowing his breath out in exasperation. Camden stood to his feet. He needed to end this, yet even the pictures of his siblings lining the wall seemed to glare at him in disapproval. This all felt so very familiar, and he hated it. The family business was a "family matter," and he'd refused that as well. Unfortunately, his answer to this ridiculous proposal was the exact same as it had been in the other matter, leaving Camden once again in the position of hurting his family because of something he felt strongly about.

He spied a few sheets of paper on the corner of his desk and had the absurd urge to pick one up and start folding. Maybe an origami puppy for Chloe could make all this yucky tension go away. Tension couldn't exist in the same room as origami puppies, right?

Instead, he ran his fingers through his already-rakish hair and pleaded. "Mom, please don't do this. I cannot grant Selby's request. I already told her 'no.' You don't need to get involved. Just let it be."

Camden's heart ached as he watched his mother's eyes fill with tears. Hoarsely she spoke, "Camden Hutchins, you are the most stubborn man I know. I don't know why I should be surprised that you refuse to put family first."

Turning around, she walked out of the office with her head held high and her shoulders shaking in accompaniment to her tears.

Bailey rushed out to follow her, and Camden slumped down in his chair, putting his head in his hands as they propped on his desk.

Once again, at least in his family's eyes, he was a disappointment and a complete failure. And all because Uncle Wayne's friend of a friend of a friend couldn't manage to get past a first date.

Bailey listened for the sound of Camden's engine as it drove away. It had taken longer for him to leave than she'd thought. He'd worked late, which wasn't unusual, but even after he announced he was going home and stepped out of the office, he hadn't actually left. Bailey suspected that either Lydia had stopped him again to continue her lecture, or John had caught him to add his two cents regarding his upset wife and Camden's culpability in the matter.

Either way, Bailey felt just a little bit sorry for Camden. She understood that he was simply following his convictions, and she respected that. However, she happened to think he was wrong and had no such entangling ethics to trip her up.

Now, with Camden out of the way, she didn't allow herself any time to analyze what she was doing, Bailey typed in the email address for Selby. Thankfully, she'd managed to extract the info from Lydia, who had procured it from the grapevine leading back to Selby herself. Camden would have never given it to her, and Lydia might not have either if she knew Bailey planned to go behind Camden's back. Thankfully, simply saying that she wanted to contact Selby directly had convinced Lydia to eagerly hand over the intel.

Now she quickly wrote a list in the email labeled "Matches chosen by a Matchmaker." She wrote down five names, inserting links to the Betwixt profiles for each. Thankfully, Camden hadn't realized what she'd spent the last couple hours working on.

She was helping Selby and doing the contest with or without Camden's consent. In this case, it was very much without.

Wanting the contest to be fair, she hadn't even looked at Heath's algorithm results but instead had started from scratch, compiling all of the profiles in Heath's area and meticulously searching for those who may be compatible. Now she gleefully typed the names into the email, knowing they were Heath's perfect fab five.

Then she used her administrator credentials to access Heath's survey results and Camden's algorithm-generated list. Without looking at the names, she copied and pasted the top five names generated by the algorithm into the email. Then she wrote a quick note to Selby, explaining who she was and that they—as in a general "they" that actually meant a singular Bailey—had decided to give her two lists of five names to help her brother. She hoped ten total names would be enough, wished Selby good luck, and asked her to follow up with Bailey to let her know how the matches worked out and if one particular list provided more compatible names than the other. Though tempted to say more, Bailey kept it simple and quickly pressed send without a hint of regret.

Like it or not, Camden had just submitted his first entry into their contest.

And Bailey could guarantee that he wouldn't like it at all.

Seven

"Are you ready to go?" Camden asked cheerfully.

"Go where?" Bailey murmured, not even blinking as she studied her computer screen.

"Go on our date," Camden supplied.

Bailey instantly jerked and swung around to look at him with eyes wide in sheer panic and her mouth gaping open in pure shock. The fear in her eyes only increased as she took in Camden's suit jacket and slacks.

At least I got her attention! Camden thought, though careful to mask his enjoyment of her reaction.

"Not a date between you and me," Camden clarified, granting her mercy with a quick explanation. "A date that was set up by our website. But we're still going. Together. To this other couple's date."

Bailey shook her head. "What are you talking about?"

"Aren't we doing the contest?" Camden asked, still enjoying toying with her. He knew he was being vague, and if doing so focused her attention on him, then he fully intended to string this out as long as possible. "I know we haven't talked about it much these past few days, but I assumed we were each working on our entries for the contest dates. It's Friday night, and I've officially chosen my first entry. Let's go!"

"I didn't intend that we physically observe the dates as part of the contest!" Bailey objected, her expression still incredulous. "I thought we were simply judging the dates by the results. Wait a minute, are you saying you found a local couple to match up?"

"Yes, I did! Well, local as in Brighton Falls. That's why we need to hurry. Our reservations are at six o'clock."

"You made reservations? For us?" Bailey asked, apparently unable to get past being completely dumbfounded by Camden's actions.

"Yes, I did!" Camden said excitedly, not bothered by her objections in the least. "Why wouldn't we go spy on a local date if I entered it into the contest? Doesn't that sound like a lot more fun than sitting in front of the computer for yet another night and waiting for the couple to leave a review? What if they don't leave a review right away, or even at all? This way, we can observe and know for sure that I won this round."

"Keep dreaming!" Bailey said, grabbing her purse.

Thoroughly convinced that he'd just played his cards perfectly, Camden smiled and opened the door for Bailey to stride haughtily past.

Please help this to go well, Lord! Camden prayed, trusting that God would know he wasn't actually praying for the success of his part of the contest.

The past few days had been difficult for Camden, and not because of the crazy workload. For better or worse, the number of new sign-ups did not drop significantly after the free promotion. The site had gone viral, and the number of new clients continued to increase at a hectic rate. Unfortunately for Bailey's workload, many people seemed fascinated by the idea of a personal matchmaker, and many of those eagerly forked over the increased member fees in order to retain those services. Bailey had barely stopped to eat and was certainly not getting enough rest to continue functioning at such a pace for any length of time.

The day after their big fight about the bad date review and Selby's request, guilt caught up to Camden. However, he didn't feel convicted about what he said or did. Instead, he felt ashamed of his attitude and realized he was not treating Bailey as he should.

While Bailey professed to be a Christian, from Camden's perspective, she quite obviously was not. Nor did she have any idea what a true Christian was. He now wondered whether God had placed him in this situation for a reason. If that reason was to show Bailey what real love and Christianity looked like, then he'd failed miserably. While not interested in

Bailey romantically, his actions hadn't shown her the Biblical definition of any kind of love. In fact, Camden couldn't recall any interaction where he'd behaved especially patient or kind, and as the rest of 1 Corinthians 13 played through his mind, he realized there was not a single aspect of any of the description that he had demonstrated to his coworker. In fact, he'd done quite the opposite.

Over the past few days, Camden deliberately tried to back off and antagonize Bailey less. He'd also tried to do nice things for her, like bringing her coffee and look for ways to go out of his way to show her love. It wasn't always easy, and she seemed to frequently bait him into an argument. He was still honest with her, and if something were important, he wouldn't back down.

Earlier that day, he'd seen how exhausted Bailey was, and yet she still doggedly worked in front of her computer, matching up people she'd never met and hoping that with each match, she'd united a pair of soul mates. Her pale face and dark-rimmed eyes told of the work's toll, and Camden knew he must find a way to make her take a break. Suspecting that she would never consent, especially if he suggested it, he realized he'd need to be sneaky.

That's when he'd logged onto the website control panel and located a date that had been scheduled nearby. The couple wasn't special in any other way other than that they were convenient for Camden's purpose. He hadn't even bothered looking closely at their profiles except to confirm that they had been automatically matched by Camden's algorithm. Without giving himself time to think, Camden quickly booked a matching reservation at the restaurant the couple listed as their meeting place in the schedule feature of the website.

"So, who is your chosen couple?" Bailey asked as soon as they were in the car and on the road to Brighton Falls.

Camden hesitated, not wanting to admit that he actually knew nothing about this couple. "Why don't you look their profiles up yourself? It's probably easier than having me interpret everything for you."

"Fine. I will," Bailey said, taking out her phone. "What are their names?"

Camden scrambled to remember, eventually retrieving, "Trevor

Clauson and Jacee. I think it was Traveler, or something like that."

"Jacee Travers?" Bailey asked a couple minutes later.

"Yes, that's her," Camden said in relief. "I really don't know that much about them," he finally admitted. "The algorithm showed that they were a very high match. Unusually so."

"I see that," Bailey said, her voice tight.

"You say that like you don't agree," Camden said cautiously.

"Of course, I don't," Bailey shot back. "They are too similar. Looking at the questions on the survey, they answered nearly everything identically, even the questions you like to see answered differently. They are virtually the same person. I guess all that is good news for me, though. I'm going to win this round of the contest without even trying."

Camden felt slightly sick. Maybe he should have looked closer at the couple. The algorithm would place a higher degree of compatibility with matching a person who was an extreme introvert with someone who was closer to the middle of the scale. If they had answered the same, then the scenario existed that they would still appear a highly compatible match with just not receiving full points in some of those vitally important areas where differences should exist.

"It will be a good match," Camden insisted stubbornly, not admitting his sudden case of nerves. "No two people are *that* similar."

"We'll see," Bailey said, smiling sweetly.

Love is patient and kind... It does not insist on its own way.... It is not irritable or resentful... Camden recited the verses over in his head several times, battling the urge to return Bailey's attitude with a snide comment of his own.

They arrived at the restaurant and quickly bypassed the line to retrieve their reservation. After being seated, they were handed menus. However, as soon as the waitress left, both Camden and Bailey dropped pretending interest in the menus and looked around eagerly.

"Do you see them?" Camden whispered.

"Right there," Bailey responded, nodding covertly to a couple seated in one of the booths directly across from them.

Sure enough, the couple looked vaguely familiar as Camden tried to mentally match them with the profile pictures he'd glanced at. They really couldn't have asked for better spectator seats. Their position at a table in the center of the room gave them an unobstructed view of the couples sitting in booths along the wall. The only thing Camden would change is that he wished their positions were swapped. Even watching unobtrusively felt conspicuous when attempting to conduct your spying operation from the exposed middle of a fancy restaurant.

"It's kind of a fancy place for a first date," Camden observed, looking around the tastefully decorated restaurant. He'd anticipated it being a nice place, especially with the need for reservations. He'd even dressed accordingly, trading his usual shorts for a pair of nice pants and even a suit jacket atop a more casual collarless blue shirt.

"I don't know," Bailey said. "I think it's kind of nice. I like the romantic atmosphere."

Of course, she does, Camden thought with a touch of humor. *She'd disagree no matter what I said. It's just on the principle of being disagreeable.*

Fortunately, Bailey always looked nice, wearing dresses and stylish outfits as if working at a high-class business office and not just his parents' house. Donned in a dress that was somewhere between orange and red, Bailey looked like she belonged here in an atmosphere that was, as she put it, "romantic." Being fair, Camden had to admit that the twinkle lights strung in just the right places created an almost magical lighting that made the startlingly white tablecloths gleam and the high-quality glass and china glisten.

Camden and Bailey eventually turned their attention back to the menus long enough to order, but as they waited for their food, they didn't converse with each other at all. Instead, all of their focus stayed glued to the couple across from them. Unfortunately, Camden soon realized that watching another couple speak and eat did not make for thrilling entertainment, especially when you weren't seated close enough to hear or interact with them.

Camden's glances Bailey's way grew more frequent, noting that she still seemed highly engrossed in the scene before them.

"It looks like it's going well," Camden finally said softly. Any conversation would be better than watching a pantomime.

"It's not," Bailey said flatly, her focus still on the mind-numbing scene she apparently found highly engrossing.

"What do you mean?" Camden asked incredulously. "They've been talking nonstop!"

"They are both bored out of their minds," Bailey explained.

I can relate, Camden thought ironically.

Completely oblivious, Bailey continued, "They talk, but do you notice that they're not looking directly at each other? They look at their food or at the waitresses or other people in the restaurant, but not at each other. They aren't happy. Their eyes aren't sparkling. Their bodies aren't turned toward each other, eagerly hanging on every word the other speaks. They aren't excited in any way about being here. Instead, they are simply passing the time until they can finish their meal and be done."

Camden watched a few minutes, noting the accuracy of every one of Bailey's observations, but doubting her interpretation.

Camden and Bailey's food arrived, momentarily distracting Camden as he began eating his seafood platter of shrimp and lobster. A few minutes later, he looked back up to check on Trevor and Jacee, and his heart sank.

Something wasn't right. Jacee seemed to be studiously rearranging her silverware and Trevor attempted a subtle check of the time on his watch. As Bailey's words replayed through his mind, he suddenly realized the missing element. Smiling. Neither one of them were smiling.

Bailey is right.

"How are your shrimp?" Bailey asked, saying something conversationally for the first time that evening.

Camden shrugged. "They are okay. Scampi isn't my favorite. I prefer fried. How is your steak?" he asked, attempting to return the polite conversation ball to her court.

The corners of Bailey's mouth turned down distastefully. "It's okay. I'm not a big fan of the seasoning rub they've used. It has a little too much pepper in it."

Camden's gaze went from Bailey's delicious-looking steak to his own plate and back again. "Bailey, do you like shrimp scampi and lobster tail?"

Bailey nodded. "I do. I just wasn't sure about ordering it here since they don't technically specialize in seafood."

"It's actually pretty good," Camden said. Then, with sudden

inspiration, he continued. "Hey, the more I think about it, the more I realize I'm in more of a steak mood tonight, and I don't mind spicy pepper at all. Do you want to trade?"

Bailey's eyes brightened, and a slow smile dawned. "I'd love to trade, if you don't mind."

"Nope, not at all." Camden eagerly switched her plate with his, pierced a bite of steak, and popped it in his mouth appreciatively. "Mmmm, that's better. I think that's a much better match."

Bailey suddenly paused with her second bite on the way to her mouth. "Better match?" she murmured. Then she dropped her fork to her plate and swung back around to the booths on the wall.

Camden followed her gaze, realizing that Trevor and Jacee were finishing up their date. Their plates were crowned with their napkins, clearly announcing their status as finished and waiting for the waitress to come by and retrieve them. Jacee even had her purse slung over her shoulder, clearly eager for the waitress to come with their check and release her to make a quick exit without a backward glance.

Bailey hopped up from her seat and headed across the uncharted territory, weaving through the tables and chairs between their table and the wall. However, instead of approaching Trevor and Jacee's table, she walked up to a couple who was clearly just leaving and standing up from a booth a few down from the other one.

Stunned by her actions, Camden watched as Bailey spoke to this mystery couple and then motioned them to follow her. She led them to the other booth where Trevor and Jacee awaited the waitress's return with a credit card.

After a smiling Bailey spoke excitedly for a few moments, something amazing happened.

Jacee sat back down in her chair, and a man sat in the chair across from her. But it wasn't Trevor. Instead, it was the other woman's date. Then Bailey led the way back over to the other booth and happily deposited Trevor and the other woman into it.

She'd just performed a seamless date-swap.

On her way back across the minefield to their own table, Bailey stopped the waitress and said a few words before sliding back into her seat across from Camden and picking up her fork to eat as if nothing happened.

"What just happened?" Camden asked expectantly.

"I just saved two dates for the website and proved that I'm a better matchmaker than you," she said, smiling before popping a bite of shrimp into her mouth.

"You switched the dates?" Camden asked, annoyed that she simply wouldn't explain. "You chose another random couple and flip-flopped the dates? Exactly how is that proving you're a better matchmaker?"

"The other couple wasn't random," Bailey said, her face expressive in its excitement. "They are Betwixt clients as well. I recognized them because I'd reviewed their profiles. They were a couple that was also matched by your algorithm, but I had checked them out when seeking matches for my matchmaker clients. After all, now that the free promo is over, paid clients are eligible to be matched with others even after they receive their own match. After I recognized them and realized they were also on a Betwixt date that just hadn't been formally scheduled on the site, I started watching them as well. Unfortunately, they weren't faring much better than Trevor and Jacee."

"If you knew they were Betwixt clients, why didn't you tell me?" Camden asked, unable to keep the irritation from his voice.

"I was trying to be nice," Bailey answered simply.

"You? Nice to me?" Camden raised a brow skeptically. "That's a first."

Bailey rolled her eyes. "Yes, I was trying to be nice. Clearly, your algorithm is lousy. I didn't think it would help to point out that it had screwed up two dates in one evening and not simply one."

Camden scowled. "I suppose this other couple was bored, too?"

Bailey shook her head. "No, not at all. But they clearly annoyed each other. In this case, the discrepancies are too much in all the wrong areas. Susie thinks Darrin is an idiot. He's a lot more adventurous than she is, and she likes the kind of adventure that's safe behind a white-picket fence. She thinks he's a thrill-seeker, and he thinks she's boring."

"You got all of that from reading their profiles and watching them eat dinner?" Camden asked, not sure if he felt skeptical or impressed.

Bailey shrugged. "Some things are obvious. Susie barely managed not to roll her eyes every time Darrin spoke, and Darrin kept checking his phone. Your algorithm got it right that there were discrepancies in the personalities and preferences, even though they both seem to share the same core values, but it got it wrong that the discrepancies would be appreciated by this particular couple."

"So, you thought you could switch the couples like we switched our plates and have equal success?"

Bailey smiled confidently. "Yes. Yes, I did. Jacee will be a better match for Darrin. She's introverted and shy, but she longs to be more adventurous than she is. Trevor is a better match for Susie because he's more of a traditional kind of guy who would appreciate Susie's no-nonsense dependability."

Camden looked over at the couples, secretly hoping to see that Bailey's new dates were crashing and burning. Unfortunately, that was not the case. As they enjoyed dessert, each of the four people eagerly hung on his or her date's every word.

And all were smiling.

"So, what did you do?" Camden questioned irritably. "Did you simply march up to them and announce that they belonged with someone else and that you'd like to introduce that someone right now?"

"Pretty much," Bailey said, seeming to enjoy Camden's obvious irritation. "I explained that I was a matchmaker for the Betwixt Two Hearts website. I asked if they were on a date set up by the website and told them that I recognized them from their profiles that I reviewed. Then I said that if they didn't mind experimenting with something strange, I'd like to ask them to swap dates with another couple for dessert, just for fun. We'd do our own little speed dating version, just for tonight, and I really thought these other clients would make for great matches."

"Here you go!" their waitress said brightly, handing Camden the check for their dinner.

"Thanks," Camden accepted the bill and glanced at it. "Wait a minute, there are a bunch of desserts on this. We didn—"

"I did!" Bailey said, snatching the bill from Camden's hand. She then handed her credit card to the waitress before Camden could recover from his shock.

"What?" Bailey said in response to Camden's look of accusation. "It was the least you could do. After all, you screwed up their dates. I told them that the website would treat them all to dessert."

"What do you mean, it was the least I could do?" Camden paused, a sudden light of suspicion flickering in his gaze. "Wait a minute, was that my credit card?"

Bailey smiled sweetly.

"Bailey, where did you get my credit card?"

"From your wallet."

"Where did you get my wallet?" Camden fumbled around all of his back pockets, searching but found no familiar wallet-shaped bump.

Bailey extended the wallet across the table, offering it back. She quirked an eyebrow. "Call it a business expense. It really was the least you could do."

Camden snatched the wallet back and shoved it into his suit jacket pocket. Only has hand went further than it was supposed to, the wallet extending out the bottom and into the open air.

"Problem?" Bailey asked innocently. "My guess is that suit jacket is pretty old and doesn't get worn that often. Otherwise, you'd know there is a massive hole in the bottom of one of your pockets. When you moved to switch our plates, your wallet fell under the table and hit my foot. It was like providence telling me I needed to use it to fix those poor mismatched couples."

"None of my shorts have holes," Camden grumbled.

Bailey laughed. "I bet they don't!"

The waitress brought back his receipt.

After signing it, Camden stood to leave. "At least it looks like it was put to good use," he said, looking at the two happy couples so engrossed in each other that they didn't even notice their departure.

"Very good use," Bailey agreed. "Your money just saved the website some bad reviews, matched two happy couples, and helped me beat you with winning two points in our competition."

"Two points? Trevor and Jacee were my chosen couple. I'll give you credit for them, but not any more than that."

"Nope. I get two points for sure. I made two matches. I took your one bad match and made two wonderful matches out of it. I'm magical. I deserve both points."

Camden looked at her in amusement as he held open the restaurant door for her to pass through. He may have made two bad matches, courtesy of his algorithm. He might have just dropped a load of money to fix those matches and use Bailey's silly competition as a ruse to get her out of the house. He may have lost to Bailey by two points, just on this round. But somehow, those sparkles dancing in Bailey's eyes made him firmly believe he'd just maneuvered a very good deal.

Bailey's phone lit up with the incoming call, and she quickly snatched it up. "Hi, stranger!" she answered teasingly.

"Hi," the tired voice greeted on the other end. "I saw I missed your call last night."

Out of the corner of her eye, she saw Camden look at her sharply, get up and immediately leave the office. She didn't know what his problem was. They'd actually gotten along well for the past week, and yet every time she mentioned or took a call from her boyfriend, Camden acted irritated and usually just left.

Maybe he just didn't want to be disturbed by her side of the conversation while trying to work. Not that Bailey really cared. It was a Sunday, after all. Camden had just popped his head in the office for a few minutes while he waited for his mom to be ready for church. With his dad out of town, Camden had offered to be his mom's escort to church this morning.

"Yes, I tried to call. Several times actually," Bailey said to Dekker, careful to keep any reproach from her voice. While she had been bothered that her boyfriend hadn't at least texted her to say he wasn't available for a call, they had never had a relationship requiring them to check in with each other. Hinting at any hurt feelings because Dekker wasn't at her beck and call would not be received well.

"Yeah, we decided on Friday night to make a quick trip down to Vegas." Dekker's dull voice mumbled, slurring the words in a way that made them difficult to understand. "We got back early this morning."

Immediate questions raised their hands high in Bailey's mind. Who was "we"? What did "we" do in Las Vegas?

Dekker continued, "I haven't slept yet, but I wanted to call you first."

At his last phrase, Bailey's question vaporized. "That's thoughtful of you," Bailey said, somewhat surprised.

"Yeah, I didn't want you to try to call and wake me up after I went to sleep."

"Oh," Bailey said, realizing he hadn't been considerate of her after all. "Well, did you have a nice time in Vegas? What did you do?"

Dekker wasn't exactly the type to enjoy a good conversation, but she hadn't seen him in almost a month. Though they talked on the phone, Dekker always seemed eager to put in his phone call duty and be done and off on another adventure, and Bailey couldn't really blame him for that. Dekker's adventurous personality was one of the things she loved about him.

Trekking off to Vegas for an impromptu getaway was not unusual for him. He had a pilot's license, his own plane, and money to burn, which left the world at his fingertips. Though Vegas didn't top her list of fun destinations, she did enjoy the romance of Dekker suddenly deciding to take her to a fancy restaurant in Portland or even Vancouver, British Columbia. All told, his good qualities far outweighed his lack of communication, making Bailey feel so very proud that he'd chosen her.

"Vegas was a blast," Dekker reported, a sliver of life returning to his voice for the first time. "You should have been there. If you hadn't decided to take off on this stupid website scheme of yours, you could have been."

Bailey gritted her teeth. Maybe he was just overly tired and irritable, but would it kill him to at least pretend to be supportive every once in a while? "If I had known you were going to Vegas, maybe I could have joined you there. I can't exactly read your mind, especially when there is zero communication."

Dekker didn't need to know Bailey wouldn't have met him in Vegas even if she'd wanted to. She just didn't have the time or money, and she certainly would never allow him to pay for it. The point was that he didn't bother telling her anything. If he expected a better relationship, he needed to put some amount of effort into it.

"Look, Bailey," Dekker groaned. "I'm really tired. Can I just go to bed, and I'll catch you when I can see straight?"

"I need to be going anyway," Bailey said brusquely. "I have a date with Camden. We'll need to leave soon."

"You have a date with Camden?" Dekker's voice suddenly sounded more alert than it had been the entire conversation.

"No. Not really a date," Bailey rushed to explain, realizing she'd misspoken. "I'm going with Camden to observe one of the dates set up by the website. That's what I meant."

"You're going to spy on another couple's date?"

"Kind of," Bailey hedged evasively, annoyed that the man who'd just enjoyed himself in Vegas seemed to be taking issue with her innocuous chosen activity. "I know you're tired, so I won't keep you. I'd just like to reserve some time in your busy schedule to talk to my boyfriend."

"None of this is my fault, Bailey," Dekker snapped, apparently still very alert. "If you don't like it, just catch the next flight to Seattle, and you can come back home and see me in person."

Great. And now we're back to this. Would it kill him to be just a little bit supportive?

She knew from previous experience that it would do absolutely no good to explain to Dekker yet again about how this business venture was important to her and why working for him as a secretary in his company wasn't something she would ever consider doing as an alternative.

"I know this hasn't been easy," she said, choosing to be encouraging. "But I'll be back to visit in a few more weeks."

"Yeah, when is that? I know you told me, but I don't remember."

"Valentine's Day weekend. I fly in on Valentine's Day, and then I get to stay through the weekend and leave Sunday night."

"Okay, I'll make sure there's room for one more with whatever I have planned for that weekend."

"Okay," Bailey said slowly, not sure she liked the sound of that. She wanted to spend time with Dekker and do things together. Tagging along for his usual extreme adventures didn't sound like the romantic weekend she had in mind.

Before she could mention her reservations, the office door opened, and Camden stuck his head in to wave goodbye.

"I'll let you get some rest," Bailey told Dekker quickly. "Why don't you give me a call after you wake up? We can talk more then."

Without waiting for a response, she ended the call, grabbed her purse, and jumped from her chair to chase after Camden.

"Hey, Camden!" she called down the hallway. "Is it time to leave for church?"

Camden turned around and nodded. "Mom is already in the car. I just wanted to let you know we were leaving. I didn't mean to interrupt your call."

"Let me grab my coat, and I'll meet you in the car," Bailey said, hurrying to retrieve her coat from the hall closet.

Confusion clouded Camden's face. "You know we're going to church, right? Do you need me to drop you off somewhere?"

Bailey shrugged her coat on and beat Camden to the door. "Yes, church. I thought I'd go with you this morning. Why do you look so surprised? It's not like I'm a heathen. I've been to church before, even if I don't go as regularly as you."

Camden didn't say a word but followed her to the car and held open the door to let Bailey slide into the back seat behind a beaming Lydia.

Lydia kept up a steady, one-sided conversation all the way to church, which was good. That meant Bailey and Camden didn't need to pretend a semblance of a polite dialogue.

Camden let the ladies out close to the church before parking, and Bailey kept hold of Lydia as they traversed the potentially icy sidewalks and into the sanctuary.

The church wasn't large by any city standards. Instead of pews, the sanctuary was lined with rows of dark green, cushioned chairs that hooked together into long strips. A center seating area was flanked by two aisles and more seating on either side.

Lydia let Bailey choose where they sat, and Bailey was grateful. She carefully studied those already seated in the congregation. With relief, she found just the right spot in the center about three-quarters of the way back, and they were in their seats before Camden could arrive to protest.

He slid into the seat next to Bailey, and she suddenly wished that she'd sat on the other side of Lydia. With the seats hooked together, Camden's arm brushed her arm, sending spider-web tingles spreading from the contact. Why did it bother her so much to be close to Camden? It was like his presence created some kind electrical field that made her highly uncomfortable if she got within that zone.

As the service started, Bailey tried to ignore the discomfort. She heard the music and stood in all the right places, but her focus remained elsewhere. More specifically, her gaze took in every movement of the couple two rows in front of where they sat.

"Who are you looking at?" Camden's voice whispered in her ear. His warm breath against her hair and neck sent shivers down the length of her body.

Bailey shot an irritated glare his way, snatched up her church program, and jotted a few words on it.

Couple two rows down, she wrote before passing the bulletin to Camden.

Camden read her words and jotted back one word, *Why?*

Bailey wrote again, then proudly showed Camden. *My choice for the contest.*

Camden frantically scratched letters on the paper. *You set up a date at CHURCH???*

"It isn't really a date," Bailey hissed back. They'd run out of room in the margin of the program, and she couldn't really explain herself with such limited space anyway. "I just emailed them and suggested church might be a great way to casually meet."

Camden stopped talking, but she felt the tension like rubber bands tightly winding every muscle in his body.

The words of the sermon flowed around her, but none of them brought any meaning. Her focus was instead divided between a thorough observation of the two people in front of her and an intense awareness of Camden beside her.

About halfway through the sermon, Bailey felt Camden tug insistently on the sleeve of her cardigan. When she looked at him with irritation, he nodded his head to the side, clearly indicating that he wanted her to follow him. Though she didn't want to leave, she also didn't want to cause a scene.

When Camden stood and made his way down the aisle to the back of the church, Bailey followed.

"What?" Bailey asked, already exasperated when Camden swung around after reaching the foyer area.

"Are both those people out there Christians?" he asked tersely.

"Of course," Bailey answered. "Why do you even ask?"

Camden pointed back to the sanctuary. "The woman just took out a tissue and looks to be crying. The man looks extremely uncomfortable and keeps squirming in his seat as if he doesn't quite know what to do. Haven't you noticed?"

Bailey's forehead puckered in uncertainty. "I thought that it was just a good sermon."

Camden laughed and took out his phone. "What are their names, Bailey?"

"Gage Anderson and Sasha Meeker," Bailey replied, her eyes still on the sanctuary as if she could see the couple's movements from this distance.

A few minutes later, Camden groaned. "Bailey, he's a devout Christian, and she's a Christian in name only."

"What? How do you know that? It doesn't say that!"

"You have to read between the lines. Gage is a Christian who attends church at least once a week. He lists someone who shares his faith as a top priority. He recently moved to Crossroads, so I haven't yet met him, but I do recall that this isn't his first visit to the church. Sasha listed Christianity as her faith, but she indicates church attendance as only occasionally and doesn't place a high priority on finding someone with a similar faith. Taking all of that into consideration, Gage and Sasha aren't compatible at all."

Bailey shook her head. "She can't be that incompatible. She lives in Brighton Falls, but when I emailed both of them about the possibility of attending church together, she seemed eager, even with the drive."

"Bailey, did you look at their algorithm scores? They aren't compatible spiritually, but it's more than that. The numbers show they aren't a good match on other issues as well. I don't even think they will like each other much."

"You're definitely entitled to your opinion," Bailey said stiffly. "I saw their differences but thought them just enough to light a spark. On the appearance side, they make a striking couple."

Camden groaned again. "Physical appearance and attraction don't matter if you can't stand who a person is!"

"Like I said, we'll just have to see." Before Camden could protest, Bailey pushed the door and slipped back into the sanctuary to find her seat once again.

The rest of the sermon passed quickly, and unfortunately, quite painfully. After Camden's interpretation, Bailey now keenly noticed Sasha repeatedly dabbing her eyes with a crumpled tissue while Gage shot her helpless looks of concern and shifted uncomfortably as if his chair were situated on constantly shifting roller skates.

No matter how she looked at it, Bailey couldn't shake the reality that Camden was right.

She'd made a horrible match. Her mind sifted through different possibilities for how she could salvage the situation, but every potential solution reflected badly on both her and the website.

They stood for the final prayer and song. Despite sitting through the entire service, Bailey couldn't recite a single thing that was said, let alone remark on the spiritual significance of the message.

The second the pastor dismissed the congregation, Camden turned to Bailey with eyes blazing. "Stay here with Mom. Don't move. Don't try to fix anything. Just stay."

Without waiting for a reply, Camden made a beeline across the sanctuary. Following him with her eyes, Bailey saw him heading to where his sisters sat at the back. Bailey hadn't noticed them before and figured they must have snuck in late after the other seats were occupied.

Lydia busied herself speaking to some friends, and didn't seem to notice Camden's exit and Bailey's preoccupation.

Bailey looked back to Gage and Sasha, seriously considering whether she should just walk up, introduce herself, and apologize. She wished there was something she could do to fix it. Gage and Sasha still sat in their seats talking, but judging by the frequent use of Sasha's tired tissue, she couldn't manage to stop crying. Gage awkwardly patted her back, looking like sitting in a dentist's chair would be preferable to his current task.

Just as she decided she just couldn't take it anymore and stepped forward to talk to them, two women approached the couple from either side of their row.

With a start, Bailey realized that the women were Camden's sisters! Geneva immediately approached Gage, and Brooke sat next to Sasha. Gage stood to meet Geneva, his expression one of pure relief at the welcome interruption. Sasha's face remained turned away from Bailey, but she did see the woman melt into Brooke's arms as they quickly came around her in comfort.

"Let's go," Camden said, appearing again at her side. Bailey blinked and looked around to see Lydia had already left and was making her way up the aisle to the doors at the back.

"Shouldn't we do something?" Bailey asked, extending a hand to Gage and Sasha before letting it drop helplessly.

"No, Geneva and Brooke will take care of it."

After making it to the back of the church, Lydia introduced her to several people, and Bailey managed to smile in all the right places. They eventually made it to the car and drove home. Though Camden kept up a conversation with his mom, Bailey remained silent, berating herself over the unfortunate match and analyzing what she could have done differently.

Bailey helped Lydia prepare a quick lunch of sandwiches while Camden set the table. They had just sat down to the table and said a prayer when they heard the front door open. A few seconds later, Geneva and Brooke walked into the kitchen.

Geneva marched up to Camden, clicked her heels together, and saluted. "Mission accomplished," she said officially.

Camden grinned up at her. "What is your official report, agent?"

Right then, Lydia's phone rang. "It's your dad," she said, her tone sounding slightly disappointed. With one last look that said she really hated to miss any of the action, she resigned herself and hurried out of the kitchen to take the call.

Geneva took a seat at the table and snagged a half-sandwich off Camden's plate. She shrugged. "I did what you said. I introduced myself to Gage and invited him to the singles Bible study at church. He seems like a good guy. I then introduced him to several of the other singles in the group."

"Did you manage to escape without him falling halfway in love with you?" Camden asked, munching on a few chips.

Geneva nodded. "It shouldn't be a problem. A few of the others invited Gage to go out to lunch with them at La Bonita Sombrero. I begged off, saying I was coming home for lunch. I think he's more Melody's type anyway. With any luck, she'll snag him before they've finished the chips and salsa."

Geneva reached for some of the chips on Camden's plate, and he playfully slapped her hand away. "Get your own food, Gen. Just because you did a favor for me doesn't give you permission to eat all of my lunch!"

Geneva sighed dramatically and stood. "Fine. I'll make my own sandwich. All of my good deeds are completely wasted on you, Camden."

"Thank you, Geneva," Bailey said, speaking up for the first time. "Camden was actually trying to fix my mistake, and I appreciate you ending the situation on a good note."

"Of course!" Geneva said, smiling graciously before turning to rummage through the refrigerator.

"And what do you have to report, Brooke?" Camden asked as Brooke slid a plate of salad that she made onto the table and sat in Geneva's vacated seat.

"Sasha got saved," she said casually, spearing some lettuce with her fork before bringing it to her mouth.

Camden dropped the chip in his hand and looked at his sister in surprise. "Are you serious?"

Brooke nodded. "She was already there at the gate. That's why she was so emotional. She just needed someone to listen to her and hold the gate open so she could walk through."

"What exactly do you mean, she 'got saved'?" Bailey asked, feeling like she was missing some vital information. "Sasha was already a Christian. I read it on her profile."

"She may have said she was a Christian, but she'd never had a personal encounter with God," Brooke explained. "She'd never repented of her sins and recognized that Jesus's sacrifice on the cross paid for those sins. I guess she'd been doing things her way, and now she accepted God's plan of salvation, giving her life over to Him and letting Him be in charge of it."

"She got all of that from listening to the sermon this morning?" Bailey asked, awed that she'd sat there in the same room and completely missed something that had been so life-changing for someone else.

"I don't know that the sermon made the difference," Brooke clarified. "It was a good sermon, but it was God who called Sasha's name. And she answered. Sasha realized this morning that she was woefully inadequate to be deserving of heaven. She also realized that God really is real and that Jesus died on the cross for her sins. Many people know the story of the Bible, but until you personally encounter the living God and come away changed and belonging to Him, you don't really know it at all."

"So, what did you do, just talk to her?" Camden asked.

"By the time I sat down, she was already ready and desperate to find peace. I don't want to tell any of the personal details she mentioned, but she told me she wanted God to save her and asked me to help her pray so she would belong to God. That's exactly what I did. We talked for a while afterward, and I took her to meet the pastor. We exchanged phone numbers, and I'll follow up with her. When she left, she said she'd never felt so at peace. She is eager to learn more about God and is planning to come back to church on Wednesday night for the Bible study."

"Should we find her a church in Brighton Falls, so it's closer to where she lives?" Camden asked in concern.

"I mentioned that to her," Brooke said thoughtfully. "She said she'd look, but she also said she doesn't mind the drive and felt comfortable here in Crossroads. Who knows? Maybe she'll decide to move to Crossroads. I'll keep track of her and make sure she gets plugged in somewhere. I really don't think it will be a problem. There's no way Sasha will ever want to go back to who she was yesterday."

Bailey felt a strange twinge of longing. Maybe she really should have paid attention to the sermon. After all, it seemed to have directly led Sasha to find an enviable peace. The whole situation made Bailey feel somehow empty, and she tried to tell herself it was simply because she'd screwed up the match so badly.

"Thank you, Brooke. You really did an amazing thing today," Camden told his sister warmly.

Brooke shook her head. "Nope. I don't get the credit. It was all God. I just got to be there to open the gate. And that was an honor. Thank you for asking me to go check on Sasha."

Lydia glided back into the kitchen having finished the call with her husband, and with the utmost politeness, insisted that both Geneva and Brooke repeat everything they'd just said. Not feeling up to hearing it all again, Bailey excused herself, quickly washed her dishes, and escaped to the office to hide. Though she felt grateful to Camden's thoroughly amazing sisters, she still couldn't help but think of herself as a failure. They wouldn't have needed to step in if she hadn't messed up the match. What was she thinking? Camden was right in that she'd been crazy to try to set up a date at a Sunday morning church service, even if she didn't officially call it a date.

Maybe he was right about other things, too. Maybe she really was just a farce. She only impersonated a real matchmaker, and pretending to be one apparently wasn't working nearly as well as she'd anticipated.

Bailey sat in front of her computer screen and stared without actually seeing it. She only roused when the door creaked open. Turning, she once again saw Camden stick his head inside the room.

With a smile, he held up one finger. "I have one point. You're still ahead, but if I can score off your dates, then this contest should be over in no time."

"I'm not sure what you're talking about. You only get a point if you create a successful match. Obviously, Gage and Sasha didn't work out, but you didn't actually set them up to find another love. Maybe they'll even still get together. If they're both single and attending the same church, it could still happen. It's too soon to tell. I admit it didn't make for the best experience today, but you don't get to steal a point. Nobody gets one on this attempt."

"But I did facilitate a match," Camden insisted proudly. "The best match there ever is! Sasha found her one true love after all."

"Did your sisters say something after I left?" Bailey asked, confused. What did she miss? "I didn't think Sasha found anyone."

"Didn't you hear what Brooke said? Sasha did find Someone. She found God—her one true love. There's no better match than truly finding your

Savior and realizing His amazing love for you. Though she didn't find the romantic match she anticipated, today she found her ultimate match in God."

Bailey opened her mouth to object, but then she closed it, completely speechless. Then she opened her mouth to try again. Still grasping nothing to actually mount a reputable argument, she aborted the mission yet again.

"I'm still ahead," she finally insisted, resigning herself to reality.

Camden laughed. Then he flashed two fingers up, followed by one. And then again. "You may be ahead, but I'm coming for you!"

With a wink, he once again shut the door, leaving Bailey with an unfamiliar feeling. Bailey usually didn't lack confidence in any task. If it was worth doing, she firmly believed herself capable of accomplishing it.

Now, for the first time, she doubted herself and feared that maybe she wasn't as capable as she thought. Worse, maybe Camden and his methods were more effective than she'd given them credit.

With a sickening feeling, Bailey considered what it would mean if she lost this contest. Losing control of doing the website her way would be difficult. But if she really were wrong in everything she believed about herself and romance, she would be left not even knowing Bailey Whitmore at all.

Eight

Camden heard an insistent knock on the door and ignored it. He was so close to figuring out this one problem. Just a few more minutes, and he'd have it.

The knock sounded again. This time it banged louder, as if someone rammed the door from the other side.

"Camden! Open the door!"

Camden blinked, realizing the shout had included his name.

He stood stiffly to his feet and rubbed his neck, wondering why his muscles cramped after sitting down at his computer for only a few minutes.

"Camden, it's Bailey! I know you're in there! If you don't open the door right NOW, I'll call the police to open the door for me!"

Camden swung the door open and rubbed his eyes, trying to get them to adjust from the bright glare of the computer screen.

Even as his vision cleared, he could clearly see Bailey was furious. Why was she mad, and more importantly, why was she at his apartment? She'd never been here before.

"What?" Camden asked with irritation. If she hadn't shown up and interrupted him, he could have solved the issue and been done with it. "I told you I was working from home today."

What he'd actually told her was that he couldn't focus to get any real work accomplished with his mom's constant interruptions and Bailey's incessant berating. Though he hadn't told the complete truth, at least he'd managed to achieve his goal of not working under Bailey's watchful eye for the day.

Instead of getting easier, maintaining the website along with everything else was becoming more difficult. Bailey's proximity still made him highly uncomfortable, and while the website's popularity far exceeded their expectations, the workload involved in that success didn't make fulfilling any of his other obligations and projects any less challenging.

"Yes, you said you were working from home," Bailey said, eyes still flashing angrily. "You also said that you would meet me at your parents' house at five o'clock sharp so we could leave for our date. By 'our date' I mean—"

Camden jerked his arm up, gawking at the time on his watch. Five-thirty. "Ugh! I'm sorry, Bailey," he said with sincerity. "I didn't realize the time. Is it too late? You didn't tell me where we're headed, but I can leave right now."

Camden hurriedly patted the pockets of his shorts, looking for his wallet, keys, and phone. Bailey waited at the door, but with it now wide open, there was no way to hide the books and papers scattered across the floor and fast food wrappers crowding his desk. Hoping it didn't look as bad as he feared, Camden spun around, frantically looking for what he needed before Bailey could make some snide comment. Revolving in a full rotation, he finally spotted his things on the desk, snatched them up, and turned back expectantly to Bailey.

She looked him up and down in obvious disapproval.

"You didn't tell me where we are going," he said defensively. "If this isn't appropriate, let me know, and I'll go change. You could also just tell me where we're headed."

Bailey let out a long-suffering sigh. "You're fine, but we need to leave now."

Somehow Camden knew if they hadn't been crunched for time, the words "you're fine" would have never crossed her lips to describe his attire.

Camden obediently followed her out the door and turned around to lock it. Unfortunately, she'd already seen the chaotic mess that crowded his apartment, and shutting and locking the door now couldn't remove that memory.

Camden opened the passenger side door of his SUV for Bailey before sliding into the seat on the opposite side and starting the engine. "My dad must have dropped you off," he surmised, noting that Bailey didn't have a car waiting out front. Obviously, he was her intended ride.

"Yes, he had to run to the store to get a few things for your mom anyway."

"So, when I didn't show up, did you just decide to come hunt me down?" he asked, backing out of his parking space and heading to the main road.

"I tried to call. Multiple times, but you didn't answer," Bailey replied stiffly.

Camden winced, feeling bad that he'd messed things up. "I'm sorry. I got busy trying to fix an issue and lost track of time. I didn't want the interruption of a phone call either, so I ignored my phone entirely."

"I'm not surprised," Bailey shrugged. "When you didn't show up, that's exactly what your mom and I guessed happened. I was even more certain when we pulled up to your place and saw your car out front. I knew you were here."

"I really am sorry, Bailey. Forgetting wasn't intentional."

"It never is."

Camden sighed, wishing she'd make things a little easier for him. "So, are you going to forgive me, or will this be an attitude that lasts the entire evening? You're free to go either way, but I'd like to prepare myself. And if you could let me know exactly where we're headed, that would be great too. I'm not much for blind dates, even if the girl hunts me down and forces me to go with her."

Bailey glared at him, causing Camden to grin back triumphantly. He loved getting under her skin.

Bailey told him to turn left, though she still didn't reveal their destination. "This isn't a blind date," she clarified. "It isn't really even a date, and you know it."

"I'm not sure what your definition of a date is. So far, you've kidnapped me from work and are taking me to an unknown location for the evening." Camden pumped his eyebrows in relentless teasing. "By definition, that's either a crime or a date."

Bailey rolled her eyes and finally admitted. "We're going to the basketball game in Brighton Falls."

"Really?" Camden asked excitedly. "It's not my birthday, is it?"

Bailey folded her arms across her front and fixed her gaze straight out the front window. "See? That's why I didn't tell you. I didn't want you to get too excited that I got tickets for us. It's completely professional. I already told you we were going to observe my second choice for our contest. Since you have refused to make a selection, I decided to make one myself."

Camden glanced down at the time. "Well, if we have tickets to the game, we'd better hurry. We don't want to miss the tip-off."

Bailey playfully smacked Camden in the arm. "Hello? Being late is not my fault!"

Camden replied innocently, "If you'd simply told me we had tickets to the game, I would have known this qualified as more of the romantic-type date and would have planned accordingly."

Bailey glowered, "Camden Hutchins, why do you delight in aggravating me?"

Camden just grinned. He really did enjoy teasing her. After the fiasco with his first contest selection, Camden really had no desire to make another entry in the contest at all. To him, it had only ever been a game, and he simply didn't have time for it. He'd put Bailey off for the past couple weeks, idly hoping she'd simply forget about it. Unfortunately, she had not. When he'd announced that he was working from his apartment today, she'd also announced that she'd made her second contest selection, and he was required to go with her on the observation of that selection this evening.

He'd only ever participated in the contest to amuse and hopefully aggravate Bailey, and now it looked as if tonight would involve the exact same entertainment goal. At least they were going to a game. Camden preferred a game to a fancy dinner at a restaurant any day of the week.

While driving to the stadium, he amused himself the entire time by bantering with Bailey and generally giving her a hard time. In his mind, their teasing banter qualified as affectionate in nature and seemed to alleviate some of the tension that perpetually existed between them. He found it to be much preferable to the outright fighting when the tension built up so much that the volcano erupted.

Fortunately, they arrived late enough that some of the crowd had thinned as people found their seats right before the start of the game. Though Bailey wanted to bypass the concessions, Camden wouldn't hear of it and managed to quickly load them down with enough food to feed their entire row.

They climbed down the stairs right as the game started and found the blue plastic chairs marked with their numbers. Bailey had purchased good seats for them, and Camden was impressed. Basketball tickets weren't cheap. If she hadn't been motivated to find the best angle with which to observe the couple she'd matched, Camden would have been flattered. He enjoyed basketball but rarely took time away from work to do something just for enjoyment.

Bailey settled into her seat beside him, and their hands brushed when both reaching for the popcorn.

Watch it, Camden warned himself. If he weren't careful, it would be very easy to slip into pretending that this really was a date, and Bailey really had been thoughtful enough to plan a date she knew he would enjoy.

Camden soon got caught up in the game and didn't even notice until after the first quarter that Bailey was unusually quiet. Turning his attention to her, he saw her eyes weren't even watching the action on the court.

"Don't you like basketball?" he finally asked.

"I like it just fine," she replied, but her glance never shifted.

Camden drew an imaginary line from Bailey's eyes to the couple she observed across the aisle and two rows up from where they sat. However, Bailey's agitation was more distracting than both the couple and the game itself.

Bailey's brow was furrowed, and Camden doubted that her lip would survive the whole game if she continued to chew it so relentlessly.

"Relax, Bailey," Camden urged. "So what if the date doesn't go well? You should know by now that we get both bad and good reviews. The good always outweighs the bad, and the website is just fine. As far as the contest, losing to me wouldn't be the end of the world, would it?"

"It's not that," Bailey said, the worry on her face not easing in the least.

"I know him." She pointed to the man across the aisle.

"You set up a man you know personally?" Camden asked.

Bailey shrugged. "I don't know him well. I met him at the airport when waiting for you back in December. He's a nice guy."

Halftime ended, and the noise level in the stadium once again increased to where holding a conversation became impossible. Unfortunately, Camden couldn't watch the game with the same enjoyment. He couldn't block out Bailey from his senses, and he was very much aware of her continued distress. Giving up watching the game, he turned his attention to the couple to figure out what exactly had her so upset.

A man with glasses and a shirt buttoned to the very top sat in his seat looking perfectly miserable. By contrast, the woman next to him stood to her feet and cheered loudly, thoroughly enjoying every play of the game. Camden watched for several minutes, noting that when something didn't go well in the game, the woman screamed at the officials and the man looked as if he wanted to melt into the floor. The whole thing was quite painful to watch, and Camden suddenly understood why Bailey felt so miserable, knowing she instigated such an uncomfortable scene.

Having seen enough, Camden sat in his chair and took out his phone.

"What are you doing?" Bailey asked when he didn't quickly finish with his phone and return to his feet.

Camden held up his hand, hoping to stop any further questions while he focused. "Just give me a minute, Bailey. I'm trying to mount a rescue operation."

Bailey's worried gaze alternated between Camden pushing buttons on his phone and Jeff Schwartz sitting miserably beside his cheering date. She'd really messed this one up.

When she'd come across Jeff's profile on the website, she'd immediately recognized him as the shy man she'd encountered at the airport. She also remembered how his sister, Kari, had explained how awkwardly Jeff behaved around attractive woman and how much she'd wanted to help him find his perfect match. She immediately knew she wanted him to be her second selection. After all, she already had an advantage because she'd met him.

From that brief encounter, she already had a good idea of the kind of woman she should set him up with. He was such a nice guy, but he really needed someone outgoing who could get him out of his shell to enjoy all life had to offer. When choosing Jeff a match, she didn't even bother looking at the results from Camden's algorithm. Instead, she did it all on her own, selecting him a perfect match who seemed really nice although opposite him in many ways.

She'd watched carefully, not reading their messages back and forth, but closely monitoring if and when they set up a date. When the basketball game popped up on their schedules, Bailey knew she had the ideal opportunity to observe a fantastic date and get credit for it in a win with Camden. As luck would have it, Ashley had also posted their seat numbers on the schedule so Jeff would know which entrance to meet her at. Bailey had then bought the tickets that would give her the best view of observing their date. While the tickets hadn't been cheap, she knew it was worth seeing her hard work pay off with witnessing a successful match.

The second they'd arrived at their seats and she found Jeff's face, she knew she'd been terribly wrong. It wasn't that he didn't care for basketball. Maybe he did. However, his nicely pressed and starched shirt and slacks made for a sharp contrast to Ashley's blue face paint and head-to-toe, brightly colored fan apparel. Maybe even that could be tolerable under the right circumstances.

However, these circumstances were far from right. Ashley's exuberance shocked and embarrassed Jeff to such a degree that his poor face continually shifted from blazing red to deathly pale. Even his popcorn sat untouched beside him. That is until Ashley grabbed it to stuff some in her mouth. Then someone on her team got called for a foul, and she launched the whole bucket in a geyser of protest that rained buttery fluff all over mortified Jeff.

Ashley wasn't heartless. She tried to get Jeff involved, even tugging him up to attempt to dance during one of the time-outs. That incident only succeeded in dousing the front of Jeff's shirt with ketchup and mustard when he tripped and fell against the hotdog Ashley held in her other hand.

Bailey couldn't take watching the scene any longer, and yet she couldn't look away. Tears pricked her eyes as her mind sorted through possibilities. Camden was right. Jeff really did need a rescue. She just wasn't sure how to go about doing it.

Camden suddenly stood and turned around as if looking for something.

"What is it?" Bailey asked, trying to speak over the stadium's uproar.

Camden leaned close to her ear and whispered, his breath tickling her hair. "Over there. She's a client."

Bailey looked at him in confusion. What did that have to do with rescuing Jeff?

"Stay here," Camden whispered again before climbing up the aisle toward the woman he'd just pointed to.

Bailey looked at her more closely. It looked like she was with a group of friends. Though she was enjoying the game, cheering and clapping in all the right places, she lacked Ashley's face paint and overwhelming exuberance. She was happy but calm and didn't seem to be at all upset no matter who scored, fouled, or what.

Bailey watched as Camden walked right up to her and spoke while she and her friends eagerly listened. When he stepped away, the young woman followed. Feeling an inkling of what Camden was attempting, Bailey hurried over to the aisle to intercept. She arrived right as Camden got Jeff and Ashley's attention and began speaking.

Flashing a charming smile Ashley's way, he said, "Hi, I'm sorry to bother you. I hope you don't mind, but we're going to steal Jeff away for the rest of the game." Gesturing to Bailey, he explained. "He's a friend of Bailey's, and she'd really like to spend a few minutes with him and introduce him to one of my friends."

At the sight of Bailey, recognition dawned in Jeff's eyes, and he leaped to his feet.

"Sure, whatever," Ashley said, barely turning to respond before jumping up and cheering for another basket scored. "See ya, Jeff. It was nice meeting you. Maybe we can do this again sometime. Do you like hockey?"

Thankfully, Jeff didn't need to respond before someone committed a foul, making Ashley completely forget that she'd even asked a question.

"Bailey, it's good to see you," Jeff said eagerly, following the small group up the steps.

"Jeff, there's been a mistake," Camden said, preventing Bailey from responding. "It turns out Ashley isn't a strong match for your profile. According to your answers, you should have been paired with someone on a different list, and it just so happens, one of those ladies is right here. Jeff Schwartz, I'd like to introduce you to Julie Davies."

Jeff's gaze swung from Julie back to Bailey as if seeking to confirm the accuracy of Camden's statements.

Bailey nodded and confirmed. "Jeff, this is my business partner Camden Hutchins, and he's right. You should have never been matched with Ashley. She's a great gal, she just isn't for you."

Camden nodded. "If you want, Julie said there's an extra seat right by where she and her friends are sitting, and you're welcome to join them."

"I don't know. I think I may have already exceeded my basketball quota for the night," Jeff said nervously, not even looking at Julie. After all, she was quite pretty.

"That's okay," Julie said with an easy-going smile. "Now that we know each other's names, maybe we can connect on the Betwixt website."

"Hey, Julie!" one of her friends yelled. "That was your guy who made that basket. Make sure you mark it down."

Julie immediately took out her phone and began pushing buttons.

"Is that an app?" Jeff asked, looking at the screen of her phone with interest.

"Oh, yeah," Julie said self-consciously. "It's just a game my friends and I play. When we go to any kind of sports game, we each pick a player or a team. We then keep track of every stat that player logs in the game and put it into this little app I created. The app assigns varying values to each task and scores the player accordingly. At the end of the game, the losing friend buys the other friends' ice cream. It's kinda silly, but it's fun."

Julie ducked her head as if embarrassed that she'd even bothered to explain it. "Sorry, I probably should have just said it was a game and left it at that," she amended.

"You created the app?" Jeff asked with equal amounts of interest and awe.

Julie nodded. "It's a pretty simple one. Just for fun."

"Who are you?" Jeff asked as if completely mesmerized.

Practically, Julie responded. "I'm a graduate student at the university. My focus is math with an emphasis in technical engineering. My master's paper is on statistics, so this app was a precursor to that project."

"My background is in technology," Jeff shared. "I'd love to see how your app works."

"Julie, your guy just scored again!" Her friend yelled. "You're ahead in points."

"Come on!" Julie invited with a delighted smile. "I'll show you."

Stunned, Bailey watched Jeff happily follow Julie to the seats near her friends.

"It worked!" she said. "It really worked!"

Then, remembering the other half of her original match, she spun back around in concern. "What about Ashley? Shouldn't we find her someone more compatible?"

Camden shook his head, an amused smile lifting the corners of his lips. "No. Look at her. For all Ashley knows, it was a great date. She's having such a wonderful time that she automatically assumes Jeff feels the same way. It doesn't even occur to her that he didn't enjoy the game as much as she did."

Watching Ashley's fist-pumping cheers, she knew Camden was right. Even as she watched, Ashley high-fived multiple other fans in her vicinity, and Bailey saw that she wasn't lacking in social interaction to pass the evening.

She turned back to see Jeff and Julie's heads bowed over her phone, and a slow smile of satisfaction spread through her body. That's what she'd been looking for. Even if she hadn't been the one to arrange the match, she was still thrilled with seeing Jeff find a special someone.

"That's interesting," she heard Camden say right before the crowd cheered again.

Before she could be heard to ask what he meant, Camden looked up from his phone and headed to the doors leading out of the arena. Bailey followed, inhaling with relief as the doors shut behind her, cutting off the noise.

"How did you know Julie was a Betwixt client and was on Jeff's list?"

she asked Camden eagerly, her words sounding loud in the concrete network of hallways encircling the arena.

Camden didn't pause to talk. Instead, he walked down the hallway as if looking for something.

"Are you going to answer me?" Bailey demanded when he didn't respond.

Camden turned to face her, warily looking either direction. "Can't you just let it go, Bailey? Isn't it enough that I found a match for Jeff and that he's happy? Why do you need to know the how?"

Bailey lifted an eyebrow, not willing to back off. "Tell me how," she ordered.

Camden sighed and motioned her to one side of the hallway. Though there was no one else close in proximity, he still spoke quietly. "Given a specific set of circumstances, I can track the location of Betwixt app users. Of course, on the website, we call it a safety feature when users grant permission for location tracking."

Bailey's eyes narrowed. "What are the 'specific set of circumstances'? I doubt users realize they can be tracked when not on a date. Julie clearly wasn't on a date, so how did you find her?"

"She didn't close the app," Camden said. "Even if the app is in the background, it remains active and can be tracked if needed. Kind of like a 'find your phone' feature, but in my case, I can pull up a map for a certain location and see all of the active Betwixt users in that area. If they close the app, it doesn't work, but you'd be surprised how many people don't actually close their apps."

Bailey immediately took out her own phone. Pressing the home button twice, she groaned, seeing that she had at least ten different apps still open. She ignored Camden's laughter as she quickly swiped each of them upward to close.

"There she is!" Camden said suddenly, hurrying over to a concession stand.

Bailey followed, wondering how he could possibly still be hungry after eating the massive amount of food he'd bought earlier.

With no customers at the booth, it looked as if the single employee was working to close up shop for the night.

"Hi," she greeted as Camden approached. "I'm just shutting this one down since the game is almost over. I have a few things still available, but they have more choices at the booth near the front entrance. That one will stay open after the game."

"Actually, I'm not interested in buying anything right now. Are you Fiona Maxwell?"

"Yes, I am," she answered, surprised.

Camden extended his hand with a charming smile in place. "Hi, I'm Camden Hutchins. I'm sorry if this sounds weird, but I'm one of the owners of the Betwixt Two Hearts matchmaking website. Your profile came up as a strong match for one of my other clients who is here at the game this evening. When I saw that you actually worked here, I thought I'd take the chance to find you. My client friend just survived a nightmarishly bad date. He's currently visiting with someone he just met, but on the off-chance that you wanted to meet one of your matches, I thought I'd just mention that he was here."

What is he doing? Bailey tugged on Camden's sleeve. When that didn't work, she leaned into his arm, trying to get him to back off and leave. Everything was perfect with Jeff and Julie, and now he was going to ruin it!

Fiona's eyes grew wide. "He's here? I mean, I signed up for the site, but I haven't actually dared to contact anyone. Maybe it would be easier if I just kind of ran into him. But you said he was already meeting someone?"

Camden nodded. "He is. His name is Jeff. There are no guarantees, but there also isn't a problem with you taking some concessions by where he's sitting and slipping him your number or telling him to contact you on the website. Maybe he will. Maybe he won't. Looking at your profile, I saw that you signed up on the first day but haven't even contacted your free match."

"No, I haven't," she acknowledged nervously. "Is this Jeff a nice guy?"

"A very nice guy." Camden turned to Bailey and captured her hands in his. The gesture probably looked affectionate, but it was really to stop her from pinching his arm. "Bailey here knows him better than I do. You want to add anything, Bailey?"

Bailey scowled. She was not helping him with this. Not trying to hide her reluctance, she reported unapologetically, "He has glasses and is a bit of a nerd. He gets extremely nervous around pretty women and may not even speak to you."

"Not because he doesn't want to," Camden assured quickly. "You just may be too pretty for him to feel comfortable right away."

Fiona's face lit up with a beautiful smile, not seeming to be scared off in the least. "That's really cute. Okay, I'll do it. Where is he sitting?"

Much to Bailey's dismay, Camden happily gave Fiona the section number and also provided a thorough description of where the seats were located and Jeff himself. The entire time, he held tightly to Bailey's hands, preventing her from inflicting any more physical proof of her objections.

"He's sitting with a woman and her friends," Bailey added sternly. "He might not even notice you."

"I understand," Fiona said brightly. "I really don't have any expectations. It probably won't work, but at least I tried! Thanks for the tip, Mr. Hutchins."

Camden nodded and headed back the way they came while Fiona worked to put together a last-minute concession tray. Dragging Bailey along with one of her hands still trapped in his, he didn't turn to her until out of Fiona's sight.

"What did you do?" Bailey demanded, finally managing to wrench her hand away only to reach over and use it to lightly smack him in the chest. "Jeff and Julie were perfect. Now you've wrecked everything! There's no reason to do that!"

Camden captured both her hands in his once again. Holding her still, he looked earnestly into her eyes. "Bailey, it will be okay. I mentioned it to Fiona because she needs someone, too, and I believe she would appreciate Jeff. Obviously, Jeff was impressed with Julie, but it wasn't clear that Julie felt the same about Jeff. A little competition for his affections might make the whole situation better. Besides, Jeff seems like the type of guy who really deserves to have two amazing women vying for his affections. I just did him a big favor, and I don't understand why any of that is wrong."

Bailey opened her mouth to respond, but then she closed it when words failed her. Camden made a lot of sense. They'd been honest with Fiona about the situation. Maybe it really wouldn't be the train wreck Bailey feared. In fact, presenting Jeff with a choice actually seemed like an awfully good idea.

Bailey looked at Camden, feeling a little lost in his blue-gray eyes as she spoke. "I'm sorry, Camden. I guess I jumped to conclusions. It's been a really rough night, and it's easy to assume you're always trying to sabotage me. Yet tonight you really saved the day. Thank you. You have no idea how much I appreciate it."

Camden looked surprised, almost as if he'd never heard her apologize before. But, of course, she had. Hadn't she?

"Bailey, I would never try to sabotage you," he said, his eyes shining with sincerity. "I know I don't do a good job of communicating, but I really only want good things for you. You should know that I didn't step in and find Jeff a match because of Jeff or for the sake of the website. I don't know Jeff, but I assume one bad date wouldn't kill him, and I'm totally fine with the website getting an occasional bad review. I don't even care about the stupid contest. I did it for you, Bailey. I couldn't stand you being unhappy, and I couldn't enjoy the game knowing you were miserable."

Bailey swallowed with difficulty, intensely aware of his presence and the warm hands still holding hers. Everything around them seemed to fade away, and she longed for something. The sparks in his eyes drew her like magnets, and she wondered if his lips were warm, too. Mesmerized, she reached up to touch the stubble on his cheek. At the contact, electricity shot from her fingers all the way through her body, ending with her lips tingling in anticipation.

Camden turned his head, lightly brushing her hand with his lips.

Bailey stood to her tiptoes, longing for those lips to meet hers.

A loud ringing shot panic through her heart, and she stumbled backward, the spell broken.

Camden fumbled for his phone and pulled it up to his ear. "Hello?" he asked, clearing his husky voice even as he spoke.

"Hi, Gen," he greeted. Suddenly his voice changed, fear threading through it. "Yes, I'm in Brighton Falls. What? Gen, slow down."

Camden's fear was contagious. Bailey watched him in concern, instinctively knowing something was wrong. She knew Camden's sister, Geneva, was a doctor. If she'd called with bad news, then it could be serious.

"Ok, give me fifteen minutes," Camden said tightly. "I'll be there."

He hung up the phone, grabbed Bailey's hand, and took off running down the hallway.

"Camden, what happened?" Bailey asked, panicking. "What's wrong?"

"Israel needs me," he explained shortly. Reaching the stairs, he hurried down, Bailey barely managing to keep up with his legs on fast forward.

"Where's Israel? Camden, please tell me what is going on!" she begged.

Reaching the bottom of the stairs, Camden suddenly stopped and turned to her, his eyes so filled with pain that they took her breath away. "Israel is working late at his office, and I need to go be with him. That was Geneva on the phone. Israel's wife, Marissa, is there at the hospital. Bailey, Marissa is dead."

Nine

Camden watched the lights blink over the elevator door and clenched his teeth tightly. *Lord, help me! I don't know how to handle this! Help me to be there for my brother!*

He hadn't stopped praying since Geneva had called, and still he didn't know what to do when those elevator doors opened.

Marissa was dead. He knew that for Israel, it wouldn't matter that she had left months ago and he hadn't even heard from her since. His grief in losing her would be just as intense, just as fresh, and only compounded by guilt.

Camden glanced at his watch, catching Bailey's gaze as she stood beside him. Thankfully, she hadn't asked a single question since he'd told her what happened. She'd simply held his hand tightly before and after he'd driven like a maniac to get here.

Geneva would be calling in about four minutes. He'd made the drive from the stadium to his brother's office in record time, and he'd be there when Israel heard the news. Geneva had called Camden first. She hadn't wanted Israel to get the news when he was alone and had purposely bypassed hospital procedures to make sure someone was there for her brother. Strangely, Camden had been her first call. Maybe their mom had mentioned that he and Bailey were headed to Brighton Falls for the evening. Maybe she knew that no matter what, Camden would drop everything and move mountains to be there for the brother who seemed to despise him.

Whatever her reasoning, Geneva hadn't called Mom and Dad. She hadn't called Dallas or any of their other siblings. She'd called Camden. Though he didn't know how to do any of this, he would be there in the room when Israel learned his wife was gone.

The elevator doors opened, and Camden and Bailey stepped out into the plush office waiting room.

Bailey squeezed his hand and murmured. "I'll wait here if you need me."

"I need you to pray," Camden whispered.

Bailey nodded soberly and took a seat on one of the chairs overlooking a view of the city.

Camden walked to a large door in the corner behind the front desk.

Lord, I don't know how to pray. Please help me and comfort Israel.

Camden knocked firmly. Without waiting for a response, he turned the knob and opened the door.

Israel looked up from his desk in surprise and immediately stood.

"Camden?" He suddenly turned and looked out the wide windows behind him, shielding his eyes as if searching for something in the city lights of night. "Wait just a minute, Camden. You're stepping foot in the office, which means I need to make sure pigs aren't flying around out there."

"Israel," Camden said, his voice cracking painfully.

At his tone, Israel turned around, and his face blanched as he took in Camden and his hesitant steps toward him.

All of the oxygen left the room. Camden couldn't breathe.

"Camden, tell me. What's wrong?"

Camden didn't answer, looking helplessly at his brother. Geneva should be calling now. Why wasn't she calling?

"Tell me, Camden," Israel begged.

Camden hesitated.

"Tell me!" Israel shouted, the noise stark and startling in the empty office.

Camden swallowed, then he spoke quietly, his voice raspy. "Israel,

Geneva called. Marissa was taken to the hospital. Israel, she didn't make it. She's gone."

Israel let out a choking sob and shook his head adamantly. "No. You lie. Marissa isn't dead." He reached out and shoved Camden hard, sending him stumbling across the room "You're lying. Do you hate me that much?"

Tears squeezed out of Camden's eyes, and he couldn't speak.

Israel's phone rang.

He stared at Camden as it rang one, two, three times.

Finally, he picked up and answered hoarsely, "Hello."

After listening about ten seconds, Israel's face crumpled, and the phone dropped from his hand. He would have fallen to the floor if Camden hadn't met him with open arms, catching him and holding him close.

"No!" Israel screamed as sobs claimed him, shaking his body in great convulsions.

Camden supported Israel's weight, getting him safely to a couch against one wall. He then retrieved Israel's phone and held it to his ear while he knelt before his brother.

"Gen, it's me," Camden said. "I've got him."

Though Geneva struggled mightily to maintain her professional composure, her thin voice was difficult to understand, and Camden knew without seeing that silent tears coursed down her cheeks.

"He needs to come down to identify the body," she said tightly. "I recognize her, of course, but it's still a formality."

"Ok, I'll see that he makes it," Camden assured. "Give us a little time."

Geneva spoke brokenly, "Camden, there was nothing we could do. They found her in her car at the side of the road, and she was gone long before then."

"I assume it was—"

"Drugs," Geneva confirmed. "I don't have toxicology reports back, but it's a classic overdose. There were drugs in the car beside her. Even knowing her history, I doubt that makes it any easier for Israel."

"No, I doubt it does. We'll be down as soon as we can." Camden signed off, set the phone down, and wrapped his arms around his brother's hunched-over, shaking shoulders. Right now, it didn't matter that Marissa's drug problem was well-known, or that her death by overdose wasn't shocking. It didn't matter that she had left Israel and Chloe months ago and hadn't bothered to keep any contact or let anyone know where she was. Drugs had consumed Marissa's life, and even though it wasn't surprising that it ended with an overdose alone in her car, that didn't make the reality of it any easier.

"It's all my fault. It's all my fault," Israel murmured over and over.

"No, it isn't," Camden said firmly, pushing his brother upright so he could look him directly in the eye and make him understand. "You didn't make Marissa's choices, she did. You weren't the one who left, she was. You didn't refuse to go into rehab or turn your back on everyone who cared."

"You don't understand," Israel moaned. "I'm not saying that her choices from the past few months were my fault. I'm talking about before that. If I had handled things better back when her drug problem started, I could have prevented everything."

"Israel, you can't know that," Camden protested. "And playing the 'what if' game doesn't solve anything now."

"Marissa first started taking prescription painkillers after Chloe was born," Israel confessed, struggling to regain a semblance of control. "She'd had a difficult delivery, and prescription painkillers were prescribed as a matter of course. If I had been more attentive when Chloe was a baby, I could have alleviated some of Marissa's postpartum depression and stress, and I would have noticed that she never stopped taking the pain medicine. She always seemed to give the doctor a valid reason for why she needed it, and I didn't realize until too late that she was addicted. Even then, I didn't handle things as I should have. I thought she'd get better when she wanted to have another baby, and she did. But when she didn't get pregnant right away, she became even more depressed. She quickly went back to her medicine. I got rid of all of the pills and tried to keep track of when she'd go to a new doctor to get a prescription. She wouldn't consent to treatment, and when I cut off her legal drug supply, she turned to the illegal variety. Things spun out of control from there. I should have forced her into rehab, but at the time, I couldn't legally do it without having her arrested on drug charges. It got to the point that she couldn't take care of Chloe, and when I threatened to call the cops and have her committed, she left."

Camden had known the outline version of Marissa's story, as related by his mom, but Israel had never spoken to him about it until now. He didn't know how to ease the agony straining his brother's features. It was a pain he couldn't imagine, and he felt he lacked any words of comfort.

Camden gripped his brother's shoulder tightly, and spoke, willing comfort and strength in his touch. "Israel, looking in the rearview mirror, you always think what you should have done. I'm so very sorry you're going through this, and I have no words to ease your pain. However, I am sure that God knows exactly what you're going through. He loved Marissa, and He loves you. He's the one to give you comfort and strength for the days ahead. None of this took Him by surprise, and He has a plan to get you through it."

"Camden, I don't even know that Marissa was saved," Israel whispered, his eyes wide as if revealing a shameful secret. "At the time we married, I thought she was. But she became so obsessed with getting her next high that she left Chloe and me. She wasn't the woman I married. The Marissa I loved has been gone much longer than today, and yet no matter what she did, I always hoped that my Marissa would come back to me. Now that hope is gone."

"Israel, you can't know Marissa's heart or God's work in her," Camden said firmly, bending to keep eye contact. "All you can do is trust who God is. You know He loved her and never abandoned her, even at the end. Because of His faithfulness, you can still have that hope that you will one day get to see your Marissa. Don't let your hope be in Marissa. Let it be in God. If she ever belonged to Him, He wouldn't have let her go easily."

"But I can't know for sure."

"No, you can't. But you can hope."

Camden prayed with Israel, and after a while, he calmed enough that Camden mentioned that they needed to go to the hospital.

Israel stood, resigning himself to the task and the one after that— telling his daughter that her mommy wouldn't be coming home.

Camden and Bailey went with him to the hospital, and Camden stood alongside him as he said his final goodbyes to his wife. Geneva was her usual professional self and guided them through the process quickly and easily.

Camden watched her in amazement. He knew Geneva felt the brunt of grief as much as he did, and yet she remained cool and calm, yet compassionate. Though her teasing, fun personality was quite different when not wearing her doctor's jacket, when on duty, Camden knew there was none better than Dr. Geneva Hutchins.

Camden offered to drive Israel back to Crossroads, but he insisted on driving himself so as to have his own vehicle in the morning. Camden and Bailey contented themselves with following his brother's taillights all the way home.

"Is Israel planning to tell Chloe tonight?" Bailey asked after they'd been driving a while.

"No. Mom will already have Chloe in bed when we get there. It's too late tonight. Israel will stay at my parents' house tonight and tell her in the morning."

"Poor little girl," Bailey said sympathetically, sounding close to tears.

"It's difficult to know how she'll take it," Camden said grimly. "Marissa leaving really threw her off, and she isn't the same happy little girl she used to be. I don't know what this will do to her."

Bailey hadn't asked for the details of Marissa's story, and Camden appreciated that. However, he thought she deserved to know the truth. As factually as possible, he told the story. By the time they pulled into his parents' driveway, Bailey was brushing at tears that streamed down her face, devastated at the tragedy of it all.

Seeing her distress, Camden grabbed a tissue, leaned over, and tenderly began dabbing her tears.

"I'm sorry," Bailey gasped softly. "I should be comforting you, not the other way around."

Camden shook his head. "Don't be sorry. Marissa's tale is a sad one deserving of grief. I appreciate you tagging along tonight. I know you tried to stay out of the way, but knowing you were there was still a comfort to me."

Bailey looked at Camden steadily. "I don't know what to do with you," she confessed. "You are the most aggravating and yet the kindest man I know. I didn't hear everything you said to your brother, but I heard some of it. I also watched the way you interacted with him and tried to help. I think you're a little bit amazing."

"Please don't put me on a pedestal, Bailey," Camden said hoarsely, pretending interest in the landscape outside the window rather than meet the admiration in her gaze. "I'll fall off. You are familiar with my faults. I honestly had no idea what I was doing tonight. I was simply trying to hold it together. It wouldn't have helped Israel if I melted into a blubbering mess."

Bailey reached over and touched his shoulder, asking him to look at her. "Camden, I've come to realize just how much you give to help others. Please make sure you take care of yourself, too. It's okay for you to feel the grief of Marissa's loss as well."

Does Bailey really think so highly of me?

Reaching out, he cautiously touched her cheek, letting his fingers trail down to her chin. Her skin was just as soft as he imagined. She seemed to beckon him, and his defenses were down. The touch of her lips promised a momentary escape from the stress and grief, and the reasons why kissing Bailey would be a bad idea quickly departed. He leaned closer. The hand on her cheek tangled in the hair against her neck, and he drew her closer.

A shrill ringing echoed through the car. Camden jerked back as Bailey scrambled for her phone.

"Seriously?" Camden asked, amused that a phone call had startled them twice in one night. Then again, it was probably all for good. The ringing brought with it sanity, and within two seconds he knew that kissing Bailey would have been a horrible mistake.

"It's Dekker," Bailey explained, looking at the name on the screen of her phone.

"Of course," Camden nodded. "Dekker the Wrecker at work again."

Bailey's eyes swung toward him, the phone in her hand still ringing. "Did you say, 'Dekker the Wrecker'?"

Camden scowled and shrugged in answer. At the risk of making her angry, he really should keep any commentary on her boyfriend to himself.

Bailey burst out laughing, startling Camden with her response.

"Good night, Camden," she said, opening the passenger door to step outside. "I'm off to deal with 'Dekker the Wrecker'!"

Camden watched her make it up to the front door with the phone to her ear. Israel had already headed inside as soon as they'd arrived. Camden

131

backed out of the driveway and drove home, mulling over, not Marissa's death, but what had just happened with Bailey.

Guilt quickly set in as he realized that he'd almost screwed up and kissed her twice this evening. He needed to be stronger. He couldn't let that happen again. Now that sanity prevailed, he knew that kissing her would destroy their friendship. Besides that, it would just be wrong. What kind of Christian guy would he be if he romanced someone he knew did not believe as he did? Not to mention that she had a boyfriend who she was "pretty much married to"!

Camden, you're an idiot, he told himself. He wasn't the kind of guy to kiss another guy's girl, and he couldn't risk getting involved with a non-Christian. End of story.

As hard on his pride as it was to admit, he now realized that he'd only escaped making a serious mistake because of the grace of God and Dekker the Wrecker.

Ten

As Bailey stepped off the airplane in Seattle, the past two weeks faded into the background, and suddenly, Crossroads seemed very far away. Bailey shuffled her bags around and pressed the send button on her phone, responding to Camden's text and letting him know she'd arrived.

She hurriedly weaved her way past security and pushed open the doors leading to the greeting area.

"Dekker!" Bailey squealed, seeing him standing against a column looking at his phone.

At her call, Dekker looked up and grinned, opening his arms as she came rushing in. His lips covered hers, sending Bailey's heart fluttering. Even after all this time, the sparks between them still took her breath away.

"Your flight is late," Dekker said, lifting his head and taking her arm to lead her toward the escalator.

"I know!" Bailey said, shaking her head in exasperation. "I'm sorry you had to wait. At least I didn't check any baggage." She lifted her sole carry-on bag as evidence.

"I was beginning to think you'd never come home, and I'm not just talking about your late flight." Though he was teasing, a hint of real criticism tinged his voice.

"You could have always come to see me in Crossroads," she pointed out.

"Why would I want to go visit the middle of nowhere?" Dekker shot her an irritated look.

"I would think you could find at least one thing worth seeing in Crossroads." Bailey quirked her eyebrows up and own.

Dekker shook his head and scoffed, "Yah, I love you, Bailey, but even that is not enough to get me to suffer through the boredom of Hicksville, especially when you can come back to Seattle."

They made it to Dekker's Porsche, and Bailey hopped inside with a sigh of relief. It felt good to be back home in Seattle, especially after the last couple of weeks. With Marissa's death, a curtain of grief had hung over the Hutchins house. Even though Bailey had never met Marissa, she deeply felt the impact. Those she cared about were grieving, and she sought to do everything she could to alleviate some of the stress. She and Camden got their work done, but it had been difficult and stressful. On the plus side, they hadn't fought nearly as much, and Camden had shown Bailey more of the ropes of the internal workings of the website so she could take up some of the slack while he helped Israel with planning a memorial service and giving extra play time to Chloe.

They were still so far behind that Bailey probably should have canceled her trip this weekend. After all, Valentine's Day promised huge returns for the website, and she needed to spend a large portion of the weekend on her computer anyway. But Camden insisted she keep her plans. He said she needed a break and promised that he would contribute extra hours so she could get a breath of fresh air away from the stress.

"Are you hungry?" Dekker asked, pulling out of the parking space and heading to the airport exit.

"I am," Bailey said, putting a hand to her gurgling stomach. "I haven't eaten anything since I left Crossroads."

"I've already eaten, but if you want, we can go by a drive-thru," Dekker said generously. "What are you in the mood for?"

"You already ate?" Bailey asked, glancing at the clock. Her flight wasn't *that* late. "I thought we were going to have dinner together."

Dekker shrugged. "My parents were going to Giovanni's and asked if I wanted to go. I'm glad I did. The Chicken Parmesan was incredible. I had to hurry to come pick you up, so I missed dessert. Maybe I'll grab an ice cream when we get you fast food."

"But it's Valentine's Day!" Bailey protested, shocked that he'd eaten dinner without her. "I was looking forward to Giovanni's this weekend, if not tonight. Maybe we can still go Saturday night."

"Oh, that's right," Dekker said, surprised. "I forgot that Giovanni's is your favorite. What is it you like there?"

"The Chicken Parmesan," Bailey replied with just a hint of a bite to her tone.

"Well, I'm at my Italian food limit after tonight," Dekker said, leaving no option for discussion. "It's not the kind of thing you want to eat multiple times a week, you know? Maybe they do takeout. We can get you an order to go on Saturday night." Dekker looked proud of his idea.

"Yeah, takeout doesn't sound nearly as good as the real experience," Bailey said dryly, still ticked that he'd gone without her.

"Burger? Chicken? What do you want tonight?" Dekker asked, oblivious to her attitude.

Bailey sighed. "Maybe we should just go home. If we stop somewhere, we'll need to get back in to battle the traffic. Do we have anything to eat at home?"

Of course, it was raining, and traffic was backed up horribly. Bailey hadn't missed the rain or the traffic of Seattle, and strangely, she found herself longing for the quaint Crossroads Main street where the biggest traffic congestion occurred when you were unfortunate enough to get behind a slow-moving tractor or a flock of sheep being herded from one location to another.

Dekker scratched his head as if she'd just asked him a difficult, thought-provoking question. "Well, didn't you buy some cans of soup before you left in December? I think we still have those."

"Fine," Bailey resigned herself. "Let's just get home."

She told herself that it really was fine. It didn't matter that it was Valentine's Day and her boyfriend had chosen to have dinner with his parents rather than her. The important thing was that she and Dekker get to spend quality time together. It shouldn't matter that he ate without her. He hadn't purposely done it to hurt her. He just hadn't considered that she might want to have a special dinner with him. Getting home would be best, and she wouldn't mind eating soup if they snuggled up on the couch with a movie or just got caught up on each other's lives. They would have other opportunities for actual dates this weekend.

"Come on!" Dekker yelled suddenly, laying on his horn as another car changed lanes in front of him. The traffic stood at a standstill with a long line of brake lights glaring through the multitude of water droplets covering the window.

Still grumbling colorful terms for other drivers, Dekker reached over, took her hand, and squeezed it. "I have big plans for us this weekend."

"Oh, really?" Bailey said, smiling, touched that he'd made the effort of planning something special for her visit. She rubbed his hand in hers affectionately. She really was lucky to have him. Looking over at him, she admired the way his dark hair fell across his forehead at just the right angle. The strands bounced as he spoke, almost adding their own cocky expressions to whatever he said. He was more sophisticated than rugged, and what he lacked in muscle mass, he made up for in sheer charisma. All he'd ever had to do is flash his perfectly white, rakish grin her way to set her heart to leaping.

Changing lanes to maneuver into one that seemed to be moving slightly faster, he flashed that grin her way and continued. "Tomorrow we have a date with a few other friends at that new rock climbing venue. It's supposed to be awesome. Then in the evening, we'll head over to my parents' party. Don't worry, I already told them you were in town, and they gave their okay for you to join me. Saturday we'll take my new boat out on the water, and then we'll take the plane to Portland for a night on the town with a few of my college friends. We'll stay the night there, then we'll head out for a quick skiing trip Sunday and be back in time for your flight. What time did you say you were leaving?"

Bailey's mouth dropped open in shock, and she couldn't find the words to respond. He had the weekend completely booked, and not a single thing sounded like something she wanted to do. "Dekker, I'm not sure that's going to work for me. It sounds like you have every moment planned, and I have a lot of work to do. I was looking forward to spending some down time together."

"We will be spending time together, but we'll be doing fun things and making memories," he said, seeming flabbergasted and a little hurt that she didn't act excited.

"Really? I'm not sure those are the kind of memories I want. You had mentioned take-out Italian food on Saturday, but even that isn't an option with your schedule. It sounds like we'll be doing a bunch of things with other people, but not so much just you and me."

"Are you really going to be like that, Bailey?" Dekker snorted in derision. "Since when did you get boring? I made the effort to plan a phenomenal weekend for us, and you're turning your nose up at it?"

"Come on, Dekker! I'm not an idiot. You didn't plan the weekend for me. None of it is for me. You're doing what you want to do, and I'm just tagging along." Even as the words bubbled out, Bailey realized their shocking truth. Nothing was ever for her. Dekker only ever concerned himself with Dekker, and she was only an accessory that suited him when she complimented his wants.

Had she ever enjoyed doing those things? Or was the thrill of being with him what she enjoyed?

"Bailey, what's wrong?" Dekker asked, soothingly, suddenly changing tactics. "I thought you would enjoy seeing everyone again and doing some fun things. Your life in Crossroads sounds terribly boring, and I wanted us to have some fun together."

Bailey felt herself softening just a little. Maybe he really wasn't as selfish as she'd feared. With his personality, maybe he simply didn't know any better and was loving her in the way he knew best.

"Look, if you don't want to do everything that's fine," Dekker offered agreeably. "You are more than welcome to stay home, and I'll go by myself. I'd really like you to come to my parents' party, though, and I want to take you out on Saturday to see my new boat."

That sounded more realistic, though Bailey still wasn't sure about the "going by myself" part or his parents' party. The fact that they said it was "okay" for her to come wasn't exactly putting out the welcome mat. His parents didn't like her, and she didn't look forward to the thinly-veiled insults and awkwardness of feeling like she didn't belong.

Realistically, she didn't belong at all. Dekker came from a wealthy family who didn't appreciate their son's interest in a poor librarian hailing from a broken and quite colorful family.

"You have a new boat?" she asked, trying to be supportive. Of the things he'd mentioned, tolerating a boat ride in February seemed the most preferable.

"Yes!" Dekker said, his eyes lighting with excitement. "I got a fantastic deal on it. Even my dad was impressed. When I was at the marina a couple weeks ago, I started talking to this old man. He showed me his boat, and it was a beauty. He mentioned that he'd just admitted his wife to a memory care facility, and he wouldn't be taking it out much on the water anymore. He said he was thinking about selling it, and I asked how much he wanted. He wasn't sure but said he'd talk to his son. In a moment of genius, I threw out a number and told him I'd give him that much if he wanted to sell it to me. He had no idea what he had or what it was worth, so the number I tossed at him sounded good. He agreed and signed the papers right there! I've never known of a craft like that to go for so very little!"

Bailey looked at him in shock, feeling like she was missing something important in his story. From his description, it sounded like he'd just taken advantage of an old man and was now bragging about it!

"It doesn't bother you that he was elderly and didn't know any better?" Bailey asked.

"Why should it?" Dekker asked with a shrug. "His loss is my gain. I will tell you, though, that his son wasn't happy at all! When I showed up to take possession of the boat, his son was with him. He knew what it was worth, and was ticked off that his dad had sold it for so little, but no way I was going to let him out of the deal. It was done. End of story. At least for them! Maybe his son will keep a better eye on him next time!"

Dekker's cackle sent chills down Bailey's spine. Was this for real? Was her boyfriend really that horrible of a person to take advantage of another person like that?

"But he could have used the money for his wife's care!" Bailey protested.

Dekker cocked his head to one side, thinking. "I'm sure he did. When you put it like that, I probably did him a favor by buying the boat."

Had she ever admired or even liked this man?

Bailey kept her silence as Dekker finally turned off onto one of the side streets leading to their apartment. She thought about protesting, labeling his actions as unethical and claiming that they took advantage of someone weaker than him. But she knew it would do no good. Dekker was proud of his actions and carried not a trace of guilt or regret. His dad had even given his stamp of approval, showing pride that Dekker had used another's weakness to great financial advantage.

Now that she thought about it, she realized this wasn't atypical behavior. This wasn't the first time he'd taken advantage of someone. After all, it was a trait glorified in the business world. With a sickening feeling, she realized it wouldn't be the last time either.

Her mind wandered back to the night she went shopping with Camden, and she remembered the snowflake wreath. He didn't need to give that snowflake wreath to that elderly woman. He'd gotten it first, and there wasn't anything unethical about him keeping it. But he'd given it to her anyway. Then he'd gone above and beyond and paid for it just to be kind and bless her. When faced with a choice that would either benefit him or benefit a stranger at great personal cost, he put someone else before him. He'd done it so nonchalantly, without a hint of pride or desire to be recognized in any way.

Unfortunately, Bailey had also been privy to Israel's reaction to the fact that Camden had not secured the wreath. Camden had walked out with him to his car the next day, and Bailey had unashamedly watched the private conversation. Israel had been very angry, while Camden stood and simply took the full force of his wrath. Of course, this was prior to Marissa's passing, and Bailey held hope that through this tragedy, the brothers could find a measure of peace between them. But at that time, tears streamed down her face at seeing such undeserved anger directed at Camden and his beautiful act of generosity. Her only consolation had been in privately telling Lydia what Camden had done. Because of it, Lydia had loved the wreath even more when Brooke had finally delivered the back-ordered treasure two days late for her birthday.

Bailey sighed. Clearly, sacrificing for someone else wasn't new behavior for Camden any more than Dekker's selfishness was new behavior for him.

Who did she want to be? Did she want to be the spoiled princess who lived life for the purpose of fun and enjoyment at the expense of all else? Or did she want to be the person who was willing to sacrifice for someone else, getting life's greatest joy out of serving others?

Maybe Dekker wasn't the one who had changed in the past six weeks. Had she really worn blinders all this time, not realizing who the man was she claimed to love? Could you really be in love with someone you didn't even like?

I love the way he made me feel.

I don't love him.

Dekker parked the car in their apartment's garage, and they both got out. Bailey got her suitcase while Dekker led the way into the place she and Dekker had called home for over a year now. Dekker turned on the lights and began rummaging around in the freezer for ice cream. Bailey set her suitcase down in the middle of the floor and turned a full circle. All of her familiar things were right where she'd left them. Yet it didn't feel the same. It was like she no longer belonged in her own house or felt comfortable in her own skin.

Her gaze found its way to where Dekker wolfed down a bowl of ice cream while on his phone, talking to a friend about how great rock climbing would be tomorrow.

She didn't belong here.

As if the world she'd seen in black and white was suddenly painted with color, she realized the truth of what Camden had been telling her all along. Attraction and chemistry weren't enough. Dekker wasn't a good person, at least not good according to her current values. He was plenty good according to his own values. She didn't admire him, and he didn't challenge her to be a better person.

Dekker was selfish and superficial. He always had been, but her feelings had completely blinded her. With the Hutchins family, she'd just experienced a depth of emotion that made everything that came out of Dekker's mouth seem silly and shallow. The plane rides, the new boats, the parties, the fun—all of that existed on a level that didn't really matter in the long run.

All of Bailey's jumbled thoughts led to one inescapable question.

What did matter?

She walked over to Dekker and pulled on his sleeve. He shot her an irritated look. He hated when she interrupted him.

"I need to talk to you," she whispered.

He held up a finger indicating that he'd talk to her in a minute, even as he laughed into the phone at something his friend was saying.

She tugged on his sleeve again. "I need to talk to you *now!*" she insisted.

He stood from his stool and turned his back on her.

Bailey went into the bedroom, found an empty box, and began emptying her clothes from the closet.

"What is it?" Dekker demanded, finally appearing in the doorway with his arms crossed over his chest and his eyes flashing angrily.

"You're never going to marry me, are you?" Bailey asked, continuing to put clothes in the box.

Dekker's face twisted comically. "What are you talking about? What's gotten into you, Bailey?"

"I just want to know. Do you ever plan on marrying me?" Her voice sounded strained and upset, even to her own ears.

Dekker held his hands out as if trying to literally push the situation back down. "Hold on, Bailey. Where is this coming from? As far as I know, we are having a good time together. We talked about marriage, but we both decided that we didn't need a signed document defining our love or relationship."

"You decided, Dekker, not me." Bailey speared him with her gaze, pouring out all of the frustration from the past two years that she'd kept carefully hidden behind the fun and butterflies. "I always hoped for something more, yet I believed your flowery words. Now I realize all of that fancy, post-modern talk sounds pretty and means absolutely nothing. You're not planning to marry me, and I now think that is actually a good thing since you don't really love me."

Dekker's hair flipped angrily across his forehead as he spoke. "Bailey, I'm lost. What happened? We've always had the best chemistry. How can you say that I don't love you?"

"Nothing about your actions says you love me," Bailey insisted. "As soon as we arrived home, you got on your phone. And that was after you went out on a Valentine's date with your parents and not me. This entire weekend is about you, not me, and definitely not us. I can't do this Dekker. I'm leaving. I'll come by to pack my things up tomorrow and have them moved to storage."

"Is that it then? You're not even going to give me a chance?" Dekker came close, his hand outstretched. "Come on, Bailey, we've had fights before. Just stay the night. We'll talk it out, and things will be better tomorrow. Don't throw all we have away. Two years, Bailey. Don't toss out two years."

Bailey looked at him and recognized his tactics. He was trying to charm her away from the cliff. If he had his way, he'd be kissing her within five minutes and then all would be forgotten as he showed her that he loved her.

But that wasn't love, and she refused to be manipulated any longer. Even her physical attraction to him now seemed greatly diminished, overpowered by her strong disgust for who he was on the inside.

"Not this time, Dekker," Bailey said firmly, yet she felt a tinge of guilt. Dekker hadn't shared her experiences of the past few weeks. He didn't know her thought processes. To him, Bailey's change of heart probably seemed very sudden and crazy.

"I'm sorry," she continued sincerely, wanting him to understand her decision and know that this wasn't a fickle tantrum she'd wish to undo tomorrow. She would not be back. "I admit that I'm not the same woman who left Seattle in December. I feel like my eyes have been opened to myself, to you, to our life together, to what love actually is, to my values and priorities. Everything has changed for me. I feel bad about the two years, but not in the way you think. Two years is an awfully long time to be wrong."

"There's someone else, isn't there?" Dekker gritted out fiercely. "You wouldn't do this if you didn't already have someone else. It's that Camden guy you work with, isn't it? I knew there was something strange going on."

Bailey struggled to find words to explain. She couldn't honestly deny that she had feelings for Camden, and yet that had nothing to do with this situation. "I haven't cheated on you, Dekker. Whether or not I have feelings for someone else is no longer your business. I have never acted on feelings for anyone but you. Now I realize that we no longer share the same values.

I don't like the way you took advantage of that elderly man and bought your new boat. I don't like the way you treat me. It's my feelings for you, and who you are as a person, that are the issues here, and those have nothing to do with anyone but you."

"Fine. Go then." Dekker reached for an empty box and threw it on the bed with the others. "I won't beg you to say. You'll be the one begging to come back to me tomorrow. You can have your high and mighty values and your stupid dreams about a paper tying me to you in the prison of marriage, but when it comes right down to it, you're nothing without me. You'll soon figure out that you miss the free handout you've had for the last two years. I'm the best thing that's ever happened to you, Bailey, and you're not going to like life very much without a sugar daddy to pay your way."

Dekker's words pierced her heart, and she knew she needed to leave now. She'd get her things later. She walked past him into the living room, picked up her suitcase and walked to the door.

"Goodbye, Dekker," she said simply. Then she left.

She made it down to the apartment parking lot before reality caught up with her in the form of pouring rain. She didn't even have a car with which to leave. In December, when Dekker had objected to paying parking fees on a car she wouldn't be using, she'd leased her car to a friend for three months.

Lacking any other option, Bailey pulled her hood up and began walking, wanting to get as much distance as possible from her former boyfriend. Her tears joined the rain as the past six weeks came rushing over her in a wave. As it retreated, the riptide pulled her back under, washing her with wave upon wave of overwhelming emotion.

Conversations with Camden replayed themselves in her mind. She remembered how he'd accused her of not knowing what love really was, and he'd been right. She couldn't recall ever feeling the kind of love Camden had described, either romantically or otherwise. The only hints she'd had of it had been in the last few weeks under the Hutchins' roof. They knew how to love each other, and even Bailey had been included in both witnessing and receiving the love of people who truly cared for her with no ulterior motive.

If Camden was right about love, was he right about everything else, too? Was his method of making matches far superior to hers? The dates she'd arranged for the contest flashed in front of her mind as if on a movie screen, and Bailey felt embarrassed. She should have paid better attention to matching people with similar core values and put less emphasis on chemistry. She'd likely made matches that mirrored her own relationship with Dekker, and clearly, that didn't lead to happily ever after all.

Shame washed over her. She was ashamed of the way she'd handled other people's love lives, but more than that, she was ashamed of her own. She now saw herself for who she truly was.

She was not a good person.

Until today, she'd agreed with Dekker's view on everything, at least on the superficial level. She had lived just as selfishly as he, only caring about people to the extent that they benefitted her. She'd seen nothing wrong with her life and had instead felt proud of all of the money, prestige, and things she'd gained with Dekker.

Nothing had changed. That is, nothing but her. It wasn't as if her life was suddenly wrong. It had always been wrong. She's been blind to the truth, assuming that the goal in life was to be happy with love as her god. If she did something and labeled it with the word "love," then it had to be right. The problem was in her definition of love. She'd never bothered to check with love's original author.

She'd created her own god based on what she thought he should be like. She'd assumed she already knew and didn't bother trying to know someone who existed independent of her beliefs. She now realized that God's existence and His attributes did not depend on her perception. It was up to her to know Him as He was, not as she wished Him to be.

Right before Camden had left her to break the news of Marissa's passing to Israel, he'd asked her to pray. She'd sat in the chair in the office and tried to pray, but she couldn't find the words to say. Standing, she'd walked over to the floor-to-ceiling windows and gazed out at the city lit up in its night time glory, and yet she still couldn't pray. Of course, she'd prayed before, tossing a petition up to heaven in a desperate time of need. Yet, this was different. It was as if she'd been talking into a phone, thinking there was no one actually on the other end. Now she couldn't escape the suspicion that someone really was on the line with her, listening to what she said. The biggest problem was that she didn't know who that Someone was.

As she walked, her misery only grew as she encountered herself, in all her faults and sins. She wasn't good enough. She couldn't save herself, and she'd spent her life ignoring the only One who could.

Dear, God, she cried. *I've lived life on my own terms and not yours!*

But beyond that, she didn't know what to do to get herself out of the quicksand where she found herself trapped.

Somewhere in her tortuous thoughts, she'd come to her senses long enough to take out her phone, open the app, and order an Uber. When the designated vehicle pulled up to the intersection where she stood, she climbed inside, completely miserable and fully soaked. Thankfully, the driver didn't press her with questions but compassionately asked if she had friends at the address she'd given.

Bailey nodded through her tears, providing the driver with enough to keep silent.

He pulled to the curb of a house, and Bailey felt a moment of hesitation. Maybe she should have gone to a hotel. However, she felt so desperate for relief that she couldn't imagine a long night without it. She'd instead come to the one person she knew could help and wouldn't turn her away.

The hour was late, and she hated just showing up on the doorstep. Nevertheless, she did it anyway. Standing hunched in the rain, she bravely pressed the button to ring the doorbell.

The door opened, and a beautiful, dark-haired woman looked at Bailey with eyes wide in surprise and concern. "Bailey, what are you doing here? Come in! Come in!"

She eagerly reached for Bailey, pulling her into the house out of the rain and shutting the door behind her.

Bailey's broken words brimming with emotion drew the other woman up short.

"Help me, Elise," she cried hoarsely "I'm so very lost!"

Eleven

The business line rang, and Camden looked up from the computer, irritated that a call had made it through. He had purposely buried the phone number on the website. If clients needed assistance, they first had to jump through options to send an email or even, in extreme cases, do an online chat during business hours. Finding the actual phone number to talk to a live person was purposely difficult. Fortunately, his methods were effective, and they didn't receive too many calls. Usually, they were able to successfully handle any customer service issues with one of the other avenues.

"Betwixt Two Hearts, how may I help you?" Camden answered formally. As much as he didn't like interruptions, he really should give props to anyone dedicated enough to locate the number.

"Detective Drisklay. Boston Police Department. Get me your boss."

Startled by the demanding, gravelly voice that sounded straight out of a *Godfather* movie, Camden responded. "Umm... ok. You're in luck. I am the boss. How can I help?"

Impatience drew out a distinctive Boston accent as the man shot back, "Look, kid. This is grown-up stuff. Get me your boss. Better yet, get me your boss's boss. Not your kid brother. Not your uncle. I need to talk to the big guy. I'm working on a murder investigation."

Murder investigation?

Camden swallowed, trying to balance the lightning bolt of horror with the sudden burst of anger at Drisklay's insults. With a calm to be proud of, he responded. "I'm the guy you need to talk to. I'm Camden Hutchins, co-owner of Betwixt Two Hearts, website designer, and operator in charge of data, delivery, security, customer service, and everything in between."

The other line was silent other than the sound of Drisklay taking a drink. Finally, he replied, "You memorize that entire speech or do you have it written out?"

Camden gritted his teeth. "I'm the one you want to talk to. How can I help?"

A two-second silence was quickly followed with more words that lashed out as if seeking their own victim. "I'm investigating a woman who was murdered while meeting a so-called 'date' she found on your website."

Camden's breath caught. This was bad. Really bad. If Bailey found out...

"What is the client's name?" Camden asked briskly. Drisklay didn't seem to want to waste time with an emotional response and protests of how the website couldn't possibly be involved. Instead, Camden sat up straight with fingers poised over the keyboard.

"Rebekah Harrison from Boston. Your guy apparently met her for the date on Valentine's Day, kidnapped her, then dumped the body thirty miles away."

Camden winced. Drisklay really could have done without the details.

Finding the profile, he clicked on it and brought up a blonde woman in her twenties who smiled beautifully as she looked up at him from the computer screen. She looked nice. Young. Innocent. Camden felt nauseated to think that that smile no longer existed on earth.

"It looks like she signed up a while ago. She had pretty narrow specifications, and a match wasn't found until right before Valentine's Day."

"What were her narrow specifications?" Drisklay asked.

"She was a Christian," Camden's heart twisted a little more. "She wanted someone to be just as dedicated as she was."

Drisklay let out a scoff that almost sounded like he was choking on spoiled food. "So dedicated Christians are now kidnapping and murdering their Valentine's Day dates?"

Camden barely managed to hold his tongue, somehow knowing that if he said anything in defense of Christianity, it would only add fuel to Drisklay's hatred.

Just stay on task.

Finding the profile of the man she'd been matched with, Camden clicked on it, bringing up the info on a man named John Paul.

"It's a fake account," Camden said, shock running through him.

"Figures," Drisklay said flatly.

"My security measures labeled it as fake and terminated it forty-eight hours after it was created, which happened to be the afternoon of Valentine's Day. I'm guessing it was too late for Rebekah to see the notification."

"So, you flagged it as fake. What else did you do then? What can you tell me about where it originated?"

Camden breathed deeply, wondering what he should do. If he revealed all the information he could glean, that put himself at risk. But a woman was dead. If he could help find her killer, wouldn't it be worth it?

"Just give me a minute," Camden muttered, clicking through a few more screens.

Clearing his throat, Camden explained. "I have the IP address where the account was created. Unfortunately, it traces back to the Copley Square branch of the Boston Library. A single user in a public place won't be easy to track down."

"Obviously not," Drisklay said dryly. "Okay, let's talk about user profiles in general. How did my victim end up matched with your murderer?"

Answering his question as he worked, Camden explained, "The client completes a detailed questionnaire, and the website uses an in-depth algorithm to make the matches along the specifications requested by the client. There are multiple options as far as the client's level of involvement and how many matches they want. In Rebekah's case, she selected one match and had very narrow parameters for that one date."

"Would it be possible for someone who knew Rebekah's answers to create a profile with the goal of being matched specifically to her?"

Camden hesitated. He hadn't considered this, simply assuming the murder had been random. However, by the way Drisklay spoke, it almost sounded like he had a theory which involved someone Rebekah knew. Camden didn't know whether this idea was more comforting or not. Either Rebekah met her murderer randomly through his site, or someone who knew her used the site as a tool to target and kill her.

"Normally, that would be very difficult," Camden explained, not at all liking the answer he must give. "In this case, it is very possible. The algorithm places a high degree of value on a person's religious preferences. Rebekah very adamantly refused to date someone who was not a dedicated Christian. She actually registered as a client a while ago, but up until this match, she had refused every name sent to her. With each one, she submitted her objections to the person prior to contacting them in any way and requested a different match. Most of her rejection reasons had to do with faith, but she also didn't seem open to anyone adventurous or overly outgoing. This was the first match she willingly accepted and agreed to meet. Unfortunately, if someone knew Rebekah and the type of man she was interested in, it is possible that particular someone designed the profile to specifically appeal to her."

Waves of guilt washed over him. He thought he'd been so careful with safety and security, and yet someone had used a weakness in his site procedures to end the life of someone else.

Seeming oblivious to Camden's emotional state, Drisklay pressed, "So does your website specialize in fake people?"

"No," Camden replied adamantly. Why was everything this man said at least mildly offensive?

"What about the account made you realize it was fake?" Drisklay pressed. "I can check out security footage from the library, but are there any other clues from the profile that stand out?"

Camden sighed, leaning back from his computer and running his hands wearily through his hair. "I already checked the library footage from that day and time of the account's creation. I didn't recognize anyone suspicious. You might have some of your department tech guys take a look and see if they can extrapolate any faces, but the camera angles seem to be good at getting the back of people's heads."

"What do you mean you checked the security footage?" Drisklay demanded.

"I mean while we've been talking, I accessed the library's security footage on my screen and checked through the cameras in the computer area." Hurrying to change the subject so that Drisklay didn't push on that point further, Camden backtracked to answer his other question. "I don't know that the profile contains any more helpful details. Whoever created it did a good job. The profile pic, the occupation, and all of the interests look quite real and match up eerily well to Rebekah's. Their algorithm score of compatibility was very high. The only points they didn't get were for areas where differences are scored at a higher value."

"If the account is so perfect, how did you identify it as fake?"

Camden resigned himself to the fact that he was going to need to explain every single procedure involved in the site. "Verifying accounts is automated. I designed a system that runs background checks, internet searches, and a few other checks on every profile that is created. If the person cannot be proven to exist, then the account is immediately locked and pulled from public view. This profile took a little longer to identify it as fake. Usually, I get notification of them quite soon. John Paul's profile was done well and also belonged to a name that is quite common. Verifying the name of John Paul is easy. Trying to find a specific John Paul and verify that he is who he says he is becomes more complicated."

"So, all a killer has to do is make a fake account and make sure he gets the deed done before you figure it out." It wasn't a question. Drisklay was taunting him by stating it as already a proven fact.

Camden winced. He really didn't need this man adding to his guilt. "When we first launched the site, we needed matches fast, and it didn't seem necessary to wait for account verification. Our website provides more security than any other site out there, and we have other security measures already in place. I didn't think it would matter if the verification came through an hour after notification of the match was sent. Rebekah's case seems to be a combination of a few rare events. I will be making changes today to ensure that nothing like this can ever happen again. All accounts will need to be verified before they are placed publicly on the site and any matches made. You have no idea how sorry I am that I didn't already do so on February thirteenth."

"I need you to send me all the info from her profile and from her date's. And I need it yesterday," Drisklay said flatly.

"I can do that," Camden answered. "I just need some kind of verification that you are who you say you are."

The detective uttered a few choice words. "You're serious? What, you want me to sing you a song just so you can give me the info you have on the screen in front of you?"

"I cannot grant private information to everyone who calls claiming to be a police detective." *Never mind this is the first. And hopefully the last.* "If you simply send me a department email with your badge number, that should be enough verification, and I'll respond with the info you need. I won't be making the same mistake of releasing any information, for anyone, without proper verification."

"Fine. Where should I have my assistant contact you?"

Camden rattled off the email, and with that, Drisklay was done.

Camden hesitated, not sure if he should mention anything else. "I assume you know the time of Rebekah's kidnapping?" he said quickly, right before Drisklay could hang up.

Seeming a little irritated that the conversation was continuing at all, Drisklay answered. "The last she was seen, she was getting ready for her date at her home. That was in the evening around six-thirty. We don't know yet exactly where or when the actual kidnapping occurred. We're not sure where she was meeting her date, just that she was. Now, if you'll excuse me, I need to—"

"6249 Waterford Street at 6:53 p.m.," Camden said swiftly.

"What?" Drisklay sputtered. "You're saying that's where and when she was kidnapped? How can you possibly know that?"

"Like I said, the website has some unparalleled security measures. Rebekah had her phone, and she'd apparently left the Betwixt app running. I have a tracking location for her at that address at the time, but nothing after that. Either her phone was disposed of, turned off, or the app disabled at 6:53. It looks like that street number is a parking lot."

Drisklay's tone was thoughtful. "Yes, that area has restaurants within walking distance of that lot. That's probably where she was planning to go but never made it. You'll send me the tracking information, I assume."

"I will," Camden confirmed, already adding the needed pieces to an email draft.

"What did you say your name was? Hutchins?" Drisklay asked, now openly curious.

"Why?" Camden asked warily.

"Because I know a sixteen-year-old internet quack from a guy who knows his stuff. Your tracking methods and security are unconventional, to put it mildly. Exactly who are you, Hutchins?"

Camden swallowed, his throat tight. "That's not something you want to know or pursue, Drisklay." Keeping his voice calm but infusing it with steel, he continued. "I'm not your investigation. I helped you, but that's the end of it. Please don't reveal where you got any of the information. Let me repeat, who I am is something you can NOT know. Do you understand?"

"Yes, I believe I do," Drisklay said, his tone turning back to brisk and irritable.

"Not even an internet search," Camden clarified.

"Understood. You get me the info I need, I'll pretend not to be curious. Deal?"

"Thank you. I can't tell you how sorry I am about Rebekah and any role Betwixt Two Hearts played." Camden paused. Drisklay's disdain for Christianity was apparent, but Camden couldn't sign off without adding, "I'll be praying for your investigation and that you find whoever is responsible. I'll also pray for Rebekah's family. I can't imagine the pain they're feeling."

Drisklay's voice was dry and scratchy, and Camden couldn't tell whether it was threaded with actual emotion or the usual scorn. "I'm not sure your prayers will do them any good after the fact. See ya around, Hutchins."

The line went dead. No thanks or expression of appreciation. He was gone as suddenly as the random ringing of the phone, and Camden doubted he would ever talk to the man again.

Camden took a few minutes to pray for Drisklay's investigation, Rebekah's family, and for Drisklay himself, though he'd not had the guts to mention that one to the surly detective. After a few moments, he felt a little relief from the guilt. It was the nature of the fallen world for good things to be used for bad purposes, and Camden wasn't responsible for someone else's sin. Though he couldn't predict the future or prevent bad things from happening to his clients, he could take steps to make sure his website was the safest possible.

A few minutes later, he'd changed website protocol so that no profile was made public or matched with another before making it through the verification process. He called it the Rebekah protocol.

He checked his inbox and saw an email come through from the Boston Police Department. He was putting the finishing touches on his reply email when the door to the office opened. Seeing Bailey, Camden startled, quickly pressing send and switching tabs on his computer screen before turning to greet her as nonchalantly as possible. Unfortunately, he could only imagine Bailey's fury if she found out about Rebekah Harrison. He also knew it would hit her hard emotionally, and he didn't want to cause her to bear the guilt and pain.

"Hi, Bailey! How was your weekend?" he greeted as if he wasn't hiding anything at all.

This was one burden he'd shoulder alone.

Bailey tried to smile, but she knew she looked tired and pale. "My weekend wasn't as expected, but it was still good. I got to see Elise."

Hopefully, Camden wouldn't press her for a full report. She knew she'd eventually need to tell him everything that went on in Seattle, but she wasn't emotionally up for it yet. She just didn't know how to casually say, *So I broke up with my boyfriend and got saved this weekend. How was yours?*

"Did Dad pick you up at the airport?" Camden asked. "I wasn't sure what time your flight arrived."

"And that is the exact reason why you weren't the one picking me up," Bailey remarked dryly as she walked over to her computer and turned it on.

Her full weekend had included staying with Elise and moving out of her former apartment with Dekker. Even though Dekker kept his plans and didn't stick around much, Elise and her husband had spent the whole time helping and acting as a buffer between them the few times when he showed up. While she had succeeded in moving everything into storage, it left neither her nor Elise any time to work on website tasks. They were currently extremely behind and needed to put in long hours the next few days to get caught up.

"Israel actually picked me up," Bailey informed. "He was in Brighton Falls for work but then needed to head back to Crossroads to take Chloe to an appointment of some kind. I was originally supposed to fly in yesterday, but I had to finish a few things in Seattle and moved my flight to today."

Bailey brought up her email account and felt daunted by the number of messages she needed to sort through. Seeing one from Selby, the sister whom she'd sent the lists of potential dates for her brother, she quickly clicked on it. Selby had kept her updated on Heath's journey through the lists as he plowed through them like a speed dating session gone very wrong.

Bailey eagerly awaited the email announcing that Heath had made some progress, but it hadn't happened yet. Now she worried that, once again, Camden had been right. Maybe she shouldn't have sent those lists. Even though Selby had specifically wanted names for Heath to practice dating, Bailey had hoped he would magically find the right one—on the list she had created, of course. Instead, she had essentially doomed each woman on there to a date that was, at the minimum, an unforgettable experience.

"I would have picked you up if you'd asked," Camden said, his hurt voice coming from right over her shoulder.

Bailey startled, quickly minimizing the email so Camden wouldn't see it. If he found out that she'd broken company policy and gone behind his back to disobey his wishes, he would be very upset.

Would he even forgive her? The thought chilled Bailey, and she couldn't handle the idea that it might ruin their relationship.

Trying to answer as if she weren't hiding anything at all, she turned to Camden and said, "Don't feel bad, Camden. I know where your talents lie and where they don't. Even with your best intentions, a decent possibility still existed that you'd get involved with work, and I'd be left waiting at the airport again."

"I would have made sure I was there on time," Camden grumbled, his tone still matching the hurt feelings of a three-year-old.

Bailey shook her head. Poor Camden didn't realize that the fact that he couldn't keep track of time when working in no way lessened Bailey's opinion of him. The man was wonderfully smart, wonderfully quirky, and all-around wonderful as well. She really didn't care who picked her up at the airport, just as long as she was picked up.

"Don't feel bad, Camden," she urged. "The change in my schedule actually worked well with Israel picking me up. Plus, when I arrived back in Crossroads, we picked up Chloe from the daycare so she they could head directly to the appointment after dropping me off. She showed me the origami cat family you made for her. That was definitely an added bonus."

A smile quirked through Camden's sour expression. "Apparently, I need to now figure out how to fold a unicorn family as well, at least that's Chloe's next request."

"Whatever you're doing seems to definitely be helping. She was very excited about that cat family. She seemed almost happy."

"Chloe is doing amazingly well," Camden said, his expression full of gentle love. "I guess in a three-year-old's mind, mommy going to live in heaven is easier to understand than mommy left and doesn't want to be with you anymore. Israel, on the other hand, will probably struggle with both for a very long time. One explanation is definitely not better than the other in his mind since they both involve a great deal of guilt."

Bailey nodded. "Israel did mention how much he appreciates all of your help. I think picking me up gave him a small sense of satisfaction to feel like he was doing something to help you."

Camden nodded sadly. "For the first time in a long time, things are good between my brother and me. It's just sad that it took a tragedy to draw us to this point."

Bailey watched him as he turned and pushed a few buttons on the printer. Grief still tinged his stormy eyes. It wasn't his own grief, though. It was a grief of empathy for his brother. His strong jaw was tight, and a few more lines of stress marked his face. Bailey could read the exhaustion from shouldering much of the burden his family was going through. Israel had been so upset by Marissa's passing that Camden took over most of the prep for the memorial service, which had turned out beautifully. He'd also taken extra time to play and give attention to Chloe, helping her work through just about the worst thing a child could experience.

Camden was an amazing man, and she now realized why. Over the last few weeks, she'd also witnessed the depth of his faith. She'd seen and heard him pray with Israel, Chloe, and other family members, seeming to draw his strength from the Lord.

He gave of himself so much that Bailey wished she could do something for him. He really deserved to find someone as wonderful as him. He needed someone who would love and care for him in the same way he loved and cared for others.

Slowly, an idea began to form.

"Camden, I know who I want to use as my last selection for the contest," she said suddenly.

"What?" Camden asked, not seeming to remember that they even had a contest.

"You know, the contest where we each arrange dates and get points if they are successful? Remember? We are tied now. I have two points from the date you arranged, and you have two points—one from the church date I attempted, and one for the basketball game. I still don't know if that last one qualifies since you matched Jeff up with two girls. I don't even know which one he ended up with, but I'll go ahead and give you a point anyway."

"Both," Camden grinned rakishly. "I checked. So far, the guy seems to be thoroughly enjoying dating both women. They seem to be very well aware of each other and have even gone on a few group dates with all of them. They use the app a lot for scheduling, so I've been able to keep track. The jury is still out on which one he'll end up with."

"That's actually probably a very good thing for Jeff. That will give him experience with women, even if they don't ever go beyond the friendship level."

"So we're tied," Camden granted, folding his arms across his front and looking at her with speculation. "Who is your final pick?"

"You," Bailey announced gleefully.

"What? No," Camden said, suddenly realizing that she was actually serious. "Absolutely not. No. I refuse to be one of your guinea pigs. No."

"Why not?" Bailey pleaded, not put off in the least by his adamant and lengthy refusal. "You're a great guy. This whole time I've known you, you haven't gone on a single date. Let me set you up on a date. Please?"

"No," Camden refused flatly, walking away from her as if the matter were closed.

"Come on, Camden. Just one date. One evening. It's not like you have to marry the girl. If you think about it, this is your greatest opportunity to win. You're my toughest critic. If you like the date I arrange, then that will really be a win. The results of the whole contest will rest entirely in your hands."

Camden paused as if seriously giving her request consideration for the first time. "One date? And I don't have to like it?"

"Nope," Bailey said. "Not at all."

"Do I still get my choice for an entry into the contest?"

"Absolutely," Bailey replied confidently. "I've attempted more contest entries than you, so if you want, you can even select two entries."

"No, I think I'll just choose one last match as well. Since we're tied, we can call it quits after this round."

"Okay," Bailey said, suddenly hesitant. She wanted to make sure the contest was fair, but if Camden didn't want to do more than one match, then she guessed that would be fine.

Camden grinned. "I choose you."

"N-no," Bailey startled. "I'm not—"

Camden held his hand up to stop her words. "I know what you're going to say. You already have a boyfriend. You know I don't think he's right for you, Bailey. Just think of it as a business arrangement, not necessarily a romantic one. If you let me make a match for you, I'll let you make a match for me." Camden flashed her a self-satisfied smile as if highly pleased with himself. "If you're a 'no,' then I'm a 'no.'"

"Okay," Bailey said slowly, returning to her computer.

"W-What?" Camden asked, shocked. "Is that a 'yes'? Are you sure? I mean, are you really sure?"

Bailey smiled, amused. Obviously, he hadn't expected her to say yes. He'd thought she would refuse, which would give him permission to also refuse and get her to leave him alone.

"Yes, Camden," she said firmly. "You can arrange a date for me. Just one. And I'll arrange a date for you."

"What about Dekker?" Camden asked. "Will he be okay with you going on a date with someone else?"

Bailey shrugged. "It doesn't really matter how he feels about it. Dekker lost any right to an opinion on my life or actions."

Camden startled, his blue-gray eyes wide with shock. "You broke up?"

Bailey nodded.

"I'm sorry," Camden said sympathetically.

"I'm not," Bailey said, lifting her chin up in determination. "I never should have been with him in the first place." She paused, a thoughtful look coming into her eyes. "I can't wish that it hadn't happened, though. The whole experience and then breaking up with Dekker and realizing how wrong I'd been about everything is what caused me to realize how wrong I'd also been about God. It's the direct reason why I turned my life over to God on His terms."

"You what?" Camden asked, turning pale and sitting down in his chair.

Bailey hesitated. This wasn't the elegant way she'd wanted to tell Camden. It just seemed too casual to mention something so life-changing like this. How did she explain what had happened?

"Camden, you were right," she said quietly. "After I broke up with Dekker, I realized how very lost I was. I went to Elise's house, and she helped me pray. I found the one true God, and He saved me. I know I won't be perfect, but I will try to spend my life getting to know Him and living my life in a way that serves Him."

"Bailey, I can't tell you how happy that makes me," Camden said thickly. Taking a deep breath, he continued, "Are you sure you're okay with going on a date? I know it still must be difficult. If it's just too soon, I understand."

Bailey appreciated his thoughtfulness, but she wasn't going to wallow. "It is too soon, but that's okay. It's fair. Like I said, it's not like I have to marry the guy. I don't even need to like him. I just need to endure one date you set up."

"Your confidence in me is staggering," Camden said wryly.

Bailey challenged, "Prove me wrong. I'll fill out the survey on the website, just like I'm a client, and you do the same. You can use your algorithm for my match, but I'll use my methods with your profile."

Camden looked suddenly wary. "I'll only fill out the survey if we don't actually post it to the website. You just need the information, so you shouldn't need the website at all."

"I guess that's okay," Bailey said. "It's only one match. I guess I don't need the website if you're that shy about your info being made public."

"Thanks. You're welcome to pull your profile after you go on the date, if you want," Camden offered.

"It's not a big issue to me either way," Bailey said. "The important thing is that we have a deal."

"Yes, I guess we do," Camden replied.

While Camden returned to his computer, Bailey turned back to hers, determined to finally make some progress. Even so, it was several minutes before she could halt herself from daydreaming of winning the contest by setting Camden up with someone as wonderful as him.

"Camden, I FINALLY have your perfect match!" Bailey danced into the kitchen and made the announcement in a singsong voice.

Camden groaned. This was exactly why he'd taken so long to fill out the survey for Bailey. He hadn't wanted to, and he'd only completed it after weeks of enduring Bailey's incessant pestering. He'd never wanted to do it in the first place. He thought he'd found an out when suggesting that Bailey let him set her up as well. He hadn't counted on her actually letting him. Before he knew what was happening, she announced her breakup with Dekker the Wrecker and agreed to his deal. Lo and behold, he was trapped into going through with a date arranged by Bailey. Dragging his feet and hoping Bailey became too busy and simply forgot seemed his next best option.

While Bailey's past few weeks involved her deciding she liked Crossroads and wanted to move here, signing a lease on an apartment in Crossroads, becoming involved in church, and maintaining a huge workload, she hadn't forgotten in the least bit. Just to avoid the nagging, Camden had finally filled out the form.

Unfortunately, Bailey's current announcement was officially worse than the nagging.

"Ok, send me the info, and I'll see what I can do," Camden said noncommittally. Ignoring her, he continued calmly assembling a sandwich as if she weren't in the room at all.

"Oh, no! I'm not going to fall for that trick again!" Bailey laughed. "Your date is tonight. I won't risk allowing you time to back out. You're to meet her in Brighton Falls in an hour and a half. You'd better head home and get ready. The clock is ticking."

Camden sputtered indignantly, "You can't do that!"

"I already did," Bailey replied nonchalantly as she snatched a potato chip off his plate. "I've corresponded with her already, pretending to be you, of course. Don't worry, she's great. You agreed to meet her for dinner tonight. You can't back down now."

Frozen in shock, Camden stared at her for several seconds. Finally, he calmly responded one word. "No."

"You can't say 'no,'" Bailey protested. "You agreed to go out with a date of my choosing."

"Yes, I did. But I didn't agree that you could impersonate me and schedule the date for the day and time 'of your choosing.'" Camden calmly finished assembling the sandwich and took it to the table. Sitting down, he began eating it as if he had all the time in the world.

Bailey crossed her arms and looked at him as if convinced he would acquiesce to her demands if she just waited.

His crunching of potato chips put her over the edge. She came over to the table and sat beside him. "Come on, Camden. Please? I'm sorry. I shouldn't have scheduled anything without your approval. I was just afraid that if I didn't spring it on you, you'd always find a way to put me off and get out of it. If you want, you can schedule my date for me in return."

"No, Bailey," Camden answered, shaking his head sadly. "I'm not going to treat you badly because you treated me badly. I don't like being manipulated. The whole point is that I wouldn't do that to you."

Bailey hung her head. "You're right. I'm sorry."

Her lip trembled, and she seemed to be genuinely repentant to the point that Camden felt a little sorry for her.

"That wasn't a very Christian thing to do, was it?" Bailey mused. "Here I am trying to do the right thing, and I screw it up."

"Bailey, everyone screws up. That's kind of the whole point. Ask for forgiveness and ask for God to help you be more like Him tomorrow."

"You make it sound so easy," she said softly.

"It isn't easy at all. It's insanely difficult," Camden consoled. "But I think the hard part isn't that it's tough to do the right thing. I think it's harder to listen and allow God to show us what that right thing is. I'm sure you were honestly trying to do something nice for me. You just went about it wrong."

Bailey nodded. "Unfortunately, I've now involved someone else. I know you're not happy with me, but could you please consider meeting your date anyway, for her sake, not mine?"

Camden felt bad for Bailey. He'd watched her the past few weeks and been impressed by the changes he saw in her. Her conversion couldn't have been more genuine. Bailey now possessed a real faith and an eagerness to learn everything she could about the God who'd saved her. She attended every service offered by the church, studied her Bible, and had spiritual discussions with anyone who would listen. Camden also saw in her a heart to serve others, even in the little things like helping Lydia with the dishes or eagerly playing some imaginary game with Chloe. Instead of the selfishness he'd seen in Bailey before, her actions revealed more of a selflessness that Camden admired.

However, even with all of the changes, Bailey was still Bailey—full of determination and spice, and willing to break a few rules in her confident plan to "help" someone else.

"Yes, I will meet her. But not tonight."

Bailey's eyes actually filled with tears. "Please, Camden. You don't understand. Please don't take my mistake out on her."

"I would meet her if I could, Bailey, but I can't. I'm supposed to meet Israel at his office this evening. He asked if I could help him with something at work. Then Mom and Dad are bringing Chloe over to Brighton Falls, and we're all going to a restaurant for dinner."

Bailey looked as if she really wanted to argue but couldn't actually do it.

"I'm really sorry, Bailey," Camden said gently. "I don't want to cancel on Israel. Things are finally good between us, and the fact that he asked for my help with something is pretty big."

"I understand," Bailey said. "I didn't realize you already had plans.

Usually, your Friday nights consist of you sitting and working in front of the computer the same way you do every other minute of every day. I wouldn't want you to cancel on Israel. He needs you, and I'm sure it will do him and Chloe good to have a special family dinner tonight."

"Thanks for understanding." Camden reached over and touched her hand laying on the table. "Hey, don't look so glum. Why don't you come with us? You can ride over with Mom and Dad. I think Geneva is planning to meet for dinner, too."

Bailey smiled sadly. "I actually think I'll pass." She glanced up at the clock. "It's too late for me to cancel on Shaya. She doesn't live or work in Brighton Falls but was planning to drive into the city to meet you. I'm sure she's already left. I'll just go and meet her myself. I'll explain the situation, and we'll do a girls' night."

"Oh, Bailey, I'm sorry. Isn't there a way to contact her?"

"All our correspondence was through the site, and I don't want to stand her up. It will be fine. She's super nice, and I know we'll be great friends. It'll be like an interview. I'll check her out and make sure she's a good match for you. It'll increase my chances of winning." Bailey smiled and winked.

Camden knew she was trying to put on a good front, but he didn't know how to make the situation better. Helplessness settled in as Bailey stood from her seat.

"Let me run upstairs and get ready really quick. I need to leave right away. I've never been to where I'm supposed to meet her, so I'll need to leave with extra time."

Camden watched her leave, feeling a nagging sensation that he really needed to do something, but he couldn't figure out what that something was. Feeling at loose ends, Camden washed up his plate and wandered back to the office.

Ten minutes later, he heard Bailey speaking to his mom on her way out the door. When Lydia asked where she was headed, Bailey happily explained that she was meeting a friend in Brighton Falls. Lydia eagerly let her borrow her car, happy that Bailey was going to do something fun. Then he heard the door open and close, and she was gone.

As soon as the sound of the car's engine melted down the street, Camden ventured out of his office. He grabbed his coat and debated if he really wanted to trade his shorts for a pair of long pants or not. Deciding that any restaurant they visited wasn't going to be that formal, he donned his coat, told his Mom he'd see them later, and headed out to his car.

Camden felt restless the entire drive to Israel's office. Try as he might, he couldn't get his mind off Bailey. He only found a little relief when he got the idea to swing by Bailey's date in between meeting Israel at his office and dinner. Bailey had said they'd contacted through the website, so it should be easy enough to look up their messages. Camden could at least show up and say hi to Bailey's date for five minutes before meeting his family.

When he arrived at the office, Israel was speaking to someone in one of the other offices. The receptionist looked ready to leave but welcomed Camden to wait in Israel's office.

Not one to be content twiddling his thumbs, Camden helped himself to Israel's chair, desk, and computer. Logging in on his brother's machine wasn't too difficult, and Camden quickly brought up the Betwixt site. Once there, he suddenly paused, unsure of where Bailey's messages were located. He could log into her account, but she'd admitted to impersonating him. How exactly did she do that? He didn't have a Betwixt account, so how could she impersonate him and communicate with another Betwixt client?

"Hey. Camden." Israel said, hurrying into the office. "Thanks for coming. Sorry I had to finish up with Doug."

"No problem," Camden said, turning to his brother. "I hope you don't mind, I helped myself to your computer."

"No, not at all." Israel came around the desk and stopped still. "Wait... How did you? Camden, you don't have my login info. How did you log on to my machine?"

Camden looked up at him and lifted one corner of his mouth in a knowing grin.

"Seriously, Camden? You hacked my computer in the two minutes since you got here?"

"No," Camden assured. "It didn't take two minutes."

Israel groaned. "And that's why I need your help! I need you to look at some of our company security. I'm not entirely convinced that everything is adequate to keep all our information secure, and the fact that you just hacked my computer confirms it. We're working on some big deals right now, and I need to limit as much corporate espionage as possible. I've already talked to the board, and they agreed to admit you access to take a look. I can show you the basics tonight, and we can set you up with an office if needed. We'll reimburse you for your time, of course."

At Camden's scowl, Israel rushed to explain. "I'm not trying to manipulate you into working here, Camden. I promise. You'd just be a contractor. You don't even need to fix everything, just take a look and identify the problems. We can take it from there, and you'll be done. I really could use some help with this, and you're honestly the best computer guy I know."

"Okay, Israel," Camden nodded. "I'm happy to help." If his brother needed his help, he'd do it, no matter if he didn't have time and didn't really want to.

Israel grabbed another chair and scooted it close to Camden. "Let me show you the basics, and I'm sure you can take it from there."

Israel started to click on an icon when a strange beep sounded.

"What was that?"

"That sounded like a message for the online chat option on my website," Camden said, his tone puzzled. "Since I was logged on the site, it would have shown the help option as available. Just give me a sec to look what it's about and log off."

"Sure," Israel said, handing over the computer controls.

Camden brought up the chat screen and read.

SHAYA YANZIK: Hi! I got an email with a Security alert that said there was a login to my Betwixt account using a different device. It was wanting to make sure it was me. The problem is that I haven't logged in using a different device, and when I tried to log in just now, it said I didn't have the right password. I'm wondering if I was hacked. Can you help me access my account?

All the blood in Camden's body suddenly turned to ice.

Shaya.

"What's wrong?" Israel asked, suddenly concerned.

Not bothering to respond either to Israel or the chat message, Camden hurriedly used his administrator controls to bring up Shaya's account. He went straight to the messages. Several entries came up to and from Shaya to another Betwixt account. The account was labeled with the name "Camden Hutchins."

Camden felt ill. "No, no, no. That isn't possible. I never created an account."

But Bailey had.

A few more clicks and Camden confirmed his worst nightmare. Bailey had found his survey and submitted it to the website, creating a public profile bearing his name. And his picture.

"Camden, tell me what's wrong," Israel demanded. "You look like you're going to pass out."

Still ignoring him, Camden clicked on the messages again. Shaya Yanzik contacted Camden Hutchins today, saying she'd seen his profile and wanted to meet. Fake Camden had responded that Shaya wasn't on his list of matches, but after seeing her profile, he thought he'd like to meet her. It went on from there. All the messages were from today after Camden's security measures had sent Shaya an email flagging the new login.

Camden stood so suddenly, he knocked his chair down. He ran to the door with Israel on his heels.

"Camden, I need to know what's wrong!" Israel shouted.

"Bailey is in trouble!" he said, making it to the elevator and hitting the down button repeatedly.

"What's going on? Should I call 911?" Israel asked in alarm.

Camden shook his head. "They won't get there fast enough or know what to do." Watching the lights above the elevator climb up to their floor in a painstakingly slow rhythm, Camden explained hurriedly, "Bailey had me fill out a Betwixt survey so she could send me on one of her stupid dates. I filled it out but told her I wouldn't submit it and make it public. She apparently submitted it anyway."

"Why is that a problem?" Israel asked as the elevator finally arrived with a happy ding.

When the doors slid open, both men rushed in, and Camden repeatedly pressed the button for the first floor, trying fruitlessly to get the contraption to move at a faster pace.

Camden shook his head. "It just is. Long story short, someone hacked a Betwixt profile today and set up a date with the Camden Hutchins profile.

When I refused to go on Bailey's date tonight, Bailey insisted on going herself. Israel, the person Bailey went to meet is not who she claimed to be."

As if understanding the gravity of the situation without getting all the details, Israel remained silent until the doors slid open on the ground floor.

"I'm coming with you," he said adamantly before both of them sprinted for the front doors of the building.

They ran through the dark parking lot until they reached Camden's SUV.

"You drive," Camden said, tossing Israel the keys. "I need to make a call."

They slid into the seats, and Camden recited the address listed in the Betwixt messages.

Israel took off with foot pushing the accelerator to the floor, paying no attention to the speed limits.

With his hands shaking, Camden pushed a few buttons on his phone, making a call he'd hoped to never need to make.

He looked at the clock gleaming an evil glow from the center console.

It's too late.

It's too late.

With all of the emotions churning through his body, the worst was the stark fear that despite everything, he wouldn't be in time to save Bailey.

Thirteen

"Hi!" Bailey greeted the host brightly. "I'm supposed to meet someone here, but I'm not sure which one of us arrived first. My friend's name is Shaya Yanzik, and she is expecting Camden Hutchins."

"Please have a seat while I check, Miss," the host replied, indicating one of the empty seats placed between the front door and his little podium.

"Thank you," Bailey answered, obediently taking a seat. The restaurant wasn't crowded, and she was the only one waiting. It didn't seem to be an overly fancy place, though Bailey couldn't see many of the seats past where the dining room opened up.

Bailey didn't like waiting. It gave her too much time to think, and in this case, feel guilty about what she'd done. She hadn't made a full confession to Camden, and she worried what he'd think if he knew exactly how manipulative she actually was. With painful clarity, she now realized that she was guilty of exactly what she'd criticized Dekker for. She used people just as much as he did, trying to arrange life the way she thought best.

I'm so sorry, Lord. I know I'm not the one in charge. You are. Yet I'm struggling with seeking to manipulate things to my will instead of even asking for Yours. Please give me the courage to tell Camden what I've done. And help him to forgive me.

Trying to distract herself, she took out her phone and logged onto her own Betwixt client account. Unfortunately, seeing her own public profile and checking her messages and the matches garnered through Camden's algorithm only reminded her of what she'd done when she'd created the profile account.

She remembered working at her computer a few days ago when Camden left to refill his coffee. Bailey had already filled out the questionnaire for the website but hadn't yet pressed the "submit" button. Instead, she waited for Camden to complete his survey before she submitted hers to be run through the algorithm and her profile made public for other members on the site. She wasn't willing to fulfill her end of the deal if he didn't intend to fulfill his.

After all of her nagging, he'd finally irritably claimed to be "working on it." After Camden left, Bailey printed out a form and stood to retrieve it from the printer. Her gaze caught on Camden's computer screen, and she paused. His completed survey glowed back at her like forbidden fruit. Unable to resist, she hurried over to the computer and scrolled up and down, making sure it really was complete. Then she saw the submit button and hovered the little arrow over it.

Camden didn't want his info submitted. She knew he intended to simply send her the survey without creating an account. However, though she wouldn't admit it to Camden, his algorithm really did make her job easier. Narrowing the options down to a few names made finding matches much more manageable than starting from scratch with the thousands of profiles on the website. Camden wouldn't need to know that she'd used his algorithm and created an account, and as soon as she found a match, she could delete it. He'd never know.

Bailey glanced at the door. Camden would return at any minute. She couldn't let him catch her messing with his computer and his survey.

Before she could change her mind, she clicked submit. She filled in a few more blanks with Camden's info and created a password. She then printed out the survey results and was just retrieving them from the printer when Camden walked back into the office.

"I hope you don't mind, I saw you left your survey up on your computer, so I printed it out for myself," she announced casually.

Camden looked mildly perturbed, but then shrugged. "I was going to do that anyway. At least now maybe you'll leave me alone."

"You can always hope!" Bailey replied blithely.

Later, she added a profile pic of him to his profile. When he wasn't looking, she'd used her phone to sneak one of him working on his computer. He had a strange aversion to having his picture taken, but she'd actually gotten a nice shot of his face with him none the wiser.

She'd immediately began looking through the names on his algorithm list of matches but hadn't narrowed it down when Shaya's message had arrived in Camden's inbox this morning. Shaya Yanzik hadn't been on Camden's list, but that's probably because her location was a bit outside the radius of Bailey's search. As soon as Bailey looked at Shaya's profile, she felt good about setting up the date. Bailey wouldn't call Shaya Camden's perfect match, but Bailey was realistic enough to recognize her bias. No one would ever be perfect enough for Camden, but Shaya was pretty, accomplished, and a Christian. She was worth a try.

When Shaya wanted to meet Camden this evening, Bailey impulsively decided to go for it. She'd hoped that a quick turnaround would give Camden less time to protest. Obviously, she'd been wrong.

Trying to appease her own guilt, Bailey had also submitted her own profile and made an account on the website. So far, Camden hadn't officially selected her date, but the whole process was rather interesting to view from the client's perspective.

She brought up the app and checked her messages. She saw five new ones from when she'd checked earlier. Apparently, her profile was attractive enough that multiple men had already attempted to contact her. With each message, she had the option of whether to accept the message and start a conversation or ignore it. The prospective suitors could not send her another message until she accepted the first one. Bailey idly scrolled through the messages, noticing that several of the men were actually on her list of algorithm matches.

Bailey didn't like this much popularity, though. Camden better hurry and choose her date so she could delete her profile. Her breakup was still too fresh. She'd consented to one date, but that's all she was ready for at this point.

"I'll take you to your table now," the host said, arriving at her elbow.

Bailey hopped up from the seat and followed the host through the main dining room.

"Your table is in one of the back rooms," the host explained.

Bailey looked around curiously. Why were they in a back room? There were a few diners here and there, but overall, the main dining room didn't look crowded at all.

The host opened a door for Bailey. The minute she stepped through, she knew she'd made a horrible mistake.

With a push to the back, Bailey stumbled the rest of the way through the doorway into the cold, outside air of a dark alley. The door clanged shut behind her with a deafening bang. Catching her balance, she swung around and tried to open the door, yanking on it with her full weight.

But it was locked.

Screaming, she lifted her hands to pound her fists against the unmoving barrier.

"You're not the Camden Hutchins we were expecting," a raspy voice spoke calmly.

Afraid hands would grab her at any second, Bailey whirled around with her back to the door. Heart pounding, her eyes searched the shadows, but not even a shimmer of light broke the darkness, and her eyes hadn't yet adjusted to distinguish various shades of black.

"Who is she?" Another voice, this one deeper and more threatening, asked.

"I don't know. Maybe she knows Camden Hutchins. I told you we should have taken a little time to find the guy and watch him. This trap was a bad idea," the original scratchy voice complained.

"Neither one of us made that call. Now we need to figure out what to do."

This set the men to arguing and Bailey to panicking. They were after Camden, and she'd just walked into their trap.

Bailey turned her back to the two voices and tried the door one more time, but the knob wouldn't turn. Letting her body shield what she was doing, she pulled her phone out. She wanted to call 911, but she didn't know if the men were speaking loud enough to be heard. It wasn't as if she could talk and give 911 her location. With no response, the operator would likely just assume it was a prank call and disconnect.

With shaking hands, she unlocked the screen. The Betwixt app came up where she'd left off. Quickly, she pushed the button accepting all of her messages at the same time.

"Who are you?" The deep voice demanded. "Why are you here instead of Camden Hutchins?"

Bailey found one more button and pushed it before slipping the phone in the pocket of her coat and turning back around.

Her eyes began to adjust to the darkness, and she could make out the shapes of two large men standing about eight feet in front of her. She couldn't see their faces and didn't want to. They'd intended to meet Camden here to do him harm, and the sound of their voices was more than enough for Bailey to know these men wouldn't hesitate to kill her if she said the wrong thing.

"I made a fake profile on the dating site and made up a name," Bailey's voice shook with the lie. "I had no idea there was a real Camden Hutchins." If they wanted Camden, there was no way she would give them any information that might help them find him.

"Why on earth would you make a guy's profile to meet a chick?" the raspy voice asked.

Bailey swallowed with difficulty, her mind fumbling for some kind of plausible explanation. She had to come up with something and keep them talking. The longer they stayed here, the greater the chance of help arriving.

"Shaya Yanzik is a friend," Bailey finally said. "I was pranking her. I thought it would be hilarious to have her show up for a date that was actually me."

Bailey held her breath. She'd taken a chance, and it could very well backfire. She wasn't in this situation because she was an idiot. She'd tried to be careful. When Shaya had messaged Camden, Bailey had searched through her profile with a fine-toothed comb. She wasn't a new client, and her account had been active for weeks. Shaya had even gone on a few dates with her matches and seemed to be enjoying the site. No rule stated that clients couldn't contact other clients not on their lists, and Bailey thought Shaya was brave for reaching out to someone she found attractive. If Shaya's account were fake, then Camden would have snuffed her out long ago with his security measures. That meant that the account was not fake but hacked, in which case, she could potentially claim to know the real Shaya.

If her theories were wrong, Bailey had just announced she was lying.

"You mean to say, we just got screwed by someone who doesn't even know this guy?" raspy voice growled. With a kick, he launched an empty box Bailey's direction, and she had to duck as it hit the door behind her.

"If it was fake, where did you get the profile pic?" deep voice asked calmly.

So far so good. They weren't onto her yet. She hadn't seen their faces. Maybe if they thought she knew nothing, they'd let her go. "It was a random pic I found on the internet," Bailey explained confidently.

"She lies," deep voice hissed, stepping forward threateningly. "There is only one picture of that man anywhere on the internet, and that was the one you claim to have used as Camden Hutchins' profile picture."

"How do you know that man in the picture?" raspy voice stepped forward. Moonlight glinted off something in his hand, and Bailey whimpered, backing up along the wall away from the approaching knife.

"I don't know him. I promise," Bailey whispered.

"She obviously knows something." Deep voice came around to the other side of her.

Bailey knew they were about to close in with no way for her to escape. "What should we do?"

"We'll take her. The boss wanted the guy, but he'll need to be satisfied with getting the information out of her. I'm sure he has his ways."

"You're right. She knows too much as it is. She'll need to come. If the boss doesn't want her, we can dispose of her."

"No, please. Leave me alone! Leave—"

Multiple hands grabbed her at once. Bailey screamed and kicked, writhing as the hands pinned her to the wet concrete. A smelly hand drew a piece of tape across her mouth, silencing her screams. They turned her over with her cheek biting into the hard ground, and she felt her hands tied securely behind her.

"Grab her phone and wallet," deep voice ordered. "We'll make it look like a mugging gone wrong."

Then her body left the ground as she was picked up and slung over a shoulder that smelled strongly of body odor.

"This would be a lot easier if you'd actually parked in the alley and not the lot!" deep voice accused.

"We're fine," raspy voice assured. "There aren't any security cameras. I couldn't park back here. The alley has no exit. If anyone showed up, we wouldn't have an escape route."

Bailey's legs were the only body parts left unsecured. With all her might, she jerked them, every once in a while landing a blow with her knee or her foot that elicited an accompanying, "Oomph."

"I wish the boss would have let us use some drugs for this operation," raspy voice growled. "Why did he insist Hutchins be awake when we delivered him?"

"Apparently he needs to extract as much information as possible out of Hutchins ASAP. He won't be happy that the guy matching the face didn't show up, and we brought him this girl instead."

Bailey jerked her knee into what she assumed was a jaw.

Raspy voice groaned and cursed, tightening his hold on Bailey until she feared her insides would be crushed.

"My rate just went up," he growled. "My kidnapping services don't include bruises."

Deep voice laughed. "Then you should be thankful this itty-bitty gal showed up and not the real guy in the Camden Hutchins' picture."

"Hurry, get her in the van! You see all those cars? We need to get out of here!"

Bailey heard doors screech open right before she was thrown onto a rough carpeted floor, knocking the wind out of her.

"Hey, I'm looking for someone!" a friendly voice greeted. "My date was supposed to meet me here, but I can't seem to find her."

"Sorry. Can't help you," raspy voice said. One of the van doors slammed shut.

Though she hadn't regained her breath, Bailey recognized this as her only chance. She squirmed and rolled her way until she came up against the hard side of the van. She then began kicking it with all her might. The resulting thuds seemed pitiful, but still, she kept kicking.

"Maybe check the restaurant," she heard deep voice say. "Now if you'll excuse us, we need to go."

"She's not in the restaurant. She sent me her location, and it says she's right here in the parking lot," the man insisted. "You see this little blinking light on the map. Maybe you've seen her. She has long brown hair and is quite beautiful."

"Haven't seen her," raspy voice insisted. "We've gotta run."

"I'm looking for my date," another voice said. "I'm supposed to meet her here. Pretty gal. Long brown hair. In her late twenties. Have any of you seen her?"

"Hey, is her name Bailey Whitmore?" the first voice asked.

"It sure is! Do you know her? Where is she?"

"I'm looking for Bailey Whitmore. I'm supposed to meet her for a date here!" The first voice was not happy.

"Did I hear you guys mention Bailey Whitmore?" A third new voice asked brightly. "Have you seen her? I'm supposed to meet her here for a date."

"We'll let you gentlemen figure it out. We've gotta go."

The other van door slammed shut, and the voices now sounded muted. Bailey could no longer understand what was being said. Tears burned Bailey's eyes, and she kept kicking, the dull thuds sounding repeatedly but not seeming to garner any attention.

The van's engine started.

She knew if the van left, there was no chance of her being found alive.

Dear, Lord, help me! I don't want to die!

Giving up on gaining anyone's attention, Bailey rolled and scooted, making her way to the rear doors. Amazingly, the van hadn't moved yet when she made it there and struggled to her knees. If she could just open the door, she would take her chance falling out of a moving vehicle. If these men delivered her to their boss, she knew she was dead.

The door contained a latch built into the door itself, meaning there was no way for Bailey to use her head or even her mouth to get hold of it. Turning around so her back faced the door, she pushed her tied hands into the door and wiggled and maneuvered them, working her fingers upward until they connected with the metal latch. She pulled it, feeling the door give slightly right as she heard the front doors slam.

With all her strength, she laid her shoulder into the door and flung her full weight at it. The door opened as Bailey launched out and landed hard on the concrete several feet away.

The world erupted in sirens and lights, and Bailey looked up to see multiple men staring down at her, their mouths gaping open in shock.

Obviously, this was not the way they'd expected to meet their date.

Camden jumped out of the moving vehicle as soon as it entered the parking lot. He paid no attention to the sirens arriving behind him but sprinted to the group crowded around a van with the engine running.

Pushing his way through the circle of men, he saw Bailey on the ground, tied up, and with duct tape over her mouth. Right then, the van's engine revved, and the brake lights blinked off. With no time to think, Camden rushed forward and scooped Bailey into his arms right before the van backed up and sent all the other men scrambling out of the way. Not able to completely escape, the rear of the van hit Camden in the back as it braked. The momentum pushed Camden off balance, throwing him to the concrete parking lot with Bailey in his arms.

The van gunned the engine, its tires screeching only to slam on its brakes as police cars blocked the exit.

Camden rolled over and picked himself up enough to look around and make sure his people had the situation in hand and the danger was past. Then he turned and looked anxiously at where Bailey lay flat on her back beside him.

"Bailey, are you okay?"

His heart broke to see the overwhelming fear in Bailey's eyes. Reaching out, he grabbed the edge of the duct tape across her mouth and pulled. It ripped away painfully, a whimper the first sound coming from her raw lips.

Then he realized that her hands were tied behind her back, and he felt ill. Taking a knife from a pocket in his shorts, he cut off the zip tie and freed her.

"Camden," she cried, reaching for him.

Camden folded her in his arms, feeling her shoulders shake with sobs as tears made trails down his own face.

"Shhh, it's okay. You're safe now. I'm here." He murmured the phrases over and over as he gently rubbed her back.

An ambulance arrived on the scene, and Camden pulled away enough to look Bailey over. Unfortunately, the dim lights from the streetlights and the flashing colors of the emergency vehicle lights didn't provide much illumination for a thorough inspection.

"Bailey, are you hurt?" he asked, his tone gentle but demanding she answer.

"My shoulder feels a little strange," Bailey answered with uncertainty.

"You hit pretty hard when the van knocked us down," Camden said, not surprised that she was injured.

"No, I didn't hurt it then. I landed on it when I jumped out of the back of the van," Bailey said.

"You jumped out of the van?" Camden asked. "With your hands tied and your mouth taped shut?"

"She sure did," a man said, speaking up from the circle of onlookers surrounding them.

Camden looked up, realizing for the first time just how many men were gawking at them and wondering where they'd come from.

"If she hadn't jumped out, that van would have been gone before you arrived, and none of us would have ever known she was in the back," the man explained.

Bailey struggled to stand to her feet, and Camden stood to help her.

"Hi, I'm Bailey," she said, reaching out with her unhurt arm to shake the hands of each of the men around them. "Thank you so much for coming. If you hadn't come and delayed them, then we would have been gone long before I could have escaped or the police arrived. I'm sorry. I know this wasn't the kind of date you expected when I sent you my location to meet."

A murmur went through the crowd.

"Are you kidding?" another man said. "This is the most excitement I've had in years!"

"Was that you making that knocking sound?" Another man asked. "When I asked the two guys from the van about it, they got upset. That's when they got in the front to leave and told us to get out of the way."

"Yes, I was kicking the side of the van, but I couldn't get anyone's attention. When I heard the van's engine start, I rolled over and tried to open the door. Somehow, I managed it and jumped out."

The men shook their heads in amazement.

"I'm a little behind," Camden said, taking in all the other men. "All of these men showed up to meet you for a date?"

Bailey nodded. "As soon as I realized I was in trouble, I wasn't in a position to make a call to 911 or anyone else without the kidnappers knowing. I had about five seconds where I could hide my phone and push a couple of buttons. I already had the Betwixt app open. The only thing I could think to do was to approve all of my incoming messages and send my location. Since all of the messages were selected, it sent my location to each one of them. I hoped that at least one would show up thinking I wanted to meet for a date."

"It looks like you got a few more than one," Camden said dryly. "How many dates did you have?"

"It looks like at least ten of us," a man answered with a smile. "Obviously, we had good reason to show up. Bailey is not only beautiful, she's smart and resourceful. What a brilliant way to get help!"

Camden scowled at the man who spoke. Bailey was brilliant, and her quick thinking in sending her location to all those prospective suitors had saved her life. Unfortunately, the other man had stolen his thunder, and if Camden said anything now, it would just sound like he was copying.

"Bailey, I'm Cody," said the man Camden disliked. "I'd really like to reschedule our date for as soon as you feel up to it."

"Get in line, buddy," another man growled. "Bailey, I'm Liam. Could I take you out tomorrow?"

"Bailey, I'm Andy. I'm a nurse. If you're not feeling well, I'd be happy to offer my services. Maybe I should take a look at your shoulder."

Camden held up his hands. "Guys, I'm sure Bailey will get back to each one of you as soon as she can, but right now, I will be the one to take her to the hospital."

"And who are you?" one of the men asked with a scowl. "Two guys just tried to kidnap Bailey. I'm not sure we should trust any guy without a badge."

"How about me?" A woman walked up to the group with her arm outstretched. "I'm not a guy, but I do have a badge."

After flashing her badge around for all to see, she announced. "Thank you all for your help tonight in saving Bailey. If you wouldn't mind, there are a few officers right over there by the patrol car blocking the entrance. They are waiting to take your statements, after which you are free to leave."

The men turned to obey, but not before many of them flashed Bailey a smile and passed her cards or slips of paper with the admonitions to give them a call.

As soon as the men reluctantly trailed off, Camden turned to the woman with the badge. "I know you need to speak with her, but she's hurt. I need to get her to the hospital. Can we meet you somewhere after that?"

"I'll just come with you to the hospital," she answered easily. "We'll make sure it's secure. It'll be fine. It's as good a place as any."

"Do I really need to go to the hospital?" Bailey asked. "I really think I'm fine. I probably just bruised my shoulder. Can't you just take a quick look at it here, Geneva?"

Israel arrived in time to hear Bailey's words and Camden's accompanying laughter.

With a smile lifting the corners of his lips, Israel said, "You spend so much time trying to not look like your real twin that now you look like your older sister. You can change your hair all you want, Syd, but that still doesn't change the fact all of you share the same face!"

Camden turned to Bailey and introduced. "Bailey, this is my sister Sydney Hutchins. She and my sister, London, are identical twins, but as you can tell, both of them also resemble Geneva a great deal."

Seeing Sydney's scowl, Bailey rushed to apologize. "I'm sorry, Sydney. I saw your face and assumed Geneva had changed her hair."

"Don't worry about it, Bailey," Sydney said, recovering with a friendly smile. "I'm happy to meet you. I've already heard so much about you from my family. I love how you keep my brother on his toes."

"I could have done without this last episode. I don't think my toes will ever be the same," Camden complained.

The paramedics checked Bailey out briefly, but she refused to ride in the ambulance to the hospital. Instead, Camden put her in the back seat of his SUV and turned to hand Israel the keys to drive once more.

"I'll take those," Sydney said, swiping the keys as she approached.

Camden looked at her warily. "Is everything okay?"

Sydney nodded. "Just taking precautions until we verify that no one else is coming after you. I'm fairly certain of who hired those men to kidnap you, and I know we can handle it. Until it's actually handled, though, I'll be your chauffeur."

Israel clapped Camden on the back. "Sorry, dude. It's gotta be a special moment when your little sister becomes your bodyguard."

Camden looked at Israel seriously. "You have no idea. Sydney's the only person I'd ever want as a bodyguard."

"Cam," Sydney said, warning in her voice.

"I know. I know," Camden said, walking around to take the seat in the back with Bailey.

They were soon on their way. Camden tried to relax, but his senses were still on high alert. Every flash of light caused him to startle, and he continually glanced through the back window to make sure they weren't being followed.

Reaching out, he covered Bailey's cold hand with his, and she didn't pull away. She was hurt. Camden knew it, even if she didn't. The guilt felt overwhelming. He was the target. They'd wanted him, and Bailey had gotten in the way and paid for it.

If the real Shaya hadn't responded to the automated message and contacted him, if Sydney hadn't answered Camden's emergency call, if Bailey hadn't thought to send her location to a dozen men, if she hadn't found a way to open that van door and throw herself out...

Thank you, Lord!

Camden knew that God's divine intervention was the only reason he held Bailey's hand in his own right now.

Unfortunately, he still didn't have the assurance that the danger was past. Would Bailey always be in danger if he stayed in her life? How would he explain any of this to her or Israel?

He tightened his grip on her hand, his eyes roving over her worriedly. He couldn't stand to put her in danger, and yet he couldn't stand more the thought of not having her with him. What if she was hurt worse than she realized?

Bailey seemed to feel his eyes on her and looked up, her face relaxing into a smile that set Camden's heart to pounding.

A new terror sliced through him as he realized the truth.

Lord, help me!

I love her!

"It's broken," Geneva said, pointing to the X-ray of Bailey's collarbone as proof.

Bailey's mouth fell open in surprise. "How is that possible? It doesn't even hurt!"

Geneva laughed. "Bailey, honey, you have so much adrenaline running through your system right now, it's like you have superpowers. Trust me, the shock to your system will wear off in a few hours, and then you will definitely feel it."

"Does she have any other injuries?" Camden asked worriedly from where he hovered on the other side of Bailey's hospital bed.

Geneva worked to immobilize Bailey's arm in a sling as she spoke. "I think she'll have some significant bruising to her entire torso area, and she'll need to see a specialist for her collarbone. It looks to be a good, clean break in the right position, though, so I don't think it will require surgery. Other than that, she's fine. We will not be admitting her. With pain meds on board and her sling taken care of, she'll be free to go."

Geneva turned to Bailey. "You're still staying at Mom and Dad's, right? I want them to keep an eye on you. I don't want you to be alone."

Bailey nodded. "Even though I signed a lease, my apartment isn't ready for me to move in yet."

"Don't worry. She won't be alone," Sydney said, entering the room. "I'll be at Mom and Dad's house tonight to keep an eye on things. We'll all make sure she's comfortable."

"I didn't even know you were in town, Sydney," Geneva said, her tone slightly disapproving.

"I suspect it's more unusual for Sydney to tell us she's in town than to come and go as she pleases," Israel observed from his chair on the other side of the bed.

Sydney shrugged. "Just happened to be at the right place at the right time, I guess."

Geneva finished up with Bailey's sling and said she'd be back with some pain meds.

"Gen, if you think she can wait on the pain meds, I really need about ten minutes to speak to Camden, Israel, and Bailey alone."

Geneva sighed, seeming to understand that Sydney wanted her out of the room. "Sydney, one of these days, you're going to need to make a full confession to your big sister."

Sydney looked at her seriously. "You have no idea how much effort I put in so that doesn't ever happen."

Geneva ignored her and turned back to Bailey. "Let me know if you need anything. Bailey. I'll come back in a few minutes with the meds, and then I'll stop by Mom and Dad's house tomorrow to see how you're doing."

"Thank you, Geneva," Bailey replied with Camden immediately echoing his thanks.

The door shut behind her, and Sydney looked at them, her expression serious. "What I'm about to tell you stays in this room, and you never breathe a word of it to anyone. I have a guard posted out front, and we have about ten minutes."

She nodded to Camden. "Camden is not at liberty to reveal any information about himself. If you ask him a question, he will not answer. Not today or tomorrow. In fact, he hasn't been able to answer any questions since he was recruited to do government work before he graduated college. However, I do have the clearance to reveal some of the reasons behind what happened tonight."

Bailey looked at Sydney, feeling like this woman must not be real. Her face was like Geneva, and she was beautiful. Yet her hair was darker, and her presence somehow demanded that you follow exactly what she said.

"Camden works for the government?" Israel asked, the color draining from his face.

"Yes, he does. He has long worked in technical areas, providing security and technical espionage."

"Camden is a spy?" Bailey gasped.

"Not in the traditional sense, but in many ways, yes. However, his spy work is usually restricted to a seat behind a computer. He identifies threats and provides security to make sure any of our activities stay invisible."

"You've been doing this since when?" Israel's voice sounded strained, and he looked as if he might need Bailey's hospital bed more than she did.

"They recruited him before he graduated college," Sydney replied, looking at Israel knowingly. "Camden was well established in his position before I even came on the scene. I've often wondered if it was because of him that I was on their radar for recruitment, but some secrets Camden and I can't even share with each other."

"That means...," Israel choked on the words. "That was the reason you didn't join the business. You were already committed to a classified position."

Camden didn't answer, but the tortured look in his eyes was confirmation enough.

Israel's eyes clouded with tears. "But all this time I thought.... Camden, I'm so sorry," Israel grabbed Camden and pulled him into an embrace.

"It's okay, Israel," Camden responded huskily. "There's no way you could have known. I understood that."

Israel stepped back and shook his head. "That's no excuse. I treated you terribly for years. I should have known that you didn't refuse just for spite. I know you better than that, and yet I believed the worst."

"Do your parents know?" Bailey asked, wondering if they, also, had believed the worst of Camden all this time.

"No, they don't," Sydney answered firmly. "And they never will. The only reason you are getting any information is that it's unavoidable. The more people who know, the more it puts everyone involved at risk."

Bailey felt tears clogging her throat. It just seemed so unfair. How could it be right to let Camden's family dynamic be completely changed because he wasn't at liberty to reveal the important work he did?

"If Camden works with technology and security, what do you do?" Bailey asked, wondering what other secrets hid in the Hutchins' family.

"I work for the FBI, I think." Sydney reached in her pocket and pulled out the badge to check. "Yes, today, I work for the FBI."

"Please don't ask her what she does all other days of the year," Camden grumbled. "She won't tell you the truth, but she very well may spin a series of fantastic lies just for the sheer entertainment."

"That's not true," Sydney said defensively. "I only ever lie with purpose. In this case, it's enough to say that I am occasionally employed by various government agencies."

"The family knows enough not to ask Sydney what she does," Israel filled in. "Though no one talks about it, we've all assumed she does some kind of secret government work. We just had no idea Camden did as well."

"Camden has always worked with a cover company," Sydney explained, "He's had legitimate nongovernment work that he uses to mask his top-secret work. He ran into a snag when his picture was leaked through a security breach in an unrelated division. For the most part, even in the government, Camden is a ghost. His boss knows who he is, but his exact identity is closely guarded. His picture as a government agent with the security task force was compromised along with a few other agents. However, it was just the photo and didn't contain a name or any other personal info other than a few of his assignments. Camden does quality work and has made enemies, even though no one knows his name. There are many who would seek to stop his work, extract information, and then kill him if only for revenge."

"That's why he was supposedly laid off," Israel groaned, putting the pieces together.

"Yes, it was. It was too dangerous to keep Camden where he currently worked. He was sort of ordered into hiding, but in this case, his hiding place was his real identity. Any name he'd used when conducting government business had been fake, so his own name should have been safe. He could continue to do work, but only if he had a different, seemingly legitimate, cover and kept his face off the internet."

"A cover?" Bailey whispered. "Do you mean the website? Camden has been using Betwixt Two Hearts to conduct his secret work?"

It has all been fake? Everything?

Camden held up his hand to stop Sydney from responding. "Please,

Syd. You don't even know what I've done on this project. She's involved. At least let me answer her this."

Sydney nodded.

"The website is legitimate," Camden said, meeting Bailey's gaze directly. "Everything we've done is very real. But also real is the fact that I agreed to do the website primarily because I recognized it as the perfect cover. Not only that, I used it as a tool in some of my government projects. My security investigations aren't simply for the purpose of keeping clients safe. I also use them to search and identify those who the government might have a need to investigate."

"You used our website?" Bailey asked, her tone hurt and disbelieving. "You used me?"

Camden looked her in the eye, his gaze unwavering. "Yes, I did. I wasn't given the choice, but that doesn't make the website or anything we've experienced any less real."

Bailey wanted to be angry with him. She felt duped. She felt used. She felt stupid that she hadn't figured it out.

Then, at the same time, she felt ashamed that she was even upset when he hadn't been given a choice. Camden was a hero. He probably saved lives on a daily basis, and yet, she was offended about his untruthfulness and ulterior motives with their website.

"I'm sorry," Camden said, coming close enough to reach down and take her unhurt hand. "I can't even promise that I won't do it again."

"I can guarantee that he will," Sydney assured. "The government isn't going to let one attack compromise Camden's work."

One attack.

Bailey gasped, jerking her hand from his and covering it over her mouth. "It's my fault!" she whispered, wide-eyed. "You said Camden's picture had been leaked. I posted a picture of him on his public Betwixt profile. He didn't know I'd taken the picture or that I submitted his info in an account. He'd explicitly told me not to do it."

"Facial recognition?" Israel asked, concerned.

"Yes, certain people have very sophisticated technology that can search the web, doing facial recognition on anything that is posted to the internet. Passwords don't even matter. If it's posted to the web and not within a government security wall, it can be viewed."

Camden explained, "I only have that level of security around the website's payment information, and my government work is completely separate and stored elsewhere. That level of security is a hassle, and at the time, I saw no reason to heavily blockade pictures and profile information for a matchmaking website."

"They found you because of me," Bailey moaned, overwhelmed with regret.

"Bailey, you didn't know," Camden comforted.

"Why do I have to be such a rebel?" Bailey felt sobs rushing up to take control. "I should have done what you instructed instead of going behind your back to manipulate you."

"Bailey, what's done is done. The important thing is that you're safe."

"I wasn't the one they wanted!" Bailey's eyes blurred with tears. "They were after you! I compromised your real identity and put you at risk. I got in the way tonight, but you are the one in danger, not me!"

"Bailey, Camden will be fine," Sydney spoke soothingly, coming closer to her bed. "Nothing you did is irreparable. In fact, because of you, we caught some really bad guys tonight. Those two thugs bribed the restaurant host to lead Camden Hutchins to the alley. Now that we arrested them, they will, in turn, lead us straight back to one of the criminals we have been after for years."

"So, you'll arrest him, and Camden will be safe? "Bailey asked, barely daring to hope.

"Not exactly," Sydney stipulated. "The man we have in mind may not even be in the country right now, but we'll still be able to amass evidence against him, ready to take him into custody as soon as the opportunity arises."

"Aside from you adopting the role of permanent bodyguard, how do you plan to keep Camden safe?" Israel asked.

"We will kill off Camden's face," Sydney said with obvious enjoyment. "Nobody knows that the name attached to Camden on the Betwixt website was actually his real name. All we need to do is release an obituary with a fake name attached to Camden's picture. This will be widely circulated on the web and state that you were killed after an attempted kidnapping.

Camden can go back to work with the website and should be fine as long as he keeps his picture off the web."

"By the way, Cam," Sydney, said turning to look at him directly. "How do you feel about facial hair? It might serve as an extra precaution to make yourself a little more unrecognizable from the pretty picture Bailey posted on the website."

Camden scowled in answer but didn't outright refuse.

"Is his profile still up?" Bailey asked, suddenly panicking. "If so, I need to delete it right now!"

"We already took care of it," Sydney assured, walking to the window to spread the blinds and take a peek out. "A few of Camden's computer friends had the profile removed before we even located you. Thankfully, you didn't list Camden's location as Crossroads but as Brighton Falls. There should be a few Camden Hutchins to keep busy around here, even if Camden's enemies decide to pursue it. We may even add a few fake Camden Hutchins' social media profiles just to stir the pot."

Camden groaned. "I hate it when I have to die."

"You've had to do this before?" Bailey asked, aghast.

Camden shrugged. "Well, it usually isn't my identity that dies, just a fake alias. But, yes, I've been erased from existence multiple times from multiple locations. Am I even listed as a college graduate at the university anymore?"

Sydney shrugged. "I doubt it. Being a ghost is a high-maintenance job. We need to make sure you stay dead."

A knock sounded on the door, followed by Geneva poking her head in the room. "Everyone, cover up your secrets. I'm coming in."

The room immediately fell silent as Geneva entered.

"Bailey, I have your medicine and your discharge papers," she announced briskly.

Before she made it to Bailey's bed, she stopped and glared at the others accusingly. "You made her cry!"

"It's okay," Bailey blubbered, unable to stop the flow of tears once they'd started. "They didn't mean to."

Even though Sydney assured her that Camden was safe, and it really did sound like everything was in control, Bailey couldn't seem to stop the tears. She knew that she was likely suffering the overwhelming release of tension and adrenaline. As if to confirm her theory, her shoulder suddenly felt like it was on fire.

Geneva hurriedly got her the medicine and had her sign the papers while Camden perched on the bed beside her.

She really wished he wouldn't look at her like that. It only made her feel worse to see concern for her in his eyes. What if he wasn't safe? It certainly sounded like Camden would continue working a potentially dangerous job. Though she felt proud of him for his sacrificing work to keep others safe, she didn't know that she could handle the danger he put himself in. She wanted him to stay safe.

Her mind spun images of tonight and mixed them with her imagination, creating horrifying scenarios where Camden was kidnapped, hurt, or tortured, and she wasn't able to find him. A fresh wave of tears washed over her, but it wasn't caused by the scary images. Instead, she realized that in each of her what-ifs, her heart was the victim.

With sudden clarity, her tear-blurred gaze swung to Camden, and she realized that even though he didn't know it, her heart had forever stowed away with him. She cried because she knew that, after tonight, nothing would ever be the same. And she cried because she realized she completely, unquestionably, and irrevocably loved Camden Hutchins.

Fourteen

"Camden, I'm planning to disagree with you," Bailey said.

"Since when do you give me notice?" Camden laughed, glancing over his shoulder to where she worked across the room on her own computer. Though her left arm and shoulder remained in a sling, that hadn't slowed her down from working, even if she could use only one hand on the keyboard.

"I just wanted to warn you," Bailey answered seriously. "I don't want you to get too upset when you see what I'm about to do," Bailey cautioned.

Now that sounded more serious. Abandoning his work, Camden immediately hopped up from his seat and hurried to look over her shoulder. The last time Bailey had taken matters into her own hands it had come with severe and dangerous consequences. Though he'd noticed her trying especially hard to be cautious and considerate the past two weeks, she was still Bailey. Her attempted kidnapping had in no way broken her, and Camden held his breath in both excitement and terror for the next adventure her natural spunk landed them in. In his mind, his top-secret work ranked as far less dangerous than spending a day with Bailey.

"Don't push the red button," Camden teased, nodding to the screen.

Bailey laughed. "It's the blue 'submit' button I'm interested in. You've screwed these matches up so much, I've got to try to fix it before we lose clients."

Camden scowled. She still had a knack for ruffling his feathers. "Exactly how have I screwed things up?" he asked.

Bailey brought up a profile picture and explained, "Mark has gone on several dates using algorithm matches, and they've all gone horribly. He even paid for the most expensive matchmaker version, but he chose to only use the algorithm. Now he requested a matchmaker, probably as a last-ditch effort before he gives up completely."

"Who do you want to match him with, and why will that make me upset?" Camden asked, hoping to skip to the end of Bailey's tale.

"I want to match him with her." Bailey brought up a second profile and placed the two side-by-side on her screen. "Her name is Casey, and it looks like she's had a very similar experience. She signed up for the algorithm match option and has gone on several dates, all of which ended terribly. She did the reviews to prove it. Now she requested a personal matchmaker. If we don't provide her with a date that is at least mediocre, I know she will close her account."

"Why would I be opposed to them as a match?" Camden asked cautiously. So far, nothing in this idea seemed objectionable, which begged the question why Bailey thought Camden wouldn't approve.

Bailey sighed as if resigning herself to admitting the unpleasant details. "Well, Casey recently adjusted her search radius. She must be traveling and wants a date that is in a different area. The problem is that, according to your algorithm, she and Mark aren't a good match."

"What do you mean?" Camden pushed, well aware that when Bailey danced around an issue, she was trying to hide something. "What number are they for each other?"

"Um... well... let's just say they're quite a ways down." Bailey clicked off the profiles and began checking her email as if no longer interested in the discussion.

"Bailey," Camden groaned. Reaching over her shoulder, he placed his hand over hers on the mouse, maneuvered the cursor back to the profiles, and hovered over the button he wanted.

"One hundred!" Camden coughed as if literally choking on the number. "He's number one hundred on her list! I didn't even realize you knew how to expand the algorithm search down that far. The automated settings only provide you with ten!"

"I figured it out easy enough," Bailey assured casually, though her eyes held a proud gleam. "Remember, her search area is expanded because of her travel. It's really not that bad. She's not as far down on his list."

Camden didn't trust her. She was trying to sell him on this, which meant she was all too eager to tell him what he wanted to hear.

Keeping her warm hand under his, he found the second list and clicked it. "Ninety-nine!" he gagged again. "She's number ninety-nine on his list! Oh, yes! That's much better!"

"Hmmm... I guess I didn't remember it that well," Bailey murmured distractedly. "I just knew it wasn't as far down. Mark's search radius must be wide, too. I think he lives in a rural area, so he's probably fiddled with the radius some to try to include more urban areas as well."

Camden released her hand and straightened, folding his arms in front of him. "Why is it you think they would be a good match when the algorithm results show at least ninety-eight to ninety-nine better matches out there?"

As if given permission to deliver a rousing closing argument, Bailey eagerly jumped in to explain. "Neither one of these people knows what they really want. In a way, it isn't your fault. The algorithm must assume a client knows himself or herself. There's no way to account for clients who consistently pick the wrong person. They think they know the type of person they are looking for but don't realize that's the exact problem. They want the person who is completely wrong for them. In this case, Casey thinks she wants a certain type of guy, so that's who the algorithm matches give her. But it never works out. I want to give her someone who is the opposite of what she thinks she wants. Same for Mark."

Camden looked at her thoughtfully, scratching at the five o'clock shadow turned stubbly beard he'd allowed to grow for a few days. "You've never seemed to let my opinion bother you before. If they requested a matchmaker and you want to make the match, do it. You don't need my permission or approval."

"But I want both," Bailey said, looking up at him with big brown eyes that did strange things to his heart. "I know I don't always act like it does, but your opinion really does matter to me. In this case, both your permission and your approval are important."

"Then you have them," Camden replied firmly. Placing his hands on the armrests on either side of her chair, he leaned forward. With his face inches from hers, he spoke, quietly studying her every slight change of expression. "You're an excellent matchmaker, Bailey. If you believe these two people will make a good match, then I believe you. It doesn't matter what my algorithm says. Click your little blue button."

Seeming slightly troubled, Bailey's gaze flickered down, breaking the eye contact.

He straightened as she swiveled back around. With a single click, the button disappeared, and Bailey approved the match for client notification.

"Thank you, Camden," Bailey said. Rising from her chair, she reached out and took his hand. "That means a lot."

Her quick squeeze of his hand sent heat radiating from his palm.

As if feeling the sudden warmth, she immediately dropped the contact. She turned back around and busied herself organizing office supplies that really didn't need organizing and then remarked brightly, "Today is the day, you know?"

Camden mentally fumbled, suddenly trying to remember what he'd forgotten. Two weeks since the incident and Bailey's injury. Nothing on the calendar but work.

He was still drawing a blank when Bailey laughed. "You mean to tell me that you've already forgotten about your date? Today is the day we finally find out who wins the contest!"

Camden groaned, wishing she hadn't reminded him. Immediately mounting a retreat, he returned to his desk and got busy, hoping she'd let the subject drop. A week ago, Bailey had approached Camden with the idea that they agree to set each other up with a date on the same night. Then, they could meet each other afterward and decide the contest results once and for all. Still riddled with guilt that Bailey had gotten hurt because of him, he'd agreed. If they did the dates the same night, then he could keep better watch on her anyway. To ensure no possibility of a repeat of their previous experience, they'd agreed to verify each of their matches with Sydney. If Sydney gave the okay, then they'd each arrange the date.

Unfortunately, their previous agreement declared tonight as

doomsday.

"Everything approved on your end?" Bailey asked.

"Yes," Camden replied stoically, his gaze holding steady on his screen. "Sydney approved, and I'll give you the address of where to meet your date right before you leave. I don't want to ruin the surprise."

Bailey nodded. "Same here."

"Then may the best matchmaker win," Camden said, turning around in his chair and extending his hand out to shake Bailey's. Unfortunately, he offered his left hand, and Bailey couldn't shake since her corresponding left hand was currently tied up in a sling.

"Oh!" Camden said, teasingly drawing his arm back. "I guess that makes it clear, doesn't it!"

Bailey looked around for something to throw at him with her good arm. Realizing his imminent peril, Camden quickly hunkered down in his high-backed chair and tried not to chuckle too loudly while turning his attention back to his computer screen.

They both returned to working silently, but it took Camden about twenty minutes to get back into the zone with his focus in place and his surroundings fading into the background.

"Yes!" Bailey suddenly shrieked, jumping up and fist pumping the air with her good arm.

"What?" Camden asked, startled.

"I win!" she celebrated. "I win, I win, I win!"

"What are you talking about?" Camden asked, thinking she'd finally lost it.

She stopped her little dance just long enough to assure Camden, "I'll still go on the date you planned, of course, but it doesn't matter. I'm ahead of you, so the most you can do now is tie!"

Camden turned back to his computer. "Let me know when you actually want to tell me what's going on and not just shout cryptically. Until then, I'm going to focus on work. Please keep the cheering down a bit."

Bailey reached out and swung his swivel chair back around to face her.

"Remember when that woman contacted you to ask if you'd send her lists of dates for her brother?" she asked, her eyes dancing.

Camden nodded. "I remember. You and Mom tried to convince me to break policy and do it. She called it a family matter and was not at all happy when I refused, but there's no surprise there."

"I sent the lists."

"What?" Camden asked, standing from his chair to look at her in exasperation.

"I sent a list of five names from each of us," Bailey explained without a hint of regret. "It was too perfect of an opportunity for our contest. For you, I sent the first five names of the algorithm results. For my list, I compiled five personal matches without even looking at your algorithm results. Then I copied and pasted both lists and sent them to Selby. I always intended to tell you what I'd done. I just needed to wait until I had some results to report."

"I can't believe you did that, Bailey!" Camden didn't even try to mask his anger. "You went behind my back and broke company policy, all in an effort to manipulate people into doing what Bailey thought best. Didn't you learn anything from what happened two weeks ago?"

"I know I shouldn't have done it." Bailey faltered, breaking eye contact for the first time. "But that was before two weeks ago, and before I was saved, so it doesn't count, right?"

Bailey looked up, a sheepish smile lifting one corner of her mouth.

Camden's shocked expression ended in laughter as he realized she wasn't serious.

"You little minx! What am I going to do with you?"

"Forgive me?" she suggested, batting her eyes in an innocent look that rivaled four-year-old Chloe in cuteness.

"I need a little more information first," Camden adopted a hard line, looking at her disapprovingly in a mighty attempt at false bravado. "Are you sure we aren't getting sued?"

"Not at all!" Bailey assured. Then, seriously, she added, "Just so you know, I would not make the same decision if presented it today. I will not go behind your back again, at least not intentionally."

Camden's expression softened, but before he could respond, Bailey excitedly spoke again.

"While the ends don't justify the means, if there ever were an exception, this would qualify." Lights danced in her brown eyes, and she seemed tempted to launch into an actual cheer. "Camden, he found a match! Can you believe it? The guy who'd never managed to land a second date now has an amazing girlfriend! His sister, Selby, has been keeping me updated on his progress. Honestly, every email she sent read like a comedy or a horror movie, or maybe a combination of both. I haven't heard from her for a few weeks, though, and then just now, I got an email that says Heath has been happily dating the same woman for weeks now. Selby was so excited, she forgot to let me know earlier. Camden, she really thinks they're meant to be together!"

"Let me guess, the woman he ended up with is one from your list," Camden said wearily. "That would certainly account for the cheering and yelling about how you won the contest."

"Yes, she is!" Bailey squealed excitedly. "I found the worst dater ever his forever match!"

"Show me," Camden instructed, indicating her computer screen.

Happy to prove her accomplishment, Bailey brought up the email from Selby. "See, it says her name right there, and she was one I chose on my list. There's your proof!"

"Wait a minute," Camden murmured. "I recognize that name. Show me your original email to Selby."

With a few clicks, Bailey brought up the email from a couple months ago. Camden took over the mouse and scrolled down.

"There," he said, highlighting two words and throwing his hands up in triumph. "Do you see that name, Bailey? Tell me whose list that name is on."

Confusion crowded Bailey's face, and she scooted closer to the computer. "That doesn't make sense," Bailey murmured

"That's my point! I'm the winner, not you!" Camden then launched into a rousing rendition of "We Are the Champions," waving his arms to the rhythm in celebration.

"That's your list. But how? I know she was on mine." Bailey grabbed the mouse and scrolled back up. "Right there. She's right there on my list."

Camden positioned his head right behind her shoulder and looked at the name in clear black and white. "You mean, she's on both of our lists? We both had her on our lists? That's hilarious!"

Bailey scrolled up and down. "She's the only one that is the same on both lists," she sighed sadly.

Launching into a remix of his victory song, he pulled Bailey out of her chair and danced her around the room until she joined in the laughter.

"I guess we both win!" she finally relented.

Camden explained happily, "When Selby asked me for the lists, I remember looking over the names of the algorithm matches, trying to decide if there was any way I could help her but not break company policy. I finally decided it was a no-go, but when I saw that name, I recognized it."

"I wish you hadn't," Bailey sighed dramatically.

"I know! I snatched that victory right out of your eager, little hand!"

"You just delayed it a little bit," she retorted impishly. "We're still tied. Tonight will be the finals with winner take all."

Camden looked at her steadily, the humor draining from his expression. "Are we really going to do this?"

Bailey looked uncertain at his words, and truthfully, Camden didn't know if he was referring to the contest or the dates tonight. Maybe both. Were they really following through with setting each other up on dates with other people in the effort to formally cut the other out of input in their business?

Camden swallowed and backed off, clarifying, "The winner gets control of the website to design as he or she pleases?"

"Of course, that's what we agreed," Bailey said easily, showing no clue that she may share misgivings.

An uneasy tension settled over them, and Camden said awkwardly, "Well, then I probably need to get some work done before then."

"Yeah, me too," Bailey replied, returning to her chair and sitting with her back to him once more.

A few minutes later, Camden was attempting to locate his focus yet again when his phone vibrated with a text message.

ELISE: HAVE U TOLD HER YET???

Camden threw a glance behind to reassure himself that Bailey's attention remained elsewhere and quickly texted a response.

CAMDEN: NOT YET. WORKING ON IT.

ELISE: COME ON, CAMDEN. 2 WEEKS IS LONG ENOUGH!

After Bailey was injured, Camden had spoken several times with a very concerned Elise. With Sydney's help, he'd managed to come up with a plausible cover story behind Bailey's attempted kidnapping and injury. Somewhere along the way, however, Elise had figured out Camden's feelings for Bailey. She then proceeded to encourage, or in this case outright hound, Camden to tell Bailey how he felt.

Camden winced, knowing that he wouldn't do himself any favors by trying to explain to Elise about tonight and how he and Bailey intended to set each other up on dates. Instead, he kept it vague.

> **CAMDEN:** NO WORRIES. I HAVE A PLAN.
> **ELISE:** LOL. FAMOUS LAST WORDS.

He certainly hoped not. He'd spent the last week praying, asking God to show him if he needed to leave Bailey alone. He still couldn't stand the idea that being with him might put her in more danger. However, instead of his feelings fading with the adrenaline, he only became more certain that she was the one for him.

Lord, please help me not to screw this up. I have no idea how Bailey feels, and yet, I'm risking everything. If I say anything and she doesn't have feelings for me, our friendship will be ruined, and maybe even our business. But I can't go on like this. If anything, that awful night showed me that life is short. I don't want to waste any of it without her. Please help me not to make a mistake! Amen!

Taking a deep breath, Camden opened his eyes and looked at the clock.

In so many ways, tonight determined whether he won or lost. Strangely, he didn't care whether or not he won the contest. His hopes were instead pinned on winning something far more valuable.

"Shouldn't you be getting ready?" Camden said, nodding up at the clock before he took another bite of cookie. "Your date is at five o'clock, you know."

"Five!" Bailey choked around a mouth full of cookie. It took more chewing and a full glass of water before she could sputter intelligently again. "I thought it was at six o'clock! Yours is at six."

"Yours isn't," Camden said with infuriating calm. "Didn't I tell you? You're supposed to meet your date at five."

Bailey looked at him in open-mouthed exasperation, but there was nothing she could do. She'd agreed to go on the date, and she couldn't back out now, even if Camden switched the time at the last minute.

"Fine, but you aren't getting your location until I leave with mine!" she said as if that even mattered.

"That'll work," Camden said mildly, choosing another one of his mother's warm chocolate chip cookies to sample.

Bailey marched upstairs and didn't realize until she stood in front of the mirror that the change in schedule might actually be a very good thing. She hadn't yet figured out how to be at both her date and Camden's date at the same time, but if the times were staggered, that meant that she could wiggle out of her own date with enough time to be able to spy on Camden as he arrived at his.

Bailey's phone beeped with a text. Putting her eye shadow down, she picked it up and read.

> **ELISE:** HAVE U TOLD HIM YET?
> **BAILEY:** TOLD WHO WHAT?
> **ELISE:** IF U WANT ME TO SPELL OUT THE WHOLE MUSHY TRUTH,
> I WILL. HAVE U TOLD CAMDEN THAT U R CRAZY IN LUV WITH HIM
> AND ASKED HIM TO CHECK THE BOX IF HE LIKES U BACK?

Bailey smiled. Elise was rarely so direct, but she had been relentless since she'd figured out that Bailey had feelings for Camden. It hadn't taken her long either. The day after she was injured, Elise had called to see how Bailey was feeling. Within the first five minutes, her friend had deduced from Bailey's emotional state that she was in love with Camden. Bailey hadn't bothered to deny it, which then sent the expert matchmaker on a mission to see her two friends together.

Bailey insisted that she handle it without Elise's help, and Elise reluctantly agreed. Now, however, Elise's patience was obviously wearing as thin as wet paper.

> **BAILEY:** I WILL TELL HIM. I HAVE A PLAN.
> **ELISE:** EVERYONE SAYS THAT. I NEED DATE AND TIME DETAILS.
> **BAILEY:** TONIGHT. I WILL TALK TO HIM TONIGHT.
> **ELISE:** U BETTER. OTHERWISE CUPID MIGHT NEED TO MAKE A
> SURPRISE VISIT.

As much as Bailey would love for Elise to come to Crossroads, she didn't want her to do anything to influence Camden. She wanted Camden on her own terms. She wanted to know that he shared feelings for her not because of some romantic or even dangerous situation. Camden definitely knew her at her worst, and if he could still manage to care for her, then Bailey knew it would be genuine.

> **BAILEY:** WILL UPDATE TONIGHT.

Just seeing it there on the screen sent her heart into palpitations. Even though she hadn't figured out all the details, tonight she would know if Camden loved her.

Bailey finished her hair and checked how she looked in a full-length mirror. Camden hadn't shared anything about the actual date, so she didn't know how to dress. She'd finally opted for a dusky blue dress with a pair of black leggings and a cardigan. It didn't look like church attire, but it also wasn't revealing in any way. Gray slouchy boots and some swingy earrings completed the look.

Glancing at the time, she knew she needed to hurry, or she'd be late. She rushed down the stairs, finding Camden waiting at the door.

"You look nice," he said, though his eyes declared he'd just made an understatement.

"Thanks," Bailey replied briskly. "Where am I going?"

"I just sent you a location on a map to your phone," he said, holding up his own phone as evidence.

Bailey looked at the incoming text. "Isn't that the ponds south of town? Here in Crossroads?"

Camden nodded, "Yes, your date is in Crossroads. You are to meet him at the gate to the walking trail. Don't worry. With the nice weather, plenty of people are enjoying the trail. Besides, Sydney approved of your date when I checked with her."

"Your date is also in Crossroads," Bailey supplied, opening the door to leave. "You're to meet her at La Bonita Sombrero at six o'clock."

"Will do," Camden said easily.

"I guess we'll touch base with each other later this evening," Bailey said, her confidence wavering.

Camden nodded. "Let's plan on it."

Bailey walked down the sidewalk to where Lydia waited in her car. With her arm in a sling, Bailey didn't feel up to driving one handed. Camden had offered to take her to her date before his, but that just felt too awkward. Lydia had readily agreed to be her taxi, saying that she planned to do some shopping anyway and would stick around until Bailey let her know if she needed a ride home.

Bailey couldn't seem to shake off the melancholy of walking away from Camden. Though she had agreed to date someone of Camden's choosing, it all felt so wrong, especially since the one she wanted to choose was Camden himself!

Just get through the next hour, then you can talk to Camden, she told herself. But instead of encouraging herself, she only seemed to make things worse.

Why, oh why, didn't I tell Camden how I feel before he set me up with another man?

Thankfully, Lydia didn't seem to notice Bailey's mood or her silence and kept a constant monologue that covered topics like her brother, Wayne, church activities, and her excitement over the upcoming weddings in the family.

By the time Lydia pulled into the parking area, Bailey had a speech prepared. As soon as she met this man, she'd launch into telling him that she really wasn't interested and that her heart belonged elsewhere. She hadn't decided if she should attempt to end on a happy note of friendship or just abandon the guy and take off right then and there to find Camden.

Is that fair to Camden? She asked herself. She'd promised to give his date a fair try for the sake of the contest.

I don't care about the contest! she argued with herself impatiently. *If skipping out on this date gets me that much closer to Camden, I'll let him win!*

Lydia dropped her off with the admonition to call her if she needed her. Telling herself that Lydia probably wouldn't make it to the store before Bailey called to ask for her retrieval, Bailey waved goodbye and headed toward the gate at the entrance to the walking trail. With each step, she rehearsed her speech.

Should I introduce myself first or just get the speech over with? She wondered as she arrived at the gate.

She waited impatiently, turning back around and scanning the parking area for her date. Though evening, warmth from the day still clung to the earth with the lengthening days. It really would be a nice evening for a walk. Spring was pouncing quickly with many of the trees boasting their early gossamer skirts of green buds. A few more weeks and the blossoms of spring would be in full bloom, clothing those debutante trees in full-flowered ball gowns.

Bailey waited for several minutes, eventually resorting to tapping the toe of her boot against the black concrete of the trail.

He isn't going to show! Bailey thought irritably. *This date Camden set me up with is standing me up!*

Eventually, even the caress of a breeze through the trees couldn't calm her, and her toe became more insistent in its dull patter of impatience.

Then, she heard something. Thinking that the sound came from a few feet off the trail, Bailey scanned the area, expecting to see a little chipmunk or ground squirrel seeking some food after hiding out through the winter. Strangely, she didn't see any animal, but something bright red lay amongst the rocks. Walking the short distance, Bailey reached down and picked up the red scrap. Only it wasn't a scrap. It was a small origami paper heart.

Rocks crunched under footsteps, and Bailey turned to see someone step out from the trees to the side of where she stood.

"Bailey," Camden called, his voice sounding hoarse.

Bailey blinked, thinking she must be seeing things. But the man in front of her was definitely Camden—rugged good-looks, dreamy blue eyes, and a pair of cargo shorts sticking out the bottom of his jacket. Why was he here? Did something happen to her date?

Camden came forward, a nervous smile on his face as he handed Bailey a red origami heart matching the one in her hand. "Hi, I'm Camden Hutchins. I'm your date this evening. Sorry I'm a little late. I have a slight problem being on time, so it's best if you know that up-front."

Bailey shook her head, thinking the man before her was too good to be true. "How...? Why...?"

Camden reached out to take her hand in his, closing the two hearts in between. "Bailey, I don't want you to date anyone but me. Ever. I couldn't set you up with anyone else when I wanted it to be me. It doesn't matter if we aren't a perfect match. It doesn't matter if we don't share all of the same likes and interests, or if we aren't the perfect couple on paper. I choose you. You drive me crazy, so much so that I'm crazy in love with you. I don't want anyone but you."

Bailey let his hand go, transferring the origami hearts to her other hand resting where the sling positioned it. Then she reached out to touch his face. At the contact of her fingertips on the rough stubble of his cheekbone, butterflies raced through her body.

But beneath the breathless excitement lay something even more profound. She loved him. She loved him for who he was. Even if those butterflies didn't always visit, she loved the man. Even when he aggravated her, she loved the person. She loved the way he viewed the world, acting with deep conviction in all he did while prioritizing God and others. She loved the way he loved, and she couldn't imagine anything better than being loved by him.

"Camden, I love you so much," she whispered.

She stood to her tiptoes to meet Camden's lips. In that moment, she knew that everything that had come before was false by comparison. It was like she'd spent her whole life thinking sequins were real diamonds. The warmth of Camden's lips on hers launched fireworks through her heart, but it was the love beneath the surface chemistry that lit a deep passion with an unquenchable thirst.

The kiss ended with tears running down Bailey's face, and she held Camden as if afraid he'd disappear. "I don't think I've ever felt this kind of love, but I was so afraid that you couldn't love me back."

Camden held her close, pulling back only so she could see the sincerity in his face as he spoke. "Oh, Bailey, I intend to spend every day proving how much I love you. I want to be your best friend, but more than that. I want to date you, but not live with you until after I put a ring on your finger and we have a big party on a Saturday. Yes, Bailey, I want you to get used to the idea of me loving you, but you also need to know that I very much intend to marry you."

Bailey's face crumpled in tears. *He wants to marry me! Dear Lord, you gave me someone who wants to marry me!*

"Hey," Camden said in concern, lifting her face up so he could read her better. "Is this a good cry or a bad cry? I didn't mean to upset you."

"Oh, Camden!" Bailey gushed, throwing her arms around him. "It's a very, very good cry. The dream-come-true type. I'm just so overwhelmed that you feel that way about me and that God has so blessed me with you."

Camden laughed. "You have no idea what a relief that is! I was worried that you wouldn't want to be with me because of my job, and I wouldn't blame you. It's probably selfish of me to ask you to be involved with me. At first, I didn't think I could do it."

"What changed your mind?" Bailey asked, curiously. He certainly didn't seem hesitant, not that she'd let him go now even if he wanted to.

"Israel," Camden said simply. Taking her hand in his, Camden began walking down the trail as he spoke. "After everything that happened, Israel recognized that I was in love with you and encouraged me to not waste any more time. When I told him my doubts, he said something that shocked me. He told me that, even with everything that Marissa put him through, he wouldn't trade one day with her. He'd loved her, and out of that love, he'd gotten Chloe. Even though things didn't turn out how they expected and his grief seems insurmountable right now, he is glad that he loved Marissa and wouldn't take it back for a second."

"It is better to have loved and lost," Bailey murmured, thoughtfully watching two ducks at the edge of the pond.

"That's very true when God is the one coding your life's program," Camden grinned. Turning serious, he continued. "Bailey, I don't know what tomorrow brings. Sydney assures me that everything is taken care of and that we're safe. I know that my job comes with some degree of danger, and I cannot ever discuss any of it with you. I also know that nothing in life comes with any guarantees. For everything God has for us tomorrow, I intend to stay just like this—walking at your side if you'll let me."

"I understand, Camden." Sliding a teasing glance up his way as they walked, Bailey continued. "I think we'll have enough to talk about with the website and plenty for me to give you a hard time about without ever mentioning your super-secret identity as a spy. I intend to hold you to that promise of being by my side. I'm not going to let you go, no matter what God brings our way."

At her words, Camden turned and took her in his arms once again. He kissed her, this time dipping her down and out of the way of a young boy riding his bike like a daredevil down the path.

Suddenly, he straightened and let her go. Snatching her hand in his, he hurried down the trail. "Oh, no! We need to go to the restaurant to meet the date you arranged for me! Or maybe you could contact her and cancel? I hate to make her meet me just to tell her my girlfriend decided she really didn't want me dating other women after all!"

Bailey's feet slowed despite Camden's insistence. "Um... well, I think it's definitely too late to cancel," she said, casually taking out her phone. "I'd still like you to go to the restaurant and meet her."

"Huh?" Camden asked, dumbfounded and coming to a complete stop.

"Oh, I'll go with you, don't worry," Bailey assured. Then she smiled sheepishly. "I have a confession to make. Over the past few months, I've completely changed my idea about love and what makes a good match. I still see the value in a personal matchmaker who can see the picture behind the numbers, but I also see the value in your algorithm and its method. When arranging a date for you, I wanted to see the algorithm results. That's why I submitted your profile and got us in so much trouble two weeks ago. In a way, I was cheating because I knew your method would at least narrow down the options for me to use my method. When I saw your algorithm results, I didn't decide on a match right away. Then when Shaya contacted me, I decided to go that route because I honestly didn't know what to do with your actual results. Now I do."

She clicked through her pictures on her phone, selecting the one she was looking for before handing the device to Camden. "These are your algorithm results, Camden. I took a picture as soon as I saw them. Your

Betwixt profile no longer exists, but I still have those list results in a single pic. When we decided to set each other up tonight, I never considered setting you up with anyone other than the number one match on your list."

Camden accepted the phone in his hands. Bailey watched as he zoomed the screen in to see the words and saw the instant he could read the name. His eyes grew round, and he looked up at her in shock. "This says my best match is Bailey Whitmore."

Bailey nodded. "I submitted my profile at the same time I submitted yours. I intended to meet you at La Bonita Sombrero tonight as your date. Apparently, no matter how you match us, we're meant to be together."

Camden laughed. Then he drew Bailey back in his arms, kissed her, and laughed again. "I love it! We both used each other's methods and came up with the best match possible—each other! I knew I did a fantastic job on that algorithm!"

"So, what does this mean in terms of the website?" Bailey asked, pulling him along to continue their walk as she quirked an eyebrow up at him in speculation.

"It means that it's running perfectly. Our clients get their best matches with you and I working together as a team. We'll keep it the same, compromising and working together on everything."

"Agreed," Bailey smiled in satisfaction. "I think we can say that we both won the contest, though this last round was definitely the grand prize."

Camden squeezed her hand, letting her know he wholeheartedly agreed.

After having made a full circle around the pond, they ended up back at the gate, right where they'd started.

"Let's go do my date now," Camden said, moving to where he'd parked his car out of sight. "I'm hungry after all that walking and kissing."

Bailey laughed. "Who knew confessing your undying love could make you work up such an appetite?"

A phone rang suddenly, sending both of them scrambling to find it. Though Bailey came up empty, Camden's hand finally appeared with the ringing phone.

Seeing who it was, he grinned and answered it. "Yes, Elise? You're on speaker."

"So?" she asked pointedly.

Bailey leaned over and very loudly kissed Camden. "Do you hear that, Elise? That's the sound of me kissing the man I love who just happens to love me back."

Excited cheering erupted on the other end, though it was so muddled they couldn't exactly understand Elise's actual words.

Finally, Elise's cheers melted down into a self-satisfied sigh, "I love it when a plan comes together!"

Camden and Bailey looked at each other, and a thousand thoughts and questions ran through Bailey's mind.

"Elise, what do you mean?" Bailey asked hesitantly "Did you...?"

"I'll let you two go, and we'll talk later," Elise said quickly. "I don't want to interrupt your time together."

Before either of them could object, Elise abruptly ended the call.

Camden looked at Bailey. "You don't really think...? All these months... The website... Sending you out here to Crossroads... Everything... It couldn't *all* be a setup, right?"

Bailey swallowed. She wished she could answer Camden with certainty, but she couldn't. Unfortunately, she knew Elise too well, and she wouldn't put a long-term, intricate matchmaking setup past her. Maybe Elise really had created Betwixt Two Hearts and sent Bailey to Crossroads in an elaborate matchmaking scheme to set Bailey up with Camden. Elise had never liked Dekker anyway. It was just like her to concoct a scheme so wonderfully devious and then pray it through to the end. While Bailey was familiar with Elise's undercover cupid scheme, she never thought that she'd be on the receiving end!

If Elise really had set them up, then Camden and Bailey had played right into her hand. Of course, Elise couldn't have known everything and Bailey and Camden went through, but she could have hoped and prayed that they would eventually end up together.

Was it really possible that they'd spent this entire time working to play matchmaker for others, not realizing that it was all a setup by someone playing matchmaker for them?

Bailey shook her head. "I don't know," she answered honestly, still stunned about the possibility. Knowing Elise and her tendency to hide a vague answer behind a sweet smile, they probably never would know for sure.

Camden tipped his head back and laughed, the sound of pure joy sending tingles all the way to Bailey's fingertips. Without expressing the words, Bailey knew his thoughts must be identical to hers.

Realizing she still carried something clenched in the palm of her hand poised in the sling, Bailey looked down at the two origami hearts nestled close to each other and smiled. She didn't know if science, romance, or Elise deserved more credit for bringing them together. However, she did recognize God's hand orchestrating all those pieces to bring their two hearts together.

And for that, both Bailey and Camden were forever grateful.

The End

The book you just read exists because I made a mistake. After you've written about twenty-five books, you start to run out of character names, or you simply don't remember the ones you've used. They all meld together a little, and your mind tends to follow the same patterns. I have to be careful, or my bad guys all end up with the same first name. Pretty soon, every time a reader comes across a "Bruce," they'll know right away what that means!

When I wrote the first Crossroads book, *Out of the Blue Bouquet*, I created the Hutchins family. They were so quirky and fun, and I envisioned the entire series following the characters and the town they called home. Only after *Out of the Blue Bouquet* was finished did I realize that I'd made a mistake. Hutchins was not a rookie name in the world of Amanda Tru.

I'd used the last name of Hutchins before in a book—a fun one I'd written a few years ago called *The Random Acts of Cupid*. The main character in it is Elise Hutchins, with the last name of Hutchins spelled exactly the same way. Had I realized my mistake earlier, I would have changed it in a heartbeat. A quick find and replace would have renamed the Hutchins family forever. However, with the first Crossroads Collection published, it was too late.

As those who read my stories know, I can be a bit intense about the details. I work my plots like a puzzle, tying off loose ends and making sure everything fits just right. While I try never to make such mistakes, I also believe that at least some part of writing is like art. When drawing or painting, mistakes are frequent. For as long as I can remember when I've made an artistic mistake, I've told myself that little smudge was meant to be there and that I could use it to make the artwork even more beautiful. I can't claim as to have had a one-hundred percent success rate with this philosophy, but I still hold dear the ideal that there are no mistakes in art.

As soon as I realized what I'd done, my first instinct was to write my way out of it. If characters from two different books had the same last name, then that must mean they were related, right? I've loved *The Random Acts of Cupid* since the story appeared in my imagination, and I've always liked the idea of turning it into a series of some sort. But, with so many demands and book deadlines, I shelved that idea along with countless others.

After writing *Under the Christmas Star* and *A Cinderella Christmas*, I fully intended to take some time off. However, my friend and formatter asked if, given the popularity of the Crossroads Collections, I intended to organize another set for Valentine's Day. The instant he said, "Valentine's Day," I had a sinking feeling. I immediately recognized what book needed to be written, and unfortunately, that meant I wasn't going to get a break!

I very quickly outlined an entire plot that completely exonerated me. My secret mistake was safe, and readers would assume I'd brilliantly tied the two stories together in a plan I'd crafted from the beginning. No one would ever know. Unless I told them, of course!

Betwixt Two Hearts was born, and less than two chaotic and stress-filled months later, it was written. I hope you enjoyed this book-that-was-never-supposed-to-be-written and that it blesses you in some way. Like Bailey, may you encounter the real and living God, and may He carry you through the minefields of your own making. After all, when God is the artist, there truly are no mistakes He can't make beautiful.

If you would like to read Elise's story in *The Random Acts of Cupid*, visit the following link: amazon.com/dp/B00B3EHCAI

Amanda Tru

Author of *Betwixt Two Hearts*

Questions

An author should like the heroine in her own book. Unfortunately, I did not like Bailey much at all at the beginning of the book, and there wasn't a whole lot I could do about it. My characters are quite real in my own mind, and I couldn't change Bailey on the page to make her something she wasn't in "real life." Luckily, Bailey didn't stay the same person as she was at the beginning, and I hope I did her story justice as she encountered who God really is and she gave her life to be dictated on His terms.

As the story went on, I grew to love who Bailey was becoming. I felt relieved when she realized how wrong she'd been about Dekker and God. I cheered her on as she bravely and intelligently protected Camden at risk to her own life. I was touched as she asked Camden's opinion on a decision she normally would have made herself. And I felt proud as she took the risk of using Camden's methods, rather than her own, to claim her own match. She was still spunky Bailey, but her life had new purpose and value.

Just as God deals with us, He didn't intend Bailey to stay as she was. He guides us through our experiences in a way that ever changes us to be more like Jesus. The moment of salvation doesn't make us perfect, but it sets us on the path to better glorify and serve the One who created it all.

Though Bailey's story was a focal point, it isn't the only spiritual message in the book. The characters struggle with deep spiritual issues that don't necessarily have easy right or wrong answers, but it is still good to think them through. None of the characters in "Betwixt Two Hearts" stayed the same, but grew in their understanding of love and forgiveness.

Maybe it's a ridiculous hope, but I wish for you the same. I don't want you to be the same person who read the first lines of this book. My prayer is that you connected with some spiritual truth embedded in a fictional story and that it spoke to you in some way, drawing you closer in your walk with God as you better understand the relationship betwixt your heart and His.

I challenge you to read through the study guide below with a group, or simply on your own. May these questions below prompt you to, like Bailey, make your exit more memorable than your arrival!

1. Did you like Bailey and Camden at the beginning of the book? What did you or didn't you like? How did Bailey and Camden change in the book? What caused the changes?

2. How has God changed you? What were you like before, and how has God brought about the changes?
Ezekiel 36:26, 2 Corinthians 3:18, Romans 12:2, 2 Corinthians 5:17

What do you think you still need to work on for your life to better reflect Jesus?
Philippians 1:6, Psalm 139:3-4, Ephesians 4:22-24

3. In the book, Bailey thinks she is a Christian, but later discovers that she doesn't know the real and living God. Have you or anyone you've known had a similar experience?
Matthew 7:13-4, Matthew 7:21-23

Many people claim to be Christians. Even different religions claim to be "Christian." What do you think is the true definition of Christianity?
Ephesians 1:12-14, Colossians 1:8-23, Romans 10:5-13

4. Love is another big theme in this book. What is Bailey's view of love? What is Camden's view of love? What is your definition of love? What examples of God's kind of love do you see in the story?
1 Corinthians 13:1-8, Romans 12:9-10, Mark 12:29-31

5. Bailey lives with her boyfriend, and Camden objects for spiritual reasons. What are Camden's feelings about couples living together before marriage?

What are Bailey's?

Today's culture has no problem with couples living together before or instead of marriage. What do you think the Bible says about this issue? What are your feelings on the subject? Do you think the same values should apply to our culture today as they did when the Bible was written?
1 Corinthians 6:18, 2 Corinthians 12:21, Colossians 3:5-8, Galatians 5:19-20, 1 Thessalonians 4:1-8

6. Israel's story is a tragic one, in both his relationship with his wife, Marissa, and his brother, Camden. With Camden, Israel was upset for years over something he later learned involved circumstances he'd never realized.

Have you ever been upset with someone, only to learn later that you didn't know the full story?

How did you react?

Marissa's death leaves Israel devastated on many levels, plagued with guilt and haunted by the knowledge that it is too late to make things right with his wife. This is a common sentiment with death, as we wish for more time for a "do-over." Looking back on your own life, is there anything you've ever wished to do over? How did you handle the feelings of guilt and grief?
Philippians 3:13, Psalm 34:18, Psalm 73:26, 1 Peter 5:7

7. The story contains multiple examples of deception and withholding the truth. Was Bailey wrong to deceive Camden, going behind his back to send Selby the names of Heath's matches, and then again, posting his profile after he told her not to?

Camden was required by his job to not reveal information, but this withholding had a devastating effect on his family. He also had ulterior motives for the website which involved his job. Yet his job was directly involved in serving his country and protecting others. Were Camden's deceptions wrong?

Is there a difference between Bailey's deception and Camden's? What is that difference? Where is the line? How much, if any deception is okay? Does the end ever justify the means?
Colossians 3:9, Acts 5:1-9, Jeremiah 17:9-10, Romans 13:1-7, John 15:13, Philippians 2:4, 1 Timothy 5:8

Tell of a time when you have been deceived or have deceived others. Was it ever justifiable?

8. Was there anything that spoke to you in the book or that you found spiritually significant? Did you have a favorite part or something you found the most touching?

Amanda Tru loves to write exciting books with plenty of unexpected twists. She figures she loses so much sleep writing them, it's only fair she makes readers lose sleep with books they can't put down!

Amanda has always loved reading, and writing books has been a lifelong dream. A vivid imagination helps her write captivating stories in a wide variety of genres. Her current book list includes everything from historical, to action-packed suspense, to inspirational romance, to a Christian time travel/ romance series. Amanda is also the author and organizer behind the unique, multi-author Crossroads collections.

Amanda is a former elementary school teacher who now spends her days being mommy to her four young children and her nights furiously writing. Amanda and her family live in a small Idaho town where the number of cows outnumbers the number of people.

Newsletter:

Newsletter Sign-up

Website:

www.amandatru.com

Email:

truamanda@gmail.com

Facebook:

facebook.com/amandatru.author

Twitter:

@TruAmanda

Crossroads Collections:

Out of the Blue Bouquet

Yesterday's Mail

Under the Christmas Star

Betwixt Two Hearts

The Wedding Dress Yes

When Snowflakes Never Cease

Crossroads Companion Books:

The Random Acts of Cupid

The Night of the White Elephant

Yesterday Series:

Book 1: Yesterday

Book 2: The Locket

Book 3: Today

Book 4: The Choice

Book 5: Tomorrow

Book 6: The Promise

Book 7: Forever (coming soon)

Tru Exceptions Series:

Baggage Claim

Point of Origin

Mirage

Rogue

And many more titles...

Introducing

Are you ready to find out about all of those dates Bailey and Camden set up through Betwixt Two Hearts? The rest of the books in this set follow the stories initiated through those website matches, and I'm thrilled to introduce the next book in the set, *The Swedehearts Glory Quilt* by Cathe Swanson.

When I initially imagined this set, I knew I needed to recruit some fabulous authors who could write a wonderful story on a short turnaround and had the communications skills necessary to work closely with me to tie our stories together. Cathe's name came up more than once, though I'd never actually met her. By reputation, Cathe is very conscientious, organized, and works hard. She is also great at communication and writes wonderfully. Hearing that, I arranged an introduction with a mutual friend, hoping I'd found a kindred spirit.

The good news is that I definitely had! Cathe is great, and I've enjoyed working with her. She is very detailed-oriented, and we worked closely to get everything just right. Besides all of that, given my own Swedish heritage, I'm thrilled with how she brings that aspect into her writing. In the end, I love the way our stories connected, and I'm really excited about her book.

Remember in *Betwixt Two Hearts*, when Bailey and Camden first argue about matching a couple? Camden wants her to approve a match, and Bailey doesn't want to, thinking that there is more to Eleanor's story. Now you'll find out what all that more involves!

In *The Swedehearts Glory Quilt*, Eleanor signs up for Betwixt Two Hearts because she wants a date for her parents' party. Her life is in limbo, and she's not sure what she wants. David, on the other hand, has his life planned out. He signs up for the matchmaking website, looking for the woman he can marry and start a family with. However, this story is so much more than a matchmaking date, and a boy meets girl scenario. It is in part a family saga, full of extended relationships, genealogy, Swedish heritage, Minnesota history, and so much more. It is funny, sweet, sad, and a story you surely will love.

Off you go! Read Cathe's story and the rest of those in this set. Find out how God touches multiple hearts and lives, creating something wonderful Betwixt Two Hearts.

Amanda Tru

Author of *Betwixt Two Hearts*

THE SWEDEHEARTS *Glory* QUILT

By

CATHE SWANSON

Copyright Notice

Eleanor Nielson looked around the table at the familiar, beloved, beautiful, perfect people and wondered if she was adopted. Her parents, like reigning monarchs, smiled benevolently at their well-behaved family. Even the twins, newly promoted from high chairs, sat upright in their boosters, neatly eating moderate portions of turkey and stuffing. A perfect family of blond, blue-eyed, Minnesotan Swedes.

She hadn't come prepared to dress up for dinner, and when Soren came downstairs sporting a striped shirt and bow tie, she laughed at him. Then Zack and Laurie arrived, bearing pumpkin pies, flowers, and grandchildren. Zack's suit looked like it was made for him. Laurie wore a long corduroy skirt and ivory cashmere sweater, loosely belted around her slim middle. Her floral scarf draped gracefully into elegant folds. If Eleanor wore that, it would collect crumbs like a bib, like a chipmunk, saving morsels to consume later. It might, however, protect her sweater from gravy stains.

"There are bound to be openings for the spring semester, not just at Westerfield but other schools in the area, too. Or you could do substitute work for a while. Eleanor!" Kathy Nielson didn't raise her voice; she just changed the pitch. "I was talking to you."

"Sorry, Mom. I did hear you. I'm going to stick it out up north for a while, though." Lather, rinse, repeat. She'd given up on explanations and discussion. Just say no and take advantage of her mother's refusal to engage in a quarrel at Thanksgiving dinner.

"You may change your mind in January, though," Soren said. "Winter up there is different from being in the city. You could get snowed in at that cabin and no one would find you for weeks."

"And that would be bad because...?"

Her brother ignored the comment and continued. "Uncle Gary will want the cabin, too, like this weekend, for hunting and fishing. You can't leave town every time he wants to have a party."

"You won't want to stay there while the cabin is full of his friends," her mother said. "And he won't want you there."

"I'll stay at his house in town, or I can probably stay with Uncle Carl and Aunt Constance. They've got a lot of room there now. It would be fun to see Penny and Lisa." She rather liked the idea of a nomadic existence, but that sentiment would undermine her position. "I'll be looking for a place of my own in the spring."

"You'll be back here by then." Zack handed a napkin to his daughter. "You'd miss Tara and Tyler too much to stay away that long."

"I don't imagine they'll change much by Christmas." Cold, Eleanor, Cold. She tried again. "I probably wouldn't see them again before Christmas even if I lived here!"

"I haven't seen the Anderson cousins in years," Rob said. "Probably since Jeremy's wedding. Uncle Carl said we're welcome to come for a visit whenever we want."

Eleanor smiled gratefully at her oldest brother. "They're really nice." She turned to her mother. "Did you know I used to be afraid of him?"

"Afraid of Carl? Why on earth would you be afraid of Carl?"

"It was a long time ago, when we were on our way back from some family event. You said he didn't care about any children except his own. You were mad about it."

Kathy stared at her. "I never said any such thing."

"Yes, you did. I remember that," Rob interjected. "It was some political thing. He didn't support something you did, or you didn't support something he did. It was probably about homeschooling."

"Well, if I said that—and I don't remember it!—I didn't mean you should be afraid of him. He just sees certain things differently than we do.

He has a limited view of the world, from up there in the country." In other words, they were all united in their enlightened views, and her brother was a backwoods hick.

This Thanksgiving, Eleanor was most devoutly grateful she'd been away from home over the election season.

"Anyhow, at Westerfield, you'd be able to substitute whenever you like, and you'd have a foot in the door when they hire for the new campus this summer." Kathy held up a hand to prevent interruption. "I know you want a break, but if you wait too long, you'll be set back another year. They'll have openings for every subject and grade level.

Eleanor broke off another forkful of pie. She didn't want to teach at all. She'd tried to tell her mother that, but she'd made the mistake of over-explaining it, talking too long, with not enough resolve.

"Westerfield's going to be in demand," her father said. "You'll do well to get in at the start."

"I'm going to stay up north." She hoped she didn't sound as desperate as she felt. She still had two days before she could go home. Back up north, away from her dear family.

"You won't like it up there for long," Zack said, "and you aren't getting any younger. You're going to want to be near Mom and Dad and the rest of us once you get married and have kids." He chucked Tyler under the chin. "You'd like a couple cousins, wouldn't you, fella?"

Zack and Laurie, having efficiently completed their family with only one pregnancy, had recently turned their attention to Eleanor's biological clock. They—and her other brothers and parents—had introduced her to a parade of teachers, politicians, and other suitable bachelors. She knew they meant well. They were genuinely concerned about her professional career and anxiously listening to that ticking clock. She ran a hundred miles away, and they could still hear it.

"Wouldn't it be fun if they had the same nanny?" Laurie asked.

Eleanor blinked. "The same nanny?"

"Well, when the twins are in school full-time, Ilse will be available."

"So," Eleanor said, "if I got married next month, got pregnant a few months later, had the baby and stayed home for at least a few months, that timing would work out for you?"

Laurie shook her head, not responding to the sarcasm. "Weddings take at least a year to plan, and the kids won't be in kindergarten for another two years." She sipped her coffee. "It was just a thought."

"Not to mention the fact that she doesn't have a boyfriend," Soren said, "but I suppose she could go ahead and start planning the wedding now."

"She's twenty-seven." Zack cut open a roll and spread cranberry butter on it. "She'd better start planning something."

"I don't need this." Eleanor stood, pushing her chair back. "I don't know if or when I'll get married, or if I'll have kids, but I've made one decision: I won't be returning to school in the fall. I am not going back to teaching." She almost enjoyed the moment of stunned silence. Even Tara, who'd been running a finger through the whipped cream on her pie, stopped and looked at her. "I don't know what I'm going to do, but I don't think I'm cut out to be a teacher."

"Not cut out..." Kathy Nielson's appalled voice trailed off.

"You're a good teacher," her father said. "Maybe you should look into high school or even college. Middle school can be rough."

"No, Dad. I'm just not good at it." She gestured widely, to encompass all of them. "That's you. Just because it's what you do, doesn't mean it's for me. I'm not like you."

"What else would you do?" Her mother asked.

"I don't know." She picked up her phone from the table and stuck it in her pocket. "I need some time to think about it."

They didn't give her time. They tag-teamed her, nagging and lecturing and reasoning, until she threatened to apply for a job as a Walmart greeter.

"You're a little overqualified for that," her mother said.

"I think I'd be rather good at it."

"I hope you're joking."

"Really," Eleanor insisted. "You say hello when they come in, help them with their carts, give stickers to the kids and then wave goodbye when they leave. It sounds like the perfect job."

Her mother reached out and caught Eleanor's hands. "Sweetheart, I'm sorry we've been pressuring you, but we just want the best for you. You are a good teacher, and it's important, meaningful work. You're making a difference in the lives of children. Investing in the future of America. The world!"

Was that supposed to be encouraging? It sounded like more pressure. "I don't think I was making a difference, Mom. I never felt like I was accomplishing anything at all. The world had better not count on me."

The older woman hesitated as if approaching a delicate topic. She shifted closer, still holding Eleanor's hands, and gazed into her eyes. "Your father and I have been talking. You've been going through a hard time, and maybe you should talk to someone. We'd be happy to pay for a counselor."

"Because I don't want to be a teacher?" Eleanor stood. "Come on, Mom... there are other careers in the world!"

Her mother's tender mood evaporated. "Maybe there are, but I don't see you pursuing any of them. You've just run off to find yourself, without thinking of anyone else."

Eleanor took a step forward. "I'm sorry, Mom. I'm not a teacher."

"Oh, Eleanor."

Their embrace felt hollow, as if nothing had been mended, but it had been an embrace. She wasn't leaving in an open quarrel. Hopefully, things would be better at Christmas. Or maybe there would be a blizzard, and she'd get snowed in at the cabin.

She should have listened to her mother. Eleanor leaned forward, clutching the steering wheel as if afraid it might jerk away and throw the Subaru Outback into the ditch. She'd left early enough to get home before dark, but at four o'clock, dusk hung in the trees. At least it wasn't snowing. A gray shadow flashed in her peripheral vision, and she flinched. She hadn't hit a deer since she was 18, but she still remembered the sick feeling.

The road narrowed to a tunnel, overhung with tree boughs, pines pressing in on both sides. Soren was right; she could get snowed in here.

Uncle Gary said he'd keep it plowed, but what if there was a big storm or, like last year, new snow every day? She could never shovel her way out.

Relief lightened her spirits as she passed the sign and motion-activated floodlights lit the driveway. She'd become fond of that fish-shaped sign since moving here. Its incorrectly-placed apostrophe used to niggle at her, until her mother pointed out that since her brother was single, it was the proper usage. Currently single, her mother had clarified. Eleanor wondered if he kept a sign that said The Andersons' in storage for his married phases.

She pulled into the garage and shut off the engine. She couldn't stay here through the winter. She'd be a basket case by December—even worse than she'd been six months ago, when she'd finally made the decision to leave her job and set out to find herself. She'd never find herself out here. She was lucky to find the cabin.

Cabin was a misnomer. Uncle Gary didn't seem to grasp the concept. This place was larger than his house in town and more luxuriously appointed. She tapped in the security code and pushed the door open. The hallway light came on automatically, flooding the great room with comfort. Through the glass wall of windows, security lights illuminated the backyard—front yard? Eleanor wasn't used to thinking of the road access as the backyard. The front yard was the one on the lake.

She switched off the exterior lights and went into the kitchen. In the evenings, now that it was dark so early, she felt exposed in the great room, with its massive glass wall. She preferred the interior spaces and the dining room, where blinds offered privacy from anyone skulking outside or on the lake.

Eleanor wrinkled her nose at the faint fragrance of cigar smoke. The refrigerator was probably full of beer, too, if her uncle and his friends hadn't drunk it all. He griped about city hunters who came up, drank themselves to sleep and then went out hung over, but he wasn't exactly abstinent himself. Eleanor cleared out for the long weekend, according to their agreement, so they could have their annual hunting trip. She hoped she wouldn't see deer carcasses hanging from trees in the morning.

They'd been tidy, at least. The furniture wasn't in exactly the same position she'd left it, and the mudroom was... muddy. Cleaning was her responsibility—even cleaning up after a hunting party. Free rent came with a price.

The trill of her phone, unexpected in the silence, startled her. Her mother, of course. Eleanor picked up her coat and rummaged for the phone.

"Hi, Mom. I made it safely."

"Good! I've been worried. How was the trip?"

"Uneventful—the best kind."

"No deer? Was the traffic bad?"

"It was all going in the other direction. Hunters heading home with dead deer strapped to the tops of their SUV's. I had the northbound road to myself. And it's not exactly an expedition across the country." It sure felt like it, for the last 20 miles, though. Eleanor rolled the stiffness from her neck.

"Far enough, during hunting season, in the dark."

True. "Well, I just got here and dropped my bag in the hall. I'm going to put your care package in the fridge and get unpacked. I have work in the morning." She could hear her mother's disapproval in the brief silence. "It was fun to spend Thanksgiving with all of you. Tell Dad I love him and I'll beat him at chess when I'm there for Christmas."

"That reminds me." Her mother ignored Eleanor's attempt to end the conversation. "After you left, we started talking about our anniversary. Laurie wants to have a party for us."

"On Valentine's Day?"

"The fifteenth. Valentine's Day is on a Thursday. It was all her idea, but your dad and I are looking forward to it."

Her sister-in-law had jumped right into the Nielson family, not only adding another female to their male-dominated family but producing grandchildren. Twins. Laurie was an overachiever. Eleanor, still single with no prospects in sight, was a failure in more ways than one. It hadn't even occurred to her to throw a party. She would have called, of course, and maybe even remembered to send a card.

"That will be nice! I'll be there." They all knew she didn't have any other plans for Valentine's Day.

David Reid inhaled the cold air, welcoming the fresh bite after the clamor and heat of the gymnasium. Cars clogged the street, unloading returning students stuffed with turkey and hurrying back to cram for tomorrow's exams. There were always exams on the Monday after Thanksgiving weekend.

His own teachers were just as sadistic—he pictured them cackling and rubbing their hands in glee—but he'd come back in time to study before worship team practice on Friday. It was his turn to choose the songs, and he'd sneaked in one of his Russ Taff favorites. Not many of today's congregation had known it, of course, but the "Praise the Lord' choruses were easy to pick up. The older members of the church—the Jesus People generation—sang it with gusto.

"Hey, David!"

He turned and waited for his friend. "Hey, Larry. What are you doing out here?"

The other man trotted to catch up. Not built for trotting, he puffed at the exertion as he came to a stop. "Hoping to find you. I texted a couple times, then I called, and left a voice message, and then I remembered you were here and probably had your phone in a locker. I was afraid you'd get all of it at once and think it was an emergency, so I thought I'd run over and talk to you at the gym."

David chuckled. "But it's not an emergency?"

"Not really an emergency—not for me, anyhow. Cal asked me to ask you to take the presentation to the city council tomorrow because his daughter had her baby early, and he and Meg are flying out there."

"He asked you to ask me...." His boss was notorious for sliding out of awkward situations. "Are his daughter and the baby okay?"

"I think so. He was in a hurry and asked me if I'd talk to you. He said you knew all about the proposal and could present it as well as he could."

"You do know I have to wear a suit and tie for that, right?" David asked darkly.

Larry sighed, looking like a deflating balloon. "Sorry."

"Not your fault." David slapped him on the back. "Cal does that—makes other people do the dirty work. He should have called me himself, but there you were... all sympathetic and wanting to be helpful. He's an engineer, not a people person like you."

"That's me... a psychologist has to be a people person."

"Hey, it pays well, right? And there's job security. The world gets crazier all the time, so psychologists will always be in demand."

Larry scratched his nose. "That's not exactly how it's supposed to work. Do you need a ride home?"

"That would be great, thanks. I'd better review the proposal and iron my good shirt."

David ran a finger around the inside of his collar. Associate pastors didn't have to wear dress shirts and ties, did they? These days, even head pastors dressed more casually. As an engineer, he usually wore whatever was clean and comfortable. It was a good job—just not his calling.

This had been a futile attempt, just like the last one, and just like the next one would be. Cal's technology was miles ahead of everyone else, but he couldn't back up his claims with years of successful application, and no one would give him the opportunity to try. The city council members were interested and liked the proposal; they just couldn't put taxpayer money into something that might or might not work. When they did, Ridgewell Mechanical would be ready to go. They'd bring big jobs to the community, too—big for St. Cloud, anyhow.

He tugged the tie loose and shoved it into the pocket of his wool coat, his fingers touching his cell phone just as it vibrated. He answered without reading the screen.

"David Reid, Ridgewell Mechanical."

"Hello, David. I'm so glad I caught you!"

Angela. He'd let her last few attempts go to voice mail, feeling guilty for not answering her calls but conflicted about how to respond.

"Hi, Angela. Sorry I missed your calls. It's been hectic." He glanced back at the building he'd just left. "I'm at city hall right now, working. Is there something I can do for you?" Wrong question. He tried to think of an excuse, but she jumped in ahead of him.

"How about lunch? Engineers have to eat, to keep that brain fueled up." Her tone was flirtatious. "Or if you're stuck at work like you usually are, how about dinner? At my place, or we can go out."

"I have classes most evenings." He'd told her that a dozen times. He softened his voice. After all, she knew he was a Christian. He ought to be winning her for Christ, not driving her off. "It's just a busy time for me."

"Not too busy to eat," she insisted. "We could grab a bite right after you get off work."

"I can't." He tried to sound regretful. Cal's much-younger sister was like a bulldozer. She'd already driven over two of his coworkers, and he was the next man in her path. David had no desire to join her list of victims.

"What about Sunday? I'd love to visit your church, and we could have brunch afterward."

He stopped and pulled the phone away from his ear, staring at the screen as if he could read her mind through it. Surely, she had no desire to go to church. She was probably just willing to sit through 90 minutes of boredom if it would get her what she wanted. Right now, that appeared to be David.

Church. She'd found the golden ticket. He couldn't say no to taking her to church.

"Okay, do you know where Grace Chapel is?" David held the phone between his ear and shoulder while he buttoned his coat.

"How about if you just pick me up?"

Oh, no. That wasn't happening. "I have to be there early. Really early, for music practice and prayer meeting."

"Prayer meeting? Is that open to the public? I could do that."

He grinned at the optimistic note in her voice. Under different circumstances, he'd admire her persistence. "It's really just a small group of guys—mostly older men. The service starts at ten."

"Sounds good! I don't know anyone there, so I'll sit with you."

The old ladies of the church would eat that up. They were always trying to introduce him to their granddaughters and nieces, convinced that a single man with a steady job must be in want of a wife. So far, none of the granddaughters and nieces had been at all interested in becoming a wife.

"And we'll go out for brunch afterward," Angela finished triumphantly. "See you then, David!"

Maybe Pastor Jack would have a good sermon on Sunday. Something scholarly that David could expound upon through brunch. He'd bore her into abandoning him. Guiltily, he winced as he slid the phone back into his pocket with the despised necktie. Jack did like to preach Old Testament exposition, but it would be better to have an evangelical message for Angela. How could he be so self-centered and conceited? That girl needed Jesus.

The phone rang again almost immediately, and he checked the caller name before answering.

"Hi, Mom."

"Hello! I just called to see how your presentation went. Any luck?"

"Nope, another rejection. My ego is suffering."

She chuckled. "I doubt it. It'll happen eventually, even if it's after you're gone."

He headed toward the parking lot, glad to have a normal conversation after what he could only describe as an assault. "Hey, you want to come to church with me this weekend?"

"I don't think we can, this weekend. Is something special going on?"

"No, just wondering."

"How about next weekend? We could do that."

David opened his car door and climbed inside. Out of the wind, he relaxed in the sun-warmed interior. "I bet you just need a weekend to recover from Thanksgiving."

"Well, your dad did suggest a vacation was in order. That was quite a day."

"There must have been a hundred kids," David said. "All of my cousins are reproducing like rabbits."

His mother laughed. "No one person had more than two or three kids... there are just a lot of you! We've never had everyone from both sides of the family all at once before—at least, not since you were little. And it wasn't a hundred kids."

"It seemed like it."

"There were 13," she said, "and Ian is 16, so you really shouldn't count him with the children. But five of them were under five years old, and it was pretty hectic."

It had been great. David spent most of Thanksgiving Day playing games with the older kids and tickling the little ones. He looked out the windshield. A young woman waited at the intersection, pushing a stroller and holding another child by the hand. The little girl was hopping up and down and appeared to be singing. "Maybe you'll have a grandchild of your own next year, if Nick and Heather finally get around to starting a family."

"Maybe."

"I was looking at all those kids," David said, "and I realized that none of them are Reids. I'm the only Reid descendant. Grandpa Ken was the only boy in his family. Uncle Kenneth had all girls."

"That's right. Does that worry you?"

"I just hadn't thought about it. I also realized that I'm the only unmarried cousin on either side of our family, Except for Uncle Kenneth's girls, and they're all still in school." Everyone was paired off in happy couples, families with babies and full lives. David, the thirty-year-old engineer, was still single. Loser.

"You'll find the right girl in God's timing, David. Right now, you're pretty busy with work and school."

"But I don't think there's ever going to be a time when I'm not busy. You're busy, and all your kids are grown and gone."

"That's true," she agreed, "but it will happen, David. Yes, we'd love to have grandchildren, but we'll be grateful for whatever God sends us. On Thanksgiving, He sent us 13 great-nieces and nephews, and that was a bit overwhelming."

"It sure was." David started the car. "I need to get back to work, so I'll talk to you later. Plan on next Sunday, though. Love you."

"I love you, too. Be careful."

"I always am. Don't forget next Sunday."

At least he'd have backup if Angela wanted to attend the following weekend, too.

Three

I don't know if you saw the weather forecast or not, but we're supposed to get some snow tonight."

Gary Anderson, a lanky man with the blue eyes and prominent brow of his Scandinavian ancestors, peered at Eleanor over the reading glasses he wore in the office.

Her heart sank. "How much?"

"Just a few inches. Maybe three. Do you want me to come and plow you out in the morning?"

She shook her head. "I'm sure it'll be fine. The Outback has all-wheel drive. I'm a Minnesotan, remember? We can drive in snow."

"You can drive in city snow," her uncle retorted. "Have you ever been out of town in the snow? A little wind can drift the snow right over the road, and it's hard not to slam on the brakes when something jumps out in front of you. That's when accidents happen."

"I know not to slam on the brakes and to watch for other cars that may not be able to stop at intersections. I'm sure I'll be fine if I go slowly."

"I'll come out and plow, just to make sure. Better safe than sorry."

He went into his office, and Eleanor spun on her stool, tapping the blueprints she'd been examining. He wouldn't like having to plow all the way to the cabin every time it snowed this winter. Last year, they'd had three feet of snow in April. She could shovel, or even learn to use the snowblower Uncle Gary kept in the garage, but the road to the cabin was a mile long and not high on the county's plowing priority list.

She couldn't afford to move. The use of the cabin was part of her pay. Even if Uncle Gary was willing to pay her a bit more, rentals were scarce. And why should he pay her more? She was slow as molasses at her job, and he had to double-check everything she did. The last take-off had been perfect, though, and she was studying the manuals he'd given her. She'd get better.

The work absorbed her attention. It was like a puzzle. The answers were right or wrong, unlike teaching, with its subjective nature and results that might not be seen for years—if she was making a difference at all.

Three hours later, Eleanor stretched and slid from the stool. Lunchtime. Peanut butter and jelly was good for you, right? It had been one of her favorite lunches, when it was a special treat instead of a steady diet. For the last few years, she'd wolfed down microwaved frozen meals and hurried back to her classroom to prepare for her next class—and to make sure the dear children didn't come in and steal her stapler.

Her uncle looked up as she passed his desk. "How's it going in there?"

"Good! The electrical is the hardest part, and I'm nearly done with that."

"Great. Can you do me a favor after lunch?"

"Sure." She'd gladly be his girl Friday if it meant he could keep her employed. There wasn't a lot of work in the winter, for his construction company or anyone else in the area.

"I've got some old blueprints for Aunt Violet. I have no idea what she wants them for, but I don't need them. Can you bring them out to her at the farmhouse?"

"I haven't seen the farmhouse since she moved back there," Eleanor said. "I wonder if Penny will be there. I haven't seen her in ages."

"Maybe. Your uncle Carl said she's there nearly every day." He shook his head. "I don't know how well a bridal shop will do all the way out there."

"It'll be fine. Penny's a smart woman."

"Mmhm. I hope that's enough."

No one appeared to be home. Eleanor considered the old farmhouse from the comfortable warmth of her car. Her only memories of the place were of kittens she'd found in the barn and playing shadow tag with her cousins. The barn was gone now. The driveway was paved, with a little parking area and a walkway that curved around the house, rising gently and ending at a side door. An elegantly-disguised wheelchair ramp. Uncle Carl's landscaping business at work, no doubt. The yard, sparse and frozen, would be beautiful when he finished it in the spring.

The gray and white house managed to look contemporary without denying its farmhouse roots. The blue door—not the ubiquitous red—gave it distinction. Still... would brides really drive all the way out from the cities to get their dresses made by an unknown young woman with no credentials? In a farmhouse?

Eleanor put the car in gear. She'd drop off the blueprints at the Andersons' house after work. Maybe she could catch Penny or Violet there. She hadn't seen any of them yet. Aunt Connie's invitation to Thanksgiving dinner, delivered through Uncle Gary, had been a matter of form. They knew she had to go home. Now, she wished she'd accepted.

A red car whipped into the parking lot even as Eleanor started to back up, a blond girl emerging, waving, almost before the car stopped.

"Hi! Did you have an appointment with Penny? She's running late. She got a flat tire and didn't have a spare, so her aunt and the handyman went out to help her. Can you wait?"

Eleanor opened the car door. "No appointment. I'm her cousin. I just came to drop off some stuff for Aunt Violet."

"Oh, it's nice to meet you! I'm Brittany. I do Penny's marketing and social media."

"Eleanor Nielson. I just moved here. I haven't even seen Penny in years. Aunt Violet, either."

"Violet will be back in a few minutes."

On cue, a blue Buick turned in and parked on the other side of Brittany's car. Eleanor hurried to meet her. Aunt Violet didn't look any different than she had last time Eleanor had seen her. Thin, with snow white hair and faded blue eyes, she leaned on a cane as she rose from the car. There was something very comforting about elderly relatives. They made her feel like she had roots. An odd thought, but true.

"Nellie!"

An unexpected lump grew in Eleanor's throat as Violet embraced her. No one else had ever called her that—fortunately—and even though she'd never been close to her aunt before, she felt like she'd come home.

"Nellie Nielson! That's a terrible name," Eleanor said. "I used to get called Ellie sometimes, but Mom's always said Eleanor, and it stuck."

"I called you Nellie when you were a baby," the older woman said. "You were a sweet little thing, with big blue eyes and always waving your arms around."

"Mom says that's how she knew I'd be good at volleyball. I've got some blueprints for you, from Uncle Gary. Can you show me around? I'd love to see what you've done here."

"The main part of the house is Penny's, but you can see my little home in the annex."

"I'm going to wait in my car for Penny," Brittany said. "I've got some calls to make. It was nice to meet you!"

"Yes, nice to meet you, too." Eleanor shook hands with the girl.

"I'm sure we'll meet again."

That would be nice. She could use a few friends here. Eleanor grabbed the rolls of paper and followed her aunt to a back door. "So, are you all moved in? Penny's going to live upstairs, over her shop, right?"

"Not yet." Violet twisted a key in the lock and pushed the door open. "We're moving in at the beginning of the year, but then I'm leaving at the beginning of February, for Florida. I'll stay with your grandma and Aunt Colleen until the weather improves."

"That's a good plan." Eleanor shivered dramatically. She looked around the spacious kitchen. "This is nice. Is this where Mom lived when she was little?"

"Oh, yes, she did. I'll make some coffee."

It would be rude to leave right away. Eleanor shrugged out of her coat and hung it on the rack. Uncle Gary wouldn't mind.

Violet talked while she filled an old-fashioned percolator coffee maker. "It's plenty big for me. I'll have two rooms for my sewing. One's just an ordinary sewing room, and the other will have the long-arm quilting machine in it. That leaves me with one bedroom for myself and a spare. Would you like a look around while the water boils?"

"Yes! You have four bedrooms here?"

"They were always full, until we all left and closed the place up. We even had some boarders for a while, but then it was abandoned until we decided to put the bridal shop in here." Violet looked around with satisfaction. "Now it's all mine—this part, anyhow, and that's enough for me."

"So, you've come home." The idea was... heartwarming.

"Yes, I have. But it's the people who matter, you know, and I was always with family." Violet pushed a door open. "This was the master bedroom, but I'm putting the quilting machine in there. The previous owner will be here tomorrow to assemble it for me."

"That makes quilts?" The electrical equipment and metal pieces, including several long pipes, looked like something from one of Uncle Gary's work sites.

"It quilts them. A great improvement over doing them by hand. This room opposite is mine, and that's the sewing room."

She pointed, and Eleanor obediently moved to look inside. It didn't exactly look like a tornado had gone through it, since everything was still piled up, but she wondered how her aunt could accomplish anything in such a jumble. The rest of the house was so clean and orderly.

"I keep most of my material and other supplies in totes in the laundry room. It used to be a sort of mudroom, but now it's just laundry. I was going to keep them in that room at the end of the hall, but your uncle Carl said I should keep it for guests." She sniffed. "I suppose your grandma might come, but she'd stay with them, especially now that I'm moving out and they'll have more room. But Brian—Penny's young man—fixed up a lot of shelves in the laundry room, and I didn't want to hurt his feelings."

Violet turned back toward the kitchen, and Eleanor followed. "I saw you have patio furniture out back. It'll be a nice place to sit when it gets warmer."

"We used to sit out there, a long time ago, before all those trees got too big and blocked the view." She opened a cupboard and took out cups and saucers. "I have some sandbakkels, too. Do you like those?"

"I don't know. What are they?"

"Cookies! Swedish cookies. Doesn't your mother make them?"

Eleanor shook her head. "She makes sugar cookies and gingerbread men at Christmastime. And sometimes others, but I don't think I've heard of sandbakkels."

"Hmph. She used to love making sandbakkels, even when it wasn't Christmas. Have a seat."

Eleanor sat. It was odd to hear of her mother spoken of as a child, so casually, by this woman who was nearly a stranger. "Then I'm sure I'll enjoy them. Can I help with anything?"

"No, it's all done." Violet set the filled cups on the table and returned for a plate of cookies. "Penny will want to show you the rest of the house herself. She's been working hard on it." She transferred a cookie to her plate. "The annex will do nicely for me."

"It's larger than I thought," Eleanor said, "but it still seems cozy. The cabin is so big and empty. It's strange to be there alone at night. I've been playing music, like white noise, to drown out the wind and coyotes."

Instead of filling the house with warmth, though, the music made it worse. If it was quiet, it disappeared, swallowed up in the vastness of the great room. When she turned up the volume, it echoed off the walls and ceiling.

Aunt Violet frowned. "All by yourself. I don't like that. Are you driving back and forth every day?"

"Yes, for now." Eleanor took a cautious sip of the black coffee. "I'm a little worried about winter. Uncle Gary says he'll plow, but he's so busy."

"And he's not going to plow you all the way to town! What if the power goes out or your car breaks down? Or if there's a lot of snow and he can't get out, either?"

Eleanor blinked. "You aren't exactly reassuring me, Aunt Violet."

"Has anyone ever lived there over the winter before?"

"I don't know," Eleanor said, "but Uncle Gary said it's all winterized. It's not exactly a rustic cabin. It's bigger than my parents' house and a lot nicer."

"It's a cabin, and isolated. What would you do in an emergency?" Violet snapped. "That boy doesn't have a lick of sense. Why are you staying out there?"

"I... It's sort of a perk of the job. I'm not all that helpful at the office, so I don't expect a lot of money. If I stay at the cabin, I don't have to pay rent or utilities."

Her aunt narrowed her eyes speculatively. "You're keeping it clean and lived in. Empty houses are a target for bugs and rodents and vandals. You're doing him a favor."

"No, not really. It's a beautiful place. I'm grateful." She ran a finger around the cup's handle. "It's just a bit remote, and with winter coming, it does make me nervous. But it'll be fine." She took a bite of cookie, mostly to put an end to her protests.

"I don't like the idea of you all alone out there. Why don't you get a place of your own, in town?"

"I've been thinking about it. I'll check the buy-sell-trade groups on Facebook. Maybe someone wants a roommate." Eleanor sighed. Just like college. The garage apartment her parents fixed up for her was nice, but it wasn't like being independent. She'd stayed long enough to pay off the student loans, and then, instead of looking for a place of her own, she ran away and ended up in a remote cabin without a real job.

"I don't care for the sound of that at all." Violet set her cup down, clinking against the saucer. "You're going to meet up with someone online and live with them?"

"I'd ask for references," Eleanor said meekly. "Or at least I could look for rentals cheap enough to get without a roommate."

"You can move in with me." The offer sounded more like a declaration. A command.

Eleanor bit her lip. Living in the back bedroom at her elderly aunt's house was a step in the opposite direction of independence. At least she had privacy at the cabin. "I don't know... I didn't mean to put you on the spot.

The cabin is so luxurious. Even if I was snowed in for a day or two, I'd be comfortable. There's even a wood-burning stove in the rec room downstairs, in case the heat goes out."

"You know how to use a wood stove?"

"I'll get Uncle Gary to show me." Eleanor smiled at her aunt. "Really, I'm fine. Have you been out there? It's like a resort."

"No, I haven't. I know cabins, though, even nice ones, and they're still cabins."

"You could come out and stay with me," Eleanor teased. "At least until you're ready to move in here."

"No, thank you. I'd rather move in here now, but Carl doesn't like the idea of me being here alone. I wonder if he knows you're alone out at the cabin."

Her uncle Carl wouldn't worry about Eleanor falling and breaking a hip, though. Someone as frail as Aunt Violet should be closer to other people, in case of emergency. She stood up. "I'd better get back to work before Uncle Gary docks my pay."

Her aunt didn't move. "I don't understand what you're doing for him, anyhow. I thought you were a teacher. Didn't you get a master's degree? Sit down."

Eleanor complied. "I decided to try something else for a while."

Violet gave an unladylike snort. "Working for a construction company?"

"I'm actually enjoying it. One of the things I'm doing is taking off project plans. That means I go through the blueprints or plans and make a list of all the items we'd need to buy to build the project." She pressed a finger against the cookie crumbs and licked it clean. "I know it sounds dumb, but it's kind of satisfying. I figure out how many eight-foot, 6-inch pipes we need, and how many six-inch, ninety-degree flanged elbows and how many bolts it would take to join all of the pipes. Or electrical wiring and outlets. That's more complicated, but I'm getting it."

"But you're a teacher!" Her aunt didn't sound impressed with her new skills. "You sound like Brian, with your wiring."

"Brian?"

"Penny's young man. The one who set up my storage. He's been redoing all the electrical work and anything else he can think of, as an excuse to hang around."

"Oh. Well, I don't know anything about electricity—just adding up the length of wires and components. Same with the rest of it. I'm in the office, not out doing the work."

Violet tipped her head to one side. "If you come now, Carl couldn't have any objection to me moving in early. And it would be safer for you than living out at the lake."

Eleanor looked at her. She didn't want to be manipulated. She'd just run away from that and was enjoying the freedom. "I don't think I can. I've made a commitment to Uncle Gary. And like you said, the house shouldn't be left empty. If I get snowed in, I'll do a lot of reading and be cozy in front of the wood stove. It sounds kind of fun."

It sounded terrifying. The cabin was more cavernous than cozy, with its prow front wall of windows, massive stone fireplace, and high ceilings that peaked at twenty feet. The logs were bigger than any pine tree she'd ever seen.

"Well, I think you'll be ready to move to town sooner than later." The old lady stared at her for a few seconds. "In fact, you could be helpful to me."

"Helpful?"

"I've been working on some little books, to go with my family history quilts. I thought they were good, but I started rereading them a few months ago, and they're terrible. They need an English teacher to go over them. Editing. There are some that still need to be typed up, since I didn't have a typewriter or computer when I started."

"You write books to go with quilts?" Interested, Eleanor sipped her coffee. It was cold.

"I make family history quilts. Didn't your mother tell you?"

"Um, no. She didn't mention it." Why hadn't she? Eleanor was beginning to wonder if she knew her mother at all.

"I've been making them for years. At least fifty years. Penny says they're like a scrapbook. I write books—stories, anyhow—to go with them, to explain what they are and why I did different things with them. I could use your help with that."

And move in early. Yep, Eleanor recognized manipulation when she saw it. "I don't think I should, right now. Would you be willing to keep the offer open for a while, in case it does get too hard out there? And if I did move in," she added hastily, "it would be temporary, while I look for a place of my own." She reached across the table and patted the blue-veined hand. "But thank you."

Four

"Did you hear Jack say that the church is booked with weddings every Saturday this month?"

"You wouldn't think January would be a big month for weddings in Minnesota." Larry paused, his cup halfway to his mouth. "But it's cold and dark, so maybe people are looking for a partner then. One person can't stay warm alone, you know."

"No," David said, "it doesn't work like that. According to my sister and cousins, weddings take at least a year to plan. It's ridiculous. Once you get engaged, you should just get married."

"I heard that. One of my clients is engaged. Her wedding is over a year away, and she's in a constant state of anxiety about it."

"Why? The wedding or the marriage? Don't get me wrong, Larry, but if my bride was so stressed out by the wedding that she had to see a psychologist, I'd wonder if she really wanted to marry me. And how would she do with married life?" David demanded, warming to his topic. "And kids?"

Larry shrugged. "Don't know."

"And a year! Larry, I'm thirty. If I found a girl tomorrow, dated for at least a few months before proposing and then had to wait a year to get married, I'd be nearly thirty-two. And even if we start a family right away, I'd probably be thirty-three or so when the first one is born. If we have two or three..." He broke off, offended. "What are you laughing at?"

"Only an engineer would do the math like that."

"I want to have a family, and I want to do it young enough that I can enjoy my retirement with an empty nest."

Larry chuckled again, getting his whole body involved. "In other words, you want to have kids and get it over with, skipping all the parenting years, and enjoy the grandchildren."

David grinned. "That's not exactly what I meant, but my folks are in their fifties, and Heather and I have been out of the house for ten years. They're done with kids and seem to be enjoying themselves. My aunt and uncle are nearly sixty and still have two daughters in college and one who's a high school senior. I'd like to have my kids while I'm young enough to enjoy them—and enjoy life after they're grown and gone, too."

"But babies don't come on a schedule—at least, not usually—and you're not married yet. You don't even have a girlfriend. I've never even known you to have a date."

"Thanks for making me feel good, Larry." David pointed his fork at his friend. "I don't see girls hanging on you, either."

"Nope." Larry scowled at the grapefruit wedges on his plate. "I'm not good husband material right now. The doctor said if I don't lose at least fifty pounds, this might be my last birthday. I'll either have a heart attack or get diabetes."

"You're doing great. You didn't cave to peer pressure and order French toast." David ran the last piece of sugar-dusted bread through a puddle of lingonberry syrup.

His friend eyed the morsel with regret. "I don't have a death wish. The weight just piled on, a bit at a time. The doctor says that's what it'll keep doing unless I make drastic changes. So, grapefruit and celery are my new best friends. I'm getting a gym membership, too."

"Good for you." David returned to their previous conversation. "I've had a few dates, set up by the matchmaking grannies at church, but none of them clicked." He set his fork on his plate and pushed it toward the edge of the table. "I don't even know any girls. I'm too old for college students."

"I know what you mean." Larry nodded. "I get older and they get younger every year."

"Right now, after a family Christmas that looked like something out of Norman Rockwell, I feel like everyone around me has this wonderful life and I'm sitting at home alone. Everyone else my age is married with a family."

"Except me," Larry said. "You really feel strongly about this. I'm sorry I laughed."

"It's okay. I'm just feeling sorry for myself after the holidays. Everyone says to wait... that God will bring me the perfect wife, but I'm not sure that means I should sit home, waiting for her to show up on my doorstep. We don't have any women in the office, and there aren't any single young women at church. My seminary classes are online. I don't know where I'd meet the right kind of woman."

"Oh! Hold on." Larry reached for his coat and dug into the pocket. "I just saw something this morning on Facebook. It's a new matchmaking company."

"Oh, no." David shook his head. "I'm not doing online dating. I've heard too many horror stories, even from those Christian sites."

"It's the way everyone meets people these days. I know several people who met online."

"Not me."

"I don't think this one's like a regular dating site." Larry flicked his finger against the screen, scrolling through posts. "It sounded more like people looking for relationships, not dating. You can get a professional matchmaker."

"Matchmaker. A professional matchmaker? Is there a college degree for that?"

"Didn't you tell me you did Fiddler on the Roof in community theater? There was a matchmaker in that." Larry continued his search. "I wish I could remember the name of the company."

"Yenta?" David scoffed. "Is she on Facebook now?"

"Here it is. Betwixt Two Hearts. There. I shared it with you."

"You didn't post it on my page, did you?" David picked up his own phone, alarmed. "I can just imagine what my family would say. They're ruthless."

"No, I sent a message. See?" Larry held up his phone. "Computer-matching or a personal matchmaker. Not professional."

"I'm not interested in computer dating."

"Look at it. You can tell them what you want. So, tell them you want a wife."

Exasperated, David dropped the phone face-down on the table. "Like ordering one from Amazon? A modern version of mail-order brides?"

Larry shrugged. "Or like Abraham, sending his servants out to find a wife for Isaac. It says here you fill out a questionnaire and they match you up with someone. You don't go through a list of people like you do on those other websites."

"I think I'll just wait for a real girl. Woman."

"How long you gonna wait?" Larry leaned back, still reading the website. "You might have kids at home till you're eighty. If you get any at all."

"I'm not that desperate."

Larry peered over the phone, brows raised. "Really? I saw Angela at church a few weeks ago. I wasn't going to mention it, but..."

"What am I supposed to do? Tell her she can't come to church? I think she's given up on me, though. We went out to brunch afterward and I told her I'm in school to be a pastor. She wasn't impressed." He slid from the booth. "I've got to get going. Happy birthday. Hope you enjoyed your grapefruit and yogurt."

"Thanks. But really, man, it's okay to check this out. Everyone's doing it. It's hard to meet people once you're out of college or in a church like ours, where almost everyone's over forty or already married. Someday..." Larry patted his stomach. "I may just look into it for myself, once I've got in shape. No girl's going to look at me like this."

"The right girl will. You probably won't find her on a dating website, though."

"That's awesome." David watched the ball spin, spiraling around the pole. It had a hypnotic effect, probably because of its silence as it traveled up and down. "But I'm getting dizzy watching it. Did you have any practical application in mind, or is it just for fun?"

His boss smirked. "Just for fun, so far, but I'll find something to do with it. Some of my best machines started out as toys." He pointed the controller and the ball fell to the floor.

"Now you can make toys for your grandson," David said. "He must be about six weeks old now, right? Did you know they make Tinker Toys for babies?"

"Really?" Cal tapped his watch and raised it to his face. "Tinker Toys."

"Are you making a Christmas shopping list already?"

"Mostly Legos, so far. Meg likes to add things like baby dolls and teddy bears, just to pull my chain. She says he'll need lots of warm fuzzies to compensate for the engineering gene."

"She might have a point. Has she forgiven you for the vacuum system you gave her for your anniversary?"

Cal hunched his shoulders. "It was a great design. She could use it for everything, even things she drops down the drain, like the cap from the tube of toothpaste, or for getting the crumbs under the heating element in the oven. I made a dozen specialized attachments, all personalized just for her."

"And she didn't think that was romantic?" David smiled sympathetically. Cal had spent weeks on that, ignoring the warnings of his friends, determined to make it a perfect, one-of-a-kind gift for his wife. It was a true labor of love, the most romantic thing Cal could think of, and after twenty-five years of marriage, Meg ought to have understood that.

"Not really, but she's using it, or makes me use it. I'd have been in real trouble if Angela hadn't been there."

"Angela?"

"Yeah, she dragged me aside, forced me to give her my credit card, and came back an hour later—still during the party—with a diamond bracelet. A very expensive diamond bracelet, in a gift-wrapped box and a card signed with my name. She told Meg the vacuum cleaner was just a joke, and this was her real gift."

"I didn't hear that part." Angela probably knew her brother pretty well.

Cal rubbed the back of his neck. "I'm not sure she believed it. She loves the bracelet, though, and she says I should shop at that store for all her gifts from now on."

"That will simplify your shopping," David said, concealing a smile.

"But it's so impersonal," Cal complained. "Meg's the most amazing woman in the world, and it seems kind of cold to just buy jewelry instead of making her something really special." He regarded his new invention. "This would make a great mobile for a baby. You'd have to keep it out of their reach and make sure the batteries don't die. I should ask Meg about it."

David watched him wander in the direction of his office, already talking to his wife through the blue-tooth earpiece. That, with all its weirdness, was what he wanted in a marriage. Cal adored his wife, convinced she was even more brilliant than he—with his genius IQ— would ever be. To him, Meg was the most beautiful, desirable woman in the world. Meg, despite her reaction to the vacuum cleaner, loved her husband. She laughed at his jokes and teased him about the baby gifts. Cal was an odd duck. Meg saw that and liked it. She didn't try to change him into someone else.

They'd been high school sweethearts. She'd supported him in their early years, working so he could go to college and then start his own business instead of taking a high-paying job in another company. As soon as Cal made his first big sale, she quit her job to become a full-time wife and mother. They were living happily—if a bit strangely—ever after.

He caught his reflection in the glass wall. He was a nice, ordinary-looking guy. Clean, polite, kind to children and small animals... Not nearly as odd as Cal, but Cal had a great marriage, and David was single. Why hadn't he had the foresight to get a high school sweetheart?

Brittany breezed through the door of the coffee shop just as Eleanor ended the phone call. How did the girl do it? Eleanor couldn't breeze through a doorway to save her life, but it looked natural on Brittany. Brittany had flair. Style. Personality.

"Hi, there. Sorry I'm late. You already got your coffee?"

Eleanor held up her cup. "I couldn't wait. I was freezing."

"It's cold out." Brittany tilted her head, concern creasing her brow. "Is something wrong?"

Perceptive, too. Eleanor took a sip of the too-hot coffee before responding. "No, I'm fine. I was just talking to my sister-in-law. She's throwing a party for my parents' anniversary."

"That's nice." Brittany tugged off heavy mittens and shoved them into her coat pockets. "How long have they been married?"

"Thirty-five years. It's not even like it's fifty or something! Why do they need such a big deal for their thirty-fifth?"

"Um... I don't know. Thirty-five years is a long time, and it's always fun to have a party." Brittany pointed. "There's an empty table."

Eleanor slid onto a stool. "But this is a big party, and way more... fancy than I expected. She's having a string quartet and a wine bar!"

Brittany's mouth fell open. "A wine bar? Is that like an open bar with just wine? No beer or mixed drinks?"

"I think so. And she's meeting with a caterer to taste finger foods that will cost more than a sit-down meal." Eleanor propped her chin on her hand, elbow precariously near her cup. "Laurie can afford it, but still... it's their thirty-fifth. An accomplishment, no doubt, but still..."

"Let me get something to drink, and you can tell me about it. It sounds like fun."

Not fun. Eleanor watched her new friend chat with the barista. Her unexpected friendship with Brittany was one of the best things in her life here. It reminded her of college days, when no one expected anything of her except that she do her schoolwork and be a friend.

Brittany set her coffee on the table and shrugged out of her coat before settling on the other stool. "So, this party... what are you going to wear? Can you sew like Penny?"

"I don't know. I mean, no, I don't sew, and I don't know what I'm going to wear." Would Brittany understand? Their friendship hadn't progressed to the soul-baring level yet.

"You don't look very happy about it."

"It's just... the thing is, Laurie expects me to come with a date. They all expect it."

"Oh. Is that a problem? I suppose it's down in the cities. Do you know someone down there to invite? It might be awkward to ask someone from up here, especially if you have to spend the night." Brittany leaned forward. "Do you really need a date? I mean, they know you'll be driving in from out of town.

"I don't think they care about that. They expect a date. A good one."

"A good one?" Brittany's eyes widened.

"Someone presentable, preferably a professional of some kind," Eleanor said. "Someone who fits in with their crowd. And preferably someone who will convince me to return to civilization and get a real job."

"Wow." Brittany stopped stirring sugar into her coffee and stared. "That's... interesting. I didn't realize your parents were so different from Penny's."

"Totally different. It's hard to believe they're related. Uncle Carl and Gary are so down to earth. My mother acts like they're backwoods hicks. But she grew up here, too." The words burst out on their own.

"She's their sister, right? Will they be invited to the party?"

"Probably. They might even go." A happy thought occurred to Eleanor. "Maybe Aunt Violet will go, and I can say she's my date. I need to take care of her, so I can't have a man tagging along."

"Your aunt isn't that frail, and she'll whap you with her cane if you imply she is."

"True. If I carpooled down there with some of the family, I wouldn't need a date," Eleanor mused, "but it would be better if I had a date."

"But you don't?"

"No. The thing is, when she started talking about table arrangements and invitations, Laurie assumed I'd be bringing a 'plus one.' I didn't correct her. It kind of snowballed, and now everyone is looking forward to meeting my date." She hadn't exactly lied... she just hadn't corrected them. "If I have a date, maybe they'll believe I have a real life up here."

"You do have a life up here! You said you like your job, and you've got family here." She flashed a bright smile. "And a friend."

That did sound like a real life. "Thanks."

"They just want you closer to home?" Brittany asked.

"Sort of. They do, but it's more than that. I need some time to decide what I want to do." Eleanor smiled tightly. "What I want to do when I grow up. I just always assumed I would do the same things they do. I was born to be a teacher. But now, I'm not sure. Or rather, I'm pretty sure I'm not a teacher. I quit my job and came up here to find myself."

"Okay, but it's not like you backpacked to Tibet. You're only an hour away, in your mom's home town, and you got a job with your uncle. You're surrounded by family."

She didn't get it. Eleanor tried to find words that wouldn't make her parents sound like conceited snobs. "Mom and Dad believe in what they do. They think it's so important that nothing else really matters. Their friends are all like them or are in a position to help them—usually in politics. It's not that they look down on people like Uncle Carl and Gary. They just sort of see them as… outsiders." She shrugged. "They raised my brothers and me to follow in their footsteps. Sports and education. Music lessons, the right social activities. I was a member of the same sorority my mom was, even if I did go to an out-of-state school."

Brittany looked fascinated. "I had no idea. I assumed you were like everyone else here. I mean, like Penny and her siblings."

"I am! I'm making them sound bad, but my parents are great people. They're involved in every kind of charity, especially for education. My brothers, too. They're all teachers or started as teachers. Really good people." Eleanor's cheeks burned with embarrassment. "I'm the one who didn't fit in."

"And if you go back without a date, you'll be answering questions and they'll feel sorry for you. And probably pressuring you to move back there, I suppose." She sipped her coffee. "There must be someone in the area who'd go with you. Didn't you have a boyfriend there? You said you lived there for three years after college."

"I did, twice, but nothing ever came of it. They were both nice guys. Mom and Dad approved of both of them, and it was convenient to have a date for things," Eleanor said. "In the end, both times, I got dumped. I wasn't ready to get serious, and they started wanting more than I was willing to give. I can't think of anyone down there who'd be willing to take me to the party, when it would be a one-time thing. I'm coming back here the next day."

"And you haven't met anyone here?" Brittany asked. "I don't suppose any of the guys who work for your uncle would do?"

Eleanor covered her face with her hands. "That sounds so bad. I'm not a snob, really! Most of the guys who work for him are married or older. I haven't met any young, single guys there, and even if there was one, it would be awkward."

"What about church? You go to Riverdale with your aunt and uncle, don't you?"

"Well, I will when I have time. So far, I've been busy or just want to relax and sleep in after working all week. I plan to get there soon, though."

"I don't know if there are a lot of single guys there, though," Brittany said. "You could try a church in St. Cloud."

That made Eleanor laugh. "Go to church in St. Cloud in hopes of meeting a man? I'm not that desperate."

Brittany settled herself more comfortably on the stool, considering the question. "You could go out to a nightclub. That's what single people do, right?"

"Not me," Eleanor said. "Do you?"

"No, but I have a fiancé."

"Can I borrow him for Valentine's Day?" Her question was only half in jest.

"No!" Brittany slapped at Eleanor's hand. "You can not. Oh! What about a dating website?" Brittany picked up her phone and tapped on the screen. "There are Christian ones. You might find someone there."

"He doesn't have to be a Christian," Eleanor said, "as long as he's not something weird."

"I just meant that it might be safer. Guys who sign up there will be expecting a girl with some moral standards. They're not just looking for a hook-up."

"Oh, right. Still... I don't think that sounds very safe, and if my parents found out, they'd kill me." Eleanor stood up. "I'd better get back to work. Thanks for listening to me whine, and thanks for the coffee break. It was good to get out of the office and have a little female companionship for a change."

Five

David looked over the top of his laptop screen and contemplated his feet, propped on the coffee table. His mom's handknit socks never quite matched each other, but they were warm. Would his wife knit socks? She might, or maybe she would be more interested in fishing or hiking. Or playing the violin or driving a race car. Or flirting with other men and shopping for things he couldn't afford. You couldn't order up a wife like a sandwich on a menu.

His gaze returned to the computer. He'd read every page of the website at least twice. It looked decent, and there was a free trial. It wasn't specifically Christian, though—just founded on "Christian principles." Still, the goal was traditional marriage, and he was pretty traditional. He clicked on the privacy tab and scanned the fine print again. They promised to destroy his information if he requested it.

What if it was a train wreck? What if it was a success? What if people found out about it, either way? Would it damage his chances of entering the ministry if a church knew he'd found his wife online? David closed the computer and shifted it from his lap to the couch next to him.

"O, Lord. I'm not hearing Your voice here. I don't want to do anything outside of Your will." David fell silent and waited. Nothing. Was he overthinking it? There was no commitment—no harm in just filling out the application and seeing what they said.

He set the computer on the coffee table and opened it. The website opened with a tap of the mouse. Betwixt Two Hearts. Silly name, but it was better than Virtual Dreams Digital Dating. He'd backed out of that one right away and been afraid to google for more options. Betwixt Two Hearts would have to do.

David scooted forward and hunched over the computer. He flexed his fingers and began to fill in blanks.

The coffee house had been transformed overnight, from Christmas to Valentine's Day, nearly six weeks ahead of time. David carried his coffee to a small table in the corner and checked his email for the third time since entering the building. Nothing from the matchmaking agency, of course. He'd only filled out the form last night. It would probably take a while, even if there were any girls in the area. He winced. What if there were a lot of college students on their list?

"Hey there. What's that look for?" Larry pulled out the chair and sat.

"Just borrowing trouble from tomorrow. I filled out a profile on that website you showed me, and now I'm getting cold feet."

"That's great—that you filled it out, I mean. I hope it works out. You never know about those places."

"Now you're skeptical? You were all for it two days ago." Indignant, David dropped his phone on the table. "It just occurred to me that the only available women in this area might be college kids."

"Oh, yeah, that could be," Larry said. "I hope your new social life doesn't interfere with our lunches."

"Work and school are starting to interfere with our lunches," David admitted. "I only have half an hour today. We had our monthly meeting this morning, and it ran late. I don't know how we can spend two hours discussing stuff and not have anything significant to say or change."

"Those things are just to keep in touch. Employee bonding or something like that. There's my number." Larry shoved his chair backward, jostling the table behind him.

The blonde girl seated there grabbed her computer before it could slide off the table, but the mouse escaped, hitting the floor and tumbling under Larry's feet. He stepped on it and staggered like a slap stick comedian, clutching at their own table. David prudently lifted the coffee cups.

"Oh, man, I'm sorry." The big man picked up the remains of the mouse. "I think it's dead."

She regarded the bits and pieces. "Yes, it looks dead."

"Let me pay for it." Larry put the mouse on the table and pulled out his wallet. "I don't have any cash." He turned to David. "Do you have any cash?"

David shook his head. "Sorry, I don't." He looked around. "No cash machine in here, but you could probably go buy something and get cash back."

"No," said the girl. "Don't bother. I can afford a new mouse."

"No, I broke it; I'll pay for it." Larry stomped off, calling over his shoulder. "Hang on. Don't leave."

The girl stared after him, clearly exasperated, before standing to put the tables and chairs back in order. David jumped up to help. "Sorry about that."

"I don't know why they put these tables so close together."

"They can squeeze more people in this way," David said. He sought words to fill the awkward wait. "Sorry about your mouse."

"Not your fault. I think I'm the only person who still uses one. I just can't seem to get the knack of using the pad."

Her eyes were denim blue. Not sky blue, or like sapphires or forget-me-nots, but like denim. Like his favorite jeans or the jacket his dad wore on his motorcycle. David had never seen eyes quite that color.

The eyes disappeared as she dropped her gaze to the table, and he realized he'd been staring, not listening to her words.

"Um, I use one, too. I'm an engineer, and the mouse works better for drafting."

She nodded, not meeting his eyes. She probably thought he was a creep. David dropped into his chair. No wonder he had to use an online dating service. No social skills at all.

"Here you go." Larry reappeared and dropped money on the girl's table.

"I am really sorry."

"It didn't cost that much." She picked up one of the bills and handed the rest back to him. "Please. Thank you for covering it."

Larry wavered briefly before putting the bill in his pocket. "Sorry." Reseated, with his back to the girl, he grimaced at David, obviously aware of the girl's proximity and finding it difficult to resume normal conversation. "So, how'd your prayers come out? Any better than last time?"

"No, not really. I had some questions, and I haven't got a response yet." Behind his friend, he saw the blond girl lift her head from the computer screen, blue eyes wide and surprised.

Before he could think of a way to rephrase his answer, Larry went on.

"Why is it taking so long?" He forked a bite of salad into his mouth and continued talking around it. "Oh, right. You said he was getting married. Maybe he's been busy with his new bride."

The absurdity of the conversation and the girl's fascinated expression—she wasn't even pretending not to listen—suddenly struck David as hilarious. He burst into laughter, immediately regretful when she snatched up her computer and stalked away. She left the broken mouse on the table.

"What?" Larry raised his brows.

It wasn't worth explaining. "It's harder than you'd think to write out prayers."

"I didn't think there was a right or wrong way to pray."

"There's not, really," David said, "but Professor Neresen says we should understand all the elements if we're going to be able to help other people learn to pray."

"That's what I mean. You're saying there's a certain way they have to learn."

David rubbed his chin. "But what would you say if someone asked you how to pray?"

"I'd tell them you just talk to God like you would a person."

"That's right, but there's more to it, too. Adoration, confession, thanksgiving, supplication... those are just words we made up to remind us, but he says we shouldn't ignore them, because Scripture says to do them.

Praise God, confess your sins, give thanks, pray for the needs of others as well as our own. You don't do all of those things every time you pray, but you do need to be doing them. It sounds easy, but this is a really intense class."

Larry didn't look convinced. "If you say so. Hey, you're late. Sorry about the interruption." He cut his eyes to the side and gave a small backward jerk of his head.

"She's gone. She heard you say that God was busy with His new wife and took off." David chuckled.

It was the free trial that sucked her in. The respectable dating sites—if there was such a thing—were expensive. The cheaper ones—and especially the free ones—gave her the willies. According to one website, nearly 30% of single Americans were using online dating apps. That same website informed her that over half of their members lied on their profiles. Caveat emptor. Buyer beware.

Eleanor drummed her fingers on the keyboard as she read the Betwixt Two Hearts website: Christian principles, traditional marriage, not required to have a certain faith, treat others with respect, terminate account at any time. Perfect. She didn't want to get married, but otherwise it looked good. She clicked back to the registration page, grinning as she typed in her name with a flourish. Whatever would her mother say?

Ten minutes later, she leaned back in the leather recliner and considered the computer screen. She'd done the easy part; now she had to come up with creative answers, to attract the kind of man she needed. The matching was done by computer, unless you asked for a personal matchmaker. A computer would be better. She could game the system, work the algorithms...

She couldn't do it. Eleanor picked up her phone and tapped a text to Brittany.

> **ELEANOR:** WANT TO MEET FOR COFFEE TOMORROW? LUNCH?
> DINNER AFTER WORK?

The reply was immediate.

BRITTANY: SURE. LUNCH WHERE WE HAD COFFEE? NOON?

That was easy. Explanations would have taken forever by text. Eleanor made a smiley emoticon and typed.

ELEANOR: THANKS! SEE YOU THEN.

"Teachers are used to eating fast. And working while we eat." Eleanor pushed her plate aside and opened her laptop. "I tried to do it at home, and it was... I just need some ideas."

"Ideas?" Brittany peeled back the top of her cup and stirred her coffee with the little plastic stick. "Isn't it just a matter of answering the questions?"

"Yes, but they aren't true/false or multiple choice. I have to come up with answers that get me matched up with the right kind of guy."

"I hadn't thought of that," Brittany said. "It's not like you're going down a list and picking the guy you like best. You have to fit their criteria, too."

"Right. A computer will match me up with a man like myself—similar interests, for example—so I need to list the right kind of interests."

"Huh." Brittany stood up and dragged her chair around so she could see the computer screen. "Nice profile pic. You look professional, which seems appropriate, because this looks a lot like a job application. You said you're a teacher?"

"Yes, I think that'll work better than 'take-off technician.'" Eleanor chuckled. "I'm not sure I'm even qualified to be called that, but I am qualified to teach. More than qualified. And Evergreen Services sounds like it might be some kind of educational service provider, right?" She clicked and scrolled. "Some of these questions are so open-ended! What is the most important thing you are looking for in another person? What do you notice first when meeting someone? I don't know!"

"Like you said, it's not true/false. Just put something generic in there. Kindness, a sense of humor, and honesty are important."

"Oh, and reliability. I like that in a person." Eleanor entered the response. "So, for the first thing I notice?"

"Eyes, smile, laugh."

"Okay, and then this one." Eleanor pointed at the screen. "What are you looking for in a relationship? So far, I have 'an honest, sensible man with a stable job, between the ages of 27 and 39.' Can you think of anything else I should add?"

She looked up hopefully and found the other girl staring at her.

"Eleanor, you sound like you're ordering something from a menu. A medium-well burger with ketchup and pickle on a whole wheat bun with a side of fries."

Eleanor frowned. "Don't you think it's best to be straightforward when you want something specific?"

"Maybe, but not for this. You're looking for a relationship, not a hamburger."

"I'm looking for a date," Eleanor corrected. "I tried to think of someone in the Cities or here. The only people I know are my cousins, and I can't ask them to take me." She kicked the table leg. "Laurie keeps texting and calling me and sending me links. This thing sounds more like a wedding than an anniversary party. It's bigger every time I talk to her, and she wants to tell me every single detail. And the way she talks... it's almost like she knows I don't have a date and is trying to make me admit it."

"Would that be so bad?" Brittany asked.

"Yes. And this part—what do you think? I said I prefer a Protestant Christian. My parents don't have a problem with other religions, but it would be easier if he's Lutheran or Methodist or something."

"How about you? Do you have a preference?"

Eleanor shrugged. "Well, if I was really looking for a husband, he'd have to be a Christian, of course, as long as he was in a normal denomination. I was here yesterday, and there were these really strange guys at the next table. They said God was married. I moved away so I wouldn't get hit by lightning."

"Seriously? God got married?" Brittany asked. "Wow."

"They sounded serious. But then one of them laughed, so I didn't know if they were just playing a joke on me or what."

Brittany leaned forward. "Are you a Christian?"

"Yes, of course. I was practically raised in the church. I was baptized and did confirmation and the whole thing. I haven't been in a while, but you don't have to go to church to have a relationship with God." She hoped she didn't sound as defensive as she felt. Religion was on the list of things her mother said shouldn't be discussed in polite conversation, along with politics and something else. Probably money.

"Well, no, but..." Brittany looked troubled. "It's easier if you do, and you might meet some nice people there."

"You said there weren't any. I'm going to give this a shot. What do you think about divorced men?"

"I don't know. I'd have to know more about him. But if you're just looking for a date, it probably doesn't matter."

Was that sarcasm in her friend's voice? She didn't want to offend Brittany. She was the only person she'd met here, outside of her family, and they were all busy with their own lives.

"I'm not opposed to pursuing a relationship if we like each other. I guess I've been so focused on this stupid party that I can't think that far ahead. I've got to get through this." Eleanor rubbed her temple. "Anyhow, I said I'd prefer no kids."

"Don't you like kids?"

"Yeah, but they'd probably get sick on Valentine's Day, just when I need him."

At the other girl's expression, she said, "I know... I know. I need to get this out of the way first. You should have been there, at Christmastime. Laurie was working on seating charts. She seems to think I'd feel left out if she didn't share all the planning with me."

"Because you're the daughter and she's just the daughter-in-law?" Brittany suggested.

"Maybe. I hadn't thought of that. I'm perfectly happy to have her do it. It wouldn't even have occurred to me to have a party. I'm a failure as a Nielson daughter, so I'm glad she's there. She can keep my mother distracted with parties and grandchildren."

"I'm sure you're not a failure. You're just different, and it may take them a while to realize that."

Eleanor shook her head and pointed at the screen. "This is what I wrote for my interests: Reading, music, theater, art museums, classical music concerts, and travel."

"Seriously?" Brittany whooped with laughter. "How's that working out for you here? The high school has a band and drama club, but otherwise we're a little lacking in those things."

"Well, I'm not limiting them to this area. I said to search within a 50-mile radius. That will include the cities, too. Here." She turned the computer toward her friend. "Can you just proofread it for me, please? I really don't want to turn it in with typos!"

If it was all computer-generated, it shouldn't be taking so long. Eleanor refreshed her email page twice before closing the laptop. She wiggled her feet into her slippers and stood up, stretching, stiff after a day spent nestled in the overstuffed leather sofa. It had been a beautiful day, spent reading and watching the snow fall in big globby puffs. If all her winter days at the cabin were just like this one, she'd stay forever. She hadn't felt so peaceful in... ever.

The familiar scraping of a snowplow broke the quiet of the midafternoon dusk. Even better. Eleanor didn't really want to be snowed in. She opened the door, and a knee-high drift of snow fell on her feet. How had so much snow accumulated so quickly and quietly? Gary waved as he pushed a swath across the front—the back—of the house. Eleanor waved back, smiling. He was a good guy. She grabbed the stiff broom and swept the steps and walkway. The snow was heavier than she had expected, though, and fuzzy slippers were not an adequate substitute for boots. Her teeth were chattering by the time she finished the short path to the garage. She hurried back inside, stomping snow from her slippers before pulling them off. Maybe Uncle Gary would like some coffee. She looked out the window in time to see his tail lights vanish into the distance. He wasn't even coming inside?

The happy feelings evaporated, leaving her cold, wet, and a little lonely.

And it was dark already, before five o'clock, so she couldn't even see the beautiful snow. What if it started snowing again overnight, and she really was snowed in? Dejected, she dropped onto the couch and covered herself with the fleece throw before pulling the computer onto her lap.

Still no mail. Maybe this whole business was a scam. It could be identity theft; they had a lot of information about her now. She navigated to the website and clicked on her profile. Still pending. She clicked on the About page, hoping for reassurance. Nothing new. She googled Betwixt Two Hearts and found mentions of it on a few blogs, but it was too new to have any reviews. She clicked on her profile again and sat up straight, nearly knocking the computer off her lap. Match found.

"No!" Appalled, Eleanor gazed at the picture of David Reid. The man from the coffee shop. He was presentable, even good-looking, but could she trust him to carry on appropriate conversation? Her mother would drive to Milaca and pack up Eleanor's belongings herself if she thought her daughter was involved with a religious nut.

She continued reading. Mechanical engineer. He'd said he was an engineer. Eleanor wondered if he ever worked with Evergreen Services. She'd have to ask Uncle Gary. David was 30 years old, played the guitar, liked being outdoors and doing photography.

"A seminary student? What kind of seminary does he attend?" She curled her legs underneath her and tugged the throw closer. He'd seemed normal before that conversation she'd overheard. Aside from the religious angle, he might work out. She could hint him away from church talk.

He was exactly what she needed, otherwise. Her parents would probably approve of him. He had a respectable job and was continuing his education. She scrolled, and there it was... he coached basketball and worked with underprivileged kids. Her parents would love him. Laurie would probably plan a wedding, pleased that the matter of the nanny would be resolved.

Six

And there it was. Despite his previous impatience, it suddenly struck David that the matchmaker couldn't have spent much time on it. He circled the email link with the cursor, reluctant to click, as if opening the email would be making a commitment. It was just a suggestion, right? The matchmaker had a girl for him to meet. That was all.

He clicked on the email and again on the link inside. Then he had to sign in. Each little step seemed to be a little closer to commitment. He paused—again—before clicking on the little heart. What about her? Was this woman—his match—expecting him to contact her immediately? Did she think of this as a direct path to marriage? What if she was all wrong? He didn't want to hurt her. What if he liked her and she rejected him?

"Stop it." He'd never thought of himself as insecure before, but this whole business was tying him up in knots. "Everyone's doing it. It's just a suggestion." His words didn't reassure him. Talking to himself was probably a bad sign, too.

He clicked on the heart and saw her picture. His breath caught in his throat. The girl with the denim eyes. The one whose mouse Larry had broken. The one who'd been so shocked at their conversation that she'd run away. David groaned and leaned back against the couch cushions.

Under different circumstances, he'd be thrilled. She was gorgeous, with thick blond hair and blue eyes, a smooth complexion and rose-pink lips.

Rose-pink? David shook his head in disbelief. Where did that come from? But none of that mattered. Last time he'd seen her, she'd been practically running away from him.

Eleanor Nielson, teacher. She looked elegant in her profile picture, but no prettier than she had in denim leggings and a long plaid shirt. Not that he'd noticed her clothing, of course. Not really. Was she a local teacher? She liked classical concerts, art museums, and reading. David frowned. None of those things had been on his list, unless you counted playing the guitar in the worship band at church.

She was a Christian. Maybe that's why they'd been matched. Or maybe there was no one else in the neighborhood. Why would a woman like her need to use a matchmaking service? And what was he supposed to do now? She must have received his profile, too, and recognized him. What was she thinking? Would she give him a chance, or would she email the company and tell them to try again? It would be rude to ignore her, though. He could email the company first, to see if they'd heard from her, or wait a day or so to see if they emailed him.

David stood up and stretched. He had to pull himself together. He wasn't a nervous adolescent anymore. He could handle a date with a woman. Or rejection. Whichever came first.

Almost there. David lengthened his stride to avoid the appearance of running, but Angela had no such scruples. The girl was fast, and she knew he wasn't really deaf.

"David!"

He stopped, hand on his car door, beaten but not defeated. "Hi, Angela. You just caught me. I'm on my way to the Y for basketball."

"You forgot this." She extended his phone.

"Oh, Thanks."

"You have a UMD bumper sticker. Is that where you went to college?"

"Yeah. School of Engineering."

"I went to Van Bramer."

Years of his mother's training prevented him from escaping into his car. "Um... is that around here?"

"No, in Connecticut."

Something was off. David shifted his weight from one foot to another, relieved when she broke the brief silence. "You've probably never heard of it."

"No, I haven't." If he'd ever thought about it—which he hadn't—he would have guessed community college, for a degree in cosmetology. She always looked nice. "What was your major?" It would be beyond rude to ask if she graduated.

"Most people go there to get their MRS. My degree was in applied data management."

Computers. Huh. "Well, I'd better get going. Thanks for the phone." He raised it in farewell.

She turned and walked away before he finished. Had he offended her? He hadn't meant to do that... he just wanted to get away. He was inside the car, starting the engine, before he realized the difference in their conversation. He'd never heard her talk about herself before. He knew practically nothing about her, except that she was Cal's sister and always hanging around the office.

He might not be a psychologist, like Larry, but even he knew she probably craved male attention because she was insecure. Their father died when she was a baby, and Cal wasn't exactly a nurturing big brother. David sighed. He should invite her to church. But Eleanor...

"I'm glad you came. You're really moving since you lost so much weight. There usually aren't so many guys here, and I was running late. I stopped by the office after church, and Angela caught me. I mean, I forgot my phone inside and she ran it out to me."

"I've only lost twenty pounds so far," Larry said. "How's Angela doing?"

"Fine. Have you ever heard of a Van Bramer College, in Connecticut?"

"I don't think so. Why?"

"Angela said she went there. She got a degree in applied data management. I assume it's a bachelor's degree, but she said they have an MRS program. Do you have any idea what that is?"

Larry gazed at him, head tipped to one side, until David had to break the silence.

"What?"

His friend reached around him and used a gloved finger to write "Mrs." on the back window of David's car. "Those credentials are usually listed before a woman's name instead of at the end of it."

David blinked. "Oh. Well, then. Angela didn't get that degree. She studied computers."

"You need to get out more," Larry said. "You engineers have a very limited knowledge of the world outside your workshop."

That stung. He was going to be a pastor. He needed to be in the world.

Larry continued. "Our receptionist has a degree in applied data management. She's a bit overqualified, but she's waiting for the administrative assistant to retire, so she can move into that position. A secretary. With another five or six years of experience, she'll be looking for a job as an administrative professional. Then she'll be running the place, but the world will still think of her as a secretary or bookkeeper."

"I wonder why Angela can't find a job, then. It seems like everyone's hiring right now."

Larry frowned. "She has a job. She works for Cal."

"Doing what? We have a woman who manages all that stuff."

"I dunno, but apparently she's pretty important. Meg says Angela's the real genius behind Ridgewell Mechanical Engineering."

David reluctantly quelled the smart-alecky comments that occurred to him. Too bad... there were some real zingers. Self-control, subdue the tongue. It wasn't the first time he'd jumped to conclusions based on incomplete evidence, in science and in human interactions. He changed the subject.

"Hey, I got a response from the Betwixt Two Hearts agency, and you won't believe who it is."

"Angela?"

"No! It's that girl from the coffee shop. The one whose mouse you broke."

Larry laughed. "Really? That's a coincidence. Have you talked to her yet?"

"Not yet," David said, "but she's seen my picture, and I'm sure she remembers us. Her name's Eleanor Nielson, and she's a teacher. She's from Milaca."

"That sounds promising. So now what? Do you exchange emails, or meet up, or what?"

"The website has a kind of messaging system. I'm hoping she'll initiate that, but I don't know. She got up and left, remember? You were talking about my professor being married, it sounded like you were talking about God. I think you scared her off."

"Sure, blame me. Let me know how it works out. Maybe I'll try it myself." Larry looked up at the heavy sky. "I think we're going to get more snow tonight."

"All day tomorrow, from the sounds of it. I went out skiing on Platke Lake yesterday, but it was a pretty wet snow. A few more inches and some colder weather will help."

"I hope to get back to skiing," Larry said as he tossed his duffel bag into his car, "but it won't be cross-country. That's more work than fun. Does your Eleanor ski?"

"I don't know. I hope so." But her profile hadn't listed outdoor activities. David hoped that was an oversight. He didn't have anything against classical music and art museums, but that kind of thing wasn't his first choice for how to spend his limited free time. "She likes music."

"Music is good. Does she know you play guitar?"

"I put it on my profile. I wrote that I play on the worship team at church."

"Speaking of worship," Larry said, "you've got the over-sixty crowd singing louder than I've ever heard before, with those old songs of yours. Where do you get that stuff?"

"The sixties, man." David pointed upward. "The great revival of the seventies. The Jesus People. That's where contemporary Christian music began."

"I hadn't realized it was that long ago."

"My grandparents were in it. Jesus People, Jesus Freaks... My mom says Grandma was a Keith Green groupie."

"I've heard of him," Larry said. "We spent a lot of time studying that whole time period in my last year of school. It wasn't just the Jesus People... there was the Back to the Land movement, the hippies with free love and communes, new secular music, drugs, student protests, Vietnam and all sorts of rebellion, set against the backdrop of space exploration, the invention of the computer, the assassinations of President Kennedy and Martin Luther King, civil rights, Watergate, Cuba, the Cold War." He shook his head. "That's what will keep me in business for a few more generations."

He'd never seen Larry so animated. "I hadn't really thought about it in that bigger context," David admitted. "Just the revivals and the Jesus music. I'm glad my grandparents went that direction instead of into LSD and free love, but I have a feeling my grandpa would have been one of the men in horn-rimmed glasses, building giant computers in bunkers rather than wearing bell bottoms and beads at Woodstock." The image made him chuckle and then laugh out loud. "I can't imagine that at all. Grandma, maybe, but not Grandpa."

"Paradox," Larry said with relish. "It was an age of exploding ideas and change. Psychologists were the new super scientists, experimenting on prisoners and college students with exotic drugs and weird tests. MK-Ultra."

"Yeah, those were the days," David said. "Now, you just listen to girls complain about their wedding planning."

Eleanor pulled the phone away from her ear and stared at the screen in disbelief. Seriously? She tapped the speaker button and tossed the phone on the passenger seat.

Her sister-in-law continued, as placid as ever. "I wanted a cruise to Alaska, but Zack insists they'd rather go to St. John. It'll have to be in the summer, though, and who wants to go to the Caribbean in the summer?

That's definitely a winter vacation."

"A cruise? For a thirty-fifth wedding anniversary?"

"No, that's what I'm saying." Was there the faintest hint of impatience in Laurie's voice? "Zack didn't want the cruise. We found a good deal at an all-inclusive place in St. John. And now Soren's mad because he was just getting them a weekend in Chicago, to see Wicked and that Japanese exhibit at the Art Institute."

"What's Robert getting them—a new car?" She regretted the sarcasm even as the words escaped. "I can't afford an expensive gift, Laurie."

"The biggest gift you could give your parents would be to come back -"

"Stop!" Eleanor shouted at the phone. "No, I'm not doing that. Not now, anyhow. I didn't know we were going to be giving them gifts at all."

"It would be strange to have a party in their honor and not give them gifts. We wrote 'no gifts' on the invitations, of course, but that doesn't apply to us. But if you don't have a gift for them, they're not going to be upset. They'll just be glad to have you at the party."

Eleanor wished she could afford a new phone. She'd throw this one out the window, just for the satisfaction of watching it smash into a thousand pieces. She'd been home three times since leaving three months ago, including extended visits at Thanksgiving and Christmas.

"Okay, Laurie. I'll come up with something. I'm driving now. Talk to you later. Love you. Bye." She jabbed at the disconnect button on the last word. Would the party issue be better or worse if she lived there? Just different, she decided. Her parents would be happy, but she'd be coming home with headaches after school every day, wishing she'd chosen a different career. Anything. She'd make a good mechanical contractor, like Uncle Gary, if she didn't have to work in the field. She could have been an engineer, like David. No, she liked what she saw of Gary's job. He didn't just design things; he built them. He made them happen. Her mother would have a meltdown if she knew Eleanor liked the idea of going into construction.

Her amusement faded at the sight of her uncle. Gary sat with his back against the picnic table, his head down, leg extended, arms were wrapped around his midsection.

He looked up as she slammed the car door and ran toward him. "What are you doing here?"

"I work here." The idiotic response slipped out.

"It's going to snow again. You should have stayed home." He started to shake his head and groaned. "I fell, getting out of the truck. Slipped on the ice. I think I broke my ankle." He gave an unexpected snort. "Just like Aunt Violet. She'll love that."

"Did you call for help?"

"Phone's in the truck. I just needed to sit down for a minute."

"Wait here." She winced, glad she couldn't see his reaction to that as she hurried to her car. She tapped in 911 on her way back to him.

"Give me that." Gary reached for the phone, and his left arm fell to his lap. Moaning, he curled forward, cradling it against his body.

Eleanor conveyed all the information to the operator, ignoring her uncle's interruptions.

"The ambulance will be there in 15 minutes, ma'am. Can you stay on the phone?"

"No, I can not. I need to get my uncle some blankets and something hot to drink." She was freezing, and Uncle Gary had been out longer than her, injured.

He looked terrible, all pink and white, shuddering with every breath, and he hadn't spoken in several minutes. Eleanor tried not to jar him as she tucked her emergency blanket around him. "I know it's not very warm, since it's been in the back of the car all winter, but it's all I have. I'll be right back. I'm going to get you some coffee. Is the office locked?"

He grunted. "Keys. Under truck."

Eleanor squatted, glad the truck's big tires lifted it higher than her SUV. She couldn't see the keys in the shadows; they must have skidded across the ice when Gary fell.

"Couldn't reach the phone. Couldn't reach the keys. I'm just going to rest my eyes until the ambulance gets here."

"No!" Eleanor grabbed the door handle as she rose, sliding on the ice. They'd be in trouble if both of them got hurt. "Don't go to sleep." What if he had a concussion? He could have internal injuries, too, and he was on his way to hypothermia.

She turned back to the truck and took a deep breath of icy air. "Okay, I can do this." She got down on her hands and knees and then scooted forward on her stomach, groping blindly for the keyring. It was here somewhere.

She jerked upward at the sound of a car engine, banging her head on the undercarriage. Her shriek was lost under the call of the new arrival.

"Hey! Are you okay?"

Too soon for the ambulance. Eleanor caught sight of the keyring and stretched. Her bare fingers, wet and cold, pushed the keys further away. She growled.

"She's under the truck. Ambulance coming."

Suddenly Uncle Gary could talk? A bubble of hysterical laughter rose in her. The man would think Gary had run her over. Eleanor wiggled sideways and hooked the edge of the ring.

"Can you hear me?"

The voice was uncomfortably close to her legs. So embarrassing. "I'm fine." Eleanor tried to scoot backward, but the man grasped her boot.

"Don't move. The ambulance is on the way."

"I'm fine! I'm freezing!"

"The ambulance will be here in just a few minutes. You shouldn't be moved until they get here, in case you have back or neck injuries."

"I don't!" Eleanor kicked free of his restraint. "I'm not hurt." She gasped as a drop of blood fell on the ice in front of her. She must have cut her head. A shudder of revulsion went through her at the flow of warmth on her forehead. She was bleeding, and she was freezing. "Pull me out!"

"But..."

"Now! Pull me out!"

The stranger complied. He squatted in front of her, a silhouette against the white sky, as she rolled to a sitting position. She pushed her hair off her face and jumped up, horrified at the blood.

"Sit down! I thought you said you weren't injured!"

"I'm not. I was just getting the keys." Still clutching the ring, she wiped her hands on her wet jeans and turned toward the office. Out of the corner of her eye, she saw blood in her hair. Her head hurt. Her legs trembled.

"Wait." The man reached for her and she stepped away from him.

"I can't wait. I need to go inside and make some coffee." Her voice rose on the last three words. She really was hysterical now.

"You're bleeding." The man grasped her arm. "And... you're Eleanor Nielson."

"Uncle Gary needs something hot to drink!"

Even as she yelled at him—actually yelled—she was conscious of a new horror. She drew herself up as tall as possible, composed, in control. Calm. Authoritative. "No, I'm not."

His mouth curved in a smile. "Yes, you are. I have coffee in my car—a latte, with milk and sugar. Come on." He took her elbow and led her to the table. "I'll get the coffee."

Seven

"See, now, you'll be much more comfortable here." Violet's voice was smug.

She'd have no privacy, and she'd be spending all of her time with her elderly aunt, who seemed to have plenty of jobs lined up for the two of them to do together. Eleanor missed the cabin already.

She dropped onto the bed and smiled at Violet. "It's good of you to have me. I hope I can be helpful." White lies and good manners. "I know you've been looking forward to living alone, so I'll stay out of your way as much as possible. Let me know what I can do to help out with cooking and cleaning—or whatever you need. I'm sure I'll have enough money saved by spring to get into a place of my own."

"There's no hurry. Like I told you last time, I have some projects I need help with. You'll be doing me a favor."

"Great." Eleanor looked around the bedroom. "I'll just get my clothes unpacked, and we can make some plans."

Aunt Violet sat down in the rocking chair. "I can talk while you work. I can even talk while I work, if you need a hand with that."

"No, thanks, I can do it. I don't have much with me." Resigned, she unzipped the smallest suitcase and opened the top dresser drawer. Lilac-printed paper lined the drawer, an unexpected and old-fashioned touch in this modernized house. "That's pretty! And what a nice dresser. Is it a family heirloom?"

Her aunt nodded. "It was mine, but I have a new one I like better. Your mother used this one, I think, right here in this very room. Maria put that paper in it for her, because she loved lilacs."

Eleanor paused. "My mother? This was her room?"

"She shared it with Colleen, but the dresser was hers. Does she still like lilacs?"

"I think so. We have some in the backyard. She used to cut branches and bring them inside."

Violet pointed through the window. "See those over there? She made your uncle Olof plant those. Kristina said apple trees would be more practical, but Kathy wanted lilacs, and she had Olof wrapped around her little finger. He got a dozen suckers from the neighbor and planted them right under Kristina's nose." Violet chuckled. "It was just about the only time anyone ever stood up to Kristina. Anyhow, your mom watered them every day all summer, even if it had rained overnight. Olof fertilized them when he did the garden. Oh, they adored each other."

Eleanor tried to imagine her mother as a little girl, hand-in-hand with a doting uncle. Impossible. Mom seldom talked about her family at all. She walked to the window. "Those are lilacs? They look more like trees."

"They still bloom pretty good in the spring, but they could probably use some pruning." Violet said. "Maybe she'll come out and see them. That would be nice. She'd probably enjoy seeing the annex, too. It was always a nice place, not old like the rest of the farmhouse, but it's even better now that Carl fixed it up for me."

Aunt Violet missed her—a young niece she'd known since infancy. Why hadn't Mom been out to see her? She should have been. Eleanor would invite her—would insist.

"I had the impression she was really little when they moved into town. A preschooler."

"No, she was nine or ten, I think." Violet shook her head. "Colleen was a chatterbox, but Kathy was quiet. She liked reading and being outside by herself or with Olof. The farm was better for her than town. I'm afraid she was teased in school and didn't have a lot of friends."

Interesting. "She said she had a good teacher here, who inspired her to become a teacher herself."

"Oh, yes," Violet said. "Maybel Furster. She was a fine woman."

"She died recently, didn't she?" asked Eleanor. "Mom was upset."

"She did. Cancer. It was sad, but a beautiful Home-going. She'd picked out all her favorite songs. 'Lots of singing,' she said. We nearly took the roof right off the building with In Christ Alone."

Eleanor blinked. A beautiful Home-going? She'd never heard that expression. It must mean going to heaven. Going home?

"She never had a husband or children, you know," Violet continued. "She just poured herself into her students at school and the Sunday school students at church. She had hundreds of people at her funeral, and only good words spoken or thought of her."

"That's lovely." A lump blocked Eleanor's throat. Was that why her mother felt so strongly about teaching, with a role model like that? How wonderful it would be, to have such an impact and reputation. "Did my mother have her as a Sunday school teacher, too?"

"Most likely. We all went to that church until they moved to town. My grandfather helped build it. That's what they did back then. They moved to America, built Lutheran churches and farmed. That church burned down about thirty years ago, and there weren't enough young people to rebuild it, so the rest of us either moved to the Methodist church or the new Riverdale one."

"Your grandfather! That would be my..." Eleanor ticked off the generations on her fingers. "Great, great, great grandfather?"

"Your second great-grandfather. I can show you on the family tree."

"I'd like that." At least, she might. Something about the gleam in Aunt Violet's eyes made her wary. "That's sad about the church, to split up after all those years together."

"There weren't many of us left. We still see each other."

Eleanor returned to her unpacking, eying Violet. The old woman had seen so much of this community, for so many years. More than almost anyone else in the area.

"Is it hard to adjust to all the changes?"

Her aunt shrugged. "Most of the time, change doesn't just happen all at once. It's gradual, and you don't realize it's changing until you look around and realize everything's different. She looked out the window. "Change is normal. It's usually fine, but sometimes it's bad—or just sad."

Eleanor sat on the bed, ignoring the suitcase full of clothing. "What do you mean?"

Violet twisted her fingers together in her lap before looking up at Eleanor. "When Maybel died, that was sad, but it wasn't bad. And it wasn't even a change. She was 95 years old and ready to move on. It's not bad at all, and just sad for us. She's doing fine."

"But some things are bad and sad, like when your church burned down. And wars."

"True enough." Violet rocked forward and pushed against the arms of the chair to stand up. "Change just happens, Nellie. Life moves on, never stopping, and we change with it. In the end, we go Home to the only eternal and unchanging God. That's really all that matters, in the end."

Eleanor watched her leave, wondering if she'd said something wrong. Their casual conversation had taken an odd turn. She pulled the plastic bag off the pile of clothes on hangers and started filling the closet. She'd not had opportunity to wear any of her good work clothes. Maybe she should just pack them away with everything else she had in storage. More things in storage, waiting for Eleanor to make up her mind. Would she discard them, use them, or leave them in storage—in limbo?

She walked to the window and tried again to picture her mother as a little girl, determined to have lilacs of her own. Stubborn and determined. Yes, that fit. And it fit her, too. If she wasn't stubborn and determined, she wouldn't be here now.

What was she going to do? Uncle Gary needed her, as many hours as she could work while he was in the rehab center, but when summer came, they'd be pressing her to come back for the start of the new school year. They truly believed that would be the best thing for her. They thought it would make her happy, because it made them happy.

But she wasn't like them. She didn't share their interests – their priorities. Teaching was a noble calling. Shaping young minds, inspiring them to learn and grow, being someone like Maybel Furston. Why didn't it make her feel fulfilled?

No, she thought. It wasn't even a matter of fulfillment. She just didn't like doing it. And that made her feel terrible. What kind of monster didn't like helping children?

Her parents would be horrified and convinced she needed a counselor. Or an exorcist.

Still tall and erect, even in his wheelchair, Uncle Olof reached out to take her hand. "Hello." He had a full head of thick white hair, and unruly eyebrows over blue-gray eyes that matched his chambray shirt. They were like hers, Eleanor realized. A little lighter, maybe, but similar.

"This is Nellie, Olof. You've never met before, but she is Kathy's daughter. One of Soren's granddaughters."

His tentative, pleasant expression grew into a broad smile. "Nice to meet you, Nellie."

"It's nice to meet you. I'm sorry we interrupted the football game."

"Vikings were losing. No point in watching that happen again." He turned to Violet. "That nurse, the one with long hair, she says Gary's coming here. He's too young."

"Oh, it's just for a few weeks, for rehab." Violet said. "He slipped on the ice getting out of his truck. Somehow, he managed to dislocate his shoulder and also break the shoulder bone. His ankle's pretty bad, all broken up inside. They did one surgery already, and he'll need at least one more." She sat down on one of the wing chairs. "He has to come here because of his hip. He fell on it pretty hard and did something to the joint. It's not broken, but he can't walk on it yet. It might need surgery too. Oh, and he has a concussion and was in the early stages of hypothermia when the ambulance got there."

"He fell on the ice and did all that? He must have looked like Dick Van Dyke, with all those falls he used to do, on TV."

Eleanor grinned. It probably had looked a bit like that. The aftermath hadn't been so comical. "We're going over there to see him in a little bit. I work for him, you know, and he's making a list of everything I need to do while he's gone."

"Make him give you a raise," Olof said.

"Good idea." Eleanor sank onto the chair in front of him. "Aunt Violet's been telling me about you. She showed me the lilac bushes you planted with my mother, Kathy. They're so big now, like regular trees."

"Lilacs?" He looked at Violet. "What lilacs?"

"The lilacs you planted with Kathy, Olof. Do you remember those? It was a long time ago."

"Oh, a long time ago." He looked relieved. "I don't remember that."

"I'm looking forward to seeing them in bloom." Eleanor broke off when Violet shook her head.

"Lilacs." Olof nodded slowly. "A row of lilacs, right where Kristina wanted apple trees. Do you know..." He bent forward and lowered his voice. "I had to replant those things? She ran the mower over them. Accidentally, she said. Ha. Don't tell Kathy, though."

"Okay." Eleanor looked to Violet for guidance.

"No, of course not." Violet stood, pulling on her gloves. "How was your dinner tonight, Olof? Meatloaf, right? Was it any better than last time? I told them you didn't want the onions in it."

He nodded. "It was better. Thanks for coming by." He looked at Eleanor. "Thanks for coming."

"It was nice to meet you. I'm sure I'll be back."

"Good, good." He wheeled himself to the door, waving as they left.

"I made him confused." Eleanor glanced back to where he was still sitting, watching them through the glass doors He waved. She waved back.

"He gets confused. He had a good spell before that, though. He knew who Gary was, and even Dick Van Dyke." Violet sounded pleased.

"He's still waving." Eleanor waved back. "Is he sad that we're leaving?"

"Maybe. Are you buckled up?"

"Yes." Eleanor gave a final wave and saw him wheel the chair away as Violet turned the car onto the street. "Does he get many visitors?"

"I get here nearly every day, but it's going to be harder now that I'm not in town anymore. Carl and Constance go, and they usually bring little Sarah. She plays checkers with him. Gary's there at least once a week, and your uncle Scott and his wife come when they can. They're up in Bemidji, and she's not in good health." She sighed. "It's hard."

"Well, Uncle Gary will be there every day, now! That will make Uncle Olof happy, won't it?"

"On his good days, yes. They can watch football games. They're all reruns, but Olof doesn't care. A game is a game. Baseball in the summer and football in the winter."

"What about his bad days?" Eleanor asked.

"Well, your uncle Gary will probably stay out of his way on those days, or just pretend to be a stranger."

"Pretend to be a stranger?" Shocked, Eleanor stared at Violet. "You mean, just act like they've never met? Wouldn't it be better to help Olof remember? Give him reference points, like you did today, when you said I was Kathy's daughter and one of Soren's granddaughters."

"He was having a good day today," Violet said, "and I started by telling him you'd never met before, so he wasn't afraid that he should already know you. We used to try to make him remember things. He'd be all worried about getting home, and we'd remind him that he lives here now, or he'd say he had to go help Papa in the barn, and we'd remind him that Papa passed away forty years ago."

She stopped at a traffic light and fell silent. Eleanor waited, hoping she'd continue. What would it be like, to be responsible for Soren or Robert or Zack in that situation?

"We tried. Then one day, a little girl—a CNA who couldn't have been more than five feet tall—came up and tugged on my elbow. I followed her into the hallway and got a lecture on how to treat people with Alzheimer's. She even printed up a list of guidelines for me."

Someone dared to lecture Aunt Violet? Eleanor hid a grin. "What did it say?"

"First of all, you don't insist they're wrong. They're anxious and afraid all the time, and it only distresses them when you confuse them more. If they do get upset, you distract them."

"Like you did when you asked about the meatloaf!" Eleanor said. "It seemed to work."

"If I hadn't distracted him, he would have worked himself up about the lilacs. And the biggest thing is that you don't tell them people are dead," Violet snapped. "How would you feel if you were upset and worried about your father, fully convinced he was looking for you, and someone kept insisting he was dead?"

"Oh. Yeah. But... it seems kind of like lying."

"So, lie," Violet said wearily. "Olof isn't going to get better. He doesn't need to be corrected. He needs to be loved and taken care of. I would have done it at home if I could, but he kept wandering off or doing dangerous things at home. This is a good place, and he's fine."

The argument, too distant for the words to be discernible, was obviously heated. Was that Uncle Gary? Easy-going, kind Uncle Gary? Eleanor cast a glance at Violet. The older woman rolled her eyes.

"Oh, for goodness sake. Men are such babies when they're sick."

But Uncle Gary wasn't sick. Eleanor followed the voices, walking faster than her aunt, and reached the room in time to hear the sweet coaxing voice, full of laughter, say "Oh, yes, you are. Come on, I'll give you another gown to cover your backside. You know how it is when you fall and break your hip. You have to get up and walk again, right away."

"It's not broken." He broke off at the sight of Eleanor. "If I'd known she was here, I'd have gone to a different hospital."

"Oh, Cheryl!" Aunt Violet pushed past Eleanor to embrace the therapist, who hugged her more tightly than seemed advisable with a frail, elderly woman. Violet didn't seem to mind. She drew back and patted the woman's cheek. "It's so good to see you again."

"You always did take her side," Gary muttered.

"Oh, stop." Cheryl held out her hand—to hold, not shake. "You must be Eleanor. I know your mom—knew her when she lived here, anyhow. How is she?"

"She's good." Did everyone here know her mother? This woman must be the same age, but she seemed more youthful, with a mop of blond, corkscrew curls and sparkling blue eyes.

"I'm Cheryl Anderson." She ignored the patient's rude snort. "Not a blood relative, but one in spirit."

"Not in law."

Gary must be in pain. Eleanor moved closer to the bed. "How are you?"

"I was better twenty minutes ago. I've been making a list for you, but she took it away."

"Therapy is on a tight schedule," Cheryl said, "and we've already wasted a lot of time." She held out a hand to Gary. He took it, and she helped him sit up and turn to the side of the bed. He used his free hand to pull the blanket across his lap.

"What about my ankle? I can't walk on that."

"Oh, I have a cart for that. It's just like a scooter. Do you ladies want to come with us?" She beamed at them, and Eleanor got it.

"Are you…"

"Your aunt!" Cheryl said triumphantly.

Gary moaned. "Ex-aunt."

"Oh, Gary." Cheryl sank onto the bed next to him. "I'm teasing you. I have a wheelchair in the hall. We're going down to the therapy room to do some measurements, and then they want to do an MRI on that hip. It'll take about an hour, all together."

"We can wait." Eleanor looked at Violet. "Is that okay?"

"Oh, yes. We can wait."

"I hope you can work a lot of overtime, Ellie." Gary rubbed his hand over his face. "I'm glad you're here. I'm going to need you."

He needed her. The words felt like a gift. An accolade. Eleanor nodded, hoping her face wasn't all scrunched up. "I'll be here."

She followed Violet into the hall, feeling better than she had in years. She wouldn't let him down.

"I can't believe she's here." Violet sounded exceptionally happy, too. "I always liked her. She was good for him. Stupid boy."

"Gary was a stupid boy?"

"They were too young to be married. I'm glad she's back." Violet stopped. "You know, I should visit my friend Josie while I'm here. Can you occupy yourself for an hour?"

"Yes, of course. I can meet you in Gary's room at…" Eleanor consulted her phone. "Ten o'clock."

"All right. I wonder if Josie knows that Cheryl's back."

Eight

Of course, his motives were mixed—no use pretending otherwise. Eleanor Nielson, after her determination to save her uncle, didn't seem like the kind of person to neglect him in the hospital. She might be here. Still, her sudden appearance, framed by the elevator doors and looking much happier than she had last time he'd seen her, rocked him back.

"Hi there!"

She blinked—in confusion?—and then smiled.

David blinked back, stunned. He'd seen her professional headshot, and he'd seen her soaking wet and blood-streaked, and even for those few minutes in the coffee shop, but he'd never seen that smile. He should have worn sunglasses.

"Hello! We meet again—and again, even without the help of that agency. If I didn't get the free trial, I'd ask for a refund."

"A refund?" It took him a minute to understand her statement. "True. It's been more providential than professional. We haven't corresponded through the agency at all."

"Right, and we don't need to do that now, do we?"

"No," he said. He tipped his head toward the elevator. "I was on my way to see Gary. How's he doing?"

"He's a mess, and his therapist is his ex-wife, who seems awfully cheerful to have him at her mercy." She clapped her hand over her mouth, her beautiful denim eyes widening. "Forget I said that. I guess I'm just so relieved to see him... that wasn't very discreet. Anyhow, he's gone for therapy and an MRI and won't be back for an hour."

"That must be an interesting situation. So, are you free until then?" David hoped she'd say yes. It would be so much easier than making a formal date, with time to work himself up into a nervous wreck.

She nodded slowly. "Yes, I am. We could get some coffee in the cafeteria."

"Perfect." Better than perfect. His lingering reservations vanished as they walked together. "I'm glad to see you again, without my good but clumsy friend. That was an awkward way to meet."

"It was," she said, "and the next one wasn't much better, with me a bloody mess, screaming at you. I can't imagine how you recognized me."

"I'd know you anywhere." Woah... way too fast. "I'd seen you at the coffee shop, too, not just the picture from the agency."

"I don't know... I looked pretty scary. The paramedics insisted I come in the ambulance."

He'd stayed until they left. She'd been too stressed to notice. "I'm glad you're okay. No concussion?"

"Just a typical scalp wound." She shivered. "And cold. That was the worst part. I was so cold, and shaking so hard, and all I could think about was how much worse it must be for Uncle Gary. I didn't know how long he'd been out there. He still doesn't remember anything after he fell, like how he made it to the bench."

"Probably just as well. It must have been painful." He watched her as she ordered and paid for her coffee. Why would a girl like this need to use a matchmaking agency?

"Have you ever done this before? Online dating, I mean." She sat, sipping her coffee and wrinkled her nose. "This is awful."

"No, have you?"

"I haven't. A friend talked me into it. I mean, she showed me the website and encouraged me to fill it out, because she knew I... I was having trouble meeting people here. Brittany's the only person I know, outside my family. Even at work, I only ever see Uncle Gary."

David set his cup on the table. "You work for your uncle?"

"Yes. I'll be putting in a lot of overtime while he's in the hospital."

"But you said you were a teacher."

Eleanor wrapped her hands around her coffee cup and looked into the murky brew. Had she lied? Why?

"I am a teacher. I mean, I'm a certified teacher. I'm just taking a break to work for my uncle while I decide what I want to do with the rest of my life. While I find myself."

The air quotes and her droll tone might have been meant to hint him away from the topic, but he had to know more.

"You don't want to teach?"

"I don't know. I don't think so. At least, not right now. How about you? Your profile said you're in seminary. You're an engineer, but you want to be a minister?"

"Yes, eventually. It's an online master's program, with a few retreats and other hands-on activities."

"Is it for a particular denomination? I... uh... heard a bit of your conversation with your friend the other day."

"The part about God being married?" He grinned. "I got the impression we'd shocked you."

"Maybe I needed some context," Eleanor said. "I assume you were just joking."

"Not joking, but we were talking about my professor, not God. I think I said I'd sent some questions and not had an answer, and then Larry said it was taking a long time because the professor had just got married."

"Oh, that makes sense!" She looked relieved. "That will teach me to eavesdrop, right? I was afraid you might be a member of some strange cult."

"Nope, just a good, old-fashioned, Bible-believing, fundamental Christian. Fundamental with a lower-case f, I mean."

"Got it. So, is it a Lutheran or Methodist seminary?"

He shook his head. "Just a Bible school without affiliation with any major denomination. Protestant, of course. More reformed than not, but not Calvinist."

"But not some cult where God is married and too busy to answer prayers." She smiled, more mischievous than dazzling this time.

"No, it's pretty basic. How about you? Your profile said you live in

Milaca. Do you go to church there, or here in St. Cloud?"

"My family goes to Riverdale in Milaca, and I go with them." She took another sip of coffee and set the cup on the table. "I haven't made it to church as often as I should. I've only been here a few months, and I was living out at my uncle's cabin on Tasker Lake until yesterday. I went back to the cities to spend Thanksgiving and Christmas with my parents."

"Minneapolis?" He tried to remember... had the profile covered that, or did it just list the current residence? "I thought you said your family was here."

"I grew up in Minneapolis. My parents and three brothers still live there—and a sister-in-law and a nephew and niece, too, and my dad's parents and siblings." She rolled her eyes. "A crowd. My mom grew up in Milaca, and some of her family is still here. Now that Uncle Gary's in the hospital, I've moved into the annex of the old family farmhouse, with my cousin and great-aunt.

"You didn't like the cabin?"

She picked up a stir stick and whirled it through her nearly-empty cup. "I couldn't live at the cabin without someone to plow, and... well, it was pretty isolated.

"Did it have indoor toilets and running water?"

Eleanor laughed. "It's definitely not a primitive cabin. It's one of those big prow-front places with a massive stone fireplace and enormous logs. It has everything, even internet and cable TV. Jet skis, a nice boat, snowmobiles... he has all the toys."

"It sounds great." He needed an uncle like that. His uncles had the cabins without indoor plumbing. "But you got lonely out there?"

She responded pensively. "It wasn't so much the loneliness as the emptiness. It was so vast, and the whole front of it's glass. I'm sure it's better in the summer, when days are longer. I worked all day, and it was dark by the time I got home, so I didn't get to enjoy the scenery except on the weekends."

"Did you get outside on the weekends?" Tasker Lake had a good reputation for ice fishing, but Eleanor wouldn't want to do that alone.

"No, not much. Saturday was nice, with that pretty snowfall. I just curled up with a good book and watched it snow. Later, I did some shoveling while Uncle Gary came by and plowed. Three days later, here I am, living with my great aunt. It's not in town, though—about ten minutes outside of Milaca." She grimaced. "It's going to be a longer commute to work every day."

That gorgeous day, on the lake, and she stayed inside to look at it through the window? "Do you ski? I went out on Platke Lake Saturday, cross-country."

"Are the lakes frozen enough for that?" She looked alarmed.

"Platke is, and Tasker would be, but not all of them."

"I went cross-country skiing a few times, back home," Eleanor said, "but more downhill. Nothing impressive... just Minnesota mountains." She grinned. "It's not like going to Aspen or Vail. Anyhow, I probably would have moved to town soon, even if he hadn't been hurt. He likes to use the cabin. He and his friends used it for opening weekend—deer season—and I went to visit my parents, but I can't do that every time he wants to use his own cabin. He stayed out there when I was in the cities for Christmas, snowmobiling and maybe ice fishing. He put out his ice fishing house, so I knew he wanted to go fishing. I felt guilty."

"I can see how that might get awkward," David said.

"He kept telling me I didn't have to leave, but... Aunt Violet wanted me to come live with her, and now I have a bedroom in her house, with not much privacy at all, so I kind of miss the cabin."

"Are you there long-term?" Was that a sufficiently-tactful way of asking if she planned to stay around? He wanted someone ready to settle down. "In the area, I mean?"

"I'm... well, I want to stay here. I think I'll like it here, once I get settled in." She met his eyes. "Part of the reason I signed up at Betwixt Two Hearts is that I haven't met anyone but Brittany and my family. I love them, but I need some other friends."

Friends. He appreciated her honesty, but... friends? Maybe she found it awkward to talk about looking for a husband with a stranger. "You like it here?"

"I do. To tell you the truth," she said, "I didn't know if I would, but I wanted to leave the cities and do something different. Not teaching."

"Not teaching? Couldn't you not teach there?"

"No, I couldn't not teach there." She propped her elbows on the table, resting her chin on her clasped hands. "I come from a very academically-inclined family. They all think education is the only worthwhile occupation in the world. When I left my job, my parents—and my brothers—took it personally. They even wanted me to see a counselor. I love my family, but I needed to get out of town if I wanted to not teach."

"They wanted you to see a counselor?" David asked. "Just because you didn't want to be a teacher?"

She hunched her shoulders in a shrug. "They figured I must be depressed or have some other issue. They kept suggesting things like changing schools or grade levels or finding another job within the system."

"But you didn't want to do that?"

"No."

David needed time to think. She certainly didn't sound settled; she sounded like she ran away from home and didn't know what she wanted to do next. He pulled his phone from his pocket and tapped the screen. "Hey, it's after ten. I hope your uncle won't mind if you're late. At least he can't fire you, right?"

Nine

"I heard you had an accident!"

"Hi, Brittany." Eleanor tapped the speaker button. "Not me. It was Uncle Gary. He fell, getting out of his truck."

"I heard you were bleeding and near hypothermia."

"Aunt Violet?" Eleanor asked.

"Nope, my friend Amy is on the EMT squad. I was a little hurt that I had to get the news from someone else."

She did sound hurt. Eleanor lifted a stack of books from her stool and sat. "I'm sorry, Brittany. I would have called if I was hurt, but really, I just sort of scraped my head, and it bled all over the place. Or rather, all over my hair and face, so I looked like the victim in a horror film. But it didn't need stitches or anything. And hypothermia... that one might be true. I was crawling around on the wet ice under Uncle Gary's truck, trying to find the keys to the office."

"Brrr. That must have been awful. How's your uncle?"

"Not bad, all things considered," Eleanor replied. "He's moving to a rehab facility tomorrow. But I do want to tell you what else happened on Monday. You won't believe it."

"Tell me! Or would you rather meet for lunch and tell me there?"

Eleanor picked up the list Uncle Gary had dictated to her. "I've got to stay here to accept some deliveries and answer the phones. Why don't you come here? I can show you what I do!"

"Okay. Did you bring a lunch, or should I stop for something on the way?"

"Aunt Violet packed me a lunch. I have peanut butter sandwiches and apple slices, like a second-grader."

When Brittany's eyes glazed, Eleanor took pity on her and rolled up the blueprints. "I suppose it's not wildly exciting, but I enjoy it."

"You do? You'd rather do this than teaching?"

"Yes. I'm really enjoying it. There's something satisfying about it. Uncle Gary can do anything. He does a lot of energy projects, and plumbing and pipes and metal construction... making things work. Look at this." Eleanor picked up the photo from her uncle's desk. "This is a little pavilion out at Meyer Park. It uses solar and wind power together for lights and to operate this little sculpture thing."

"I've seen that. That's more interesting than plumbing, anyhow."

"This one was designed by David Reid." She waited for the name to register. Apparently, it didn't. "David Reid! My match from the Betwixt Two Hearts agency!"

"Oh! He works with your uncle? Have you met him yet? Again, I mean?"

"I did, right here, on Monday morning, when I was soaking wet and covered with blood!"

Brittany dropped her McDonalds bag on the table. "He was here?"

Eleanor nodded. "He had an appointment with Uncle Gary. He got here before the ambulance did. And he recognized me, even like that!" She lowered her voice. "And when I mentioned that yesterday, he said, 'I would know you anywhere.' I couldn't decide at first, if that was creepy or romantic, but he's a nice guy."

"Wait, wait. What happened yesterday? It's only been about three days since I talked to you last, and you've moved into town, nearly died of hypothermia, met your guy twice, and started running your uncle's company! You move fast!"

"Me?" Eleanor laughed. "I'm not a fast mover, but it has been an eventful week. And don't let Uncle Gary hear you say that about his business. He's all worked up. He gave me a list of things he wants me to bring him at the rehab center. It's going to look like mobile command center."

"That should go over well with the staff. You want some french fries?"

"Thanks. We met again at the hospital yesterday and had coffee. He's a nice guy."

"Okay," said Brittany, "you've said that twice. Are you trying to convince me or yourself?"

"No, really, he is. He seems like just a nice, ordinary guy." Eleanor unwrapped her sandwich, folding the waxed paper into quarters before putting it back in the lunchbox. Any discomfort she'd experienced was her own fault. Hedging the truth on an online questionnaire—gaming the algorithm—had seemed so simple before she had to sit down with David and explain things.

"Was he very analytical? Penny says engineers can lack people skills that way—Brian being the exception, of course."

"Of course." Eleanor sipped her water. "How can two people, who've known each other all their lives, be so besotted?"

"Right? I'm trying to think of a really sappy wedding gift for them. His & Hers embroidered bathrobes or something like that."

"Oh, that reminds me! You won't believe this." Eleanor broke off self-consciously. "Sorry. You don't want to hear my family drama."

"Sure, I do!" Brittany pointed a fry at her. "I'm saving up credits. My family is pretty drama-free at the moment, but our time will come. I'm all ears."

"Laurie called on Monday morning. She's talking about presents now, like they're getting married, only bigger."

"Bigger than wedding gifts? Like what?"

"Trips to the Caribbean."

Brittany dropped her hamburger and stared. "Trips...plural?"

"No, only one to the islands. I believe Soren is sending them to Chicago, to see a show and visit the art museums."

"Cheapskate."

"No, that would be me," Eleanor said. "I wasn't planning to give them a gift at all."

Brittany picked up her hamburger. "So, what are you going to give them?"

"Not a clue. A dozen roses might be in my budget. Maybe."

"How about making them something?"

"Like what?" Eleanor asked. "I'm not real crafty. I could look on Pinterest, but really... it's hard to compete with sandy beaches. Not that I want to compete," she added hastily. "I just don't want to look like an idiot or an ungrateful, rebellious daughter."

"Can you paint? How about photography? You could take a nice picture of scenery or something from your mom's childhood and have it framed."

"I don't have a camera." Eleanor picked up her phone. "This takes pretty good pictures, but I'm not sure I could print anything really big."

"How about a quilt? Your aunt could help you. Or you could knit or crochet an afghan if you don't want to do a quilt."

"Knitting and crocheting were not included in my extensive education. In fact," Eleanor said, "I don't think I had any really creative classes. Academic classes, some music and sports. I can play volleyball and the piano. Soccer and basketball, too, but I went to school on a volleyball scholarship."

"I didn't know that!" Brittany leaned forward and propped her elbows on the table. "Where did you go to college?"

"Rockland University."

"Oh, I know where that is! It's a big engineering school, isn't it?"

"That and education. Guess which one I went to." Eleanor smiled tightly. "After a few months here, I'm beginning to think I should have gone into engineering. Doing take-offs isn't the same thing as engineering, of course, but it's related, and I think I'm better at that than I am at teaching."

"Did you have a boyfriend down there?"

"A boyfriend? No."

"No? None at all?"

Eleanor wrinkled her nose. "Like you said, it was a lot of engineering. Penny's absolutely right about them. Have you ever dated an engineer or scientist?"

"No, I haven't," Brittany said. "I think Brian's the only engineer I know."

"Well—except for Brian, of course—they aren't the most romantic men on earth. I went out to the theater with one guy, and he whispered through the whole performance, telling me which color lights were being used and why. I mean the whole performance—not just a few comments. Not only was it annoying, but our neighbors were furious. I can't remember the last time I was so embarrassed. Then he asked me to go to a concert the following weekend. I figured that would be okay, since it was outdoors— no lights. But then he just talked about sound waves, through the whole thing."

Brittany grinned. "Did you go out with him again?"

"No, but he kept trying. He said he'd really enjoyed our time together."

"So, don't date an engineer."

"Actually," Eleanor said, "the scientists were just as bad. My roommate set me up with her boyfriend's roommate, thinking that would be convenient for them. He was a good-looking guy, and I thought a zoologist would be interesting, but he spent the entire date talking about the life cycle of the dung beetle. Not kidding. I didn't ask about dung beetles. We didn't see a bug that inspired conversation. We sat down at the restaurant, got our water, and Heath said, 'Have you ever seen a dung beetle?' I thought it was a joke at first, so I said no and waited for the punch line. There wasn't one."

"A dung beetle? What's a dung beetle?"

"Just what you'd expect. He started at conception and worked his way through the beetle's life until the poor thing died and dried up. Seriously, the entire meal. It was like he couldn't help himself. He just kept talking. I could tell he was miserable when he said goodbye and dropped me off."

Brittany laughed. "Poor guy. He was probably nervous."

"I hope he became a professor, because he was a good lecturer. To this day, I remember most of what he told me. I didn't have a lot of time for dating, though. Like I said, I was there on a volleyball scholarship, and we practiced off-season, too. I had a heavy class load, because I wanted to get through my double master's degree in five years, and my sorority activities, too. I didn't have time for other socializing."

"I only went to the community college," Brittany said. "It was fun. I got an associate's degree in marketing and business by the time I was 19, and I've been doing this ever since. I worked for the newspaper for a while, but now I'm keeping busy and making more money freelancing. I like it." She held out the carton. "Want some more fries? I got the large one, to share, and then I ate almost all of them myself."

"No thanks. Where did you meet your fiancé?"

"At school. He works at the car dealership south of town, in the shop."

"When are you getting married?"

"No hurry." Brittany popped the last fry in her mouth and rolled up her garbage. "We haven't set a date. We were planning on Christmas—this coming Christmas—but not a specific day. That's how I met Penny. I took my wedding dress designs to her, and she asked me to do her social media and marketing. Where should I put this?"

Eleanor pointed to the garbage can. "So, you have a dress but not a wedding date?"

"Well, I told Penny to hold off on the dress, too."

"That doesn't sound good."

Brittany sat and looked at her. "My sister just got a divorce. It made me take a good look at what I wanted in a man—in marriage. I asked Andy if we could go to premarital counseling, and he laughed. He wouldn't do it." She shrugged. "I decided I wanted a man who was willing to go to premarital counseling. Our pastor says that it's an investment in marriage, and if a man isn't willing to make that small investment ahead of time, he might not be willing to invest much later—to do whatever it takes to fix things if there's a problem. When Andy made a joke of it and said it would be a waste of time... well, that was a red flag. I'm not breaking off the engagement—at least, not now—but I'm praying for wisdom. And maybe some courage.

Ten

"Well, that stinks." Eleanor sat in the hard chair next to the bed. "I mean, I understand they have to have a deadline, but it was a big project, and your bid was good. All that time wasted!"

"You did a good job on it," Gary said, "and it wasn't a waste of time, because you learned while you worked. Each project is more practice, like playing the piano."

She laughed. "Like playing the piano?"

"Yeah. You play the piano, don't you? I seem to remember your mother talking about your recitals when I was down there for her fortieth birthday party."

"I haven't done it in a while, but yes, I can play. Why?"

He plucked at the blanket. "I have a favor to ask. Don't be afraid to say no." He paused. "Well, if you say no, you'll have to explain it to Aunt Violet, but if you'd really rather not, I'll figure something else out."

"What?"

"On Tuesdays, over at the nursing home where Uncle Olof is..." He stopped. "Actually, it's a rehabilitation center, and I'll be there, too, while this leg heals up. So, on Tuesday mornings, they have sing-alongs. They sing old songs, from when they were younger."

"Okay." She waited. Did he want her to play accompaniment?

"Well, I'm not going to be able to play for a while, with this shoulder, and I'd very much appreciate it if you'd fill in for me." The last few words came out in a rush.

"You mean, you play the piano for their sing-alongs?"

"Yeah. It's not hard. I can't do concertos, but Cheryl had a piano, and she taught me how to bang out a few songs. They aren't a picky audience."

She smiled at him, amused and a little surprised by the affection she felt for this uncle she hadn't known until a few months ago. "And you want me to do it?"

"I'd be grateful if you would. I'd still pay you for 8 hours on Tuesdays, plus all the overtime you'll be collecting for the next few weeks. If you have an early lunch, you could be at the office by 12:30."

"Well, what songs would I have to play?" Did she really want to do this? Did she have a choice? "I haven't played in a while."

"I have songbooks. It's old stuff—'When Irish Eyes are Smiling', 'Don't Sit Under the Apple Tree', 'When You Wore a Tulip', 'Yellow Rose of Texas'.... "

"I don't know any of those," Eleanor objected.

"You will," Gary said darkly. "They're the kind of songs that get stuck in your head, and the next thing you know, you're humming 'A Bicycle Built for Two' on the job site."

"Good morning!" Cheryl rolled a wheelchair ahead of her as she entered. "Hi, Eleanor. No need to leave. I just want to see him get in and out of the wheelchair."

"I thought I wasn't supposed to do that." Gary sat up, pivoting to dangle his legs over the side of the bed. "I thought I had to wait for assistance."

"That is correct. Both here and at the nursing home, you must wait for a CNA or nurse to assist you in or out of your chair or bed."

"Then why do you want me to do it now?"

His exaggerated patience didn't put a dent in her cheerful demeanor. "Because, Gary, you are going to do it anyhow, and I want to make sure you know how to do it without injuring yourself all over again."

Eleanor giggled. No wonder Aunt Violet liked this woman.

Gary grinned ruefully. "Oh, no. I'm going to follow every rule to the T, so I can get out of that place and back to work."

"I don't think so. Have you seen the CNA's at the nursing home? You're going to have to call them when you want to use the bathroom, Gary, or just to get out of bed in the morning."

He scowled at her. "Would you please stop calling it a nursing home? It's a rehabilitation center."

Cheryl pursed her lips and tilted her head, considering. "No, I don't think so. I like calling it a nursing home."

"You could call it a rehab clinic, Uncle Gary," Eleanor said, "but then people would think you were there to break a drug habit."

"In and out of the chair, Gary. I'm not signing off on your discharge until I see you do it."

He heaved a sigh. "Did you come back here just to torment me?"

"No," Cheryl said, "that's not why I came back. It is a nice little bonus, though. Just wait until we get to the nursing home, where we'll have more time together." She smiled with all her teeth. "We'll get you fixed up in no time."

Later that afternoon, as she drove out to the office, Eleanor realized she was humming "A Bicycle Built for Two" and burst into laughter. All those years of piano lessons were finally going to be put to good use. What would her mother think?

"Your mother will be pleased." Violet beamed at Eleanor she set a cup and saucer on the table. "You remember, I told you how fond of him she was. They sang songs together, possibly some of the same ones you'll be playing on Tuesdays."

Eleanor still had trouble believing in that relationship. If her mother had ever mentioned Olof, it was only in passing or in connection with the rest of the family.

"And she read to him. He'd work while she read, or sometimes he'd sit with her and look at the pages as if he could read, too. He couldn't, you know. He has dyslexia, like Penny, but no one ever knew that back then. Teachers just thought he was lazy. It wasn't until Penny was diagnosed that the doctors tested him."

"I didn't know that."

"Your mother—as far as I know—never asked him to read to her. She read and he listened." Violet tipped her head and looked at Eleanor. "Does anyone else in your family have dyslexia?"

Eleanor shook her head. "No, not that I know of. The twins are just three. Of course, they'll be starting preschool soon, and Laurie will want them reading by the time they're four, so I guess we'll find out. Dyslexia is hereditary, isn't it? I wonder if Mom worried about that."

Violet spread butter on her roll. "It's hereditary, at least a bit, but it's hard to tell how much, because when you go back a generation or two, we didn't know about it. We just thought people weren't smart enough to learn. They were just labeled illiterate."

"That's sad." Eleanor stirred sugar into her coffee. She might as well take advantage of her aunt's good mood. "Speaking of my mother... are you going to my parents' anniversary party?"

"Oh, I don't think so," Violet said. "I'll send them a card."

That seemed an appropriate response to a 35th anniversary. Eleanor wished she could do the same. "Laurie, Zack's wife, thinks we should give them gifts. Us kids, I mean."

"What kind of gifts?"

"Expensive gifts. Soren's giving them a weekend in Chicago, to see a show. Zack and Laurie are giving them a vacation in the Caribbean."

Eleanor blew out a sigh. "I don't know what to give them."

Violet sat upright. "A vacation in the Caribbean! What will you give them for their fiftieth—a new car?"

"Thank you. I agree, but I'm stuck. I can't afford something like that. Brittany suggested making a quilt for them, but I don't know how to do it, and from what I've seen here, it requires a lot of tools I don't have. Would you be willing to help me make one, if it's even possible to get one made by Valentine's Day?"

Would this be a good time to start humming "A Bicycle Built for Two"?

"Do you think they would like a quilt?" Violet asked.

"I think so. Mom likes handcrafted things as long as they aren't too hokey. I saw some quilts on Pinterest that looked kind of modern. Is fabric expensive?"

"Sometimes," Violet said. "We can find a sale and coupons. I'll help you if you're sure you want to do it. And I'll show you how to use the quilting machine."

"That's a little intimidating!" Relieved, Eleanor leaned back in her chair. "I appreciate it. It won't be as nice as the other gifts, but at least it's better than a bouquet of flowers or a gift certificate to a restaurant they could afford better than I can."

"I'm sure she'll like it. They both will. Do you have time to look at patterns after work today?"

"Yes, I can do that." She picked up her phone and navigated to Pinterest. "Let me show you what I found. I'm completely open to suggestions, though."

"Can you get my reading glasses from my nightstand for me? I can't see those little screens."

When Eleanor returned, her aunt was reading her text messages—apparently without the aid of her readers. She looked up without a trace of embarrassment. "Brittany wants to know how your date went. Were you on a date? I didn't know you have a young man here."

"I didn't go on a date." Not yet. Eleanor reached for the phone.

Violet released it. "You don't have to keep secrets from me. I'm not your chaperon. At your age, you ought to be dating. You're even older than Penny."

Amusement swept away Eleanor's irritation. "I'm not that old."

"You're not that young, either," the woman said tartly. "You don't want to be my age and still have kids underfoot."

The idea staggered the imagination. Eleanor couldn't help laughing. "No, I don't. But I still have a few good childbearing years left." She tapped in a quick message to Brittany and closed the text window. "Here's the first quilt I saw. It's called a double wedding ring, so it seemed appropriate."

"It would take six months and a lot of skill," Violet said. "You need one that can be rotary cut and machine pieced quickly."

"I don't know which ones those would be. How about this one?"

"We could do that one." Her aunt took the phone and scrolled down the page. "Do you have certain colors in mind?"

"The house is pretty neutral. A lot of white now that us kids are all gone. I thought maybe I could make it for Valentine's Day, but not too country-style."

"The style won't matter as much as the fabrics you choose," her aunt said absently. "Since you said seasonal, are you talking about a wall hanging or a lap quilt instead of a bed quilt?"

"Yes. I don't want to interfere with their bedroom decor." Eleanor fought the urge to snatch her phone back. "Something for the couch or to hang on the wall somewhere."

"How about this? It looks like Swedish paper baskets." Aunt Violet turned the phone so Eleanor could see it but didn't let go. "It has hearts, so it would work for Valentine's Day or a wedding anniversary. We could look at different fabrics, but I like the moderate contrast here."

Eleanor looked up at the suddenly authoritative voice. Aunt Violet knew what she was doing.

"Not beige, since you said their house is white, but maybe in grays? With some pink or blue?" She handed the phone to Eleanor. "I'll draft it out, and we can go shopping tomorrow."

Now that she'd given her spare room to Eleanor, there wasn't space to dedicate to this project. Violet dragged the last tote into the middle of the quilting room. The annex, with four bedrooms, should have been more than enough space for her, but after years of living in other people's houses, she reveled in being able to spread out.

"Hey! I can do that!" Eleanor sounded more alarmed than the circumstances warranted. Violet appreciated help; she didn't like being treated like a frail old lady.

"Thank you, Nellie." She pulled off the lid of the tote and straightened, rubbing her hip. "I thought maybe you could use this room for the transcriptions and editing. We can bring in a desk and chair for you."

Eleanor walked to the quilting machine and ran her hand over Violet's current project. "This one is smaller than the other ones I've seen. I like the colors."

Too small. This quilt had been the hardest. It should have been bigger, to record a long life with a wife and family. Instead, it was small and... lonely. Who would want a quilt made for a boy who'd died at 19 years old, nearly 75 years ago? She joined Eleanor and touched at the small flag and cross.

"Karl didn't live long enough to fill up a bigger quilt. He died in 1944, in Normandy." She pointed. "Those blocks record the rest of us, and our parents and grandparents, but there wasn't much to say about his own life."

"He was your brother?"

"Yes, my favorite." She smiled, remembering the many kindnesses of her older brother. They'd etched themselves into her mind—her heart—over the decades, and she'd written them in his book, not wanting Karl to be lost. She and Olof were the only people who remembered Karl now, and poor Olof's memories grew fuzzier every day.

She turned to Eleanor. "This is what I need your help with. All these journals..." Violet gestured at the tote. "They need to be typed up. I wrote those out by hand, before I had a typewriter. The blue tote has typed pages that need to be re-typed into the computer, and what's already in the computer needs to be edited and organized."

Eleanor's eyes widened. "All that is family history?"

"We've been around since 1908," Violet said. "In America, anyways. I didn't record much about the time before that. Do you think you can do it?" She couldn't leave it in this kind of mess. She'd been entrusted with these stories, and even if no one else cared, she had to get them recorded for posterity—whether posterity wanted them or not.

"I'll do my best. That's a lot of history!"

"Four generations of Anderson family life," Violet said. "But the fourth generation is starting to multiply faster than I can sew or write, so I'm falling behind. Will this room work for you?"

"This is your quilting room! Can't I just do it at the kitchen table or in the living room? I can carry my laptop computer anywhere."

"Are you sure?" Violet asked. "If you're sure, we could keep these totes in a corner of the living room and you can just take out what you need." Relief lightened her spirits. As important as the written history was, Violet craved the time alone in this room, with God and her history quilts, rolling back and forth along the quilt, guiding the head of the quilting machine, humming and praying silently—and sometimes, not so silently. She'd have to remember there was another person in the house. She didn't want to startle Eleanor.

"It's working out great. I'm loving Aunt Violet. She's telling me all sorts of stories about you."

Violet leaned in, grateful for the annex's modern doors, so unlike the solid wood ones in the main part of the farmhouse. Eleanor was silent for a few minutes, and she eased back, hoping she hadn't been detected. It must be Kathy. Too bad the girl didn't use speaker phone.

"No, really. It's nice here. I have your old bedroom, and even your old dresser, with lilac shelf paper in the drawers. You should see the lilac trees that you and Uncle Olof planted. They're huge! He remembered planting them, too."

Eleanor continued after a shorter pause. "He's good. Aunt Violet says it was one of his good days. He looks like a much older version of Uncle Gary."

Kathy must have had more to say this time. Violet could hear Eleanor moving around the room, opening and shutting drawers, sitting on the bed and walking over the squeaky floorboard by the window.

When she started talking again, her voice was sharper. "That's why I have to stay here, Mom. My job didn't go away because Gary's not there. He needs me now, to do a lot more than just the takeoffs and some office work. I'm getting to do some of what he usually does. He's teaching me about the business, and I'm liking it!"

A brief wait this time. "I know you love me, Mom, and you want what's best for me, but I like it here. I like my job, and I like this part of our family. Oh! I forgot to tell you. On Tuesday mornings, I'm going to be playing the piano for the golden oldies sing-along at the nursing home where Uncle Olof and Gary are. Did you know Gary was doing that until he got hurt?"

It sounded like the call was ending. Violet stepped away, ready to slip into her own room, just catching Eleanor's next words.

"I'll be there. I wish you'd come here for a visit, though. Everyone would love to see you. Just think about it, okay? I love you. Bye."

"Good morning, Aunt Violet!"

She leaned in to receive a hug from Constance. "Good morning, dear. Eleanor's parking the car. She dropped me off in front."

"There she is." Brian smiled at Eleanor. "I'm glad the two of you made it, in this weather."

"Oh, yes," Violet said. "We wouldn't miss church." She was going to make sure Eleanor didn't miss church, as long as the girl was staying with her.

"The church is always full when there's a blizzard," Penny said. "Everyone has to demonstrate their hardiness and devotion."

"And they're not above calling the slackers to ask why they missed church," her fiancé put in.

"It's pride." Violet handed him her tote bag so she could shed her coat. "It's not just going to church in the blizzard, but making sure everyone sees you strapping on your snowshoes."

"I'd be pretty proud of myself if I had to wear snow shoes to get to church," Eleanor said. "Aunt Violet was telling me about going to the old church in the winter, when everyone lived in the farmhouse. It sounds a lot harder than just driving my nice warm car down a plowed highway, and they had perfect attendance!"

Everyone looked at Violet, and she felt her cheeks warming. Maybe she'd exaggerated a teensy bit, but it wasn't pride to take pride ... er, to be glad that one's family had a good attendance record.

"Anyhow, whatever their true motivation, the church is present and on time during bad weather." Penny hooked her arm through Brian's.

The sermon was on pride. Penny leaned across Eleanor to point out the information in the bulletin and jerked her hand away when Violet slapped it.

"Shh. Sit still." She heard the stifled giggles and was tempted to pinch them, as she had their parents for such behavior.

"Hello, Olof."

"Hello." He extended a hand, and Violet shook it. Another one of those days. The good ones were getting further apart. At least he'd been able to talk to Eleanor last week. Maybe, if Kathy came, he'd remember her.

"Would you like to go down to the living room? There's a little girl looking for someone to play checkers with. Do you like checkers?"

"She cheats." Olof handed her a book. "Have you read this?"

"Yes, it's a good book." It was an old TV guide. She set it on the dresser and wheeled him to the lobby, praying he wouldn't be overwhelmed by the visitors. Most of the elderly residents lacked company; Olof had enough for all of them.

He spied Sarah, of course, and ignored the rest of them. "Violet! What are you doing over there? We need to go home."

"I want to play checkers."

He wavered. "We need to go home."

"Come on." Sarah got behind the wheelchair and pushed him toward one of the game tables. "Let's play checkers."

"Okay, but no cheating." He placed the checkers in one long row on his side of the board. "Is that right?"

"Let me fix it." Eleanor stepped close and tried to adjust them. "They alternate, on the black squares."

He slapped at her hands. "I can do it! Violet and I are playing checkers. Go away. Go home."

Violet hoped Eleanor's feelings wouldn't be hurt. She'd had to grow an extra layer of skin herself in the last year or two, as Olof's filter deteriorated. "Be nice, Olof. This is Eleanor. We're going to watch TV for a while."

"Bye." He didn't take his eyes off the board.

"Why does he call Sarah Violet?" Eleanor asked. "Does he think she's you? I read a bit about Alzheimer's after our last visit here, and the article said what you did—he thinks he's a child, looking for his mom or wanting to go home."

Eleanor had researched it. Violet patted her arm. "Exactly. He's not always in the past, though. Sometimes when we come, he recognizes me but not her, so I introduce her as Sarah, and he's nice to her. Sometimes he doesn't remember either of us." She nodded at the wing chairs. "We can keep an eye on them from here. Carl and Constance went down to check on Gary. On days like today, he's eight years old. If I tell him I'm Violet, he doesn't believe me, because I'm an old lady. To him, Violet is his little sister."

"And Sarah just plays along? That's kind of... creepy."

"Ha." Penny spoke from behind Violet. "You don't know Sarah. She would play games with anyone—any game—24 hours a day, if she could, and she's always loved Uncle Olof."

"She loved him because he couldn't get away from her," Violet said. "She'd push him around in his wheelchair or climb in his lap and read books to him, long before she could actually read the words. It's just how she knew him." That was a while ago, though. He was so unpredictable now.

"It's my turn. You just went." Sarah pushed at Olof's hand. The old man grumbled but complied, waiting for the girl to move her checker.

"Okay, you can go now."

"She's competitive, too," Penny commented. "She's not going to let him win."

"Is it always this empty?" Eleanor asked.

"Most of the residents take a nap in the afternoon. Olof doesn't." Violet shifted in her chair, avoiding the stare of an elderly man in high-waisted jeans and suspenders. The collar of his plaid shirt stood out around his skinny neck, not shifting with the movement of his head as he strutted toward them. He'd stalked her last time she was here, too.

Sarah jumped two of Olof's checkers, and her crow of triumph rang through the room, drawing indulgent smiles and a few sleepy mutters.

"Hopefully, I'll never have to be here," Violet said. "Thanks to Penny, I have a home at the farmhouse as long as I need it. She and Brian are going to live there for a little while, and then they might rent it out to one of his sisters. So, there will be someone around."

"We won't leave you there alone," Penny said.

"When are you getting married?" Eleanor asked. "I haven't heard a date yet."

"We wanted a spring wedding, so we can have it outside, but the more I'm around brides and their mothers, the more I want to elope."

"Too many mosquitoes in the spring, and you can't trust the weather.

"Violet turned a shoulder to the man, praying he was just passing by. "And you can't elope. You've put too much into this bridal business of yours. You have to have a nice wedding. It won't hurt you to wait a few months."

"The shop is amazing." Eleanor glanced at the man and back to Penny. "You'd never guess from the outside what it's like inside. I went with my college roommate to a bridal shop in Chicago. It was so elegant we were afraid to touch anything. Yours is elegant, but it's more comfortable.

"Country chic." Violet said. "That's what she calls it. It does look nice."

"Thank you. Dad will finish up the landscaping in the spring, and in a year or two, when it's all grown in, it'll be a showcase. First impressions matter, you know, especially with mothers of brides, who are expecting to pay a thousand dollars for a wedding dress."

"Ole, what are you doing over here?" A middle-aged woman in Tinker Bell scrubs hurried toward them. "This is Miss Anderson. She's Olof's sister."

"Ja." He spit the word out. "It's her... da sister. Da hussy. Traitor." Violet pressed back in her chair, frightened by his venom. His toothless mouth and thick accent garbled the words, but there was no mistaking the hate. He leaned closer. "Tramp! You're out dere in da field, consortin vit Jerry -"

"Ole! Stop that! I'm so sorry, Miss Anderson. Come on, Ole." The aide raised her voice. "Mary! Can you come help me?"

Violet's breathing slowed as the man turned his anger on his caregivers.

"What was that about?" Eleanor stared after them. "Do they have violent patients here?"

"Are you okay, Aunt Violet?" Penny crouched in front of her.

No, she wasn't okay. She'd never been called a tramp before. The absurdity of the accusations finally brought a chuckle. "I'm fine. I don't know who Jerry is, but I promise, I'm not consorting with him or anyone else, especially in a field in January."

Twelve

David picked out the elegant, simple melody of "King on a Donkey" as the ushers passed the communion plates. Angela Ridgewell sat at the end of the back row, alone, staring out the window. Had she heard the message about extravagant grace? He should mention her to Pastor Jack, so he could follow up.

Or was that his responsibility? He could ask one of the women to do it, but a pastor couldn't shirk fifty percent of his work because he didn't want to minister to women—or more specifically, a particular woman. In public, in the company of the rest of the church, he couldn't use discretion and "best practices" as excuses. He just didn't want to do it. Honesty counted for something, right?

He brought the song to an end as the ushers returned the plates. The closing song, *"Grace Greater Than Our Sin"*, with its catchy waltz rhythm, might touch Angela, unless the bloody parts bothered her. He caved in on the last line. The woman was here, all by herself, and he had the Gospel to share.

"We'll meet you at Charcoal Grill. We know you've got people to talk to, and your dad and I could use some coffee."

Confirmation. David made his way down the side aisle and stopped at the sight of Angela in conversation with Larry. His friend sat in the aisle ahead of her, turned around, listening to whatever Angela was saying.

Maybe he'd be at the restaurant sooner than he'd thought. Even as he turned to go, she stood and strode away. Larry, rose, brows drawn together, rubbing the back of his neck.

"How'd it go?" David waited for Larry to exit the row. "What did she think of the service?"

"Angela? She didn't say."

"She was talking to you!"

"People do that," Larry said. "Even people who aren't my clients."

"She must have said something about it." David looked at the other man, exasperated. "I was hoping she heard the sermon. She really needs the Lord."

Larry stopped walking and turned around. David rocked back, to avoid a collision.

"In all your classes, at UMD and in this seminary, do you have any classes in human psychology? How do you plan to be a counselor? Just read Bible verses at people and tell them to suck it up and trust God?" He grabbed David's elbow and pulled him through the crowd, into the library. "She needs Jesus, but I think she needs something else, too."

David opened his mouth to argue, but Larry held up a hand. "He is sufficient, but guess what... He uses me, too, and other kinds of doctors."

He'd never seen Larry angry before. David dropped into a chair. "Yes, He does. What do you mean about Angela?"

"Something's going on. I don't like to interfere, and if she was my patient, I couldn't. But I've known her since we were kids. I might go talk to Meg. Cal won't get it, and I don't know if Meg will. They're both pretty single-minded." He sat opposite David. "Their mother was a mess. Still is, as far as I know." He chuckled. "That's not a professional opinion—just my childhood memories of her."

David leaned forward. "You mean she's suicidal or on drugs or something? A mental illness?"

"I don't know." Larry stood and extended a hand to pull David to his feet. "You going to lunch with mom and dad?"

"They're waiting for me at Charcoal Grill."

"By the way, have you met your match yet?" Larry grinned at his joke. "Were you able to overcome that unfortunate first impression?"

"Yes! It's a long story, but we have a date for Tuesday night. I think it's going pretty well."

"How can it be a long story? Didn't you just get her information a week ago?"

"It's been an eventful week." David pulled on his coat. "Don't worry. I'm not rushing things." He shrugged. "There are a couple things—not red flags, but maybe yellow. Like a traffic light."

"My mom thinks a yellow light means you should accelerate to get through before it turns red," Larry said. "Personally, I step on my brakes at that point."

"I'm somewhere in between. I'll proceed with caution." Maybe it would be better to step on the brakes, though, and wait for a green light. God's green light.

David liked scholarly Old Testament sermons, but this professor managed to turn vibrant, God-breathed history into dusty lists and statistics. He closed the laptop and propped his feet on the coffee table. It was all important, even the genealogies and numbers, gruesome deaths and family history—much of it dysfunctional. God included it in Scripture, after all. He wrote it all out, in great detail, and then He repeated it in Chronicles. Professor Voe expected David to memorize all of it.

Tomorrow night, he'd talk to Eleanor about her faith. She'd been vague, and Christians weren't supposed to be vague. Had his profile made his intentions clear enough? Being a pastor's wife would be different from being an engineer's wife. He tried to picture her as a pastor's wife and himself as a pastor. The two of them, with a quiverful of little PK's, all dressed up and shiny on Sunday morning.

It didn't float, and he didn't think the children were the problem.

David leaned back and covered his face with his hands. He wanted to serve God, more than anything else, with all of his being. He wanted it more than he wanted a wife and family... more than he wanted anything the world could provide. But lately, whenever he worked toward that goal, there was something in his path. His grandma would call it "a check in his spirit." Pastor Jack might call it spiritual warfare.

Which was it? Was he going down the wrong path, with the Holy Spirit trying to redirect him, or was he on the right path, with Satan trying to stop him?

"Even the ones who don't talk were singing!" Eleanor lifted a stack of papers from a chair and set them on her desk. "You can sit here. I'm trying to stay on top of the things I can do here. Uncle Gary is so positive and encouraging, but he must be worried. We missed a deadline the day after the accident, and now we're trying to coordinate things between here and the nursing home and the job sites."

"Are you going out to job sites?" Brittany grinned. "I can just picture you with a yellow hard hat. You could take a selfie and send it to your sister-in-law. But tell me about your sing-along. I've read about music therapy for dementia patients. How does it work?"

"I play the piano and they sing. I thought I'd have to lead singing, but Gary did it. They all came into the living room in their wheelchairs, an aide handed out songbooks, and I played. They're all songs from the 20's, 30's, and 40's. We sang all the songs, and then they left.

She'd loved it. The best part—the very best—was Uncle Gary. He sang with gusto, waving his good arm as if directing a choir. He helped people turn the pages in their songbooks and introduced each song with enthusiasm. She could see why women were attracted to him. Gary Anderson was generous, easy-going, kind, and chivalrous. That's probably how he'd ended up married so many times. He'd given her this job even though she wasn't qualified and let her stay in his cabin. She had no doubt that if she'd made a mess of the take-offs, he'd have found her something else to do.

"Are you going to do it every week, then?" Brittany asked.

"That's the plan, until Uncle Gary is healed up."

"So... have you seen any more of David Reid?" Brittany took a bite of her salad. "Did you set up a real date?"

"Yes, as a matter of fact, we're going out to dinner tonight." She sat down opposite her friend. "I really like him, Brittany. He seems intelligent and sensible, and he's a good listener. He's good-looking, too, in a clean-cut, all-American kind of way."

"Meets all your qualifications, huh?"

Eleanor ignored the edge of sarcasm. "He does, and not just for the anniversary party." When he'd called to invite her to dinner, she'd forgotten all about the party. "I started thinking about that last night. It might be nice to get to know him and maybe even go out together, but I don't want a husband right now." It had kept her awake, listening to the wind, worrying about David's expectations. "He must have filled out the application because he wants a real relationship."

"Ya think?"

Eleanor dropped her gaze. "I know... I didn't think about him at all. I was so wrapped up in my own situation."

"How are you going to introduce the topic of your immediate need for a date on Valentine's Day, in Minneapolis? An overnight date, since I assume this party will last until at least midnight. You can't come back here that late."

"Sure, I can." She hadn't been planning to, though. She couldn't just take off like an ordinary guest.

"David may not want to drive back here late at night, especially in winter," Brittany said.

"Then he can stay at my parents' house or get a hotel." The words lacked conviction, even in her own ears. Eleanor bit her lip. "It's a dinner. It can't go later than nine, can it?"

"I don't know how you folks do things down there in the big city," Brittany said with an exaggerated drawl, "but around here, we can stay up till midnight for a good party, especially if we're having a string quartet and a wine bar."

"Maybe I should just be honest with him," Eleanor said. She picked up her apple and set it down again. "But what if he gets mad and leaves?"

"Then you'll be right back where you started and have to decide whether or not you should just go to the party without a date. It wouldn't be the end of the world." Brittany wrinkled her nose. "My parents would rather have me come alone than get a date with a stranger just for the party."

"They wouldn't have to know he's a stranger," Eleanor muttered. "I don't need a date. It'll be fine. I'm making my family sound like monsters, and they aren't. Not at all. They're sincere, well-meaning people who love me and want the best for me."

"They sound egotistical and manipulative." Brittany bit into her sandwich.

"No, they're not!" But maybe a little, subconsciously. "I'm pinning my hopes on a blizzard. Let's talk about something else. Anything else."

"Oh, tell me about your quilt. Did you get the fabric?"

"Yes, and I like it. Aunt Violet really knows her stuff. She's got it all charted out and even printed out a picture of what it will look like. She has a program for designing quilts."

"I didn't know she was so computer-savvy," Brittany said.

"Oh, yes. She knows enough for what she wants to do—the quilts and her genealogy and writing. We're making a quilt with hearts on it. She's calling it a Swedehearts Glory Quilt."

"Swedehearts, like Swedish hearts? Why the Glory?"

"I'm not sure. She made one she called Christmas Glory for my aunt in Florida." Eleanor folded her paper napkin in half and then into quarters. "I don't always know what she's thinking. Sometimes she dithers around like an ordinary old lady, but she's sharper than most people give her credit for. She talks a lot about the family in her generation and the one after that—my mom's generation. I hadn't realized that my mom grew up there in the farmhouse, at least until she was ten. Aunt Violet's always talking about her."

"And then your mom went away to college and never came back. That's a common story in rural areas. Kids can't wait to leave the farm and move to the big city." Brittany licked her fingers. "Not me. It's fun to visit the cities for shopping or a special event, but I get all tense in traffic. And I like being able to see the stars at night."

"It's nice out here," Eleanor agreed, "especially in the winter. The snow stays whiter."

"We've had so much snow this year that it probably stays pretty white in the cities, too. It gets freshened up every day. Maybe you'll have your blizzard after all."

Thirteen

He always scanned both sides of the road for deer, watching for eyes reflecting the truck's headlights, but David never saw the one that raced from the woods straight into the side of his SUV. He recognized the jolting thud. Of all the rotten timing... why now? Grateful the plow had cleared the shoulder, he eased the truck to a stop.

The animal was nearly invisible in the dusk—a gray-brown lump in the middle of the road, where the next car was bound to hit it. Pulling on his gloves, he examined the damage to his truck. Stupid deer. Hopefully, it was dead, because he didn't have a way to put it out of its misery if it was suffering.

David pulled his phone from his pocket and turned on the flashlight app as he walked back toward the deer. He squatted by the still animal and shone his light over it. No visible blood; it must have broken its neck. One eye opened and glared at him. David groaned. Another time, he would have felt more compassion. Right now, he just wanted to drive away and not be late for his date with Eleanor.

He couldn't do it. David turned off the flashlight and put a hand on her heaving ribcage. Her eye closed. He stood up when the dispatcher answered. "Hi. This is David Reid. I hit a deer out here on HWY 23, about 5 miles west of Milaca. Actually, she hit me. But I don't have a gun or anything, and she's still alive. Do you have someone who can come out and take care of her?"

The doe lifted her head and stared at him as if outraged. Three seconds later, she staggered to her feet, took a few dizzy steps, and then leaped off into the woods.

"Uh, never mind. She took off. She looks okay. Thanks anyhow."

Shaking his head, David got back in the SUV. He'd be late. Not a good start for a relationship, but surely Eleanor would understand; even in the city, people hit deer. He tapped out a message.

> **DAVID:** HIT A DEER. I'LL BE ABOUT TEN MINUTES LATE.
> **ELEANOR:** ARE YOU OKAY?

Nice.

> **DAVID:** THE DEER AND I ARE BOTH FINE. THE TRUCK HAS A DENT.
> **ELEANOR:** BE CAREFUL. SEE YOU SOON.

He smiled as he restarted the SUV. His mother said that—"be careful"—every time he left. He wished the Betwixt profile had some information about what kind of family Eleanor wanted. 2.5 children? Six? Maybe they could talk about that tonight, in a casual sort of way. No, there was nothing casual about conversations when you met through a matchmaking agency. Everything mattered.

Eleanor was drop-dead gorgeous and seemed like a nice person, but there was something confusing about her, too. He didn't even know if she was a Christian—at least, not really. She'd talked about church in a positive way and knew enough to be concerned about his doctrine, but... He'd have to ask her more openly tonight.

And what about her job—her career as a teacher? Was she just passing through here, restless and still trying to decide what she wanted in life? If so, why did she sign up for the matchmaking service? The goal of the agency was traditional marriage, not casual dating. Not friends.

David pushed the CD into the slot, and the sweet voice of Larry Norman filled the air. Edgy songs, more so than most contemporary Christian music, with blunt words of truth and calling Christians to love one another.

To lift up the fallen and lost, instead of stepping over them. When some people were talking about free love, the Jesus People were telling everyone about the only real free love. David wished he'd been there, to see the Christian hippies and the men and women of the Jesus People movement, revolutionizing Christian culture in America. Evangelizing with abandon, his Grandma said. A grand adventure.

Eleanor sat on the bench to stop herself from pacing. He'd said he was fine, but how could you hit a deer and just continue on to a dinner date? She'd be a wreck, whether the deer was hurt or not. But if David hit it hard enough to put a dent in his truck, how could it be okay? At least he wouldn't arrive with it strapped to the top of his truck. She jumped to her feet and peered out the window.

"Are you sure he's coming?" The lone waitress, hands on her hips, joined Eleanor and scanned the parking lot. "You can sit at a table if you want to."

"No, thanks. He'll be here soon."

"If you say so. You can seat yourselves whenever you're ready. Menus are on the table." She sashayed toward the kitchen, and Eleanor resumed her watch.

How did wives and mothers do it... worry and wait for their children to get home, when something didn't feel right? Even little things, like this, when you knew it was really all right, but you just had to see for yourself?

Fifteen minutes, not ten. Eleanor ran into the parking lot to meet him as he stepped out of the black SUV. "Are you okay?"

"Hi! I'm fine. It wasn't a big collision."

Eleanor examined the front end of the truck. No broken glass. The parking lot lights reflected from the shiny paint and smooth chrome. She looked at David, who'd followed her. "I don't see a dent."

"Keep going." He walked around the SUV. "It's on this side. I hope I don't have to replace the whole door."

"The door? The back door? How did you do that?"

"I didn't do anything," David said. "I was driving along, minding my own business, and this dumb deer ran out and threw herself at my truck. Just ran right into it."

"No way. You were driving in a straight line and it ran into you from the side?" Eleanor asked, incredulous. "What happened to the deer?"

"I think she heard me calling the sheriff's office, asking them to come out and kill her, and she got up and ran away."

"Asking them to kill her?"

"She was lying in the middle of the road, but she was still alive," David said. "I didn't want to leave her suffering."

"Oh." That made sense, but it sounded horrible. She couldn't imagine having to kill an animal you'd just hit with your car. "I suppose she was just stunned." Eleanor looked at the dent. Did deer get concussions? "I hope she's okay."

"She ran off just fine once she woke up. I wouldn't have left if I thought she was really injured."

What a nice guy. Eleanor nodded toward the restaurant door. "Should we go in? It's cold out here."

He glanced at the flickering "open" sign in the window. "Do you come here often?"

"Never been here before. I found it in the yellow pages."

He raised his brows. "The yellow pages? As in, a real phone book?"

"Yep. There was a phone book on the shelf in the office, and it seemed easier than searching online." She bit her lip. "It is kind of a dive. I don't know my way around here yet."

"Well, I saw a Subway and a Dairy Queen on the way into town, but I'd rather have a hot meal. I'm sure this is fine." He opened the door. "After you."

"He showed up!" The waitress's voice was loud enough to catch the attention of everyone in the restaurant. "You folks sit wherever you want. I'll be right there."

"Sorry," Eleanor said. "Next time, we can find something in St. Cloud." Would there be a next time?

"Larry said there's a good place on 169 north of town—Rough Cut. He says it doesn't look like much from the outside, but it's got the best food in town."

"I go by there every day! I thought it was mostly just a bar and liquor store." Eleanor sipped her water. "I live a few miles north of there."

"North? You really do have a long commute."

"It's a pretty drive, though. I'll have the Milaca Burger without cheese, with the chicken dumpling soup instead of fries, please." Eleanor handed her menu to the waitress, who tossed it on the next table.

"That sounds good to me," David said, "but I'll have the cheese on mine, and fries, too."

"Soup and fries?" The waitress accepted his menu and put it with the others. "Both? Are you sure?"

"Right now, I could eat a horse."

If he'd smiled at Eleanor like that, she'd have melted into a gooey puddle. The waitress just rolled her eyes and walked away.

"I wish they'd pay waitstaff a regular wage," Eleanor said. "They could just add it into the price of the food. Then a tip would mean something instead of being an obligation."

"And the absence of a tip would mean that you got bad service, instead of meaning that you're a jerk."

"Exactly!" She beamed at him. "As the system works now, the tip reflects the quality of the customer instead of the quality of the service."

"Huh." David nodded. "You're right. I hadn't heard it put that way before. I always try to extend grace and maybe give a little more when the service is bad. I fold it up inside a tract."

A tract? She kept forgetting he was in school to be a pastor. They'd spent most of their last conversation talking about her, as he peeled away her half-truths and evasions. It was his turn.

"Have you always lived around here?"

"Yes. I grew up in Mora. It's only about an hour away, so I can go home pretty often, to see my family."

"Mora's that little Swedish town, right?" Eleanor asked. "The one with the big Dala horse?"

"That's the one."

"Are you Swedish?" He didn't have the classic icy blue eyes of the Andersons and Nielsons. His were warm. Hazel eyes, brown and green and gold. Warm, with dark brown lashes and eyebrows.

"...grandpa. I think we're mostly northern European, but not all Scandinavian."

With a start, Eleanor brought her attention back to the conversation.

"I've never thought of myself as specifically Swedish... just American. Aunt Violet is all about our heritage and family tree, but Mom and Dad aren't interested in that kind of thing. They're pretty proud of being Minnesotan, though." She stretched the third syllable, and he laughed.

"Minnesota nice?" He suggested.

"They made up that term to describe my parents," Eleanor said. "They epitomize Minnesota nice. They make Canadians look rude."

He really did have a nice smile. When his lips turned up like that, he had little parentheses curling around the corners and just a hint of a dimple in his left cheek. What on earth was he doing with the matchmaking agency? There must be something wrong with him... something she just hadn't seen yet.

"Here you go." The waitress set a large tray on the next table and began unloading it. "Two Milaca Burgers, two bowls of soup, and one order of fries. You want anything else?"

No, Eleanor wouldn't need anything else to eat for three days. The hamburger had four patties, separated by ruffly lettuce and thick slices of tomato and onion. Bacon strips protruded from the top and bottom. No toothpick would have held it together; the cook had stabbed a knife through the top bun.

"Wow. How big is this thing?" David gazed at his burger, apparently awestruck. His had cheese between each patty, too, just melted enough to ooze off the edges. He pulled out the knife and set it on his plate, not taking his eyes off the hamburger.

"A pound. It was on the menu. Didn't you read it?" The waitress picked up one of their discarded menus and flipped it open. "Four quarter pound patties. You do the math, it adds up to one pound." She snapped the menu shut. "Anything else?"

Eleanor shook her head. "I think we're good."

"Thank you," David said. "It looks great."

Oh right. He was going to be a pastor. He had to be nice. She pulled a fry from the basket and held it up. "This is the biggest french fry I have ever seen."

"There must be four whole potatoes here. You'll have to share them with me." He pushed the basket toward her."

"Are you kidding? They must super-size everything. Look at this soup!" She picked up her spoon and dipped it in the bowl—the tureen—of chicken dumpling soup. "I hope they have take-home containers."

"Would you mind if I say grace?"

Eleanor let go of her spoon, and it slid to the bottom of her bowl. So much for impressing him with good table manners. She used her fork to fish it out. "Sure. That would be nice."

She hesitated, uncertain of the protocol, but he started without ceremony. She caught up quickly—chin tucked into her chest, eyes closed, and hands clasped like a child's, on the edge of the table.

"Oh, Lord our God, how great you are."

Eleanor's eyes flew open. She hadn't expected such... volume. David looked relaxed. At least his eyes were closed, so he hadn't seen her reaction. She closed her own again, squeezing them shut, hoping he prayed fast. What was wrong with "Come, Lord Jesus"? She knew that one.

"Thank you, God, for this food, an abundant provision for us. You are so good to us. Thank you for this time Eleanor and I can spend together, getting to know each other."

What was he doing? Eleanor peeked at him. He still looked calm. Comfortable.

"We know that your hand is on this situation, Lord, and you knew that we would meet like this. It's a part of your plan, and our heart's desire is to live out that plan according to your will and glorify you. Help us to see what your will is, God. Show us what we should do and help us stay on that path. Be close to us and guide us, moment by moment, every step of the way, into the relationship you want us to have."

Why was he talking about this now, out loud, praying in front of everyone in the restaurant? She rubbed her fingers, numb from being clenched so tightly.

"Be with us this evening, God. Help us to keep the words of our mouth and the meditations of our hearts clean and acceptable in your sight, Oh

Lord, our rock and our redeemer. In the name of Jesus, we pray, Amen."

"Amen." She untangled her fingers and flexed her hands under the table. How was she supposed to respond to that?

"Here. Take my spoon." He reached across the table and set it down. "I'll get another one after I finish this amazing hamburger." He turned the plate, admiring it from every angle. "I feel like I should take a picture and post it on Instagram."

"You use Instagram?" Eleanor laughed. "Really?"

"No, but my sister and cousins do. At our family meals, they're allowed to have their phones out long enough to take pictures of the food and post them on Instagram."

"Every meal?"

"It seems like it. I don't know how it started, but now it's a bona fide Reid family tradition—at least for the girls. The guys just want to eat."

"Oh, my goodness -" Eleanor broke off. "I'm sorry, I didn't mean to interrupt you, but this soup is delicious. The dumplings are perfect, and look!" She scooped up a spoonful of soup. "It has real chicken and carrots in it. They must have made it from scratch. Get a spoon and try it."

"Not yet." David handed her a french fry. "These are great." She watched him, enjoying his happiness. Her mother would have pursed her lips and looked away as he made happy, appreciative noises as he chewed. Good manners meant ignoring other people's bad manners. Eleanor liked it.

David wiped his mouth with the paper napkin. "This burger is incredible. How's yours?"

She set down her soup spoon, carefully, and bit into the burger. Perfect. She swallowed and wiped sauce from her chin before opening her mouth to comment.

David didn't wait for her response. He waved both arms in the air. "Hey, Susan!"

The waitress's name was Susan? Eleanor remembered a name tag, but she hadn't read it.

"What do you need?" The waitress approached, surveying their table. She frowned at David. "Something wrong with your soup?"

"I took his spoon," Eleanor said. "He needs a new one. The soup is delicious. I love chicken and dumpling soup, and this is the best I've ever had. Ever."

The waitress lit up, transformed by a broad smile. "Thanks! It's my dad's recipe. I usually just chop things, but he let me make the dumplings this time. I can't wait to tell him!"

"The burger is awesome. The fries, too." David took another one. "Do you make them, too?"

She shook her head, laughing. "I'm nearly forty years old, and Dad still won't let me near the grill or fryer. People do like my pies, though. I'll get you a spoon."

Eleanor stared after her. David returned to his burger.

"That was really nice of you."

"What was?" David raised his eyebrows. "Complimenting her on the food? It's true."

"It... it made her so happy."

"It's true," he repeated. "'Pleasant words are a honeycomb, Sweet to the soul and healing to the bones.' Another version says 'Kind words are like honey—they cheer you up and make you feel strong.' "

"It did cheer her up." Bible verses and praying. She didn't really mind the praying. She just hadn't been expecting it. Otherwise, he was easy to be around. She liked him.

Eleanor set her hamburger on the plate. She wasn't here for a relationship. David was kind, open, friendly, caring enough to stay with an injured deer—and in search of a real relationship. A wife. Instead, he got a selfish woman who only wanted a temporary fix. God hadn't made their match. This wasn't His plan. It was Eleanor's plan. She was using him.

"I had a good time tonight. Thanks." David glanced at his truck. "At least, dinner was good. I'm glad we didn't go to Dairy Queen or Subway."

Eleanor held up her stack of Styrofoam boxes. "I'll be eating leftovers for a while. I can't believe you actually finished yours and ate the pie, too."

"I didn't have much choice, when she gave it to us for free, and it was excellent pie."

She couldn't see his face in the shadows, but she heard the smile in his voice.

"You know," he said, "we really should talk about this Betwixt Two Hearts business."

Yes, they should. "Would you like to have lunch together one day this week?"

"That would be great. How about tomorrow?"

She chuckled. "How about Friday? Uncle Gary has me booked solid for the next two days. I'm getting a crash course in mechanical contracting."

"We'll have a lot in common. I can imagine it, and you can make it happen! A match made in heaven."

No, it wasn't.

Fourteen

Eleanor wiped sweaty palms on her jeans and breathed deeply, trying to get air into her depleted lungs. She couldn't do anything about the drumming in her chest, but she had to remember to breathe steadily.

She scooted forward in the chair, positioned the fabric under the presser foot, and carefully lowered the foot. The fabric slid away. She caught it before it fell to the floor this time. Wordlessly, Aunt Violet handed her another pair of perfectly-aligned strips.

"Are you sure I shouldn't pin it? Just one or two pins? Even if I can get them started, I'm afraid they're going to slip apart while I'm sewing."

The older woman leaned over her. "Your left hand goes here, holding these threads." She hooked the threads and laid them across Eleanor's fingers. "Hold on to those, but don't pull too hard. You just want to get the seam started smoothly and not get the threads tangled underneath. Once it's going, you'll use your left hand to hold the strips loosely together here and your right hand to steer them through the machine."

"And I just sew the whole thing without stopping? The whole strip?" Impossible.

"When you get to the end of the first pair of strips," Violet said, "you'll start the next one without breaking your threads. I'll help you when you get there."

"Okay." Eleanor tried to position her hands, but it felt like she had too many of them—or not enough.

"Stop."

She lifted her foot from the pedal and looked at her aunt. "What did I do wrong?"

"You're getting off your quarter inch."

Eleanor looked at the fabric. She'd practiced on scrap fabric, but maintaining a straight seam allowance was harder on the real thing. "Okay," she repeated. "Should I take it out or can I just sew over it?"

"Sew over it. Start from the beginning."

Great. She'd sewn six inches and had to start over. The cutting had been bad enough, especially after Penny took her aside and said that under no circumstances should she leave Aunt Violet alone with a rotary cutter. Apparently, Violet did just fine with cutting as long as she had good lighting, wasn't tired, took frequent breaks and had someone nearby to apply tourniquets if necessary.

"Stop now."

She only had an inch left. Eleanor slumped back in the chair. "Did I mess it up?"

"You're doing fine. You need to start a new set now. Just like this." Aunt Violet set another pair of strips behind the ones she just sewn. "You're chain-piecing, one piece after another, without cutting the threads in between, so you'll end up with one long chain of them. Just keep going."

"Got it." Eleanor embarked on the second set of strips. As soon as the first was clear, Aunt Violet cut the threads between them.

Eleanor stopped. "Why did you cut them?"

"I'm going to press while you sew. If you were alone, you'd just keep going and press when you were done with that sewing step." Violet carried the strips to the ironing board and spoke over her shoulder. "Keep going."

ELEANOR: I HATE QUILTING.

Eleanor typed out the text and deleted it. Brittany wouldn't understand unless she went into detail, and it wasn't nearly as scary in the telling as it had been in the doing. Besides, Brittany was probably tired of hearing about the perils of Eleanor.

She flopped back against the stack of pillows. How could quilting be so exhausting? Maybe it wasn't, once you got used to it, or if you didn't have such an exacting teacher, but this was definitely not a relaxing hobby. She'd never finish before the anniversary party. Maybe she should have taken out a loan to buy her parents a new car.

Or perhaps she should just pray harder for a blizzard. Maybe if she could pray like David did, God would answer her prayers. He didn't, usually, or maybe she just didn't usually pray. She didn't even think about God, most of the time, so how could she go running to him when she had a problem? You couldn't just ignore people for months at a time and then start asking for favors.

"Dear God, I really don't want to go to this party alone, but I will, if you want me to." She thought about mentioning the blizzard and decided not to. "I don't want to hurt David. I don't want to lose him, either. Or rather, lose the chance to get to know him, or something like that. Mostly, I don't want to hurt him. In Jesus' name, Amen."

Nothing happened. She rolled over, burying her face in the pillows. She couldn't just rush right in and tell him she'd only joined the agency to get one date. She didn't want him to despise her.

"Well, here we are again." Eleanor smiled as she slid into the booth opposite David. "I meant to ask you. Have you heard from that matchmaking agency at all? Are we supposed to report in or anything? I didn't know if there was any kind of follow-up."

Her vivid eyes reflected the blue sky and white snow outside the window. Not denim today—she was pure Scandinavian. David brought his attention back to her question. "Not that I know of. It sounds like it's up to us to initiate contact if we have questions or want a new match or to cancel."

"A new match?" Eleanor raised her brows. "You know, this is a lot more awkward than I thought it would be. I thought meeting a stranger would be the awkward part, but this 'what now?' stage is worse. I mean, what if one of us didn't like the other person?"

"Or what if you wanted to date a few different guys before making a commitment to the first one?" asked David. "Or what if you had different objectives in signing up for the service in the first place?" If their relationship was going to end, he'd rather have it happen now than later.

"Right." She toyed with her straw. "Why did you sign up for it, David?"

That was blunt. David suddenly wished he hadn't brought it up. He'd tried to formulate this explanation, muttering under his breath as he practiced it, but there didn't seem to be any easy way to explain he didn't want to keep looking for a woman who might not show up—and then have a long courtship and engagement before getting married and having a bunch of kids.

Eleanor sat, watching his face.

"What about you?" He asked. "What made you decide to sign up?" Her gaze dropped to her hands, and he went on. "Are you looking for an exclusive relationship? A long-term relationship?" He took a deep breath and used the M word. "The goal of the agency is traditional marriage. That's what I want."

At her continued silence, he pressed. "Is that why you signed up?"

She hunched her shoulders in a shrug and then relaxed. Instead of answering, she repeated, "But why the agency? Why not a nice girl from your church or a friend of a friend?"

"You're a good volleyball player." She looked up, startled, and he continued. "You keep throwing the ball back into my court."

She smiled. "My next question was going to be about the church. How do they feel about internet dating?"

"That would be spiking the ball." David smiled back at her. "I don't know. I didn't ask. I prayed about it, though, and I think it's a fine thing to do. Some people might object to it, I guess, but it's becoming pretty mainstream. The difference with Betwixt is that it's not a dating website. It's a matchmaking service."

"But why use the agency instead of finding someone local? Waiting for

God to send the right woman?"

Eleanor's persistence and his conscience forced him into the truth. "I'm nearly thirty years old. When my parents were this age, they'd already had all their kids. Now, in their early 50's they're enjoying life without us. They should have grandchildren while they're still young enough to enjoy them."

"You're worried that your parents will be too old to enjoy your children?"

He sounded like an idiot. "No, I'm worried that I will be too old to enjoy mine."

She shook her head as if to clear it. "You... Are you saying that you think you're getting old and you want to get married and have children right away, before you get too old to enjoy them? So, they'll grow up and leave home, so you can have an empty nest and then grandchildren right away after that?"

"Um..."

"That requires the cooperation of a lot of people, David, starting with your wife and then your children and their spouses—all so you can dandle grandchildren on your still-functional knee?"

Was she outraged or laughing at him? He couldn't tell. David opened his mouth, hoping something good would come out.

"A hundred years ago, you could have sent for a mail-order bride."

Definitely laughter. He felt the heat in his face and knew he was turning red.

Eleanor sobered and reached across the table to touch his hand. "I'm sorry. I shouldn't tease you. You're doing exactly what the website offered. Exactly."

He relaxed his grip on the water glass. "That's what I said, when Larry showed me the ad: mail-order brides. He reminded me that Abraham sent his servants out to bring back a wife for his son. Not exactly the same thing, but similar." David grinned. "My mom has a bookcase full of historical romance, and I'm pretty sure there are some mail-order bride books in ,there."

"I wonder what she'd think if she knew you sent for a mail-order bride," Eleanor took a sip of her water. "Personally, I think it's a practical idea."

"Personally, you sent for a mail-order husband." David looked at her.

"Or why did you sign up?"

She set down her cup. "I wanted a date for Valentine's Day."

He waited, but she didn't continue. "And?"

Silent, she picked at her cuticles, glancing at him from under her lashes.

"A date for Valentine's Day?" David asked, incredulous. Eleanor had signed up for a matchmaking agency for just one date? "That's all? Just a date for Valentine's Day? Why?" His voice was too loud. Angry. "That's... I'm sure you could get a date for one night without having to sign up for a matchmaking agency!" He stopped and moderated his tone. "I feel like that's deceptive." He felt hurt and angry and humiliated, too. "Betwixt Two Hearts isn't an escort service."

"Yeah." The word was a sigh. "I realized that the first time we talked, at the hospital. Then, at dinner, I just... it was nice. Fun. I shouldn't have signed up." She kept her gaze on her hands. "I didn't know what else to do."

"Why?" he asked again. How could a girl like Eleanor be that desperate for a Valentine's Day date? Had he completely misjudged her?

She rubbed her eyebrows with her fingertips, covering her face. "It's in Minneapolis. An anniversary party for my parents, and they're expecting me to bring a date. I didn't want to go without a date." She lowered her hands and finally looked at him. Clouds had drifted over the sun, and her eyes were denim again, and worried. "I've already decided to go alone. I wasn't going to ask you. It was a stupid idea."

"Yeah, it was." David heard the roughness in his voice. He hadn't expected her to be looking for an instant husband, but she should have been looking for a relationship, at least, open to romance. That's what the agency was for.

She slumped. "I am sorry." Eleanor pulled her purse onto her lap and dug through it. She laid a twenty-dollar bill next to her plate, smoothing it carefully, not meeting his eyes. "I'm truly sorry, David. You're a really nice guy and I hope you find a wonderful wife."

He watched her pull on her coat as she walked out the door. He wanted to say something, but not the wrong thing, so he said nothing.

Fifteen

"Hey, Sis! How are things going up there in the frozen tundra?"

"Hi, Soren." Eleanor tapped the speaker button and handed the phone to Aunt Violet. "I'm putting you on speaker, because I'm driving. Is everyone okay there?" She couldn't remember the last time she'd talked to Soren on the phone.

"Everyone's good. Missing you. When are you coming back to civilization?"

"I'll be there for the anniversary party! I'm looking forward to it." That wasn't what he meant, of course.

"I called to let you know there's a professional development workshop coming up on Saturday, in Minnetonka. I'm not sure of all the details, but you'll be able to pick up some of the clock hours you need in mental illness, suicide prevention and positive behavioral intervention. I'll email you the link. It's sponsored by Westerfield, so you'd be able to meet some of the administration there."

Eleanor rolled her eyes. "Golly, Soren, that sounds like a lot of fun, but I don't think I'll be able to make it."

Aunt Violet snorted.

"I'll send you the link. I know you have a couple years before renewal, but it would be a good opportunity to make some connections."

"I'm going to be busy all day Saturday," Eleanor said. "Soren, we just arrived at church, so I'm going to hang up now."

"Who's with you?"

"Aunt Violet. You're on speaker phone. Say hello, Aunt Violet." Eleanor grinned, wishing they had time for a nice long discussion of family history. It would serve him right.

"Hello, Aunt Violet! How are you?"

"I'm very good, Soren. How are you?"

"Never better. I hope you ladies have a good Sunday. Eleanor, don't forget the workshop. You can sign up at the door, but it's best to register ahead of time."

"I'm not going, Soren."

"Just think about it, Ellie. Talk to you later. Bye!"

Had Aunt Violet told the pastor what to say? A spurt of outrage subsided when she remembered that her aunt didn't know about Betwixt. The whole message was obviously aimed specifically at her, though.

She wasn't arrogant—not proud, like the pastor said. She knew she didn't always do the right thing, but she tried. She was an honest person, except for little white lies like telling Soren she wasn't available on Saturday, or telling Brittany her new sweater was pretty. Or shading the truth on that matchmaking agency application, trying to game the algorithm. It had worked. She got exactly the kind of man she wanted.

But the Lord weighs the heart. Not only had it been bad because it hurt David, it was wrong because God saw her heart and knew her intentions. She was so self-centered that she hadn't considered how her actions would affect the man she was matched with...

"A person may think their own ways are right, but the Lord weighs the heart." The pastor leaned over the pulpit. "Let's say you've done something. Something kind of bad... it doesn't have to be terribly wicked. You failed to send your mother a birthday gift. On the day of her birthday, you only remember because you see it on Facebook!"

A ripple of amusement stirred the congregation. He continued. "At this point, you should probably post a birthday greeting on Facebook, preferably one of those long messages about having the best mother in the world. That's a good starting point. You can call her. You can call a florist and have flowers delivered. Probably, you're coming up with some good excuses for the lack of a present. You had to work late and couldn't get to the store. You're low on cash. You didn't know what she wanted. She always tells you not to get her anything, anyhow.

"But where was your heart? You just plain forgot, maybe because you didn't care enough to put it in your phone. Or, if you thought about it earlier in the week, it never became a priority. Maybe you were saving your money for a new television. Maybe you're mad because she did something you didn't like. God sees your heart. He weighs it. He knows the truth—and your mom probably does, too."

The pastor chuckled. "That's a pretty silly analogy, but I think you can see what I mean. A person may think their own ways are right. Those excuses you came up with? They weren't only for her. You were busy justifying your behavior. Coming up with rational reasons for your actions. But the Lord wasn't interested in your excuses. He's weighing your heart. Very few of us have pure hearts. The heart is deceitful and desperately wicked. Who can know it? God can. He knows your heart.

Eleanor gathered up her belongings as soon as the last song ended, smiling brightly at Aunt Violet. "I'm going to use the bathroom, and then I'll bring the car around front."

"No hurry, Dear. I'm going to talk to Constance for a few minutes."

How could that pastor make assumptions about her motivations? He didn't even know her. She shook her head, suddenly aware of the absurdity of her attitude. If anyone had told the pastor what to say, it must have been God. Had she thought her own way was right when she filled out that application? Yes, it made sense to her. Had her heart been pure? No. And God knew.

But it was pretty hypocritical of the pastor to say doing the right thing was more acceptable than sacrifice just before he passed the offering plate.

"How are you ladies doing?"

Uncle Carl reminded her of his brother—cheerful, energetic, and kind. Eleanor wished she'd known them better, earlier in life. She liked it here.

"We're good," Violet said. "I was just telling Constance that we're not going to the nursing home today. Olof's getting a lot of company today, and I didn't sleep well last night. I'm going to treat myself to a Sunday afternoon nap."

"Good idea." Carl turned to his wife. "Can I do that?"

"Certainly, right after we get home from seeing Uncle Olof."

Carl turned to Eleanor. "Gary tells me you're keeping the business afloat while he's in there."

"I'm trying. He's very patient with me."

"He says you're doing great." He clapped her on the shoulder and looked at his wife. "Every time I go there, he complains about Cheryl. He says she's abusing him."

Constance chuckled. "Physical therapy is hard work. I'm glad she's back. We should have her over for dinner one night soon."

"Larry!" David hurried across the parking lot. "Are you going to be at the Y for basketball this afternoon?"

"I wasn't planning on it. Did you need me?"

"I'd be grateful if you'd come." David said. "There's a boy there... I'm a little worried about him, and I don't have time to talk to him while I'm coaching. I was hoping you could come by and chat with him."

Larry shook his head. "I should just set up one of those booths like Lucy had in the Peanuts cartoons. 'Psychiatric help. Five cents.'"

"I've got five cents." David made a show of digging in his pockets. "Maybe even a dollar. Most of those guys could use a listening ear. I thought the basketball would be a good outreach, and I'd be able to help the kids, maybe draw them in to some of the youth activities at church, but now I'm running the program and don't even have time to talk to the boys."

Larry looked at his watch. "How could I resist that appeal? Sure, I'll be there. But if you want to help them, get yourself some volunteers to help with the coaching, so you can have more one-on-one time with the kids."

"Thanks, Larry." David hesitated. "You know, I haven't seen Angela at work in the last few days. Do you know if she's okay? I thought I'd ask you before asking Cal."

"You should ask Cal."

That was interesting. David nodded. It might mean that Angela had become a client, or Angela might be in trouble, or maybe Larry just didn't want to gossip. Maybe he just didn't know. David hoped she was okay.

Sixteen

"Encore, encore!"

Eleanor grinned. It was a sing-along, not a performance. They just wanted to keep singing. She looked at Gary. "Do we do encores?"

"It's up to you, kiddo."

She leafed through her songbook. "How about 'Michael, Row Your Boat Ashore' and then 'Take Me Out to the Ballgame'? I know those pretty well."

"Sounds good. We'll get everyone good and riled up before lunch."

Uncle Gary didn't believe in paperless offices. Right now, his office was a tiny bedroom in a nursing home — a rehabilitation center. In addition to his tablet and laptop, he had a printer/fax machine, a portable scanner, and a wastebasket. A dry erase board leaned against the window, and a small file cabinet had replaced the original bedside table.

"Did you bring me that phone book?"

Eleanor pulled it from her bag. "I did, and the portfolio, too."

"Thanks. Set the phone book over there by the catalogs and bring me the portfolio."

"You know, Uncle Gary, you never used half this stuff when you were in the office." She picked up a pad of sticky notes. "I've never seen you use a sticky note. I don't know why you wanted a calculator, either; you always use the one on your phone or computer."

He peered over his glasses at her. "You young people are so disrespectful. I might need it, and I can't be calling you in the middle of the night to bring me a sticky note."

"In case you need a sticky note in the middle of the night?"

"Be prepared." He closed the portfolio and held it on his lap. "Would you be willing to take this out to a job site for me? The guy's only going to be in town on Friday, and I want him to see these projects I've been doing with Ridgewell. You met David Reid in the hospital."

"He came to help us when you had your accident, remember? I've met him a few times, now."

"Really! He seems like a good guy. So, the man at the job site is John Frans. I'll give him a call to tell him you're coming."

Ten minutes later, Eleanor hitched her computer bag over her shoulder and accepted the portfolio from her uncle. "Do I need a hard hat at the job site?"

"Yes, you do. I've got a few of them around. Maybe we should just order you one of your own."

She'd like a hard hat of her own. Pink would be silly; maybe a light blue.

Gary spoke as she stopped in the doorway. "You're doing a great job here, Ellie. If you're still here by summer and want to stick it out, I've got a permanent place for you. It's like this—mostly take-offs in the winter and office work in the summer, but if we start getting more of the Ridgewell projects, or things like that, we'll be working with new materials and suppliers. More crew. It would pay a little more than what you're getting now." He grinned. "Nothing like you'd make as a teacher, and the benefits aren't that good, but think about it. I'd be glad to have you.

Eleanor hummed as she rounded the corner of the house and let herself into the annex, pretending she was the 10-year-old Kathy, returning to this big crowded house after school every day. Instead of Aunt Violet, Grandma would have been here, ready to greet her children with cookies and milk.

Actually, Grandma was probably busy sewing when they got home, just like Aunt Violet was doing now. Eleanor found her in the quilting room, removing Karl's quilt from the frame.

"Is it all done?"

Violet nodded without speaking. She folded the quilt and carried it across the hall to the sewing room. Eleanor hesitated. Did Violet want to be left alone, or did she want company. It would be better to have company when you wanted to be alone—after all, you could send people away— than to be alone when you wanted to have someone there with you.

Her phone rang. Eleanor sighed. Having reached such a philosophical conclusion, she couldn't send her mother to voice mail.

"Hello, Mom!"

"Hi, there. How are you? I haven't talked to you in a while."

"Oh, busy. Gary's still laid up. He's supposed to be there for at least another four weeks, so we're running everything from two locations. I'm glad he's able to do his rehab in Milaca instead of St. Cloud." Eleanor poured herself a glass of water and sniffed at the beef stew Aunt Violet had made for dinner. "The nursing home is between here and the office."

"That's nice," Kathy said. "I was calling to let you know that Westerfield is hosting a Professional Development workshop. It's on Saturday, and it looks good. I thought we could go together."

"Soren told me about that. I'm not planning on going, Mom."

"You're going to need the clock hours for re-licensure. This would be a good place to get some of them."

Eleanor sat and propped her elbows on the table. "Mom, I still have two years on my license. If I decide to renew it, I have plenty of time to get the credits I need."

"You don't want to wait until the last minute," her mother warned her. "Look it up online. I'll send you the link."

"Are you sure we're going to finish this in time?" Eleanor rose and stretched. It should have been a comfortable chair, but she sat with every muscle tensed, hunched ten inches from the sewing machine, not blinking as she sewed. "We haven't finished a single block yet, and we only have three weeks left. I wish I had more time to work on it." At the nursing home, Gary made lists and scheduled her day, and she was still busy at the office, keeping track of everything. One of his crew had quit, and the staff at the nursing home had flatly refused to let him do job interviews in their conference room.

Here at home, she worked on the quilt under the gimlet eye of Aunt Violet and tried not to think about her wretched treatment of David.

"We'll finish it on Saturday," Violet said, "so you'll be busy all day Saturday. Hand me those scissors, will you please?"

Busy all day Saturday. Eleanor handed the scissors to her aunt. Violet didn't meet her eyes.

"This old rayon doesn't hold up very well. The armholes are already frayed." Violet laid the pink dress across the cutting table.

Was she really going to cut that up? Eleanor started to object and then fell silent. If Marlys didn't want it, who would?

"That was Molly's wedding dress?"

"Yes." Violet's terse response didn't invite further comment. "You need to press those outward now."

Eleanor complied, watching her aunt while she waited for the iron to get hot. It would be natural for an elderly, unmarried woman to care about her extended family. Her nieces and nephews were the closest thing she had to children of her own. She'd even lived with them from the time they were born.

"Marlys sent all sorts of things in that box," Violet said. "Some of it must have come from her mother's family. I think she was just downsizing and unloaded it all on me."

She was probably the only one who would take it. Eleanor walked over to the table. The limp fabric didn't look like a wedding dress. If she hadn't seen the photograph, she wouldn't have been able to imagine it as a dress at all.

"She must have been tiny."

Violet nodded. "She was, but she was a spitfire. She could hold her own with Axel. I always felt sorry for her students."

"She was a teacher?"

"For nearly fifty years," Violet said, "until they sold the feed mill and moved to Florida."

"Three years was enough for me. Was she a mentor for my mother, too, like Maybel Furster?"

"Oh, no. Molly wasn't a mentor to anyone, and she was especially strict with your mom and the others. Maria tried to get them reassigned, but there was only one classroom for each grade level. Of course, it was probably hard on Molly, to have her twelve-year-old nephews in her classroom, too." A fond smile curved Violet's lips. "Those boys were mischievous."

"Gary and Carl? I bet they were."

"And Scott," Violet said. "Colleen could be a handful, too, but your mom was always well-behaved. Is that your phone?"

"It's Laurie. She can leave a message."

Aunt Violet raised her brows. "You can take a break to talk to her, if you want to."

"I don't. I know exactly what she's calling for. The same thing Mom and Soren called about—a continuing education workshop there in the cities. I'm not going."

"I see. The iron should be hot now."

Eleanor obediently returned to the ironing board. "What else was in the box? Did you get the pictures?"

"Yes, but I had most of them already. There were some letters and a notebook that belonged to Kristina, but I set those aside for now. Then she sent some other things that couldn't have belonged to us: a packet of postcards, a little wooden box with cigarettes in it, a pocket watch and a locket with an old picture of a man and woman. No one I know. There were some other things, too, that might have been Axel's after he moved to Florida."

"But you don't think the postcards and cigarettes were? And the pocket watch?" Eleanor used the side of the iron to push open the triangles. The pink and gray fabrics were perfect for her mother.

"No. They look older—from the 40's, maybe, and I think the inscription on the pocket watch is German. The postcards have churches and towns that look German, too."

"Maybe they're souvenirs of the war," Eleanor said. "Soldiers brought home all sorts of stuff after both world wars, didn't they?"

"Not our soldiers."

Eleanor shut her eyes. That was probably the single most insensitive comment she'd made in her entire life.

Violet went on before she could think of a way to apologize. "Axel was very prejudiced against Germans. He would have burned these things, not saved them." She sighed. "The war was hard on Axel. He was just 13 when Hans and Karl died. His big brothers. All his life, he wouldn't even be polite if he thought someone might be German. He wouldn't shake their hand or wait on them at the feed mill. No, these things belonged to someone else."

Eleanor tipped the hard hat onto her head, wishing she'd tried it on before she left the office. It still didn't fit. No matter how she adjusted the straps, it still perched on top of her head, making her feel like one of those bobblehead dolls her brother had on a shelf in his library. With a scowl at her reflection in the rear-view mirror, she jammed the hard hat down as far as it would go and opened the car door.

She'd had trouble deciding what to wear, but jeans and plaid flannel seemed a safe choice. Eleanor looked at her feet doubtfully, hoping tennis shoes were adequate. She didn't own any steel-toe boots. She wasn't staying long, but as a representative of Evergreen Services, she wanted to make a good impression on Mr. Frans.

"Hey, lady. You can't park there."

Why not? There weren't any signs, and the small lot already held half a dozen trucks. He should have been clued in by the hard hat; she was there on official business. "I'm looking for John Frans."

The man shook his head. "No one here by that name. This is private property."

"I'm looking for a job site next to the old schoolhouse." Eleanor looked at the assortment of construction equipment. Now what?

"Is that the one you're looking for?"

She followed his pointing finger. Four men, two of them in suits, and one lone backhoe. The ground wasn't even broken yet. Suits.

Oh, God, please, no. She'd been sending up more of these silent prayers lately, usually in the office, when she was stressed. She hadn't felt any response, but at least she hadn't had a full-blown anxiety attack.

And she wasn't going to have one now. "I'll only be here about ten minutes. Can I leave my car that long?"

"The boss'll be back from lunch in half an hour. He'll want to park there."

"I'll be gone by then. Thank you."

Clutching the portfolio, she walked across the frozen ground with her most confident stride. One of the men raised a hand in greeting, and as she responded, she realized she still wore the yellow hard hat. She sent another panicked prayer heavenward. It was becoming a habit.

She pasted a bright smile on her face as she neared them, but it dimmed when she recognized the man on the end. David's smile looked a little forced, too. She'd never seen him in a suit before. He looked amazing, and she looked like a slob. A slob in a hard hat and tennis shoes. She smiled harder.

"You must be Eleanor. Gary told us you'd be coming. I'm John Frans, and these are my partners, Jake and Luke Brown." The tallest man reached out to shake her hand. "David was telling us you've worked with Ridgewell before."

Eleanor nodded. The hard hat slipped over her eyes. She pushed it back, and it tumbled to the ground behind her. She was putting on a comedy act, not impressing them with her professionalism.

David retrieved the hard hat and turned it over, examining the interior. Maybe he'd fix it for her. She handed the portfolio to John and gestured toward the larger construction site. "Gary said the job site was next to the old schoolhouse. I thought it was that one. Are you just getting started here?"

"Just checking out Ridgewell's proposal so far. We got sidetracked by the POW camp." He gestured toward the row of cabins at the wood line. "I never knew this was out here."

"I never knew we had POW camps in Minnesota," one of the other men said.

"Fifteen of them," Eleanor said. She'd taught her middle-school students about it, for three years in a row. She found it fascinating; they just wanted to know if the prisoners were tortured. "They came as agricultural workers, because the men were gone to war."

"Slave labor camps!" The comment came from the third man. "Were they tortured?"

"Didn't the locals object to having the enemy there?"

"No, not tortured. They were treated in strict accordance with the Geneva Convention, which meant that they had better housing and food than many of the local people did, during the war. People did object to that." She needed to leave before the sight of her car being towed away put a cap on her less-than-stellar performance. "You can look it up online. It's very interesting. It was nice meeting you."

She shook hands with each of the men, ending with David, who returned her hard hat. She wasn't prepared for the warm smile that accompanied it, or the sympathy in his hazel eyes. If he was going to be a pastor, though, he'd have to forgive people, right? And feel sorry for them when they made fools of themselves.

Worry replaced depressing thoughts of David as she drove into the office parking lot. Some of the crew, even more dirty than usual, lounged outside the office, smoking or talking on their phones. The crew supervisor, Tim, stood with his back to her. She closed her eyes and sent up another prayer. Soon, she'd have to make time to say more than "help me" when she talked to God.

She gathered her tote bag and Gary's books, plonked the hard hat on her head, and pushed the car door open with her foot. The hat fit.

"Ellie." Tim came toward her, followed by several of his men.

She gasped. "What happened?" The odor made her eyes water. Resisting the temptation to close the door and roll up the window, she stepped out of the car and surveyed them. They looked like they'd climbed through a fireplace, with ashes and soot, and then rolled in... a bean bag chair. "Is that insulation? Blown-in insulation?"

"That's the least of it." Tim brushed at the tiny white balls on his jacket. "We were just setting up to take out the old ductwork over on Harris Street, and half the ceiling came down on us."

"Is anyone hurt?"

"Nah, it just crumbled away. Apparently, there's been bats living in there for a long time."

"Oh." She couldn't help it. She took a step backward. "You're all covered with bat... er, guano."

"Yeah, bat guano." One of the men snorted and then coughed.

"Histoplasmosis."

Eleanor turned to the speaker. He held up his phone. "I googled it. It's a lung disease you get from inhaling bat... guano."

She groaned. "Okay, you'd better all go over to Occupational Health and get checked out. Let me grab the paperwork. Umm... how about if you guys wait out here. I'll be right back."

Tim gave a bark of laughter. "Hurry. By the way, you have company."

Eleanor stopped at the sight of her visitor, a fatalistic sort of acceptance rendering her speechless.

"She's says she's your sister-in-law."

"I can get you a job." Laurie stood in the middle of the entryway while Eleanor printed out copies of accident reports and claims forms. "A real job."

"I have a job, Laurie, and I need to do it right now. All those men are waiting for me. Then I need to call Uncle Gary and see if I need to call our lawyer."

"But, Eleanor, this isn't what you went to school for. I know you wanted a break, but this..." Laurie swept out her arms, encompassing the noisome men as well as the utilitarian office. "Wouldn't you rather have a job in my office, or as a substitute somewhere?"

"No, Laurie." She didn't have time for this. Of all the rotten timing... Eleanor straightened and stared at her sister-in-law. "I am not going to your workshop tomorrow, Laurie."

The other woman stiffened. "It's such a good opportunity for you, Eleanor. Tomorrow's Saturday, so you won't miss any work here."

"I'm busy all day tomorrow." Eleanor couldn't help smiling at the words. She set the stapler on the desk. "Can you take a paper from each stack, in that order, and staple them together, please?"

Laurie complied, continuing her appeal. "You know, you could probably get a job up here, if you just want to get out of the cities."

"I have a job up here." It was an improvement over the usual insistence that she live near the rest of them. Eleanor tried to soften her voice. "I like my job, Laurie. I really do. I know you don't understand that, but it's true. It's not always like this. Most of the time, it's just interesting work, building things. When it's not so busy, maybe I can show you what we do."

"No! I don't want to see what you do!" Laurie stomped her foot like a child. "I want you to come to your senses and come home where you belong! And can you please take off that stupid hat?"

Seventeen

"Make sure you get some of my mom's chicken hotdish," Sarah said. "Everyone loves it. She always makes three pans full, and there's never any leftovers."

"Thanks for the tip." Eleanor smiled at her young cousin. "Anything else I should know?"

The little girl beckoned her downward and whispered. "Mrs. Jessin makes cookies with whole wheat flour and doesn't add sugar to them."

"Good to know. Thank you."

"They're pretty bad," Sarah said seriously. "They're nutritious, though."

"Well, I'm not eating them." Eleanor shuddered dramatically. "What kind of cookies are made with whole wheat flour and no sugar?"

"We call that whole wheat bread," Jeffrey said, "but it's worse because it's masquerading as a cookie."

Eleanor turned to smile up at him and nearly dropped her plate. "What happened to you?"

"Sarah beat me up."

His sister heaved an exasperated sigh. "Will you stop telling people that? It's embarrassing."

Jeffrey shook his head. "Not for me. It's a lot less embarrassing to be beat up by your eight-year-old sister than to tell people what really happened." He touched the strip of tape over his nose. "With that gash in my forehead, I might have a scar like Harry Potter. At least only one of my eyes is swollen. I can still see out of the other one."

"It's very colorful," Eleanor said. "What did really happen? Will you tell me, if I promise to keep it a secret?"

"Yeah, it's not really a secret. I just like to tease Sarah." He looked over the fellowship hall and pointed. "There's Penny over there. Come on, Sarah. You know mom won't let you eat all three of those brownies. You'd better give me one."

She loved this place. The whole church treated her as if she belonged there. She'd never lived there, but they treated her as if she'd come home. Maybe she had.

"Hi, Eleanor!" Penny stood to give her a hug. "We live in the same house, and I never see you. We'll have to make an appointment to get together soon."

"Yes, let's do that, this week," Eleanor said. She sat next to Sarah and looked at Jeffrey. "Okay, I'm ready."

"It's really Penny's fault. She wanted Mom to go to some Bridal thing in the cities, so I had to milk the goat and take care of the chickens. And you know how that goes. That little Rhode Island Red took off." Jeffrey shook his head in disgust. "How can something with six-inch-long legs outrun a human being? I almost had her, in the yard, because the snow slowed her down, but she made it to the driveway and went crazy, running back and forth. I started thinking of 'why did the chicken cross the road' jokes, and was laughing so hard I didn't see Rocky coming."

"That's the red rooster," Sarah informed Eleanor. "He's mean."

"I grabbed that big coaster sled and was using it like a shield, to keep him back," Jeffrey continued.

"What were you using for a sword?" Penny asked.

Jeffrey grinned. "A snowshoe. I didn't want to hurt him—much. Anyhow, he kept coming on, and I was backing up—"

"Getting closer to the hill?" Penny asked innocently. She was already giggling. "You slid down the hill, didn't you?"

"Don't ruin my story. It's marginally less humiliating if I made a dramatic telling of it." Jeffrey made a face at his sister. "So, I was busy fighting the rooster, and out of the corner of my eye, I see the hen coming at me from the other side, right under my feet. I kind of twisted around, trying to avoid her and Rocky, and I fell on the sled, sort of sideways." He wiggled in his chair to demonstrate. "I swear... Rocky pushed me down the hill. I didn't get far before I rolled over and whapped myself in the face with the edge of the snowshoe." He held the side of his hand to his face. "A straight line down the middle of my face."

"You hit yourself in the face with a snowshoe?" Sarah sounded disgusted. Then she laughed. Eleanor couldn't help laughing with her.

Jeffrey looked resigned. "Well, it's all true."

Eleanor reached across the table and patted his hand. "Corroborative detail, intended to give artistic verisimilitude to an otherwise bald and unconvincing narrative."

They all stared at her.

"Say that again?" Jeffrey asked.

She repeated it. "It's from 'The Mikado.' Gilbert and Sullivan."

"Corroborative detail, to give artistic verisimilitude to an otherwise bald..." Jeffrey broke off.

Eleanor said it again, and he practiced it until he could quote it smoothly. She laughed at his pleasure in the quotation. "You homeschoolers do know how to have a good time."

"It's a great quote," Jeffrey said. "I'm going to use it. You're a good teacher, Eleanor."

"I found you a coach," Larry said. "A police officer who played basketball in high school and college. He's committed to every Sunday afternoon through the end of the school year. So, you'll be able to be more of an assistant and work with the boys."

David slid into the booth. "That's great! When can he start?"

"He's going to come and just hang out today, but if everybody's happy, he can start officially next weekend." He lifted his coffee cup in salute. "I'm paying him."

"Paying him? It's supposed to be a ministry!"

Larry propped his elbow on the table and rested his chin on his hand. "David, this is your ministry, but it got too big, and now you don't have a ministry. You have a nice secular program. You just organize and supervise."

"But you can't go on paying him indefinitely, and I don't know how much I can contribute, if I -" David broke off. If he became a pastor. Not when. A check in the spirit or spiritual warfare? The more he thought and prayed and read, the more conflicted he became.

Larry waited patiently, drinking his coffee and looking out the window.

"Do you think I'm wrong? About being a pastor?" David hadn't meant to ask him, but what was the point of having a Christian psychologist for a best friend if you couldn't get free advice? He tried to think of something funny to say about that, but he couldn't. "I just don't know anymore."

"Have you tried making a list with pros and cons?"

David paused. "That's your best psychiatric advice and spiritual counsel? Make a list?"

"I'll try to come up with something profound if the list fails." Larry set down his cup. "I see you wanting to serve God in an active kind of capacity. You like the one-on-one of working with the boys at basketball. You get pretty pumped up about the Jesus People kind of ministry." He held up a hand. "I am not telling you to run away and become a hippie. Please don't. And I'm not saying you shouldn't become a pastor. I'm just saying— because I know you're already praying about it—make a list or two, with pros and cons, about what you would do as a pastor, or in some other kind of ministry, or even doing what you do now with worship music and activities for the kids. Look at it analytically. You're an engineer." He grinned. "That'll be five cents, please."

Cal leaned over David's chair and peered at the computer screen. "How's that going? Did you find a way to make it lighter?"

"Maybe. I tried this." David clicked to a different window. "And it works, but I don't like the aesthetics. It's not quite right. But we can use it if I don't come up with something else."

"Take your time. We're not out for the quick buck." Cal put a hand on his shoulder. "You do good work, and even though you don't like them, you're my best guy for presentations. I think you got Frans Brown hooked."

"Excellent!" David grinned. "It's not so much doing the presentation as wearing the suit and tie. Why do we have to do that?"

"No idea, but it is what it is. I like it better when you wear the suit. You're better with people, anyhow. So, I fully expect to be signing a contract next week, and I'd like you to come along." He scowled. "Angela quit."

"Quit! I didn't know that." David leaned back in his chair, watching his boss. Cal looked like a sulking baby. I don't know what I'm supposed to do now. She says she'll come back this summer for a while, to train someone new, but I don't know how to find someone to replace her. I don't even know what she does."

"Maybe you could get her to write up a job description and help with the hiring," David suggested. "Or ask Andrea." Andrea was the office manager, wasn't she? Or maybe she was the administrative assistant.

Cal pulled over a chair and sat down. "Andrea does different stuff. You know what Angela was?"

David shook his head. "No," he said truthfully. He hadn't even realized she was an employee until Larry told him.

"Angela was the CEO."

Wow. That was a shocker. "I thought you were the CEO."

Cal lifted up his glasses and rubbed the bridge of his nose. "I am. I mean, that's my title, but you know I'm not CEO material. I just want to be an engineer. I nearly ran us into the ground. When Angela graduated from college, Mom insisted I give her a job. I didn't think I'd have anything for her to do. I didn't even know if I could keep the business afloat." He gave a reminiscent grin. "A month after she got here, she had all the books in order. Six months after that, she was running the place and we were making a profit. She's a genius.'

"But she quit." David hoped that didn't mean his job was in jeopardy. "What's she doing now?"

"Larry took her away, and he won't tell me or Meg where she is." He leaned back and crossed his arms over his chest. "I think she's in some kind of a sanitarium or something. Like I said, she'll come back here in the summer, but then she's going back to college. She wants to be a doctor. Not an ordinary doctor, like you go to when you're sick. She wants to do something with 'bacterial research'." He said the last two words in a sneer. "She already had a useful degree."

David looked at Cal. A genius with no people skills and little concern for the health of his sister. He'd skimmed right over the sanitarium and on to his own grievance. David hoped Angela found work that would fulfill her—and work for which she'd be recognized.

"If we weren't all Christians," Penny said, "I'd say Aunt Violet's part witch. She's got this uncanny ability to read people and tell the future. You know those quilts she makes?"

Eleanor nodded. "Yes, they're all over the house."

"She made a block for me, of course. You know what was on it? Clothes from Brian's childhood. All those years ago, she'd decided that I'd eventually marry him."

"You're kidding!" Eleanor sat up straight.

"I'd show you, but she still has it." Penny laughed. "She's probably adding my children as we speak. I wonder if I'm having boys or girls."

"Hmm... I wonder if she's started mine yet. I'd like to know the future." Would she? Yes, Eleanor decided. She would.

"I've been wondering... do you think she's doing okay? Mentally, I mean?" Penny twisted the cap of her water bottle. "It might be my imagination, but she seems quieter lately."

"I don't know what she was like before I came here," Eleanor said. "She's really sharp with things that matter to her—the genealogy, quilting, and things like that. She knows what she wants to do for a garden this year."

"Maybe she's hoping to dig up more family treasure. Last year, she found—or rather, Brian found—an old Swedish bridal crown that her father made for her mother before they were married." Penny smiled. "And a love letter to go with it. Brian read it to me when he proposed."

"I saw a picture of it," Eleanor said, "and a copy of the letter. It's so romantic, and sad, too, knowing that she died in childbirth."

"They did have some time together. They were friends for ten years before they got married, and they were married for nearly twenty years. That's pretty good by today's standards."

"True." Eleanor snuggled back into the corner of the couch, tucking her stockinged feet underneath her. "Why do you think Aunt Violet never married? Kristina never did, either, but she sounds awful."

"I don't know," Penny said. "Violet worked for the phone company, you know, as an operator. Maybe she just never met the right man."

"Their lives don't seem to have been very happy. Linnea escaped at the first opportunity. I think if I'd been Violet, I wouldn't have been too fussy about finding Mr. Right."

"Aunt Violet? Are you in here?"

"Hello, dear."

Eleanor turned on the light, and her aunt blinked. "Sorry, I didn't mean to blind you. She turned on a table lamp and flicked off the light switch. "I forget how bright that one is."

"Brian put daylight LED bulbs in everything. Penny and I have been quietly replacing them with soft whites, but I keep forgetting to do that one."

"Are you okay, sitting here in the dark?" Eleanor dropped onto one of the old-fashioned wing chairs.

"Praying. Thinking about the past, praying about the future. Trying to give it all to God to worry about instead of taking it on myself." Violet smiled. "And praying for you. We really haven't talked about God much, have we? You come to church and sound like a believer, but I don't know much about your faith."

"Yes, I'm a believer." Eleanor said the word again. "Believer." It sounded like belonging. She believed in Jesus, belonged to Him.

"So, did you grow up in a Christian home?"

"We went to church most weekends, when I was little, but we got busy with sports and things later," Eleanor explained. She hated making her parents sound bad—and Aunt Violet would think poorly of her parents for skipping church in favor of sports—but she needed to be honest. "And I went to youth group for a while in junior high. I did confirmation."

"But were you saved?" Violet pressed. "I don't know the terminology people use today. Were you born again? Converted?"

Eleanor furrowed her brow. "Well, yes, but… you mean, was there one time that I did all of that at once and understood it? I sort of knew it, growing up, and then we went over it all again in confirmation classes. We had to say if we believed it or not, and then we could join the church."

"Did you—do you believe it?"

"Yes, I do. I think I understand what you're talking about. There was a little girl in one of my classes who told me she invited Jesus into her heart. I asked a friend about it, because I was afraid it might be something weird." That memory reminded her of meeting David at the coffee shop.

"Yes. Did you have a time like that?" Violet asked.

Eleanor shook her head slowly. "I don't think I had any one magical epiphany moment. Was I supposed to? It just kind of clarified over time, over the last few months. I knew all the basic facts, and it's like things just clicked into place a bit at a time. I started understanding sin more—if you know what I mean. Not like the little girl who was seeing sin as being naughty or telling a lie. So, then I could see the holiness of God. Salvation wasn't a light thing—not a quick, cheap forgiveness."

"The gift of grace is very precious," said Violet. "His blood, poured out for us."

"Right. And then when we were at church, and later, when I did some reading on my own, I just kept seeing the bigger picture. And I realized I'll never see the whole picture until I'm in Heaven." She smiled at her aunt. "Until I go Home."

"Glory, glory." Violet's words were just a whisper.

Eleanor continued. "I knew the words since I was little—saved by grace through faith, the grace of God that brings salvation, if we confess our sins, he forgives—even though I hadn't thought about them in a long time." She tapped her chest. "They were still 'in there.'" She tipped her head to one side, considering. "It's almost like they were big words. I knew what they meant all along, but as I got older—mostly in the last few months—my vocabulary and comprehension skills increased, and they started to make more sense."

"And the better you understand God's word, the more you know Him and love Him. You can't have a close relationship with someone you don't know."

"Very true." Eleanor stood up. "So that's where I stand, Aunt Violet. I'm reading and praying and listening at church. The Holy Spirit keeps pretty busy, convicting me of something new every time I turn around, but it's all good. God's good." She dropped to her knees by the old woman's chair and hugged her.

"Glory, glory." Aunt Violet's words made Eleanor think of the quilts. She'd ask her about that later.

David knew how to pray. He did it all the time. He was doing it now. Larry was right… why did he need a class in prayer? David worked his way through the test. The definitions were all so similar, each with just a small difference in nuance. But those differences mattered.

He wondered what Eleanor was doing. She'd been… adorable at the job site last Friday. She'd been trying to be professional, of course, and she really was. But with the hard hat sliding all over her head, she did look a bit like a bobble head doll. A beautiful bobble head doll.

Outside the testing room, the reference librarian stamped books with vigor, branding them for return if they tried to escape. A little girl skipped back and forth between the rows of books. When she stopped and made a face at him through the window, he made one back. She ran away.

He had to focus. This final exam, unlike most of the tests for his online classes, required paper and pencil, a proctor and a ticking clock. He bent over the test, completing and reviewing the answers until the librarian tapped on the door. "You have five minutes left."

"I'm done." David stood up and handed her the sheaf of papers. "Thank you."

"You're welcome." She led the way to the reference desk. "I'll just sign off on this and seal up the envelope for you. You have the postage ready? There you go! It will go out with the morning mail." She beamed at him.

"Mostly, we get homeschoolers in here. College students usually use the university library."

"My classes are online, through a school in Virginia," David said. "And I'm almost done."

"Well, I hope this goes well for you." She held up the envelope.

"Thanks." He cracked open one of the glass doors to inhale fresh air. The black sky and bright stars promised a cold night outside the overheated library. Slipping on his coat, he turned back to nod goodbye to the librarian. She stood outside the other testing room in conversation with a young blond woman. Eleanor.

He pulled on one of his gloves. He should leave before she saw him, avoiding embarrassment for both of them. He should do it quickly. Just walk out the door.

He stepped toward Eleanor.

"David." She held out her hand, not surprised to see him. She'd probably seen him through the glass of the testing room earlier. "Nice to see you. Do you come here often?" She laughed at the cliché pickup line. "Let me rephrase that. Do you use this library frequently?"

"No, hardly ever. What are you doing out here?" It felt good to talk with her again. "What's a nice girl like you doing in a place like this?"

She tipped her head toward the testing room. "My cousin Jeffrey has a test. He does some online courses, and he didn't get to the Milaca library before they closed. We raced out here." She glanced at her phone. "He's barely got enough time to finish it here."

"Ah. One of the homeschoolers the librarian mentioned. He takes college classes online while he's finishing high school?"

She nodded. "It's a smart plan. I wish I'd done that."

"I'm surprised you didn't, coming from a family of educators."

"I took a lot of AP and Honors classes instead, another year of Spanish and some music electives. All very useful."

He raised his brows. "Do I hear sarcasm? What would you have liked to take, other than early college credits?"

"Auto repair, for one thing. My car is making a squealing noise. Uncle Gary said I can use his, but I'd rather not. I need to ask Uncle Carl or Jeffrey." She scowled. It was a cute scowl. "Everyone should take a class in auto repair."

"I agree. Would you like me to take a look at it?" He hadn't meant to say that, but it was too late to take it back. "I'm a mechanical engineer. Mechanical, mechanic, auto mechanic? Engineer, engine? I'm not making any promises, but I could take a look."

Her eyes had a faint wash of green over the blue tonight, probably from the fluorescent lights. "No. I can't ask that of you. David, I am so, so sorry. I was wrong, and you were all right. I wish... I wish I hadn't done that."

"Please let me." David moderated his eager tone and responded to the apology. "No hard feelings. I can at least take a look, to see if it's safe to drive. Is it in the parking lot now?"

She shook her head. "No, we took Jeffrey's. He can drive at night with a licensed adult driver. I feel old."

It was just as well. In the cold, dark night, with only the few tools he kept in the truck, he wouldn't be able to see or do much.

"I could take it to work tomorrow, but I won't get there until nearly one o'clock." She smiled. A warm smile, not the dazzling one or the mischievous one. "On Tuesday mornings, I play the piano for the Golden Oldies sing-along at the nursing home where Uncle Gary and my Uncle Olof are."

"I bet that's fun!"

"It really is. I only agreed to do it because Uncle Gary's shoulder was broken, but I love it. He still leads the singing."

Maybe he should go visit his good friend, Gary, in the nursing home tomorrow. "I didn't realize he was still there."

"I think they have to chain him to the bed at night, so he doesn't escape. He's ready to leave, as soon as they release him."

"I'll come out at one o'clock tomorrow and take a look at it." David sat down, compelling her to do the same, not above taking advantage of her good manners. "Look, Eleanor. There's no reason we can't be friends. Not every relationship has to end in traditional marriage. Not all relationships should." He wished this one had been going that direction, though.

"I was at fault, David. It was selfish of me. I'm sorry." She pushed a strand of hair back from her face. "I'm upset with myself and embarrassed about the whole thing."

"Well, it's over. We can have a good laugh about it someday. Maybe not this week, or this month…"

"Or this year," Eleanor interrupted. "Thank you. I appreciate your willingness to let bygones be bygones. I didn't mean to -"

It was his turn to interrupt. "Let's just drop it. Let's pretend we met at the coffeehouse that day Larry broke your mouse."

A genuine smile lit her face. "Okay. I got a much nicer mouse with the money he gave me."

"Good. You should have kept all of it. Larry can afford it. He makes about three times what I do, and he's always looking for opportunities to do good."

"I'll keep that in mind," she said.

She was smiling. He should leave while the going was good. "I'll be there at one tomorrow."

"I'll pack a lunch for both of us. Do you like peanut butter?"

"Of course I like peanut butter. I was a poor starving college student for five years. I did get enough of ramen noodles, though, so don't bring those."

"I ate in the cafeteria," Eleanor said, "so I didn't have those. I was going to stock up on them in case I stayed at the cabin, but now that I live with Aunt Violet, I've been eating pretty well. I just like peanut butter sandwiches, so that's what I normally bring for lunch."

"Works for me. See you then."

Eleanor watched David leave the library, hastily, as if afraid she'd change her mind. He'd been gracious about the matchmaking business. Had he told the people at Betwixt Two Hearts about her deception and requested another match? She hoped he'd find one. He would make a good husband.

"Who was that?"

"A friend." Eleanor waited while the librarian sealed up Jeffrey's test. "How do you think you did?"

"Oh, fine. Piece of cake." Jeffrey zipped up his hoodie. "I didn't know you had any friends."

"Thanks a lot!"

"I didn't mean that. I just didn't think you knew many people here. You work for Uncle Gary in the office and you live with Aunt Violet."

"That does sound pretty pathetic, doesn't it?"

Jeffrey cast an anxious glance at her. "Sorry. I didn't mean it like that."

"Well, don't keep explaining. It gets worse every time. Are you driving?"

"Absolutely."

She followed him outside, marveling at his bare legs. Did boys around here wear cargo shorts as some kind of macho symbol? "Aren't you cold?"

"The car warms up pretty fast."

"I mean, your shorts. Aren't your legs cold?"

He glanced down as if surprised by his attire. "Oh, no. I'm good. I thought you meant you were cold. The car gets warm fast. It's not one of those new ones with heated seats, though."

"Just wondered. I've seen a lot of teenage boys with shorts on, all winter."

"Yeah, we're tough." Jeffrey smirked. "We only wear jeans when we're doing stuff outside, not just going in and out of buildings."

The boy drove competently, as he did most things. She wished she could ask him about his education. Her parents made a point of not discussing the homeschooling Andersons, tight-lipped and tactful. They probably saw it as a rejection of the very things they devoted their lives to. That was probably how they saw her behavior, too. A rejection.

"So, are you ever going to be a teacher again?"

The question startled her. She glanced at his profile. He looked relaxed, with hands at ten o'clock and two o'clock, his slender neck revealing his youth even in silhouette, in the dark.

"Maybe. I don't know yet."

"Did you like it?"

"No." Her answer startled her as much as his question had. It was easier, in the dark car, on a quiet road, to be honest. And Jeffrey wouldn't pressure her to be something he wanted her to be. He didn't care what she did. It was a refreshing change. "No, I didn't like it."

"But you thought you would?" He asked. "That's what you went to school for? You got all the way through college and then found out you didn't like it?"

"Sort of." She tried to find helpful words. These were important matters for a boy his age. "By the time I graduated, I was beginning to think I'd made a mistake. Then I taught school for a few years, and I was sure of it."

"All my siblings are in the medical field. Mark is on his way to med school. He wants to be some kind of surgeon."

And it made her mother crazy that they were all so academically successful. Eleanor smiled in the dark.

"I thought I might want to be a lawyer," Jeffrey went on. "Probably because it goes with doctors. I told Mark I'd defend him when he cut off the wrong body parts and got sued for malpractice."

"You could give him a family discount," Eleanor said lightly. "Handy to have a lawyer in the family."

"According to my mom, it would be more handy to have a plumber. She's thrilled that Penny's marrying Brian, because he's an electrician. Well, an electrical engineer, but he has practical skills, too."

Eleanor laughed. It was the funniest thing she'd heard in ages. Brian had gone to college for five years, to earn an advanced degree in engineering, and his future mother-in-law was glad he had some practical skills. "The degree isn't worth much if it doesn't come with some useful skills, is it?"

Jeffrey ignored her hilarity. "I liked speech and debate, and I didn't want to be a politician or economist, so I thought maybe law..."

"Jeffrey, are you really interested in law?"

"I don't think so." He stopped to wait for another car and glanced at her. "I think I'd really like to do landscaping. Maybe do some more nursery stuff, too."

"I think that sounds like interesting work." He wanted to follow in his father's footsteps; she didn't want to follow in hers. "You've done a lot of it, right? So, you probably have an idea of what's involved."

"All my life. Dad says he'll take me on as a junior partner if I still want it after I go to college."

"Would you take business classes? Horticulture?"

"Yeah." He drove in silence for a while and then said, "Dad didn't make Penny finish college, but that was different. I think I'll go for all four years."

"A business degree would be helpful," Eleanor said. She wasn't qualified to give educational advice. Or was she? She turned in her seat to face him more fully. "Business and horticulture would both be useful, but talk to people who are actually successful in those fields—not just a college counselor. Get advice on what works best for you in your own situation, with a family business. You don't want a cookie-cutter education. Everyone's needs are different."

"Uh, Eleanor, we're homeschooled. Not a lot of cookie-cutting going on in the Anderson household. But thanks. My brothers and Lisa have all complained about the classes they had to take—and the ones that looked interesting but they weren't allowed to take, or didn't fit into their schedules."

"One of my friends took a class in internet security," Eleanor said. "I asked my counselor about it, and he said I couldn't take it. I wasn't in the program, or I didn't have room for an elective, or something like that. Someday, when my email gets hacked, I'm going to go back and find that guy."

"Everyone should know internet security," Jeffrey said seriously, "but there's thousands of people at colleges. I suppose they do the best they can, trying to get everyone the classes they need for their degrees. My friends in the public schools say the same thing. They get on a certain track and then can't do anything else."

The best they can. She almost wished her parents were able to hear this boy's comments. He should get on a committee for education reform.

"It must drive Aunt Kathy crazy that she can't solve all those problems. She really cares about kids and education."

Eleanor felt a tiny—very tiny—twinge of guilt. Her mother did care. She was single-minded because she cared about kids and education. She devoted all of her time and attention to her work because she cared about kids and education. She thought Eleanor should be a teacher because she cared about kids and education more than she cared about what Eleanor wanted. Eleanor would rather plant trees with Jeffrey. Or learn how to plan and build structures with Uncle Gary.

"So, what do you want to do if you don't want to be a teacher?" her cousin asked.

"Well, I've been thinking about that a lot."

"What do you like to do for fun?"

"Fun? I'm not sure." That was a good question. Eleanor thought about it. "I like music and concerts and art museums."

"Really?" He sounded skeptical.

"Really! I wish I got outside more."

"Why don't you?" asked Jeffrey. "You can always just go out for a walk."

"It's cold out!"

"It's Minnesota!"

The absurdity of her objection struck her. Unless she moved south, she should find something to do outdoors even when the weather wasn't warm. "What do you do in the winter?"

"Skiing and snowmobiling and fishing. We go sledding sometimes, sometimes with chickens." He made clucking noises and continued. "We've got snowshoes, as you know, but we haven't used them much. There's a skating rink in town, in the park, but you can just get outside at home. When my brothers were around more, we used to make labyrinths of tunnels in the snow. Last week, my friend and I made forts in the backyard, for a snowball fight, and then Sadie wanted to turn one of them into an igloo." He chuckled. "Mom turned it into a science experiment and social studies lesson, of course, but it was still fun. She made the igloo, and then her friend came over and wanted her own house. So, they made her a little house and then they wanted a bigger one. So, they're building an entire neighborhood in the backyard, with paths for roads and little snowmen people."

Fascinated, Eleanor asked, "and they just play out there?"

Her own childhood had been enriched by team sports, music, clubs, and other scheduled fun. If her brothers had ever played like the Anderson kids, she hadn't seen it. Of course, they lived in town, and they were all so busy. Her mom said it was good to keep kids busy, to keep them out of trouble.

"I guess I could take up snowman construction," she said.

"Hey! You could make a giant bride in the front yard of the farmhouse, with a fancy wedding dress. I bet we could give it a lot of detail. You can use water to help shape the snow. That would be awesome!"

Jeffrey's enthusiasm was tempting, but Eleanor shook her head. "Your sister's worked awfully hard to overcome the farm image for her bridal salon. She likes the snow in the front yard to be smooth. We stay on the sidewalks. But we could do it in the backyard!"

"Not nearly as much fun," Jeffrey said. "So, do you think you'll keep working for Uncle Gary, then?" He took a turn a little too fast and cast a guilty glance in her direction. "Sorry."

"I think so. I like it," she said, "and I think I'm good at it."

Nineteen

Eleanor turned her back to the wind, holding her hair out of her face with mittened hands. A hat would have been sensible, but they always made a mess of her hair. David leaned over the engine, apparently oblivious to the January cold.

"Can you tell what's wrong with it?" Her teeth were chattering, bringing memories of the first time she met him here.

"I think so. Go start it up."

Eleanor opened the car door and slid inside. "Okay, step back." She waited for him to move.

"Start it up," he shouted.

She leaned out the door. "I'm waiting for you to move. I don't want you to get hurt when I start it."

He walked around to where she was. "Okay, I'm here. Now start the engine."

Was he laughing at her? Eleanor complied and sat in the car while David examined the running engine, unable to watch him poking around the moving parts. Odd... She'd been willing to let Uncle Carl do it.

He closed the hood and she turned off the engine. "Is it terminal?"

"Only in the battery."

"The battery?"

He grinned. "Terminals, battery, get it?"

She shook her head.

"You can't tell me you don't know how to use jumper cables," David said.

"Oh! Battery terminals. Yes, I've done that! My roommate and I had to jumpstart her car when she left the lights on. We found a YouTube video."

"A YouTube video. Well, that was resourceful."

"That's the real thing we need to teach people," she informed him loftily. "How to find the information they need to know. Always start with Google."

"It's a good place to start." He tossed his tool bag in the back of his truck. "Where can I wash up?"

"Inside. We can eat at the conference table." She chuckled. "That's what Uncle Gary calls it, but it's really just one of those collapsible white plastic tables. We keep it in the closet and bring it out for special occasions."

"Like lunch with your favorite mechanic." David gave a little bow and held up his greasy hands. "Where's the washroom?"

"So, is it going to be expensive?" Eleanor opened a container of grapes and set it between them. "Please tell me it won't be expensive."

"I don't think it will be expensive. It looks like your fan belt's loose. I can put a new one on for you. If that doesn't fix it, it might be one of the other belts."

So, it's something that can be changed at home?"

"If it's a belt." He took a sandwich and peeked under the top slice of bread. "Crunchy or creamy?"

"Crunchy, of course," Eleanor said.

"Of course. It's awfully nice of you to make lunch for me," David said.

"It's more nice of you to look at my car. I really appreciate it. I'm always asking Uncle Gary to do favors for me. He says he doesn't mind, but... I don't like being indebted to people."

"Well, this makes us even." David held up the sandwich. "Thank you."

"You're a cheap date." Eleanor bit into her sandwich, wishing she'd not said that.

"I like peanut butter sandwiches. They remind me of youth and college."

She rolled her eyes. "You aren't exactly middle-aged." Ugh. They had to get off the topics related to the matchmaking agency. "Aunt Violet and I are still learning how to handle meals. She's never lived on her own before. She grew up in the farmhouse and lived there with the entire family—about 15 people—until she retired, then she moved into a house in town with her brother, and then she moved in with my Grandma, and when Grandma moved to Florida, Aunt Violet moved in with Uncle Carl. Now she's nearly 90, and she's living alone, back in the farmhouse. In the annex, anyhow. Penny lives upstairs in the farmhouse, but they both have separate entrances."

"But you're living with her," David pointed out, "so she's still not really living alone."

"She says she is, because it's her house. She invited me as a guest. A temporary guest." She laughed at the expression on his face. "Yes, that's what she said: a temporary guest. I wonder what she'll really think of living alone, when she does it.

"She never married and had kids of her own?"

"No, never." Eleanor folded up her paper napkin. "But she's always had nieces and nephews—and grand-nieces and grand-nephews—living with her, and she was like another grandma to them. I never knew her very well, of course. I'd only met her a few times."

"And here you are, living with her."

"She seems to think it's normal," Eleanor said, "and my options are pretty limited right now. I needed something in a hurry, when Uncle Gary went in the hospital, and she took me in. I need to find a place of my own soon."

"Does that mean you're staying here?

"Yes," Eleanor said. "I am. I'm going to take a permanent job with Uncle Gary. I like it here."

He smiled, creases forming at the corners of his brown-green eyes. "I'm glad."

When she said it was the original family farmhouse, he'd assumed it looked like most midwestern farmhouses: two-story frame houses with shabby white paint and a peeling porch with overgrown shrubbery and a rutted driveway leading around back to a pole barn twice the size of the house.

This was bigger and looked more like a business than a home. The Penny Anderson Designs sign hung from a wrought iron frame. A bridal shop. David stepped from his truck onto smooth blacktop. Two other cars sat at the end of the little parking lot. Brides? He grimaced, glad he wouldn't have to go inside. Eleanor said it was an annex, with a separate entrance.

The back yard was friendlier, with a patio and fire pit. Trees and piles of frozen leaves edged the lawn, still bare and muddy in February.

"Can I help you?"

David turned to see a blond woman in a blue and white plaid coat. "I'm looking for Eleanor Nielson. Is she here?"

"No, she's out of town. Can I help you with something?" Her expression conveyed annoyance rather than any desire to be helpful.

"Are you Penny?"

The girl shook her head. "Brittany Green. I'm a friend of Eleanor's."

"She's mentioned you." David took a step forward, hand outstretched. "I'm David Reid."

"Oh." She walked forward slowly and shook his hand. "Eleanor's gone to Minneapolis for her parents' anniversary."

"Already? I'd hoped to catch her before she left."

"Were you going to go?" Brittany tipped her head and regarded him with interest. "She said you weren't."

He shook his head. "I ran into her uncle at a job site, and he said she was going alone. He's worried about her car and asked me to drop off a charging kit."

"Drop it off? Don't you live in St. Cloud?"

He rubbed his jaw. "Gary's busy, after being out of work for so long. I had some spare time." He'd offered to do it, pretending to believe that Gary's thinly-disguised attempt at matchmaking was a genuine request for a favor. He wasn't as sure of his own motives or feelings. Now he'd wished he'd come yesterday, just in case she really did have car trouble.

"You missed her."

He did miss her. Even with their brief acquaintance, with few conversations and the issues between them, he missed her. "Can I leave the charging kit here? It's in my truck."

"Sure." Brittany gestured for him to precede her. "You never know... she might really have a need for it." Her tone indicated skepticism.

"I've never been here before," he said over his shoulder. "It's not what I expected from an old family farmhouse."

"It's mostly the bridal salon, and Penny's family can do anything. Gary has the construction business, and Penny's dad is a landscaper. Her fiancé is an electrical engineer and all-around handyman," Brittany said. "The inside is beautiful. Would you like to see it?"

He shook his head. "I'd probably better get back to work."

"Oh, come on. You drove all the way out here. You might as well come inside for a few minutes." She grabbed his elbow and tugged. "There aren't any brides in there—just Penny and Violet. We were eating lunch and saw you come in the yard. Violet wanted to point a shotgun at you for trespassing."

Brittany, Penny and Violet. He'd rather face the shotgun. "I don't think so."

"They don't know about the online dating. They think you and Eleanor know each other through Gary and her work there." She smiled. "You're just friends."

Well, that was what Eleanor had wanted: friends. No, she'd wanted a date for a party, as if Betwixt Two Hearts was an escort service. He'd been mad, hurt, humiliated, and disappointed. And the next time he saw her, in that ridiculous hard hat, all of those things melted away.

She tugged again. "Come on. Look—there's Violet, peeking out from behind that lace curtain." She waved at the old woman, who beckoned in response.

He gave up. "Okay, but just for a few minutes. I don't think Eleanor would like it." The word 'stalker' occurred to him, but he was on a semi-legitimate errand for her uncle, after all, and he'd met Violet in the hospital. It would be rude to ignore her.

That hadn't taken long. The old lady's interrogation techniques should earn her a place in the FBI. The younger women sipped their coffee politely and murmured encouragement as he told Violet about his family, his faith, his goals, and everything else she wanted to know. So far, she hadn't asked about Eleanor.

He shot a harried glance at Brittany, who smiled blandly and tucked a stray strand of hair behind her ear. "You know, you're lucky to have such a supportive family. I'm feeling bad for Eleanor right now." Her limpid blue eyes met his. "Those people will eat her alive."

"Nonsense!" Violet set her cup on the table, missing the saucer. "They're a fine family. You've never even met them."

"I know what Eleanor tells me," Brittany retorted.

David admired her courage and hoped she survived the discussion. Her desire to throw barbs at him—totally unjustified—had led Brittany to disparage Violet's family. He resisted the urge to smirk at her.

Brittany continued. "She keeps saying, 'I know they love me', 'I know they want what's best for me', 'they're really nice people', and so on, over and over, but they don't understand her or respect her."

Violet frowned. "What do you mean, they don't respect her? Of course, they respect her. They love her."

"They call her all the time," Brittany said, "and they send her emails with job openings—teaching jobs, in the cities. She's told them she doesn't want to be a teacher, and they treat her like an obstinate child, humoring her for a little while and then dragging her back into good behavior."

"They are kind of pushy," Penny said. "Aunt Kathy used to quiz us, as if she thought we might be behind in school. I ran away and hid whenever she was here. Lisa always got stuck with her, because she was too nice to avoid it."

"Kathy was a nice girl," Violet said. "She was."

"Mom finally told her to leave us alone. She said we weren't trained seals." Penny chuckled. "Later, Aunt Kathy sent her a list of private schools in the area, 'just in case.'"

"And this," Brittany put in, "is where Eleanor would say 'I know they just want the best for me.'"

They seemed to have forgotten him. He took a drink of his coffee and kept quiet.

"I know she was upset with Laurie about this party," Penny said. "She said she was praying for a blizzard."

"So, she wouldn't have to go. Laurie's the worst of the bunch. She's one of those super-achiever, perfect people who make everyone else look bad." Brittany snorted. "She insisted on having this big party with expensive gifts for a 35th wedding anniversary, and she called Eleanor every other day, telling her all the details."

"That girl has a whole nest of issues," Aunt Violet said. "She's the most insecure person I've ever met."

"Insecure?" Penny asked. "I've only met her once. She seemed more than confident. She's got some high-powered job with the Minnesota Department of Education, doesn't she?"

"That doesn't mean anything. She thinks she has to be perfect, and she can't—none of us can—so she tries harder and harder. She's going to have a nervous breakdown one of these days." Violet slapped the table for emphasis. "She's one of those who blames herself for her parents' divorce—and her mother's next divorce, and the one after that. And her mother is one of those who let her do it. And now Laurie's making Nellie feel guilty for not being a better daughter."

"How do you know all that?" Penny asked.

"She told me." Aunt Violet smiled complacently. "People like to confide in me."

And have their confidences betrayed. David cleared his throat. "I should get going. I hope Eleanor enjoys the party anyhow."

"She's not going to enjoy it," Brittany snapped. "She's going to be spending the entire evening with her family and a hundred of their friends, all of whom are wondering where she's been and why she's not teaching. She'll have to talk about it and listen to their opinions, all night. She won't have a single person on her side, for support, or just to be a buffer."

David looked at her. She'd worked the entire conversation around to that single statement. She wanted him to know that.

"Why didn't she just say so?" He asked Brittany, ignoring the other two women. Eleanor had said she was desperate for a date, but she hadn't explained. Maybe he hadn't given her a chance.

"She felt guilty," Brittany said. "She liked you, and she knew she'd been wrong to... you know."

David ignored the fascinated stares of Penny and Violet. "Do you think... would it help if I went there? Or would that make it worse?"

"It would be good," she said. "If nothing else, she could use a friend there." She smiled. "A masculine friend. It would be nice if he was well-dressed, handsome, intelligent and charming, especially if he stayed close to her and gave people the impression that she's happy and healthy."

He nodded. "I can see that. Is a tuxedo necessary or will a suit be good enough?"

Twenty

The dress was just a little too short. Not immodest, but about one inch shorter than she'd like. She loved it, otherwise. After four months in blue jeans, Eleanor hardly recognized herself in the midnight blue velvet and lace sheath. Had Laurie remembered how much she liked the style, with a bateau neckline and three-quarter length sleeves, or was it a lucky guess? She tugged at the hem, turning in front of the mirror. At the last minute, she'd pulled the bobby pins from her updo and brushed out her hair. She liked the way the long silver earrings peeked when she moved her head.

The dress was gorgeous, but the shoes... Eleanor tottered over to the bed and picked up her purse. Brittany would appreciate this. She snapped a picture in the mirror and sent it before she could change her mind.

> **ELEANOR:** WHAT DO YOU THINK?

The answer was immediate.

> **BRITTANY:** NICE! NEW DRESS?
> **ELEANOR:** BIRTHDAY GIFT FROM ZACK AND LAURIE. EARRINGS AND SHOES, TOO!

She propped a foot on the bed to take a picture, nearly falling over in the process. Brittany responded before she could send it.

BRITTANY: WHEN IS YOUR BIRTHDAY?

Eleanor sent the picture of her shoe and tapped a reply.

ELEANOR: NOT TILL APRIL, BUT THEY DECIDED TO GIVE IT TO
ME NOW SO I COULD WEAR IT TO THE PARTY.

She waited a few minutes, but Brittany didn't reply. She didn't have to. They were both thinking the same thing: Laurie wanted to make sure she was dressed appropriately for the party.

"You look beautiful!"

Her mother had said it at least six times, but the mournful note in her voice detracted from the compliment.

"We all look beautiful!" Eleanor gathered Laurie and her mother into a hug. "Thank you for the dress. I love it. And I'll try not to break my neck in these heels. That would ruin the party."

"No ruining the party," Laurie said. "I think we're all ready."

Eleanor surveyed the elegant banquet hall. The musicians were warming up and the caterers, in their black and white uniforms were putting the final touches on the food. "Laurie, this is incredible. The flowers, the tables... and that ice sculpture! I can't believe how perfect it is. You should be an event planner!"

Laurie laughed. "I'm pretty happy with my real job." Her pink cheeks and sparkling eyes betrayed her pleasure.

"I think the guests are starting to arrive," Eleanor's dad said, "but it's only six o'clock.

"Oh, no! We aren't ready!" Laurie's voice rose.

Kathy put a hand on her shoulder. "It's perfect. You have it all set up, and now you need to enjoy it. Don't fuss."

"I don't think I know him."

Eleanor turned at her father's voice and looked at the man strolling toward them. She caught her breath.

"Do you know him, Eleanor?" Laurie glanced at her.

"Yes, I do." She hastened toward him, warm with gratitude and pleasure.

He reached out to take her hands, and he smiled.

It was the smile that did it. Eleanor stumbled, staggered, and fell.

She never hit the floor. David scooped her up and cradled her in his arms. "Are you okay?"

His voice was low, and he was asking about more than her ankles. She smiled into his warm, deep, wonderful hazel eyes. "I am now."

"Can you walk?" Her family was nearly upon them, calling anxiously.

"I think so." She slid to her feet. Before she could move away or respond to her parents, he drew her close and kissed the top of her head. He held her like that as the others fell silent.

"Thank you." She breathed the words, hoping he'd understand all of her gratitude. A few seconds later, he released her, leisurely, and turned to meet her family.

He held out his hand. "I'm David Reid, the man your daughter has fallen for."

"This is nice. The fireplace** and couches remind me of Uncle Gary's cabin." Eleanor glanced back at the dining room. "And that area's so elegant, all crystal and china. I think I like this better." She dropped onto the couch. "Laurie does know how to throw a party."

David sat next to her, close enough that she could feel his warmth. "The food was amazing."

Eleanor turned to look at him. "I can't even begin to tell you how grateful I am. If you hadn't been here, it would have been one long series of questions and criticism, and not just from my own family." She waved a hand toward the dining room. "All of those people share my parents' priorities. They seem to think we're some kind of scholarly dynasty."

"But you like the work you're doing now, don't you?" David asked.

"I really do. Uncle Gary says he'll pay for me to take a couple classes at the technical college if I'm sure I want to stay."

"Are you sure?" His voice, deep and quiet, gave the question a deeper meaning.

"Yes." Her own voice was a whisper.

He tipped his head toward the party. "Will they be very upset?"

She nodded. No point in denying it. "When I quit teaching, they took it as a personal rejection. And it's not fair. I'm walking on eggshells, trying to make them see I still believe in what they do, but they don't think my work—what I want to do—is as important, and they don't hesitate to say so." She leaned against the cushions. "They've never even asked me about what I do. They're just upset because I'm not doing what they think I should do."

They sat without speaking for a few minutes, gazing at the gas fire. Music and laughter drifted from the dining room, filling the silence.

David stirred. "It's easy to assign relative values to work. People have been doing it forever, even in the church. There's a whole chapter in 1 Corinthians devoted to that problem." He pulled his phone from his jacket pocket and handed it to her. "I've been dealing with some of my own issues there. I made a wallpaper for my lock screen, for when I start second-guessing myself."

Eleanor tapped on the phone and read the words aloud.

"There are different kinds of gifts, but the same Spirit distributes them. There are different kinds of service, but the same Lord. There are different kinds of working, but in all of them and in everyone it is the same God at work."

David took the phone and slid it back into his pocket. "I'm going to finish my seminary classes, but I don't think I'm going to be a regular pastor. I'm not sure what my ministry will look like, and I'm not going to jump into anything until I'm positive."

"What about the rest of it? Do you still want to get married and have children?"

He nodded. "I do. That hasn't changed."

"So..." Eleanor ran a finger across the nap of her velvet skirt. "Are you going to ask the agency for another match?"

He shifted, bringing their shoulders into contact. "No, I don't think so. That was an awful lot of work. I think I might just keep trying with the match I got."

Eleanor caught her breath. "You didn't get a very good match," she whispered.

"I think I did." He turned her to face him. "I think I got a perfect match. I know it's not what you were looking for, but I think we are a good match. We can be friends, and I think we can be more than friends. I want to try. Will you give me a chance, Eleanor, please?

His eyes, warm and earnest, searched her face. She pushed back a strand of hair, tangling it in her earring, and he worked it free, smoothing the hair behind her ear and moving his hand to cradle the back of her neck.

Eleanor gazed up at him, into those beautiful warm eyes. They held promises of things she'd not dared to hope. He saw her for who she was, not who he thought she ought to be. He'd seen the worst in her and still saw the good. And David Reid was the best man she'd ever known.

"Yes. Let's try." Eleanor touched his cheek with her fingertips. "I'd like to try. I'd like that a lot." She moved her fingers to touch his lips. "And we are friends already. I think we can start working on the next step."

He drew her closer and kissed her. Happiness and anticipation flowed through her. The future was bright. She'd met her perfect match.

The End

Questions

1. In the beginning of the book, Eleanor feels like she can't measure up to the rest of her family, all of whom are successful and confident. It's not a deep, soul-crushing sense of failure but a nagging inferiority complex that prevents her from believing she really fits in. Have you ever felt like that?

   How did you get past that self-doubt and take your place in your family, church or group of friends?

   If you are still feeling that way, how are you trying to change the situation?

2. All her life, Eleanor has expected to follow in her parents' footsteps, as her brothers did, but now she's realizing it's not what she wants to do. They don't understand—they think she's absolutely wrong—and put pressure on her. Eleanor knows they care about her and want the best for her. She doesn't want to hurt their feelings or be estranged from them. She values their work and wants to honor them. It can be hard, as a child grows into adulthood and chooses to "disobey" or reject their parents' values and guidance.

How can we—as the child or the parent—work through these situations in a way that glorifies God and preserves relationships?

3. Eleanor has run away to "find herself," but David has his life mapped out. He's working as an engineer, going to seminary, and intends to become a pastor. He wants a wife and children, and he wants them now! Those are all good things.

   Have you ever made plans—all good things—and later realized that you should have been more open to God's direction?

   How could David—or you—have done that?

4. Eleanor dreaded the prospect of her parents' anniversary party because she knew she'd spend the evening answering questions from a hundred guests. Even though she knew it was really a matchmaking agency, she signed up for Betwixt Two Hearts just to find a date—a presentable man to act as a distraction and buffer, so people wouldn't keep telling her she should come home and go back to teaching. She let her desperation lead her into deceit.
   How would you have advised or helped her?

   Can you think of any examples from Scripture in which a person acted rashly because they were afraid?

5. Once she fully understood how wrong it was, she knew she had to tell David the truth. It was hard, not just because she had to confess to her sin, which is always painful, but because she liked him. She knew that when she told him the truth, their budding relationship would be over. He would leave with a poor—but accurate - opinion of her. Our sin has consequences.
   Have you ever experienced lasting consequences from a sin that was forgiven by God?

   How do you deal with that situation? Does living with the consequence ever cause you to worry that the sin wasn't really forgiven?

6. David formed a lasting opinion of Angela's character based on her behavior. Afraid that she was pursuing him, he avoided even public, casual conversation with her. Even when she wanted to come to church (admittedly, to impress and be with him), he only thought of how he could evade her.

   On the surface, this was a sensible precaution. We think it's wise. But no one in her life was seeing her. Larry listened to her—not even for very long—and realized she needed help.

   How can we, as ordinary Christian people, watch for people who are hurting, in trouble, or who might need professional help with mental health issues?

   How do we listen to people like Angela, who look like they might be trouble?

7. David eventually realizes that he may not be called to be a pastor. He still plans to live a life of service and ministry, but he's more open to God's leading, realizing that although his gifts might not be what he thought they were, they are the ones God gave him and still important for God's kingdom. **I Corinthians 12:4-6**

   Sometimes, we value one job or gift over another. This was true in David's mind as well as for Eleanor's family. It can lead to discouragement or pride.

   How can we respond when we see this happening in our church, family, or community?

8. Violet Anderson values family history as well as living relationships. It grieves her that the younger generations only look forward and aren't interested in their ancestors. She's never married or had children of her own, but she tries to hold the extended family together. They are all getting married (gaining in-laws) and having babies, too busy to make the extended family a priority.

Is the extended family a dying institution?

Looking at Scripture, what instances can you find of this?

9. Many families have an Uncle Olof. Do you? Alzheimer's and dementia are common problems, painful for the victim and their loved ones. Eleanor is uncomfortable with lying to Uncle Olof instead of encouraging him to remember people. She finds it "creepy" that little Sarah doesn't mind him thinking she's his sister and calling her Violet while they play checkers.

Do you have a loved one with dementia or Alzheimer's?

How would you engage with a person in Uncle Olof's condition?

Cathe Swanson lives in Wisconsin with her husband of 34 years. They enjoy spending time with their grandchildren and being outdoors, kayaking, birdwatching, hiking, and fishing, but summer is short in Wisconsin, so it's important to have indoor hobbies, too.

Cathe has been a quilter and teacher of quiltmaking for over 25 years, and she enjoys just about any kind of creative work, especially those involving fiber or paper. The long winters are perfect for writing and reading books!

Cathe enjoys writing stories with creative plots and eccentric characters of all ages. Her books will make you laugh and make you cry—and then make you laugh again.

Newsletter:	www.catheswanson.com/newsletter
Website:	www.catheswanson.com
Twitter:	twitter.com/CatheSwanson
Facebook:	facebook.com/CatheSwanson
Pinterest:	www.pinterest.com/catheswanson
Instagram:	instagram.com/CatheSwanson
Goodreads:	www.goodreads.com/CatheSwanson
BookBub:	www.bookbub.com/authors/cathe-swanson
Amazon:	www.amazon.com/author/catheswanson

The Great Lakes Series

Baggage Claim
Snow Angels
Hope for the Holidays
Christmas at the Unity Plenkiss

The Glory Quilts Series

The Christmas Glory Quilt
The Swedehearts Glory Quilt

Introducing

Thank you for reading my story, *The Swedehearts Glory Quilt*. I've enjoyed telling the Anderson family's stories in the Glory Quilts series because, while the characters are fictional, the Swedish Minnesota culture and traditions are part of my own heritage.

I had so much fun meeting Kari Trumbo, another native Minnesotan, through this Crossroads collection! Kari's historical and contemporary books have themes of forgiveness and renewal, strong characters and vivid settings.

Her contribution to this collection, *Whole Latte Love*, is about seeing ourselves the way the Lord does—as a precious child of the Most High—and not as others see us. No one knows our innermost being better than our Father.

When best friends Drew and Addi are matched up by *Betwixt Two Hearts*, they need to overcome self-doubt and past hurts and just believe that truth.

> See what great love the Father has lavished on us, that we should be called children of God! And that is what we are! The reason the world does not know us is that it did not know him. Dear friends, now we are children of God, and what we will be has not yet been made known. But we know that when Christ appears, we shall be like him, for we shall see him as he is.   1 John 3:1-2

I think you'll be blessed by *Whole Latte Love*. It's a fun story with profound spiritual truths that will stay with you long after you finish reading it.

CATHE SWANSON

Author of *The Swedehearts Glory Quilt*

WHOLE *Latte* LOVE

By

Kari Trumbo

INKED IN FAITH

Copyright Notice

One

Addi Merrick had spent her life waiting for *him* to show up, or so it seemed. For months he'd come in every day The Bean was open. Mr. Dependable. Not that he'd ever really noticed her. Oh, he requested she make his coffee, but he never talked to her beyond a hello and a thank you. He only had eyes for her boss, Kaylie.

Addie froze in her spot by the table where she watched for him. The gray cement floor gleamed with a polish that accented the rustic, rough wood walls and booths of The Bean on Main. Two of the corners boasted comfortable seating arrangements, and one corner even had a fireplace, not that they usually needed it in Texas. Her spot created the perfect vantage point to watch him come around the corner and into the little shop he used as his morning office.

Perfectly on time, he swept inside with a burst of cool Texas winter air, the scent of cloves, and a smile... directed at her boss. Kaylie gave him a face that resembled a baby tasting peas for the first time, then turned her attention to Addi, giving her the *I'm going to be in back* look. She shoved away from her spot at the till and rushed through the swinging door to the small storage area and lounge at the back of the coffee shop.

Drew set his laptop at his usual window booth, then hung his front-zip sweater on the peg she'd come to think of as his. Tall and lanky, he never seemed to put forth much effort in reaching for anything. He was always the same, yet took her breath away every single day.

"Can I get you your usual, Drew?" She ventured from her spot across the room where she'd been wiping off a perfectly clean table. It hadn't even been used yet that day, but he wouldn't know that. Always kind and warm, he treated her nicely, just not with any affection or even friendliness. She could feel his lack of interest with every interaction. It didn't stop her from hoping. One day he might just notice her.

"Sure, thanks. Must have been Kaylie's break time? Guess I'm later than I thought." He strode back over to his seat, his fitted maroon, button-down shirt hugging his frame. The sun shone through the window, gleaming on his dark hair and beard for just a moment as he settled into his spot.

"Yeah." It wasn't actually Kaylie's break, but she couldn't tell a customer, especially not this customer, that her boss would rather have her teeth pulled than to socialize with him. "She had a long morning, so she took her break a little early. But I'm happy to help you." If she made her voice sound chipper, she might force her mood in that direction. It wasn't fair. She was always the buddy, the friend, the confidante, never the girlfriend. Never the main attraction. Sidekick syndrome, all the way.

He nodded and didn't give her another glance that she could see. He soon opened his computer and clicked various keys, happily ignoring her.

Addi made his coffee—which wasn't even on their menu—a straight-up black coffee with a hint of mint, and brought it over to his table. He gently removed the lid she'd just put on it and took a deep sniff, closing his eyes. "I needed this, thanks. Now, time to work." He opened his eyes long enough to hit her with their deep-blue depths, then flicked his attention back to his laptop, her cue to leave.

She took one step back, then another, her face getting hotter by the second. Why couldn't she act like a normal person around Drew? "I'm, um, just going to be in the back for a minute. If you need anything—," She tripped over her own foot and gasped. "Bye."

He flicked her a glance as she spun and raced from the room. The swinging door hit her in the rear as she made her escape. "If you need anything— Bye?" she mumbled. "I'm so stupid."

Kaylie rolled her eyes. "Why do you let yourself get so flustered over him? It's just Drew. He's more annoying than anything." She crossed her arms and legs in an abrupt movement from where she sat on the checkered couch she'd picked up from Goodwill.

Addi flinched at Kaylie's assessment. "Says you. You go out all the time. I never do." Though her hands weren't dirty, she wiped them on the towel hanging near the washstand by the door. Drew always made her so nervous her palms got sweaty.

"Yeah, says me. He's asked me out twice because the first no wasn't enough." Kaylie's head slid back and forth to accent every word, and each one lodged deeper in Addi's wounded heart.

"Good for you. He's a nice guy. You don't need to be mean." Not to Drew, or her.

"I'm not. I've got someone. I don't need him asking me out all the time. It's weird. Is he coming in here every day to stalk me or something?"

Addi had hoped *she* was part of the reason he kept coming in, but it couldn't be true. He rarely gave her a second glance and never really talked to her. Certainly not like he tried to engage Kaylie. "I really don't think he's the stalker type. He looks more metro bus than van by the river."

Kaylie rolled her eyes again. "If you like him so much, you go out there. Make yourself available. Wouldn't hurt to get your hair done or maybe wear some makeup." She gestured to Addi's leggings and belted shirtdress, then sighed. "Never mind. You probably wouldn't even know what to look for. I'll be back in for the lunch rush. You've got the floor. I'm going home." She stood, flung off her apron and tossed it on the couch, then grabbed her purse. "He needs to find a new coffee shop. Seriously."

If he did, Addi would never see him again. Even though he didn't care for her, she cared about him and wanted to know him more. She'd lose that chance. "But he likes this one. We cater to him." Addi bit her lip, but the words couldn't be taken back.

Kaylie's eyes lit up, and she gave her first genuine smile since Drew had walked in. "Perfect. I'll stop ordering the mint, and he'll stop coming in. Problem solved." She swung out the back door and let it slam.

Drew Tanner stared at his screen and tried to type up a proposal for a new client. He was a freelance marketing consultant, and The Bean on Main provided a perfect place to get work done. Finding new ways for businesses to interact with the public and attract attention was his specialty, but not when he couldn't focus.

Kaylie had intentionally avoided him since he'd asked her out for the second time the week before. He hadn't even planned to do it, but she'd been smiley for a change, joking with him. It had just come out. Kaylie's coworker, Addi, had looked mortified, but not as much as Kaylie herself. He didn't stand a chance. She acted and looked so different from the last woman he'd dated, so out of his league. Different from the woman who walked away. That had to make her better, more his type, didn't it?

The door swung open, and he hoped to see Kaylie coming off her break, but Addi came through instead. He sighed, unable to contain it. Addi was nice but too soft-spoken, too girl-next-door, too much like Lauren. So, she had to be wrong for him. Wrong in every way. Sometimes, he couldn't even stand to look at her, because she acted too much like what he'd lost.

Addi had soft, brown hair that she always tied back in a tail with the end stuck in the ponytail holder to form a loop. Her casual clothes always fit nicely but didn't scream for attention. In fact, none of her screamed for attention. He jumped as she slid into the booth across from him. He hadn't even seen her coming, and she'd never done anything like that before.

"Oh, sorry. I didn't mean to scare you. Can I get you a refill on your coffee?" Her warm, brown eyes smiled at him, yet her face remained placid as usual.

He glanced down at his coffee, still full and steaming. "I'm good. Thanks." She seemed nervous, but she had no reason to be. "Is everything all right?" He'd never seen her sit with patrons and definitely not him. He'd done his best to keep her just the barista who made the perfect coffee. Sliding into his booth was too much like a friend, and that's just how Lauren had started.

Addi rubbed her arms against the cool air seeping through the nearby window. "I'm just not used to handling the whole shop alone. Kaylie had to run some errands and won't be back for a few hours."

He always hoped to get a word or two with Kaylie, but that wouldn't happen if she'd left. He often only stayed until lunch, so he didn't take up a table during their rush. "Oh, I'm sure you'll do fine." He closed his laptop. He had no reason to stay if he couldn't see her.

"You're leaving?" Addi's eyes widened. "But you never leave this early."

He popped the lid back onto his coffee, surprised she kept track of when he usually left. "Well, I really do hate the quiet of my apartment, but even your shop is a little too quiet for my taste today."

She drummed her fingers on the table and searched out the window, then gazed at him, not that it lingered. "You doing anything for Christmas?"

He had half a mind to lie and tell her he didn't believe in Christmas, but that would be mean, and she'd never been anything but kind to him. Just like Lauren, right up until she walked out of his life, leaving him to explain to their wedding guests why there would be no wedding. He swallowed the memory back. One day he'd even throw out the suit he'd bought for that day. No other man he knew bought a suit for their wedding, but he had because he and Lauren had planned to renew their vows every five years and try to do as many of those in the same clothes as possible.

"I," He paused to consider his words, "don't really celebrate." He slipped his laptop into its case and stood to get his sweater. He turned to avoid Addi's brown-eyed stare as he slid his arms into his sleeves. Small talk wouldn't get his proposal written. He shouldn't feel like a jerk for leaving a coffee shop, but he did. Addi might be exactly like Lauren, or nothing at all like her, but he wasn't willing to find out.

"Well, see you tomorrow, then." She wiped down his table, though he'd left nothing on it, and turned to head to the till.

He followed as he pulled out his wallet. Coffee every day, a luxury he couldn't live without. He handed her the money and waited for her to make change, then dropped a few coins in the tip jar. "I'm sure you'll do just fine on your own."

Her jaw stiffened slightly, and she nodded. "I've managed so far."

It struck him as the first thing they had in common; so far, he'd managed just fine alone, too.

Two

Christmas parties were the worst. Addi caught a glimpse of her light-up, ugly Christmas sweater in the mirror that ran along the whole back wall of the gilded ballroom. The deep-red, flat-weave carpet clashed with the bright red of her sweater, not that she'd ever witnessed a single piece of clothing in the entire world that wouldn't clash with it. Kaylie had asked everyone from all three of her locations to wear ugly sweaters, but, as Addi glanced around the room, the only ugly sweater belonged to her. Now, she looked like a fool amid the nicely dressed guests.

She knew no one else at the party besides her boss, who made her way around the room to each little group of people, smiling and laughing loudly. Her current date, Julien, hid behind a huge potted fern with one of the girls from Kaylie's uptown location. Uptown would give Kaylie a run for her money in style, and apparently in her taste in boyfriends as well.

If Kaylie's trajectory stayed true, she would miss the scene playing out for all of her employees. If she shifted just a bit, she might catch him, though Kaylie could be somewhat oblivious. Either way, she wouldn't make it to Addi for a while because Kalie always dealt with her last, and if she took about five minutes per group, she would barely have time left to talk to Addi before the party ended. She should've just stayed home. Kaylie acted like a friend, sort of. She talked to Addi at work when it suited her. But when it came down to it, Kaylie wouldn't give Addi the time of day, even at a work party.

Addi turned off the blinking lights on her sweater just as Julien emerged from the other side of the plant, his paramour tagging along behind, tugging her skirt down slightly. The side of his mouth bore a grotesque pink slash of bright metallic lipstick. Kaylie froze in the middle of her obnoxiously loud giggling when she realized just what had happened right in front of all her employees. She strode to him, grabbed him by the tie, and dragged him over to the wall.

Everyone in the room backed away and tried to look busy, glancing away from the scene or suddenly worried about their clothes. As Addi swept over the room with a quick glance, everyone surreptitiously watched Kaylie with varying degrees of interest. Uptown lady made a beeline for the door, grabbed her shawl, and disappeared through the large doors. Kaylie's voice rose as she blasted Julien for embarrassing her in front of everyone. He dodged out from behind her and loosened his tie as he, too, made for the door.

Part of her wanted to feel sorry for Kaylie, but she attracted people who used others because that's how she, herself, treated people. Kaylie strode to the center of the room and crossed her arms. "I think that about wraps it up. Hope you have a *great* holiday." By the end, she could barely be heard over her angry huffs. The sarcasm dripped from her words.

A few people made a mad rush for the door; others gave Kaylie guilty glances, but left. After just a few minutes, Addi and Kaylie were the only people left, not that she wanted to stay. If she wanted Kaylie as a friend, she had to treat her like one, and that meant being there for her when she was down. As far as she could tell, Kaylie didn't have any real friends, so she prayed Kaylie wouldn't verbally slap her like she'd done with Drew.

"Want to come to my apartment and talk about it? I've got rocky road." Addi never knew what to do with her hands, so she held on to her elbows and felt like a turtle in the desert. She rarely invited anyone to her place, but Kaylie needed a friend. Unfortunately for her, she'd have to settle for Addi.

Kaylie scowled at her; her ice-blue minidress matching her cold eyes perfectly. "Rocky road? You think ice cream is going to make me feel better? Do you have any idea how good he was for me?" She wiped under her eyes, but neither her mascara nor her eyeliner budged an inch.

"Maybe. Have you ever tried it?" Addi headed slowly for the door and the two remaining coats hanging on the rack. Kaylie followed a few steps behind.

"No. I guess I never saw the point. Nothing has ever been solved over a pint of ice cream." She yanked her tiny fur shrug off the hanger.

"That's why I don't do pints. I do gallons." Addi laughed, but her boss just rolled her eyes.

"Okay, what other option do I have? I planned to be here late into the night, then Julien was supposed to take me out. He certainly can't now."

As always, she was the last resort. Addi mentally kicked herself for the pity party. Kaylie had just gone through a nasty and very public breakup. She had a right to feel angry and hurt.

"We'll talk, eat ice cream, and make a plan."

Kaylie narrowed her eyes and took her handbag from the top of the rack. "Plan?"

"Yes, what to do about tomorrow when you have to go to work."

She couldn't fire the girl; it wasn't legal. But Kaylie would have to be prepared to deal with her, assuming Uptown didn't quit.

"I don't ever work in that location. I have a manager over there. I do payroll and deal with out-of-hand issues, which are rare." Kaylie waved a jeweled hand. "I suppose I should thank her. If he did that at my own Christmas party, what was he doing behind my back?" This time her jaw quivered just slightly. Perhaps the woman Addi had always assumed was made of ice, actually had a heart. Maybe Drew saw her deeper than Addi had.

Addi slipped her coat over her arm. She'd planned for cooler evening weather, but it hadn't grown late enough to be cold. The horrible sweater made it too warm to wear both. "Good. I'll lead the way." She opened the door and held it for her boss.

"No, you'll give me your address. I'll drive."

She hadn't even been in a car in a long time, and she smiled, despite the state of affairs. A terrible situation could be turned to good. She could make Kaylie a friend yet.

Drew stared out the window of his fifth-floor apartment. The city twinkled in Christmas lights below and reminded him of what Addi asked him at the coffee shop. He didn't have any plans, not for this holiday or the next. His life, even from the vantage point of the window with the Currier and Ives view, didn't hold much hope.

Kaylie had made it abundantly clear she wanted nothing to do with him, and he didn't see many other women since he worked so much. The dating scene just wasn't happening. Even the few times he ventured to church, he sat in the back row and escaped before he could talk to anyone. His brief conversation with the barista had been the closest to a friendly chat he'd had in a very long time. For as much as he wasn't the chitchat sort of guy, it had been nice. Almost friendly. Perhaps the one person he'd blocked from his life needed a place in it, if only to slake his minor need for some semblance of companionship. Too much of his life was wasted on social media instead of face-to-face conversation.

He would have to draw a boundary with her though. She would have to understand that they could never be more than friends, and she'd have to understand it without his explanation. It was just too personal. He'd failed, and it had been on display for all his friends and family to see. Never again.

A *ding* from his phone distracted him from the window. As he picked it up, the little image of his mom showed on his screen. He swiped it to see what she had to say.

MOM: MARYANN WANTS TO KNOW IF YOU'RE FREE FOR AN EVENING NEXT WEEK. HER DAUGHTER IS HOME FROM COLLEGE.

Drew sucked in a deep breath and squeezed the bridge of his nose. His mom just didn't understand he wanted no part of the setup. He couldn't just relinquish control. Not now. There was too much at stake. He hadn't dated in over a year, and even though he'd asked Kaylie, there was no urgency, no great desire for her to agree. Not really.

397

DREW: SORRY, MOM. I'VE GOT PLANS ALL NEXT WEEK. BIG
CONTRACT. MAYBE SOME OTHER TIME.

He fired off the text knowing that it didn't matter how often MaryAnn's daughter came home, he wouldn't make time. Mom probably knew it, but the text would give her a valid excuse, one that sounded better than, "my son isn't dating because he was left at the altar by an amazing woman." The pressure between his eyes hammered him harder.

Just what was a guy to do? He'd made it all the way through college and hadn't met any woman who wanted a quiet guy. Now he had his own company, doing well, and had thought he was on the road to wife, house, and family. Yet, the whole castle of cards had collapsed right on top of him.

His phone *dinged* once again.

MOM: I KNOW YOU AREN'T BUSY ALL WEEK, BUT I UNDERSTAND.
I KNOW YOU'VE NEVER BEEN ONE TO JUST DATE, BUT MAYBE IT'S
TIME TO PUT THE PAST WHERE IT BELONGS AND START FRESH.
DON'T LET ONE DAY RUIN YOU.

His mother had always given sound advice, sometimes harsh, but usually wrapped in chocolate cookie sweetness that was as genuine as a diamond. Start fresh. Maybe he could do that, let go of a little control and start with someone he'd never met before. He smiled as he grabbed the pen and paper on his kitchen counter and jotted down a slogan: Past failures are still partial successes.

He'd learned a lot from Lauren. Now he knew where to begin.

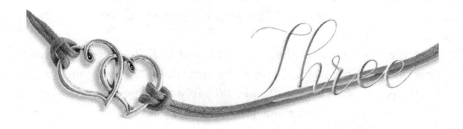

Three

Kaylie dug a huge spoonful of rocky road from the carton and closed her eyes with a groan as she sucked on the spoon. Its sweetness obviously more enjoyable to someone who never ate it than for Addi, who almost felt like she should leave the room to give Kaylie her private moment with her spoon.

"I've never tried this before, but you're right, it's amazing." Her eyes rolled skyward once again.

They seemed to do that no matter what her mood—as if they had a mind of their own—and a little of the edge Addi had felt over that action lost its sting. "Yeah, me and rocky road have a long history." Every time she'd set up a friend with a guy she'd wanted to date, every time she watched that same guy fall madly in love with her friend. Too many times to think about when Kaylie needed her. This wasn't her night to reflect on past failures, but Kaylie's. That's exactly what would eventually happen with Kaylie and Drew. It was inevitable. Bring on more rocky road.

"So, what will you do now? You're never single during the holidays." At least Julien hadn't left her on Christmas, but a Christmas party in front of all her employees could be construed as just as bad.

"I've been thinking about that. A friend of mine just signed up for a new dating site. They are doing a trial membership where if you sign up, you get access to the site for three days. That would be fast enough to find a

.

Christmas date. If they have anyone signed up in this area, I could try. At least it's new enough where the creepers won't have signed up yet."

A dating site wasn't exactly how Addi had pictured her model-beauty boss would find her next victim. "But what about Drew? He's right there and you already know him." Though a big part of her wished he didn't notice Kaylie at all.

Kaylie dug out another huge spoonful, and Addi flinched as she stuck it in her mouth and started talking at the same time. "I'm not going to date him. Simple as that. He's a customer. Probably doesn't even make as much as I do. Honestly, I want a husband who makes enough that I can hire managers at all three store locations and just be an owner. I'm tired of trying to run the shop and do everything else."

Addi would be the last to point out that Kaylie's parents *really* owned the store and managed the money, Kaylie was just their face in the office. She always said she did payroll, but her father's signature adorned the bottom of the checks. Would Kaylie need someone wealthy enough to buy out her parents?

"How are you going to find a guy like that on a brand-new dating site?" She'd had enough of the ice cream and tossed her spoon into the sink, finally making Kaylie flinch. Addi's favorite ice cream would never be the same.

"It's all in the way you answer the questions. You might only get matched with one guy, but he might be the perfect guy. I don't really care about personality, I just want a guy who has the means to help me maintain or even grow my business, and who won't cheat on me."

A sick, swirling feeling did a hula dance in Addi's belly. "And what about you? Would you be restricted from cheating too, or just him?"

Kaylie rolled her eyes once again. "Whatever."

That didn't come close to answering her question, but she couldn't make it any of her business. They weren't close enough friends yet to push the issue. At least she wouldn't ever treat Drew with such disdain. He didn't appear to make enough money to satisfy Kaylie.

"I'd better go home. I may even sign up for that site tonight. Thanks for the pep talk. I owe you one. Maybe I could even set up a date between you and Drew."

Addi's heart rolled over itself. "No. I don't think he'd go for that. I don't even think he remembers my name."

"It's sewed on your apron. How could he not know it?" Kaylie stared at her, mouth slightly agape.

Good question, but she was still pretty sure he didn't. She couldn't remember him ever saying it. "I don't know. He's just not interested in me. Especially not when you're in the room." Addi grabbed the tub of ice cream and pushed the lid onto it. If conversations were always this uncomfortable with her boss, she wanted fewer of them, not more.

"It wouldn't take much to make you look presentable, you'd almost be pretty with a little work."

Heat stormed up Addi's neck and into her face. "I work in clothes that are comfortable. I have to do more cleaning and lifting than you do, so I wear different clothes." Not to mention most of her budget went to tuition. She'd been surprised her boss hadn't mentioned the tiny size of her apartment, the scary guys that ogled and commented to them on the way in, or the gorgeous view of the next building over, three feet away from her own. The only thing to look at was the collection of alley cats that roamed between buildings.

"Well, if you ever want to attract his attention, let me know. I'd be glad to help you out." She clicked her nails as she stood and grabbed her shrug.

"What was the name of that site?" Maybe she could sign up for it herself. If she got three free days, she could make use of them. Someone had to be out there for her, a match.

"Something cute and short, let me think, maybe Betwixt2Hearts dot com? I'll write it down for you tomorrow at work. Why? You thinking of joining? I wonder if I'd get a discount for giving you the name?" Kaylie laughed. "If not, I should. Free advertising."

"I thought you said it was a free trial?" Her budget left her with no extra, tight, like ramen-dinner every night, tight.

"It is, but only for three days. You might need more time than that, but it seriously couldn't hurt you. You need to get out more." She grabbed her clutch and headed for the door. "Oh." Kaylie turned back and took a deep breath. "Not a word about this to anyone else. I wouldn't want it to get out that I was hanging around with my coworkers. It wouldn't be fair." She turned and left, the echo of the closing door as much a slap in the face as her words.

Addi slumped into her overstuffed couch and let her shoulders fall. "Don't worry. I have no one to tell."

A cool wind blew Drew's jacket, and he shoved his hands in his pockets to keep it lying flat, his over the shoulder computer case bounced against his hip. Only a week until Christmas, and a cold front had settled over the little suburb of Grand River, Texas with well below normal temps, leaving the usually busy street barren. If he hadn't needed his routine just to get work done, he'd have skipped going outside like everyone else.

As soon as he opened the door to The Bean on Main, the scent of fresh-roasted coffee warmed his nose. The Bean was one of the few stores in town that roasted on-site. While some people couldn't stand the smell, he craved it. He closed the door and noted Addi in the exact location she always stood when he arrived. She was as much a creature of habit as he, and that satisfied him. Kaylie, on the other hand, couldn't be found in her normal queenly perch behind the counter.

He took a moment to wave and offer a hello to Jack, another regular there in the morning. If he didn't force his path away from Addi, she might suspect he'd noticed her, and he'd been doing his best to make certain she *didn't* know.

Addi shot him a nervous smile, then went back to wiping the gleaming table. With the unseasonably cool weather, only two other people besides Jack sat huddled in comfortable chairs near the small fireplace in the corner, earbuds in, ignoring the world as they worked on their computers. Drew took off his jacket and hung it by the door as he always did, and by the time he made it back to his table, Kaylie waited for him with a strangely warm smile.

"Well, Drew. It's been a while. How are you?" she gushed as if they were best friends and she hadn't been avoiding him for over a week. It felt like a setup and his neck prickled to life.

"I'm, uh, chilly. Can I get a cup of your finest?" Not that he really wanted whatever was their finest. It probably consisted of some frou-frou concoction with caramel something-or-other that he would hate.

"Addi, you heard him. Get the man a coffee." Kaylie waved a regal hand, and poor Addi scurried off to do her bidding. He'd never noticed just how Kaylie treated people around her. He'd thought she just treated him that way.

"Isn't she just the cutest thing?" Kaylie tilted her head and cocked a smile like she would at a puppy, not her employee.

He glanced over at Addi, and her face couldn't possibly have gotten redder. He wasn't even sure how to answer her question. He couldn't be honest and keep Addi at arm's length where she needed to stay. Once you told a woman you didn't find her hideous, you were practically dating. "Uh, sure." He sat and unzipped his computer case, hoping that, like Addi, Kaylie could take a hint. For once, he didn't want to chat with her.

"You know, she's single."

Danger!

His skin prickled to life as he felt Addi's eyes lock onto him. Drew didn't miss the audible gasp from the other side of the counter, even though she stood a good fifteen feet away.

"Are you trying to set me up with her?" The cold should've kept him at home. If it had, he could've avoided this mess. He hated confrontations like this, the kind where someone would end up getting hurt. Jack glanced his way, with wide eyes, and nodded for the door as he grabbed his coat and made a run for it. Smart man.

Kaylie held up one manicured finger. "Well, *she* certainly doesn't have any other options—" She held up a second matching finger on her other hand. "You're obviously single, or you wouldn't keep asking me out." She slowly moved the two fingers together. "It seems like the perfect solution to me." Kaylie let her hands fall and drummed her long nails on his table, the clicking shivered up his spine. Addi appeared a second later and gingerly set his coffee down on the table. He couldn't miss the extra sheen to her eyes, nor did he miss that she dashed away and into the bathroom before he could even thank her.

"That wasn't very nice, you know." While he didn't know Addi personally, their conversation had been enjoyable last Friday, and he owed her for reminding him what pleasant conversation was like.

Kaylie rolled her eyes. "Tell you what. If you're so tired of being single but have no interest in Addi, you should try that new dating site, Betwixt2Hearts. It's new, and I think your first match is free, or something like that. The rules are on the site." She stood up and fixed him with her icy-blue eyes. "Never know, might find someone just like me, only" she raised perfectly plucked eyebrows, "interested." She winked and sidled off behind the counter, pushing all the way to the back room.

It was so silent in the little café he could hear the faint music from the earbuds of one of the other patrons. When Addi emerged from the bathroom about ten minutes later, red-faced and hunched, he motioned her over to his table. He couldn't let her go through the rest of her day feeling embarrassed over something she couldn't control, namely, how her boss treated her.

She took much longer than usual to reach his table and gripped her little order pad tightly in front of her, pulled a pen from her apron, and refused to look him in the eye. She'd never even used that pad before. He hadn't even realized she carried it.

"Can I get you something for lunch?" Her voice rang a little too high—crackly—and she cleared her throat as she glanced at the other two people in the shop.

"You don't have to worry about them. They didn't hear a thing, with their music on. I can practically hear what they're listening to from here." If a small joke didn't work to make her less anxious, he'd just have to try a little harder.

Addi pursed her lips and tapped on her pad.

"Right, lunch." She was such a nervous sort. He'd have to get her to sit for a minute and talk. "Yeah, I'll have two ham and cheese sandwiches, with pickles. You pick the chips. The second sandwich is for you since I'm guessing you take your lunch soon, before the actual lunch rush." He tried to catch her glance, but she kept scratching away on her pad. Her eyes didn't even widen. Hadn't he shocked her at all?

"I'm not allowed to eat out here. It's against policy." She met his eyes for just a moment, long enough to know it wasn't that she *couldn't* eat with him, she was just hesitant.

"I have a feeling if you asked your boss today, she'd let you. Since she just tried to set me up with you, apparently without your foreknowledge. I just want to talk to you for a minute. This isn't a date." Boundaries. He had to keep a wall up. A friendly wall, no barbed wire or anything, but it still had to be there. Fences made good neighbors. Why did making friends have to be so hard?

"Of course it isn't." She chuckled, but it sounded more like a strangled sob.

She ducked in the back but only for a minute before she reappeared and headed over to the sandwich-making station. He didn't really want to eat at The Bean, but if it got Kaylie off Addi's back, he could sacrifice one lunch with his new almost-friend.

Addi came over and laid down the two baskets, the chips, and a fruit juice. She'd chosen plain potato, his favorite if he had to choose. Salty, with nothing extra. Perfect. As she slid into the seat across from him, he noticed the soft dimples that accented her cheeks—and that when she allowed herself to smile, even in nervousness—it changed the shape of her whole face.

"You didn't have to do this. I know you didn't want to, so I paid for mine." She picked at her sandwich but didn't lift it from her plate.

"I don't usually do things I don't want to do."

"You barely spoke to me before today." She slid back in her seat, far away from her lunch, and him. He *had* kept a distance there—had been less than nice to her—simply because of her looks and demeanor. Too close to his past.

"Well, I guess that's one good thing about your boss's behavior, it got me to finally talk to you." He smiled, but she didn't return it. She twisted the top off the juice and took a long drink.

When she set it down, she held the bottle like a lifeline. "I'm sorry she embarrassed you. She had a tough weekend."

Whether she did or didn't, the woman didn't have the right to treat her employees like the paperboard boat his sandwich came in. "A tough weekend? So, you're friends outside of work?"

She stiffened, then frowned. "Does that surprise you? That I would have a friend as pretty as Kaylie?"

He knew she channeled her hurt at him because she couldn't let it off anywhere else. Lauren used to do just the same thing when he'd meet her after a hard day at work. It was enough of a reminder to keep his feelings in check. Addi was cute and sweet, but he couldn't get close to her. He wouldn't allow it. "It doesn't surprise me at all. People like her tend to need people like you, people who will let them be alpha yet take care of them when they get their feelings hurt."

Her shoulders relaxed slightly, but she still made no move to eat. "Well, maybe her loss is your gain. She and her boyfriend broke up. Kaylie is officially single. But not for long. She's been working on her profile at Betwixt2Hearts since she came in this morning."

He couldn't imagine someone like Kaylie using a dating site. Unless she was desperate, but if so, why not at least accept his offer? "That dating site?"

"The same. You know, you should go and put up a profile, but leave your picture blank. She's looking for someone rich, someone to take care of her business." Addi glanced to the back of the shop where the door hid the boss they were talking about.

"I don't know that I still want to go out with her. What if she treats me the way she treated you?" He hated to point out the obvious, but he wasn't exactly infatuated with Kaylie. He just wanted a few relaxing evenings. Someone he could tell his mom about so she wouldn't pester him anymore about dating, and grandbabies.

"It was just a suggestion." She pushed the pickle to the other side of her sandwich.

"I'll think about it. I've never done anything like online dating." He picked up his own lunch, hoping she would then join in.

"I haven't either. I've been afraid to put myself out there. I've never really done much dating. My friends all get married, but I only seem to make friends." Her eyes widened slightly and she pursed her lips.

"Don't worry," he joked. "I won't take the 'only friends' comment as an insult."

She finally picked up her sandwich and took a tentative bite. When she finished chewing, she glanced up at him. "Good, it wasn't meant to be. I really can be a good friend. I've had a lot of practice."

That was another thing she could teach him. He hadn't allowed any friends in his life for a long time. He worked during the day, camped out in front of the television at night. Some life. He picked up his coffee, and it was now the perfect temperature. As he took a drink, the scent of the coffee mixed with a hint of mint warmed him to his very heart. Addi always got it just right.

"Thank you for the coffee. You know, you've never messed it up."

She laughed, and he mentally patted himself on the back. He'd cheered her up. At least he'd managed that.

"It isn't all that hard."

Maybe not, and neither was talking to her when he let himself do it.

Four

It wasn't like Kaylie to be late. Addi stood in the front picture window of The Bean and searched the sidewalk for her boss. She'd gotten there on time, prepped everything as she always did, but without Kaylie, she couldn't open the till and the store was supposed to open in ten minutes. People would want to come in right away.

Her phone buzzed in her pocket and Addi yanked it out, praying for once that Kaylie would call her. She hit the answer button when Kaylie's picture appeared. "Hey, where are you?"

"I'm taking the day off. Maybe the week. I've got some shopping to do. I sent over Liberty from the college location to help you out."

"But what about the till? The money?" Her head felt light, and she reached for the window. How could her boss be so careless?

"The till money is where it always is, in the safe. The combination is under the counter in the black book."

"You seriously leave the combination right where anyone could find it?" It should've been surprising, but her boss never thought things through.

"Yes. For times like this. You'd best unlock that door. Hop to it." Kaylie hung up, and Addi slipped her phone in her back pocket. Now that Kaylie wasn't coming in, Addi could order an extra bottle of the mint mix for Drew's coffee. She'd forget by the time she got back anyway.

She had no idea who Liberty was, but she hadn't arrived yet. Just so she didn't have to pull out the book with the combination in it while customers were standing there, she didn't unlock the door first. She'd just taken care of the safe, when Liberty came in the back door and met her with a huge grin, like sunshine after a storm. Liberty had bright, expressive eyes and curly, dark hair that looked a little too perfect to be real.

"Morning! I'm Liberty Dryden, and Kaylie tells me I'll be working here at this location for at least a week." Liberty had dark blue eyes and a bohemian style that Addi loved, but could never pull off. She had a dimple in her right cheek that made her look plumper than she really was. Her fuzzy boots slid across the floor as she walked.

Addi unlocked the front, but no one waited to get in just yet. "I'm glad you're here. I was worried Kaylie wouldn't think of finding a replacement. Not that she does much while she's here."

Liberty laughed so hard she needed a tissue. When she finished, she collapsed onto a barstool near the counter. "I didn't catch your name?"

"I'm Addi Merrick, and I'm a student out at the Rooster, Counseling Psychology."

Liberty's eyes widened. "I thought I recognized you from somewhere when I saw you at the Christmas party! I wanted to go and talk to you, but it ended so abruptly."

"It did. But Kaylie seems to be over it."

"He was so not good for her. Or, anyone really." Liberty stood and went behind the counter, collected an apron, and tied it on. "So, is this store busy? The Rooster location is hopping all the time and" she glanced around the shop and grimaced, "it's only a week until Christmas. Why isn't this store decorated?"

They kept just busy enough that she'd never had time to do it. "We have a few regulars in the morning, and they should show up soon. It gets really busy between ten and two with the work crowd. I don't know about after that, I leave at two, so I can get to campus for an afternoon lecture and time to research in the library. I do most of my classes online, but I try to get to the campus as much as I can."

Liberty frowned and started slipping the coffee cups between her fingers. "I wish I was a student. I made it through the middle of my first semester. Master's of Business program. But I had some major life upheaval and couldn't attend anymore. Kaylie let me keep my job at that location, even though I'm not a student anymore because it's closest to my home. I guess that's why she felt she could ask me to work here while she's gone. I owe her."

Addi bit her lip and immediately felt bad for saying anything about Kaylie. "That's great. I'm glad she could help you."

Liberty smiled like it was the only way her face wanted to be. "At the Rooster, we turn on KJRS. We've never gotten any complaints. Can we turn it on here?"

KJRS was the Christian music station, and while Addi listened to it at home, she'd never asked Kaylie to allow that. "If Kaylie doesn't mind."

"Nope, she goes to the same church my sister does." Liberty turned and pushed through the back door to turn on the radio.

Church? Addi had always assumed Kaylie didn't believe, because of how she acted. It was also possible that she went to church, but never let it go farther than skin deep. But who was she to judge? She didn't know Kaylie's heart, only her actions.

"What church do you go to?" Addi asked as Liberty began prepping the sandwich station.

"The one on Fourth. You?"

In all the years she'd worked in that store, her faith had never come up. Addi had left it at the door. Why had it taken a stranger to get her to admit she was a believer? Kaylie probably didn't know she was a Christian, either.

"I go to Harvest." It was the first she'd even mentioned it within the walls of the shop. Her favorite song began playing over the radio. "I'm kind of hoping you can stay on here."

Liberty smiled and her shoulders raised just a bit. "It would be fun to work with someone I get along with."

Maybe Christmas wouldn't be a total bust. She'd had a nice long chat with Drew the day before, and now a new friend. What had started as a pretty horrible week, had turned downright peachy.

Drew stared at the screen and groaned. Why had he convinced himself this was a good idea? Hadn't he watched Kaylie treat people worse than dirt? Why did he continue to feel some strange attraction to her, like he could redeem her in some way if he could just be nice to her? The chances of this service even matching him up with her were slim. He hoped, literally, there wouldn't be other wealthy men in the area signed up for the service. Normally, he'd never divulge accurately what his bank account looked like. He didn't want to be loved for his money any more than anyone else.

It seemed like there were a million questions, and while they made sense if they were trying to match him up with the perfect woman, it still took more time than he'd planned to invest. As it was, he was late for the coffee shop. He checked his phone for the time. Yup. He needed caffeine, and he needed it ten minutes ago. Drew shut his laptop and went for his jacket. He'd finish the application at The Bean, then get his work done.

He stopped mid-shrug with his jacket stuck on his forearms. Kaylie would be there and if she saw him, might question why he was applying on the site. She told him to do it, but that didn't mean she really wanted him to. If they were matched, she might get angry with him.

Wrestling with his jacket, he finally got it on his shoulders. He could keep his work open in one tab, then switch back and forth if she came over, which wasn't all that likely. She didn't come talk to him often. Grand River was a big place, a college town with lots of business and industry, but Main Street felt like a small town. It gave the illusion he might have a chance, though they might be very small, there was still a chance.

It only took about ten minutes to walk to the little shop. When he pushed open the door, it was like he'd walked into a new world, not his familiar Bean. Addi and a woman he didn't recognize were putting up Christmas decorations, and a Christian hits music station played in the background. Instead of the quiet he was used to, people laughed and chatted over their coffee. While he'd always enjoyed the smell and feel of The Bean on Main, the changes made it even cozier, and less likely he'd get work done.

Addi turned from hanging bunting and smiled at him. She called from across the room, "I was beginning to get worried about you. I don't even know your last name to send out a search party."

He laughed and realized it felt really good to be missed. He set down his computer at his table and took a minute to glance over the whole store. They had put up a tree, hung garlands, and put out coffee mugs with various festive items spilling over the tops, all over the shop.

"Tanner. I'm Drew Tanner." Instead of hanging his jacket, he tossed it over the back of the booth seat. Today seemed to be the day for change. "Who's this?" He nodded to the other woman.

The stranger popped forward with all the energy of a Category 5 hurricane and thrust out her hand with a smile as big as Lake Erie. "I'm Liberty. What can I get for you?"

He hated to be rude, but Addi always made his coffee just perfect. He glanced at Addi to save him, and she laughed. "The usual, coming right up."

He started to turn back to his seat, then paused. "You know, I don't know your last name, either. Might be important. In case I ever need to send a search party for you."

Her eyes widened slightly, followed by the expected slight pink tinge to her cheeks. "Merrick," she mumbled so quietly he had to strain to hear over the music.

Liberty linked her arm with his and led him back to his seat. "So, you're a regular here? That's great."

He opened his computer and nodded, taking the extra step of plugging in, in the hopes this new exuberant barista would go find something to do so he could get his work done. In that instant, Addi arrived, setting his coffee down gingerly. "Can I get you anything else?"

He picked up the cup and cradled it in his hands, the mixture of coffee and mint soothing the rough edges even before he took a drink. "No, I've just got a lot of work to do today."

Addi swung her gaze to Liberty and tilted her head back toward the till in a silent command to go. Liberty stood with a slight pout that disappeared in an instant and brushed off her apron. "It was nice to meet you, Drew."

He held up his cup in salute. "Likewise." Though not really. Liberty, and especially Addi, were a distraction. He'd spent his evening wishing he had Addi's phone number to call or text her to see how she was doing. The friendlier he got with her, the worse it could get for him. Sweet, friendly girls hid things, like who they really were. Lauren had never come right out and told him how she felt, she'd just disappeared. In so doing, she'd ripped his heart out. No more sweet, quiet women. They hurt too much.

Without Kaylie to distract him, he got the application to Betwixt2Hearts set up and sent off. Hopefully soon, maybe even before Christmas, he could get his mother off his back about getting into dating. If he was really lucky, he'd find someone he could care about. His gaze slid over to dark-haired Addi, with her leggings that hugged shapely legs, and her messy ponytail. Maybe he'd already found someone he *could* care about, but only if he allowed himself to be open to that kind of hurt again. Not likely.

Five

Two days after Drew submitted his application, Christmas day, a response sat at the top of his inbox. One. As he stared open-mouthed at the screen, he almost couldn't believe his luck. There, at the top of the email, Kaylie Viro. Her profile picture was sultry, as expected, with a perfectly painted pout, hair too platinum to believe, and her usual smirk. Drew had the strangest urge to pray for her. With the number of other men who would see the not-quite revealing, yet revealing in so many ways, image, she might need it.

Would she agree to meet with him? It was the final hurdle in getting the date he'd wanted for months—yet, other than a sense of shock— his brain refused to get excited over it. Probably because she would never agree, but maybe because his brain remained stuck on Lauren. *He* had to move on.

With a click of the respond button, he sent Kaylie a request to chat and gave her his personal email. He only had one day left of free access, and that wasn't enough to talk with her. Though it was dishonest, he didn't let on that he knew her. If she put it together by his first name and his super-old profile picture, then it was done, and he'd put up with the storm at the coffee shop. She might even ask him to never darken their door again.

Before he could even flip to a new screen, Kaylie replied.

Hello Drew,

> IT TOOK ME A MINUTE TO MAKE SURE YOU WEREN'T SOMEONE
> ELSE. I'D LOVE TO MEET UP WITH YOU. HOW ABOUT THIS NEXT
> WEEK?
> KAYLIE

He hadn't seen Kaylie in about four days. It had taken him two days of putting together his profile and another two for Betwixt2Hearts to respond. In that time, he hadn't seen her. She'd been absent from the coffee shop, replaced by Liberty.

The coffee shop had completely changed in Kaylie's absence. Not only had the arrival of Liberty brought music and décor into the shop, but Addi had also changed. Instead of huddling in her shell, she talked more, smiled more, and even her usual messy ponytail had changed into more of a styled bun on the back of her head with pretty tendrils that curved around her face. The changes were subtle, but he'd watched for whatever she would change next. He'd missed Kaylie much less than he'd thought he would.

That would change once they were dating though. If they made it to that stage, it had to. She'd realize he was a great guy, worth more than his money. He'd see that she wasn't snarky like she acted at work, because, really, who was? Kaylie had a heart too and deserved someone who would be willing to treat her well, not like the last guy. Addi had told him about what had happened at the Christmas party, but she'd left out why it had induced Kaylie to use the dating service. No matter. God knew he could take care of Kaylie, or He wouldn't have orchestrated the connection. Only God could do that.

Drew hit reply.

> KAYLIE,
> SOUNDS GREAT. LET'S TALK A LITTLE BIT IN THE NEXT FEW DAYS
> AND GET TO KNOW EACH OTHER, LET ME KNOW WHEN YOU'RE
> FREE, AND I'LL CLEAR MY SCHEDULE. CAN'T WAIT TO SEE YOU.
> DREW

If he were really a stranger, he would've written "can't wait to *meet* you," but he wouldn't outright lie to her. She might take it hard at their first meeting. There had to be some give in her, or the meetup wouldn't have been scheduled at all. Even though she'd had to make sure he wasn't the Drew she knew from The Bean. Except he was. Only time would tell if the shock would wear off quickly.

The day after Christmas—not nearly a long enough absence—Kaylie swept into the shop wearing a Pinterest-worthy outfit and gathering Addi and Liberty around her like a mother hen. The heavy feeling that accompanied her settled over Addi's shoulders and hit like a hammer at her temples. Kaylie gently pushed them both toward the back room, even though customers sat in the front, and shouldn't be left alone.

"But," Liberty tried to speak up, but Kaylie cut her off.

"Quiet, I've got news!"

This behavior wasn't new to Addi, Kaylie often hid in the back room and wanted to chat. Addi indulged her if the shop was close to empty, but not usually when they were so packed. Drew hadn't even arrived yet, and many of the booths were taken. The Bean had seen a surge in customers in the last week. It was likely that the employees at the other stores had no idea what their boss was really like though, and the open-mouthed confusion on Liberty's face confirmed it.

Liberty piped up first, with some hesitation. She always liked to guess. "You've gotten back together with Julien?" Her eyes were wide, yet confused. Addi ducked and hid her face behind her hand to keep from saying anything. Kaylie never wasted time on the past, and they both knew Julien was long gone.

"No, of course not." Kaylie scrunched her face and blinked a few times, then sighed and went on with her story. "I signed up for that dating site and got a match! We'll be meeting this week." She squealed loud enough for jets flying above to hear.

"Oh, that's wonderful!" Liberty clapped her hands together, then fidgeted with her sleeve, probably doing her best to keep from hugging her boss, which Kaylie would never find acceptable. Addi found it refreshing, and more than a little funny.

"Nothing to say, Addi? This is all thanks to you." Kaylie smirked.

Addi popped up straight and shook her head. There was no way she would take on that stress. "No way. You are not pinning this on me. If your date is a failure, you'll blame me. I never suggested that site. I only asked how you were going to deal with working alongside the employee who led your boyfriend astray." Or, maybe it was the other way around; who could tell?

Kaylie flipped her hand in the air to stop Addi. "She quit the next day, and I haven't seen either of them since. Wait," She stopped and glanced around the room, her plucked and preened brows slanting inward. Addi could've warned Kaylie about the changes around the shop, but hadn't. She was too worried Kaylie would put a stop to all they had done. "What is that?"

Addi wasn't sure which *that* Kaylie could be talking about, they'd changed so much. "What's what?"

"The music. I've never allowed music in my store, and I don't even recognize this."

Addi tried to think quickly, which wasn't something she was good at where Kaylie was concerned. Everything she said always seemed to come out wrong.

Liberty laughed. "We've been playing it since I came, it's the same music we play at The Rooster. I've had so many comments about how nice it is and how it improves the ambiance." Kaylie nodded, her eyes wide and bright blue, with her mouth slightly open.

"Well, if the customers want it," Kaylie let her words trail off. She didn't know the first thing about running a business or what brought people into the store. If she'd had to start from the ground up, she probably wouldn't survive. Her parents had created the brand, built the stores, hired the employees and trained them, then turned all three sites over to Kaylie.

"What's your news?" Liberty collapsed onto the sofa and crossed her legs. Addi stayed near the door in case someone rang the bell, and chewed her fingernail. Something didn't sit right. Kaylie never bothered to go out of her way to tell her employees anything, unless she was bragging.

"As I said, I submitted my application to Betwixt2Hearts, and I've already gotten a response. He's excited to meet me, so excited that he wants to meet right away."

Liberty flounced to the front of the seat. "Do you know his name? Is he hot? Can we see his picture?"

Kaylie slipped her huge phone out of her purse and made a show of opening it with her long nails. It had been so nice to have someone working with her who could actually work, thought Addi, instead of sitting there because she couldn't wreck her nails or get dirty. Kaylie held out her giant phone, and the screen was so large it was like looking at a photo. "His name is Drew Tanner and here is his picture." She batted her lashes and showed it off like a prize. "I was worried at first that it was creepy Drew, but he doesn't seem to know me."

Addi's heart did a flip and acid filled her stomach. "Drew... Tanner?" She grabbed the phone to get a closer look. It couldn't be. She squinted at the profile picture. It was old but definitely Drew. Addi glanced up to make certain Kaylie wasn't joking with them, but she maintained her superior appearance. Liberty took the phone next and swept a glance toward Addi, then motioned almost imperceptibly to the door. Addi nodded, and Liberty handed Kaylie her phone back.

"That's great, Kaylie. Hope you enjoy your date. What day are you going?" They would need to make sure Kaylie and Drew stayed apart until then. Obviously, Drew wanted the date, but Kaylie wouldn't have agreed to it if she knew.

"Sometime in the next few days, we didn't discuss particulars. I don't want to seem too eager. Rich guys don't like that." Kaylie was already fixated on something else on her phone.

Liberty got behind Addi and shoved her out the door. Once they'd immersed themselves in the noise of the shop, Liberty stopped and went to the till pretending to work so she could talk to Addi without attracting notice. "Didn't you tell me Kaylie had turned our Drew down twice?"

Addi bristled at Liberty's *our Drew*, but let it slide. "Yes. Only a few weeks ago."

At that moment, Drew walked in and waved. He was later than usual. If he'd come on time, he would've been in the shop when Kaylie had come in, and it might have ruined everything for Drew. She rushed to meet him before he sat down.

"Drew, you need to go. Right now. Maybe come back in an hour." He'd already set down his laptop, and she grabbed it, shoving it into his hands. He was so handsome in his green sweater and fitted jeans. He'd trimmed his beard over Christmas, and it framed his lips perfectly. Life just wasn't fair. Why did he have to be attracted to her boss?

"Why?" He stood there, unmoving. The man would finally get what he wanted if he would just listen. She could feel all the potential scenarios she'd worked out for meeting Drew outside of the coffee shop slip away.

"Kaylie is here," She hissed between her teeth and glanced over her shoulder to make sure Kaylie hadn't appeared behind her.

"Oh, well it isn't like I'm not going to see her."

Only after Addi rolled her eyes did she realize she'd learned that behavior from her boss. "Drew, if you want that date to happen, leave now. If she realizes it's you, she'll never agree."

He set down his computer. "I'm not going to lie to her, but she doesn't think it's me. Plus, I wanted to talk to you. I'm sorry you got to hear about my date from Kaylie."

Why was he worried about where she'd heard the news? "Yeah, well, I guess you'll finally get what you want. Just remember who makes the best coffee in town." Her heart cracked a bit. At least he'd come and see her to make coffee when he was blissfully married.

His face fell slightly. "You do."

Her chest tightened. He was so good, so handsome, and so much more likely to go for someone like Kaylie. There would be no walks in the park or basketball games. Best friends forever wasn't just a cute saying for her, it was her curse. "I hope you have a great time. If you're not leaving, I'll get your coffee." She wondered if Kaylie would even bother to learn how he liked it.

Six

Though Drew had tried to hold out for as long as possible in meeting Kaylie for their date, she pushed to meet him. He'd wanted to talk to her by email and text for a bit before they met in person, mostly so she could see he wasn't such a bad catch before she realized she already knew him. The problem was, she didn't want him to talk at all. She wanted to go dancing and see things, to go for drives in the countryside and go shopping. She would be disappointed when she found out he didn't drive anything bigger than a scooter, mostly because everything he needed was within a few blocks. Where he couldn't walk, was only a cab ride away.

His phone buzzed for the third time in a row. Kaylie had been so short on words at the coffee shop, he hadn't been prepared for the thesis-length text strings she liked to send, but hated if he responded with more than a few words. He'd learned after the first one that she would get angry with him if he tried to respond before she was done. She took it as personally as if he'd verbally interrupted her. Drew scratched his temple and wished he could go get a coffee to prevent the headache lurking behind his eyes, but the weekend crew was at The Bean, and they just didn't make his coffee quite right. Too much mint making the whole brew too bitter to drink.

A vision of Addi in his kitchen making coffee for him flashed in front of his eyes. Without thinking, he pulled up his computer and opened a search, then typed in Addison Merrick, Grand River, Texas. Nothing came up, but under suggestions, it read: Were you searching for Addi Merrick? He clicked the link, and her social media profile came up right on top. He'd recognize that dark hair and shy smile anywhere.

He could see she was online at the moment and he sent her a friend request. If he had to guess, it would shock her that he'd found her, but she *had* given him her name in case he needed to send out a search party, and he did. Lack of coffee was an emergency. His messenger lit up with one unread message.

When he clicked it open, it was from Addi and just one line, he didn't even have to open it to read all of what she said.

ADDI: IS THIS REALLY YOU?

Such doubt. He laughed and opened up the box.

DREW: YES. IS THIS REALLY YOU?

He could see her typing something, and he waited. When it seemed like she'd been typing for about five whole minutes, he figured she'd just walked away. Maybe their friendship was only at the shop. Just as he'd suspected, she and Lauren could be twins. He reached for the top of his laptop to close it when the message finally popped through.

ADDI: IT IS. I DIDN'T REALLY EXPECT YOU TO ACTUALLY LOOK FOR ME.

He stared at her comment for a minute. She was so shy and unassuming, yet completely blunt when asked a direct question.

DREW: YOU SAID I COULD SEND OUT A SEARCH PARTY IF I WAS EVER IN NEED. YOU ALSO TOLD ME TO REMEMBER WHO MAKES THE BEST COFFEE IN TOWN. I CAN'T SEEM TO BREW ANYTHING BUT A MONSTER HEADACHE. ARE YOU FREE TO COME OVER AND MAKE SOME COFFEE? I'LL BUY, MAYBE EVEN SPRING FOR PIZZA.

Would she go for it? Having Addi all to himself, without the pressure of other customers and the shop and without Liberty to come over and chat too, had him staring at the screen bouncing his leg while he waited. Finally, after what felt like three lifetimes, Addi began typing.

ADDI: YOU WANT ME TO COME OVER TO MAKE COFFEE?

He laughed again because, in his mind, he could see the doubt on her face, the questions in her eyes.

DREW: AND EAT PIZZA. DON'T FORGET THAT. IT'S A PRETTY IMPORTANT PART.

He got a notification that she'd accepted his friend request. Oddly, that felt like more of a success than scoring a date with Kaylie.

ADDI: I SUPPOSE I COULD. I HAVE SOME HOMEWORK TO DO, SO I'LL NEED TO LEAVE SHORTLY AFTER PIZZA. HOW DO I GET THERE?

He gave her the address and decided that, unless she drove to get there, he'd bring her home on his scooter or rent her a cab, whichever she felt more comfortable with. At least he would know she made it back home all right.

ADDI: I NEED TO STOP FOR A FEW THINGS ON MY WAY. GIVE ME ABOUT FORTY-FIVE MINUTES.

That meant he had some time to wipe the dust off the top of the television, make sure pizza got ordered, and wipe down his kitchen. He wasn't a slob, but he just didn't use his apartment all that much except as a place to crash and watch his television. A quick look around and he realized he hadn't done much with the place since he'd dated Lauren. The throw pillows she'd made him buy were still on his couch, just where she'd left them. The painted canvas with the word Together in a scrolling font was still in its prominent spot on his wall, not to mention the pictures.

He had a few on the wall showing the two of them, and a few more on tables around his living room. He hadn't realized how often he saw Lauren every single day, without ever noticing that he did. He pulled the photo off the wall in the entry hall and stared at it. It was an engagement photo, and

A Crossroads Collection

he realized it felt like he'd lived a whole life since then. He collected all the photos of Lauren and put them in his room. Maybe he'd put them back up, maybe not, but he couldn't have Addi asking about her. Lauren was a subject best left to his past.

After all the pictures were put away, and he was reasonably certain there was nothing embarrassing for Addi to find, he gathered what he had for coffee supplies and set them out on the counter. Nothing he had looked anything like the machines they used at The Bean and that was probably how they managed to make regular coffee taste so good. But then, when anyone but Addi made it, it wasn't quite right either.

He patted his hand against his thigh. How much longer would he have to wait, and why was he so anxious to see her?

Addi stared one more time at the address she'd copied down and still couldn't believe it. Drew had messaged her. She'd pinched herself to make sure she wasn't dreaming, then he'd told her the reason he'd found her. It wasn't just to hang out or even to be friends online outside of work. He'd needed coffee, of course. He was all about the coffee, and he had a date with Kaylie coming up. She shouldn't have gotten her hopes too high, but she had as soon as she'd seen his name.

She stopped at The Bean and picked up some ground beans and the mint extract used to make Drew's coffee taste just right. She had her French press in a box, and with a few other things from the store, she was ready to make Drew his preferred drink. She'd walked ten blocks, with a box, so she could make him a cup of coffee, and she wasn't done yet. From The Bean, she had another six blocks to go. And she would do it again because Drew had asked. She'd do about anything for him.

She reached his apartment complex and buzzed his apartment. He came down and let her in, then grabbed the box from her arms. She'd expected him to be more relaxed on the weekend, but he wore what he usually did, a pair of jeans that fit him far too well and a button-down shirt that was about a third unbuttoned to reveal a fitted tee in a complementary

423

color. The man was more coordinated than herself.

"What's all this?" He eyed the inside of the box.

"It's everything I need to make your coffee. I can't have you thinking I'd failed. Plus, if I'm going to walk that far just to cure your headache, I want to be sure it will work."

He smiled, and her feet suddenly didn't hurt anymore. She smiled back as he led the way up five flights of stairs. He stood in front of his door and tried to open it, but couldn't get a good grip as he tried to balance the box. It shifted, and she grabbed for it before it fell.

"Why don't you let me open the door, so we don't lose that?" She laughed but didn't want her coffee press to get broken—not that she drank coffee, but her mother did when she came to visit.

He nodded his approval and Addi opened the door. She'd expected bachelor-white walls and no décor, considering he didn't seem to have much interest in that sort of thing. He hadn't even noticed the changes at The Bean, or hadn't said anything.

"Don't look too closely at anything. I haven't really done anything with the place in over a year. I work too much to care." Drew came from behind and set the box gently down on his kitchen counter and started pulling things out for her.

"It's nice. You have more paint on the walls, pictures, and matching furniture than I do."

"I've also had a few years of running my own business. You work at a coffee shop and are in college."

How had he known she was in college? She couldn't remember telling him, but if she did, it meant he paid attention. Her life wasn't meant to be broadcast to just anyone. She didn't want him thinking she was just a brainless college kid with no goals outside of making it through the semester. That stage had come and gone years before. "I'm not just in college. I'm working toward my Master's, in Counseling. The classes that require I attend, I do after I get off work, but many I take online."

She arranged everything she needed in the order she'd need it on the counter, then got busy making it. It took longer, because she didn't have the specialty equipment available to her at work, and while she could've just made him a coffee when she'd been at work, it wouldn't have been hot by the time she got it there.

Drew hovered behind her, watching her, and she could feel his presence, his every movement. Though she thought he'd make her nervous—like Kaylie—he didn't. Having him there soothed her, which was unexpected.

"So, what caused your monster headache?" She turned to look at him as she grabbed the large mug he'd left out for her use.

"Dare I say?" He raised his eyebrows and smiled, drawing her attention to his lips, that were just the right fullness for his neatly trimmed beard, or kissing... she turned back to her task to hide the heat climbing up her cheeks.

"Well, I should know what to prepare for. If I have to come over here often, I need to know." She laughed but hoped he would invite her to do something that didn't involve coffee at some point.

"It was Kaylie. She's more than I ever expected."

That woman was about as high-maintenance as they came, but Drew had to have known that from seeing her at The Bean. She wasn't any different there than she was outside of work, the little that Addi had seen anyway.

"And this surprised you?"

He chuckled as she handed him the cup. He did his usual embrace of the mug and lifted it to his nose, took a deep sniff and closed his eyes as he breathed a sigh. If only she could make someone that happy with something other than a drink.

"Yes, I guess I thought maybe her work self was different than reality. We're going to see a play, then I'm taking her out to eat after. It's something I wanted to see anyway, but wouldn't go alone."

Addi had never been to a play, not that she wouldn't love to. Tickets were expensive, and she'd rather eat. "Sounds like a great time. I'm sure Kaylie will enjoy herself. Though, snap a picture if you can. I've never actually seen her eat anything but ice cream." Addi shivered at the memory.

Drew took a sip of the coffee. "It isn't quite the same." He paused to think, then took another sip. "It may be even better." He took a deep breath and just enjoyed it for a second, then replied, "Are you insinuating my date is a vampire?"

The thought was preposterous and too funny to ignore. Addi laughed and leaned against the counter, amazed at how comfortable she felt there. Drew just wasn't much of a stranger anymore, even though they hadn't talked all that much.

"Not at all. I think she absorbs nutrients from her phone. I rarely see her touch anything else. Though she does leave the store for lunch."

He glanced behind her. "Aren't you going to make one for yourself?"

She never drank coffee. It was one of the benefits of working where she did; there was no need to burn through her paycheck on a product she didn't consume. "No, I'm good. No headache." She tapped her temple, and he laughed as he turned to leave the kitchen that was literally three times the size of her own.

He didn't push the subject and led her out to his couch, offering her a seat on the far end, and he sat on the other side. Whereas the kitchen felt like the perfect place to talk and joke around, the living room had a different feel, like she had intruded on someone else's space. Even though Drew hadn't ever mentioned a girlfriend, her touches were all over his living room. There were far too many to ignore. If Drew had a girlfriend already, why had he asked Kaylie for a date, and why was she, herself, there?

"Now that you have your coffee, is your head feeling better?" She was at a loss for another topic, since asking about the throw pillows would be strange.

He rubbed his temple and set his cup down on the table next to him. "Yes, I believe it is. Thank you. I know it was crazy to seek you out, but I'm glad you answered."

She stood back up and made her way to the patio door. He had a good view, but that's not why she was there. There was an oppressive feeling she couldn't shake, and the hair on her neck prickled to life. "It isn't like I had much else going on today. I should probably go, now that you're taken care of, though. Homework." She made for the door. Her feet still throbbed from the walk over, and her coffee pot was still hot, but she could get it later.

"Addi, you don't have to run off so quickly. Remember, pizza?"

Were his eyes hopeful, or was that just her imagination? Could she ignore that gut feeling like she didn't belong there? "Right, pizza." What could she possibly lose by staying a little longer, besides her heart?

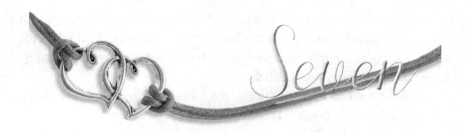

Seven

He could tell himself till he was blue in the face that he wanted her to stay so he didn't have to eat a whole pizza by himself, but he could probably do it if he had to. What he *really* wanted was to talk to Addi. Talking with her in the kitchen as she'd made his coffee, watching the expressions wash over her face like the waves on a beach as he joked with her, was so refreshing. It certainly wasn't anything like chatting with Kaylie over text. Addi had managed to dispel his headache even before she'd handed him the cup.

When they'd finished a few slices of pizza, Addi had allowed him to pull her back into conversation. Now she sat back in her seat on the sofa, contemplating what she needed to say. Addi eyed him, pursing her lips slightly like she did before she was about to be brutally honest with him. He braced himself but didn't want her to stop.

"I know I shouldn't be here. My boss is going on a date with you. This week. You might have invited me over as a friend, but if Kaylie wants to date you, she won't see it that way. Not that she would see me as competition, but she would be angry, and she'll take it out on me, not you."

He'd managed to keep her there for about an hour already, but he'd hoped she would stay longer. Addi stood and threw her paper plate in the trash. He hadn't really considered she might feel that way when he invited her since he wasn't dating Kaylie yet. After talking with her by text, he doubted Kaylie would want a second date. He wasn't even sure she'd want to go with him on the first one once they met up.

"She might, but we were friends before the dating site. We'd talked a little bit at The Bean. It isn't like I'm trying to date both of you."

Addi flinched from across the room. "But we never spoke enough that we could be called friends. I don't mind if we talk outside the coffee shop. I actually had a really great time here, but I don't want to make Kaylie angry. She's hard enough to work with as it is."

He hadn't seen her at The Bean, and he realized he hadn't even been looking for her. "Is she back? I hadn't noticed."

Addi laughed briefly, and for a moment he felt better. "No, I don't think she plans to come back. She replaced herself with Liberty, which is just fine with me. Liberty is amazing and actually helps me. Not that I'm talking about your girlfriend behind her back." Addi's eyebrow rose in challenge. He would be the first to admit, talking about Kaylie would be easy, almost too easy, and he shouldn't do it. But if she was so negative, what did he see in her? Was it only that he thought he could change her, give her something she needed? Or did he hope to gain something too? He didn't want to cancel the date, he'd waited for it. Too long. Now that it was on the horizon though, he wasn't as excited as he'd thought he'd be.

"Liberty's great, and she certainly talks more than Kaylie. That woman would talk your ear off if you'd let her. And with a smile, no less."

Addi sat back down on the couch, and he pushed the pizza box out of the way on the coffee table, glad that for the moment anyway, she'd decided to stay.

"She would. She's a small-town girl, who hasn't let the big city change her. She's friendly to everyone who comes in and treats them like she's known them her whole life."

"And she treats you better, which is why you started talking more, smiling more." He cut his words off quickly. He couldn't list anything else or she would realize just how closely he'd paid attention to her flourishing outlook the last couple weeks. Far more than he'd paid attention to the missing boss who he was supposed to be attracted to.

"Well, Liberty and I see each other as equals. Kaylie never did. She was the boss, and that was fine. Because she is." Addi shrugged her narrow shoulders.

It bothered him that she would just stay at a job with a boss who treated her the way Kaylie did, just because she didn't see the issue. "Just because she's the boss, doesn't mean she should belittle you. I've been a boss for three years; I don't treat my employees that way." It didn't matter that he was his only employee.

"I needed the job. Her parents offered me one. I had no skills because I was focused on school through my ninth-grade year up until I got my Bachelor's degree. Then I needed to work to continue. I didn't realize until it was too late that Kaylie would be my boss. I can't just quit, I have bills to pay."

"I'm sure you do." Who didn't, and he still wanted to see her at the coffee shop, so having Kaylie take some time off was good for everyone.

"What do you hope to do with your degree, once you finish?" He sat back and got comfortable. She hadn't made any further move for the door, so he could relax.

"I want to go into co-counseling at my church. There's a psychologist there already, but he needs help."

He'd never wished that Great River was smaller until that moment. It was great having everything he ever needed close by. But if it were, he might be able to find her church easily—without even asking—and surprise her some Sunday. But not in a city this big. "Where do you go?"

She chuckled slightly. "Grace, uptown. I have to take the bus, but it's worth it."

He nodded, he'd heard of that one, but had never been there. He liked his church, so it made no sense to hop around. "I go to Shiloh."

She nodded enthusiastically. "That's where Liberty goes! I'm surprised she hasn't cornered you yet."

He was too. It was probably only his penchant for showing up just on time and leaving immediately following that saved him from talking more to Liberty. While she was much better for Addi than Kaylie, she was too talkative for his taste.

"What will you do if Kaylie doesn't want to go with you?" Addi's voice lowered to almost a whisper.

He hadn't wanted to face that, but he should make a plan. "I'm hoping she'll go just because she won't have anything else planned for the evening. I'm certainly a better prospect than that fern-kissy guy."

Addi's laugh burst from her lips. He'd never heard her relax so much and he couldn't help smiling at the sound.

"'Fern-Kissy Guy'? You're far better than him, but that nickname will now live in infamy."

He couldn't stop staring at Addi's lips after that glorious laugh. "Meaning, you'll tell Liberty, and you'll both laugh about it."

"For hours." She giggled some more. "But, now that you've kept me longer, I really do need to go. Homework calls." She stood and closed the pizza box, then took it to the fridge. He weighed his options, cab or scooter? He wanted to take her himself, but wouldn't be able to carry her box with her coffee equipment. If he sent her by cab, she'd have no reason to come back.

"Let me wash up your coffee pot. It's the least I can do."

She came out of the kitchen and glanced around his living room like it was a cage. "I don't need it. I don't drink coffee so I can get it some other time."

"Well, if that's so, can I give you a ride home?"

She bit her lip. "I don't usually tell people where I live."

He took a step closer to her. She didn't have to worry about him, didn't she know that yet? "I'd feel much better if I knew you made it home safely. You trusted me enough to come here."

Addi sighed and turned her head away from him, but it did nothing to hide the blush that crept up her cheeks. "It isn't that I don't trust you. It's just, embarrassing. I live in the low-rent district."

He smiled, hoping she understood he didn't judge her. After all, it wasn't like a barista—putting herself through a Master's program—had a lot of extra money. "All the more reason for me to do it. It's getting dark out."

"I should've left sooner, but—" She bit her lip, cutting off her own words.

He understood, far too well. Lauren had that same pull. He could've talked to her for hours and then still called her before bed to talk some more. He usually hated to just sit and chat, but with the right woman, maybe?

No.

Addi wasn't the right woman. She was only a friend. Because if she became more, he'd have to face more heartache. She would realize whatever Lauren had, and leave. He couldn't do that twice in one lifetime.

Drew handed her a helmet that looked much like a bike helmet and helped her tighten the chin strap properly. She felt positively silly as he slipped on a matching one.

"I'll need your address." He stared into her eyes, but surely he had to see how ridiculous she looked. "410 Appleton," she mumbled.

"Great. I actually know the way. Climb on." He swung his leg over and slid forward to give her enough room.

Addi hesitated for a moment. She would have to hold onto him, maybe even hold tight to him depending on traffic. She took a deep breath and swung her leg over just as he had, then arranged her feet on the floorboard and tentatively put her hands on his waist. He turned slightly and looked at her through the corner of his eye, then turned the key to start it up. The machine sputtered to life under her. Drew pushed it for a few steps with his feet, then they were off.

It never really felt terribly cold in Texas, especially to a girl originally from Michigan, but as they drove down side streets and wove their way through one-ways, she was thankful she'd worn a sweater. Within a few minutes, she realized he wasn't taking her directly home, but there was no way to ask him unless she got even closer to him. Addi held tight to his shirt and inched forward on the seat.

"Where are you taking me? I thought you said you knew the way."

He turned his head slightly to acknowledge her. "I know the way. I'm just giving you a little ride. Thought you might enjoy it."

He cut through some traffic and buzzed up a bicycle path through a park.

She laughed and pointed at the signs that clearly read No Motorized

Vehicles.

He shrugged. "It's late, and I see the police on their Segways all the time. I slowed down."

He had, but her heart hadn't. It felt just right sitting behind Drew on that scooter, letting him drive her around town, holding on to him. But when the night was over, Cinderella would turn right back into a lowly barista, and the pretty boss would get the prince.

Drew pulled over and parked near a bike rack. He slid off his helmet and hung it on the front handlebars. "Want to go for a little walk?"

Hadn't she daydreamed of just that? But she couldn't. As it was, she would have to stay up most of the night, writing her paper. "I really wish I could, but I do have to get home."

He nodded but didn't climb back on. "It's just that," He rubbed his nose and glanced off down the trail they'd just come down. "I want you to know you're welcome to come over whenever you want. I feel, uh, comfortable with you."

Her heart shriveled at the word. Comfortable. She was just another friend. She was no Cinderella, and he didn't want to find her slipper. No one ever would. "Right. Got it. Now, can you bring me home?"

Tears pooled behind her eyes, burning the sensitive corners, but she blinked them away and thanked the Lord it was too dark for him to see. Once he had his date, he wouldn't be a friend anymore either. If Kaylie realized how good he was, she would want him all to herself and Addi couldn't fault her for that. She'd want it the same way.

Drew slid back on the scooter and fixed his helmet, then drove her the few blocks left to her apartment. The closer she got to home, the more the world seemed to close in. Tighter housing. Dirty streets. Police cars parked every few blocks. Until they'd neared her home, the afternoon had felt like a date, and now she didn't want him to go any further, didn't want him to see how she really lived. Addi let go of her hold on his shirt and touched his arm. Drew pulled the scooter over.

"Is something wrong? We're almost there."

"I think I can walk the rest of the way." This way, she wouldn't have to be disappointed by the goodbye, because it would never be anything like what her heart desired. Drew had never led her on. She was the one who put importance on his every word.

"I thought we already talked about this. I'm taking you all the way home. I kept you out later than you planned, so I need to make sure you get home all right."

She bristled. "This is my neighborhood. I live here. I think I can manage to walk a few blocks." Addi slid back on the seat to get off, and he took off again. The engine sputtered and revved to keep up with his demand. Addi wrapped her arms tightly around him to keep from sliding off the back. He pushed the little engine harder as it zipped down the darkening streets. A little later, he pulled up in front of her apartment building.

Her heart still pounded in her ears, but she wasn't sure if it was the ride or clinging to Drew that made her breath come fast. She fumbled her way off the back of the scooter, and with shaking fingers, tried to unfasten the helmet. Drew didn't laugh, bless him, but reached up and quickly squeezed the clasp, releasing her from it. She pulled it off and handed it to him, still not sure how she should say goodbye or if she should be angry that he'd just taken off when she'd still been talking.

"There, you're home. Now I don't have to worry about you."

Why did he have to say things like that? To make her question whether he would've indeed had any thoughts about her at all after she'd left his apartment.

"Yes, no worries." The idiotic words tripped off her tongue before she could stop them.

"I'll see you Monday then?" He stood, flipped up his seat, and stored the helmet underneath.

"I'll be there." She backed away, sure he would just want to leave.

"It was good to hang out with you." He sat back on the scooter and backed it away from the curb.

"Yeah, you too." She waved and forced her feet to remain planted instead of running to her room and slamming the door shut on her life. Why couldn't she ever be the one to get the great guy? Why was she always the one who got to hear about the great dates and fabulous kisses, but never the one to experience them?

He pushed the scooter in a U-turn, then took off in the direction he'd come. He never even actually said goodbye. She'd let her expectations ruin a perfectly wonderful and completely unexpected afternoon. Once she got into her room and leaned against her door, she batted away the tears threatening to spill down her cheeks, but finally settled on closing her eyes.

Why Lord? Why am I always the friend and never anything more? Will I be alone forever?

Eight

As Drew slid his tie to his neck, he swallowed the dread he couldn't shake. Kaylie would be angry. He'd tried to fool himself since he got the original notice that maybe she would change her mind, but he'd had enough time to think about every possible scenario—and none of them were good.

His phone buzzed from its perch on his dresser, and he slid it forward. Kaylie had sent him a message.

> **KAYLIE:** I CAN'T WAIT TO SEE YOU! I'LL MEET YOU BY THE
> STATUE IN MIDDLE PARK.

The same park he'd taken Addi the night before. He'd wanted to take her on a walk and talk more. Keep her for every minute and just enjoy being with someone who didn't judge him in any way. Addi was about the closest thing to a close friend he'd had in a long time, and he craved time with her. Craved the way he felt when he was with her.

He quickly typed in the best response he could, then called a cab to pick him up. He would meet Kaylie at the park and then she would ride with him to the Center for the Arts to see a show. When that was done, if it seemed like Kaylie wanted to, they would go to his favorite sushi bar and eat. It would all be low-key, without any pressure on her to see him again if she didn't want to because he couldn't imagine her wanting to.

The cab ride flew by, and suddenly he arrived at the park. He asked the driver to wait and pushed open the door. Kaylie arrived by another cab a few minutes later. Her face, in picture-perfect pout, flashed surprise, then she turned from him, searching all along the sidewalk. Drew took a deep breath and approached her.

"Kaylie, I'm the Drew who came here to pick you up."

She whipped around to face him. "You lied to me. There's no way you could've seen my profile picture and not known it was me."

He had known from the moment he opened the email from Betwixt2Hearts exactly who she was, but why hadn't she recognized him? His picture wasn't *that* old.

"My profile picture was there too. You never asked if it was me. Look, this doesn't have to be a waste. Just come to the show with me, we'll go out to eat afterward, then I'll bring you home. We don't even have to tell anyone if you don't want to."

"And I won't." She strode off toward the waiting cab. At least she was coming, and he wouldn't have to scramble to find someone else to take the spare ticket. Addi was at school in the evening, so he couldn't even ask her.

He rushed ahead and opened the door for her. As Kaylie slid into the cab, she gave him a scathing glance. "I suppose what you put in for your income was a lie, or you wouldn't be using a cab."

His ego wanted to defend himself, but he felt a soft prodding in the area of his conscience. "I don't have my own car because I don't really have a need for one. I didn't lie to you, except by omission. I'm sorry that I didn't come right out and say that I'm the guy from the coffee shop. But Betwixt did set us up. We must have some things in common, or they wouldn't have."

She crossed her arms and this time pouted for real, with sullen eyes and pursed lips. "I guess I'm the one who told you to apply, but I haven't gotten any other notifications, and I did pay even after setting up a date with you. It's just not fair."

The few other business owners who were in his circle would never use a site like Betwixt to find a date. They would rely on friends in their sphere to set them up before letting a stranger do it. Until Kaylie found a way to break into those groups, she wouldn't find the rich guy she wanted.

"I'm sure you'll find someone. Give it time."

"I haven't got time. I want to quit now. Do you have any idea how stressful it is to run three stores? I just want someone else to handle it. I've even considered giving them back to my parents, but then I wouldn't have an income at all."

He'd wondered why she was insistent on a wealthy husband, but he had no desire to run coffee shops. "What if the man you find doesn't want to take them over? Would you just sell them?"

Kaylie's ice-blue eyes softened just slightly. "I don't know. I'm not cut out for it. That much I know. If I have to work, I want to be in fashion, not coffee. I guess I was just hoping that a wealthy man might be able to hire someone to manage the businesses for me. It isn't like they aren't profitable. They are."

Sure they were, thanks to people like Addi who knew the customers, made excellent coffee, and acted like she wanted to be there even when she didn't.

"Why didn't you go out with Addi?"

Kaylie's question shocked him right out of his thoughts. Had she realized he'd been thinking about Addi?

"She isn't my type." Except she was far too close to his type for comfort.

"And I am?" She stared at him with that hard set to her face.

"I thought so." He *had* thought so, weeks ago. That seemed like a long time ago, and he wasn't so sure now.

"I think you're wrong, but I'll give you the benefit of the doubt. I'll go to the show and out to eat, then we can go back to the site and leave our feedback on our first date."

"And you'll give me a chance? You pretty much had me pegged as a loser the moment I walked into The Bean."

Kaylie huffed and slid over a few inches farther from him. "You have a lot to overcome. It will be almost impossible for me to shift how I think of you, but you can try. You are a client, one who didn't take no for an answer. You don't hang out with the right people. The only thing you have going for you is that you like my shops enough not to sell them off."

"Maybe. I'm in marketing. I have no interest in going into coffee right now. I'm not asking about our futures beyond the next four hours. Will you give me a chance?"

Her blue eyes burned into him like lasers. "I will do my best."

It was more likely that he could survive a swim across an ocean. She would let him pay for a fun night, but she had no intention of changing how she thought of him. He let the cabbie know they were ready and settled back in his seat as Kaylie slid farther away.

Addi stared out the bus window as it pulled down the dark streets toward Main. The Belltown Theater Performance Center for the Arts was on Main, exactly where Drew and Kaylie were at that moment, enjoying a production of *Oklahoma!*.

As the bus neared the theater, the flashing lights and people drew her attention. Would she glimpse Drew, and if she did, what if he was happy? Wasn't that what she wanted? His happiness was the most important, not that he chose her. He could choose her and be completely unhappy for the rest of his life; that wasn't worth thinking about and wasn't what she wanted. Though, he would never know he didn't want her unless he actually tried, which he wouldn't.

They passed the theater, and Addi pulled her phone out of her bag to check her email. Still no new messages, which meant the dating site couldn't find anyone for her, either. The free three days had yielded nothing. Big surprise. *She'd* been trying for years. The idea some site could fix her problems in three days should've been laughable, except it wasn't funny at all. There just wasn't anyone for her. She'd be alone forever.

A text pinged through from Liberty.

LIBERTY: YOU HOME YET?

Liberty was the closest thing she had to a best friend, but sometimes Liberty was just too happy. Addi had a good funk going on, and she was ready to be miserable for at least the whole evening.

ADDI: NO, STILL ON THE BUS.

The reply came back almost instantly as if she'd already had it typed, waiting for the reply.

LIBERTY: GOOD. GET OFF AT MY STOP.

Addi let out a groan loud enough that people turned to gape.

ADDI: BUT I HAVE HOMEWORK TO DO.

Again, she'd had a comeback ready.

LIBERTY: NO BUTS. YOU NEED ME TONIGHT.

Fine, but she refused to enjoy herself. She yanked on the cord to indicate she needed to stop at the next bus stop and slid the strap of her backpack over her shoulder. If she went to Liberty's, she'd have to catch a later bus, and that would end up costing even more money she didn't have. Being poor was harder and harder to manage by the day.

Addi's feet were like lead as she tromped off the bus in front of Liberty's apartment. Addi had never been there, but they had shared addresses when Liberty had learned she attended Central Texas University. She lived in a nicer area of Grand River. There was even an attendant at the door to hold it open for her. He asked who she was and buzzed Liberty, then punched in the code to unlock the door and let her in when Liberty answered.

"Have a good evening, miss." He smiled as he held the door for her, but it was one of those smiles people offer to everyone, a work smile that didn't even warm his face.

Liberty already had the door open and waited for her in the hall as the elevator opened. "I wasn't sure you'd remember where I live. I only told you once. I was ready to run out to my car to come pick you up in case you'd already passed this stop."

"I can't believe you guys have your own bus stop. How many people who live here even ride the bus?" Addi asked, her foul mood causing her to lash out at her friend.

Liberty let it slide without even noticing. "Not all that many. Doesn't the bus stop near your house?"

"No, only four blocks away. The bus only goes around the periphery of my neighborhood, even though a lot of people ride." When she'd started riding, she was almost sure they arranged the stops like they did to actually deter people in her neighborhood from riding.

"Well, don't worry. I'll drive you home."

"You don't have to do that." Addi had told Liberty the route she rode home, but not the actual location. Drew, her parents, the college, and now Kaylie were the only ones who knew her real address. She'd used her school PO at The Bean when she'd applied, so even Kaylie hadn't known before the Christmas party.

"Well, you're welcome to just stay. We could hang out and eat supper, chat, and then I could go do my thing while you do your online classes. I have super-fast internet." Liberty's eyebrows rose along with the sides of her mouth.

The offer was generous and sounded like fun, but she had no clothes, and she would have to get up earlier to go home for clothes in the morning if she stayed. "I'll just catch a bus. Don't worry about it."

Liberty pulled her into the kitchen. Like Drew, Liberty had a real kitchen, not just a hallway with cabinets, a stove, and a refrigerator. It was bright with stainless steel appliances and white cabinets, an actual room. "I'm baking cookies. Sit here at the island and talk to me."

They had been friends long enough to know that when Liberty asked you to talk, that meant give her a topic suggestion and she would run with it.

"I'm tired of being single." Her raw mood refused to be filtered. After spending the afternoon with Drew yesterday, holding onto him on the ride home, and thinking about him all day, she felt inadequate. He'd still chosen to keep his date with Kaylie. A day with her hadn't been enough.

"So, do something about it. Did you sign up for that site?" Liberty picked up a wooden spoon and stirred something in a big stainless steel bowl.

"Yes, and they have no matches for me. Not, 'we're working on it.' Not, 'you have these choices which match a few of your traits.' Just none. No matches."

"Hey." Liberty slammed the bowl down on the counter and the huge

440

lump of whatever was inside bounced once. "Pity, party of one. Your table is in the corner. Knock it off."

Addi set her backpack on the floor. "What? You asked what's up, I told you. That's exactly how I feel right now."

"Have you ever heard of God leaving a vessel empty?" Liberty turned back to her bowl and attacked the contents with fervor.

"What do you mean?" She was so tired from worry, hurt, and filling her mind with things she'd had to strain to recall in class. There was no room for thinking about all the possible things Liberty could mean.

"I mean, if God's going to take the time to make you, shape you, direct you, and place you. He will fill you. It may not be with a relationship. Maybe He'll suddenly fill you with a need to be a missionary in Zimbabwe, but if you ask Him to fill you, He isn't going to ignore that request. Not having a boyfriend doesn't make you any less of a person."

"But I'm lonely, Liberty." All the hurt Addi had collected from years of being everyone's friend, but not special enough to date, finally burst. "I love that we're friends, don't get me wrong. But I'm probably the only twenty-six-year-old in the entire town of Great River who has never been on a date." She was teased for being 'sweet sixteen and never been kissed.' If she'd known back then that a whole decade would pass and she still wouldn't have had the experience, maybe she would have made different decisions.

"You aren't." Liberty smiled softly, and unlike usual, let the room go silent.

The tension grew between them, and Liberty dug a pan out of a lower cabinet. Addi rested her elbows on the counter, suddenly feeling about two inches tall. "You too?"

Liberty nodded and didn't answer until she had the pan sprayed with cooking spray and the oven turned on to preheat. "About a year ago, I lost one hundred pounds. Not because of any special diet, but because I had cancer. It robbed me of a lot. I was so sick that I couldn't eat. I had a really posh job at an advertising firm. About midway through my treatment, they claimed I wasn't doing my job and fired me. Luckily for me, I didn't have a husband and kids. All the extra money I'd earned had gone into savings, which let me keep my insurance plan, even though it cost me more than three times my rent every month."

Addi took a deep breath and let her anger and hurt leave her as she exhaled. There was no way to feel sorry for herself in the face of someone who'd gone through what Liberty had.

"Is it in remission?"

Liberty plopped a gob of dough onto the pan. "Yes, fully. I still have to be checked in six months, but I just had my one-year checkup, and I'm clear for now. If my next six-month check is clear, I don't have to be seen for a year."

"But your job? Why do you work in a coffee shop when you could have an amazing, high-level career?" And how did she manage to be so positive, friendly, and energetic all the time?

"I don't want to. At least, not right now. The people at The Bean don't give me more stress than I can stand. I was able to heal because I could work full time without the stress of the agency. When I had to quit my Master's, the first place I thought of to apply was the place I spent the most time, The Bean. My first few months there were pretty horrible, I was so sick, but Kaylie never fired me."

The mention of Kaylie turned Addi's stomach a little. "She's been nice to you this whole time. I don't know why she treats me like she does."

"I can tell you. If you want to hear it." *Plop.* Liberty let more dough fall on the cookie sheet.

"Have at it. This has already been a horrible day. A review can only make it better."

Usually, Liberty either didn't get sarcasm or ignored it. This time, she raised her eyebrows, took a small plate out of the cabinet by her head, flopped a cookie's worth of dough on the plate, and then handed it to Addi. "You need this. Seriously, it's like medicine only it tastes good."

With the chocolate chip cookie dough before her, Addi pinched some off of the dollop and licked it off her finger. It was wonderful and sweet, with hints of brown sugar.

"Ready?" Liberty glanced at her over her shoulder but didn't wait for Addi's answer. "She treats you like she does because you let her. You don't stand up for yourself. You don't push back, and you never show her any personality. She doesn't even realize you have one. You don't have to be mean to have a backbone. But next time she snaps her fingers at you, ignore it until she asks you like a boss should."

Addi popped another bite of the dough into her mouth and considered Liberty's words. Because she'd thought she was completely replaceable at the coffee shop, she'd never said anything to Kaylie, only resented how Kaylie treated her. She'd set the expectation.

"So, you invited me over for cookies?"

Liberty smiled. "No. I invited you over for cookie dough. Whatever amazing ingredient is in the dough that makes people feel better, evaporates in the oven. They're still good, but the magic is gone."

She'd met Liberty just when her Rocky Road had lost its power, maybe the Lord had known all along she would need Liberty. "Thank you. This was exactly what I needed tonight."

"Good. When these cookies are done, you can let me drive you home."

After hearing Liberty's story, she couldn't refuse. There were no excuses left. Liberty wouldn't judge her for her situation, and friends like that were too rare.

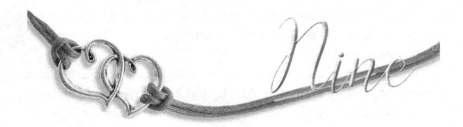

Nine

Drew had all he could do to stay in his seat. Kaylie yawned her way through the show, leaning away from him with arms crossed. She hadn't welcomed any conversation during intermission. Now, she sat across from him at the table, fully engrossed in her phone, and probably complaining about the wasted evening to whoever would listen on social media. At least she hadn't taken a selfie at the table.

"Would you like me to order you anything?" Drew sent the waiter away for the third time because he hadn't been able to get Kaylie's attention.

She finally glared up at him. "This is a sushi bar, so, no."

She hadn't mentioned a fish allergy or anything when he'd offered to take her to supper so he couldn't figure out what was wrong with the restaurant. "Help me out here? What am I not seeing?"

She rolled her eyes but didn't look up from her phone. "I'm vegan."

"They have vegan options here. The menu is right there." He nudged it closer to her.

"You know, I just requested a cab." She clicked a button on the side of her phone and slid it into her purse. "Drew, you're not a bad guy, but you're not for me. I just can't—" The words died abruptly on her lips as she gazed up at someone over his shoulder approaching their table.

"Hey, Drew! How are you?" Tom Higgs, the owner of one of the local radio stations, stopped at their table. He was a long-time acquaintance, and they worked together often since he was one of Drew's advertising contacts. They had also gone to a few basketball games, but other than a friendly greeting, wouldn't normally go out of their way to get together.

"Good, just wrapping up an evening after seeing *Oklahoma!*. This is my friend, Kaylie Viro."

Tom reached out to shake her hand, and she pasted on a hasty smile. "Kaylie, this is—"

She interrupted Drew, "I know the owner of KDWJ when I see him, Drew." She slipped her hand into Tom's and stared up at him. "Care to join us?"

He laughed and slid his hand away, shoving them in his pockets. "Thanks, but the guys are waiting for me over by the bar. I just wanted to say hello. Have a good evening." He nodded to each of them and went on his way.

Kaylie released her breath, and the smile slid back to her normal sulk. "You know him?"

"Well enough. We go out for drinks after work sometimes."

"Is he single?"

Drew held his tongue. She was supposed to be on a date with him, not asking for dating advice or a phone number of one of his friends. "I don't know, that usually doesn't come up."

She rolled her eyes again. "Fine. My cab should be here shortly anyway. I guess you can go up to the bar and join your friends." Kaylie stood and strode out, and he wasn't sorry to see her leave. The evening had been the worst date he'd ever been on as far as comfort level. Even awkward was better than hostile. Betwixt had asked for a review of the first date and as much as he hated giving any business a negative review, there wasn't anything positive he could write. How had they even matched he and Kaylie, and how had he seen anything in her to begin with?

Addi might've had fun. She would've joked with him about the costumes during intermission, accepted the flowers he'd offered to buy, and would've sat here talking to him, even if she didn't like sushi. She would've at least looked at the menu. He sighed and glanced at his watch. It was still early. She might be available to talk if she was home from school. Then his whole night wouldn't be a complete bust.

He waved to Tom and the guys as he made his way to the counter and ordered two plates of California Sushi rolls to go. It was ready for him to take out in a few minutes, and after he paid, he went out to hail a cab. His phone buzzed as he waved one down, then climbed in.

KAYLIE: CAN I PLEASE HAVE TOM'S NUMBER? IT COULDN'T HURT TO TEXT HIM. DO YOU THINK HE WOULD REMEMBER ME?

He wouldn't normally ignore a text, but he'd had enough Kaylie for one night. Since he already had his phone out, he messaged Addi.

DREW: YOU HOME? AND DO YOU LIKE SUSHI?

If she answered fast, he could redirect the cab to her place. Since he had two rolls, he could share.

ADDI: YES. AND YES. WHY?

He smiled and tapped on the glass, then gave the driver the address.

DREW: JUST HOLD ON. YOU'LL SEE IN A FEW MINUTES.

The driver let him off in front of Addi's apartment building. About a half dozen men stood by the door smoking and mumbling to one another. None of them moved out of Drew's way, forcing him to weave between them to get inside. There was no one at the door to let people in. He pushed on the button marked Merrick.

Addi's voice crackled over the aging system. "Yes?"

He pushed it again. "It's Drew. Let me in? I have sushi."

A loud buzzing sound signaled that the security door was unlocked and he pushed through. The buzzer at the front didn't have her apartment number on it, so he just started up the stairs and hoped she would find him. Addi appeared at the top of the stairs on the second floor. She had her hair pulled all the way up in a messy bun, with soft pieces loose and framing her face. She was in fuzzy PJ pants and a loose, long-sleeved tee.

"I wasn't expecting you to actually come by. I don't know what I thought, but this wasn't it." She shoved her hair behind her ear and bit her lip. His heart melted at her sweet, unpolished self. Even completely casual, she was pretty.

"I had sushi to share and no one to share it with." He held up the bag to prove it.

"Why are you always trying to feed me?" She laughed and pushed open a third-floor door that didn't sit on its hinges well. Inside, her apartment was sparse but clean. She had an old sofa that at one time had a floral pattern, but was now covered in saris, giving the room a colorful and foreign look. She had a lamp and two other mismatched chairs. The whole room felt comfortable.

Addi stood staring and squashed both lips between her teeth, her cheeks flaming. "I'll get us some plates." She motioned for him to find a seat, then dashed off to the small galley kitchen.

He shrugged off his suit coat and laid it over one of the chairs, then opened the bag and pulled out the cardboard box with the rolls inside. When Addi returned with the plates, he felt the need to explain, because she was obviously confused as to why he was there. He wasn't even completely sure.

"The date with Kaylie was pretty bad. Did you know she's vegan?" He glanced over at her.

"I had no idea. Wait, she can't be. She ate ice cream with me. Plus, why would a vegan own a coffee shop where there's cream in almost every drink we serve? Then again, I've never seen her drink any of the coffee, not even straight without milk or anything else. She always eats her lunch elsewhere."

"She lied about it?" He took a deep breath. That shouldn't surprise him, she'd needed an excuse to leave and grabbed a plausible one. "I shouldn't be surprised, but to find out at the restaurant that she wouldn't eat anything there? It was important knowledge." He hadn't even thought about asking, which was exactly how she'd used it against him.

"I don't know what to say, except, I'm not all that surprised. I don't have chopsticks." Her brow furrowed.

"I don't think anyone will mind if we use forks." He laughed at her concern over providing the proper utensils, which was more than his date had offered all night.

"I'm sorry it didn't work out," Addi mumbled as she stared down at her plate. "I know you wanted it to. You'd hoped you and Kaylie would be a thing."

"Maybe. I was glad when the matchmaking company set us up, but the more I got to talk to her, the less I wanted the date at all."

Addi's warm brown eyes met his. "Really?"

It was difficult to look forward to going out with someone so cold after he'd met someone so warm. "Sure." He picked up one of his rolls with his fork, ready to be done with all things Kaylie. If Addi didn't work at The Bean, he might not even go in there again.

"I'm sorry. I shouldn't have talked about her. Your feelings for her might not have changed without my negative attitude. Liberty talked to me about that tonight, that I let her treat me the way she does, and then—instead of telling Kaylie how I feel—I turn around and tell others. It's the wrong way to deal with it."

"Hey." He reached out and touched her arm. He hadn't even thought about touching her until that moment, but it felt so right to comfort her. "Sometimes, bullies just need to be told no. Other times, they'll just get worse. She uses you, and she tried to do that to me tonight. I don't think the fault lies completely with you for not sticking up for yourself. She has a character flaw."

Addi sighed and laid her fork down, sushi untouched. "Ever since I started working there, I've compared myself to her. My hair was never as pretty, my clothes never as nice, but I tried to be friendly to everyone to make up for it. You know what that got me? Exactly nowhere. No one comes into that shop and remembers Addi Merrick, but everyone remembers Kaylie."

"I remember you." He had a fierce urge to gather her close and kiss her, but he couldn't do that. She wasn't his girlfriend, though his reasons for keeping her away were getting thinner and thinner by the day.

"Only because Kaylie shoved me at you. You'd still be sitting in that booth, hoping for a date with her if she hadn't."

He wanted to argue that it wasn't true, that he'd noticed her far before Kaylie had been rude and tried to get him to ask Addi out. Now, he almost wished he had. The pain over Lauren was so far in the past now, it was hard to remember just how badly it had hurt to be left on his wedding day.

Almost. He'd convinced himself that nice quiet girls couldn't be trusted, but could he be wrong?

"So, what will you do? Will you try again with the dating site?" Addi's voice pulled him from his thoughts.

"I don't know. I have to give them a review of my first date, then they'll send me more information. So far, my confidence is low, but I think that's pretty normal for most dating sites. If they matched you the first time, they'd never make any money."

"Everyone is entitled to their pay. I doubt they have someone sitting there physically matching people. If they did, maybe things would go smoother." Addi still hadn't eaten any of the sushi, and he searched her face looking for some reason she might be ill or uncomfortable.

"Maybe. Are you okay? You've been sitting there picking at that food since we sat down."

She laughed and picked up one piece. "Like I said, I wasn't sure why you were asking me about sushi. I ate cookie dough at Liberty's a few hours ago. There's only so much rich food a girl can handle in one night. Especially when shrimp ramen is the closest thing this girl gets to a delicacy."

Drew couldn't help cringing. Dried shrimp in dried noodles, reconstituted, was not a delicacy. "In that case, I'll leave these here so you can enjoy them when you're hungry. I should get home and let you finish your homework." He stood back up and grabbed his coat. "Thanks for letting me come hang out with you for a few."

She stood and nodded at him, but didn't smile. Addi's fire seemed to have burned out sometime during that day, and it bothered him.

"I hope it cheers you up a bit."

Addi cocked her head slightly. "Why? Do you think I need it?"

"You could definitely use a good cheering." He shoved his worry to the back of his mind and gave her an awkward side hug. He'd never been very good at those, and her eyes widened at his apparent lack of finesse.

"I'll see you in the morning." He waved.

She smiled slightly, her eyes a few degrees warmer than they'd been a minute before. "See you."

Ten

He'd given her a hug. Sort of. Addi stared at her sagging, textured ceiling above her bed and sighed as she let the warmth of the remembered almost-embrace fill her. She had to convince herself it meant nothing because he was just a friend. He'd made that clear from the start. He was a friend who needed some comfort after a bad date. Yet when the day was over, she'd ended up being the one who got comforted.

There was no way to know how she should act the next day when she saw him at The Bean. After seeing Drew privately two days in a row, her mind started to play tricks on her. She wanted to think of him as more, but that would be dangerous. If she pushed anything, he could just walk away. Hadn't every other guy in her life? Usually with whoever she was close friends with at the time. He'd discounted the idea of dating her when Kaylie had suggested it. He didn't want her in that way. If she didn't get a handle on her feelings, she would end up hurt *and* friendless.

A loud argument broke out in the apartment next door. It was a common occurrence in her building. The longer she lived there, the easier it became to ignore it. The people in her building had just become noise on the other side of the wall, just like all the other noise. When she'd first moved in, the fights would keep her up, and she'd struggled with worrying over every person and situation. The weight of the world was heavy, and night after night, she'd had to deal with it. Until she couldn't anymore.

That's when her heart had hardened to the plight of the people around her, because she couldn't do anything to help them, except pray. There was no way to know if her prayers were answered because there would be new fights the very next night.

Addi's phone buzzed, and she reached for it. It was too strange an hour for it to be anything but important.

Drew's name appeared at the top of her phone.

DREW: YOU UP?

She was, but why was he talking to her so late at night? Was something wrong? She squinted at the little clock in the upper corner of her phone. 1:15 a.m.

ADDI: YES, WHY?

It seemed like she was always asking him that. At some point, she would have to come up with some real questions for him, and then he'd have to answer with something other than food.

DREW: I WAS UP. CAN'T SLEEP. I MADE IT HOME OKAY, IN CASE YOU WERE WORRIED.

She smiled, then chuckled. She hadn't been worried. He was just so charismatic it never crossed her mind to worry whether he got home, she just assumed he would. With style.

ADDI: I'M GLAD, AND I'M SORRY YOU CAN'T SLEEP.

He replied quickly.

DREW: I SEE YOU'RE HAVING THE SAME PROBLEM.

She stared at his statement for a minute, but couldn't think of anything witty to say. She always thought of those well after the moment had passed.

ADDI: MUST BE A FULL MOON. AND JUST BECAUSE I'M AWAKE DOESN'T MEAN WE CAN GET TOGETHER FOR FOOD.

She rolled her eyes but hit send anyway, hoping he would think it was funny.

> **Drew:** What? You don't want to go get coffee and cinnamon rolls in the middle of the night?

How was she having this conversation? She couldn't even understand why he was talking to her at all, much less in the middle of the night.

> **Addi:** Nope, I'm not changing out of my fuzzy pants. And how do you stay healthy if you're eating pizza and rolls all the time?

Not that she minded. She'd had more yummy food in the last two days than she'd had in a year.

> **Drew:** I'm pretty sure there's no sign on the coffee shop that says 'no fuzzy pants.' Wouldn't that make an interesting sign? No shirt, no shoes, no fuzzy pants = no service.

Addi snorted and typed her reply as quickly as her fingers could manage in the middle of the night.

> **Addi:** Maybe you should make up an ad campaign: No fuzzy pants!

Not that she would stop wearing them. She didn't buy yoga pants, but if she was at home, she wore PJs. She'd been that way for years.

> **Drew:** I can't do that. My clients would lose most of the college-age customers, and I might make some of those angry. Wouldn't want that.

Addi stared at the screen with an open mouth. Was he *flirting* with her? She was too out of practice to even be sure.

> **Addi:** I don't think you have to worry. I'd better go to sleep. See you in the morning, assuming you don't sleep

IN.

He only took a few seconds to reply.

DREW: WOULDN'T MISS IT.

Addi stared at the three words as her heart raced and the little voice in her head wouldn't leave her alone. It shouted at her to pay attention to what was happening. No matter what he'd said, he was paying attention to her. Wasn't that all that mattered? Who cared what anyone labeled it? Except a friend would never end up a bride.

Drew sat at The Bean sipping his mint coffee and staring at his screen. He'd just gotten an email from Betwixt2Hearts. They had literally replied in minutes after he'd sent his review of his first date. The woman who replied offered him a complimentary match, but not through the algorithms on the site that had set him up with Kaylie to begin with. She proposed a more personal touch.

What did he have to lose? They wouldn't set him up with Kaylie, and he needed a distraction from Addi. He'd gotten far too used to turning to her whenever he thought about her—which was becoming more and more. He agreed to the suggestion and hit send. Another email came through, and he didn't recognize the address. The email preview said: *Do you remember me from High School?*

He glanced at the email again, and it gave him no clues. Drew clicked into the email, and a short letter came up.

> Do you remember me from High School? You took me to the junior prom. I've done a lot of soul-searching, and I've come to think of myself as a man. My therapist says that it's healthy for me to come out to those I've been intimate with in the past. Since there aren't that many, I wanted to reach out and let you know.
> Ray (Rea) Zale

A woman he'd asked to prom didn't consider herself a woman

anymore. He thought back and could remember Rea's soft, blonde hair, her quiet smiles, the way she clung to his arm and danced with him all night, not wanting to share him with anyone else. The only reason he hadn't continued to see her was because her family had moved two weeks later.

Drew clicked out of the email and stared at Addi. While he didn't believe there was any chance she would ever change that drastically on him, it just proved that those quiet women, those who he would never expect to change, always did. He shut his computer and Addi came over to the table, her soft, shy smile making his heart thump.

"Leaving so early? Going home to take a nap?" She giggled, and he held his breath. He'd never heard her do that and it was beautiful. This had to stop; he had to stop their friendship from getting any closer, or he'd be lost.

"Yeah, I have a few things I need to do. On a good note, I got an email back from Betwixt. They're going to give me another setup. On the house."

The smile slid off her face like a mask. "Oh, that's wonderful. I hope this time they find someone who won't make you seek out food for comfort afterward." She gathered his cup and wiped his table everywhere except where his computer lay.

"I didn't seek out comfort. I was looking for a friend." He picked up the computer and headed to the till. Liberty stood behind the counter and turned her thousand-watt smile on him.

"Hey, tall, dark, and handsome, you're just as good as any coffee we make." She winked at him, and he laughed, though he didn't feel very handsome at the moment. One dud date, one woman who left him at the altar, and one ex who had switched sides made a guy wonder just what he was doing wrong.

He took out a few bills and handed them to Liberty. "Have a good day, Liberty." There was no good comeback for her comment. She was just fun, and they had play-flirted since she'd started working there. He just didn't feel like playing along anymore. He didn't feel like doing much of anything anymore. He obviously had some massive character flaw that left him unable to make good decisions about people, especially women. All the more reason to avoid Addi. They'd both get hurt if he didn't.

Eleven

The psychology book lying in front of Addi held little interest. Though it was one of the courses she would need the most, the book itself distracted her. She'd picked it up at the off-campus used bookstore, and it had been turned back in at least three times. There were many colors of highlighter all over its pages, and wading through the chapters always gave her a headache, though it could also be the leftover sushi she'd eaten when she got home. It hadn't tasted quite as good as it had when Drew had been there with her. At least she hadn't had to eat ramen. Again.

Her phone lay a few feet away, but it had been silent all night. Drew hadn't texted. Maybe he really only needed her after his horrible date to make him feel better. He probably knew she would date him in a heartbeat. She was good for his ego. Plus, he seemed to know she was always there, available. It wasn't like he had competition for her time.

Her professors would tell her it wasn't healthy to always be available for someone who only needed her for support, but was that really the case? She thought back over the past forty-eight hours. First, he'd found her online to ask her to make him coffee. That was needy. Then, he'd texted and told her he was coming over after his date because it had been so bad. Needy again. Last, he'd sent her a text in the middle of the night because he couldn't sleep. Strike three.

She wasn't his friend, she was his fallback. Addi yanked out a piece of paper from her notebook and wrote the names of all the guy friends she'd ever had who she'd crushed on. There weren't all that many. As she thought about each one, the great majority of them had been friends with her only because she'd reached out to them, in the hopes that they would see her. Retrospect put her pitiful, less-than-stellar love life in DSLR focus. No one cared; not really.

Addi flopped off of her bed and strode into the bathroom. The light above the mirror was permanently a yellow hue, and she always looked sick, but even if she ignored that fact, she could no longer even pretend she found herself pretty. Not after so much rejection.

An email pinged through on her phone, and she ran to get it, stupidly hoping it was Drew. The unread message was a no-reply email from Betwixt2Hearts.com, just an automated message.

> Dear Addi Merrick,
> We are sorry to inform you that we were unable to match you with any candidates in your search area. Don't give up, your perfect match is still out there. You can keep your profile active for a small fee. Please visit us at www.betwixt2hearts.com to set up a plan perfect for you.
> Thank you

She focused on keeping her breathing even. Her father had always said that in the weakest moments, that's when Satan would strike. She did feel weak, very weak, and alone, and inadequate. Addi grabbed her phone and slipped it in her back pocket, shoving her key in the other. Her own church was far away, and if she wanted to go there, she'd have to pay for bus fare, which she couldn't afford. There was a chapel a few blocks from her apartment, right in the middle of one of the poorest neighborhoods of Great River. It stayed open twenty-four hours a day for prayer and worship. She'd never been there but had heard about it.

No one was out and about as she made her way down the dark streets. The closer she got, the louder the music from the little building became and when she opened the doors, a calm soothed over her. She took a deep breath, and the scent of candles and incense filled her nostrils. A woman stood up front, singing a worship song. Some people joined with their hands raised. Others raised their hands and just swayed to the music, but didn't sing. Some people knelt by the front in prayer.

Addi took a few steps in, and a woman came up to her. "Is this your first time?"

She couldn't answer, couldn't form words. Her body felt full, from head to foot. She managed a nod.

"I assumed so. You have that look about you. There are no set rules here. Pray or worship in your own way."

The room had a vibration, a hum, that she couldn't explain. She stumbled forward and slid into a pew by herself. The heaviness that had held her captive all evening released, and tears coursed down her cheeks. "You will not win, Satan. I am a child of God," she whispered.

The words Liberty had spoken to her the day before came to mind. She was an empty vessel that needed to be full. She couldn't give love from an empty well. "Fill me, Lord. Fill up all my empty places. Make me see me, how you see me."

Her eyelids drooped, and for the flash of a second, Heaven gave her a glimpse of herself—but nothing like her human form—and she fell to her knees as the tears came in earnest. "I'm so sorry, Lord. I'm so sorry I believed the lie."

She remained on her knees while she listened to the songs of worship at the front of the chapel, but she had no more words. There was no doubt in her mind that the Lord had drawn her to that spot to meet with Him. He wanted her to know she was a princess of the most high King and she needed to act like it.

There was no clock on the wall, and she didn't check her phone, but when the singer in the front changed, Addi pulled herself off the floor and made her way to the door. She looked for the woman she'd encountered on her way in, but no one was the same as when she'd entered, or she simply couldn't remember them.

The cool night air brushed over her face as Addi made her way back to her apartment. She pulled her phone from her back pocket and realized she'd been in the chapel for over two hours, but it hadn't seemed that long. She'd missed a text at some point, and she opened it up. It was from Drew, only one line.

DREW: BETWIXT GOT BACK TO ME WITH A MATCH. I'LL BE SET

UP WITH A SURPRISE DATE SOON.

Drew paced back and forth in his living room. Hadn't Addi gotten his text? She'd never ignored him and certainly not when it was so important. Though, perhaps she'd gotten the same email he had and already knew what *he* did, that they'd been matched. Not just put together by some arbitrary computer program, but matched by a human who had combed through a bunch of profiles to find him the perfect one. That's what his email had said. She was his perfect match.

He hadn't been able to think of a good response when they'd told him, and had just closed his email instead of agreeing to the date right away. He had to talk to Addi about it. How was it possible that the two people this company had matched him with were known to him? It had to be because it was so new, they didn't have a large pool to pick from yet. The first had disastrous results, but did he dare risk a date with Addi? What if he enjoyed himself and she proved to be just the girl he had hoped for, then changed on him? Worse, what if they had a great time and one of them wanted to continue, but the other didn't? What if she was even more perfect than Lauren, but left him anyway? He'd have to go through that crushing loss all over again.

Two agonizing hours had gone by since he'd sent her the text. Now he didn't know what to say, and even more, what to think. Was she ignoring him because Betwixt had contacted her, or had she already changed and moved on? He raked his hand through his hair and fell limp onto his sofa, all the pillows Lauren had left behind lumpy underneath him.

No more Lauren. That was the first step to clearing his mind. He'd let her ghost ruin his life and his thinking for too long. He gathered all the pillows and wall hangings, every knickknack and scented diffuser. He put every last piece into boxes for donation. Someone else could enjoy them, but they'd hung around his apartment long enough, reminding him of his failure.

His phone buzzed, and he leaped to it where he'd left it on the sofa.

Addi's message was short and to the point.

ADDI: I HOPE YOU HAVE A GREAT TIME.

She didn't know. They hadn't told her yet, or she hadn't checked her email. He punched in a quick reply.

DREW: WE NEED TO TALK. CAN I COME OVER?

He stared at his phone, willing her to respond quickly. He had to stop her from reading that email. If she did, and he said he didn't want to date her, he'd have to explain why. He would have to admit that he wasn't anything special. He was the guy that love left behind. Maybe that had been his real worry all along. Not that Addi would change, but that she would discover *he* wasn't all that great. Certainly not great enough for Lauren and maybe not enough for Addi either.

ADDI: IT'S LATE, AND I'VE HAD A LONG DAY. CAN WE TALK TOMORROW?

No, they couldn't. He needed her now. He rested the side of his head against the back of the couch. If Betwixt didn't send her an email until he responded, then he was safe. There was no guarantee that would happen. How would he get Addi to skip over that email, without telling her an outright lie?

DREW: I REALLY NEED TO TALK TO YOU RIGHT NOW.

He sounded desperate, but desperate times meant he had to pull out all stops.

ADDI: IT'S TOO LATE FOR THE BUS, AND IT'S NOT SAFE TO LEAVE YOUR SCOOTER OUT HERE AT THIS TIME OF NIGHT. TALK TO ME TOMORROW AT THE BEAN. I'M HEADED TO BED.

All logical, but when had Addi been logical? Something was wrong. Unless she had read the email and denied the match. Maybe she had denied it because he'd already turned down a date with her and she just didn't want to talk about it. That had to be the case. Otherwise, she'd want to talk to him, they'd hardly spoken all day.

DREW: ALL RIGHT. I'LL SEE YOU IN THE MORNING, BEAUTIFUL.

He clicked off his phone and slid it onto the coffee table. He'd been worked up for hours over that email, but now it was over, and he could rest. He closed his eyes, and an image of Addi appeared. She had her hair down, and in his mind's eye, it was softly curled. She had a gentle smile on her lips, but very little makeup. She didn't need it; gorgeous women never really did.

A man approached her and held out his arm. She waved to Drew, and the image disappeared. Was that what he was destined for yet again? To watch someone he cared about just walk away? But why wouldn't she; he had no hold on her. He sat up and rested his head in his palms. Love meant risking a lot. It meant he might get hurt, again. Would losing Addi to another man be worse than losing her because he couldn't keep anyone?

His phone buzzed once more.

ADDI: GOODNIGHT, DREW. SORRY FOR HAVING TO PUT YOU OFF. IT'S NOT YOU; I'VE JUST HAD A LONG DAY. TALK TO YOU IN THE MORNING.

It's not you. He read that little phrase over twice more. She hadn't gotten or read the email yet. There was still time.

Twelve

There was very little to look at as Addi walked to work while it was still dark, so she stared at her phone; namely, the last text Drew had sent.

DREW: ALL RIGHT. I'LL SEE YOU IN THE MORNING, BEAUTIFUL.

After she'd gotten that text, she'd gotten an urgent email from someone at Betwixt2Hearts.com. They wanted to match her up with a local man who'd had a very bad first date. When she'd clicked on the link to find out who it was, she'd almost fallen out of bed.

Drew Tanner. The Drew Tanner she'd been talking to and praying about, the very same one who'd just called her beautiful by text. Was that what he wanted to talk to her about? Had he wanted to make sure she was okay with the match? Was that why he'd called her that? He never had before.

She'd taken extra time with her hair that morning. Her hair usually hung in soft curls, but not overly thick, around her shoulders. She could easily curl it into bigger curls which held all day, and that's what she'd done. Since she worked with food, she still put it up in a ponytail, but this time she made sure it looked nice. She'd taken time with her clothes to make sure they matched and were as flattering as she could manage. Today just might be the day she'd been waiting for. Her mother had always said the worthwhile things were worth the wait and she'd had to wait for years and years for a great guy to walk into her life, but Drew was worth it.

She pushed open the back door to The Bean on Main. Liberty usually came in about a half hour after Addi, since she didn't have a key and she stayed later. Kaylie sat on the little sofa, filing her nails.

"Oh, I was waiting for you to get here." She indicated the chair Addi should sit in. "Don't worry, I got everything set up for the day already."

Kaylie hadn't been there in so long, Addi had been sure she wouldn't come back. Everything had run so smoothly—with sales up and people happy—that there hadn't been any reason for her to come back.

"What's going on?" Addi sat in the chair and wove her fingers together to keep from fidgeting.

"I've decided to give Drew another chance. The date wasn't so bad, and he does have friends in the circle I want to break into."

Addi's heart sank to the floor. Drew had said the date was terrible, but only because of the way Kaylie acted. If she wanted to go out with him again, he would probably say yes.

"The problem is, the site asked me not to contact him after the feedback. They offered to set me up with someone else. I gave them the name of the man I wanted, but they said he wasn't a member. When they tried to find someone else for me, they couldn't find a match. I'm on a waiting list."

Of course, the day she was certain would change the course of her luck forever wasn't meant to be.

"What are you asking of me?" It wasn't like Kaylie couldn't just ask Drew. She had to have his number, and rules had never stopped her before. They had contacted each other for days before their date.

"I want *you* to set it up. If I call him, he won't answer. I've already tried texting, and he ignored it. Oh, and I want you to make him want it. The date wasn't great, but you can spin it to make it seem good, or at least that I deserve another chance."

Liberty was right, Kaylie would never ask that of any of her other employees. She asked Addi because Addi was too nice to say no. Now was her chance to stand up for herself, to have a backbone as Liberty had suggested.

"I don't want to do that to him. You had your chance, and you didn't want it. You were mean, you lied to him."

Kaylie glanced at Addi over her long fingernails. "Need I remind you that you and Liberty made a bunch of changes to my store without my approval. Your employment is at-will, and if you don't do this for me, you can leave your address in the book where we can send your final check. That nasty little hole on the south side."

Addi gripped her fingers tighter. She was barely making the rent as it was. One missed check and she'd be homeless. She couldn't even put in two weeks' notice because she couldn't work two jobs and go to school, and a new job wouldn't pay until she'd worked a full pay period.

"Fine. I'll talk to him soon. But don't expect results right away, this isn't something I can just do."

"I knew you'd see reason. Don't take too long." Kaylie picked up her phone and ignored Addi.

Liberty walked in smiling, and it faltered and died as soon as she looked at Addi. "What's wrong?"

Kaylie stood and glared at Addi. "Nothing. I just missed Addi so much I had to stop by and say hi. Have a great day you two." She grabbed her purse and left out the front.

"What was that all about? And why are you all dressed up?" Liberty came over and rested a hand on her shoulder. "You look like you've seen a ghost."

Addi's insides trembled, and she wanted to run home, but that wouldn't do any good. If she didn't face the day, she couldn't pay her bills.

"Kaylie wants me to get her another date with Drew. She's changed her mind." Just saying it out loud hurt. If there were an option to just quit and walk away, instead of doing this to Drew, she would.

"Tell her no. You aren't her little toy to push around." Liberty went over to the wall where all the aprons hung and slipped one over her head.

"I guess I am because she threatened to fire me if I don't."

Liberty whipped around to face her. "You're serious?"

She blinked to keep the tears where they belonged, instead of running down her cheeks. "I've never been more serious. Maybe if I suspend my schooling right now, I could scratch by until I find another job. I just can't take this anymore."

"Honey, you let me handle this. I'll talk to Drew when he comes in, you just stay busy back here. It's inventory time anyway."

"Ugh, I hate inventory." She hated everything about The Bean at the moment, except Liberty and seeing Drew.

"Inventory will keep you from losing a job you need. You get busy, I'll handle the floor." She gave Addi a quick smile and left her in the back room to handle the work alone.

Drew watched Liberty help the last customer in a long line to pay for their coffee. She stared at him until the jingle above the door signaled they were alone, or at least it would seem that way. Addi hadn't shown her face all day, despite telling him she couldn't wait to see him and telling him she would talk to him. Liberty slid into the booth seat across from him, clutching a water bottle.

"So, how's the dating scene?" She pegged him with her deep blue eyes.

"Uh, fine." What was she up to? He never quite knew with Liberty.

"I heard that before I started, Kaylie tried to set you up with Addi."

He sat back in his seat and recalled that conversation. It's what had started his real friendship with Addi. "Yeah, she did."

"What made you say no?" Liberty usually smiled, but not today. She was all business.

"At the time, I didn't know her."

"You didn't know Kaylie, either, yet you were happy to get a date with her." Liberty unscrewed the cap on her water and took a drink.

"Yes, but that was different. I was fairly sure I knew Kaylie. Now I can see, though, that the problem wasn't either Kaylie or Addi, it was me." At least Kaylie had seen him for what he was right away, no need to get any feelings involved.

"So, why don't you give Addi that same chance?"

He couldn't do that. If he did, he would get attached. Probably quickly, if their friendship was any indicator.

"But I like Addi as a friend."

Liberty laughed, but her smile was still absent. "I'm her friend. As her friend, I'm asking you to take a risk. She's worth it."

A risk. He'd been thinking about risks just the night before. Was God trying to tell him something with the message from Betwixt, his vision of Addi leaving, and now Liberty?

"Okay, I'll take her out. It isn't like I haven't spent time with her before."

Liberty nodded. "Good. Do you need a refill?"

He glanced at the cup, and though it had been good, it wasn't just as he liked it. "Only if Addi happens to be hiding in the back. I don't know what she does to make it better than anyone else, but she does."

Liberty laughed and grabbed his cup. "Sugar, I know exactly what she does. Hold on."

She set his cup on the counter and pushed the door to the back room. A moment later, Addi came out, and the breath yanked right out of his lungs. She was amazing. She'd worn some stylish leggings and a flowy top that made her look curvier than he remembered. Her hair was in a loose ponytail and curled so that it just nipped her slender neck. He forced his jaw to close as she collected his cup and went over to the machines.

What had he been working on? He couldn't remember, but he needed to look busy. He flipped through each of the tabs he had open on his computer, but none of them made any sense. Addi set his cup down on the table, and the aroma of the mint dislodged all the fog from his brain.

"Can I get you anything else?" she whispered, and he couldn't figure out why. They were alone in the front window of the little coffee shop.

"Sit with me? Just for a minute?" He offered the open booth across from him.

She slid in. "I'm sorry I didn't come out when you got here. I agreed to do the inventory this morning. Liberty told me she'd talked to you?"

He smiled because he couldn't help it. She was acting so shy now that he'd agreed to go out with her.

"Liberty suggested I take you out sometime. I think it's a good idea."

Addi's eyes went wide, and her mouth slackened slightly. "Oh, I didn't realize I would be the topic of conversation."

"It's just one date. I didn't figure you'd mind."

She fidgeted in her seat. "I guess you didn't get the email, then? From Betwixt?"

"I did—that's what helped me decide it was a good idea. Mind if I just pick out someplace fun to go?" He'd take her somewhere he would enjoy going because a date with Addi was more like going out with a friend and he didn't need to impress her.

"Sure. I'd better get back to work. I'll talk to you later." She got up and dashed away to the back, leaving him alone in the front of the store. He didn't know women all that well, but her response wasn't quite what he'd hoped it would be. She hadn't even smiled. Instead, she'd looked worried. He yanked out his phone and checked the movie theater schedule, ordered two tickets for that Friday night, and sent Addi a text, knowing she'd see it in a minute and hopefully it would draw her back out to talk to him.

> **DREW:** ADDI. GOT TICKETS FOR FRIDAY. I'LL PICK YOU UP AT 5:00.

He watched the door and plastered a smile on his face, praying she would be happy. She'd accepted him so far. There was no reason why she should quit right away. Of course, Lauren hadn't given him any hints that she was losing interest either.

His phone buzzed.

> **ADDI:** SOUNDS GOOD.

But she didn't come back out.

Thirteen

"What did you do?" Addi slid to the floor from her spot on the couch and buried her head between her knees.

Liberty laughed and slid a box of dark roast across the floor then marked the clipboard in her hand. "I did what you should've done when Kaylie tried to originally set you up. I made lemonade out of lemons."

"This is my job you're playing with. Do you get that? If I get fired, I have nowhere to go. I don't even have enough money for bus fare back to my parents' house in Michigan."

"Why are you under the delusion that Kaylie has to know? As Drew said, it isn't like you've never hung out before. You have. This is two friends going out for an evening. Afterward, you can tell him Kaylie wanted to see him again and let him choose. She seems to forget that he has the choice in all this. Maybe if she hadn't treated him so bad, she wouldn't have to sneak behind his back to get a second date."

Addi's stomach pitched. It was dirty and underhanded, and she didn't want to do it. Not to any friend, but especially not Drew. "I feel like I have no choice. You've been there, Liberty. You were faced with no job. Remember?" Though Liberty had enough income to live comfortably for a while, she *had* lost her job and faced a terrifying illness.

"It isn't fair for her to fire you for this. If she tries to do it, I think you should report it to her parents; they are the ones who hired you."

She'd gotten a letter right after training that the company had been turned over to Kaylie, and basically, Mr. and Mrs. Viro would be silent partners. "I don't think they want anything to do with The Bean. They sign the checks, but they have nothing else to do with the employees. The only other person in any sort of management capacity is the manager at the Uptown location, and I've never even been there. I only met her briefly at the Christmas party." Addi didn't feel like getting up, but her shift would end soon, and she'd have to go to school and pretend to pay attention. How would she go through the next two days at work, knowing she would be going out with Drew, and knowing she shouldn't if she wanted to keep her job?

"So, he really said we were just friends? He actually said those words?" Addi glanced up at Liberty and caught the brief look of pity on her face before she wiped it away with a smile.

"Who cares what you call it? It's still a date, and it could lead to more." She knelt in front of Addi.

"Or less. What if he realizes I'm nothing special?"

"What if he realizes you're the greatest thing since the stars were created?" Liberty rested her hand on Addi's shoulder and gave it a squeeze. "Believe it or not, there are people in this world who don't see you like Kaylie does. It might feel like they're rare, and maybe they are, but that just makes them all the more special. Go with Drew. Be yourself. Have a great time, and if he asks you again, go."

"And if he doesn't?" Because that seemed exponentially more likely.

"Then laugh it off and pretend like you're still friends until it's true. Good friends don't just happen, they're put in our lives for a reason. You are the reason Kaylie asked me to take her spot here. She may not have realized it, but God did. We needed each other."

Liberty stood back up and held out her hand, then helped Addi off the floor. "Let Friday worry about itself. We'll take care of the Kaylie situation next week. She can wait that long."

Later that night, Addi flipped through her closet for something to wear on Friday. She didn't own a lot of clothes. If it wasn't really a date, did she have to dress up? It wouldn't matter if Drew didn't even notice. She'd avoided going back out to talk to Drew because she didn't want to put too much importance on it, talk too much, and make him think she was as excited as she was. If she did dress up, would he think she was trying too hard? She flipped through some shirts with big flowers printed on them. She'd gone through a tropical phase years before that was pretty embarrassing now, but she couldn't get rid of the shirts either.

Her phone buzzed, and she yanked it from the waistband of her leggings and swiped across without looking at who it was.

"Addi," she answered.

"Hey, were you avoiding me today?" Drew's voice sounded tentative as if he'd considered his words for hours before saying them.

"No. I just had inventory to do." *And to keep from freaking you out about the date.*

"Okay, because I agreed to go out with you and you vanished. If you don't want to go—"

"I do!" She slapped her forehead at her haste. "I mean, of course I do. Why wouldn't I? You're a great guy. A great," she paused, flinching at the word, "friend." She swallowed hard and prayed he didn't read too much into her excitement. What if he canceled?

"Good. I was worried. I'm looking forward to it. So, in honor of the disaster that was my last date, is there anything you're allergic to or averse to that I should know about?" He laughed for a second, then let it fade to a nervous chuckle.

"No. I'm pretty easy to please. I'm sure wherever we go will be fine." She bit her lip. "So, I was sort of planning my outfit for Friday, do I need to dress up, or casual? You said tickets, but I don't know what that means, exactly." Not that she needed to know an exact itinerary or anything.

"Nothing fancy. Just be yourself, and you'll be perfect." She loved how his voice sounded over the phone.

"Then I'll just be normal if that's what you want." She flinched again. Could she ever say anything to him that sounded cool or romantic? How would he ever see her as anything but a friend if she couldn't make herself act flirty like Kaylie?

"Normal has worked so far." He laughed. "I just wanted to let you know that I've got a business meeting tomorrow with a new client. I won't be coming into the shop. Didn't want you to miss me or think I was skipping out on you."

He'd thought about her enough to tell her his schedule? "Thank you, I probably would have. But you'll be there Friday morning?" Making her nervous the whole time.

"I plan on it. See you then."

She smiled and backed away from her closet. There was no need to worry about what Drew thought of her. "Can't wait."

Fourteen

Drew asked the cabbie to wait while he ran up to get Addi. The man didn't want to, shook his head wildly in protest, but finally agreed and Drew rushed to the front door. This time, no one waited to mumble at him, but it still reeked of old cigarette smoke in the whole lobby. He buzzed her apartment.

"I'll come right down," Addi's voice crackled through the old intercom.

He would've rather gone up to her room and walked with her back down, but if she didn't buzz him in, he had no choice in the matter. Through the glass doors, first he saw heels, then amazing legs, in a knee-length purple dress that clung perfectly all the way up to beautiful shoulders. Addi's hair was completely down in voluminous curls that his fingers wanted to feel. She smiled nervously at him through the glass as she opened the locked door.

"Wow. You look amazing." He couldn't even think of any other greeting.

She blushed and tucked her chin. "I hope I'm not overdressed. This is maybe a little nicer than normal."

"It's great. You're great." He sounded like a fool. No wonder he couldn't keep a girlfriend.

He reached out and took her hand. It was warm and soft in his as he pushed open the door and held it for her. He led her to the cab, then again opened the door for her and waited until she ducked inside.

Suddenly, his planned date of dinner and a movie didn't seem quite nice enough. They could go to a movie any night. She knew where he'd taken Kaylie. Would she think he thought less of her because he didn't do something just as nice with her?

The cab driver sped off toward the theater and Addi settled into the seat next to Drew. She always smelled like coffee at The Bean, but tonight she smelled like soap and fruity hair products, not strong perfume. He slid a little closer to her, and she sent him a shy smile. Conversation had been so easy over the phone or text, or even when they'd gotten together as friends. Why did the label of "date" make it so much more difficult? He'd tried to relieve some of that tension by insisting it wasn't a date at all, but that didn't seem to be working for either of them.

The car stopped in front of the theater, and he helped Addi out. She wobbled slightly on her heels, and he slid his arm around her to keep her from falling, then didn't want to let go. When he didn't, she tentatively put her arm around him, and he led her inside the theater. When he'd booked the tickets, he'd chosen an action movie, but he'd mostly chosen for himself. That seemed like a poor choice now.

"Is there anything you'd like to see more than anything else?" He glanced at all the movie posters lining the wall. There was the typical kids' film, a YA magical film, a boatload of rom/com and chick flicks, and two action movies. They didn't have anything that might appeal to both of them if Addi was the chick movie type.

"I wanted to see *Ransom Note*. I heard it's good." He couldn't tell from her eyes if she'd just said that to make him happy or if she really wanted to see it. It was the movie he'd originally chosen.

"Are you sure? I didn't know what you'd like." Though they were now about a foot apart and looking at each other, he couldn't make himself let go of her waist.

"I actually like them, though I don't get to go often. If you don't mind, that is. We can go see something more for a date if you want." She broke eye contact with him and stared at the posters.

"No, I think that's perfect."

The conversation just wouldn't flow as he'd hoped. They waited in the snack line for a few minutes, but conversation still wouldn't come. He bought some treats to share, then he turned in his tickets, and they went down the hall that led to all the theaters. Addi carried the giant pop, and he carried the popcorn because he didn't want her to get oil on her dress. He'd also grabbed napkins so that if he put his arm around her later, he wouldn't leave a handprint on her shoulder. Movie popcorn might be good, but he wanted her to remember their first date for him, not an oily mess on her dress.

Addi settled in about as close to the screen as he usually liked and right in the middle. He sat down next to her and then she slid the pop in the holder between them. They had some time before the movie started, and small groups of people chatted all around them in the semidarkness.

He didn't want to mention his date with Kaylie, because that would bring Addi down, but even the twenty minutes they'd spent together so far was better than the other date as a whole.

"I know I would miss you at the coffee shop, but have you considered finding a job in your field, so you could intern?" He'd learned a lot when he'd interned with a huge ad agency in nearby Dallas.

Addi settled in and relaxed a little. "I have, but I'm not sure where I would go. A church counseling atmosphere is different from a standard clinic. I also don't know that I would get paid and I would need to. Right now, I don't have time between school and work."

"I can't imagine the coffee shop pays all that well and you aren't there full time." Since she was turned slightly to face him, with her knee against his, he laid his arm across the back of her seat and gently tugged at the ends of her hair. It was even softer than he'd thought it would be. "By the way, I like your hair down."

She laughed and leaned forward, out of his reach for a moment. "I can't exactly wear it this way at work, but thank you."

She'd dodged his first question by answering the second. What he really wanted to know was if she was as nervous about this as he was. Did she have doubts in herself like he had?

"You said before that you don't drink coffee, so why work in a coffee shop?" She hadn't settled back in her chair yet, so he moved his arm. He didn't want her uncomfortable around him.

473

"I needed a job, pretty badly actually, and I didn't have all that many skills. Everyone seems to like the coffee I make for them because I follow the recipes to the letter. I don't go by looks or whatever because I don't know what each drink really tastes like. So, I have to use the guides. It makes it a good job for me."

"You do make a pretty amazing cup of coffee, even when you don't have the guide to go by."

She smiled and settled back into her chair, leaning her shoulder against the backrest. "I know your coffee by heart at this point."

He wanted her to know a lot more about him by heart, but what he wanted and what would happen weren't up to him.

"I'm glad I wandered into The Bean. I might still be searching for that perfect cup of coffee if it wasn't for you." Just maybe, her imagination would take that and run with it.

"Or you would've just put up with the coffee Kaylie made because you liked her first."

His heart pinched. He would forever kick himself for making such a mistake. He'd judged based on looks, and now he couldn't see Kaylie as even close to as attractive as Addi.

"Does it help that I know better now?"

She flinched. That was unexpected. "Kaylie really isn't so bad."

No, he wasn't going to let Kaylie derail another date. "Let's not talk about her. We're here to have fun." He wanted her to look back up at him again, not down at her lap where her fingers were locked tighter than Fort Knox. He reached over and pried them apart, then held them. "Why even bring her up? What's going on?"

Addi swallowed hard, and he watched her throat constrict, then she batted her lashes and stared at the lights but wouldn't look at him.

"Hey, you can tell me." He let go of one of her hands and tilted her face down to look at him. "Please?"

A tear raced down her cheek. "Kaylie wants to see you again. I told Liberty, and she said she'd take care of it, but instead, she set you up with me. I shouldn't even be here. This should be Kaylie."

He wanted to gather Addi close, but he couldn't without spilling popcorn all over and making Addi a spectacle "No, it shouldn't. I don't want to go out with her again. Ever."

She flinched again and pulled away from him. "Just consider it. Remember, we're just here as friends. Let's have fun and pretend like we didn't set this up as a date. She's changed a lot over the last week." Addi wasn't usually one to avoid his eyes for an entire conversation, especially not something important.

"Any reason why you're broaching this now when we're supposed to be on a *date*? Or didn't you want to be here at all?" He knew it. She'd already decided to ditch him.

Addi reached out and took his hand, holding it tightly. "No, not at all. I want to be here. More than you know. But we're both nervous—can't we just go back to acting like friends and have a great time? And tomorrow, when you think back on tonight, consider Kaylie's offer?"

He wanted to forget that she'd ever mentioned Kaylie *and* have a great time, but he couldn't. Why would Kaylie want to see him again except to try to get the phone numbers of his friends? "Sure." He turned away from her and stared at the screen, and she did likewise. As soon as the ads started showing, she made fun of a few, and he explained to her why some were bad and others were good.

Soon the movie was rolling and they spent the whole show commenting on it to one another quietly. Two hours, a tub of popcorn, and about a gallon and a half of pop seemed to go all too quickly. When the lights came up, Addi's face was rosy with laughter, and her eyes were bright, not misty as they had been before. Maybe she was right. They were destined to be great friends.

"I think after I turn in my review of this date, I'm done with the dating scene for a while," Drew said. The realization that Addi would rather he go out with Kaylie than ask her again, sealed his fate. He'd thought Lauren was his only, but he'd been wrong. It was Addi.

"Think you've found your match?" She glanced at him, then back down at her feet.

"I'm sure of it. It's just too bad she doesn't really like me." He laughed because he couldn't show her how hurt he was.

"You never know. There's always your second chance." She kept walking, and he wanted to slow her down, hold her hand, keep her in that moment for as long as he could. Their date would be over before he knew it and he might never *get* another chance.

"Where do you want to eat?" He stepped a little livelier to reach her.

"I'm not really hungry after all that popcorn. Want to take a walk?" He couldn't read her in the dark of the hall outside the theater. Her face was little more than shadow and softness, but there was hope in her voice.

"Sure, the park is just a few blocks down, and we'll call a cab from there." He slid his arm around her waist again, and she let her head fall against his shoulder. The touch was so simple, so innocent and without any demands. She didn't want him for his money or his connections. She didn't want his silly comments or even his quirky need for near perfection. She wanted him, just the way he was.

"I think we should do this more often." Would she allow it, or would she think he was pressuring her for more dates? He wanted more, but he wouldn't demand her time if she wasn't ready to give it.

"Taking walks in the park was always how I dreamed dates would end. I guess that's silly." She tried to step to the side, but he gently tugged her back close to him.

"A walk in the park is a perfect end to a date, or get-together, or whatever. There are no rules posted around the park about pairs of people."

She laughed, and the soft gold of the street lamps glistened over her cheeks. There was only one thing this date would lack, and only because she'd asked him to think of this as anything but a date. If she hadn't, he'd have kissed her goodnight. He still wanted to.

Addi turned to him for a moment and searched his eyes. "Thank you. You didn't have to do this—I know Liberty sort of tricked you into it—but this was the best night I've ever had."

His breath caught, and a dopey smile took over his face until he was able to think clearly again. "It wasn't a hardship, beautiful." He kissed her forehead and directed her back to the edge of the park. He wanted her to remember that part of their date for a long time. He would.

Fifteen

Addi hummed off-key as she strode into The Bean on Monday morning. Kaylie waited on the couch, and the song died in her throat.

"Did you have a good weekend, Addi?" Kaylie narrowed her icy eyes and shifted in her seat to glare.

"I—" She'd had a fantastic weekend, filled with reliving Friday evening over and over. Especially the part where he'd kissed her ever so lightly on the head and called her beautiful. That was a memory she would cherish forever.

"Middle Park is beautiful this time of year, isn't it?"

Kaylie had seen them? But it was dark, and by that time Addi hadn't even been thinking about Kaylie anymore. "I'm sure it is," Addi mumbled. Why couldn't she ever just talk to Kaylie like anyone else?

"Did you set up my date or were you too busy enjoying your own?"

Addi couldn't catch her breath. She'd talked to Drew about it, but he wasn't interested. She couldn't force Drew to go out with Kaylie, could she?

"I talked to him about it." She had mentioned it; at least that wasn't a lie.

"So, when is the date?"

Drew had texted her that weekend that he'd like to meet up that night at Maynerd's. It was a sports bar where they could sit and talk while watching basketball on all the big screens.

"Tonight," she squeaked. "Meet him at seven at Maynerd's"

She made a mortified sound in her throat. "Really? That's the best you could do? I ought to fire you on principle."

She would love to sit with Drew and joke all night over a big bowl of chili cheese fries. It wouldn't matter to Kaylie that she was sacrificing her own time, it was time Kaylie didn't think she deserved anyway. And poor Drew. When she didn't show up, he might never talk to her again. He'd made it clear he didn't want to see Kaylie.

"You don't have to fire me. I quit." The jolt of freedom released her tongue. "Now *you* can work here all day and rush home so you can freshen up for a date that will be your last because he doesn't like you and doesn't want to see you. He'll be surprised when you show up tonight, and not in a good way." Addi turned on her heel and shoved back through the door.

Reality hit like a smack in the face. If she didn't find a job that day, she was sunk.

Drew strode into The Bean and did a quick search for Addi. He'd shown up early because he couldn't wait to see her. He hadn't thought she'd agree to meet with him that night, but she had. He'd been careful not to call it a date. If he had to slowly convince her they were meant to be together, so be it. He'd take it slow.

Kaylie pushed through the little door and scowled at everyone in the room until her gaze landed on him. It sent a chill up his spine as her look shifted from Arctic to Tropical within seconds. She slowly made her way toward him like a lioness stalking prey.

"Good morning, Drew. What can I get you?" She traced a single line from his wrist up to his elbow with one glistening fingernail.

"Uh, is Addi in?" Kaylie was about the worst at making coffee of any of the people who worked there. It almost wasn't worth paying for.

She yanked her hand back. "Addi called in sick. Very sick. She won't be in for a while. Days. She asked me to take her place with you tonight."

"Take her place?" That didn't sound like anything Addi would do, and she hadn't mentioned feeling sick when he'd talked with her the night before. "We were just going to hang out tonight. It's no bother, you don't have to." And he didn't want her to. Life was just starting to look up.

"Oh, I insist. I'll meet you at seven. Did you want your usual?" She cocked her hip out dangerously far.

"Yeah, sure." He wanted Kaylie to go away so he could text Addi and make sure she was okay. Why would she even tell Kaylie about meeting up with him? She could've just canceled. He sat and pulled his phone from his computer bag.

> **DREW:** HEY, BEAUTIFUL. HEARD YOU WEREN'T FEELING WELL. HOPE EVERYTHING IS FINE. I DIDN'T REALLY WANT TO MEET UP WITH KAYLIE TONIGHT, BUT I'LL MANAGE. LOL. CALL ME SOON AND LET ME KNOW IF I CAN BRING OVER SOME CHICKEN SOUP.

He glanced up just in time for Kaylie to bring his drink. There was probably coffee under there somewhere. It was a large cup, but had a mound of whipped topping on the top, making it look suspiciously more like an ice cream cone than a hot coffee. On top of all the cream was an artistic rendition of the coloring work of his two-year-old niece, only with chocolate and caramel.

"Wow, that's quite the coffee." He stared at it, not even sure if he was supposed to mix it or try to drink it that way. Should he ask for a straw?

"I thought it was time you tried something new. Especially since it's only five dollars."

Yikes, more than double the cost of his usual. Liberty finished what she was doing at a nearby table and came over. "Good morning, Drew."

Kaylie gave her the evil eye. "Can't you see we're talking? There are a lot of other tables, go find one that needs you."

What had he ever seen in her? "Actually, I need to get to work. Thanks for the coffee." He held it up for a second, then set it back down well out of the way. If she put mint in it along with all that other stuff, it probably didn't taste very good anyway. He couldn't even smell it under all the topping.

After he got his computer powered up, he checked his phone, but Addi hadn't responded. She'd been so quick to talk to him all weekend, but if she was sick enough to avoid work, she might be sleeping. He'd surprise her with that chicken soup later since he wouldn't get to see her like he'd planned that evening.

Liberty glanced at him once again, like she was trying to get his attention, but Kaylie scuttled her to the back room. Was Kaylie keeping something from him? Liberty wasn't usually one to be diverted, but Kaylie was in a particularly nasty mood.

Liberty shoved the back door open, and it slammed against the counter, turning a few heads her way. She marched over to his seat and plopped down on the bench, then turned to face him.

"You can't do this." She clasped her hands in front of herself on the table.

"Do what?" He was so lost about what was even going on. He glanced down at his phone, watching for Addi's reply.

"You can't go out with Kaylie tonight. I don't know what happened with Addi. Kaylie won't tell me, and Addi isn't responding when I call her."

So, it wasn't just him. "I tried to text her, too. She wasn't sick yesterday."

Liberty tilted her head down and gave him a look like he was ten kinds of fool. "I checked the chart while Kaylie was up here flirting with you. Want to know how many sick days Addi has ever taken? Zero. Zero sick days, Drew. What's the likelihood that she wasn't showing any symptoms yesterday but is so sick today that she would risk a short check?"

He couldn't answer that, but he knew Addi was money conscious. When they'd been at the movie, she'd tried to talk him into getting less food because of the cost of the tickets. "I'm guessing it's not likely."

"No. It's not. She's put up with Kaylie this whole time because she feels trapped in this job. She takes on every hour that she can. There's no way she called in sick today. I'm here until four. Can you please go check on her? I'm worried."

Now he was, too. "Yeah." He dug in his wallet and fished out a five. "Sorry there's not much of a tip, but I didn't *actually* order it or, you know, drink it."

Liberty flinched. "What is this?" She sniffed it. "Caramel chocolate mint mocha?"

"Your guess is as good as mine." He shrugged and shut his computer.

Liberty stood and rested her hands on her hips. "Addi told me you run an ad agency?"

Finally, a topic that didn't bother him. "Freelance."

She nodded and backed away a step. "If you're ever looking to take on a business partner, I know someone who's really good. I can get you a resume and references. She's suddenly really looking to get back into her old career."

If he ever convinced Addi to marry him, he just might. If for nothing else, the added security of having someone to take over if something ever happened to him. "I might be. Why don't you get me their info when you can?"

She nodded and went back to work as Drew gathered his computer. It was about ten blocks to her apartment, and he jogged most of the way. It didn't matter if he looked foolish, something was wrong, and he needed to see Addi. When he reached her apartment building, he buzzed her room, but there was no answer.

He pushed the button again. "Addi? If you're up there, please let me in."

Someone else came out from inside, and he dodged through the open door then took the stairs two at a time until he reached her floor. Pausing in front of her door, he listened. Many noises came from other apartments, but he couldn't hear anything from hers. He knocked and waited. She didn't come to the door.

"Addi?" He called through the door. "If you're okay, can you just come to the door and let me know?"

He waited, but he couldn't hear any movement inside. She either wasn't there or was just ignoring him. He took the stairs, back down and made his way through town, taking the way that took him through the park where he'd taken Addi that first day he'd asked her over for pizza. It was midday, so there weren't many couples walking around, but there were a lot of moms with baby carriages.

"Drew?" A soft voice came from behind him.

He turned and stared right into a very familiar and still incredibly pretty oval face. She hadn't changed much in a year, but he now saw her differently. He also saw the tiny infant she carried in a front pouch carrier, like a koala.

"Lauren." His voice sounded distant to his own ears.

She smiled slightly. "I'm so sorry, Drew. It's such a surprise to see you here. You were always so busy."

Too busy to see what was right in front of him, that Lauren hadn't been happy. "I don't come here often."

She smiled slightly. "I need you to know that I couldn't face you after what I'd done. It wasn't you, Drew. It was me. The week before our wedding, one of my exes showed up, and he wanted to talk to me. I probably should've said no, but I felt this tug." She sighed and laid a gentle hand on the baby's head.

"Mark was the one who got away from me, so when he came back, it was a temptation. We met up at a coffee shop and talked for hours. I realized I still had feelings for him and I couldn't marry you when I felt something for someone else."

Married, with a baby. He'd been so angry with her he hadn't been able to see her as anything more than the woman who left him at the altar, embarrassed him, proved to him he wasn't worth having.

"I should've called, but I was so mortified by what I'd done. I was so scared of what you would say to me. I still cared about you, still do, but I realized it wasn't love. I love Mark. I'm so sorry, Drew."

It hadn't been him all along. "I can't tell you what that did to me." All the other words failed him because they would be scathing, hurtful, and what good would they do now?

"I know. I'm so sorry. I shouldn't have left you to deal with everyone. I should've talked to you. I should've done a lot of things. We found out we were pregnant about six weeks after we eloped. That first year of marriage is hard, and every time I thought of calling you, I was worried what it would do to my husband, so I didn't. Wrong or right, that's what I did. I had to put my marriage first."

If he'd met Lauren in the park two weeks before, he would've been furious with her words, but he felt little more than a hollowness at them now. He'd been happy with Lauren when they were together, missed her when she was gone, but she wasn't Addi. Addi filled in all the rough places every hurt had left behind.

"I forgive you," he said without hesitation. "And congratulations."

Lauren smiled, then slid a ring off the ring finger on her right hand.

"I wore it hoping I would meet up with you someday. This belongs to you." She handed it to him. It was the ring he'd taken months to pick out. It was simple and elegant, just like Lauren, and just like Addi.

Lauren turned sideways so he could see the little cherub face of her daughter. "Her name is Gwen, and we are over the moon. Well, when we aren't trying to catch up on sleep, that is."

"Take care, Lauren." While the baby was cute, Lauren was a part of his life best left in the past, and he needed to find his missing future. He gave her a little wave and continued on his way. Seeing her hadn't affected him like he'd always assumed it would. She wasn't evil or horribly changed. She hadn't shifted her feelings for him, just realized she loved someone else more. Which meant there was hope that Addi, the one who'd reminded him of Lauren from the start, would be the perfect one. She could be the one who wouldn't love anyone else. He just had to find her and find out.

Sixteen

Addi tromped back to her apartment, the left heel of her shoe broken, adding to her disappointment. Even after rushing home to change and going to every place that might have an opening, she was no closer to finding a job. And she'd missed school, so she missed a lecture and would be behind.

The day that had started out so good had been ruined by her rash mouth. If she'd just held her tongue, but then, after she'd let Kaylie take her date with Drew, working there wouldn't be enjoyable at all anyway. But it would've still paid the bills.

She shoved open the door and stuck her key in the lock to open the lobby door and headed up to her floor. A few people lingered out in the halls, but it struck her as quieter than usual. She unlocked her door and kicked off her shoes, then trudged over to her sofa where she collapsed with a sigh.

Her phone buzzed, and she pulled it out. Twenty-seven missed texts. She'd had her phone shoved in her backpack and hadn't noticed it all day. Nineteen of the texts, including the last one, were from Drew.

> **DREW:** KAYLIE CAME. SHE STAYED ABOUT FIVE MINUTES BEFORE SHE LEFT. I THINK THAT'S TAKEN CARE OF NOW. CAN YOU PLEASE CALL ME? I'VE BEEN TRYING TO GET AHOLD OF YOU ALL DAY.

So, Kaylie had gone. Good, and even better now that the whole mess was over. But where did that leave Addi? She searched through all the texts, and he'd asked her how she felt, and he worried about her, but of course, he would. Friends cared. Friends loved to a point, then stopped. She needed more, more than Drew had been willing or able to offer. He'd never questioned her request to stay friends, to reassure him she wasn't after more than he was willing to give. He'd relaxed completely as soon as she'd suggested they make their date a non-date. Didn't that prove he didn't want to date her at all?

Liberty made up the balance of the texts and she, too, mentioned illness. Addi quickly replied to the last text.

> **ADDI:** I'M FINE. I QUIT. KAYLIE FINALLY GOT THE BEST OF ME.
> DON'T KNOW WHAT I'LL DO, BUT I NEED SOME TIME TO MYSELF.

She tried to think of some way to respond to Drew, to tell him she was fine but didn't want to see him. It hurt too much. Seeing him would just remind her that she'd been willing to sacrifice his happiness to keep her job, a job she'd thrown away.

> **LIBERTY:** PLEASE LET DREW KNOW YOU'RE OKAY IF YOU
> HAVEN'T ALREADY. I'VE NEVER SEEN HIM SO WORRIED WHEN HE
> CAME BACK FROM YOUR PLACE, AND YOU WEREN'T THERE.
> WHERE WERE YOU ALL DAY, ANYWAY?

A knock interrupted her reply, and Addi got up to see who it was. She hadn't heard a buzz. When she glanced through her peephole, Drew waited on the other side. He held a huge covered bowl in his hands. She tentatively opened the door, and he peered around it to see her.

"Thank God. I was so worried about you." He smiled slightly and raised the bowl. "Can I come in? I brought soup."

It smelled wonderful, and though she should send him away to protect her heart, she couldn't. She unlatched the chain and opened the door to admit him. He came inside and toed off his shoes, then went straight for the table.

"I wasn't sure what kind of illness you were dealing with, so I just made the most of what I had—lots of garlic, turmeric, chicken stock, carrots..."

He turned to face her and stopped.

"I'm not sick, Drew. I quit." Why was it so embarrassing to admit that? He'd probably never quit anything in his life. He always handled himself well.

"Why?"

She held back the hiccup that would have let loose the floodgates. If she let that out, she'd be lost. "Kaylie threatened to fire me, so I took away the option."

"Fire you?" His face hardened as he set the bowl down on the table. "What could you possibly have done to make her want to fire you?" He took two steps closer to her.

She wanted to collapse into him, let him hold her up. She'd had to handle so much since that morning, but he wasn't there to hold her. "Because of Friday, and because I was supposed to set you up with her."

"So, you made a date with me, then decided you wouldn't show up? You'd send her in your place? You *played* me?" She couldn't handle the anger that created a deep V-shape between his eyebrows. He'd never looked angry before and especially not at her.

"It wasn't like that. I didn't agree to meet you with the intent to trick you. She threatened me."

"Threatened to fire you, then you quit anyway. You knew how I felt about her, that I didn't want to see her again. I even told you the only reason I wanted to keep going to The Bean was to see you. When will you figure out that the only person I want to see is you? I made a mistake, I saw something in Kaylie that wasn't there, and worse, I thought I saw things in you that weren't there. But these last few weeks, you are all I think about. Are you throwing me away?"

Her heart screamed *no,* and it wouldn't be silenced. "I've watched every single guy I've ever had feelings for walk away with my friends. Every one. I figured it was only a matter of time until you figured out that Kaylie—or anyone else, really—was a better option than me."

He strode up to her, and his arm slid around her waist, the warmth of his breath on her face spread quickly down her neck and over her whole body. His lips lowered to hers. He started softly with the gentle caress of unease, but the moment she responded, he tucked her closer still. In a moment, she clung to his suit coat lapels and prayed that her kiss had the same effect on him as he had on her.

His hand slid up her back to her nape and held her there as he took his time exploring every bit of her mouth, then finally released her.

"Please don't throw me away, Addi."

"Please don't leave me, Drew." She didn't want to lose him, ever. She'd made a mistake. Holding back her anger against Kaylie had made her say and do things she didn't mean. "I'm sorry for listening to Kaylie. I was scared."

"I won't leave you Addi. I want you with me always." He dug in his pocket and held out a ring. It was the most beautiful thing she'd ever seen.

"Are you telling me that I'm going to be engaged before I ever go on a real date?"

He kissed her again and caressed her cheek, then captured her gaze and held it. "Only if you say 'yes,' beautiful."

She slid the ring on her finger, and it fit perfectly. "I say, yes."

She slid her arms around him. "I guess Betwixt was right."

"I'm going to spend my life proving just how right they were."

The End

I think all of us, no matter how pretty or popular, have felt alone at some point in our lives. Romance novels tend to focus on beauty, but what's inside is what truly matters. When we find our inner strength in Christ, the beauty within us comes forth. I hope that came through in this story. Neither of these characters was physically appealing to others in the story, but to each other, as they grew and accepted the reality of who they really are, they became even more beautiful to one another. Beloved, that is all of us in Christ.

1. What do you think is *really* holding back Drew and Addi? Do you feel that they have worked through it enough to have a future? **Romans 12:12** offers a little hint.

2. What is the difference between Drew's reaction to his first set up with Kaylie and the second? Do you think he already had some inkling of what he felt for Addi? **John 8:15**

3. The experience Addi had at the worship center is the beginning of Addi's realization of who she really is. Do you think that it's necessary to know exactly who you are to have a meaningful relationship? **1 Peter 3:1-6**

4. Kaylie was also given the opportunity to have her own special date set up by the Betwixt matchmaker. Do you think she has any hope of a happily-ever-after? What might be holding her back?

5. Liberty has dealt with a lot in her short life, making her a very strong person. What qualities do you see in her that you would want in a best friend?

6. This story was based on a few verses relating to waiting on the Lord, specifically: **Romans 5:3-5**, **Psalm 69:13** Which do you think apply the best to the situation?

7. Sometimes it is easy to let what others think of us define who we are, and we are told specifically to be watchful of our words, so we don't bring down others in **Ephesians 4:29**. Where could you put this verse to remind yourself daily to offer grace and remind yourself how our Heavenly Father sees you?

About

International bestselling author **Kari Trumbo** writes historical and contemporary Christian romance. She began her writing journey five years ago and has over thirty titles published to date. Before writing, she was a freelance developmental editor and beta reader.

Kari is a member of the Romance Writers of America (RWA) and American Christian Fiction Writers (ACFW) national group as well as her local chapter MN N.I.C.E. She makes her home in central MN—where the trees and lakes are plentiful—with her husband of over twenty years, two daughters, two sons, a cat, a bunny, and one hungry woodstove.

Follow Kari's newsletter to find out what happens to Drew and Addi in the future, and to learn when Liberty will meet her match!

Newsletter:	karitrumbo.com/contemporary/
Author Site:	www.KariTrumbo.com
FaceBook:	www.facebook.com/karitrumboauthor/
BookBub:	www.bookbub.com-authors-karitrumbo/
Twitter:	www.twitter.com/KariTrumbo/
Amazon:	www.amazon.com/Kari-Trumbo/e/B015IJOLN4

Contemporary:

Big Dreams

Better Than First

Whispers in Wyoming

Heartstruck and Heavensent
Temptation and Tenderness
Sensitive and Secure

Historical:

Seven Brides of South Dakota

Dreams in Deadwood
Kisses in Keystone
Love in Lead
Romance in Rapid

Sparks in Spearfish
Hearts in Hot Springs
Courting in Custer

And many more titles...

Introducing

I very much hope you enjoyed *Whole Latte Love*. I welcome you to join me for my new Great River Romance series. The next book features Liberty. She was such a fun character!

Join me at www.KariTrumbo.com/contemporary for updates on all releases.

Now, I'd like to introduce an amazing woman who you may already be familiar with if you've read other Crossroads Collections. Alana Terry is full of passion, not only for writing stories but for humanity. Like me, she is a homeschooling mom. She is also a pastor's wife and lives in beautiful rural Alaska. I've had so much fun getting to know her as a member of this group. Her story, *Seoul Refuge*, is about a wife away on a mission trip while her husband investigates a murder. There's more than one mystery, though.

I hope you enjoy her story and thank you so much for reading.

Kari Trumbo
INKED IN FAITH

Author of *Whole Latte Love*

Seoul REFUGE

By
ALANA TERRY

Copyright Notice

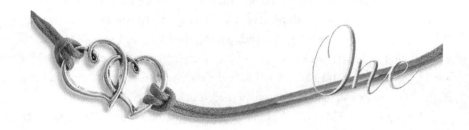

Caroline glanced up from her airplane reading when a white-haired woman stopped beside her in the aisle.

"Excuse me, sweetie." Her voice warbled but seemed to possess the strength of someone half her age. "I hope I'm not interrupting anything."

Caroline stared. There was something familiar about the woman's fiery features, the laugh lines streaming from the corners of her sharp eyes, the collar of her billowy blouse.

"The gentleman in the seat beside me insists on using the Lord's name in vain," she explained, "and the stewardess said I could move to an empty spot if I found one." She gestured to the window seat. "Would you mind?"

Caroline had enjoyed her solitude toward the back of the plane but felt it would be rude to deny the woman's request. She moved to unbuckle her seatbelt, but the old woman held up her hand.

"Don't worry about that. I'm not too big. I can just hop right over you." Which is exactly what she did.

Once settled in her seat, Caroline's new travel companion gave her a smile. "Now tell me, do you know Jesus Christ as your personal Lord and Savior?"

Caroline blinked. Never in her entire life, not in her fifty-something years as an agnostic or her three years since she became a Christian had anyone asked her a question this pointed about her faith, especially not a stranger she'd just met. She was so startled, it took her several seconds before she found her voice and stammered her answer.

The woman beamed. "I'm so glad to hear it. I'm Lucy Jean, by the way, but you can call me Grandma Lucy. And I'm just delighted the Lord led us together. When my granddaughter was driving me to the airport to catch this flight, I was just praying to God, asking him to give me a Christian to sit next to. I'm healthy for my age, which is saying a lot, but every once in a while, I get forgetful. In fact, my niece didn't want me to take such a long flight, but my grandson was recently married, and..."

Her voice trailed off when she glanced at the book Caroline was holding. "What's that you're reading? Is that one of the books by Cameron Hopewell's son?"

Caroline nodded, surprised that Grandma Lucy's smile could grow any more enthusiastic.

"What a delightful man of God," Grandma Lucy gushed. "You know, I have a grandson who was saved at a Hopewell revival."

Caroline was about to ask how many grandchildren this old woman had but didn't have time.

"What a true servant he is. Such a powerful anointing." Grandma Lucy was beaming at the author photo on the back cover of Caroline's hardback. "Is this his newest one?"

Caroline lowered the book to show Grandma Lucy the title. "I don't think so. This is the one he wrote with his wife. It's talking about..."

Grandma Lucy clasped her hands in front of her oversized collar. "The spiritually mismatched. I know this book." She gave a soft chuckle. "Wish I had had something like this when my husband was still alive."

Caroline didn't know what to say. Their flight had only left Seattle an hour earlier, and it was still a long way to Seoul. She'd hoped to get more reading done before trying to settle in for a nap, but Grandma Lucy seemed to have other plans. She stared at Caroline and asked pointedly, looking over her thin glasses, "So, is he backslidden, nominal, or unbelieving?"

"I beg your pardon?"

Grandma Lucy continued to smile. "Your husband. Your spiritual mismatch. Is he backslidden, nominal, or unbelieving?"

"Unbelieving," Caroline answered, feeling her cheeks heat up.

Grandma Lucy nodded as if she'd known the answer and Caroline was only confirming her conviction.

Caroline waited, although she couldn't have said what for, feeling mildly annoyed. After all the time Caroline had spent praying for her marriage, especially over the past three weeks, why was God pouring salt into open wounds, plunking her down on a plane next to this outspoken little firecracker of a white-haired old lady? She held her breath.

Still waiting.

Still uncertain what for.

Then, before there was time to react, Grandma Lucy's hand shot out. Her palm landed flat on Caroline's forehead, and Grandma Lucy's prayer rang out so loudly over the hum of the airplane engines Caroline wondered if the pilot locked up in his cockpit could hear.

"Dear Lord," Grandma Lucy prayed, "great and merciful Savior, we lift your name on high. Yes, sweet Jesus, for you are good and your love endures forever. You know everything, from the smallest hair on our heads to the names of the stars in the outer stretches of the universe. You know, dear Lord, for you created all these and so much more.

"You created my beautiful and sweet sister here, giving her a heart for you, saving her out of her sins. Your mercy extended to her mightily, and I know that you have already used her to advance your kingdom in ways she isn't even aware of yet. But, Lord, her heart is heavy, this sweet sister of mine. She's been united in the holy bonds of matrimony with a man who doesn't believe in you, who doesn't proclaim your name. He doesn't proclaim your name *yet* is what I should say, for you, dear Lord, are in the business of saving even the hardest of hearts.

"I do not know her husband's situation. I do not know what pain or anger he's carrying around in his spirit, but I sense a heaviness, sweet Jesus. I sense pride and arrogance that keeps him from acknowledging his need for you. Only you can show him, Lord. Only you can open his eyes. Only you can soften his heart. Only you can speak to his soul and let him realize how much you love him, how lost he is without you, great and merciful Savior.

"And so, Lord, we leave this dear husband, this lost sinner, in your hands, and we pray that you would do whatever it takes to draw his heart to yours. We ask this in the great and mighty name of our Lord and Savior

Jesus Christ, who wills that none should perish but that all should come to repentance to enjoy your glorious gift of salvation."

Caroline's forehead burned hot the entire length of the prayer, but after the old woman pulled her hand away, the sensation disappeared, along with any conviction or hope that had started to burn in Caroline's spirit. What was left was an emptiness. A longing. Was Caroline's deepest pain so obvious that even a stranger on a plane flying across the Pacific Ocean could perceive it?

She clutched her book, hoping Grandma Lucy would say something, anything, to soothe over the giant, gaping wound that had opened up in Caroline's spirit during that prayer. But the old woman simply smiled and pulled out a cowboy handkerchief from her pocket.

"These long overseas flights always make me feel sleepy." Grandma Lucy covered her face with the handkerchief, crossed her arms, and settled back in her seat without another word.

Caroline stared at her book, the one she'd meant to finish on this flight. The one her pastor's wife had recommended to encourage Caroline while she watched her marriage fall to pieces. The one that was supposed to teach her how to keep her marriage from dissolving into millions of infinitesimally small particles. Teach her how to live with a man who'd despised everything about her ever since Caroline gave her life to Christ.

She wanted to read more, but her heart was too heavy. Her eyes were dry, and even when she opened the book, she sat blinking at the words, comprehending merely a fraction of their meaning.

She glanced once more at Grandma Lucy, this strange woman whose prayer had felt so inspired and yet at the same time so depressing. Caroline had been praying for her husband's salvation for three years, sometimes spending a full hour on her knees crying tears of desperation. And God still hadn't answered her. Things had gotten worse even before Calvin moved out. Before Caroline came to Christ, her husband had been a comfortable agnostic, apathetic to religion. Now he was outspoken, angry whenever Caroline did or said anything relating to her faith.

She slid the book into the seat pocket in front of her and let out a loud breath. Her husband's last words before he moved out of their home and out of her life echoed in her ears. "Enjoy being alone with nobody but that

God of yours."

She'd known he was ready to move out. Sensed months earlier that her marriage was already dead, and yet still his departure had felt like a shock. She hadn't been ready. She'd been praying. Day and night, she'd begged God to soften Calvin's heart. It would take a miracle to save her relationship with her husband, and in spite of all her prayers, heaven was woefully out of miracles.

Drisklay swung around in his chair and reached for the pot of coffee, which had grown cold hours earlier.

"I'm taking off, boss." His junior partner Alexi sounded far too chipper, especially for this late in the day. "Have a good evening." Alexi gave a playful salute, his smile never diminishing.

Drisklay didn't look up but stared at his computer screen. There were too many unanswered questions. That was the problem. Too many unanswered questions, not enough clues.

"Why her?" he asked himself, staring at the photograph of the murder victim. Rebekah Harrison wasn't exactly the kind of nineteen-year-old Drisklay's colleagues on the force would classify as high risk. She was a pastor's daughter fresh out of a twelve-year homeschool curriculum. On her dating profile, she listed her favorite hobbies as crocheting blankets and reading Jane Eyre. By all accounts, she'd led a quiet life. Good grades, steady employment at a Christian bookstore, not so much as a parking ticket.

Now she was dead.

Drisklay turned away from his computer and perused the scribbles in his notebook. He'd already followed up on the guy she'd met on the dating website. A cold lead. Fake account set up from a laptop at a public library. Whoever he was, he wasn't making it easy to trace his steps.

But Drisklay wasn't going to give up.

With the tepid coffee sloshing around contentedly in his stomach, he grabbed a file that had been serving as a coaster for a few old Styrofoam cups and half a stale Danish. After dusting the crumbs off the envelope, he pulled out the crime scene photographs, then took a bite of the Danish, washing it down with a gulp of cold coffee. Wiping his hands on his pants, he stared at the photographs, poring over details he'd seen dozens, maybe hundreds, of times before.

"Alexi!" he shouted. His junior partner was notorious for dilly-dallying for twenty or even thirty minutes after he closed his work station for the day, and Drisklay hoped he was still around.

Sure enough, Alexi bounded around the corner. "You need something, boss?"

Drisklay opened a new Danish wrapper. "Get another pot of coffee going. And hurry."

Without pausing to watch while Alexi scampered off, Drisklay spun his chair around, tossing the photographs of the murdered young woman onto the table behind him. This secondary workstation was only slightly less cluttered than his desk, but it offered more room to spread everything out.

"I'm gonna get you," he whispered into the empty office, then glanced at his clock to calculate how long it would take before he had a fresh cup of coffee on his desk.

He'd need it for the night ahead.

"Coffee?"

Caroline glanced up at the flight attendant. "No, thanks. Just water."

The woman passed her a small cup and turned to the passengers on the other side of the aisle.

Caroline let out her breath. Ninety more minutes before they landed in Seoul. She'd never been so far from home. This mission trip would be frightening enough to undergo on her own even if she didn't have all of Calvin's taunts racing through her mind.

Which she did.

If you get arrested overseas, it can take weeks for the US Embassy to sort everything out. Remember those two college students imprisoned in China?

That was Calvin's problem. Decades of police work had hardened his heart. He didn't trust anyone, not the government, not the Lord, not even his wife.

You'll get into trouble and won't know how to get yourself out.

In a way, it was true. Caroline had rarely traveled outside of the States, spending the vast majority of her life tucked away safely in New England suburbs. She'd only been to the West Coast once, and that was for a teachers' convention almost ten years earlier.

Now she was preparing to land in South Korea to volunteer at a Christian orphanage. Caroline was grateful for the chance to fit meaningful work into her summer vacation. But her determination to head to Seoul ended up sealing the lid on the casket of her marriage. It wasn't that Calvin needed her around. He'd been so busy working the case about that murdered pastor's daughter that Caroline could have spent several months away from home without him noticing.

His problem wasn't the fact that she was traveling. His problem was the fact that she was traveling to help at a Christian ministry. Ever since she'd been saved, Calvin hated Caroline for being involved at church in any capacity. Before the fight that preceded his moving out, the two of them had come to an unspoken truce of sorts. Caroline would go church for one service on Sunday, but any other church functions during the week weren't worth the additional verbal assault from her husband.

Caroline would have loved to have joined the Tuesday night women's Bible study led by her pastor's wife, Sandy. It had been Sandy who led her to Christ in the first place, and Caroline always felt her soul rejuvenated after they spent time together. Unfortunately, that time together was hard to come by, not only because of her busy work schedule during the school year but because of her husband's ridiculous stubbornness.

Not that he had the right to care what his wife did in her free time, especially since so many of his evenings were tied up tracking down murderers throughout the Boston area. It might have been different if she'd taken up some other hobby—basket weaving or continuing ed classes for her teacher's license—but church functions were definitely out.

She took a sip of water, curiously surprised that she didn't feel better about the weeks ahead of her. She and Mrs. Cho, the director of the orphanage where she was going to serve, had connected online several years earlier. After her salvation, Caroline wanted to find something she could do to serve the Lord. It was her pastor's wife and her mentor, Sandy, who first told her about Korea Freedom International, an organization that ministered to North Korean refugees resettled in Seoul. The nonprofit needed a newsletter editor, something Caroline could do in her own home on her own computer without Calvin ever realizing it. Soon, Caroline went from a volunteer proofreader to one of the Korea Freedom newsletter's most regular newsletter columnists. Caroline loved the opportunity it gave her to speak with Christians on the other side of the world, Christians like

Mrs. Cho.

Mrs. Cho had spent the past several decades, nearly the last half of her life, caring for children in a Seoul-based orphanage where she lived, worked, and ministered. Caroline's relationship with the old woman was only supposed to last as long as it took to come up with a five-hundred-word column, but she and Mrs. Cho had shared a connection of sorts and would chat every so often by email.

Mrs. Cho didn't know anything about Caroline's marriage, didn't even realize how young of a believer Caroline actually was. Which was exactly how Caroline wanted it. Even though she'd been attending Pastor Carl and Sandy's church for the past three years, she could never walk through the doors without feeling like the newcomer. The one who didn't really belong.

It was the same feeling she saw in the eyes of students who transferred into her class from another district right in the middle of the school year.

The same feeling that swept over Caroline any time she had to drop something off for her husband at the police station, with all its sprawling hallways, dim lights, and uniformed workers she didn't know or recognize.

The feeling of being an outsider.

Caroline tightened her seatbelt when a jolt of turbulence rocked the plane. She glanced over at Grandma Lucy. The old woman was still sleeping with her colorful handkerchief draped over her eyes. Caroline had made a little more progress in her book, but she'd spent far more time wondering if there was any point in finishing it. She'd bought dozens of titles like this before and already knew what they were going to say.

Pray for your husband. Don't be a nag. Leave the changing up to God, and be such a good example that your husband will automatically fall on his knees and accept Christ as his personal Lord and Savior.

That was what all these authors said, paraphrasing or sometimes quoting each other directly in chapters that hardly varied in style or subject.

Pray. Be a good witness. Sit back and watch God work.

Caroline shut the book then reached for her phone, so she could double check her hotel arrangements. She'd wasted enough time on this flight already on books that wouldn't help, offering empty promises that could never come true.

Drisklay leaned back and let out a belch that tasted like old coffee and stale Danish. He rubbed his eyes, refusing to lift the post-it note he had placed on his computer screen to cover the time. On nights like this, it was too much of a distraction to pay attention to how late (or early) he was working.

For hours, he'd been looking up every known fact about Rebekah Harrison, searching in vain for missing links to connect her to some known criminal or suspect. Missing links that simply weren't there. He shook his head, thankful yet again for his good sense to never have children of his own. Who would want to bring anyone into a world as cruel and dangerous as this?

A few years ago, four Boston women were murdered after responding to online dating ads, but that suspect was already behind bars, waiting while the prosecution got their act together to give him the stiffest sentencing possible. Those women were all a specific type. Outgoing. Flirtatious. The kind who post photos online with their hips jutted out and their lips all pouty and their cleavage spilling over like a celebrity wardrobe malfunction just waiting to happen.

Rebekah Harrison, also murdered after joining an online dating service, was nothing like that. She was apparently the only individual under twenty-five in the state of Massachusetts who wasn't addicted to a daily social media fix. She could go weeks without posting, and the posts she did share were mostly to wish her grandparents, aunts, uncles, cousins, and homeschooling friends a happy birthday. Every once in a while, she'd also pass along one of those sappy sweet pictures of Jesus standing on someone's front porch like a vacuum salesman waiting to be let in, and that was all.

Drisklay took another sip of cold coffee. Why was she dead?

Her murder could have been completely random. Maybe not even connected to the dating website at all. Wrong place, wrong time. That's it.

Yet his gut told him otherwise.

Drisklay rapped his pencil against the side of his desk. "Who killed you, Miss Church Mouse?" he muttered to his screen. "And why?"

Caroline had just finished emailing Mrs. Cho at the orphanage in Seoul when one of the flight attendants addressed the passengers on the loudspeaker. Another twenty minutes and the plane would land at Incheon Airport. To the locals in Seoul, it was around four in the afternoon, but since Caroline's internal clock insisted it was the middle of the night, she was going to go straight to a hotel to rest up, so hopefully, when she met Mrs. Cho tomorrow morning, she'd feel at least somewhat human.

She let out her breath, trying to convince herself there was nothing to be nervous about. The uneasy feeling sloshing around in her gut was the same feeling she got when her brand-new husband was a rookie on the police force out patrolling the streets in the middle of the night. Sometimes Caroline would wake up certain Calvin was in trouble. Even though she'd spent most of her married years as a non-Christian, she would still pray. Without knowing how or why she'd beg God to keep her husband safe.

And he had.

Calvin had been involved in more dangerous and high-profile cases than Caroline could remember. He'd advanced solidly up the ranks so that now he was the most senior detective in the homicide department. In his career, he'd brought down mafia bosses, human traffickers, and would-be homegrown terrorists. He'd solved cases involving murdered politicians and kidnapped children.

But he was never happy. Maybe it was because all he saw was the darkest side of human nature, but even just a few years into their marriage, Caroline watched helplessly as her gallant husband turned even more cynical. Even more depressed.

It hadn't been easy, but she'd managed all right. She'd made enough friends with other police wives to realize her situation was normal. Somebody had to patrol the Boston streets, and rocky marriages were apparently the price that the spouses of these heroes simply had to pay.

She'd married young, but Calvin's penchant for working every overtime case meant she had extra time on her hands. As a newlywed, she'd started working part-time as a school aid, saving her paychecks until she could put herself through community college and eventually wind up with her teaching degree. Even though she'd qualified last year to retire from the district with full benefits, she had renewed her contract. It wasn't as if she and her husband would buy an RV any time soon and start traveling the country, so what else was she supposed to do but continue the job she loved?

Things would have been different—significantly different—if she and Calvin had ever had children, but a car accident when Caroline was only a child made that impossible. Well, perhaps not impossible. When Caroline was recovering from her injuries and all throughout her teen years, she assumed she would one day adopt.

She just hadn't accounted for Calvin's stubbornness.

So here she was. No children, no grandchildren. Her only family was a husband who'd regularly put in a hundred hours of work a week without thinking twice about what his schedule was doing to his health or their relationship. If you were to ask Calvin, all their marital problems began when Caroline became a Christian.

The thought would be laughable if it weren't so depressing.

A flight attendant passed up the aisle, apologizing as she reached across Caroline to tap Grandma Lucy, still sleeping in the window seat. "Ma'am, will you please raise your seat and make sure your seatbelt is securely fastened?"

Grandma Lucy removed the handkerchief from her eyes and smiled. "Are we almost to Seoul?" Her voice was surprisingly youthful. Caroline wished she could feel even partially as refreshed as the old woman sounded.

Grandma Lucy clasped her hands in front of her chest. "Thank you for such a hearty nap and such a safe flight." She was still staring at Caroline, so it wasn't until she breathed, "Amen," that Caroline realized she was praying and not addressing her directly.

"Did you enjoy your flight?" Grandma Lucy asked. "Did you finish that book you were reading? Did it bring your heart encouragement in our Lord and Savior Jesus Christ?"

Caroline was momentarily flustered by this outpouring of questions and couldn't decide which to answer first, but apparently, Grandma Lucy wasn't waiting for a response. Instead, she reached over, took Caroline's hand in hers, and began to pray.

"Lord, I thank you that every step of my young sister's life has been ordained by you from the beginning of time. I thank you that not a prayer of hers has gone unheard. I thank you that she is stronger than she knows because her faith and her hope are firmly grounded in you.

"I sense such a tremendous longing in my sister's soul, Lord Jesus, and I pray that if it has anything to do with her sadness at her husband's hardness of heart that you would be working miracles in this situation. For you are the Sovereign God who desires all men to be saved, and so we claim his salvation in the great and powerful name of Jesus Christ, who died for our sins and rose from death to deliver us from an eternity separated from you. Yes, Jesus, for this was your good will and purpose, and it's in your name we pray and ask all these things."

Grandma Lucy's voice had risen incrementally so that she was practically shouting by the time she finished her prayer. Caroline offered a weak smile and resisted the urge to glance around and count how many passengers had turned to stare. She cleared her throat, adjusted her seatbelt, so she had some way to occupy her hands, and hoped that the plane would land soon.

Her most recent argument with Calvin, the one before he finally moved out, rang through her ears. She mentioned something about Seoul, and soon her husband was lamenting that he'd lost all respect for her after she joined up with that *Jesus cult*, as he called it.

Her response had been far from gracious.

Now here she was, on a plane thousands of miles away from home, just three weeks after her husband left her, complaining about how much she'd changed since Christians "brainwashed" her.

She felt guilty about that argument, particularly her response to it. Maybe she should have tried harder to encourage him to stay. Sometimes she even felt guilty about continuing on with her plans to go to Seoul. What right did she have to work for God when the corpse of what had been her marriage wasn't even yet cold?

But more than anything, she felt guilty because when she looked deep down into her psyche, into the darkest parts that she didn't want to admit to anyone else, she was tired of life with Calvin. Tired of the angry tirades, the shouting matches where he accused her of being a brainwashed fool.

She was tired of being married to a man like that, and the past three weeks since he'd moved out had been the most peaceful she'd known in years.

She'd asked God to save her husband. She'd asked God to save her marriage. Now, she just wanted to spend her time in Seoul serving the Lord and forgetting all the heartache of her failed marriage. The chance to serve God before starting another busy school year back in the States. Was that so much to ask?

Yes, she'd loved Calvin once, and maybe if his job hadn't made him so hard and cynical, there would still be love there. Now, all she found was exhaustion.

In the end, he had been the one to leave her. It wasn't as if she'd abandoned him. There wasn't a whole lot she could do anymore. Not like she could physically restrain him to keep him from walking out of her life, leaving nothing but broken dreams in his wake.

Caroline was ready for a change. Needed a change. As the South Korean landscape zoomed into focus, her heart reached out for a shred of hope. Not hope that her husband would come to his senses and accept Christ as his Savior. Not even hope that God would work on Calvin's heart and lead the two of them toward reconciliation.

Right now, all she had left to hope for was that he'd leave her in peace. He obviously hated being married to a Christian, and since Caroline's conversion was the most real thing that had happened to her in her adult life, their marriage had arrived at an impossible impasse.

If Calvin wanted out, she couldn't stop him.

The thought brought a rush of relief she hadn't felt in months.

Drisklay jerked awake and wiped the drool off his cheek. It wasn't the first time he'd fallen asleep at his desk, but no matter how often it happened, he never quite got over the few seconds of disorientation when he woke up.

He reached for his Styrofoam cup. Empty.

Great. He glanced at the clock.

"Alexi!" he bellowed.

His partner rushed over and slapped him on the back. "Long night, eh, boss?"

Drisklay scowled and muttered, "Just sleeping off that last pot of coffee."

Alexi tried to hand him a jumbo cup. "Yeah, I figured you'd need to refuel, so I picked you up a mocha."

Drisklay stared, ignoring the sound of a few of his coworkers sniggering in the background. Alexi had been transferred to his unit a month earlier, long enough that he should know better than to offer Drisklay something as disgusting as a sugar-ridden mocha.

The nerve.

Drisklay stared Alexi down until his partner slunk away, frou-frou cup in hand.

Drisklay shuffled papers around on his desk, waiting for his brain to realize it was already morning.

A minute later, his partner returned, a penitent look on his face as he held out a Styrofoam cup of steaming black coffee. "Long night?"

Drisklay grunted his reply and turned back to his notebook. He needed the caffeine, but he wasn't thinking about that right now. Right now, he was still thinking about that pastor's daughter. Something didn't fit. He was overlooking something.

Something important.

He downed a large gulp, wincing as the liquid scalded the back of his throat.

He was going to find this murderer.

And stop this criminal madness before anybody else ended up dead.

Three

Caroline hadn't realized how long it would take just to get through customs. She was ready with her passport, but when the agent asked for the phone number and address of her contact in South Korea, she'd had to pull up her inbox on her phone and stand there in the front of the line scrolling through dozens of emails she'd exchanged with Mrs. Cho. In the end, she could only find the orphanage phone number. She gave it to the agent then used the public address listed on the Korea Freedom website, hoping he wouldn't recognize it as a business instead of a place of residence.

Finally, she was on the curb, mentally repeating the number of the bus she was supposed to take, wondering if it would be easier to hail a cab.

"I had a feeling I'd be seeing you one last time."

Caroline turned to find herself staring down into Grandma Lucy's smiling face. The two women had traveled together through the terminal, with Caroline helping wheel Grandma Lucy's small carry-on, but they'd been directed into separate lines at customs and lost track of each other.

"The Lord is always faithful to bring his children together, isn't he?" Grandma Lucy crooned as if she and Caroline had been separated for years and not an hour.

"I'd like you to meet my grandson and his wife." Grandma Lucy beamed up at a tall redheaded man with a confident twinkle in his expression. "This is a good friend of mine," she told him. "We met on the flight over."

He chuckled and stretched out his hand. "Why am I not surprised to hear that Grandma Lucy made a friend on the plane?" He stood with his arm around a young woman with long brown hair. She was pretty and quite obviously pregnant. All the while, Grandma Lucy stood by, beaming broadly.

Caroline tried to overcome her mental fog to think of something to say to the family, but the red-haired grandson was too quick. "This one's ours," he announced, and Caroline felt herself breathing a sigh of relief as he helped his wife and grandma board the bus. She usually wasn't afraid of chitchat, but something about her previous encounter with Grandma Lucy made her feel on edge. It was a sensation she'd experienced before and one that was particularly unwelcome here.

Early on in her Christian life, Caroline and her husband had come to the tacit agreement that he wouldn't harp on her *quite* so much if she limited her church going to just Sunday mornings, so Caroline needed to find alternate ways to nourish her spirit that didn't involve darkening the doors of a church. Instead of joining Sandy's ladies' Bible study or attending weeknight prayer meetings, she poured herself into Christian books and podcasts, things she could read or listen to only when Calvin wasn't home to overhear.

Most of these resources were invaluable, exactly what Caroline had needed. In her early days as a new believer, she'd been so eager to soak up whatever Bible teaching and spiritual encouragement she could find. But lately, she'd noticed something from even some of her favorite podcasts. A hint of guilt. A sense that if she were a better Christian, she wouldn't be struggling the way she was.

Like the blog post Caroline had read where an anonymous woman related her desperation after being married to an unrepentant unbeliever for over three decades. The article itself was heartfelt, echoing Caroline's own discouragement and despair. But the comments... Caroline had spent the afternoon crying and had finally called Sandy to talk through how upset they'd made her.

"These women act like if your husband's not saved, you must be the one preventing God from working," she complained. "They take one or two Bible verses and make out like it's my fault that Calvin still doesn't believe."

The other line was so quiet that at first Caroline wondered if she'd lost the call.

Then Sandy simply said, "Some people really are idiots, aren't they?"

The words were so surprising coming from her pastor's wife that Caroline didn't know if she should laugh or just cry harder.

As it turned out, Caroline had repeated Sandy's spontaneous and somewhat irreverent remark to herself on more than one occasion since then. Even though at the time it had shocked her out of her despair, it never fully took away the pain of knowing that some people blamed her for her marriage's failure.

As if she had any choice in the matter.

As if she hadn't tried everything in her power, begging God and heaven to intervene, to save both her husband and her marriage.

Some people really are idiots, aren't they? Even now, while her bus pulled to a stop by the crowded airport curbside, Caroline smiled to herself at the words.

It didn't take away the slight unease she'd felt meeting Grandma Lucy. It didn't change the fact that some Christians would consider her a failure.

Caroline boarded the bus, pleasantly surprised to discover it nicely air conditioned, and found a window seat so she could watch the city skyline loom into view. She put her bag on her lap, still smiling to herself at her memory of that phone conversation with Sandy. *Some people really are idiots...*

It didn't change the fact that her marriage was dead. It didn't change the fact that some people still would blame her for not being a perfect wife and a perfect witness to Calvin as if all her marital woes were her fault and no one else's.

But as long as Caroline could remember what her pastor's wife taught her, as long as she could remember that some people really were idiots, she was going to be all right.

Everything was going to work out in the end. She just had to find a way to hold on without losing her mind or her faith until then.

Drisklay led the dead woman's parents into the sparse room and set his Styrofoam cup on the table between them. "Have a seat." He gestured to the worn couch.

Mr. Harrison looked at his wife, and they both sat in silent unison.

"I'd like to express my condolences regarding your loss." The words rolled off Drisklay's tongue. Practiced and rehearsed. How many times had he led victims' families into this very room, sat them down on this very couch, and opened his interview with this exact line? Sometimes he'd even caught criminals this way. Figured out when a story or an alibi didn't line up, at which point the bereaved family member turned into a suspect, prepped to transport to the far less comfortable interrogation room.

Drisklay took a sip of cold coffee and nodded toward the pastor. "Is it okay if I record this?"

Harrison glanced again at his wife, and they both nodded together. Sitting next to each other, they looked as if they could have been twins.

Disgusting. And more than a little disturbing.

Drisklay hated preachers on principle even before his wife was won over by Bible thumpers. All preachers wanted was your money, and they'd use hell and damnation and any other scare tactic to get it.

Sick people.

He took one more swig from his cup, gulping loudly, then decided he'd start with the woman. The mother.

"What can you tell me about Rebekah?" He kept his voice gruff, having learned from years of experience that if you let softness or compassion seep into your words, even just a little, you'd have the victims' loved ones blubbering. Drisklay glanced at the box of Kleenex on the side table, hoping the janitor had remembered to make sure it was full, then leaned forward, waiting for the woman's answer.

Mrs. Harrison glanced toward her husband, who gave the slightest nod.

"She was always a good girl," the mother began.

Drisklay clasped his hands in front of him, trying to come across like

515

the kind of detective who has all the time in the world. Without staring straight into her eyes and making her uncomfortable, he kept his eyes focused mostly on her earrings, glancing every so often at her pupils, the biological lie detectors, nature's gift to detectives.

"She never gave us any trouble." So far, Mrs. Harrison was telling the truth. Or at least she wasn't deliberately making stuff up. Typical of any mother, whether that of the victim or the criminal. Always thinking the best about her children. Never willing to admit what kind of danger they might be willfully putting themselves into or what kind of deranged crimes they might be willing to commit.

Mrs. Harrison was wringing her hands together, and to avoid the mess of having to deal with a complete meltdown, Drisklay turned toward the husband. The pastor.

"What can you tell me about her friends?"

On cue, the couple shared another glance, and the pastor took his wife's hand. "She kept to herself, mostly. Quiet. Had some kids she graduated with that she kept up with occasionally."

"I thought she was homeschooled," Drisklay interrupted.

Mrs. Harrison straightened her back and offered the first comment of the interview that hadn't been preceded by a conjugal glance. "She was part of a homeschool co-op through our church."

The church. It figured.

"Any particularly close friends you think I should talk to?"

Mr. and Mrs. Harrison glanced at each other, all four of their eyebrows arched in matching question marks.

"Maybe Misty?" Mrs. Harrison suggested.

"Or Katie."

Drisklay already had an interview with Misty scheduled but decided to get the second girl's last name and jot it down in his notebook before moving to his next question. "Boyfriend?"

At the word, the pastor stiffened his spine, and Drisklay noted with marked attention the way his wife gave his hand a firm squeeze. She looked Drisklay straight in the eyes, the first time she'd met his stare straight-on, and answered, "No."

The word fell flat, but at the sound of it, her husband visibly relaxed.

Interesting.

Drisklay leaned forward. "You are both aware, aren't you, that your daughter had a profile up on a dating website, correct?"

His question was met with icy, palpable silence.

"You were both aware, I assume?" he prodded.

Mrs. Harrison nodded. "Yes, Rebekah told her father and me that she'd made herself a profile. I researched it online, and it looked respectable. A nice way to find young Christian men her age. I thought it was a good idea…"

Her husband tensed, and Mrs. Harrison stopped her breathy discourse, biting her lip and staring nervously at her hands.

"I take it you also were aware then of her activities online?" Drisklay asked the father.

Harrison knitted his brows and answered curtly, "Yes." He leaned forward intensely. "Now, officer, what can you tell me about my daughter's murder, and what are you doing to bring her killer to justice?"

It was at that point Drisklay knew the interview was over. Not surprising, really. Better to end the meeting early than risk further alienating the bereaved parents. He'd need more help from them later on, and it was in his best interest to keep them as cooperative as possible.

Pleasantries were exchanged. Thanks given and received. More apologies, condolences for their daughter's death, regrets for the inconvenience of a police interview.

Drisklay shook both Mr. and Mrs. Harrison's hands in turn. The pastor's grip was firm and confident, hers weak and feeble. As Harrison led his wife out the door and down the hall, it looked as if he were supporting the bulk of her weight.

Drisklay let out a deep breath.

"Get anywhere with them, boss?" Alexi asked, materializing by the open door.

Drisklay shook his head.

"Think they're involved at all?"

Drisklay didn't bother to answer. Something was going on here. He'd have to keep focusing on this family, but for now, there were other interviews to conduct.

His partner was still standing stupidly next to him, like a twelve-year-old kid totally ignorant of the concept of initiative.

"Is the friend here?" Drisklay snapped.

Alexi jerked to attention. "Misty? Yeah. You ready for her?"

"I'm ready." Drisklay thrust his empty cup into his partner's hands. "Get me a refill and lead her back."

Alexi stared at the empty cup. "You want creamer or sugar or..." He stopped mid-sentence and spun on his heel in response to Drisklay's glare.

"Be right back," he muttered, and Drisklay paced the hallway while he waited to interview the dead girl's best friend.

Four

Heavy rain started to pour just minutes after Caroline locked herself into her small hotel room. Thankful to be buffered from the traffic and city noise, she welcomed the pounding drops splattering against the windowpane.

Something about the rain reminded her of that Halloween night. How many years ago was it now? Twenty-five? Maybe more. Calvin would remember. They hadn't talked about it since it happened, but he still remembered. She was certain of that.

When it came right down to it, that night was what had changed everything. Calvin was never the same after that. Neither was their marriage.

Which was why it was stupid of her husband to blame her conversion for their troubles. Had he forgotten all the stress they endured even before she was saved?

She tried to ignore the rain and plopped her suitcase onto the bed. She'd lost track of how many hours she'd been awake at this point, but it was probably close to twenty-four if not already more.

Calvin would never change, his constitution as steady as the rain pounding on the roof. He was the same stubborn, cynical man who'd come home broken that Halloween. It was the last time she'd seen her husband cry. It was as if that one night had opened his eyes to just how tragic the world could be, and he'd vowed to harden himself so his work could never affect him in that way again.

Maybe it was the right call for a police officer. Maybe it was what anyone else would have done in his situation. But it also spelled the death of any remnants of closeness, love, or romance between them.

How do you develop any sense of intimacy with a man who's shielded himself from all emotion whatsoever?

Caroline's conversion wasn't what broke their marriage. Their doom had been written out decades ago, on a rainy night just like this. All of it—Calvin's unhappiness, his cynicism, his inability to express or receive love in any meaningful way—boiled down to that one pouring evening.

Caroline left her suitcase half unpacked on the bed and stretched out on the mattress, covering her ears with the pillow.

She hated the sound of the rain.

Drisklay didn't like the look of Rebekah Harrison's best friend from the moment Alexi led her into the interview room. Misty slouched in a vain attempt to conceal her six-foot-tall height. She was young, only twenty, and yet she was as bent over as Drisklay's grandma had been at seventy-five.

Her hand was sweaty when she agreed to shake his, and her voice held a high-pitched nasal quality that made Drisklay want to offer her an entire box of Kleenex.

Her clothing was drab, and she picked at the fuzz on her checkered knee-length skirt when she sat down.

"Misty, thank you for being here today."

Her expression didn't change. Her look was one of both fear and painfully debilitating shyness.

He forced himself to smile. "How are you doing?"

She sniffed and didn't answer.

Drisklay nudged the Kleenex box closer to her. "You were Rebekah Harrison's best friend." He hoped the statement would open her locked jaw, but this must not have been his lucky day. "I'm very sorry for your loss," he added automatically.

She sniffed again. Drisklay forced himself not to cringe.

"The reason I brought you in here today, Misty," he began, "is that I'm trying to get a picture for the kind of young woman Rebekah was. The kind of friends she had, the things she liked to do in her free time, what her family's like." He said this last part with no special emphasis but studied her carefully enough he could discern the slight movement of her head when he mentioned the word *family*.

"Can you tell me anything about her parents?" he asked, hoping he wasn't frightening the breath completely out of her lungs.

She took a deep breath, and Drisklay was pleasantly surprised that her voice carried the three feet that sat between her mouth and his ears.

"Her parents are really good people. I even lived with them once when my own..." She stared at her skirt and fidgeted with her hands in her lap. "I mean, they helped me out. They'd help anyone out. That's the kind of people they are."

Drisklay didn't comment. Once he realized she had a voice, he didn't want to risk scaring her back into silence.

"She was real close to her mom. Mrs. Harrison's a really good woman. She loves having people over. She'd drive us around when we'd be doing a sleepover when we were littler. She's been my best friend since grade school."

It took Drisklay half a moment to realize they were talking about the dead victim now, not the mother.

"When did you meet?" he asked.

She took in a choppy breath and stared at a point level with Drisklay's kneecap. "Well, we were in the same class in second grade but didn't know each other that well. But the next year our church went through a really bad split, and so my family started going to her dad's church, and that was the same year..."

"I thought you were both homeschooled," Drisklay interrupted.

She gave him a sideways glance. "We were."

She stated this so factually that Drisklay had to do a mental rewind to figure out if he'd heard what he thought he had. "You said you were in second grade together."

Misty's look of confusion morphed into a chuckle that looked awkward on her long, angular face. "I'm talking about our homeschool co-op. We'd meet once a month at Rebekah's dad's church. We've been doing it for years. In fact, it was Mrs. Harrison, that's Rebekah's mom, who started it up, and our family became members that very first year..."

Drisklay allowed his mind to wander while Misty droned on about field trips to the zoo, cooking lessons, and annual Christmas pageants, but his thoughts weren't entirely without purpose. In his years as a detective, he'd gained something of a sixth sense, an almost immediate ability to gauge the usefulness of a witness only a minute or two into an interview. Misty had something important to offer him, but her favorite memories from the fifth-grade homeschool science fair weren't going to solve his case.

"That's quite fascinating," he eventually interrupted. "I wonder could you tell me some about her father?"

"Pastor Harrison?"

"Yes." Drisklay smiled sardonically. "Tell me about Pastor Harrison." If his wife knew how much he relished the thought of gaining any sort of dirt on a Christian preacher, she would resent him for being so cynical. But Caroline was on the other side of the world, running errands of mercy, so he didn't have anything to worry about.

"Pastor Harrison's a real good man."

Drisklay immediately noted the way Misty's quiet voice became even more subdued. Any animation she'd dredged up talking about show-and-tell and homeschool picnics had vanished.

He waited for her to continue then finally prompted, "Did he and Rebekah have a good relationship?"

"Oh, yeah," she gushed, answering far too quickly, her enthusiasm entirely out of place. "They're great." She cleared her throat and stared at her lap. "Real great."

Bingo. Drisklay knew there was more to this family. Now he just had to keep digging to figure out what.

He stared at Misty, ready to hear whatever else she wanted to divulge.

Instead, she let out a girly giggle. "I don't know what else you want me to say."

"Don't worry." Now it was hard for Drisklay to suppress his grin. "Don't worry," he repeated. "You're being more than helpful. And with your help, we just might be able to nail down your friend's murderer. You'd like that a lot, wouldn't you? Alexi!" He reached out his arm and pounded on the door of the room.

"Alexi!" he was bellowing again when the door swung open.

"Yeah, boss. You looking for me?"

"Get this friend of mine a cup of coffee, would you?" He gave his partner an exaggerated smile.

Alexi's eyes darted from Drisklay to the girl and back again before he raised his eyebrows at Drisklay. "Cream and sugar?"

Drisklay was in too good of a mood to be upset. "Ask her yourself."

Alexi began blushing and fumbling over his words until Misty breathed softly, "Just sugar, please." Her words sent the young man bursting out the door in search of drinks, and Drisklay turned back to his interview.

Now it was time to get some answers.

Five

Caroline gasped, whipping her arm across the bed to wake up her husband. She came to two simultaneous realizations. Even if she were back in Massachusetts, Calvin wouldn't be in bed with her, and the sound that startled her awake was thunder and not gunfire.

She blinked at the clock on her hotel nightstand. 7:05. It took far more mental energy than she was prepared to exert to realize it was still the evening and not even morning yet. She'd only managed to eke out a short nap. What was worse, given her luck, her body would still think she was meant to function on East Coast time. Her stomach rumbled, hungry for breakfast, as if to confirm her suspicions.

Great.

Well, at least she'd managed a slight rest. Maybe if she lay perfectly still and didn't think about the rain or the thunder or the time change, she'd fall back to sleep and stay blissfully unaware until morning.

Fat chance.

Two minutes later, she was throwing on fresh clothes after taking the world's shortest shower. The hotel she'd booked was far from a five-star, but Caroline hadn't realized that meant there wouldn't even be hot water. She propped up the pillows by the head of the bed to make herself a backrest of sorts and then tried to decide what to do. She didn't feel like taking the time to dig around for the TV remote. Seeing as how she could never remember how to use the remote that she and Calvin bought three years ago, she seriously doubted whether she'd be able to figure out a new system here.

She still hadn't finished her book from the plane, but the last thing she felt like doing was sitting around beating herself up for not being a better wife, the kind of wife whose husband would automatically beg for the chance to ask Jesus to forgive his sins. It just wasn't realistic to put that kind of pressure on women. Didn't the authors of drivel like that know just how much guilt people like Caroline already carried around?

Sandy had loaned her a couple novels, two historical romances that looked good and probably offered nothing but sweet and somewhat predictable storylines, but Caroline wasn't in the mood for happily ever afters either. As if life were ever as simple as those novels made out.

Trust God. Pray hard. Marry the love of your life and never have another problem again for as long as you both shall live.

It was ridiculous. Caroline felt sorry for young Christian girls who read fiction like that and lived their lives fully expecting their husbands to act like perfect, godly, chivalrous fictional heroes. Life just wasn't like that. *Men* just weren't like that. Even Pastor Carl, the man Caroline respected more than any other, would press his wife's last buttons until Sandy would tell him to head to the den and leave her in peace. Caroline remembered the first time she heard the two of them bicker. It was about something trivial, and they scarcely even raised their voices, but she'd been shocked to discover that yes, even Christian couples have their fair share of marital conflict.

Caroline's brain definitely thought it must be morning, and since she didn't want to spend all night staring at a blank TV screen, she pulled out her Bible. At first, she hadn't planned on bringing it with her to Seoul, worried as she was about luggage fees and accustomed as she was to finding Bibles in the nightstand drawers of any hotel room she ever entered.

But South Korea wasn't America, and Caroline was glad for the women's devotional Bible Sandy had given her the day Caroline was baptized. Now in her hotel room across the planet from her friend, she thumbed through the pages of Scripture, pausing at some of the highlighted passages. Maybe it was the teacher in her. Maybe it was her love for order, but she'd even come up with a color system.

Purple highlights were for verses she hoped to one day memorize. The yellow ones reminded her of that time when she was a brand-new believer, full of fervor and zeal, certain that every single promise she read in Scripture would come true for her in a day, a week, a month at most.

Caroline reserved the pink highlights for times when she felt especially low, verses she knew she could turn to for encouragement when the Christian life got too hard for her to walk alone.

The green highlights were verses that would remind her to pray for her husband, promises she meant to claim specifically for him.

Sadly, she'd hardly used her green highlighter lately. Sometimes it looked like the pink verses were about to overtake everything else, and it was definitely the pink verses she'd need during such an uncertain time as this.

Her favorite passage lately was Romans 8. She loved all of it, especially the part that reminded Christians how absolutely nothing—not death nor life, not height nor depth—could separate them from the love of God. She also nearly always found encouragement from Psalms and Isaiah. The picture from Isaiah 40 of devout believers soaring on wings like eagles always created such vivid imagery in her mind.

Tonight, a passage in Isaiah 43 drew Caroline's eyes: When you pass through the waters, I will be with you; and when you pass through the rivers, they will not sweep over you. When you walk through the fire, you will not be burned; the flames will not set you ablaze.

She didn't recognize the verse from any of Pastor Carl's sermons or the Christian podcasts she'd listened to. She couldn't remember ever pulling out her highlighter to mark this particular passage, but the words spoke to her nonetheless, maybe even more so because she was reading them with fresh eyes.

When you pass through the waters. Well, she had certainly done that. Not just little puddles either, but floodwaters that finally engulfed her marriage, leaving behind nothing but debris.

When you pass through the rivers, they will not sweep over you. How many times could Caroline have used a verse like this? How many times had she felt swept away by Calvin's torrential tirade against her faith until she felt like she was drowning, not even able to tell which way would carry her to the surface and which would drag her down to even darker depths?

When you walk through the fire, you will not be burned; the flames will not set you ablaze. Even though she couldn't remember reading this passage before, she did remember the story of Shadrach, Meshach, and Abednego, Israelite men thrown into a fiery furnace as their punishment for refusing to bow down to a false god. And the Lord had protected them. Not even their hair was singed.

Caroline needed that. Her entire life since becoming a Christian felt like she'd been thrown into one blazing furnace with no hope of reprieve. Maybe that was why she'd clung so stubbornly to this idea of serving God short-term here in Seoul, even if it cost her marriage.

Caroline liked the picture of herself as a martyr, the zealous believer willing to sacrifice anything—yes, even her husband—for the sake of the gospel. Certain believers would look at her actions this summer and see just that. There was no doubt Caroline felt God calling her to Seoul. In fact, even before the director of Freedom Korea asked her to consider this placement, Caroline had dreamed one night about Mrs. Cho and her orphanage. It had been over a year since Caroline interviewed the old woman, and they hadn't corresponded in months. But still, it was clearly Mrs. Cho in Caroline's dream, handing her a baby and asking her if she could change his diaper.

The next day, Caroline had joked to Sandy, "I think God's telling me I should go to Seoul." Two weeks later, she was contacted by the director of Freedom Korea. The very next day she purchased her plane ticket and began the paperwork to update her passport.

Then came the fun responsibility of telling her husband about her plans.

And he acted just about as irrationally as she'd expected.

"Well, maybe you could have asked for his opinion first," Sandy told her thoughtfully one day when Caroline dialed her up to complain.

But Sandy didn't understand. God had *called* Caroline to make this trip. There was no way Calvin would have agreed to her going if she'd spoken to him about it first. This wasn't a case of asking permission and letting the cards fall where they might. This was a desperate attempt for Caroline to finally take charge of her own spiritual life for a change instead of hiding in fear, her heart pounding every Sunday morning when she had to sneak back into her own home after church.

"I just think it would have been respectful to talk to your husband about it before finalizing your plans," Sandy had said in response to Caroline's protests.

Well, that was easy for Sandy to say. She was married to a man who fit nearly every definition of the word saint. All their (usually) good-natured bickering aside, Carl and Sandy loved each other deeply. Not only that, but they respected each other. If God told Sandy to do something, all she had to do was say, "Okay, God," then go ahead and tell her husband about that conversation. There was nothing else to it.

What really irritated Caroline about Calvin's reaction was the hypocrisy. If she had said she was going to spend the summer away doing something to further her career, he would have been totally supportive. Or at least he wouldn't have made her feel horrible for even having the desire.

"Why would you spend thousands of dollars to travel to another country to help orphans? Do you know how many kids there are in a five-mile radius of our home who don't have adequate food or clothing or shelter?"

He'd flung that argument at her a dozen times, along with his typical tirades about how all Christians want to do is steal your money. Words like *cult* and *brainwashed* were shot out until she was almost immune to them.

Almost, but not entirely.

Why does this have to be so hard, God? she prayed, but like she expected, God gave her no response.

Now she stared at the words of comfort and encouragement on the page of her Bible. Maybe heaven wasn't so silent after all.

Drisklay was finishing up his second pot of coffee by the time he started to wrap up his interview with Misty. He felt more than a little pleased with himself at getting such a quiet young woman to tell him everything she could possibly think of to shed light on the Harrison family.

Conservative parents. No surprise there. Rebekah and her older brother weren't allowed to go to any dances or overnights. Because Misty and Rebekah were so close and the families shared such similar values, the two girls were allowed occasional sleepovers, but only until Misty's brother, four years younger than she was, shot up in the sixth grade and both families decided that the days of slumber parties were at an end.

"Did Rebekah have any suitors?" Drisklay finally asked. He felt like he'd been transported back into one of his wife's cherished old-fashioned TV adaptations using outdated language like that, but Misty had already spent the better part of half an hour explaining the Harrisons' church's view on courtship. Because apparently, members of their congregation viewed dating in a contemporary context as obscene.

Heaven forbid two young people would want to meet up and get to know each other over drinks. Even if those drinks were nothing stronger than the sweetened decaf coffee Misty was holding in her hand.

"There was this guy she was excited to meet," Misty began, speaking slowly. Tentatively. Eying Drisklay cautiously as if she didn't exactly trust him even after divulging so much about her church and her dead friend's family members. She took in a deep breath and went on. "They met on a dating website. That new one for Christians."

"I've heard of it," Drisklay mumbled. He tried not to let his impatience show. This was what happened in interviews like this. You sat for an hour and a half, listening while people blabbered on, giving you not only their own life stories but their grandmother's and step-aunt's babysitter's as well. But in the end, you got the answer you were looking for.

If you were lucky.

Today, Drisklay felt remarkably lucky. "Did she ever meet this man as far as you're aware?"

Misty shook her head. "No. Well, at least I don't think so. She was supposed to meet him the night she..." She lowered her gaze. "That's when she disappeared."

Drisklay leaned forward, wishing for the ability to telepathically communicate to her how important her honesty was going to be on this next question. "Are you sure she didn't meet him another time? Are you sure this was going to be their very first meeting?"

Misty sniffed. "Yeah. I'm her best friend. She would have told me if they'd met before. She told me everything." She set down her coffee cup. "He was all she could talk about. She was so excited to meet him, too." Her voice broke, and Drisklay waited for her to compose herself.

"She was nervous." Misty began sobbing. "I was on the phone with her while she was getting ready for her date, and she was about to change her mind. She said she didn't want to go through with it. That maybe she should cancel. She said her mom told her she had her blessing, but she was afraid of making her dad angry."

Another noisy sniff. Drisklay glowered at the Kleenex box, which Misty hadn't touched.

"I'm the one who convinced her to go on with it," the young woman blubbered. "I said if it was meant to be then everything would work out perfectly. And now she's dead."

"Now she's dead," Drisklay muttered to himself. He'd give the girl another minute to pull herself together, then it was time to wrap this interview up.

A minute later, fresh Kleenex in hand, an eager Alexi appeared to escort Misty down the hallway. Drisklay gave her a polite nod. "Thank you, Misty. You've been very helpful. That's all I'll be needing from you today."

It was almost midnight in Seoul by the time Caroline closed her Bible. She couldn't remember the last time God had spoken to her with such clarity. Maybe that was her problem. Maybe all the stress of living with Calvin was harming her relationship with Christ. Maybe this separation from him was really what her soul needed.

It wouldn't be easy. Especially since even as a young believer Caroline had seen the way certain Christians would shun divorcées. With Calvin out of her life, Caroline would be permanently branded.

The woman whose husband left her.

The woman who gave up on her marriage.

The woman who disappointed God.

It wasn't as if she hadn't tried. God knew better than anyone how much time and energy and prayers she'd put into saving her marriage. Maybe that was one of the reasons God told her to come here to Seoul. Maybe it wasn't just because Mrs. Cho needed so much help in her orphanage. Maybe God knew that Caroline needed this time away from the drama.

Time away from Calvin.

The thought was encouraging. Yet, nagging in the back of her mind remained doubts. Probably there would always be doubts. Could she have done something more to make things work out? Could she have been a more faithful witness? Should she have asked to pray with him more consistently? Invited him to church more faithfully? Spoken to God about him more boldly? Or maybe the opposite. Maybe she should have kept her faith less visible so it wouldn't make him so upset. Push him away.

These were answers she might never know, and questions she didn't want to dwell on. She was here in Seoul to do God's work. Wasn't that why he'd given her that dream in the first place? Mrs. Cho needed help in her orphanage. A woman at that age, she couldn't be expected to look after all those children without outside help. If Calvin was hard-hearted enough that he'd destroy their marriage because Caroline decided to obey God and spent a few weeks on the mission field serving him, their marriage wasn't worth saving anyway.

Was it?

She stared at her Bible on the pillow beside her, wondering what happened to the peace she'd felt just moments earlier. If her husband wanted out of their relationship, there obviously wasn't anything she could do to change his mind.

So why did she still feel so guilty? So unresolved?

She picked up her Bible one last time. "Okay, God," she prayed. "I really need a sign from you. Am I giving up on my marriage too easily? Or is this separation your way of protecting me from putting myself through more and more pain?"

She'd already given Calvin the best years of her life. With any other man, she might have been a mother. Maybe even a grandma by now if they'd adopted young enough. But her husband wouldn't hear of it, and Caroline didn't want to pick a fight. Not another one.

She'd stuck with him through all his career advancements and discouragements, all the unsolved cases that left him bitter, grumpy, and cynical. She'd thrown away her dreams of motherhood, of family. And for what? For a man who despised her the moment she became a Christian.

It wasn't as if she'd committed a crime. She hadn't gone out behind his back and gotten involved in some torrid affair, even though his emotional distance could have made that look like a tempting offer. She wasn't stealing money out of his account or gambling away their savings or slipping oleander powder into his food like that black widow killer he'd put behind bars a few years ago.

"God, none of this makes sense. None of this feels fair." She realized how silly the words sounded as soon as she prayed them. Since when did God promise to make her life easy and fair? But still, after all she'd been through, was it that wrong for her to grumble every now and then? Who wouldn't in her situation?

"All right, Lord. I know I'm not supposed to complain. And I really appreciate all the encouragement you gave me from your Word. But I need more, Lord. I need something I can really hold onto. I need something to carry me through whatever happens between Calvin and me, whether it's good or bad. Please, just show me what you want me to hear."

She opened up her Bible to a random page. It probably wasn't the most effective way to listen to God, but right now she didn't have the energy or will to dig through her concordance searching for the right verse on her own. If the Lord had something he wanted to say to her, he could show her this way.

She was somewhere in Ezekiel, one of the Old Testament books she'd never read before. Come to think of it, she couldn't remember hearing it mentioned on any of her podcasts or any of Pastor Carl's sermons either. She shrugged, about to reopen the Bible to something more familiar when a single word on the page caught her eye.

Heart.

She read the entire verse.

I will give you a new heart and put a new spirit in you; I will remove from you your heart of stone and give you a heart of flesh.

A wave of warmth, love, and regret crashed over her at once. It was impossible to differentiate a single emotion from the others. She was overcome with a sense of God's presence in a way she hadn't experienced since her first Sunday at church with Sandy.

"Daughter," a heavenly voice seemed to whisper, "have you forgotten that I'm right here with you?"

Yes, she had forgotten. She'd turned to Scripture for encouragement, but what she'd really been longing for wasn't just God's Word but Jesus himself, the outpouring of his Holy Spirit, filling her soul until she was certain her mortal body couldn't contain so much of the divine.

He was here. She realized now he always had been. Why had she ever doubted?

Tears streamed down her cheeks. "I'm sorry, Lord," she whispered.

Through blurry eyes, she read the verse again. How could she have been a Christian for three full years and never come across this passage in all her studying?

I will give you a new heart and put a new spirit in you; I will remove from you your heart of stone and give you a heart of flesh.

A heart of flesh. That one phrase kept pulsing through her soul like a fire.

I will remove from you your heart of stone and give you a heart of flesh.

Then Caroline understood. She'd spent years praying against her husband's hardness of heart, years praying for God to soften his spirit so he could sense the love Jesus had for him.

She'd longed for God to remove Calvin's bitterness, his cynicism, his antagonism to anything relating to Caroline's faith.

But that wasn't what this verse was talking about. Not in this case. Not right now.

The heart of stone wasn't her husband's. In fact, Calvin had nothing to do with this passage, at least not the way God opened her eyes to see it.

The person who needed a new heart, the person who'd become so hardened and calloused and so desperately in need of God's divine touch, wasn't her husband after all.

The verse wasn't a promise about Calvin's salvation or a declaration that God was planning to restore their relationship.

The verse was talking about Caroline and nobody else.

The hardened heart was her own. She'd carried it like a chain around her neck for years. Bitterness, frustration, anger that her husband hadn't accepted the gospel with the same enthusiasm she had.

The heart of stone belonged to her and no one else. But now, as tears of repentance rushed down her cheeks, the Lord replaced it with a heart of flesh.

Drisklay tossed his Styrofoam cup into the trash. Another late night. Not that he had any reason to rush home.

Alexi had left early. Something about an appointment for his mom. Family business, not Drisklay's. The smell of cheap street tacos wafted toward his desk, and he opened his box of Danishes.

Empty.

Oh, well. He had a few boxes of Cracker Jacks in his bottom drawer. He'd pull them out later. For now, he could get by on the coffee. Alexi always warned him that so much caffeine couldn't be healthy, but it had to beat the five extra shots of corn syrup and artificial flavoring in those frou-frou drinks Alexi carried around.

Disgusting.

Drisklay popped a cough drop into his mouth and held it between his teeth while he sipped at his lukewarm coffee. He'd spent several hours in interviews today. Tonight, he'd go over the files again and tomorrow probably have to hit the streets if he didn't find any more leads by then.

He chomped down on his cough drop then cleared his throat. He wanted to research that pastor's family again. The Harrisons. What was it about them that piqued his interest? Was his gut leading him in the right direction, or was he just out of any other good ideas? Intuition had solved its fair number of cases, and Drisklay was hopeful that this one would prove no exception.

If his intuition was correct, the answer lay somewhere with the pastor.

He typed Rebekah Harrison's name into the computer, finding nothing. Just like the fifteen or twenty other times he'd pulled up the search. No criminal record, not even a speeding ticket. She had an older brother, a senior at a Christian college down in Florida. Jeremiah Harrison. Tiny run-in with the Boston police several years earlier for underage drinking. Nothing else after that. But still, it was enough to prove that this family wasn't as squeaky clean as they wanted everyone to believe.

"Are you just saying that because they're Christians?" Great. Caroline was thousands of miles away on some sort of errand of mercy, saving orphanages on the Korean Peninsula, but it was still her nagging voice ringing between his ears.

When would enough be enough?

Still, he was certain that was what Caroline would say if she were here. Which she never would be. His work was his work, just like her classroom full of snot-nosed kids was hers. He never told her how to teach a class of kindergartners, and she didn't tell him how to solve cases.

Still, the fact that he could hear her voice so clearly irked him. She'd been a drag ever since she got caught up with those church folks. Religious fools going from door to door peddling Bibles and salvation to poor souls terrified of eternal damnation. He'd tried to warn her. The minute she said she was going to an Easter service with one of her student's families, he could clearly see the start of their marriage's doom. Things had been fine between them for years. No, in fact, things had been great. They hardly ever argued, they'd managed to pay off their mortgage a few years early and weren't so worried anymore about pinching pennies. Now that he thought about it, that was probably why that pastor and his family targeted her to begin with. Dual-income family, no kids, no mortgage. Nothing like a fat bank account for greedy Christians to suck dry.

He scowled as he typed the father's name on his keyboard. The pastor didn't have a criminal record, but what did that prove? All clergymen were crooks. It was just that most of them were slick enough to get away with it.

The wife's background was the only one that held even a hint of interest. Apparently, Mrs. Harrison had been married and divorced in her early twenties after filing several domestic violence charges and eventually a restraining order against her ex. Could he possibly be involved? A vengeful lover returning from the shadows of a murky history?

More clicks. More names typed into the police database.

Sadly, no. The ex had died four years ago. The obituary said colon cancer.

Poor fool.

But that couldn't be everything. There had to be more, and Drisklay would find it. He pulled up Google and looked up the name of Pastor Harrison's church. Maybe he'd find some clues there.

The answer was getting closer. Drisklay stared at his empty Styrofoam cup lying in the trash.

Time for more coffee.

Seven

Caroline woke up, her cheeks wet with tears. As the vestiges of her dream faded away, she tried desperately to clutch at the disappearing remnants.

Come back, she wanted to shout. She wanted to scream.

Come back!

But it was gone, not just the dream itself, but her conscious memory of it. All that remained was a quickly disappearing essence, fragments of an echo, half an aura of memory.

Come back. She was crying again, but these tears were different. What had she been dreaming about? Everything would make sense if she could only force herself to remember, but the more conscious energy she channeled into summoning her dream, the more thoroughly it eluded her grasp, slipping through the crevices of her mind, fading away into nothing.

Then it was gone.

She wiped her cheeks dry, uncertain now why she'd been crying to begin with. Then she looked at her hotel clock.

Oh, no.

She jumped out of bed. How could she have slept in so late? Her pajamas clung to her chest and back, soaked through with sweat, but whether that was from Seoul's humidity or the forgotten stress of her dream, she couldn't have guessed. Nor did she have the time to spare wondering.

She threw on the first clothes she could yank out of her bag, stuffed her toiletries and dirty laundry into her suitcase, and rushed down the hallway. *God*, she prayed, *please don't let me be late.*

What she most wanted out of her day was to make a good impression on Mrs. Cho. She'd spoken by phone several times with the old woman, who struck her as warm, compassionate, and gentle-hearted, the kind of gracious soul that made Caroline wish all other believers could be so refined and mature.

She had no reason to expect that Mrs. Cho would be angry or irritated if Caroline ended up being late, but as she wheeled her suitcase into the hotel elevator, panting slightly from her recent aerobics, she found herself praying even harder that God would allow her to reach the orphanage on time.

Maybe it was because Mrs. Cho was the first Christian that Caroline was close to who didn't belong to Pastor Carl and Sandy's church. Who didn't know about her failing marriage, her spiritual mismatch? This summer in Seoul would be the first time that Caroline would be recognized first and foremost as a dedicated believer. The distinction between Christians who simply showed up to church on Sunday and Christians who traveled overseas on short-term mission trips might seem subtle to some, but to Caroline, the distance between the two may as well have been as far as Boston was from Seoul.

The elevator doors opened to the lobby, and Caroline rushed out, nearly plowing into a Korean businessman adjusting his tie with one hand and swiping the screen of his smartphone with the other. She muttered a hasty apology and hurried outside. She was momentarily disoriented before she could force her still sleepy brain to remember which way she was supposed to go. She seized onto her bearings as soon as they flashed into her head and dashed toward the subway station. At least, she was pretty certain it was the right way to the subway station.

Please don't let me be late, she prayed again, envying Jesus and his companions. Were they ever in a hurry? In a society and culture that wasn't bound to digital clocks whose seconds were all in perfect sync, would Peter, James, or John have worried about arriving at their destination ten or fifteen minutes after their expected time?

She made some mental estimates. If she got lucky and didn't have to wait for her train, she might not be late at all. Caroline wondered if Korean culture was similar to America if being even two or three minutes late could cause a major inconvenience. Maybe Seoul was more laid-back than that. She certainly hoped so.

When she pulled her suitcase into the subway station, she was struck by two simultaneous discoveries. The South Korean subway stations were just as clean as all the tourist blogs made them out to be, and there wasn't a single escalator in sight. There had to be a handicap ramp or some other way to get down without having to lug her nearly-fifty-pound bag behind her, but she didn't have time to run to the other entrances to check.

Down the stairs it was.

Clunk, clunk, clunk.

If she hadn't been sweating before, she certainly was now, but strangely she welcomed the exertion. First of all, she couldn't complain anymore about feeling groggy. The adrenaline rush required to keep her and her suitcase from tumbling down a cement staircase was enough to match a pot of Calvin's strong black coffee. She also felt fiercely independent. Here she was, a middle-aged woman, traveling alone on the other side of the world. She'd managed to not only locate the subway station, but now she was hefting an extra 48.7 pounds behind her, and she was doing that while racing to catch her train.

Peter, James, and John could walk twenty miles a day through desert roads wearing sandals centuries before the invention of arch supports, but Caroline could get her suitcase to her train and still make it to Mrs. Cho's orphanage on time.

She hoped.

The train pulled up. Perfect timing.

Maybe it wasn't the same thing as running to keep up with a chariot like Phillip did in the book of Acts. Maybe it wasn't the same thing as stepping out of a boat in the middle of a storm and walking on top of the waves. But Caroline felt both thankful and triumphant when she wheeled her suitcase onto the train car, found her seat, and let out her breath.

She had made it. Now she just had to sit back, try to stop panting so hard, and let the subway whisk her off to where she needed to be.

Drisklay adjusted his headphones and reached for more coffee. Empty. Figured.

"Alexi," he shouted, holding out the pot.

Alexi hurried over. "How's it going, boss?" He glanced at the computer screen where Drisklay had been researching Harrison's church.

Drisklay paused the video he'd been watching and glowered. "I'll be doing a lot better once you bring me that coffee."

"You want any cre—" Alexi stopped mid-sentence, and Drisklay clicked play.

"The good news, brothers and sisters, is that Jesus Christ came into the world to save sinners like you and me." The father of the dead girl had started his sermon in a soft, even tone, but about halfway in his tempo and pitch both started to rise exponentially. Now, he was closing up the last few minutes of preaching, and even with the low-quality video recording, Drisklay could picture beads of sweat trickling down his face from all that exertion.

"Jesus Christ is the same yesterday, today, and tomorrow, and his word promises us that when we put our trust in him, he'll cleanse us from our sins. That's the gospel message, brothers and sisters, the fact that God demonstrated his own love for us by sending his Son to die on the cross for us. Do you know that love today? Have you experienced that great salvation? If not, I want to encourage you to come up and let me or one of the elders pray with you."

So, there it was. This wouldn't be one of those pleading for money sermons. Harrison was smarter than that. You reel them in first, make them terrified that their so-called sins are bad enough to warrant an eternity in hell, and then you make them pay. Drisklay still remembered with pride the internet preacher he'd help put behind bars for extortion. Apparently, the funds that the gullible herds sent him so he could build orphanages in Africa were instead being funneled into a jet and a private strip of beach near Cape Cod.

He shook his head. Why were the masses so ignorant, and why couldn't they learn from centuries of history? At the moment, Drisklay couldn't decide which made him angrier—listening to this fire and brimstone sermon meant to scare the gullible public into opening up their wallets and handing over their credit cards, or trying to figure out how and why he'd lost his own wife to men like Harrison in the first place.

It wasn't as if he and Caroline were struggling for years in their marriage and her conversion was the proverbial last straw. If anything, things had gotten better between them. About five years ago, she'd broken down in tears, begging him to spend more time with her, so he used some vacation days and took her for a long weekend at Martha's Vineyard. Things could have kept on just fine between them if Caroline hadn't allowed herself to get brainwashed by Christian theology.

He'd thought his wife was smarter than that. It was difficult overestimating his disappointment when he realized just how wrong he'd been.

Pastor Harrison's voice was so loud now that Drisklay had to lower the volume on his computer. "The Bible promises that if you repent today, Jesus Christ will be faithful and just and will forgive you your sins and purify you from all unrighteousness. All you have to do is ask, and the stains of your sins will be washed away, making you as white as snow. Jesus Christ died to pay the penalty for your sins, so you don't have to experience eternal separation from God, and all you need to do to receive this great and glorious gift is receive it by faith. Say, *Jesus, I know I'm a sinner. I believe that you died and rose from the dead to save me from...*"

Drisklay slammed off the recording.

"Is this hot enough for you?" Alexi's voice wavered slightly as he carried a pot of black coffee and a heating pad to Drisklay's desk. "I hope it's strong enough."

Drisklay grunted in response, then told Alexi, "Go find me the file on that church. The one the dead girl's dad is the pastor at. There's something I want to see."

Alexi leaned forward. "Is he a suspect? Is that why you're watching his sermon online?"

Drisklay glowered, and Alexi scrambled away.

Drisklay swiveled in his chair and tapped his fingers on his desk. "Harrison," he muttered to himself. Even the name sounded somehow sinister. "What exactly are you hiding?"

What Drisklay needed was an inside scoop. What he needed was a pastor he knew and trusted, a pastor familiar with other churches in the Boston area, someone he could count on to give him an insider's perspective.

"Here's that file you asked for." Alexi seemed uncertain whether he should hand Drisklay the envelope or set it on his desk. Drisklay spared him the torture of uncertainty and yanked it out of his hand.

Alexi's eyes darted nervously from the pot of coffee to Drisklay's empty Styrofoam cup. "Is there anything else you need?"

Drisklay was about to yell that what he needed was a quiet space to think, but then an idea came to him. A better idea than yelling at his partner.

"Yeah. You know that big megachurch in Cambridge, St. Margaret's?"

"Sounds familiar," Alexi offered without sounding at all certain of himself.

"Find me the pastor's phone number. Not the church office. His cell's around here somewhere. Get that for me and come back here. And get another pot started. Stronger this time."

Eight

"I miss you too, baby."

Caroline did her best to ignore the tall American standing next to her in the subway car, feeling vicariously embarrassed on his behalf. Didn't he realize how loudly he was speaking? "I sure wish you were here, too, honey. Just remember, we're doing God's work, and he's promised to take care of us both. We have to trust in his perfect plans." Caroline didn't want to eavesdrop, but he left her no choice.

"I'll be praying for you, too, sweetie. Give my love to the girls, okay? I'll see you soon. Just a couple more weeks, and then we'll be together again. It'll be just like Jacob and Rachel in the Bible. He had to wait a full seven years, but God says it only felt like a few days."

Caroline squirmed in her seat, wishing there were a way to put more distance between herself and this stranger, wondering if many people thought the two of them were traveling together. How long until the subway reached her stop?

The man sent another crooning sweet nothing into his cell phone, then hung up and looked at her with a somewhat sheepish grin. "My fiancé," he explained.

She smiled back automatically, but her heart mirrored nothing of the joy that radiated from his face. "Congratulations." She clutched her handbag, praying that she'd recognize the name of the right stop when it came through on the automated announcements. She'd been distracted listening to Mr. Loverboy and had lost track of how many stops they'd already passed.

"Where you headed?" the man asked. He was balding slightly, with a teddy-bear build.

"A meeting." Caroline didn't want to be rude, but she would have preferred to spend her time trying to connect her phone to the public Wi-Fi service to contact her hostess. Even with the train arriving right on time, she was pretty sure she'd end up late to Mrs. Cho's.

He nodded and continued to grin. "I'm off to a job interview. My fiancée is a missionary here. I'm trying to find a place to work after the wedding."

His eyes glistened when the spoke about his future, making him younger than his balding head intimated.

Caroline gave a brief nod, trying to keep her body from lurching forward as the train slowed to a stop. The stranger cleared his throat and smiled broadly. "This is where I get off. Have a nice day."

Caroline watched him depart, wondering what it would be like to be an engaged couple in a city this far from home. What it would be like to be engaged to a Christian. A believer. Someone with a heart for God. Someone who wasn't ashamed to talk about prayer or God or faith in a crowded Seoul subway.

A heavy sigh. These thoughts wouldn't get her anywhere. Sandy's voice, like it so often did, echoed through her memory to encourage and comfort her. *You sure can't change Calvin's heart,* her pastor's wife had told her in that slight southern drawl that sounded so out of place in the Boston suburbs. *Only God can do that. It's not your job to save your husband. It's only your job to pray for him.*

Pray for him. Did Sandy realize how much Caroline had already prayed these past three years since she'd become a Christian? Praying. Weeping. Fasting. Long weekend retreats when Calvin was out working a case, flat on her face before God, begging him to save her husband.

Sometimes she wondered if Pastor Carl was wrong when he preached that nobody was outside of God's reach. No heart was too hard for him to heal.

If God wanted Calvin saved, wouldn't he have done it by now? If her prayers made any bit of difference at all, wouldn't her husband have accepted Christ instead of becoming even more hardened? Even more cynical? It was that biting sarcasm of his that hurt Caroline the most. How many times had he given hardened criminals that same glare of hatred and contempt, intimidating them until he got the confession he was after? But Caroline wasn't a criminal, not unless being a Christian living with an unbelieving spouse had at some point become illegal.

Except now she wasn't even living with him. In the end, her prayers had done nothing. They hadn't saved her husband. They hadn't even saved her marriage.

Calvin was gone. Even though Caroline didn't want to admit it, even in spite of the tears and the anger and the shame and the confusion, one emotion bubbled up to the surface to rear its ugly, accusing head.

She was tired of fighting for her marriage. Tired of begging God for miracles. In her most honest moments, Caroline had to admit she was relieved he had left.

Drisklay held the phone against his ear and swiveled in his office chair. "Hello, is this Carl Lindgren?"

"Certainly is," answered back the booming, resonant voice on the other end of the line.

"This is Detective Drisklay from the Boston Police Department. We've spoken before on a few occasions."

"Of course. How are you, Detective?"

Drisklay gripped his Styrofoam cup, despising these necessary pleasantries. He'd much rather deal with suspects in the interrogation room than with a man of the cloth. Or whatever you'd call the non-Catholic equivalent. "I'm working on a case and wondering if I could ask you a few questions."

A woman began jabbering in the background, her voice so loud she might have been shouting into Carl's ear.

"Quiet," the pastor whispered. "No, it's not one of the kids. It's

Detective Drisklay... Hey, wait. Give me that phone back..."

"Officer Drisklay!" Carl's wife's voice was high-pitched and enthusiastic, with a hint of a southern drawl. It was also one of the most unwelcome sounds Drisklay could have imagined at this precise moment. "It's Sandy here. So good to hear from you. How's Caroline? Is she enjoying her time in Seoul? Did she arrive safely? Is she settling in? Do you know if she remembered to take those jetlag pills I gave her? You know, they were a lifesaver for me when we flew over to pick up Woong from that orphanage. But come to think of it, I remember that I was more tired coming back. Of course, that might have been because Woong was so young when we got him. A real handful. You probably haven't seen him in a few years, have you? We're going to have to have you over, soon. I'm getting a meatloaf ready right now. Will you be off by five? I can't wait to see you."

Drisklay glowered at the phone. Alexi, who'd been walking toward him with some paper in his hand, glanced at his face and turned the other way.

"No, don't grab it from me," Sandy chided her husband. "That's rude. I'm just inviting him over for dinner."

"He's calling on police business, woman," answered Carl, the irritation in his voice evident but not nearly matching Drisklay's.

"Whatever business he has," Sandy insisted, "it'll be better discussed on a full stomach, don't you think? Besides, his wife is out of town on a mission trip. I'm not about to let him go hungry. You know how he gets. He probably hasn't eaten anything but Danishes all day, have you?" Sandy pursed her lips in the momentary silence. "So, it's settled then? We'll see you here at five o'clock sharp. No, don't bother trying to get out of it. What kind of friend would I be to Caroline if I let her husband starve to death while she's serving God overseas? It'll be no trouble at all, and it'll be our pleasure. You still remember how to get to our house, don't you? Well, you've got Carl's number. You can just call if you need directions. I've got to pull some buns out of the oven now, but we'll see you at five. Do you like apple pie? I was thinking of doing some baking this afternoon, but with Carl's diabetes, it's hard to justify, and Woong eats so much sugar nowadays. Did I tell you that boy's already had four cavities? Four cavities. Can you believe it? I declare, he's got to start taking better care of his teeth, or they're going to fall out of his mouth one day, just like in those dreams you have. Do you ever have dreams like that, Officer? You know the ones I mean, where your mouth feels so dry and all of a sudden, your teeth start to crumble out? I declare, it's one of the most uncomfortable feelings in the world, and I told Woong if he doesn't start brushing better, that's going to be what he goes through except in real life. And eating all that sugar doesn't help either, I'm sure, but I can't seem to stop baking, and Carl can't have desserts anymore, poor fellow, what with his blood sugar and diabetes, but I'm sure you know all about that. Anyway, if you talk to Caroline tell her hello and that we're going to take real good care of you, and remember to just give Carl a call if you get lost and need help getting to our house. You don't have any allergies, do you? All right. Talk soon. Bye-bye."

Drisklay sat staring at the phone in his hand several seconds after the call disconnected.

"Who was that?" Alexi asked, tentatively slipping some papers on top of the clutter on Drisklay's desk.

"Crazy woman," he muttered in response.

"Suspect?"

"I wish."

Alexi turned to go then stopped. "Hey, you working late tonight?"

Drisklay didn't look up from the report his partner had just delivered. "Likely."

"Thought so." Alexi cleared his throat. "Well, me and the guys are gonna order takeout before long. Want us to get you anything? I mean, you wouldn't have to, but since you'll be here anyway, I just thought maybe I'd ask, you know. See if you wanted anything." He paused, clearly waiting.

Drisklay finished off his Danish and then threw his napkin into the trash. Why was his partner still here?

Alexi cleared his throat. "I think it's pizza. Or maybe Chinese. I'll find out if you want. I can just go ask..."

"I got dinner plans," Drisklay answered gruffly.

Alexi's eyes widened. "You don't say."

"Yeah. And last I checked you were a detective, not a pizza delivery guy, right?"

Alexi nodded. "Right, boss. You got that. Absolutely true. I'm getting right back to work now. Right now, right as we speak."

Drisklay didn't respond. He reached for his next Danish then pulled another page from the stack of papers cluttering his desk.

He had work to do.

Nine

Caroline's heart was racing by the time she wheeled her suitcase up to the front door. There was nothing to distinguish Mrs. Cho's orphanage from the multiple homes and apartments surrounding it. A small and tidy garden on the side of the house spilled over with fresh foliage.

Caroline wondered what her students back home would think if they realized how nervous their teacher could get. She'd ended up getting off at the wrong station, hailing a cab, and paying the equivalent of over twenty-five US dollars to get here. She didn't know how God managed it, but even after all that she was still only fifteen minutes late. A miracle, however small and probably insignificant in the grand scheme of things. And yet a reminder that God was taking care of her, looking out for her.

So, why did she feel so anxious?

The woman who opened the door was older than Caroline had expected. Older and frailer, yet there was a radiance in her face that made her instantly appear inexplicably strong and vibrant. Mrs. Cho held a child on one hip, wiggling a small rattle in front of the baby's face to make him laugh.

"Come in, come in." Mrs. Cho's smile was generous, and the moment Caroline stepped through the threshold of her front door, peace quieted her soul. Her pulse no longer surged through her veins, and she felt strangely at home. The sensation reminded her somewhat of how she felt visiting

Pastor Carl and Sandy at their house, the same hospitable, welcoming feeling, but that's where the similarities ended.

The Lindgrens' home in the States was compact and spilling over with crafts, baking utensils, and homemade odds and ends. The walls in every room were covered with family photos or crayon drawings from grandkids. Mrs. Cho's home, by contrast, was immaculate. Even the baby seats and high chairs were lined up against walls and organized by model, color, and size. Aside from a small stuffed tiger on the arm of one couch, there were no toys to be seen on the premises.

No toys or children either, apart from the infant in Mrs. Cho's arms.

"Where are the kids?" Caroline asked.

Mrs. Cho let out a sweet sigh. She smiled and maintained eye contact with the baby she was holding while she answered. "The toddlers and infants are taking their naps upstairs. The older children are at school."

Caroline had assumed the Korean schools would be closed this time of year like back in the States. There was so much about Mrs. Cho's life running this orphanage she wanted to ask about, but she wasn't here simply on a cultural exchange.

"What can I do to help?" She peered around the corner, hoping to find something she could offer to clean, but the kitchen area was as spotless as the living area, the hardwood floor gleaming in the sunlight streaming in from the skylight overhead.

Mrs. Cho acted as naturally as if she and Caroline had known each other for decades. "Maybe you will hold this little one for me while I prepare his bottle. Da is the youngest one here, and I'm afraid I've been spoiling him. He won't fall asleep without his bottle, even though he's far too old to need it."

Caroline had so many questions. How many children did Mrs. Cho care for at the moment? Throughout their correspondence, the numbers had varied from as few as eight to as many as twenty-one. How did she maintain such a peaceful, serene home with only occasional help from members of her church or people like Caroline who traveled here short-term?

But Mrs. Cho glided into the kitchen in her slippers, and Caroline couldn't find the words to ask a single question. Instead, she held the little boy Mrs. Cho had set gingerly in her hands.

"You're a chubby one, aren't you?" Caroline crooned at Da. She'd been handling classrooms of thirty rambunctious kids or wiggling preteens for decades, but she didn't want to admit to Mrs. Cho that her experience with infants was gravely limited. She hoped her inexperience didn't show by the way she held Da.

What right did a woman her age have to be uncomfortable around babies?

"Are you ready for your food?" she asked him while Mrs. Cho opened up a cupboard in the kitchen to reveal rows of perfectly matched bottles, their lids alongside them in straight lines. Caroline watched the old woman at work, trying to figure out a way to initiate some sort of conversation.

"How old is Da?" she finally asked.

Mrs. Cho squinted at her scoop of formula while she leveled the powder with a silver knife small enough to belong to a child's tea set. "Eleven months," she answered.

A salty, sea smell filled the kitchen when Mrs. Cho filled the bottle with water.

"It's a fish-based formula," Mrs. Cho explained, simultaneously answering Caroline's unspoken question and confirming her fears that she hadn't done a very good job masking her curiosity at the odor.

"More vitamins," Mrs. Cho added with a prim nod of her head.

The bottle was shaken carefully, wiped down with a rag embroidered with small red flowers, and placed into an electronic heater, which Mrs. Cho then proceeded to wipe down with a different rag, this one yellow with frilly edges. A timer was set, and Mrs. Cho gestured to the living room. "Shall we wait more comfortably?"

Baby Da had discovered his finger and was sucking at it noisily. Caroline sat down on the couch, wondering what it would be like to be this woman, to be so calm and organized even with so many children to care for. A pang of envy shot through her heart as Caroline realized that all this—the children, the babies, the peaceful home, the aura of blessing and peace, the sense of family—was a life that was closed to her.

Mrs. Cho took baby Da into her own arms when he began to fuss and crooned at him in Korean.

"I told you he was spoiled." She smiled at Caroline. "He won't take his bottle cold but doesn't like to wait for it to warm up."

She let out a sigh then turned her eyes away from the baby and leveled them with Caroline's. "Now, tell me about yourself and why it is that you felt God called you here to work with these blessed children of mine."

"I'm so glad you could join us, Officer," Sandy crooned, pulling the front door open and stepping aside so Drisklay could pass.

"He's a detective," her husband corrected. "That's different from just an officer."

"Oh." Sandy looked at Drisklay with her mouth open in surprise. "Well, come on in. Woong, baby, put your gadgets away and come say hello to our guest."

Drisklay had never been good at guessing children's ages. The Lindgren's boy who came darting in could have been eight or thirteen. He was short, but the pimples spreading out from his nose in a kaleidoscope of acne hinted at a preteen.

"Woong," his mother called out, "What do you say to Officer Drisklay?"

"Did you come here to arrest somebody?" the child exclaimed, with his eyes widening. "Because I can tell you that my parents never did anything unlawful in their entire life, except for my dad because he used to do those things where people would find restaurants who didn't like to serve black people, and they would sit there until they got beat up and arrested. My dad even got sent to jail once for this parade he was in. Except it wasn't a parade really, I guess you'd call it more like a march, but other than that, he and my mom haven't done anything against the law ever in their entire life, and that's the perfect truth."

Carl chuckled and put his hand on his son's shoulder. Regardless of the child's age, Carl was old enough to be his grandfather. Apparently, the Lindgrens were the kind of folks who weren't content raising just their own kids, but when they got their own flesh and blood out of the home, they had to go out and find someone else's brood to raise.

Drisklay stared at the Korean boy and his black father. Thank God he and Caroline never wanted children of their own. What are kids other than a twenty- or thirty-year commitment? It would be like spending a couple hundred thousand dollars just to send someone out in the world to get murdered or mugged.

No, thank you.

At least that was one thing he and Caroline had agreed on from the start. No children. Too much hassle. In a way, Caroline's childhood car accident was a huge convenience for them both. No need to worry about birth control or any sort of unwanted surprise. The thought of himself as a father was at the same time terrifying and hilarious. What did he know about kids? When his eight-year-old niece came to spend a few weeks with them one summer, he'd asked Caroline if they needed to buy baby gates for the stairs, a faux pas she hadn't let him forget.

Sandy put her hand on his back and pushed him toward the dining room. "Woong's just going to set the table for us real quick. Woong, don't drink up all that milk now. Save it for dinner, and go set the table, and then we'll sit down for a nice meal. I'm so glad you joined us, Officer. Do you like meatloaf? I can't remember if you said you liked meatloaf or not. I wanted Carl to call you, but I think he forgot. Carl, did you remember to call Officer Drisklay and ask him if he likes meatloaf?"

Carl stood behind his wife and winked at Drisklay. "Detective, do you like meatloaf?"

"As long as you don't make it like my mother did." Drisklay hadn't been trying to make a joke, but Woong laughed so hard milk sprayed out his nose.

"Oh, honey." Sandy knelt down and wiped up the spray with the bottom half of her apron. Drisklay cringed.

"How was work today?" Carl asked, ignoring the grotesque scene.

Drisklay shrugged, and Carl smiled knowingly. "Another day, another dollar?"

Drisklay had never particularly liked that expression. "Something like that."

"Hey, Dad," Woong interrupted from the kitchen where he stood stacking plates. "Want me to tell you a joke I heard at school?"

"Woong, dear," his mother inserted, "let's get that table..."

Carl plopped into a chair and interrupted. "Aww, let the kid tell a joke. Detective, have a seat." He patted the table. "All right, son, tell us your joke."

Woong smiled. He was addressing his father but looking at Drisklay out of the corner of his eye.

"All right. Here's how it goes." Woong cleared his throat then took in a deep breath. "Let me think. It starts in a bar, right? Yeah, it's in a bar, and there's these two..."

"Honey, is this a joke you'd be comfortable sharing if Jesus were sitting around the table with us?" Sandy called out from the kitchen.

Woong rolled his eyes. "Yeah, Mom. It's fine. It's just a joke."

"Well, I just want you to be careful when you're poking fun at bars and drinking. It's a very serious stumbling block for some people. You know, your sister, Blessing, she can't even walk past a bar without getting tempted to..."

"He's got the point, woman," Carl blurted out, keeping his good-natured tone. "Just let the boy finish his story."

Woong glanced from one parent to the other, and when neither spoke, he grinned again. "All right, so it's at this bar, and there's these two whales there."

"Sweetie pie," Sandy piped in. "Did you remember to set an extra spot for Officer Drisklay? We'll need four places to have enough room for everybody."

This time Woong didn't respond and continued on with his story. "Okay, so there's these two whales sitting at the bar."

"Wait a minute." This time it was Woong's father. "How does a whale sit anywhere, let alone at a bar?"

Woong looked flustered. "I don't know, it's just part of the..."

"Honey," Sandy admonished, "I really don't think you should interrupt him. Just let him tell the story so we can pray and eat, all right? I'm afraid the food will get cold if he goes much longer."

Drisklay tried to think if any of tonight was worth the scant chance that he'd get some real insider information on Pastor Harrison that he couldn't have gotten anywhere else.

Carl motioned for his son to continue.

Woong's grin had spread even wider across his acned face. "Well, one of the whales at the bar, he looks at his friend, and he says *ooooooooooooooooh-aaaaaaaaaaaaaaaaah-eeeeeeyoooooouuuuu*." He made his voice rise and fall dramatically, pausing twice to refill his lungs. After this dramatic display, he glanced at his parents, then bit his lip, probably to keep from laughing too early.

Sandy carried in a basket full of bread rolls and set it on the table. "I don't get it," she admitted.

"He's not done," Carl whispered, a slightly prideful grin on his face.

Now Woong really did start to laugh and had to take another sip of milk to try to regain his composure. Drisklay was glad he was on the opposite side of the table in case any more launched out of the child's nose.

"Well then," Woong snorted, "the other whale looked over at his friend, and he said, 'Go home, Bill. You're drunk.'"

Carl burst out laughing, slapping his knee and then his son's back. Woong took another sip of milk, hiding his blushing face behind his glass.

Sandy sat down at the table with a pout.

"Didn't you like his joke?" Carl asked.

Sandy adjusted her apron; the same one she'd used to clean up after her son earlier. "You told it quite well," she told Woong primly. "You really did sound like a whale at one point."

"Wasn't he great, though?" Carl pressed, looking to Drisklay for confirmation. "I mean, what a great delivery."

Sandy set her napkin on her lap, sitting with her spine so straight she might have been suspended from the ceiling by invisible threads. "Seeing as how members of our own family have battled the demon of alcoholism, I'm just not sure his joke was in the best of taste, that's all."

Woong looked deflated until his father leaned over and whispered loudly enough for everyone to hear, "That was hilarious, son. Good job." He glanced up at his wife, who had already folded her hands. Carl turned to Drisklay then smiled and said, "All right. Well, let's pray for this food and dig in, shall we?"

Caroline had been talking for so long, she'd lost all sense of time. She couldn't guess how long they'd spent talking about her conversion, couldn't recall the series of questions Mrs. Cho had asked to get Caroline spilling out her entire life story. She felt like she'd been talking for hours already and was surprised at how freely her words started to flow once she began.

"I had a student in one of my classes, a little boy named Woong. His mother and I became close. She's a pastor's wife and still one of my closest friends. Their family invited me to Easter service at their church. At first, I didn't want to go. I knew my..." She paused, surprised at the heat she felt creeping up to her cheeks. "I knew my husband wouldn't agree to it. Not that he wouldn't let me go," she hurried to add. "It wasn't like that. I just knew... Well, Calvin wasn't happy about it. Let's just leave it at that. But I went anyway. I told him it would be a nice way for me to support one of my students because his dad was the pastor there, and Calvin was busy working that weekend anyway so it wasn't like I was taking time away from our relationship or anything like that."

She cleared her throat, aware and again ashamed when she recognized the bitterness behind her words.

"Well, the sermon was different than anything I was expecting. I hadn't gone to church growing up, and I had this feeling that pastors spent their entire time preaching about why you shouldn't drink or do drugs or stuff like that, but Pastor Carl wasn't like that. He was…" She paused, searching for the right word. "He was inspiring. Instead of preaching at us about all the things we were doing wrong, all the reasons God had to be mad at us, he talked about God's love. It was the first time I heard the full gospel message. I knew the Bible talked about the cross and the resurrection, but it wasn't until I heard Pastor Carl's sermon that I understood why Jesus had to do those things. That it was to take the punishment for my sins."

She paused, thinking that Mrs. Cho might want to add something, but the old woman remained silent. Listening. Waiting for Caroline to finish her testimony.

"There wasn't an altar call or anything. And I wasn't saved that day, but it made me start to wonder. What if everything I'd thought about God and the Bible were wrong? What if the gospel really was true? What if this man called Jesus really was the Son of God, and what if he really did love me so much that he was willing to die on a cross to take the punishment for my sins? I still had a lot of questions, and Sandy—that's my student's mom I was telling you about—she and I would get together at her house for tea, and we'd talk. It wasn't an official Bible study or anything. But she was patient with all my questions, and then over the summer, when I had more time, we started reading the book of John together. I didn't want to take a Bible home with me. I knew that would cause problems with my husband, so I just read it there with Sandy. We went through the whole book, and by the time we got to the end of it, I realized that I believed everything it said.

"I guess it's weird because I don't have an exact day I remember coming to Christ. I think it was one of those things that happened when I wasn't really thinking about it, but we got to the end of John, and I realized I believed, and I said something to Sandy like, 'So I guess I should probably get baptized now?' That was a problem because up until then my husband didn't know how serious I'd gotten about my faith. He knew I went to church, but he's been antagonistic to the gospel for his whole life, and I kept telling him I was doing it because Sandy and I were friends and it was one of the only times during the week that we could get together.

"Well, when I decided to get baptized, I knew I had to tell Calvin everything, that I'd converted and I was a Christian now." Caroline forced out a laugh, hoping it didn't sound as unnatural as it felt. "It didn't go over too well. To this day, I swear Calvin thinks I'm brainwashed or something." She shrugged. "But what can you do?" She smiled, waiting through the awkward silence.

Mrs. Cho stared at her intently before finally stating, "I believe God is working in your husband's life for a purpose. And I'm praying for his heart to be softened so that the truth of God's love will break through to his soul."

Caroline wished she could sense some of that same hope and conviction she heard in Mrs. Cho's voice. She forced another smile. "That would be nice."

Mrs. Cho held her gaze, and Caroline couldn't maintain her fake grin. She let out her breath, feeling her shoulders slouch in defeat. "That would be nice," she repeated, her voice quiet and far less certain than she liked.

Drisklay didn't realize how hungry he was until Sandy served dinner.

"Would you like some more cornbread, Officer Drisklay?" she asked. "Or another bread roll? We have plenty, and Carl can't have them anymore because of his diabetes, so eat up. In fact, when it's time for you to go home, I'll pack you up some leftovers. That way Caroline won't have to worry about you eating so unhealthy when she's gone. Woong, sweetie, don't have your cup so close to the edge of the table. Remember what happened when your dad's friend from seminary came over, and you spilled it on that little girl's lap? What was her name, by the way? She was awful pretty, wasn't she?"

Woong shrugged and took a noisy gulp of milk. "I didn't like that big wart on her nose."

"That wasn't a wart, pumpkin." Sandy's tone didn't change as she poured her son another glass. "It's a birthmark. Her mother said she was born with it. Some people call it an angel kiss. I think that's an awful sweet name, don't you?"

Woong shrugged again, and Sandy sighed noisily. "Well, it's not what's on the outside that matters anyway. You know that, right? And I think she's a very sweet girl. You know, you're getting to the age where you'll start noticing girls before long..."

"Mom," Woong exclaimed in a whiny voice.

Carl rubbed his wife's back. "Let's let the boy finish his food, all right?"

She scooped more meatloaf onto her son's plate. "Well, I'm just saying that I think he's going to start puberty pretty soon. Officer Drisklay, don't you think he looks quite a bit taller than he did last time you saw him? And he's sleeping in every single day. I declare, we're going to have to get him a second alarm or something because I can't wake him up for school no matter how hard I try. And that can be a sign of a growth spurt too, you know, which is why I'm against these schools starting so early. It's not right for kids to miss out on that much sleep. Not good for their brains, I mean. I was reading a report that Mrs. Linklater brought up at the recent PTA meeting, and she's going to take it all the way to the school board, you know. I guess one state, I forget where just now, but they recently passed a law where the high school can't start before nine o'clock in the morning. And I know some parents got upset by that, but I'll tell you what, if this boy is so hard to wake up now and he's still only in junior high, I don't even want to guess what it'll be like when he really is starting puberty. Do you remember when Justice was that age, Carl, how much sleep he needed? I declare it was probably twelve or thirteen hours a day, and even more on the weekends. Now Woong, what did I tell you about slouching at the table? It's not good for your back. Remember when we went to that nice chiropractor lady, and she told you it was better to sit up taller? That's going to help you your whole life, you know. Some people have back problems all the way into their old age just because they slouched when they were growing up, isn't that right Officer Drisklay?"

"Honey," Carl said in a quiet voice, "I think maybe we can let him eat a little in peace."

She shrugged and absently set another bread roll on Woong's plate. "That's fine. But I'm going to scribble myself a note to write to that nice family we had over, remember the ones you knew from seminary? Because now that I think about it, their daughter really is a sweetheart, and I wonder if she and Woong would like to become pen pals. They're down in Pennsylvania, which you know isn't too far away. I think he could write a letter to her and only have it take a couple days to get to her there." She sighed. "You know, I wish more people would write letters. It used to be when I was growing up that..."

Carl cleared his throat. "This was a wonderful meal, dear, but I think the detective and I should probably retire to the den."

Sandy looked at the food still on the table and frowned. "Well, I know if I were out of town on a mission trip and my husband was eating dinner at my friend's house, I'd want to know that he wasn't going to go home hungry."

Carl set his hand on his wife's. "You've enough dinner to feed a small country. I'm sure the detective's not in danger of starving any time soon, are you, brother?"

Drisklay wiped his face and made a noncommittal response.

Sandy sighed melodramatically. "Well, now, if you two are sure you've had enough to eat. I guess Woong can finish off a little more of the meatloaf for us, can't you sweetie? And then while you two are talking in the den, I can pack up these leftovers to send home with Officer Drisklay. You need to be sure to tell Caroline when you talk to her that we're taking good care of you, all right?"

Drisklay cleared his throat. It was bad enough that these people had brainwashed his wife into their backwards cult of rituals and religion. And now this. Obviously, Caroline hadn't told the Lindgrens that Drisklay had moved out. Probably too embarrassed to admit it. Didn't want the pastor to know that his newest little protégé was on her way to a divorce.

Still, it was annoying to sit here with people who fawned over his wife and fretted over his well-being while she was gone and had no idea they hadn't shared the same roof for over three weeks. Oh, well. If Caroline wanted to keep secrets, that was her business. He was here for work. Despite what Sandy might assume in her well-meaning, overbearingly hospitable way, Drisklay hadn't dropped by for a social call.

"I think the den sounds like a good idea," he announced.

Carl looked at him gratefully and scooted his chair back quickly. "Thanks for dinner, babe." He leaned over and gave his wife a peck on the cheek, then clapped Drisklay on the back. "All right, now, Detective. We've had our fill. Let's go into the den and hear what's on your mind, shall we?"

Eleven

Caroline was so absorbed retelling details of her testimony and days as an early believer, she hardly noticed when a timer from the kitchen let out a tiny ding. Mrs. Cho held up her hand. "So sorry to interrupt you, but it's time for me to wake up the children."

Caroline still couldn't understand how the house had remained so quiet for so long. Baby Da had fallen asleep in Caroline's arms just seconds after finishing his bottle. Mrs. Cho had carried him upstairs (to keep him from getting even more spoiled, she explained), and Caroline hadn't heard a single sound that would indicate there were any children at all in this home.

She stood up when Mrs. Cho did, but Mrs. Cho waved her hand. "No, you sit. You're tired. You had a long day of travel. I will wake up the children and be down shortly."

A small fraction of Caroline's brain wanted to protest that she'd come here to help with the kids, after all, but Mrs. Cho's words carried a sense of authority that wasn't readily argued against. Mrs. Cho let out a cheerful greeting in Korean as she took to the stairs, and Caroline was impressed by her agility. If only she'd be that sprightly when she was Mrs. Cho's age. Some people said that working with kids your whole life would keep you young, but Caroline was pretty sure her over-crowded and often over-rambunctious classrooms full of kids had contributed to more gray hair than to any sense of youthfulness in her own case.

The unwelcome sense of jealousy sent another pang through her chest. How different would life have been if she and Calvin were able to have kids of their own? Maybe he would have decided to stay home more. Maybe Caroline would have even taken a few years off of work to focus on turning her house into this kind of peaceful haven, a safe and restful place her husband would want to spend time in.

Maybe if they'd had children, they would have both put in more effort to work on their marriage, to stay together. For the sake of their kids if nothing else.

But it was senseless to think about that. Why should she even torture herself? It was too late now. Too late for so many things ...

Mrs. Cho disappeared at the top of the stairs, speaking in a high, melodic tone. She reappeared moments later carrying Da and followed by four sets of miniature legs that plodded down the stairs.

Mrs. Cho stopped the small procession in front of Caroline, who still sat feeling useless and lazy on the couch, and addressed the children again. They all chanted a greeting in unison. Mrs. Cho smiled and with one more directive sent them all to their spots around the table in the dining room. Caroline wondered if spending these next few weeks here would give her some good ideas for classroom management. The two oldest children, a boy and a girl, were setting the table as Mrs. Cho pulled out two trays of food, already prepared, and placed them on the counter. Caroline hoped that before long she'd stop feeling like an intruder and more like a helper, but for right now, it appeared like Mrs. Cho had everything under perfect control.

Mrs. Cho clapped her hands once, and the children folded their hands. A prayer was offered, and then Mrs. Cho turned and asked the question Caroline had been desperate to hear. "Would you be willing to help me serve the food? The children would appreciate it so much."

Caroline hurried into the kitchen to make herself useful, thankful for something to do with her hands, thankful for some sense of purpose. A few minutes later, the only sounds to be heard were the sounds of the children eating contentedly while Mrs. Cho stood behind them, placing her hands on their shoulders or backs as one at a time she spoke to them words of encouragement that made them beam.

Caroline stood off to the corner, watching the scene with both surprise and curiosity, trying hard not to think about how life may have been different if Calvin had been willing to open their home to a child of their own.

Trying hard to force herself to stay awake for just one more hour. Trying hard not to resent Mrs. Cho and the peaceful calm surrounding her home and the children she cared for.

Trying hard not to wonder if coming here to Seoul had been the right idea after all.

Drisklay sat on the couch in the Lindgren's den. Across from him, Carl leaned forward with his elbows on his knees and asked, "Well, Detective, what can I do for you?"

Drisklay was glad for the chance to get right down to the point. "I'm investigating the Rebekah Harrison murder." He eyed Carl, paying close attention to his expression.

Carl nodded. "Thought it may be something like that."

"Her dad was a pastor. *Is* a pastor," he corrected.

Another nod.

Drisklay took the verbal plunge. "I wanted to know what you can tell me about the family."

Carl let out his breath. "Well, I hate to say anything bad about another minister of Christ."

If Drisklay wanted to hear a sermon, he would have stopped by church one of the dozen times his wife nagged him. "Anything you have to tell me will be held in strictest confidence," Drisklay assured him then lowered his voice. "It could help us put Rebekah Harrison's killer behind bars for good."

Carl paused. Drisklay knew it. There was something fishy about the pastor and his picture-perfect family, his quiet little wife who wouldn't say anything without first glancing at him for approval. He knew something was going on. His instincts had led him down the right track once more.

Carl took in a deep breath. Drisklay knew better than to rush. He would give him all the time in the world.

"Honey, do you and Officer Drisklay want some tea?"

Drisklay glared at the intruder. Sandy was balancing a tray on her hip with floral teacups, frilly napkins, and sugar cubes in a crystal glass.

Carl waved her away. "We're fine. We're stuffed like your Thanksgiving turkeys and don't need anything else."

Sandy frowned. "You sure? Officer? Can I get you some tea?"

Drisklay could use a cup of coffee but didn't want to risk it coming in a four-ounce china set and watered down with sugar cubes and cream. He forced a smile, hoping it would get Sandy to leave that much more quickly. "I'm fine. Thanks."

"Well, Woong and I are going to bake some brownies as soon as he's done clearing the table, so you make sure to talk long enough for them to bake. I usually put them in for half an hour, but all my big casserole dishes are at the church to get ready for the missions conference coming up, so I'm afraid I'm going to have to use the eight-by-nines, and I really don't know if that's going to take them longer. We better say thirty-five minutes just to be safe, and of course, Woong gets distracted so easily. I declare, he's probably out there right now checking his email on his iPad to see if that friend of his from school texted him. You know, she's a sweet one, but her mom's a single mom, and I think she's a little overwhelmed, and she lets Becky spend far too much time on her phone if you ask me. Why, if we didn't have controls set that turned the internet off at bedtime, I declare Woong would stay up until ten or eleven texting her. It's not good for your eyes if you ask me, let alone your brain. You need sleep when you're that age. Your body's still developing, and..."

Carl cleared his throat, and Sandy let out her breath. "Well, now, you two just let me know if you get hungry for anything, and I'll be in before too long with those brownies. Carl, you remember that your friend's a bachelor tonight, but that doesn't mean he doesn't need his sleep too. I wouldn't plan on staying up too late. You've got that men's prayer breakfast tomorrow morning. Don't forget that. You told Woong you'd take him for the Belgian waffles he likes so much if he did well enough on his history report, and he brought it home today. It was an 84, which is a solid B, but that teacher of his took three whole points off because he didn't have the bibliography formatted right in the back. Can you believe it? Three whole points. I wonder if maybe I should call him. You know, I looked over Woong's report, and it read perfectly fine to me. Sometimes with that teacher of his, I just don't know what..."

"I'll take Woong for waffles," Carl interrupted, a soft smile on his face.

Sandy bustled out the door, calling after her son.

"So." Drisklay was worried Sandy's interruption may have destroyed any momentum he'd gained. "About Pastor Harrison?"

Carl let out a noisy sigh. "Well, Detective, I hate to say anything bad about a brother in Christ, but since this is part of your investigation, I'll just have to come right on out and say it." He lowered his voice. "You said this is strictly confidential, right?"

Drisklay nodded. At least it was for now.

"Well, I've known Harrison for several years now. Not in a close way, strictly professional. But if you want my opinion, that's one man I'd never let stand behind my pulpit and preach to my congregation. Not if you were to pay me a million bucks."

Drisklay reached nonchalantly for his notepad. "Really?" He tried to keep his voice detached. Disinterested. "And why is that?" He was ready. He was waiting. In a way, he was already congratulating himself for following up on the Harrison lead when all he had was the hint of a hunch.

Carl bent forward, the old couch creaking in protest under his weight. "It's his theology. That man is off his rocker."

Drisklay waited. Unmoving. Frozen. "His theology?" he was finally forced to repeat.

"Harrison believes that you can't ever be sure of your salvation, for one thing. That even once you accept Jesus as your personal Lord and Savior that there might be a sin you could commit that would make him decide to condemn you to hell."

Drisklay blinked. What was this man raving about?

"Furthermore," Carl went on, "Harrison denies God's omniscience. He thinks that it's unjust for God to already know who's going to be saved, and so he thinks God's out there just as surprised as anyone else when a sinner comes to repentance, but the Word of God specifically states that…"

"I'm going to stop you right there." Drisklay had heard enough. "Aside from these…" He struggled to find the right word. "Aside from these theological debates, do you have any reason to suspect Harrison of foul play?"

Carl started in shock as if Drisklay had just admitted to the murder himself.

"Foul play? Like having something to do with his daughter's… with what happened to Rebekah? Is that what you're asking?"

Drisklay tried to mask his impatience. "That's exactly what I'm asking."

Carl recoiled as if he'd been slapped. "No, that's absurd. Just because his theology's off doesn't make him capable of murder."

Drisklay was wondering if there was any way to salvage the conversation, or any real reason to, when Woong ran in. "Dad! Dad! Becky wants to know if I can go to her birthday party next Friday night. Her mom's going to be home, and they're not showing any movies, and there's going to be boys and girls there, but everything's going to be supervised.It's nobody older than ninth grade coming, except she's got this cousin who might stop by for a little bit, and he's like seventeen or something. He's only coming by because his mom hired him to work on the car, so we probably won't even see him because he'll be in the garage. Besides, Becky doesn't even like him all that much. Mom said she'd have to talk to you about it first, but I thought that if I got all the questions…" He stared at Drisklay and stopped. "Oh. Hi, Detective. I forgot you were in a meeting."

Carl's voice was steady as he addressed Woong. "Yes, son. We're in a meeting."

"Should I ask you about it later?" He took a step back toward the door.

"Yes," Carl answered. "That's exactly what you should do."

Woong slumped his shoulders then raced out of the den.

Carl stared after his son. "Sorry about that. He's starting to notice girls now. We're in a whole new ball game than we were when…" He cleared his throat. "Anyway, what were we talking about? Oh, yeah. The doctrine of election. Come to think of it, I have a book on the subject if you're interested. People far more intelligent than I'll ever be have been arguing these points for hundreds of years. Give me a minute. It'll just take me a second to find it on my shelves..."

"That's quite all right." Drisklay stood. "I probably better head out."

Carl looked at him as if he'd started spouting off in German. "So, you don't want that book?" he finally asked.

Drisklay took a step toward the hallway. "No, thanks. But you have my number. If you can think of anyone who might have tried to hurt Rebekah Harrison, you'll let me know?"

"Will do, Detective." Carl clasped him heartily on the shoulder. "And if you want to know more about the doctrine of election, I'm teaching a whole series on it in my Sunday sermons. We'd love to have you join us."

"We'll have to see about that," Drisklay muttered. "Thank your wife for dinner. I'll let myself out."

Twelve

Caroline was surprised to discover it was mid-morning by the time she woke up in Mrs. Cho's spare room. Hadn't she set her alarm? She got dressed hurriedly, worrying that her hostess must think her the epitome of laziness.

The children were downstairs in the living room. Soft music was playing, and Mrs. Cho led the group in a choreographed song. She smiled as Caroline sheepishly walked down the stairs.

"Did you sleep well?" she asked, continuing her hand movements in time with the flowing music.

Caroline nodded, uncertain if her brain simply wasn't awake yet or if there was something deeply relaxing, almost hypnotic, about watching Mrs. Cho lead this slow dance.

"You are free to join us," Mrs. Cho said with an expression that led Caroline to doubt there was any polite way to refuse. She stood behind the children and tried to mirror the old woman's gestures, thankful that Mrs. Cho's attention had turned back onto the kids.

After one more song, Mrs. Cho gave the children some instructions in Korean, and the children scattered in different directions. Toys appeared out of chests that Caroline had assumed were simply decorative, and in a second the room was as busy and noisy as any preschool would be in the States. There was something highly refreshing about the relative disorder.

"Would you like something hot to drink?" Mrs. Cho asked, leading her into the kitchen.

Caroline felt like she should apologize for sleeping in so late but instead watched the children playing while Mrs. Cho prepared a mug of instant cappuccino.

Sitting across the table from her, Mrs. Cho asked, "Did you get enough rest last night? I hope the children didn't wake you by their noise."

Caroline shook her head. If there was one thing her years of teaching had given her, it was the ability to function perfectly well in the midst of chaos.

Mrs. Cho took a small sip of tea, smiling broadly.

Caroline felt as if she should say something and stared around the room for any cues. "Who's the soldier in that photograph?" she finally asked.

Mrs. Cho turned and smiled at the young man in the frame. "That's my husband."

Caroline studied him. The photograph was old, but the kind features on the man's face were clear in spite of the picture's age. "He must have been a very nice man," she remarked.

Mrs. Cho broke into a serene smile, and she lifted her eyes toward the ceiling. "Oh, he is. He loves the Lord so much."

"How long were you married?" Caroline asked.

"We were wed two years before the start of the Peninsula War."

Caroline did a quick mental calculation. If Mrs. Cho was a young woman at the start of the Korean War, she was even older than Caroline had guessed.

Mrs. Cho set down her teacup and let out a sigh. "It's been so long. I pray for him every single day."

Caroline was confused. Did Korean Protestants pray for their deceased?

Mrs. Cho was still staring at the man in the photograph. "My husband and I made a promise to love each other no matter what, to believe all things, to hope all things, to endure all things. When we made that vow, we certainly didn't expect God to put our devotion to the test so soon."

There was no way Caroline could have contained her curiosity at that point. "What happened?"

"When the war broke out, my husband was a pastor. We were living near Pyongyang at the time. In fact, his father and grandfather were both evangelists whose witness God used greatly during the Pyongyang revival at the turn of the century."

Caroline tried to not let her surprise show. A revival somewhere as closed to the gospel as North Korea? Maybe she should have studied more about the history of the Korean church before traveling to Seoul on a short-term mission trip. Then again, how could she have guessed that her host would be speaking about events that happened over a century earlier?

"The two of us met at church. My father was a deacon, his father was the pastor. It was obvious from the beginning that God was calling us to join our lives together."

Caroline wasn't used to hearing language like this. When she and Calvin decided to get married, they talked about what kind of house or apartment they could afford to share, what kind of potential honeymoon destinations were within their budget. Not whether or not their destinies were joined together by God Almighty.

What if Caroline had been a Christian at the time? What if she'd bothered to pray all the way back then? How different would her life have turned out...

"Shortly after we married," Mrs. Cho went on, "God blessed us with a beautiful, healthy boy. It was prophesied over him that he would grow up to lead many to Christ, to spread the Word of God's salvation to distant shores. He was colicky, a very fussy baby, and yet if he saw his father reading his Bible, he would crawl up on his lap and sit perfectly still. An anointed infant."

Mrs. Cho's voice took a nostalgic tone before it trailed off, and Caroline steeled herself for whatever was to come.

"When war broke out, God told us that Pyongyang, once a haven for the spread of the gospel, would become a danger and a snare to all believers. My husband had just become the pastor at the time. He didn't want to leave but urged me to go ahead. My sister lived near Seoul, and he wanted me to take our baby there. He meant to join us shortly afterwards."

Mrs. Cho sat as if waiting for a response, but Caroline had no idea what to say. Finally, she managed to croak, "What happened then?"

"I lived with my sister until she died five years ago," Mrs. Cho answered. "Up until then, we ran the orphanage together. Her husband's will left us this home and provisions to continue to care for the children."

"And your husband?" Caroline winced, hoping she hadn't asked the wrong thing.

"I have not heard from him since the day I took our baby and joined my sister here in Seoul."

"Do you even know if he's still alive?" As soon as she asked the question, Caroline wished she could take it back.

Thankfully, Mrs. Cho's serene expression remained unchanged. "I do not. However, God has given me a dream."

"A dream?" Caroline repeated lamely.

Now Mrs. Cho's face looked as if it were beaming, illuminated by her own faith or conviction or love. "In my dream, my husband is old, like me. His body shakes with tremors as a result of his age. His face is wrinkled, his body stooped. His eyes, Lord have mercy on the dear man, ceased seeing years ago, and yet he hides a Bible in his home, a Bible he cherishes and guards with his life, even though he can no longer read the words it contains."

Caroline stared at her hands in her lap, unworthy as she felt to witness the peaceful, glorious luminescence shining from Mrs. Cho's entire countenance. "Do you think God spoke to you in that dream?"

Mrs. Cho's smile widened. "I do. I first had this dream over fifteen years ago. I asked God if it was a message that my husband was still alive, still serving our Savior, and he answered by giving me the same dream several times since." She sniffed and stared into her tea cup. "Sadly, it has been several years since the last time this dream came to me. When I ask God why this is, he answers me only with silence."

Caroline didn't want to guess what that silence could mean and was thankful when Mrs. Cho changed the subject. "But of course, I will continue to pray for my husband until the day God calls me home. At least I know that my beloved and I will be reunited again."

"I'm glad you have that comfort." Caroline felt her heart constricting between her lungs. What would it be like if she could say those words about Calvin?

Mrs. Cho offered her a warm, sad smile. "It seems we both have hurts to lay before the throne of heaven."

"I guess we do," Caroline had to agree.

"Well then," Mrs. Cho replied, taking Caroline's hands in hers, "maybe we should pray, no? For my husband, God bless his soul, as well as yours."

Drisklay was more tired than he'd expected to be when he pulled up in front of his house.

His former house, that is.

Caroline didn't know he was living here while she traveled the world on her errands of mercy, but she'd never asked him for his key. He needed that time to pack up the rest of his things. Besides, the old house was only a ten-minute drive away from work, and it beat sleeping in his office or cheap motels.

He disarmed the security system. This was one of the first times he'd been home since he started working the Rebekah Harrison case. He was looking forward to sleeping in an actual bed and not his office chair.

He walked straight to the kitchen cupboards and pulled out the Aleve. He popped four pills then shoved the bottle deep into his pocket. Caroline never used the stuff. By clearing his junk out of here, he was actually doing her a favor. Wasn't she always the one who complained that he didn't pick up after himself? Well, now he could make up for lost time.

Before closing up at the office for the night, Drisklay had done a quick web search on various schools of Christian thought and came to the original conclusion he'd maintained before. Carl Lindgren might be one of the Boston area's most popular pastors, but his personal opinions on theology had no bearing on his current case. Drisklay still hadn't shaken the gut feeling that Rebekah Harrison's father may have somehow been involved in her death, but if so, Carl wasn't going to be the one to point him in the right direction.

Well, he'd pack up a few things, sleep off his last pot of coffee, and start tomorrow with fresh eyes. Maybe he should look into that best friend again, at least bring her in for more questioning. He'd worked on the force long enough to have developed an uncanny intuition regarding when something was about to break, like joints that flare up right before heavy rain, and he knew that this case was about to be blown wide open.

He just had to be ready, and hopefully awake, when it happened.

He turned on the TV in the living room. Caroline had left the station on to some televangelist. Figured. This guy had sleaziness dripping out of his spray-tanned pores. Drisklay switched the channel to catch the score of that night's Red Sox game—mostly to see how unruly the bars would get— then he turned to the news.

Thankfully, the media had already moved on from Rebekah Harrison's death. Tonight's headlines covered election campaigns, gay rights, and a missing teen girl. Probably a runaway, but she happened to be a skinny blond cheerleader from suburbia, which meant that her story trumped the hundreds of other missing teen cases that took place every day.

Drisklay opened one of the cupboards, trying to decide if he should make himself another pot of coffee. Probably not. He kept the TV running and headed down the hall. He'd pack up a few more things, then see if he could get to sleep.

He was surprised that nothing in his bedroom had changed since he moved out. The room was a little tidier, but his nightstand looked completely untouched. He'd half figured Caroline would have tossed his junk into boxes herself, as eager as she'd been to see him leave. Oh, well. She was probably too busy with that beloved church of hers.

He grabbed a shoebox from under the bed and swept everything from his nightstand into it haphazardly. He'd sort through it all later. When he peeked into the closet, it was similar to the nightstand, almost eerie in the way nothing had been moved or handled since he'd left.

He walked over to Caroline's side of the bed, glancing at the books on her nightstand several titles about praying for your husband, one called *Scripture Promises for the Christian Woman*, everything you'd expect from a Christian convert. Her Bible was gone, no doubt with her at that orphanage. She wouldn't have left something as precious as that at home while she went out to parade as Mother Teresa.

Well, he hoped she was happy in the life she'd chosen. Drisklay himself wouldn't be caught dead shuttling himself across the planet, posing as a do-gooder just to earn a few extra bonus points with God. He pulled back the covers, tossed off his pants and climbed into bed.

He rolled over with his back to his wife's nightstand, feeling nothing but exhausted, and hoped for a long night dreaming of just that.

Nothing.

Thirteen

"I think Da has taken a liking to you." Mrs. Cho offered Caroline a warm smile as she cleared the dishes from the children's lunch.

Caroline held baby Da and didn't know what to say. She didn't want to admit that yesterday was the first time she'd changed a diaper since she was a teenager, babysitting to earn a little spending money while she was in high school.

The children were napping upstairs, and from the looks of Da's drooping eyelids, he was going to be ready to join them any minute.

"I wish Calvin and I'd been able to have children." Caroline's admission sounded strange, almost an affront to her marriage. She'd felt this way for over a decade, but had she ever spoken the truth out loud so succinctly?

"He didn't want to be a father?" Mrs. Cho asked.

Caroline shrugged. "I was in a car accident when I was twelve, and they told me then I wouldn't be able to conceive." As soon as she realized she was talking to a woman who made it her life's mission to look after orphans, many of whom waited eagerly to be placed in adoptive homes, Caroline felt like she had to defend herself. "I always planned on adopting, but to Calvin that was out of the question."

She expected some sort of chiding remark, but Mrs. Cho just nodded her head. "Some people do feel that way."

Confronted with the grace of Mrs. Cho's response, Caroline felt suddenly even more uncharitable. "Well, I wish he'd felt a different way."

Mrs. Cho frowned. The expression looked entirely unnatural and unpracticed on her wrinkled face. "Surely if God wanted to bless you with children..."

Caroline was glad when baby Da squirmed and Mrs. Cho shifted her focus to calming him down.

"Tell me about your son." Caroline was eager to change the subject. "He was still a baby when you came to Seoul?"

Mrs. Cho nodded. "Yes, and he is an answer to the prophecy God has given him. He lives in China and spends his life training North Korean refugees, teaching them the gospel and equipping them to return home as undercover missionaries."

"That sounds dangerous," Caroline remarked.

"It is. Several times, he has been imprisoned by Chinese police."

"No, I mean for the missionaries," Caroline explained. "The ones he sends back to North Korea."

Mrs. Cho was silent for a moment then finally said, "Yes. He fears that many of them will lose their lives in service to the gospel."

Caroline wondered if she'd ever have the courage to do anything even remotely similar. It took her two full weeks to get up the nerve to tell her husband she was getting baptized. What would happen if her choice was to curse God or die? She didn't want to think about it, didn't want to know the answer. Not right now. Maybe if she was more mature in her faith, if she'd had more time to study Scripture, if she was as close to God as someone like Mrs. Cho, then it would be easier.

Wouldn't it?

"Do you worry about your son?" she asked.

Mrs. Cho chuckled. "No. I told God that I would rather have my son beaten and bruised in body than for his soul to perish in hell. He is serving the Lord, just like his father and grandfather and great-grandfather before him. What greater honor could there be for a mother?"

Caroline didn't know from firsthand experience what it would be like to be a mom, but she could imagine how great the burden must be to want to see your children walking with the Lord.

"I sometimes feel that way about my students," she admitted and thought about the kids who'd come and gone in her classroom over the years. Some were grown with children of their own now. She'd always believed in the teacher's ability to influence and encourage her students, but she wasn't allowed to talk about religion in the classroom. "I just don't know what kind of spiritual impact I can really have in the classroom," she confessed.

"What do you mean?"

Caroline explained the laws that kept teachers like her from sharing the gospel in a public-school setting.

"So, in a nation that boasts its religious freedom, you're unable to teach your students the truth of the gospel?"

Caroline wanted to explain it was more complicated than that. In fact, she'd heard other Christians, even Pastor Carl, speak out in favor of the separation of church and state. If Caroline could stand up and lead her classroom full of impressionable youngsters in the sinner's prayer, what would stop a Muslim teacher from leading her children in the tenets of Islam, or a wiccan teacher from forcing her students to participate in witchcraft? But the words froze on her tongue when she looked at Mrs. Cho, whose husband stayed behind to lead a church in spite of grave dangers and whose son trained underground missionaries to venture into the most closed nation on the planet.

"It's hard to explain," she finally replied.

"But there are no laws that can prohibit you from praying, correct? In your own heart, not forcing anyone else to join you or listen in?"

"No. There aren't any laws like that."

Mrs. Cho's smile returned. "Then that is your answer. You pray."

Was it really so simple? "I guess you're right." She looked away, hoping Mrs. Cho wouldn't perceive that she was only saying what she thought was expected of her.

"Maybe we should do that now, do you think?"

"Do what?" Caroline asked. "Pray?"

"Of course. How do you think I manage this houseful of young ones without losing my temper or my sanity?"

Caroline couldn't tell if Mrs. Cho was making a joke or not but guessed that she was. "That sounds like a great idea. Let's pray, for the kids in your orphanage and the kids in my classroom."

"And for our husbands, as well," Mrs. Cho added.

"That's right." Caroline tried to ignore the pain zinging through her heart. "We'll pray for our husbands too. Both of them."

Drisklay had almost forgotten what it felt like to sleep flat on his back, not slouched over his desk in his office or reclining in the front seat of his car.

He was exhausted enough that he didn't get to enjoy the feeling for long before he was dreaming.

Sirens. Screaming in his ears, almost drowning out the noise of the toddler in the front seat.

Almost.

"Hang in there, little guy," Drisklay tells him. His voice is on edge. His palms are sweaty.

Outside the rain pours.

And the siren wails. In the distance. In his eardrums. All around him.

"Hang in there." He says the words almost like a prayer, even as the life drains out of the child.

Drisklay isn't new to the force, but this is the worst domestic violence case he's ever been called out on. If he could get his hands on the judge that let the deadbeat out of jail in the first place...

It's Halloween. Apparently, the myriad of trick-or-treating children and their happily oblivious chaperones must assume the squad car and flashing lights are only there for display. Don't they realize this is an emergency?

Why are they all outside in this rain anyway?

"Get out of my way!" Calvin shouts, but his voice is distorted. As if he's underwater. As if the air is thickening around him, slowing him down, keeping him from speeding ahead. Doesn't the universe realize this child will die if Calvin doesn't get him to the hospital? The paramedics who should be here are held up in traffic, and this child has no time to spare. No time at all.

"Move it!" The siren wails, piercing his eardrums, but the pedestrians are

laughing and frolicking in the middle of the street, totally unaware. Deaf. Unmoving.

"Out of my way!" Drisklay lays on the horn. Nothing happens. The siren continues to wail...

He jerked himself awake. What was that sound? Was he still in the squad car?

No this was his bed. At least, it used to be. What was making that noise?

He reached out blindly until he found his phone. "Hello?"

The voice on the other end was breathy. Almost panicked. "Detective Drisklay? This is Sandy Lindgren, Pastor Carl's wife. I know it's late. I'm so sorry to bother you, but I didn't think this should wait for morning. It's about that case you're working on. The murder."

Drisklay was fully awake now, fully alert, even though the back of his shirt remained drenched in his sweat. "What can I do for you, Mrs. Lindgren?" He flipped on the bedroom light, groping blindly for his notebook.

"It's about Pastor Harrison. His wife is here with me. She has some information she thinks you should know. Can we come over?"

"Here?" Calvin had found his notebook, but where was a pen? Had Caroline stashed them all away?

"Are you at home? We can be there in ten minutes. Fifteen tops."

Calvin let out his breath. Ten minutes? Just enough time to make himself a pot of coffee and get dressed.

Get dressed and find himself a blasted pen.

"I'll be here," he grumbled then rolled out of bed.

Fourteen

"You are fitting in so well with the children," Mrs. Cho remarked as Caroline sat with two little girls on her lap, flipping the pages of some picture books.

"I'm having a great time," Caroline admitted and let out a chuckle. "I'm really glad I didn't let Calvin talk me out of coming here."

A frown darkened Mrs. Cho's countenance for a fraction of a second. "Your husband was unhappy with your decision?"

Caroline felt herself blush before her embarrassment was placed with resentment. Why should she feel ashamed if she happened to be married to the most stubborn, impossible man in the United States of America?

She feigned indifference and gave a little shrug. "Not that happy, but it really wasn't his choice to make, so..." She stopped when Mrs. Cho puckered her lips.

"You don't worry that your actions come across as disrespectful?"

Chalk it up to a cultural barrier. Mrs. Cho didn't understand that mutual respect didn't hold the same weight in the States as it did in a place like Korea. Caroline probably was coming across as the stereotypical brash American housewife, stubborn and aggressive, when in reality she'd tiptoed around Calvin and his antagonism toward the gospel for years. "He's decided to make his own path in life," she finally stated, as if that were all that was left to say.

Mrs. Cho sat down on the couch next to her. "But aren't you worried that when you return home, it will be hard to restore the harmony?"

Caroline didn't want to shoot back that if she had listened to her husband and stayed at home, Mrs. Cho would be short one orphanage worker. Not that she seemed to need the extra help, but still, Caroline felt herself bristle. "It wasn't like there was ever any harmony to begin with," she found herself saying. "Ever since I became a Christian, all he's done is ridicule me, my friends, my church..." She stopped herself. She'd been looking forward to this time in Seoul so that she could have a break from the constant berating, the constant insults. But here she was, about to pick a fight with a godly Christian woman like Mrs. Cho. What was wrong with her?

"I'm sorry." She stared at one of the little girls on her lap, straightening out her smooth hair. "I don't mean to complain."

Mrs. Cho's smile returned. "I understand that it is difficult. But I do worry that your time here will make things harder on your marriage when you return to your husband."

Caroline sighed. She should have known the truth would come out soon enough. She'd tried so hard to make Mrs. Cho think she was a model Christian, a model wife. Now the pretense was over. "Well, don't worry yourself too much about that. We separated a few weeks before I left."

There. The full truth, in all its ugly glory. The words left a bitter aftertaste in her mouth. "He's the one who left me," she hastened to explain, worrying that Mrs. Cho's silence was unspoken judgement. "I would have tried to keep on making it work, but the truth is I don't have any more fight left in me. I can't make him stay, so..." She shrugged once more.

Mrs. Cho shut her eyes. Great. She was so disgusted with Caroline she didn't even want to look at her. Was this the point where she would ask her to pack up her things? To head back home to patch things up with her husband or at least leave the orphanage where she might be contaminating the children with her western feminist sinfulness?

"The Lord's ways are not our own," Mrs. Cho finally declared. "I believe that God called you to Seoul because he's planning on working a miracle in your marriage, a miracle you wouldn't believe if he were to reveal his plans to you now."

"That sounds nice," Caroline mumbled, but in her heart, she was too tired to hope, too spiritually exhausted to put any faith in the old woman's words.

Drisklay was already on his third cup of coffee before he decided to start up his computer. If Sandy and Mrs. Harrison were going to take their sweet time getting here after waking him up in the middle of the night, he might as well be productive while he waited.

An initial google search of Pastor Harrison didn't reveal anything Drisklay didn't already know, but if there was more information coming about the case, he may as well have as many details about the family as possible.

A few minutes later, he was sipping hot coffee and browsing through blog articles on Harrison's church website. Pretty standard stuff from what Drisklay could tell. *Why Christians should abstain from alcohol... Why Halloween is the devil's holiday.*

Drisklay could at least agree with Harrison on that one even if it wasn't for the same reasons.

He spent a minute or two browsing the headings then clicked on one that looked interesting enough to peruse more thoroughly. *How Christian fathers can protect their daughters in the dangerous world of dating.*

Drisklay scanned through the major bullet points.

Fathers, at least according to Pastor Harrison's line of reasoning, had a God-ordained mission to shield and shelter their daughters until the time that God brought a righteous man into their lives who could assume responsibility for said daughter's spiritual and physical well-being.

Because apparently, Pastor Harrison had never read the memo that in the twenty-first century women had not only the right to vote but to get an education, earn a living...

He continued on.

Daughters, as descendants of Eve, who was tricked by Satan way back in the beginning of time, were naturally prone to deception, making them easy targets for seduction. Therefore, a father's role was to vet any potential dating prospect before giving his permission for a relationship to develop. As an example, from the animal kingdom, a zebra's potential mate has to fight off the father to prove his worthiness before entering into relations with the female.

Drisklay couldn't help but wonder how the female zebras felt about said arrangement.

The second half of the article grew quite rambling, but the gist seemed to be that a Christian father had the sole responsibility before God to ensure that his daughter (no matter what her age) ended up paired off with a Bible-believing man who would respect her modesty, femininity, and virginity until the day of their nuptials.

Were they living back in the days of Victorian England? These were the kind of people Drisklay's wife had grown to venerate. Was it any wonder he and Caroline had grown so far apart? At least they'd never had children. Caroline would probably expect Drisklay to act like that male zebra, fighting off his daughter's suitors until he found one worthy to act as her mate.

What a messed-up system.

So, what had a girl like Rebekah Harrison been doing setting up a profile on an online dating site, especially with such an old-fashioned man for a father? Her profile mentioned in several places that she was looking for a Christian man, but that was just the thing. She was doing the looking.

Not Reverend Papa.

Was Pastor Harrison so set against seeing his daughter dating that he might have done something to try to stop her?

Is that what his wife was on her way over to confess?

The doorbell rang, and he stood up. Whatever Mrs. Harrison had come here to tell him, he was about to find out.

Fifteen

Mrs. Cho emerged from the kitchen with a warm smile on her face, beaming at Caroline. "I appreciate you watching the children while I clean up. You are a true blessing sent to me from heaven in my time of need."

Caroline didn't feel like she was worth such profuse praise. "Really, it's easy. The kids are so well behaved. I just wish there was more I could do." As many times as she'd offered, Mrs. Cho had never let Caroline take on any of the household chores. Most of Caroline's time had been spent reading to children and cuddling baby Da while he took his bottle.

"Would you like to share the Bible story today?" Mrs. Cho asked. "We usually have an afternoon time of prayer and study."

Caroline wasn't sure which surprised her more—that Mrs. Cho actually had set aside time to pray with kids so little or that she'd asked Caroline to lead today's session.

"None of them know any English, do they?" she asked.

Mrs. Cho grinned. "If God can use donkeys, he can most certainly use any one of us in spite of our language deficiencies. Please. Use your gifts of teaching to share with us from God's Word." She called the children together, speaking to them rapidly and clapping her hands for emphasis. Caroline sat paralyzed on the couch, wondering what she should say.

"Do they have a particular story they'd like to hear?" she finally asked, glancing around to see if there were any props. Maybe if she found puppets or stuffed animals and made them re-enact something...

"Just tell them what's on your heart," Mrs. Cho encouraged. "They're very good listeners."

Caroline sighed and realized there was no way out of this. The easiest path through the awkwardness was a straight line to the end. But what should she say?

"Do you know the story about the prodigal son?" She glanced at Mrs. Cho. Maybe telling a group of orphans a story that demonstrated a father's love wasn't the best of choices. But she felt committed now. Besides, she reminded herself, the kids couldn't understand her anyway.

"Once there was a young man who was very mean to his father," she began. "He took his father's money and ran away to another town, where he wasted it all." She paused for just a moment, thinking about all the years she'd squandered as an unbeliever. Years she could have spent worshipping God, learning about his goodness, serving him. In so many ways, she still felt brand-new to the faith and wondered when it would finally seem like she had matured. Right now, she thought the children sitting around here listening politely to a story they didn't understand probably had more spiritual training that she did.

"Well, when the boy's money finally ran out, he realized what a terrible mistake he'd made." A lump caught in Caroline's throat. Why was she getting so sentimental about a simple parable? What was it about the story, about the children's wide and attentive eyes, about Mrs. Cho's silent smile that made her want to break down into tears?

"So, he decided to go back to his father. Now, he didn't think he could ever be forgiven for all the bad things he'd done, but when his father saw him returning home..." She paused, laughing at herself as she wiped her eyes dry. "I'm sorry." She glanced at Mrs. Cho. "I don't know what's gotten into me." She turned back to the children. Some had started to fidget, and they were probably wondering what this foreigner was blabbering on about.

"When his father saw him returning home," she tried again, "he ran down the road to meet him, threw his arms around his neck, kissed him and praised God for bringing his son safely back to him."

She tried to laugh again as another tear slipped unwelcomed down her cheek. "It's a story of how much God loves us, no matter how many bad things we've done." She finished her Bible lesson as quickly as she could. Then she excused herself to the bathroom and had a good cry.

Drisklay opened his front door.

"You're not Mrs. Harrison." It was all he had time to say.

A fist connected to his jaw. The adrenaline that flooded his system was far more effective than his pot of coffee in awakening his dulled senses.

"My wife's a stinking liar." Harrison barged into the house. Drisklay shoved him against the door, slamming it shut behind him.

He grabbed Harrison by the collar. "What do you think you're doing in my home?" He slammed his fist into the pastor's gut.

Harrison bent over with an *oomph*, and Drisklay brought his knee up to his nose.

Harrison was on the floor. Drisklay straddled him. The front door burst open. Another man. A glint of metal in his hand. Fire seared through his shoulder. Pain and anger and a surge of hot rage.

Someone was shouting. Both of his attackers were up now, on their feet. He ignored his right arm, inexplicably rendered useless, and swung with his left. A yell. His vision tunneled, blinding him to the assailant who attacked from behind.

Fire in his kidneys. In the muscles and flesh of his back. His vision continuing to tunnel, his pulse surging through his ears.

Was this fear, or was this rage? Drisklay surged forward. A couple of punches and the pastor was down.

He turned around and let out a roar of rage when he faced the second attacker. The man looked startled. A punch to the jaw, a knee to the groin. Drisklay lunged toward the living room. Yanking open the drawer, groping to grab hold of his Sig. Racking the slide. Taking aim.

Another stab through his side. What was that?

Hands on his throat, toppling him. His gun went off, firing straight into the ceiling.

Not good.

He was on the ground. His fist pried open. One attacker straddled him. The other stood over him, breathing hard. Holding the Sig. Aiming at Drisklay's head.

Harrison nodded. "Let's finish this." Drisklay squeezed his eyes shut instinctively.

Protectively.

Bracing.

The deafening burst of gunfire. A last millisecond surge of adrenaline.

Then nothing.

Sixteen

"You are feeling better now, I take it?" Mrs. Cho asked as Caroline emerged from the bathroom.

Caroline cleared her throat, scarcely trusting her voice after her display of tears. "Yes, thank you. I think I'm just a little tired. It's the jetlag..." Her voice trailed off as she realized how weak her excuse sounded. Maybe it was better to change the subject. "Is it time to start getting ready for dinner? Please put me to work however you'd like..."

"First," Mrs. Cho interrupted, "I want to show you something." She walked over to the photograph of her husband, her steps slower than normal. Less spry.

She opened the back of the frame and pulled out a folded piece of paper.

"Before we were separated," Mrs. Cho explained, "my husband wrote me this letter." She sat down on the couch and held the paper out even though Caroline couldn't decipher any of the writing.

"I will not be able to translate it well, but he says that he is sorry. Before our son and I escaped to live with my sister, my husband and I got into a fight. A very big one. He didn't want to leave Pyongyang. As pastor of the church there, he thought it was his duty to stay. I could understand this. What I couldn't understand is why he would send his family, his own flesh and blood, away. In my mind, there was only one choice. If he was going to stay, we would remain in Pyongyang with him to do the Lord's work. But he insisted."

She lowered her head. "Most likely, his stubbornness saved me and our son. But even now, I wonder if it wouldn't have been better..." She sighed. "Well, now, we know that God has his reasons for everything he does, and if the Almighty wanted us here in Seoul, who am I to complain? But I show you this letter because even my husband, a powerful man of God, had a need to apologize."

Caroline wasn't sure what she was expected to say.

"I mention it," Mrs. Cho explained, "because this afternoon I was praying for you. I was thinking to myself, *If I were married to a non-Christian, how would the devil use that to try to discourage my faith?* This is what I realized. If I were married to an unbeliever, I think what I would be tempted to do is look at each and every thing he did that bothered me—every fight, every little argument—and I would say to myself, *If only my husband were a Christian, my life wouldn't be so hard."*

She smiled softly. "I'm afraid that I've been around long enough on this earth to realize that there is no such thing as a perfect marriage. Even between two believers. My husband and I were both young when we married, and as much as we loved each other (and still do, I must say), we both acted selfishly more times than I could ever remember. But we learned to confess our sins to each other and offer forgiveness when necessary."

Caroline nodded, wondering what use a marriage lesson was to her now that she and her husband were separated.

"You came here against your husband's wishes because you sensed God was calling you to serve him, no?"

The pointedness of the question made the skin on the back of Caroline's neck bristle and put her instantly on the defensive.

"I understand," Mrs. Cho added before she could respond, "how difficult it must be to live with a man who doesn't share your commitment to the Lord. But even if you can't agree on matters of faith or religion, I wonder if there is still love in your heart for him. Forgiveness and grace that can carry you through the difficult times ahead."

Caroline wasn't sure how to respond. Why was she being lectured all of a sudden?

"I can see that I'm upsetting you." Mrs. Cho stood up. "I'm sorry if I've become too preachy. But my heart hurts when I think of what you and your husband must be going through."

Again, Caroline was left uncertain as to what to say.

"Let's not talk about it any more, at least for now." Mrs. Cho's suggestion was more than welcome. "But I want you to know that I will continue to pray for you, for God to show you how to be a light to your husband in spite of the hardness of his heart."

"Thank you," Caroline managed to croak, hoping to avoid another trip to the bathroom to cry behind locked doors.

Mrs. Cho straightened the pillows on the coach. "Well, now, let's see what we have in the pantry for dinner."

Sirens.

Wailing. Deafening.

Screaming to be heard.

"Out of my way!" Drisklay was shouting, just like in his dream, except this time it felt different. Less like a haunting memory. More like the real event. The original stuff from which his nightmare had been made so many years ago.

The trick-or-treaters scrambled to get out of the road. "Hang in there," he told the boy.

And then the collision.

He saw the young woman a fraction of a second before his car slammed into her body. She'd been laughing. Why couldn't he remember that detail until now? She'd been laughing. Bending over to look into her little girl's plastic pumpkin, and she'd laughed.

Next, the collision.

Slamming on the brakes, the squealing tires, the smell of burnt rubber. It flooded his senses now more pointedly than any dream from the past.

Jumping out of the car. Racing to where she lay on the pavement, shouting at a passerby to get her little girl out of the road.

This was a sight no child should see.

A sight doomed to haunt Drisklay's dreams until the day he died. His curse would be to carry the memory of this exact moment for as long as his body drew breath.

Watching the blood leaving the young mother's body pulse by pulse until there was nothing left.

Nothing left at all.

Then the dream changed, and he was the one in the ambulance. He was the one stretched out on a gurney as bodies scrambled around, trying in vain to restore him to the world of the living.

"Let me go," he wanted to tell them. "I'm not worth it."

The words refused to escape his lips.

"I'm not worth it," he repeated, this time to himself. Almost like a prayer. But not quite.

"Just let me go," he wanted to croak. And then there was the pain.

Everywhere.

His shoulder. His back. His side. His face. A fiery, aching turmoil.

Oh, his face.

Was this hell? No, the men around him were still scrambling to keep him alive. He wasn't dead yet.

Suspended, maybe.

There had been a fight. Images leaked in between the dark veil of confusion. A knife. The echo of a memory, the shadow of what happened. A gunshot. Fire in his jaw.

Ice in his soul.

Drisklay had always known he would die on the job. It was a certainty he carried around with him every day, just like he carried his Sig Sauer in its holster on his hip.

But he hadn't expected it to happen yet.

He'd hoped to solve at least a few more cases...

The case. Rebekah Harrison's murder. Her father. The pastor...

"I know who did it."

A man leaned over him. "Try not to talk. Save your energy."

"It was the father. And someone else too..."

"... Anyone we should call?" someone was asking.

My wife. This time Drisklay could only think the words as his vision faded again to black and his mind went completely blank.

Seventeen

Dinner was ready a full forty-five minutes before it was time for the children to eat, and Caroline didn't argue when Mrs. Cho suggested she run upstairs and lie down. The jetlag hadn't been quite as bad as Caroline expected, but she was still thankful for the chance to rest her eyes. *When did Mrs. Cho sleep?* she wondered as she spread out on the small mattress on the floor.

Outside her bedroom, she heard the children playing. The older kids were home now from school, and the sound of their happy conversations and laughter was comforting.

Familiar.

Caroline had been surprised by her emotional outburst earlier and was thankful for the chance to spend a few minutes alone. She didn't like to admit it even to herself, but she was also thankful for the chance to take a break from Mrs. Cho's ever-watchful, ever-perceptive presence.

Caroline shut her eyes and let out her breath, her brain heavy with exhaustion. Maybe it was the jet lag after all. Or the fact that her mind was constantly trying to decipher a new language.

Or maybe it was that she was exerting all her mental energy trying not to think of Mrs. Cho's convicting words.

Caroline still couldn't decide if the old woman had been trying to lecture her, encourage her, or preach at her. Maybe it was a combination of all three, but instead of feeling inspired or understood, Caroline came away from their one-way conversation with a sense of total isolation. That was probably the single worst factor about being married to an unbeliever, how alone she felt. The scant times she did make it to one of her church's women's Bible studies, the ladies would share prayer requests like, "Please pray for Max and me because he's been offered a big promotion at work but it would mean less time with the family, and we're really trying to seek God's wisdom." What did women like that know of Caroline's struggles, of the fact that she couldn't even tell her husband she'd sneaked out to join a Bible study without him ranting for a full thirty minutes about how she'd been brainwashed?

"I thought you were smarter." How many times had Calvin yelled something like that to her? Did he think that would win her back over to his side? Did he think it would be constructive at all?

"You've got Jesus now. Guess you don't need me, do you?" He'd spoken those words to her the day he moved out. Secretly, there had been a part of her that wanted to agree with him at the time. To be able to look into the eyes of the man she had once loved and admit, *No, I don't need you. I've lived with you for over thirty years, and you've never been there for me. So, I learned to live and survive and thrive without you.*

The irony was for so many years the biggest problem in their marriage was that Calvin never cared what she did.

Then she became a Christian, and all of a sudden, he cared way too much.

God, I don't know what to do, she admitted as she lay on her back, staring up at the ceiling. *I wish there was something I could do to change him, but I can't.*

Why don't you leave the changing up to Me? The voice that spoke to her was neither audible nor in any other way remarkable. She wasn't overwhelmed with God's presence like she'd been that first Easter Sunday at Pastor Carl and Sandy's church. Yet she knew it was God who was speaking to her.

At first, she wanted to argue. *God, if I'm supposed to leave the changing up to you, why haven't you done anything in Calvin's heart yet?*

But she was silent. Thankful. It was enough to know that God understood her pain, that he sensed her isolation. That he was with her even when it felt like nobody else understood what she was going through.

I trust you, God, she whispered to him in the quietness of her soul.

A knock shattered the illusion of peace and solitude. Mrs. Cho cracked open the door. Her voice was rushed. Almost breathless.

"Your phone... kept ringing... wanted you to get your rest... answered it myself." She stepped into the room, looking diminutive and apologetic.

She knelt by Caroline's mattress. "There's been an accident," she said, gripping Caroline's hand in hers. "A terrible, tragic accident."

Thirty hours later

Drisklay blinked when Carl opened his eyes, and the pastor said "Amen" in his booming voice. This visit was a welcome reprieve from staring at the hospital ceiling. Still, Drisklay wasn't sure the closing prayer was necessary.

Carl clasped Drisklay on his uninjured shoulder. "So, you're gonna be all right? Gonna make a full recovery?"

Drisklay nodded through a drug-induced fog. He felt both heavy and also as if he were floating above himself.

Curious.

"Well, I'm just glad Sandy came by when she did," Carl remarked. "Paramedics said if you'd been on that floor another ten minutes, you would have died. Too much blood loss. I guess that's what happens when you get stabbed multiple times and then shot in the face." He chuckled. "Hey, didn't you ever hear the joke about bringing a knife to a gunfight?"

Very funny, Drisklay wanted to reply, but the bullet wound in his jaw made it all but impossible to speak. Right now, he should probably be thankful to be alive.

Drisklay always knew he'd die on the job. Die serving the people of Boston. After getting shot in his own home, he'd thought his time was up. But he'd been given another chance.

More time.

Some men in his situation would get all poetic, would start musing over the purpose of life, the reality of death. But Drisklay had more pressing matters to worry about right now.

"Rebekah." He had to repeat the name several times before Carl understood.

"You're asking about the case?" Carl let out another chuckle, and Drisklay wondered how it was that this man could always be so cheerful.

He sat down on the stool by Drisklay's hospital bed. "Well, when I came by yesterday, I wasn't sure I was supposed to talk to you about the details, but it's been all over this morning's paper. Harrison confessed everything. Apparently, he didn't want his daughter on that dating website because he had his eye on some man named Taft. I'm afraid you had the honor of meeting him at your residence. It was Taft that Harrison wanted for a future son-in-law, but his daughter had signed up for this Christian dating service, so between the father and the hopeful suitor they hatched up what sounded to them like a great plan.

"Taft was going to create a fake account, talking about all the things he knew Rebekah loved. So of course, by the time he asked her out, she was ecstatic. Now, her dad was into this whole courtship thing. Thought that dating was too modern. So, he decided to kill two birds with one stone, so to speak, and give his daughter a good scare for trying to find a match online and throw her into the arms of Taft, the one he wanted her to end up with in the first place.

"Taft used his fake account to set up a date with Rebekah, then he was going to wear a mask, pretend to kidnap her, and throw her in the trunk of a rental car. After letting her sweat it out for a few minutes, he was going to take off the mask, become his real self, play the hero who saw the whole thing, scared off the bad guy, and saved the girl. And then, boom. They were going to fall in love and live happily ever after.

"Sadly, and this is the part where my heart breaks for everyone involved, he thought it would be a good idea to cover Rebekah's mouth with duct tape before throwing her into the trunk, and somehow she ended up suffocating. Could have been the fear. She hyperventilated and with her mouth covered couldn't get enough air, plus her mom said she'd had a little bit of a stuffy nose too. They're still figuring out the details, but according to Taft's confession, all he did was drive a few miles, and when he opened the trunk, she was dead.

"Well, this is where Daddy gets involved, because Taft wanted to rush to the hospital, but at this point, Harrison knew what a mess they'd both get into, so he made Taft dump her body, swore him to secrecy, and turned a tragic accident into a terrible cover up. What Harrison didn't realize was that this man Taft actually had half a conscience. He went over to Harrison's the night you got shot and tried to urge him again to confess. Harrison wouldn't hear of that, convinced Taft to keep it quiet, and that might have been the end of it. Neither of them realized that Mrs. Harrison overheard enough of their conversation to put two and two together. She called my wife—she knew Sandy and your wife were close. So that's why my Sandy was on her way to your place with Mrs. Harrison so they could tell you everything. Unfortunately, Harrison and Taft realized the cat was about to leap right out of its bag, and they got to you first."

He shook his head. "I didn't want Sandy to go out so late, but she insisted, and you know how stubborn a woman can be when she puts her mind to something."

Drisklay didn't respond.

Carl let out a loud sigh. "Well, I'm just glad you're all right. I mean, I'm sorry you had to get as beat up as you did, but at least you're going to be back on the streets fighting crime before too long, right?"

Maybe it was the drugs, but Drisklay felt magnanimous enough to try to smile. Based on Carl's confused reaction, however, he wasn't sure how well he'd pulled it off.

"I better go," Carl said. "I'm taking Woong to a Red Sox game tonight. I just wanted to stop by and let you know we're all praying for you. No need to get up for me," he joked. "I can let myself out."

Drisklay watched him leave. He'd interacted with Carl long enough to suspect his compassion wasn't just an act, but that flew in the face of everything Drisklay believed about pastors being manipulative con men who only wanted to brainwash their victims and take all their hard-earned money.

Carl was an enigma. A mystery.

Drisklay had always found himself drawn toward a good mystery.

Eighteen

Caroline should have been exhausted. It was hard to calculate exactly how long she'd been awake because of the time zone changes, but she knew it must have been at least thirty hours ago when the cab took her from Mrs. Cho's orphanage to the airport, where she jumped onto the first flight the agent could book for her.

Still, she didn't feel tired. Maybe it was the adrenaline. The same adrenaline that had kept her from resting for even a few minutes on the multiple flights back to the States.

God, you can't let him die. She'd lost track of how many times she'd begged God to spare her husband's life. Sandy's initial phone call had been grim. Shot through the jaw. Over half a dozen stab wounds, one straight to the kidney. Calvin was in shock when the paramedics got there, and even then, it took them quite a while to get him stable enough to transport.

Thank God Sandy had stopped by, or her husband would be dead.

Her husband would be dead...

Caroline had never spent any more time than necessary thinking about the reality of hell. She'd much prefer to focus on God's love and forgiveness and grace, but the stark reality of her husband's situation stared her in the eyes from the moment of that first phone call and refused to back down.

Her husband couldn't die. God would never let that happen.

Would he?

No, he couldn't. Thankfully, each of the updates from the hospital staff was progressively more encouraging. By the time her plane landed in Boston, doctors expected Calvin to make a full recovery.

Eventually.

The word hung in the air like fog over the city skyline. As she hailed a cab, wondering why she'd bothered packing such a big and awkward suitcase, she thought about the rest of the summer.

Another week at the hospital for certain. The doctor had pretty much guaranteed at least that much. Even after the kidney removal and initial jaw reconstruction, there were still a few surgeries to go. Still, several months before Calvin would be ready to return to work. He would be antsy. He would be anxious.

And he would need her.

It wasn't ministering to orphans in Seoul. It wasn't traveling the world for the sake of the gospel. Apparently, God's plans involved nursing her sick and cranky husband back to health.

And she was ready.

"Looks like your kidney is starting to work again." The nurse held up the bag attached to Drisklay's catheter as if the small amount of yellow liquid sloshing around inside it was supposed to make him feel proud.

He scowled. The nurse had no idea how lucky she was that his jaw still made it too painful to talk.

He still couldn't believe what the doctor told him. An entire week? Not just a week before he could be back to work, either. He'd be lucky to be wearing his badge again by the time autumn decided to roll around. No, a week here at the hospital, getting fed through his veins, peeing through a catheter.

Alexi would take over the Rebekah Harrison murder, even though Drisklay had done literally every piece of the investigation and paid for it with his blood, sweat, and one kidney. In addition to losing his organ, Drisklay would have to undergo another surgery to reconstruct his jaw.

Even once he was off the IV, he'd be drinking through a straw, maybe for months. What kind of life was that, anyway?

Then again, at least it was life.

That had to count for something.

Caroline was on her way. The nurse had held up the phone for him while his wife cried into the receiver. "I know we've had our troubles," she'd sniffed, "but I just want to put all that behind us and focus on getting you well."

It was a nice gesture, and probably a necessary one seeing as how there was no way he'd be able to take care of himself once he was discharged. But the truth remained. After his recovery, their problems would be there waiting.

Her faith.

His unbelief.

"It was God who kept you alive," she'd sobbed into the phone. Since his jaw had been shattered by a bullet not twelve hours earlier, he couldn't even argue with her.

It was going to be a long recovery.

The door to his room opened, and the nurse who'd been fidgeting with all his wires and monitors gave a smile. "You must be the missus."

Drisklay wished that he could turn to face his wife, but he had to wait until she stepped into his field of vision. Even over the sound of his annoying monitors, he could hear her tentative steps.

She reached for his hand. "How you doing?" Her voice was soft. Uncertain. He wished he could jump out of his broken body for a moment, just long enough to tell her he was glad she was here.

Yes, she was a nuisance. Yes, the next few weeks would be a bear with him being unable to talk and her keeping him as a captive audience. She'd probably try to shove Bible verses and prayer times down his throat like medicine in his IV.

Even so, he couldn't deny one simple fact.

He was glad to see her.

He was glad she'd come home.

Nineteen

Thirteen weeks later

Autumn was in no apparent hurry to arrive in Massachusetts this year. By the smoldering heat, even though it was nothing compared to the humidity in South Korea, Caroline could have assumed it was smack in the middle of summer vacation, but her calendar told her otherwise.

"You're sure you don't need me to take another week off?" she asked. "The principal already told me I could if we needed."

Calvin stared at her from the couch, mug of coffee in hand. "Do I look like I need a full-time nurse?"

She eyed his flannel pajama pants, his arm hanging in its sling, and gave him a playful smile. "Do you want the real answer to that?"

He grunted.

She inched her way toward him. Better to do it now than to lose her resolve entirely. She'd already texted Sandy, asking her for prayers. Today was the day. How many weeks ago had she resolved to take this next step?

She cleared her throat, and he glanced up from his mug.

"Did you want something?" His voice was brusque, but Caroline wouldn't read too much into that. If she did, she'd lose her courage.

She clenched her fists, hating how slimy they felt when they got sweaty like this. She reminded herself about the good times they'd had lately. She and Calvin together. Watching cop comedies on TV, where he made fun of all the procedural details the script writers got wrong. Explaining how the detectives were all bumbling idiots.

Laughing together.

Not often, but sometimes.

It was a start.

Since Calvin's return from the hospital, they'd only gotten into one fight about church. Actually, no. She couldn't even call it a fight. A snide remark when he found her reading her Bible one afternoon when she thought he was napping.

Nothing too caustic.

Certainly nothing she hadn't heard before.

Things were improving.

Which possibly explained why she was so nervous now.

"Have I grown a set of horns?" he asked sardonically. "Is that why you're staring?"

She blinked and shook her head, trying to clear her mind. "No."

"No, what?"

She sat down in the recliner across from him. Leaned toward him. Sent a silent prayer floating up to heaven.

Knowing she couldn't take this next moment back.

"I had an idea," she began. Where was her courage? Where was the confidence she'd felt when she pictured how she wanted this conversation to go?

"You don't have to say yes," she hastened quickly to add. Too quickly.

This was ridiculous.

She dug into her pockets and pulled out the brochure.

He raised an eyebrow. "Las Vegas?"

The name triggered the argument she'd planned to save until last, but now she was going to run with it. "Remember when you told me about that conference you went to?"

He shook his head.

"We were newlyweds," she explained, hating the way her voice sounded so breathy. "And I was going to go with you, but I had tests for school and couldn't reschedule. But you said you liked it. And that we'd go one day."

He eyed her suspiciously.

"You don't remember?"

Another shake of his head.

She tucked her disappointment deep into the pit of her gut. "That's okay. But listen, Carl knows this guy. He's a marriage counselor. A really good one. And he's got these conferences. They're all over, but I thought that... Well, I mean..."

She licked her lips, forcing herself to stare at the brochure in her husband's hands instead of into his hardened expression. She could do this.

She had to do this.

"I thought that maybe we could go. It's not until spring. You'll be strong by then. Back to yourself, I mean. And I thought after all we've gone through, we could use some time away..."

She paused, studying him as he squinted at the brochure like a lawyer reading the fine print of a two-hundred-page contract.

"We don't have to go," she added softly.

"You say Carl knows him?" he asked. "Carl Lindgren?"

"Yeah. They know each other from seminary. Except he's not a pastor, he's a counselor. And his conferences aren't just for Christians. It's for anybody. They don't talk about God. I actually sent them an email to be sure, because I know we're not at that point yet. But it's supposed to be really beneficial. I read a few testimonies... I mean, I read a few stories. Of people who'd gone and said it was a real blessing... Not a blessing, but a boost. A real boost to their marriage. And it just got me thinking that maybe..."

"Sure." He held the brochure out to her.

She took it with tentative fingers. "Sure?"

"Yeah. Sure." He gave the closest facsimile he could to a shrug after the injury to his shoulder. "Why not?"

"You mean it?" She glanced at the back. Had he seen the part about the cost? "It's not free."

"Do you want to go or not?"

She tried hard not to recoil when he snapped. "I do. I mean, I want to if you do."

Another shrug. "Then let's do it. But you make all the arrangements. And don't try to pinch a few pennies and put me on one of those red-eye flights. They never give you enough coffee on those."

She blinked, trying to force her brain to keep up with this unexpected turn in the conversation. "You really don't mind?" she asked. "You're not doing this just because..."

"Because why?" he interrupted when she hesitated. "Because you've put your life on hold to nurse me back to health? Of course, that's why I'm doing it."

"But you don't mind?" This time her voice was a little stronger. A little more certain.

The faintest inkling of a smile crept onto Calvin's face, rendered slightly off-centered after his reconstructive jaw surgery. "You know why I like watching those TV detective movies, right?"

She wiped her sweaty hands on her pants. "Because you like to make fun of all the writers' mistakes?"

"Besides that." The smile still hadn't completely disappeared, nor had the playfulness in his voice. "Do you know why else I like them?"

"No. Why?"

"Because it's a mystery. Who's the good guy. Who's the bad guy. Sometimes you don't find out until the very last scene."

This time she found the courage to match his smile. "But I thought you had an impeccable sense of intuition."

"I do." This time, there was nothing but seriousness in his tone. "That's why I'm so good at my job. I follow my hunches because they always lead me down the right path."

Caroline still didn't understand what any of this had to do with a marriage conference coming to Las Vegas in over half a year, but her husband looked so happy—at least compared to how he normally appeared—that she tried to keep up the playful banter.

"So, what is your gut telling you about Las Vegas?" she asked.

This time his smile faded. Had she misread his jocularity? Had she stretched out this moment of closeness, of apparent harmony too far?

"I don't know what my gut's telling me about Vegas," he replied, "but I know what it's telling me about you."

This time, Caroline couldn't read his expression. He was back to his closed, stoic self. She bit her lip, trying to swallow her disappointment, bury it deep down where it couldn't resurface. Couldn't steal her peace anymore.

Calvin set down his mug and sat up a little in his seat. "Right now, my gut's telling me that you should hate me. That you should despise me and resent the fact that you wasted your entire summer and the first two weeks out of your school year babying me. But you don't," he added before Caroline could protest.

"And that," he concluded, with just the hint of that momentary playfulness, "is a mystery to me. I have a few hypotheses I'm working on. Maybe you're just addicted to punishment, like one of those battered wives. Or maybe you're trying to earn your brownie points with God."

Caroline tried to interrupt, but he held up his hand. "I'm still trying to figure it out," he admitted. "You'd think that after all these years, you would have stopped being a mystery to me. But you haven't."

A warmness crept into his eyes. It was gone in an instant. One blink, one fraction of a second and it vanished.

Had it actually been there to begin with, or had Caroline made the moment up?

"You're a mystery to me," her husband admitted, reaching out his hand. At first, she thought he meant to take hers, and she was afraid he'd be disgusted by her sweaty palm.

Instead, he picked his mug back up, took a sip of his cold, double strength coffee, then confessed, "And you know me, Caroline. I'm always drawn toward a good mystery."

The End

Questions

1. What are some of the specific struggles a Christian faces if married to a non-Christian?

2. Why do you think Calvin was so opposed to adoption? How would a child have impacted their marriage struggles?

3. Who was someone instrumental in either bringing you to Christ or deepening your walk with him?

4. If you could spend your summer on a short-term mission trip, where would you go and what would you do?

5. Imagine you are Caroline's friend. What one piece of advice would you give her on days when her marriage has her particularly discouraged?

About

Alana Terry is a pastor's wife, homeschooling mom, self-diagnosed chicken lady, and Christian suspense author. Her novels have won awards from Women of Faith, Book Club Network, Grace Awards, Readers' Favorite, and more. Alana's passion for social justice, human rights, and religious freedom shines through her writing, and her books are known for raising tough questions without preaching. She and her family live in rural Alaska where the northern lights in the winter and midnight sun in the summer make hauling water, surviving the annual mosquito apocalypse, and cleaning goat stalls in negative forty degrees worth every second.

Newsletter:	www.alanaterry.com/readers-club
Website:	www.alanaterry.com
BookBub:	bookbub.com/authors/alana-terry
Facebook:	facebook.com/groups/126407717925552/
Instagram:	instagram.com/explore/tags/alanaterry/
Twitter:	twitter.com/search?q=Author%20Alana%20Terry
Goodreads:	goodreads.com/author/show/7048073.Alana_Terry

North Korea Suspense Novels

The Beloved Daughter

Slave Again

Torn Asunder

Flower Swallow

Orchard Grove Christian Women's Fiction

Beauty from Ashes

Before the Dawn

Sweet Dreams Christian Romance

What Dreams May Come

Kennedy Stern Christian Suspense Novels

Book 1: Unplanned

Book 2: Paralyzed

Book 3: Policed

Book 4: Straightened

Book 5: Turbulence

Book 6: Infected

Book 7: Abridged

And many more titles...

Introducing

Dear Reader,

The Christian life isn't easy. Being married to an unbeliever can be especially hard, just like you read in *Seoul Refuge*.

For more suspense featuring Caroline and Calvin and their spiritual journey together, grab a copy of *Save Me Once*, Book One in the brand-new *Safe Refuge* Christian Thriller series. These suspense novels bring you more of Calvin and Caroline and introduce you to a new cast of supporting characters Calvin helps as a detective.

A single mom whose daughter goes missing, a teen girl who realizes too late what kind of man her boyfriend really is—these are the people you will meet in the Safe Refuge Christian Thriller novels.

Fans of suspense and mysteries love diving into the adventure, while romance and women's lit readers love to follow Caroline and Calvin as they navigate the waters of a spiritually mismatched marriage.

Start this brand-new series now with Book One, *Save Me Once*. Get your copy today at this link:

readerlinks.com/l/397449

I hope you've enjoyed this bundle so far. One of the things I love most about the Crossroad Collection novels is that it gives me a perfect excuse to hang out with some of my favorite Christian fiction authors.

Carol Moncado's novel is up next. If you like royal characters, craft conventions, and quirky cats, you're going to love this one!

ALANA TERRY
Author of *Seoul Refuge*

GUARDIAN OF HER *Heart*

By

Carol Moncado

USA Today Bestselling Author

Published by

CANDID
Publications

Copyright Notice

Spring sometimes came early to the Missouri Ozarks, but rarely stayed long.

Mark Bertolini found himself wishing the warmer temperatures of Tuesday and Wednesday had lasted through the weekend. Instead, he put on his warm coat, gloves, and knit cap before going outside to double check perimeter security. At least only a couple more days of this were in the forecast. Monday was supposed to warm up again, leaving only the weekend as a return to winter.

Not that he had regular weekends.

A voice crackled over the radio in his ear. "Mark, the queen wants to talk to you when you finish your rounds."

"I'll be about twenty minutes," he told Brian, his second-in-command.

He didn't hurry through his surveillance of the grounds, but Mark made sure he didn't dawdle either. When the queen wanted to see you, you made sure you'd done your job properly then hurried to see her.

Mark made his way to the main house, the one he'd lived in with the queen for years.

He mentally adjusted the thought. He and Todd had been Crown Princess Adeline's bodyguards all the way through her years at Serenity Landing University.

That's when he'd fallen in love with a woman he could never have.

He'd known that all along, but the final nail came when then-Crown Princess Adeline met Charlie, a single father from Serenity Landing. She'd literally run into him with her car on an icy January evening.

The rest, as they say, was history.

He'd spent the better part of her first year as queen as part of her secondary detail, with the Monarch's Protection Detail taking over as primary. After she and Charlie announced that she was expecting their first child, Mark decided the time had come for a change. When the opening came available, he applied to be head of security at the queen's residence in the States. The job had since expanded to include security for a number of other homes in the neighborhood, all belonging to royalty with ties to the Serenity Landing area for one reason or another.

Mark went into the house to find Queen Adeline putting a small package into her handbag in the foyer.

"Good morning, Your Majesty." Mark bowed at the waist, more than he was required to do, but a simple incline of the head didn't seem like enough.

She sighed. "You'll never call me Addie again, will you, Mark?"

He shook his head. "No, ma'am."

"I miss those days sometimes, you know. Where it was the three of us here, and I didn't have the responsibilities I do now."

"You wouldn't trade the life you have now for the life you had then." He'd known her better than just about anyone.

"You're right. I wouldn't trade my life with Charlie and the children, but I do miss the anonymity sometimes."

She sighed, then turned, a bright smile on her face and a twinkle in her eye. "Do you remember the time we watched that late night special on the 1970s?"

Mark shook his head. "Not really."

The queen pulled something out of her purse. "An ad for one of those online dating sites came on. We joked about it, and you said if you were still single at thirty, you'd consider one."

Right. That conversation he remembered.

"Don't think I forgot your birthday." She held out the envelope. "Or the conversation."

He took it from her. "You didn't need to get me anything, ma'am."

"Regardless, take it." She shoved it toward him.

Mark took the envelope and slipped his finger under the flap. It opened easily. "A membership for Betwixt Two Hearts? What's that?"

"It's a new online dating service. They sounded intriguing when I heard about it. I remembered the conversation and signed you up. You'll need to fill out the questionnaire, but I expect you to do so this week." She gave him a mock glare. "As your boss, I can make that an order."

"That won't be necessary." He turned the informational card over in his hand. "I'll do it." Maybe he'd at least get a couple of dates out of the deal. Evenings away from work wouldn't be a bad thing.

"Good."

Lindsey, Charlie's daughter, bounded into the room. Now a teenager herself, she'd grown into a lovely young woman. "Addie, Dad says he's ready when you are."

"I'll be right there."

The teen bounced back out of the entry.

Mark smiled after her. "How are you going to survive a plane ride with a kid with that much energy?"

"She'll settle down and play with her little brother or something. It'll be fine."

"Good."

Queen Adeline picked up her purse. "It was good seeing you, Mark." She nodded toward the envelope. "I expect a report on how that goes next time I see you."

"Yes, ma'am."

With that, she was gone. Mark went back to his office at the house next door and went to the website listed on the card. He used the login information given to create his own profile and spent over an hour going through the questions.

He held out little hope that this website, as different as it claimed to be, would help him find a woman he wanted to take out more than once or twice.

As he read through the information on the website, he realized the queen had signed him up for the most expensive of the options. He would, allegedly, be getting a match made just for him by someone in an office somewhere comparing his answers to someone else's and deciding they're compatible. He opted to use the computer-generated matches, at least at first.

Once he downloaded the app to his phone, he decided that was good enough for the night. He checked in with the night crew then went to bed expecting less than nothing to come from this insane idea of the queen's.

But at least he could tell her he tried.

Casey Smithton flopped back onto her bed, her phone in one hand as the other covered her face. "You've got to be kidding me."

"Nope." Her best friend's voice echoed across a poor connection. "We're moving to Alaska."

Casey knew it was an amazing opportunity for Rachel's husband, a conservationist, but she hadn't thought the job would actually come through. After all, Joss was fresh out of college with no experience. Maybe that's why he got the job. No one with experience wanted to move to the Alaskan outback. No one sane anyway.

It also meant Casey was without a job and a place to live.

Rachel's CHUVsy shop also employed Casey and was run out of Rachel's old bedroom in Casey's two-bedroom apartment. CHUVsy was the newest, and almost biggest, online site where Custom, Handmade, Unique, and Vintage items were sold. When Rachel married Joss, she'd moved across the complex, but the business stayed. Rachel's half of the rent was the only way Casey could afford the place.

"Think about it. You could do your yarn full time again." Rachel, like always, tried to put the best spin on things. "You loved that."

"But it never gave me a full-time income." And she'd sort of lost interest over the last couple of years.

"Well, no, but it's not like the CHUVsy shop is going anywhere."

"The CHUVsy shop you run, where you make the stuff, and I handle the other details, isn't moving to Alaska with you?"

"Yes, and no. I won't be able to do custom orders without a lot longer lead time and shipping, so I'm thinking I'll do the premade stuff and ship you a box once a week. You can fulfill orders from that. I'll still pay you. Just like always, only we won't be together is all."

"It's not the same, Rach."

"I know, but Joss can't pass this up." Dishes clanked together on the other end of the line. "Look at it this way. You can travel more. You'll have to drive because you'd have to take the stock with you, but you can do the shipping from anywhere. You've always wanted to travel. Maybe go to those yarn shows you always talked about."

She'd only been to one, but it had felt like she'd found her people. Younger than the average attendee, Casey still felt at home. She'd learned to knit from her grandmother and had loved it ever since. Casey wanted to spend more time doing it, but it didn't pay the bills. She still loved knitting, but her passion for being active in that community didn't buy food or gas.

"One other thing." Rachel sounded hesitant for the first time in the conversation.

"What?"

"I'm not going to be able to attend the craft show in Serenity Landing."

Casey groaned. "Anything but that."

"There's a wool and yarn expo section of the show. It's near that one company you love. Maybe they'll be there."

"Show Me Yarn." They did great work. Casey loved their yarn colors.

"Please." Rachel turned to begging. "And I'll even pay for a couple of months of that Betwixt membership. The premium one."

Ever since Rachel met Joss through an online dating app a year earlier, she'd been after Casey to do the same. She'd tried a couple different ones but hadn't found anyone she wanted to see again. Betwixt Two Hearts was the latest of the apps. After a few horrible dates, with men she could admit likely looked like a good match on paper, Casey gave up.

Rachel hadn't.

"Fine, I'll go. But no need for the fancy matches. The computer-generated ones are fine." Give it one more shot then tell Rachel to stick it.

"One more thing."

Of course there was. "What?"

"I need you to keep Bruce for me for a bit."

"I don't want your cat," Casey groaned.

"I can't take him until we're settled. Hopefully, just a month. Maybe two. Then you can come visit and bring him with you."

Casey sighed. Rachel knew she would say yes. She always did. "Fine."

For the next week, Casey spent her time helping Rachel with the CHUVsy shop and packing. She put off reactivating her Betwixt account as long as she could, but Rachel insisted it be done before she left. Casey updated her profile, arranged for Mrs. Christian to look after Bruce for her, loaded the van, and started for Serenity Landing and the craft show.

After hugging Rachel and Joss goodbye as they started on their first grand adventure since the wedding.

Casey's trip didn't go quite as well, but she made it to Serenity Landing after a day of driving where detours and road construction made a seven-hour trip take closer to twelve.

She pulled into the Serenity Landing Lodge parking lot at 8:30 in the evening, grateful she'd forced herself to get on the road earlier than she really wanted to. Otherwise, she wouldn't have arrived until nearly midnight.

When she finally checked into her room, she looked at the Betwixt app again. She'd set her destination in the settings. That allowed the algorithm to look not just where she was but where she would be.

There was one potential match, but Casey was too tired from the trip to do anything about it. She'd look in the morning. Maybe. If she had the energy after emptying the van by herself. She'd helped Rachel with these shows before but had never done one by herself.

Casey just hoped she could wait until the designated breaks to need the bathroom.

With the phone between his shoulder and his ear, Mark clicked a few times on the website. "Todd, I'm telling you. Security is fine. I don't need

Mr. Langley-Cranston for backup."

"The queen insists. Says you need a break."

"I've already had a break," Mark muttered.

Todd laughed. "I heard you had a date last night."

"The queen bought me a six-month membership to some dating site. I made a good faith effort, I really did, but it was a disaster."

Todd had been his fellow security guard while the queen spent her college years in Serenity Landing. For six years, they'd been nearly inseparable.

But Todd hadn't fallen in love with the woman they were protecting. He'd found a young woman almost as soon as they returned home for good. They'd been married nearly two years, and she was expecting their first child.

Reminding Mark again of what he still didn't have.

"What happened?"

Mark leaned back in his chair. "On paper, I can see how we'd have been a good match, but in person, we just didn't click. She's never been to Europe and has no desire to go. The fact that I'm not an American, and I might want to return to Montevaro someday, even for a visit, was too much."

"Ouch."

"It might not have been too bad, if not for that, but she asked about my accent almost immediately, so in ten minutes, we both knew it wasn't going to work out. Then it got awkward and stayed that way."

"So, you're not going on a second date with that woman, but what about someone else?"

"It was my fifth date that went basically the same way. I have no idea if they've found me another match or not. I might give it one more shot, but I'm not holding out a lot of hope."

"Go into it with an open mind." Todd hesitated. "She won't be Addie, but I bet you can find an amazing woman out there who's perfect for you."

Todd never referred to the queen so informally, which meant he'd known far more about Mark's feelings than Mark realized. "I'll figure it out." His cell phone buzzed in his pocket. "I've got to go."

"Jonathan's crew will be over in an hour."

"Great. Thanks." Mark hung up, muttering to himself about not needing someone else looking over his shoulder as he picked up his cell phone.

A match.

He thought he'd told Betwixt they couldn't send him push alerts. He'd have to change that later. He opened the app anyway and skimmed through the profile.

On paper, this match didn't seem as good as the last one. She'd never traveled much. Said she wanted to but was apprehensive and finances were often an issue. The last woman said she loved to travel - in the lower 48 only, and then only to places with nice weather, but she hadn't mentioned that part.

After that, he'd decided to ditch the computer matches and go for the personal touch.

This new woman had semi-steady income working for a friend's CHUVsy shop. Her answers to the open-ended questions were long-winded, run-on sentences, but properly punctuated.

Something seemed off about the match and yet... the longer Mark looked at her picture, the more he wanted to at least talk to her.

He accepted the recommendation and put his phone away. Some things needed doing before Jonathan's team arrived. Not many, but a few.

His phone pinged with an incoming Betwixt app message.

> **CASEY:** HI. I KNOW YOU LIKE JUST ACCEPTED THIS POTENTIAL MATCH OR WHATEVER IT IS, BUT I'M FROM OUT OF TOWN, AND YOU'RE LOCAL, AND I COULD REALLY USE A HAND. PUBLIC LOCATION. ALL THAT. DON'T EVEN NEED YOUR PHONE NUMBER, IF YOU'RE NOT COMFORTABLE WITH IT, BUT I'M KIND OF OUT OF OPTIONS.

So, she wanted money. Great.

> **CASEY:** NO MONEY.

That made him feel a smidge better.

> **CASEY:** WELL, NOT REALLY.

So, she did need money.

> **CASEY:** WHAT I REALLY NEED IS A CAT CRATE AND SOME CAT
> FOOD.

They'd set him up with a crazy cat lady?

> **CASEY:** I'M HERE FOR THE SERENITY LANDING CRAFT FESTIVAL,
> AND MY BEST FRIEND'S CAT STOWED AWAY IN MY VAN.

Mark didn't even know what to do with that information.

> **CASEY:** I KNOW YOU DON'T KNOW ME FROM ADAM - OR EVE AS
> THE CASE MAY BE - BUT IF THERE'S ANY WAY YOU COULD HELP
> ME GET SUPPLIES FOR THIS STUPID CAT, I'D APPRECIATE IT. YOU
> CAN DELETE MY PROFILE AND THE MATCH AND WHATEVER ELSE
> AFTERWARD, BUT MY BEST FRIEND ABSOLUTELY ADORES THIS
> CAT - HER HUSBAND GAVE HIM TO HER - AND SHE'D JUST DIE IF
> ANYTHING HAPPENED TO HIM.

Mark was not a cat person. Not even a little bit. He liked dogs. Big,
manly dogs. Working dogs.
He hadn't even replied yet.
After waiting a minute to see if she was done, he messaged her back.

> **MARK:** WHERE ARE YOU? I'LL SEE WHAT I CAN DO. I CAN'T
> LEAVE FOR AN HOUR OR SO THOUGH.

She messaged back her location and implored him to hurry because the
show was starting soon, and she needed to set up.
Maybe he could start with a crate and water. Wasn't there a dog crate
around here? From when Princess Anastasia and her husband, Dr. Jonah
Fonataine, came to visit with their daughter and her dog? That and a bowl
with water would be a good start.
Maybe he could find someone who had a clue what to do with cats
before he made it to the Pond Creek County Convention Center.

"Problem, boss?"

Mark looked over at Brian, his local second-in-command. "A new friend of mine..." Mark sighed then shook his head. "I'm not even sure I believe it." He explained.

Brian laughed. "Go get what you need and go on. We've got this covered."

With a last glance around, Mark went to the garage and found the dog crate with a water dish inside.

He messaged Casey to let her know he was able to get away from work sooner than expected and was on his way.

When he reached the convention center, he drove around until he found the white van parked near a loading zone. He managed to snag a spot nearby and grabbed the crate.

"Casey?" he called, walking around and looking for the woman in the picture.

"Oh good! There you are. You must be Mark."

Her voice didn't sound anything like he expected and when he turned, he realized her photo had been a lie as well.

This woman wasn't a late-twenty-something with pretty blue eyes. She had to be at least seventy.

Two

After putting the last storage tub down in the booth area, Casey hurried back to the loading dock but stopped short when she saw Mrs. Bateman talking to one of the most handsome men she'd ever seen in her life.

Could that be Mark? If so, his photo on the Betwixt app didn't do him justice.

"Oh, there you are, darling!" Mrs. Bateman turned, still cuddling Bruce. "This young man says he brought a carrier and bowl for water for this kitty."

"Thank you for watching him for me, Mrs. Bateman." Casey trotted down the stairs. "I've got everything in there now. I need to move the van."

The man turned and smiled. "You must be Casey." He set down the pet carrier and held out a hand. "Mark."

She took it and warmth spread through her. Not a spark or electricity but warmth. "It's nice to meet you. Thank you so much for your help."

He stared straight into her eyes. "It's my pleasure." He broke the contact. "I happened to have a crate and bowl handy so thought I'd bring those over right away so you'd have somewhere to put him while I figure out what else he needs. Unless you have a list?" He seemed hopeful.

"Maybe." She pulled her keys out of her pocket. "Let me move the van. I'll be right back."

Mark held out his hand. "Let me, and you can get the cat settled."

She handed over the keys. "Thanks."

Mark drove off. She turned to Mrs. Bateman. "Thanks for holding him."

"Oh, it's no trouble at all." She scritched under his chin. "I love cats."

Casey was glad someone did. She tolerated Bruce because of Rachel, but she'd never love him like her friend did.

"Mark is cute," Mrs. Bateman whispered. "I like him."

She hadn't told Mrs. Bateman how she knew Mark. "Thanks."

Mrs. Bateman went back inside as Casey put Bruce into the crate and poured some water from a bottle into the bowl. She didn't start with much. He'd been in the back of her van, hiding underneath everything for over thirty-six hours by the time she found him. Too much, too fast would be bad, right? She'd see how he tolerated it then give him a little more in a while.

Mark returned as she latched the crate shut.

"I can't thank you enough." Casey took her keys back from him. "I can get you a list of what I need from the store, but my cash is in my bag." She blew out a breath. "But I think I buried it when I took everything in. I need to get it all set up and organized. I'll find it then. I don't suppose you know a good vet in the area I could ask a couple of questions?" Casey bit her bottom lip as she looked up at him.

Mark smiled, a more genuine smile than she'd received earlier. "I don't know one personally, but I'm sure I know someone who does. In fact, I have a phone meeting with a local friend in about half an hour and can ask him for a recommendation. He has a dog and a vet his wife loves. I know that much. I can ask him." He crouched down and looked inside the crate. "Do you not have a vet back home you can call?"

"Do you mind if we move this conversation inside? I need to get unpacked. I only have a couple hours before the show starts."

"Of course." Mark picked up the crate before she could. "I have a few minutes to help if you'd like. I have that phone meeting, but then I can go to the store. I'll bring back whatever you need."

Casey glanced up as they walked into the main room of the convention center. "You'd do that for me?"

Mark smiled at her again. "Turns out my boss thought I'd been working too hard, so she made arrangements to have my workload lightened for a couple weeks. I'm not completely off work - I rarely am - but I shouldn't be quite as busy for a while."

Never completely off work? Casey wasn't sure how she felt about that if Mark was a potential relationship candidate.

"Well, thank you. I appreciate it."

His phone buzzed as they reached her booth. The one she was manning without Rachel for the first time.

Mark pulled it out. "Jonathan asked if we could move our meeting up to right now. Do you mind if I take this call then we get the rest figured out? I should be off the rest of the day."

Casey nodded. "Go ahead. Thank you." Like she'd tell him no, that he couldn't do his job because he needed to be helping her instead.

After setting the crate down inside her booth area, Mark smiled and headed back for the door, already typing away on his phone.

With a sigh, she began moving display shelves into place. Once they were situated, she opened tubs of completed crafts and filled the squares. The cloth buckets that had come with the shelves would be filled with craft kits and placed on the tables. Samples needed to be hung up.

And Bruce meowed the whole time. Every so often, she gave him some more water. He lapped it up quickly but showed no ill effects.

When she'd first found him huddled in the only empty square out of the three display shelves, Casey knew he'd been there since she loaded up two nights earlier. He couldn't have moved into the square since then.

Why he hadn't thrown a fit, she'd never know, but she hadn't heard a single cat-like peep the whole time she drove.

Fortunately, the organizers were very understanding. They didn't have any immediate solutions but said they'd do their best to help however they could. Mrs. Bateman had been helping her daughter set up in the next booth when she'd overheard the conversation and offered to cat sit while Casey finished unloading her van.

And Betwixt had sent her a local match.

She doubted anything would come of this potential relationship with Mark, but at least he'd been able to help her this morning, so there was that. She'd take whatever small favors she could get.

Mark didn't want to discuss his potential love life with Jonathan, but it seemed he had little choice. "I just met her. She found her cat had stowed away in her van. She asked if I knew a local vet. I'm asking you."

"But *how* did you meet her if she just drove in from out of town?" Jonathan's natural curiosity wouldn't let it go.

With a sigh, Mark told him the truth. "The queen signed me up for a dating app. This woman was matched with me this morning. As soon as I accepted the ability to message, she sent me one asking for help with this dumb cat."

"Better not let her hear you say that." Jonathan's grin could be heard in his tone.

"I don't know her well enough to know if I care if she hears me or not."

"Don't shoot yourself in the foot is all I'm saying. I'll send you the number of our vet. Tell them I sent you, and they'll make sure you're taken care of."

Knowing people with money had its perks. Places like veterinarian's offices tended to give them a little better treatment since they knew money was no object. That wasn't to say they treated the rest of their patients poorly, but Mark suspected Jonathan would be able to get in on a moment's notice easier than some others.

"Thanks. Do you have any idea what a cat would need?"

"Nope. I had to ask them for a list when I found Mr. Benny."

The small Shorkie had been scared to death after being dumped in the woods. Or so the story went. Mark had heard it from Jonathan's adopted step-daughter many times.

"Maybe they can help me out, too. Casey said she'd send me a list, but there's a chance she could miss something for a cat that's been hiding out in her van for several hundred miles."

"Are you going to ask her out?"

Why must everyone want to know so much about his life? "I haven't decided yet."

"Understood." The hidden chuckle in Jonathan's voice meant Mark was more transparent than he wanted to be.

Of course, he was going to ask her out. Otherwise, the queen would wonder why. At least if they went out once, he could tell his boss they just hadn't clicked.

After ending his call with Jonathan, Mark went back inside. As expected, the call just confirmed what Mark already knew. Security was tight. Jonathan's men would supplement his for the next few weeks to give his men a much-needed break after the royal family had spent two weeks in Serenity Landing.

Back inside, Mark reoriented himself. Casey's booth was in the back middle-ish. It didn't take him long to find it.

"How'd your phone meeting go?" she asked as she hung an Easter cross stitch up then moved back to look at it critically. The only reason Mark knew it was a cross stitch was the note attached to it.

"Fine. Easy. Just like expected." He looked at his phone. "And I have the number for a vet in town. My friend said to give them his name, and they'd make sure Mr. Cat is taken care of."

"His name is Bruce."

"Okay. They'll make sure Bruce the Cat is taken care of."

"His name is Bruce the Bat, actually." Casey moved the cross stitch to the other side of the booth. "Two guesses who he's named after. He's not mine. I don't know how much money my best friend would be willing to spend if he's not quite okay."

"Don't worry about that just yet. Why don't I call them, and if they can work him in, I'll take him over? See what they say and go from there?"

She nodded. "Thank you for taking care of it." Her attention was more on the display than their conversation. Judging from the preparedness of the booths around them, she was running behind.

"What can I do to help you get ready?" That was when he realized the shelves on the tables hadn't been there before. She'd lifted them by herself. She likely didn't need his help at all.

"If you could start putting the lids back on the tubs and organizing them under the tables, that would be great."

Okay. He could handle that.

By the time he was finished, Casey had completed whatever task she had set for herself. "Thanks." She glanced at her watch. "I have fifteen minutes before we open. Would you mind watching the booth while I go to the bathroom? I won't have a chance for hours once people come in."

"Sure." Not for hours? Was she working this booth by herself? What about Mrs. Bateman? He'd thought they were together. Or did they require two people to be there at all times?

While she was gone, Mark called the vet. Unfortunately, even name-dropping Jonathan Langley-Cranston didn't help much. They had a doctor and tech call in sick and were already overloaded, but they'd see the cat about six that evening. Mark suspected they wouldn't have offered that much if it weren't for Jonathan's name.

When Casey returned, there were five minutes to go. Mark explained the situation with the vet.

With her hands on her hips, Casey surveyed the booth. "Okay. We finish at five today. I can go to the vet after that. Can you message me the address?"

Mark pulled out his phone. "I can text it to you." Except he didn't have her number. "If you don't mind giving me your phone number."

Casey shook her head and rattled off the digits faster than he could keep up. After repeating it twice, Mark sent the information.

When Casey smiled at him, he felt his heart skip a beat. She was attractive, sure, but there hadn't been the sparks he'd heard others talk about. Just a warmth, a comfortable feeling, he wasn't certain how to define.

He glanced at his watch as the doors on the other end of the convention center opened. Noon. He didn't have anywhere he needed to be.

"So, Casey, why don't I stick around for a while and help you out?" He couldn't believe he was offering to stay, but he found himself unable to leave.

It seemed he'd do almost anything to spend some time with the pretty craft shop owner and her stowaway cat.

Three

Whatever Casey had expected from Mark, staying to help her with the booth wasn't part of it. She'd gladly take his assistance though.

"Do you want to give me a crash course on all of this?" he asked. "Tell me what I need to know."

"You'll never remember all of it," she warned.

"No, but I'm usually pretty good at absorbing information quickly when I need to. It's part of my job."

"What do you do?"

"I can tell you, but then I'd have to kill you." He actually winked at her as he said it.

Casey laughed. "Seriously?"

He seemed to hesitate before answering. "I'm in security. I manage properties for several families who have homes in the area but want to keep them safe and remain under the radar as much as possible when they're here."

She blinked. That wasn't the answer she expected. "Are you even allowed to tell people that?"

"I can't tell you who, not at this point, but I can tell you that much. If you follow the news in the area at all, you could make some educated guesses. You might be right, but you might not."

Casey's eyes narrowed. She'd figure it out. "If I guess, will you tell me?"

Mark looked toward the ceiling as he thought it over. "If you just start guessing, no. If you have a rational basis for why you think so, then yes, I'll tell you if you're right or not."

"First question then. Where's your accent from?"

That made him chuckle. "Nope. Not telling you that part."

"Fine."

Customers had begun streaming into the convention center. Most started at the front booths and worked their way back, but a few decided to start at the back and work their way forward. Casey's booth was far enough back that the ones who did that were starting to get to them.

The first woman walked into the booth and began to look around. Casey smiled at her. "Good morning. How are you today?"

"I'm good."

Mark moved toward the back of the booth, out of the way, while Casey talked with the woman and several others who came after her. They each bought something. Mark surprised her by working the tablet and card reader, smiling and talking with each of them.

As soon as the small rush cleared, she checked on Bruce and gave him some more water.

"Thank you for your help, but you don't have to stay," she told Mark as the next potential customer walked up.

"I don't mind." He smiled that real smile at her, the one she decided she liked.

"Thank you. I promise I'll buy you lunch to help make up for it."

"That's not necessary but thank you."

Before she could insist, the customer asked her a question. That was followed by another customer, and though not everyone bought something, it was after noon before she really had a chance to talk to Mark again.

She had noticed him keeping an eye on Bruce in between ringing up customers for her. After a while, he also did some upselling and was quite good at it. He smiled at the older women and charmed them. The younger women, those who might possibly be interested in him, he treated with more reserve, but still made them feel special.

Whatever he did in his regular life, he was a born salesman as well.

Casey had found her bag when she set everything up. As classes started and the crowd cleared out some, she pulled twenty bucks out of it. She held it out toward Mark. "I can't offer you some five-course meal, but there's a food court on the other end of the room if you want to grab yourself something."

He crossed his arms over his chest. "I know this isn't really a first date, but it's on me. I can either get something for you and bring it back, or you can go when I'm done. Your choice."

"Cheeseburger if they have it. Pretzel with cheese if they don't."

"And to drink."

"Pepsi if they have it. Dr Pepper if they don't. Coke only if they have neither."

"Got it."

With that, Mark walked off. She watched him go and wondered what made the man tick. Who would spend their day helping a woman matched to him by a dating app? Why didn't he have more pressing things to do, like watching over those properties?

Mrs. Bateman had been helping her daughter with her booth, but with the crowds dissipating she stopped by to check on Bruce.

"That young man of yours is causing quite the stir," she told Casey.

"He's not my young man," she told Mrs. Bateman for the eighteenth time. At least. "He's a friend. That's all." At least for now. They needed a date or two, at a bare minimum, to see if there would be more.

"If you say so." She pulled Bruce out of the crate. "Did you talk to a veterinarian yet?"

"Mark did. We're doing the right things until we can get to the store or someone can bring some food."

Mrs. Bateman shoved Bruce at Casey. "Let me make a phone call. I know a lovely young woman who runs a cat rescue not too far from here. She may be able to help. Eden Animal Haven is a wonderful organization."

Before Casey could thank her, a customer wandered into the booth.

"Is that the cat?" she asked, her eyes lighting up. "In four of the last six booths I was at, I heard about a cat who stowed away."

When she turned a little more, Casey could see a cat on her shirt and a shoulder bag with cats all over the fabric.

"That's him," Casey told her with a laugh. "I didn't know he'd become famous."

"Oh, yes. He's the talk of the convention, I think." The woman ran her hand over Bruce's head a few times then turned to the booth. "Let's see what you've got."

By the time Mark returned with their food, she'd sold items to three more women, all of whom had heard about the Craft Convention Cat as Bruce was coming to be called.

But when the local news station wanted to do a story about him, she was pretty sure this was going to be the biggest weekend she and Rachel ever had.

When Mark returned with their lunches, Casey and Bruce were being interviewed by the local news station. He stayed far enough back that there wasn't a chance he'd be caught on camera. It wasn't part of his job to be in front of them anymore. It never was, but when the queen was a princess, and he was on her primary team, sometimes he'd be caught escorting her in or out of a location or while working a crowd.

He wanted to stay out of the limelight. At an out of the way table, he set her food down then ate his own.

When they finished and packed up their gear, Mark took her food to the booth. Casey put Bruce back in the crate.

"Oh, my goodness!" She reached for the burger. "Thank you! I didn't get a chance to eat breakfast this morning. I'm starving."

While she scarfed down her food, Mark tried to reorganize some of the cubbies to look fuller than they really were.

"There's more stock in the buckets," she told him. "Rachel's been working to get ready for this show for months. We've got plenty."

"What will you do with the rest?" he asked as he pulled one of the buckets out.

"She has an CHUVsy store that most of it will go into."

A note of sadness entered her voice, making Mark turn. "Why isn't

Rachel here? Was she unable to come at the last minute?"

Casey wiped her mouth on her napkin. "She and her husband moved to Alaska last week. I'm her continental US marketer now." She explained to him how they'd met in college and become roommates. When Rachel's CHUVsy business took off, Casey began helping her while she finished her Masters' degree in Business Administration, though her first love was marketing.

"Is there a reason why you two didn't become partners in the business?" He looked up from his crouched position as he put one of the tubs back under the table.

"What do you mean? Rachel's the crafty one. I just do the photography and shipping."

He stood and leaned against the back table, stretching his legs out in front of him. "It sounds like you do a lot of her marketing already. She pays you by the hour or piece or whatever, but to me, it sounds almost like you do half the work, just not the creative side of things."

"Not the crafty side anyway. I do the social media posts and banners, things like that. Graphic design type stuff, mostly." He watched the thoughts turn over in her head. "I guess I always thought of it as Rachel's company, and I help her out. The company isn't mine. It never was. Becoming official business partners never crossed my mind."

Mark decided it wasn't the time or place to press the issue. It worked for the two of them, though from the little Casey told him, it sounded like she did far more than a normal employee would in a two-person business.

In the last few hours, he'd learned more about needlepoint and other crafts than he'd ever expected to know. He hadn't been wrong in what he told Casey though. He was able to pick up what he needed to know and retain it pretty well.

The afternoon rush began to pick up, so Mark went back to his job of running the tablet register. It surprised him that Casey so quickly trusted him with the money side of things. He knew he was trustworthy, but did she? If she was too trusting, that could be an issue if they were to try a relationship. He'd have to tell her who he worked for before too long, but if she trusted that information to anyone and everyone, that would really be a problem.

If she was just relieved, she didn't have to do this alone and made a choice to trust him based on some algorithm or person in a cubicle somewhere deciding they should be matched up and her own gut feeling, that might be a little different.

Maybe.

Something they'd need to discuss.

Before he knew it, the afternoon session ended.

The minute she could close down, Casey grabbed the tablet and cash box. "Can you grab Bruce and send me directions to that vet?"

"I'll take you. You'll have a hard time finding it, even with your phone helping you."

"Thanks."

Customers had been cleared out of the convention center, but a few people he knew called to him, and almost everyone wished them luck at the vet.

Once outside, he took Bruce from Casey. He opened the passenger door for her then stowed the crate in the middle seats.

As they drove, he pointed out sites he thought she might find interesting, though there weren't many. They did cross a branch of Serenity Lake to get to Trumanville. A couple of miles outside Trumanville was the Pond Creek County Vet Clinic. Inside, the slate tile and cold fireplace couldn't offset the feeling of warmth he felt just walking in.

"Is this the famous Bruce?" the receptionist asked. "We just saw you on the news."

"Already?" Mark glanced at his watch. It was after six by the time they'd made it out there.

"Yep. Let's weigh Bruce, and we'll get him checked out."

Bruce seemed a lot more lethargic than he probably should be, but he let himself be weighed. A minute later, they found themselves in a room with the vet and one of her techs.

She ran her hands over Bruce and checked a few things, like pinching the back of his neck and watching how fast the skin went back the way it was supposed to.

"I want to do some blood tests to make sure, but I think he's going to be fine," she reassured Casey after a few minutes. "Do you have a list of what you need? You said Bruce isn't your cat, correct?"

"A new friend was supposed to have someone from a cat rescue bring me most of what I need, but I guess the lady was out of town and she's a one-woman operation. A list would be great. I know me. I'll forget something crucial, like kitty litter."

Mark chuckled. "It wasn't on the list you sent me earlier, but I knew enough to add it."

Casey's shoulders slumped. "See? I haven't even told Rachel or contacted Mrs. Christian to let her know that I have Bruce. She's a neighbor who was supposed to stop by and check on him. I don't know why Rachel trusted me with him. I clearly don't know what I'm doing."

Unable to take it any longer, Mark moved next to Casey and wrapped his arms around her. "Hey. You're doing your best and asking for help when you need it. That's all anyone can ask you to do."

The feel of her head resting against his chest was something he'd been waiting years to find. He couldn't tell her that, not yet. He didn't think finding out he worked for a royal family would scare her off, but telling her that holding her felt right in a way he never had before? That was probably too much.

Four

How weird was it that Casey didn't care that the kind vet and her assistant were witnessing her first hug with Mark?

First?

Did that imply she hoped there would be many more to come?

She didn't let herself over-analyze it. Not yet. That would come later. Right now, she just wanted to enjoy being held like this.

It hadn't happened in a long time, and she wanted nothing more than to relax into it, but their audience precluded her from doing that.

She pulled back. "Thanks. I needed to hear that."

"It's the truth."

The vet jumped in. "He's right, you know. As soon as you knew you needed help, you did what needed to be done."

"You have no idea." Mark's wry tone made her smile.

"Do I need to leave him here?" Casey asked.

The vet shook her head. "Nope. We'll take him to the back and draw the blood. We'll run it first thing in the morning. We're here until noon, but we'll call you long before that to give you an update."

"Thanks."

The vet and her assistant left her alone with Mark for a few minutes.

"Thank you again for everything today. When they're done, you can just drop me back off at my van. I can take it from there." She really hoped he wouldn't. She wanted a dinner date with him, though she wouldn't be dressed her best or have her makeup just so.

"Nope. We can drop the cat off at your hotel if you think he'll be okay there, then I'm going to take you to dinner. Nothing fancy, but some good local food."

She didn't let her shoulders slump in relief. "That sounds wonderful." Except she wasn't sure if the hotel would let her leave Bruce there. "I should probably call and explain what happened. See if the hotel will let me pay a pet deposit or something."

Before she could, the vet brought Bruce back in. "He's good to go. We'll call you in the morning. If it was mid-summer, I'd be much more concerned, but even coming from Texas, it wasn't nearly as hot as it could be. He's clearly not frostbitten or overly dehydrated, so I think we're going to be just fine."

A few minutes later, she was back in Mark's very nice SUV. She'd noticed it looked far more upgraded than any she'd ever been in before. Rather than asking, she just poked around the center dashboard-console area until she found the heated seats.

"Does this car go along with the security thing you talked about?" she asked as he pulled out onto the rural country road.

"It does. It's much more secure than your normal SUV."

"I noticed. So, the people are super VIPs."

"You could say that."

Casey pulled out her phone. She wanted to do a search for what celebrities called Serenity Landing home, but instead called her hotel and explained the situation.

They gave her the answer she most dreaded.

No pets.

No exceptions.

Tears threatened to fall down her cheeks, but she willed them back. After thanking the woman for her time, she opened her browser on her phone. "I need to find a hotel that takes pets."

"Don't worry about it. Jonathan already told me you're welcome to the apartment over their garage if you needed it."

She turned to look at him. "Are you serious? How much?" She'd pay it, whatever it was, but she was already going to be out two nights at the hotel anyway.

"He wouldn't charge you anything. He has the space. You have a need. End of story. His wife may have been at the craft show. I'm not sure if she had a booth or not. If not, she'll be shopping, I'm sure."

"What does she do?"

"When she's not pregnant, she dyes yarn."

Casey blinked. "She's not Show Me Yarn, is she?"

Mark shook his head. "Kenzie's Kreations, I think. She knows the other ladies though. Most of the locals know each other."

"I've used her yarn before I think. She does good work."

"I'm sure she'd love to hear that." He flipped on his blinker. "We'll drop Bruce off there. I'm sure their daughter would love to play with him. We'll grab some dinner then pick up your things at the hotel. I can take you back to Jonathan's then."

Before she could protest that she wouldn't have her own vehicle, he was making a call to his friend.

While he talked, she decided to do that web research. *Famous people in Serenity Landing* turned up a weird hodgepodge of unrelated articles, except for one about some HEA TV star filming a show for MyBingeFlix. She vaguely remembered the original show, *2 Cool 4 School*, a show about teenage twins in high school, but had never really watched it.

But it seemed that Christopher Bayfield lived in Serenity Landing full time, so that couldn't be who Mark worked for.

"Jonathan and Kenzie are at So Cheeeezzy already. We can give Bruce to them. We can eat there if you want or go somewhere else."

Casey blinked. "First, I need to know what kind of food is served at a place called So Cheeeezzy. Is it all grilled cheese and macaroni all the time? Because I could totally get on board with that."

Mark laughed. "Sorry. It's a New York style pizza and Italian restaurant. Locally owned and operated. Decent food."

She didn't try to hide her slight disappointment. "That will work, though an all grilled-cheese-and-macaroni restaurant would be okay, too, if you have one of those around here."

"Are those even a thing?" Mark slowed as they neared the town of

Serenity Landing. "It sounds good, I guess, but I've never heard of one."

"Pizza and Italian sounds good, too. I can always eat pasta and pizza."

He flipped on his blinker then turned right on what appeared to be a main thoroughfare. In a block, he turned into a parking lot near a house-ish looking building. They pulled into a spot on the other side of an empty one from another large SUV. A man was putting a child into a car seat as a woman helped a little girl in the other side.

It wasn't until the man turned around that Casey gasped. "Jonathan Langley-Cranston? Your friend is Jonathan Langley-Cranston?"

As he pressed the button to turn the engine off, Mark glanced over at Casey. "You know Jonathan?"

She shook her head. "Not really, but Rachel follows a bunch of the royalty websites. She was all excited about the possibility of him marrying some European Crown Princess, but I guess they broke up, and she married someone else. She made me wake up to watch the wedding."

How long would it be before she put two and two together? If her friend was that invested in Addie, wouldn't she realize it was Serenity Landing at the center of all of the stories, at least on the American side?

Rather than dwelling on it, Mark opened his door. "I'll introduce you."

Before he could make it around to the other side of the SUV, Jonathan had already turned and opened Casey's door for her and was introducing himself.

Mark worried Casey would be one of those people who didn't know how to act around someone they perceived to be famous, but she just smiled and thanked him for the offer of a place to stay and taking care of Bruce.

"Lorelai will love having a cat around for a few hours," Jonathan told her as Mark opened the rear passenger door. "She adores them, but I'm mildly allergic." He held up a hand. "I'll be fine, but we can't have one."

"Then thank you."

Kenzie walked around the back of their SUV. "She may never let you have him back even though Jonathan's allergic." She held out a hand to Casey. "I'm Kenzie."

Casey glanced up at Mark. "Mark says you dye yarn. I think I've used some of your stuff before. It's fantastic."

"Thank you." She bumped Jonathan with her hip. "This guy is almost as good as I am these days."

Jonathan laughed. "I just follow her recipes. That makes it a lot easier."

"I can't mix dye when I'm pregnant," Kenzie explained. "Jonathan does it for me when I can't."

Mark wrapped an arm around her shoulder for a quick hug. "Congratulations. I haven't seen you since the announcement." He'd already mentioned it to Jonathan.

"Thanks. I've had a lot more morning sickness this time around, but I've been craving calzones, so here we are. I can't get them to come out right to save my life."

Mark let his arm fall and pulled the crate out of the back seat. "Thanks again for taking care of him for us."

Jonathan took the crate from him. "Our pleasure."

Kenzie looked between them. "You're not from here, right, Casey?"

"I'm just in town for the craft show," she confirmed. "I've never been here before."

"Then how do you two know each other? Did you meet in Montevaro at some point?"

So much for keeping it a secret. Mark looked at Casey who'd turned a becoming shade of pink as she looked at the ground. "Addie signed me up for a dating app. Casey's friend signed her up. They matched us, and she needed help. I had the day off. The rest is history." More or less. No sense in hiding it.

"Addie?" Kenzie's eyebrows lifted. "*Addie* signed you up?"

Mark nodded. "She's convinced that since she's happily married, and Todd is happily married, and so are her brother and sister, that everyone else needs to be, too."

"It just doesn't seem like a thing she would do." Kenzie shrugged. "I've only met her a couple of times in passing, though."

"I guess she saw a commercial for this Betwixt app and had someone look into it to make sure it was legit."

Jonathan looked sheepish. "That would be me. I had no idea what she wanted the information for, though."

Casey squared her shoulders. "Well, I for one, am glad this Addie person signed him up. I don't know what I would have done without his help today, both with Bruce and in the booth at the show."

Mark wasn't sure what to think of the twinkle in Jonathan's eye. "I remember my first show with Kenzie. I didn't know much of anything, but I learned fast."

"Mark did, too."

A scream from inside the car caught their attention.

"And that's our cue." Jonathan put Bruce's crate in the back seat of their SUV. "We'll be home the rest of the night. Your code for the apartment and the front gate is today's date."

Two minutes later, they were seated in the restaurant. Mark sat where he could see everything going on and both exits. He wondered if Casey would notice he had to sit where he could take stock of things.

"Tell me something about yourself," he asked Casey. "Besides the business thing."

"I graduate in May. I have no clue what I want to do with my life except keep working for Rachel. I'm not sure I actually want to use my degree, but I do love the stuff I do for her. Not the packaging and all of that, though I don't mind, but the marketing side of things. Graphics and all of that."

"Have you thought about being a virtual assistant? I know Kenzie used one for a while, though I'm not sure what happened. She paid someone to do her graphics and post on social media and other stuff, but I have no idea what."

Casey took a sip of her Dr Pepper. "That's a thought. I see people mention it on Facebook sometimes, but I've never considered doing it myself."

"Maybe Kenzie could give you some suggestions on what people look for." He shrugged. "I don't know. Just a thought."

"No, it's a good one." She took another sip of her soda. "It's your turn to tell me something about yourself. Sounds like you're from Montevaro? Is that in Europe?"

So, she hadn't put the name Addie together with Queen Adeline of Montevaro. "It is. South of our sister country Mevendia and north of Italy. I did six years of schooling at Serenity Landing University. I have my Master's in International Relations."

When Addie had been called home following her father's skiing accident and subsequent revelation of his Parkinson's disease, they'd all been given the opportunity to finish their last semester. Mark had, as did Adeline, but Todd decided not to.

Her eyes had widened. "International relations? Well, I guess if you do security work for someone international, that makes sense. I mean, I'd guess your clients are international since you're from Europe."

Something started to work itself out in her head. He could see it happening.

"Wait. Addie. You're from Montevaro." She leaned in closer and whispered. "Do you work for the queen of Montevaro?"

Five

Though he'd known it couldn't keep it from her for much longer, Mark had hoped he might make it through dinner. He nodded. "But I'd appreciate it if you wouldn't make a big fuss over it. It's not a secret, but not something I talk about openly in public very often."

"That makes sense."

Their waitress appeared with a calzone for Casey and lasagna for him.

"Do you mind if I say grace?" he asked.

Casey shook her head. "Go right ahead."

Mark did something he'd never done on a date before. He reached out and took her hand before giving thanks for the food.

As they ate, he told her a little bit about Montevaro then promised to answer at least some of her questions about his job when they were on their way to pick up Bruce.

"I would imagine your job can make relationships difficult," she said, keeping her eyes on his.

"It was worse when I traveled all the time. Since I took over here on a permanent basis, it would have been easier when I wanted to spend more time with someone."

"Have you dated much then?"

He shook his head. "Not really. I dated several women through the app. I never went out on a second date with any of them. I could see why, on paper, they looked like a good match, but we never clicked. You?"

"A few, but same thing. Never clicked, even though we should have been compatible." She dipped her calzone in marinara sauce. "I would imagine you've traveled all over the world?"

"A fair bit, though I never did much of the tourist stuff or was able to explore on my own. I always had..." He glanced around. No one was near them. "Other concerns."

"I can't even imagine. Would you like to go back and visit on your own?"

That was a key question about whether this relationship had potential or not.

"When I can. I should be able to take more vacation now. My boss pushes me to when we talk, but I have a hard time leaving things in the control of others. What about you? Would you like to travel?"

Casey pushed the little bit of food left on her plate away. "Like to? Yes. Afford to? Notsomuch at the moment."

"If the money wasn't an issue?"

"I would love to." She leaned forward like she was going to tell him a secret. "I've never even been on a plane."

The way she said it made Mark smile. If this worked out, he'd make sure she got to ride in one sooner rather than later. He had friends he could call for favors.

While he finished, they talked about the places she would visit if she could. All were places he'd been, though he only ever saw the inside of a control room or SUV or watched the crowds for potential threats.

He paid the bill and found himself resting his hand on the small of her back as they walked back to his SUV. Mark found himself wondering what it would be like to kiss her.

When was the last time he'd wanted to kiss a woman?

He'd never even felt that way about Addie. He hadn't let himself even as he believed he was falling in love with her.

After a stop at the hotel to get her things, they drove straight to Jonathan's estate. Casey gasped as the house came into view.

"I knew he had money," she whispered, "but I never imagined I'd see it myself."

"You haven't seen anything until you've seen some of the palaces around the world. This is very nice, don't get me wrong, but compared to say, Buckingham or the Montevarian palace set in the middle of an island in an Alpine lake? This pales in comparison."

"I'm sure it does." The wistfulness in her voice told him she'd like to visit those places someday. For most tourists, even with money, they'd never get to see more than the public tour areas, and not all palaces had them. Buckingham did at times, but the Montevarian castle only did tours for very select groups.

Mark wanted to tell her that someday he'd take her, but he didn't want to make a promise he wasn't certain he could keep.

He parked the car near the outer door leading to a small entry and stairs to the apartment. Both doors were locked, so he showed her how to punch in the code, should she need it.

About halfway up the stairs, Casey stopped in her tracks.

"I don't have my van. How do I get to the convention center tomorrow?"

Mark had thought of that about the time he punched in the code for Jonathan's gate. "I'll pick you up. If something comes up and I can't, Kenzie is going in the morning. If you need to go earlier than her, Jonathan has a car you can borrow. He likely has several you could use."

She started back up the stairs. "I'm not sure I'm comfortable with that. I'd much rather go pick it up now." At the top of the stairs, she punched in the code like he'd shown her. "That is, if you really think something might come up so you can't come get me. I don't mind that as much, though I'm not sure I can define why."

"Because I'm your date for the day."

"Which reminds me. I need to get Bruce from Jonathan."

"I talked to him while you were getting your things from the hotel so he'd know we were on our way. Lorelai offered to watch him tomorrow while you're at the craft show."

"That's very kind of them but unnecessary."

Mark set her suitcase and duffle bag down near the sofa. "Jonathan already had his assistant get them everything Bruce needs. He's being fed and has a litter box." Mark sat down on the couch, right in the middle. If she wanted to sit by him, she could, or there were two other chairs she could choose.

She sat inches away from him, though she perched on the edge.

The question was, could he work up the nerve to kiss her?

As she tried to work up the nerve to lean back against Mark's arm where it was outstretched along the back of the sofa, Casey wondered when she'd get around to texting Rachel about Bruce.

"Would you like to watch a movie? Can we even watch a movie in here?" She looked around. A large television hung over the fireplace, but she had no idea if there were movies or a streaming service.

"We can find something, or we could talk some more."

She finally let herself sit back. "I'd like that."

Mark's fingers played with the hair at the nape of her neck, but he didn't try to get her to move closer to him. She could have chosen one of the other chairs, but she wanted to be next to him.

"You need to relax. I'm not going to hurt you or try to take advantage of you or do anything that makes you uncomfortable. If you'd like me to go, I will. If you want me to give you a neck and shoulder rub because that's where you're carrying all of your tension from today, I can do that."

"If I want you to kiss me?" Casey blurted the question out before she could stop herself.

Mark chuckled. A warm sound that sort of rolled over her. "I might be convinced to do that before I leave, but likely not until I'm at the door." He stood and moved the coffee table out of the way. "Have a seat on the floor and let me see if I can work some of those knots out of your muscles."

She slid onto the floor as he moved to sit behind her.

Strong hands squeezed her shoulders lightly before his thumbs began to knead right where she needed it most.

"You're good at this," Casey told him.

He kept going but didn't say anything.

"Have you ever been in love before?" She needed to know, and if this was going to work, she'd have to tell him about her old boyfriends. All two of them. The history of her love life was quite boring.

"Once. I thought I was anyway."

"What happened? Did she not feel the same way?"

"She never knew."

He didn't seem to be lacking in courage, so why wouldn't he have told her? She asked him just that.

"It's complicated," he told her with a sigh. "Or rather, it's not complicated at all. I knew there was no chance of a future with her, so why tell her something when I knew she didn't feel the same way and would never even entertain the idea of a relationship."

"Why wouldn't she? Unless she was the queen or something, that's ridiculous." Even as she said it, Casey remembered who his boss was. "That's it, isn't it?"

"I moved here with the Crown Princess and one other guard, Todd, for six years. The three of us were virtually inseparable. Everyone here thought we were chosen by our country for full scholarships. They bought us a place to live and paid our bills while we learned, so that was true in a sense. We weren't with Addie all the time like you'd expect. We all went to school. We all took classes. We all were in most of the same classes. But as time went on, we became more like friends."

That had to be hard. To become friends when you knew the friendship would be limited to a certain time and place. When they returned to Europe, things would automatically be different. She asked Mark just that.

"Exactly. When we weren't here, Addie kept a low profile for the most part. She didn't want to be seen in public much so that her pictures would make their way back to Serenity Landing and her privacy would disappear."

His thumbs worked in tandem on the tendons in her neck. Casey had to stop herself from groaning at how good it felt. "What happened?"

"She took one of the cars one night. Ice came on earlier than expected. She was in a fender bender with a single dad, one she fell in love with almost immediately. Her father and Parliament would never approve of Charlie, though, and he refused to leave Serenity Landing."

"Why? If she was a princess, he had to understand that she would be queen someday and couldn't stay here."

"Exactly, but he didn't know who she was, just that she refused to even consider the idea of staying local. He grew up with parents who lived all over the world on archaeological digs. He grew up living out of a tent or a trailer or here with his aunt and uncle. He didn't want that for his daughter. He wanted roots here."

"How did she find out?"

"Do you remember when the US President was in Europe a few years ago, and his family went skiing, but a local king had an accident and was injured?"

Casey searched the back of her mind. "Vaguely. Rachel probably told me about it."

"That was her father, King Jedidiah. She went straight home. Because the First Family was there, the news covered it here in the States. Charlie and Lindsey, his daughter, saw her on the news."

"And that's when she dated Jonathan? I do remember that much."

"Yes. But then a bunch of stuff happened. Charlie saved her from a guy who got too handsy. His parents and daughter were both given titles for finding a lost treasure. He received an Order of Merit of some kind for his actions. Her father decided to go up against Parliament if he had to, but in the end, he didn't."

"And all the while, you were in love with her."

His hands stilled. "I thought I was. I don't know for sure. I suppose when I'm in love for real, I'll be able to compare and see if I was really in love with her or if I was in love with the idea of her or the idea of something sort of forbidden overcoming the odds. Regardless, after a couple of years back in Montevaro, I decided I didn't want to be there anymore, so I came here."

"Self-exile?"

"In some ways, I suppose." He sounded sad. "I still talk to my parents regularly and visit several times a year. The queen lets them stay at the house when they come here for a visit, but it isn't the same. I always thought I'd move back and be part of Addie's detail when she returned to life as Crown Princess and eventually queen. I was but not like I envisioned. I decided it was time for a change."

Casey leaned her head against his knee. "I don't know why you ended up back here, but today I'm glad you did."

His hand rested on her head, and his fingers brushed her hair away from her forehead. "I am, too."

He hadn't kissed her.

By the time they finished talking about Addie and Mark's relationship with her, such as it was, Casey had been too tired to think clearly. He wasn't about to kiss her in that state of mind.

Maybe before the day was out, there would be another chance.

He pulled up outside the apartment and texted her that he'd arrived, just as she'd requested. While he waited, he sipped on his coffee. He hadn't been that open with anyone about his feelings for Addie, ever. Todd suspected, but Mark had never confided in anyone before.

Why now?

Why Casey?

Because instinctively he knew something was different with her?

Or he was just tired of pretending when that question came up?

A text from Casey said she'd be down in a minute. Before he could reply, his phone rang. The number wasn't stored in his phone, but he recognized it as the queen's private line.

He swiped across the screen. "Good morning, Your Majesty."

"It's afternoon here, Mark."

"It's still early morning here." He took another sip.

"I spoke with Jonathan last night. He told me about the cat and how you spent the day at a craft fair."

Mark knew Jonathan only had the best of intentions, but he wished the other man had kept his mouth shut. "Yes. All of those things are true."

"Do you like her?" There was undisguised glee in the queen's voice.

He put his coffee in the holder. "Listen, Addie..."

Before he could go on, she interrupted him. "Addie? You never call me that anymore."

No. He never did. "Because I'm not talking to my queen at the moment. I'm talking to the woman who was my friend but who, because of life's circumstances, no longer can be. Please leave it alone. Leave my love life alone. Who I date, or don't date, or if I date, is my business. Unless and until it affects my job, I need you to back off and let it go."

Silence on the other end of the line told him his words hit their mark. He never wanted to hurt her - that was the last thing he'd choose - but it needed to be said. He and Addie couldn't be friends.

Not while Adeline was both his boss and his queen.

"I understand." Her quiet words told him something had shifted in their relationship, something that had shifted years earlier but was finally being acknowledged. "I do want only the best for you, Mark."

"I know, and I appreciate that, but there comes a time where we need to maintain professional boundaries, and this is it."

"Then I will wish you well and see you the next time I come to the States."

"Yes, ma'am."

"Goodbye, Mark." There was a finality to her tone as she hung up, one he didn't quite understand. Just because he needed her out of his love life didn't mean he wanted their easy working relationship to end.

He reached for his coffee cup as Casey opened the passenger door. Shoot. He'd meant to get out and greet her, open her door for her. Be a gentleman.

"Everything okay?" she asked as she buckled her seatbelt.

Mark shifted into gear. "Yeah. Just had a phone conversation that didn't go how I would have expected but it's fine."

"You don't have to stay with me today, you know."

He made a conscious effort to shake himself out of the funk. "I know, but I want to. I mostly enjoyed yesterday, and this time I'll know what I'm doing."

"I do appreciate it."

"I'm happy to." He'd picked her up earlier than strictly necessary because he wanted to make a stop before going to the convention center.

"I know I'm new and all, but is this the right way?"

"Did you eat breakfast?" he asked glancing over at her as they passed Serenity Landing High School.

"No." She twisted in her seat. "Are those cows?"

He chuckled. "Yes."

"At the high school?"

"Yes."

"That's a thing?"

"Serenity Landing is still a semi-rural area. A large portion of the student population live on farms and want to farm or do other agricultural related jobs when they grow up. The Ag department raises cows every year. They also rotate crops in the acreage around the school. I think one is soybeans and one is hay, but I'm not sure what the others are or if soybeans is right. They've always hayed the area around the school."

"Wow. Don't have anything like that in the city."

"I'd imagine not."

She turned back to look at him. "Did you say something about breakfast?"

"Chick-fil-A is right around the corner. We'll grab something and eat on the way to the convention center because you need to eat breakfast."

"I normally do, you know. Yesterday, I overslept. Today, I didn't have anything available."

"I understand completely. Just making sure you get some." He turned into the parking lot and into one of the two drive-through lanes. An employee he didn't recognize, but whose nametag said her name was Maggie, met them with an iPad in hand. He ordered his usual - chicken breakfast burrito, no hash browns, with bacon and Chick-n-minis.

Maggie turned to Casey. "And for you, ma'am?"

Casey winced. "I have had breakfast here like once. Do you have a menu?"

The girl smiled and handed a laminated card about the size of a piece of paper through the window. Mark passed it over to Casey who studied it for a moment.

"A chicken biscuit and the biggest coffee you've got." She handed the card back to him. "Thanks."

Maggie gave him the total and told him he could pay at the window.

He pulled around, stopping two cars back from the window itself.

"Thank you for thinking of this," Casey told him. "You didn't have to."

Mark reached over and took her hand, linking their fingers. "I find I like the idea of your company in the morning as well. It's no trouble at all."

"Even though nothing happened last night?" She looked straight ahead as the cars began to move.

"What do you mean nothing happened last night?" He squeezed her hand. "I spent a lovely evening with a beautiful woman. What more does there need to be?"

Was this guy for real? Casey sure hoped so.

None of the other guys she'd met through the app - or in real life - felt that way. Or didn't seem to anyway.

As Mark eased the car forward to the window, he pulled his wallet out of his back pocket. "Good morning, Ashleigh," he said to the young woman standing at the window.

"Hi, Mark. I thought that was you! Not many people get that combo." She handed him a cup of coffee that he handed to Casey. "Do you need cream or sugar?" Ashleigh leaned around a bit, so she was looking at Casey, not Mark.

Casey lifted the cup. "This is perfect, thanks."

Ashleigh handed him a bag of food. "You know you could get your coffee here."

Mark grinned at her. This was clearly a conversation they had often. "You know I like my own blend. Thanks, Ashleigh."

"My pleasure. Have a great day!"

Casey took the bag from him as he handed it over. "You come often?"

"Often enough. She knows I get extra good coffee from home. I have a Thermos of it in the back if you want some. I wasn't sure if you drank it or not." He looked both ways then turned back down the way they'd come.

"This will do for now." She took a small sip to check the temperature. Hot, but not too hot. A longer sip followed before she put it in the cup holder. "Do you want your burrito or your other thing?" Passenger always handled divvying up the food.

"Nothing just yet. Give it a minute." He turned onto another road, one they hadn't been down before. A couple minutes later, they pulled onto a dirt road then came almost to a stop. He inched the car forward a little bit until she could see the lake spread out beyond the windshield.

"Aren't we a little close to the edge? Are we even allowed to be here?" Hadn't there been private property signs?

"This is Jonathan's property. I told him we'd be out here. Normally, there's a gate, but he had one of his guys open it for us so I wouldn't have to."

"He's quite a guy." She took her biscuit out and handed the bag to Mark. "But we're not too close?" She couldn't see the edge of the cliff.

"Nah. It's farther than it looks, but I'm still careful when I pull up."

They ate in silence as the sun continued to rise in the sky over the lake.

"It's pretty," Casey told him as she balled up her tin foil wrapper.

"I like it here. It reminds me a little bit of home, though this lake isn't quite as pristine as that one."

Casey leaned back against the headrest. "I'd love to visit the Alps sometime, maybe even learn to ski."

"Skiing is something most kids learn in Montevaro. I was on skis almost before I knew how to walk."

"Not so much in Texas."

"I'd imagine not." He finished the last of his burrito and put his trash in the bag. "Ready?"

Casey struggled to keep a straight face. "As long as you promise to back up."

That made him laugh. A real laugh unlike one she'd heard from him before. He'd chuckled or laughed lightly, but not like this. "Never fear. I've learned all sorts of defensive driving and how to escape from bad guys intent on running you off the road. I think I can handle getting us out of this." Then he winked at her.

She gave a half-shrug. "Okay. If you insist. I'll trust you."

He moved the gear shift. "R is for reverse, right?"

With a roll of her eyes, she nodded. "Yes, Mark. R is for reverse."

His lips twitched into a quirky half-smile. "Thanks for helping with that."

The SUV backed up as slowly as it had come in until he could turn them around. Casey glanced at her watch. They'd left Jonathan's house in plenty of time, but they were starting to cut it close.

"Don't worry. We'll be at the convention center in about fifteen minutes."

"Thanks."

After he turned back onto a paved road, he took her hand. She kind of liked that.

A lot.

Probably a lot more than she should, given he hadn't even kissed her yet.

Maybe later today he would.

"I don't think you've said when you head home."

And there was the damper on everything.

She sighed. "I'm supposed to leave first thing in the morning."

"Have to be at work on Monday?"

"Yes and no. I have work to do, a lot of it, this week. Mostly for Rachel's company, though I do a little bit for another friend. I don't *have* to do it at home, but I'm not sure I brought everything with me that I need to stay longer."

"That's too bad." He sounded genuinely disappointed. "What's the schedule look like today then? I'd guess you'll be packing everything up?"

"The show closes at five. I'll start packing up some before that, as long as it's not busy. I should be ready to load my van by six at the latest, but probably sooner."

"Good."

Good? "Why is that good?"

"Because then I can make you dinner." He squeezed her hand. "If you don't mind me doing so at the apartment."

"Why would I mind? It's not my apartment."

"No," he answered slowly as a sign for the convention center came into view. "But it is kind of like your home for the next day or so. I would never presume you would want me, a man you've known less than twenty-four hours, to spend that much time at your place."

She went back to her question from earlier. Was this guy really for real? "I appreciate giving me the chance to decline, but it's fine. Really. I'd enjoy it, especially since I don't cook at all."

"You don't?" He sounded genuinely perplexed.

"Nope. I mean, I *can*. I can make simple stuff like spaghetti with sauce from a jar, but I hate it. Definitely don't ask me to do something fancy."

He pulled in and parked, continuing to give her a puzzled look.

"What?" She flipped the visor down and opened the mirror. "Do I have something in my teeth?"

"No. It's just that I was very specific in my profile that I wanted to be matched with someone who loved to cook. It's something I always enjoyed when I had the time. Now that I have the time on a regular basis, I cook all the time. I wanted that to be something I could do with my wife when I have one."

Casey's heart fell a bit with every word. She'd been clear on her profile that cooking was something to be tolerated at best, and she wasn't capable of doing it.

It sounded like this could end before it even got started.

Seven

Before Mark could say anything else, Casey hopped out of the SUV.

Great.

He hadn't meant to insult her or run her off, just express his confusion over how they'd been matched when something he said was very important didn't line up with her profile.

By the time he'd turned the vehicle off, grabbed their things, including her backpack, the extra coffee and both of their coffee cups, Casey was nearly to the door of the convention center.

With the three containers, he couldn't go as fast as he wanted. By the time he caught up with her, she was pulling tubs of product out from underneath the table.

"Hey."

She didn't look up. "Would you grab the gray tub under that other table?"

"Casey, stop." He set the coffees down and lowered the backpack to the ground.

"I've got things I need to do before this place gets crazy in about half an hour." She still didn't look up as she turned to get the tub she'd asked him to grab.

"Casey."

She plopped down onto the floor and bent one knee as she pulled the bucket toward her. "I need more of the cross stitches. The Easter morning ones with the Bible verse on them sold well yesterday. So did the bunnies and Easter eggs. I think there's more in here."

So, she babbled when she was trying to avoid a conversation.

"They're not in that one." He turned and grabbed a dark green bucket from under the table where he'd handled the money most of the day before. "They got moved."

After putting the lid back on the gray one and shoving it past the tablecloth, Casey turned, lifting the other bucket and moving it in front of her rather than facing him.

Okay. She didn't want to talk about it, but that didn't mean he was going anywhere.

He'd always known that if he met the right person things like cooking together wouldn't matter, but since he could choose the characteristics, he wanted in a life partner, he'd picked someone who could cook. It was just odd that he'd been matched with someone who didn't like to.

That was all he'd meant.

Mark had no intention of letting this potential relationship end over something like that.

Rather than push her at the moment, he quietly got to work, helping to restock the rest of the booth before setting up the money box and tablet. She'd entrusted him with the password the day before.

By the time the booth was ready to go, Casey had untensed a little bit but not completely.

Maybe he should ask what she'd like him to make for dinner. But he didn't. Did she have any food allergies? Was that information in her profile?

The booth was ready, but she still didn't talk to him. Instead, she fidgeted. Straightening this, tweaking that, even though it all looked fine.

He sat in the chair behind the back table and pulled out his phone. The Betwixt app would let him look at her complete profile. Maybe he should look through it a little more closely.

Scanning the information, he noticed some things he hadn't the first time through. No known food allergies, but no cooking was also on there. He'd missed it when he'd looked before accepting the match.

A few other potential red flags stood out. She wasn't much for outdoor sports, but she did love to read. She liked walks in the park, but not hiking as much.

He'd already taken the traveling differences into consideration.

The relationship, if they were to have one, could work despite those things. It just took some shifting of expectations.

Montevarian food. That's what he'd make. He sent a text to Jonathan, making sure it was okay that they used the apartment kitchen and asking if it was stocked with utensils and such.

Jonathan responded almost immediately. Mark then texted Brian and asked him to pick up the food so that Mark wouldn't have to later. He'd follow Casey to the Langley-Cranston Estate. If she told him to shove off, he would, but he hoped she'd give them a chance.

"You don't have to stay." She still didn't look at him.

"You're talking to me? I thought we'd taken a vow of silence." The needling might not be the right way to connect with her, but how would he know unless he tried.

That earned him a glare and made him grin. At least she was looking at him.

He stood and went around the table, leaning back against it as casually as he could manage. "I have no intention of going anywhere. I told you I'd give you a hand today, and I meant it."

She shrugged. "If you want to."

What he really wanted to do was give her that first kiss.

Then spend the whole day with her and not a crowd of thousands, but that wasn't going to happen. They had just a few minutes before the show opened.

He picked up her cup of coffee. "Do you want this? Or do you want me to pitch it? It's almost cold already, but I've got hot of my blend if you want it instead."

Casey reached for it but didn't look at him.

He held it out of reach. "You at least have to look at me."

Another glare as she moved closer.

With his hand held up so it was still out of reach, he looked into her gorgeous blue eyes. "Hi."

"Yo." Those eyes could flash fire and ice at the same time. "Can I have my coffee?"

Mark leaned in slightly. The look on her face softened just a bit as her eyes darted from side to side.

To see if anyone was watching?

He didn't much care.

Leaning in slightly more, he gave her ample time to back up if she didn't want what was about to happen.

When she didn't, he did what he'd been hoping to do before the day ended. He just hadn't expected the opportunity so soon.

He kissed her.

For a split second, Casey wasn't quite sure what was happening even though she'd guessed what he was thinking before he did it.

Mark was kissing her.

Before she could make a conscious choice to kiss him back, to do more than let her lips cling to his, it was over.

She rocked back on her heels as he lowered her coffee cup.

"Here you go."

Casey took it from him. "That wasn't payment for my coffee."

"I know. That was a kiss between two people who've been wanting to do that for hours. At least I know I have. I thought you did, too."

She nodded, though it was almost grudgingly. Why was he leading her on? Why kiss her if there was no future for them? If they'd been matched on some kind of fluke?

At some point, when they weren't busy, she needed to find time to scan his profile and see what else they didn't match on.

The doors to the show opened, forcing Casey to turn her attention away from the maddeningly casual man leaning against her display table.

With that grin.

She was kind of falling for that grin, even if he was annoying her at the moment.

Before customers reached them, Mrs. Bateman wandered by. "How's

Bruce doing this morning?"

She hadn't even checked on the stupid cat.

"He's staying with a friend of mine," Mark offered. "The vet thought he was going to be just fine after his ordeal, and my friend's little girl is over the moon. Her dad's allergic so she doesn't get to play with a cat very often."

He never said his friend's name. He didn't name drop the people he knew. That made sense. A man who would name drop wouldn't be entrusted with the safekeeping of a future queen. She needed to ask him how he got into that. Was it the family business? Had his father guarded the Montevarian royal family?

She'd looked them up briefly before he arrived to pick her up. There were pictures of the queen and her family, including the man from Serenity Landing and his daughter. Casey wasn't quite sure if Queen Adeline had adopted the girl or not. Maybe it wasn't legal since she was queen, but the two clearly adored each other.

There had been two pictures of the extended family, including her parents, brother, sister, and their families. In one, they looked as formal and intimidating as you'd expect a royal family to be.

In the other, taken at a country home of some kind, they looked like the family next door, albeit with a castle behind them.

This was who Mark had spent years protecting, still protected, though from a distance.

Mrs. Bateman brought her back to the present. "We'll miss having Bruce around today. Be sure to let me know what the test results say."

"We will," Mark answered for the both of them. "I'm sure he's fine, though."

"Good."

She still hadn't called Rachel either. Normally, she texted her best friend regularly and certainly should have told her how sales went the day before. Rachel could see the app they used and get an idea of what sold and how much money had been brought in, but those numbers wouldn't give the details.

At least Casey had remembered to text Mrs. Christian to let her know she didn't need to take care of Bruce.

The first customers found their way to the booth and the day was off and running.

For the first hour or so, things continued to be awkward with Mark, but they settled into a rhythm. The vet called and reassured them Bruce was fine. By the time Mark went to grab something for them to eat at lunchtime, she was even able to smile at him.

He didn't say anything else about dinner, even when they cleaned up and packed everything away. Having his help reloading the van was fantastic. It was so much easier than doing it herself.

When he closed her door with a "see you later," Casey resigned herself to having seen the last of him.

But even as her phone directed her back to the Langley-Cranston Estate, he stayed right behind her. Maybe his house was nearby. It would make sense given who he worked for. The string of properties they'd driven past seemed to indicate a number of very wealthy families owned lakefront property along that road.

But when she turned into the short tree-lined drive before the gate, he turned, too.

Maybe he had another meeting with Jonathan.

Then he parked next to her near the garage.

She didn't say anything as he followed her up the stairs and into the apartment. Was he still going to make dinner?

"If you wanted to change into something more comfortable, go ahead," he called over his shoulder as he went to the kitchen. "And I don't mean anything by that except that you might want some sweats and a t-shirt."

"Thanks." Casey went into the bedroom, filled with furniture far nicer than anything she'd ever dreamed of owning, plus an in-room Jacuzzi tub. She'd soaked in it after Mark left the night before, even though she'd nearly been asleep. Streaming her favorite episode of *Friends* on the bedroom television helped keep her awake.

When she came out, something sizzled and smelled delicious. "What are you making?"

"A traditional Montevarian dish. Your profile said no food allergies. Is that right?" He set a bottle of water on the bar in front of a barstool.

"As far as I know, though I'm not too adventurous in my cuisine." Probably something else they didn't have in common. "What's in this dish?"

He shook his head. "I'm not telling you. Is there anything you absolutely cannot stand? That the smell or taste of makes you sick for no apparent reason?"

"I'm not crazy about beef stroganoff. Apparently, I ate a bunch when I was like two then got sick later that night. I never ate it again until I was a teenager. I'll eat it if I'm somewhere with no choice, but I don't like it. It doesn't make me sick, though. I just take small portions."

"Well, this isn't beef stroganoff like at all, except it does have some pasta." He stirred something on the stove then walked around the bar to stand next to her. "While that does its thing, there's something else I'd like to do."

Casey suspected it was the same thing he'd done earlier in the day. She nodded but didn't say anything.

With one hand, he reached up and brushed her hair back off her face then leaned down. He kissed her softly once.

Then again.

Then a third time.

Casey's arms wound around his neck as she kissed him back, far more enthusiastically than she'd managed that morning.

Coherent thought became difficult, but it occurred to her that maybe the cooking thing - and the other things she'd discovered while he grabbed lunch - wasn't a deal breaker after all.

Sunday morning found Mark feeling far more restless than he'd felt in a long time. He went to church, then worked out, but nothing could calm the restlessness he felt.

Casey texted a couple of times when she stopped for gas or to grab a bite to eat, lamenting that Chick-fil-A wasn't an option on Sunday. She'd told him she'd call when she made it home but not to expect one during the day. Apparently, she didn't like to talk to people on the phone during long drives.

When his phone rang about 2:30 in the afternoon, it surprised him.

"Hey. Where are you?"

"I don't know." Casey sounded frantic. "Some gas station in the middle of nowhere Oklahoma."

"What's going on?" He looked around his room for his keys and wallet.

"I don't know. The check engine light came on, and there was a clunking noise. Fortunately, I was near a rest stop and stopped here."

"Is there a mechanic? An auto repair shop?" Fortunately, he'd showered after his workout. He could leave immediately, but it would be hours before he reached her.

"I don't think so, but I don't know for sure. I just pulled into a parking space and called you. I know next to nothing about cars, just that this one has a lot of miles on it."

Mark stuck his wallet in his back pocket. "Okay. I'm going to leave in a couple of minutes. I'll be there as soon as I can."

"I don't know where I am." She sounded relieved knowing help was on the way, even if it would take hours.

"Go into your maps app and send me the location. I'll call you when I have a better idea of how long it'll take me."

"Thank you, Mark. You have no idea how much that means to me. But don't you have to work tomorrow? Even if we go straight back to Serenity Landing, it'll be super late."

"It'll be fine. No one's here this week, so duty is pretty easy. It's not a big deal if I need to take a day or two off unexpectedly." He headed out the door. "Let me call you back in a bit, okay?"

"Okay. There's a fast food place in the gas station. I'm going to get a bite to eat and try to lower my blood pressure."

"Great idea. Send me your location, and we'll go from there."

"Thanks, Mark."

"My pleasure." He smiled as he said it.

After ten minutes conferring with Brian, he was on the road headed toward Interstate 44. No matter where she actually was, he had a couple hours before he'd turn off of it.

His phone buzzed with her location.

He'd already texted with Jonathan who had connections everywhere there were connections to be had, so he forwarded the location on.

In a few minutes, Jonathan texted back that he had a cousin driving through the area. She and her husband would be happy to stop and stay with Casey until Mark could get there. He was also having one of his men make some calls to see about getting the van taken care of.

Mark texted Casey to let her know she wouldn't be alone as the miles rolled under his wheels.

As he drove, he thought back to the night before. Casey had loved dinner, but he could tell she remained apprehensive, so rather than watching a movie, they went through their profiles and discussed the areas where they were different and, should they give this a shot, what kinds of compromises they might be willing to make.

She offered to try to cook with him but made him promise that if it didn't work out, she'd be allowed to sit on a bar stool and make conversation like she had while he cooked. He agreed. It had been about the time together anyway.

He agreed to walks in the park, both slow meandering walks, and faster more exercise-ish ones. He convinced her to at least try hiking with him. He promised easier trails at first, but with amazing views to make it worthwhile.

After nearly two hours, he turned off the Will Rogers Turnpike, headed south toward Texas. Eventually, he found his way onto another Turnpike.

From the turn at McAlester to the travel plaza near Antlers, Mark saw a couple dozen other cars. Total. Both directions.

In nearly a hundred miles.

He'd scoped it out on the satellite. It looked like it was in the middle of nowhere, and Casey wasn't far wrong when she said that, but there was a town with better services just a couple miles away.

The van sat in the parking spot closest to the highway. Mark parked next to her then went inside. He found her laughing with a young couple.

"Mark!" Casey jumped up and practically ran to him. She threw her arms around his neck. "Thank you for coming," she whispered.

"Of course. I couldn't do anything else."

After a minute, she let go and turned to the table where she'd been sitting. "This is Gwendolyn and Adam. Gwendolyn is Jonathan's cousin.

They were in Tyler, Texas visiting family and headed home."

Mark shook their hands then slid into the booth next to Casey. "Where's Bruce?"

"In the van. I couldn't bring him in here, but I go out there and check on him every twenty minutes or so, make sure he has water."

Gwendolyn and Adam left a few minutes later. Mark sat down across from Casey.

"There's a tow truck on the way. It's going to take your van to a shop in a town not too far from here. We can stay here or a larger town like McAlester. I can drive you home, or we can go back to Serenity Landing. It's up to you."

"Back to Serenity Landing is fine, or whatever's easiest for you."

He reached across the table and took her hands. "That wasn't what I asked. What's best for you? If I could, I'd let you take my SUV home, and I'd wait here for the van, but I can't let you."

"Home would be best," she admitted. "But I need my van. It's my only transportation. My parents gave it to me when my mom upgraded a couple years ago."

"Then what if we rented a car for you? I'll wait here for your van and get someone to drive it back for you then return the car."

"You would do that for me?"

He squeezed gently. "Casey, I'm starting to think there's a lot of things I'd do for you."

Eight

Tears swam in Casey's eyes. "You've known me forty-eight hours."

Mark just smiled at her. "You know what my boss told me once?"

Casey shook her head.

"When she met Charlie, she just knew. When I met you, I just knew there could be something special between us. I want to see what that could be, but there is one more compromise we haven't talked about yet." The way he said the last part scared her.

After taking a deep breath, she asked. "What's that?"

"Eventual living situation. In my career, I have to live either in Serenity Landing or Montevaro, or travel with the queen. Are you willing to move someday? Possibly relocate to Europe? Being in Serenity Landing has served a purpose in my life, and still is, but I never planned for it to be permanent."

She'd thought about that the night before when he made her that pasta dish. "I never planned to stay where I am forever, but there was never anywhere I wanted to move either. I'm open to it, under the right circumstances."

But, on one level, the way he worded it bothered her a little, so she pressed on. "What if I wasn't? If I said I couldn't, or wouldn't, move indefinitely?"

Mark stared at their joined hands. "I don't know. This is my job, my chosen profession, what I've wanted to do since I was little. If that was the case now, then I'm afraid I'd probably have to say goodbye here. If someday in the future, we were married, and something happened with your parents for instance, and you needed to be close to them indefinitely, but they couldn't be moved closer to us, then we'd discuss it and go from there. But before making it permanent? That's a much more difficult decision."

That made sense. "I get it. Now that Rachel moved, I don't have anything keeping me in Texas. I won't move tomorrow, but if we do the long-distance thing, and it's working out, then I'd be very open to it."

"The truth is, when I get married, I'll likely be recalled to Montevaro. They prefer single men for these assignments. It's not required, but it is pretty typical."

She took a deep breath and blew it out slowly. "So, if things work out, I move to Serenity Landing to get to know you better. We fall in love. You ask me to marry you. We get married and move to Montevaro."

"Probably." He let go of her hands and leaned back. "Is that a deal breaker for you?"

Casey picked up the napkin she'd used earlier in the afternoon and started shredding it. "I don't think so, but I'm not ready to commit to that right this minute. Can we see how things go?"

She wasn't committed to Texas, but she wasn't sure she was willing to commit to moving to another continent until she knew there was a future.

"Of course. I understand not making a decision right now, but it's better to know now if it's a definite no." He reached for her hands again. "Now that we've talked about it and are both on the same 'let's see what happens' page, let's get you a rental car so you and Bruce can head home."

He pulled his phone out. "Jonathan was going to find you a rental as close as possible, but I doubt there's any in Antlers."

"Antlers? Is that a place?"

"You're not far from the exit, though it looks to be a little way off." He tapped on his phone. "Okay. Forty-five minutes to a national rental agency so you can return the car wherever you want. As soon as the tow truck gets here, we'll get them set and then head out."

She tilted her head toward the window. "There it is."

"Good. I know you need to get home." She cleaned up the last of her trash and thanked the employees she'd gotten to know over the last nearly six hours. Mark took her hand as they walked out the door.

She let him handle the tow truck driver. It wasn't a sexist thing, but she really didn't know enough to know when she was being conned.

Mark handled it as she got her personal items out of the vehicle. He handed her his keys, which she took as a sign of trust. She *could* take off with it while he was occupied, but he knew she wouldn't. Instead, as she put her things in the back, she noticed he had emergency supplies stashed there. It didn't surprise her. He was the kind of guy who was always prepared.

Casey watched as he shook the man's hand then turned to her. "Case, would you move the SUV out of the way, so he has more room to work?"

She blinked but nodded. Once inside, it was a reach to get to the pedals, and she had to scoot up to the edge of the seat, but Casey didn't want to mess with the way he had it set.

By the time she made it to another parking spot a little farther away, Casey was in love.

Maybe someday she'd be able to afford a car with all the bells and whistles.

Rear view camera.

Heated and cooled seats.

Bluetooth.

Several buttons she suspected were added aftermarket, including a button that may - or may not - have been an eject button.

Probably not.

But maybe.

After putting the car in park and turning it off, Casey hopped out, making sure to leave the windows cracked for Bruce.

The tow truck driver had her sign a couple of forms. She should have looked them over better, but Mark had, and she trusted him.

It was a good start.

A few minutes later, the man had driven off to a service station with excellent online reviews.

As they flew past the exit to Antlers, Casey shifted so her back was more against the door, and she could watch Mark as they talked.

"So, long-distance thing. How exactly does that work?"

"We talk on the phone in the evenings. Text when we have a chance and have something we want to say. Email. Snail mail. I can fly to Dallas pretty easily. You're outside Tyler, right?"

"I am."

"If you're willing to pick me up at the airport, I can be on the first flight out of Springfield and the last flight back. That would give us about ten hours together. We could do that a couple times a month if you want."

A two-hour drive. She could do that to spend the day with Mark. "You'd be willing to fly to Dallas? That can't be cheap."

He quirked that half grin at her. "But you're worth it. If this is going to work, we have to be worth it. We are."

Did the drive have to end? Mark wished it didn't. He loved the time with Casey and was loathe to see it end.

Even though Bruce insisted on yowling the whole time.

"Why don't you use my phone to book my first flight?" He unlocked it then handed it over. "I don't have anything on my calendar that can't be moved the next three weekends."

She pulled out her phone. "Let me check mine." After she scrolled a couple of times, she told him she was clear those weekends too.

They picked a date two weeks out, and she used his phone to book his ticket. He could get a direct flight out about eight in the morning. She'd pick him up before ten. The flight back left at eight at night, so they'd have ten hours to spend together.

Maybe Dallas had a grilled cheese and macaroni restaurant.

He should check.

Casey's phone rang. She groaned as she looked at the screen and swiped. "Hey, Rachel. I'm in the middle of nowhere so if I lose you, I'll call you back."

He could hear the other side of the conversation. "What's this I hear from Mrs. Christian about Bruce not being home?"

Casey winced. "Sorry. I've been meaning to call or text, but this weekend had been kind of crazy." She explained what happened over

Rachel's gasps and exclamations. "He was checked out at a local vet and is fine. Promise."

Mark couldn't quite hear Rachel's response.

The woman in the passenger seat looked over at him with a smile he hoped to get from her often. "I met some really nice people this weekend. They were a huge help. Some of them let me stay in an apartment over their garage since the hotel wouldn't let me keep Bruce with me. Their daughter played with Bruce all day yesterday. That's probably why he's howling now. He misses Lorelai."

Rachel's exclamation came through loud and clear. "Wait. You're not home yet? What time did you leave?"

Casey shifted in her seat until she was facing front. "My van broke down on the Indian Nation Turnpike. It's been towed to a mechanic. I'm headed home to get my work stuff then go back to wait for it to be ready."

She hadn't mentioned that before. It might change Mark's plans a bit. He reached for his phone to send a text. He normally used voice-to-text but couldn't this time.

"Yes," Casey continued. "I'll have the marketing stuff done tomorrow or Tuesday. Except for my van, it's my sole priority."

They talked for a couple more minutes before Casey hung up, right as they passed the exit for the car rental place.

"Isn't that where we were supposed to go?"

Mark nodded. "I can turn around if you want me to, but I can also just take you home. If you're headed back anyway, I can bring you. We'll get a couple of hotel rooms. You can work. I'll get lunch for you, or we can go out, or whatever you want. Then I'll take you to get your van when it's ready." He squeezed her hand. "Then we'll go our separate ways for a couple weeks."

"You'd really do that for me? Take the extra time off?"

"I've got the time built up, and right now there's no other way I'd rather spend it." He pulled her hand toward him and kissed the back of it. "Getting to know you is the best use of my time off if you don't object."

Her smile lit up the inside of the SUV. "I don't object at all."

That was how he ended up kissing her goodnight in her living room then getting a hotel nearby. He spent the next morning driving around her town, going into the locally owned businesses and browsing, even buying a few small items.

He picked up sandwiches from a local shop and took them to Casey's apartment. They sat at her bar because her kitchen table was covered with work.

"What's all that?" He nodded toward it.

"Work for Rachel." She took a bite of her sandwich but didn't look at him. "I've thought about what you said, and you're not wrong. I might not make the products or do the designs, but I'm working as many hours as she is, and I don't charge her for all of them. I don't have a job without her, but without me, she doesn't sell as much. You're right about it being a symbiotic relationship. I'm going to talk to her about being co-owners."

She took a deep breath. "If she says no, that's fine, but I'm going to be more diligent about tracking my hours, and I'll let her know that. If she'd rather give me a set amount she can spend and a prioritized list of tasks, that's fine, too. I can easily pick up more work elsewhere and start my own business as a Virtual Assistant. I talked with a couple people this weekend looking for them."

"Is it going to sour your relationship with Rachel?"

She picked a bit of shredded lettuce off her sandwich. "That's my concern. She's kind of mentioned some of it in the past, but I don't think she really meant it or really knows how much I do off the clock, as it were. I don't think she's shortchanging me on purpose, but I think she's relieved I do what I do for the price I charge her. Does that make sense?"

"Completely." He reached out and tucked a piece of hair behind her ear. "Unfortunately, you're going to have to be ready for her to be upset. If you're not sure..."

Casey shook her head. "No. I'm sure. I knew before you said something. I hope it'll be okay, but it needs to be done. Especially if there's a chance I'm going to be moving sometime in the not-too-distant future, plus getting my van fixed."

He'd tell her later the expenses for her vehicle were being taken care of. At the moment, he wanted to focus on the other part of what she said. "Moving in the not-too-distant future? I like the sound of that." Mark leaned closer until he could feel her breath mingling with his. "As long as it's closer to me."

"There's nowhere else I'd rather be."

"Me either."

And he kissed her.

Epilogue

Casey never imagined her first flight would be from the private section of the airport.

But the queen—*queen!*—of Montevaro had arranged for a private jet to fly them back to the capital city of Montero.

For their honeymoon.

Three months after meeting Mark, she was Mrs. Bertolini.

They hadn't started talking about marriage until the third time he flew to Dallas six weeks after the craft show. By then, they knew it was right.

She'd started to look for apartments in Serenity Landing, knowing she likely wouldn't live there long. Her virtual assistant business had grown rapidly. The discussion with Rachel had gone well. She surprised Casey with news of her own. She and Joss were expecting their first child. Morning sickness had hit with a vengeance, and she was going to have to scale back anyway. Bruce was loving their new home, but Rachel worried what he'd think about a baby.

"What do you think?" Mark sat in the plush captain's chair next to hers and took her hand before leaning in for a kiss.

"I'm pretty sure this is the only way I'll want to fly from now on."

He chuckled. "You've never flown any other way."

"I know, but I can't imagine wanting to fly commercial after this." She gave him another kiss. "You're spoiling me."

"I wish I could take credit for it, but the queen handled it as a wedding gift and to welcome you to the larger royal household." His thumb rubbed over her knuckles. "Are you sure you're okay with moving like this?"

All of their belongings that could fit were in the hold of the plane and any other cubby that could hold anything. She wouldn't be coming back to the States to live ever again.

"I'd planned to take you to visit before asking you to marry me. I wanted to make sure you'd like it enough to live there."

"I know. That would have been my preference too, but sometimes things work out differently."

Like when her parents came to her master's program graduation and told her they'd been asked to go on a six-month medical missions trip. Rather than waiting for them to get back, Mark's parents had flown over, and they'd had a small ceremony on Jonathan's property the day before. His parents had decided to spend a few days in Missouri before heading home.

"Mr. and Mrs. Bertolini, please be sure your seat belts are secured. We're taxiing and currently first in line to take off."

Casey tugged on the strap to tighten it just a bit.

Mark just smiled at her actions. "Nervous?"

"More about meeting the queen and everyone than the flight."

The plane made a turn and began to pick up speed. In a few seconds, she felt the wheels lift off the ground. Casey kept her eyes glued out the window as they went higher.

After a wide turn, she saw sort of familiar sites come into view. She hadn't been in Springfield often enough to know what the buildings were in the medium-sized city, but she recognized Serenity Landing High School, the estates on the lake, including the Langley-Cranston Estate, and the Pond Creek County Convention Center on the southwest side of the lake.

But then the little she knew about the area below them disappeared, and she settled back into her seat.

"You don't need to be nervous about Adeline. She's very excited to meet you."

Casey leaned her head against Mark's shoulder. "Your conversation with her went well?"

He'd talked to the queen early the day before, but Casey forgot to ask him how it went when they were finally alone. They'd both had other things on their minds when they made it to the apartment over the garage.

"It did. She apologized for her interference. Said she has a hard time sometimes remembering that we're not friends, not like we were when we lived in Serenity Landing. Even then we weren't the kind of friends we pretended to be. She was always the future queen, and I was always her security guard. She just wanted me to be happy."

"You can't be too mad at her. If she hadn't bought you that Betwixt membership, we never would have met."

"I know. She said she never would have considered it for any other employee, but she also thought of me as a friend. When she was in Serenity Landing last time, she thought she saw something in me that wanted a family of my own, so she signed me up. She also said she wished we could still be friends like we were during university but understands things are different now. She cherishes our friendship the way it was and my experience and expertise in security now. We're going to be fine."

"You haven't said what your new position is going to be." Casey knew it would mean more travel, and she wouldn't be allowed to go on most trips with him. His focus needed to be on his royal charge, not his wife.

"I'm going to be the head of one of the security details."

Sadness crept into Casey's heart. Selfishly, she wanted him home most of the time, but being the head of a security detail was a big deal. She wouldn't begrudge him that. "The queen's?"

"Nope."

"The prince consort?"

"Nope."

Casey looked up at him to see the Cheshire grin on his face. "Then whose?"

"King Jedidiah and Queen Alexandra's."

"Who?" Casey didn't know enough about the history of her newly adopted country.

"The last king and queen. He has Parkinson's and retired a few years ago."

She did remember that. Sort of.

"The queen asked me to take over as their head of security when their current one retires in a couple of months. The former king doesn't travel anymore, and the queen mother seldom does."

Hope began to blossom. "You'll be home every night?"

He kissed her again. "Maybe not every night, but most of them, and you'll have Thor to keep you company." The puppy they found a few weeks earlier would make the trip with Mark's parents in a few days.

"Perfect."

"That's what I thought when the queen offered it to me." He kissed her several more times, all softly. "I did realize something else when I talked to her."

"What's that?"

"I never really loved her, not romantically. I thought I did. Maybe I could have if it had been an option, but I didn't. Certainly not like I love you, Mrs. Bertolini."

Casey was glad to hear that as it set one of her minor fears to rest. "I love you, too, Mr. Bertolini."

After one more kiss, Casey pulled out some knitting as they settled back into their seats for the rest of the journey to their new home. Their first home together.

And Casey couldn't be happier that a dating app and a stowaway cat had led her to find the guardian of her heart.

The End

Questions

1. Have you ever felt so strongly about someone or something, such as Mark about Addie, but realized it wasn't God's plan? How did you handle it? How did Mark?

2. **1 Peter 4:9-10**—Who in this book lives out the hospitality and serving mentioned in these verses and how did they live it out?

3. **Psalm 37:4-5**—What were the desires of Mark & Casey's hearts? How did God provide for these desires? Or did He?

4. **Ecclesiastes 4:9-10** talks about having friends and why they are important. There are many friendships in this book. Which ones stuck out to you and why are they a good example of a friendship?

5. Casey had a stowaway cat. Discuss a time when trying to help someone did not work out the way you thought it would. What was the ultimate outcome?

6. Queen Adeline signed Mark up for the dating services. What were her motivations? Was Mark's reaction appropriate? How would you have handled it? Have you ever had a friend do something for you that you weren't crazy about?

7. If you had gotten a text from a stranger, such as Mark got from Casey, how would you have responded? What are some examples of people in the Bible helping strangers? **Gen. 19**, **Joshua 2**, & **Luke 10:25-37** are just a few examples.

8. Casey & Mark have a discussion about their future & locations. What would you be willing to change for a potential spouse? What did Casey & Mark decide to do and do you think it was a good plan?

9. Have you ever had the instant connection with someone you just met, as Casey & Mark seemed to have had? Who was it and what happened? (doesn't have to be a love interest)

10. What do you see for Casey's & Mark's future?

About

When she's not writing about her imaginary friends, *USA Today* Bestselling Author **Carol Moncado** prefers binge watching pretty much anything to working out. She believes peanut butter M&Ms are the perfect food and Dr Pepper should come in an IV. When not hanging out with her hubby, four kids, and two dogs who weigh less than most hardcover books, she's probably reading in her Southwest Missouri home.

Summers find her at the local aquatic center with her four fish, er, kids. Fall finds her doing the band mom thing. Winters find her snuggled into a blanket in front of a fire with the dogs. Spring finds her sneezing and recovering from the rest of the year.

She used to teach American Government at a community college, but her indie career, with nearly two dozen titles released in the first 2.5 years, has allowed her to write full time. She's a founding member and former President of MozArks ACFW and is represented by Tamela Hancock Murray of the Steve Laube Agency.

Newsletter:	carolmoncado.com/newsletter
Author Site:	www.carolmoncado.com
Facebook page:	www.facebook.com/CarolMoncadoBooks
Reader Group:	bit.ly/MoncadoReaderGroup

Crowns & Courtships

Heart of a Prince

The Inadvertent Princess

A Royally Beautiful Mess

The Indentured Queen

Her Undercover Prince

The Spare & the Heir

Crowns & Courtships Novellas

Dare You

A Kaerasti for Clari

Love for the Ages

The Monarchies of Belles Montagnes Series

Good Enough for a Princess

Along Came a Prince

More than a Princess

Hand-Me-Down Princess

Winning the Queen's Heart

Protecting the Prince (Novella)

Prince from her Past

And many more titles...

Introducing

Dear Reader,

'Thank you for joining Mark and Casey as they tried to figure out whether their differences were too big to overcome!

From the time I wrote their first scene together in *Good Enough for a Princess*, I knew bodyguard Mark thought he was in love with Crown Princes Addie. It would never work. I always wanted to know more about what happened to him after she found her Happily Ever After—and now I know!

If you want to know more about Addie and Charlie, you can read about them in *Good Enough for a Princess*. Jonathan and Kenzie found each other in *Discovering Home*—and you can find out more about Gwendolyn and Adam there, too.

The Crossroads Collections are all so much fun in how they intertwine! Figuring out how Mark and Casey's story fit together with Amanda's story was a blast.

Up next is the final book in this amazing collection!

When I read Chautona Havig's summary, I knew I couldn't wait to read the story!

Endless zoological facts? Check!

A cute girl who sticks around anyway? Yep!

What more do you need?

A picture of a mandrill monkey? Got that too!

Keep going to read *Random Acts of Shyness* by the amazing Chautona Havig!

Author of *Guardian of Her Heart*

RANDOM ACTS OF *Shyness*

By

CHAUTONA  HAVIG

Published by

PUBLICATIONS

Copyright Notice

One

With more care than necessary, Heath Karras pushed the door shut until he heard the soft click. Jacket off and hung by the door, his shoes followed. For half a second, he almost thought he'd done it. However, as he turned around, there stood his sister, bouncing up on the balls of her feet with the energy of a border collie and twice as cute.

"So... how'd it go? Did you like her? Was she pretty?"

Dodging the subject—futile. The moment thwarted, Selby made an English bulldog seem almost compliant and docile. Still, he tried. "I don't want to talk about it."

Heath dug his phone from his pocket and plopped down on the couch, feet propped on the arm. The intensity with which he regarded that screen should have counted for... something. Again, wishful thinking. Selby slid across the coffee table and came to rest just inches from him, concern etched in every feature—concern and dismay. "Life cycle of a dung beetle?"

"Don't I wish."

"Ugh." Selby slipped off the table and plopped on the floor beside him. A hand stole over his arm and squeezed. "Just tell me it wasn't the mating chimps."

Thank you, Lord, for that. I wondered where You were... again. But I need to remember. It could have been worse. I could have fixated on the chimps, so thanks for that, anyway.

"Um..."

Putting her out of her misery would benefit them both, but he couldn't bring himself to say it.

That's all she needed to know. "Oh, Heath, no. Not the bladders."

"It's better than chimps?" Even as he spoke, his confidence in that wavered.

"Well, that's true." Selby sat up. "It's a new year, right? We'll try something else. You don't have to be trapped in this forever. It's time to take charge."

How many times had he heard it? How many times had he wondered why he didn't put a stop to all meddling? *I'm not in junior high anymore. And she's not Mom.*

"I'll ask Kelsey about it. I mean, she knew Jordan..."

What else Selby said, he never heard. As he had many times, Heath tried to imagine a whole, rich life alone. Instead of a wife and children, he'd have his sister, the husband she'd find someday, and her children. Like every other time, it failed at the idea of a life without someone to love and cherish *because* of his issues with dating. If the Lord never chose to bring someone into his life—he'd deal with that when it came.

I just don't want my personal issues to make it impossible. Is that too much to ask?

"—learned about this phobia. It's kind of cool in a weird way. *Venustraphobia.* It means a fear of beautiful women. I think maybe if you went to a therapist—"

That caught his attention. "I'm not sure I have a *phobia* of beautiful women, Sel. I just make a fool of myself around them. I'm also *not* going to a therapist. Period. I'm just not. So..."

"Then we create your own regime. I'll talk to Kelsey and..." She shook his head at the panicked look he hadn't been able to repress. "Okay. Just remember that you promised me. You said if you hadn't had one good date by the beginning of the year, that you'd try things my way."

There was the rub—he had. He'd been so sure that having a list of topics to focus on would work this time—what, with all the practice he'd done. Still, even as he nodded his agreement, Heath's stomach churned. To get both of their minds onto a different subject, he did the only thing he could.

"Tonight's hint..."

That did it. Selby jumped up, her eyes darting around the room as if he'd hide anything where she could just *see* it. "Well?"

"January third..."

She grinned, waiting for more.

"March." Heath sat up and met her gaze with a smile—she loved him, this sister of his. Not *just* because they were related. He knew that. She enjoyed him. And if she did, someone else would someday.

Again, Selby asked, "Well?"

"It's not St. Paddy's Day without it."

She raced for the freezer, tore through it, and found the mint chocolate chip ice cream he'd thrown in for a decoy. "I've got dessert!"

"Too bad you don't have your gift."

From across their apartment, they gazed at one another. Heath almost had to gag himself not to give another hint. She peeked into the fridge and shut it almost immediately. A slow spin in the kitchen didn't help, but just as he thought she'd ask, something shifted. A second later, her head disappeared as she dug into the cabinets by the stove. Seconds later, she emerged with a wrapped cylinder.

There was his cue. While she tried to guess what was inside, Heath dragged himself across the living room and into the kitchen. "Just open it." Two bowls and two spoons. "You know what it is anyway." Ice cream scoop—the creation of two perfect bowls of ice cream goodness was underway.

"I do not! It could be a scarf, a sweater, or even a sweatshirt or hoodie."

Heath pushed Selby's bowl over to her. "Open it."

The wrapping paper peeled off in a single move—just as it always did. The girl had skills. "An oatmeal container? So help me..." She shook it. "Okay, no. No 'porridge' for Christmas. That would be cruel."

As she peeled the plastic lid from the container and pulled the burnt orange sweater from it, Heath grinned. "Thought it was time you had a proper sweater for St. Paddy's Day."

"You just want to pinch me. I know you." Though Heath thought she might throw it at him, she didn't. Instead, she flung her arms around him.

"Thank you for being the best brother ever. No one I know gets *twelve* gifts for Epiphany."

"Well, from what I read, your church should."

"Not like *you're* doing! I swear, I should have converted to Anglican years ago. Think of the *loot!*"

Only Selby Karras could make a greedy, materialistic comment like that and the true state of her heart shine through. Heath just hugged her and said, "What'd you learn today?"

She gave him a sidelong glance. "That the month associated with January third is October and not March?"

"Good thing that sweater is *orange* then, isn't it?" A spoonful of ice cream flew at him. Heath missed it with his mouth, but he managed to scoop it from his shirt before it landed on the floor. "Yummy."

"You did that on purpose!"

"When I realized that it was the *third,* I figured you might buy that I mixed it up and did March again. I also figured your little shamrock earrings would give you that spot of green to wear with it—win-win."

Once more, Selby's arms wrapped around him, but this time, she didn't thank him. Instead, she whispered. "Are you okay?"

All ground he'd gained in watching her with her gifts zipped backward at warp speed. The picture of Jordan Aylward's keen blue eyes and sandy curls filled his mind. The way her eyes crinkled when she gave him an awkward smile and shook his hand. The button nose...

His reply came out in a ragged whisper. "Selby, she had *freckles.*"

Selby's arms tightened. "I'm so sorry..."

"That man will be single for the *rest* of his life." As she drove through the streets of Fairbury, the worst date she could ever have imagined replayed until Jordan Aylward begged the Lord for mercy. "Isn't it bad enough I'll have to rehash this with mom?"

She pulled onto Primrose Lane and up to the house she called home for the last and the next eight months. Though a nice, roomy 20's bungalow,

Jordan had her eye on the houses in the "tree streets." Holly Circle would be preferred, actually. Just in case the Lord was in any doubt of that, Jordan sent up a silent reminder.

Mail—none for her and only junk mail addressed to D.C. Wright. Junk she couldn't throw away because D.C. insisted that she save every piece of mail with his name on it until he returned from a fifteen-month deployment. "Well, at least it's no bills." Thanks for small favors came to mind. Jordan offered them. It's what she did.

The entry clock—who had those things anyway? She thought it every time she looked at it, and every time, Jordan had to admit that it was handy. It read eight. "I shouldn't have been home until at least ten. And then I should have whined all the way to bed at midnight for agreeing to a Thursday-night date."

Jordan made a stop by her room to grab sleep pants, shirt, and underwear. Linen closet—towel. And in the bathroom, she stared at herself in the full-length mirror. The reflection didn't even hint that she was such a troll. "I always thought I was reasonably interesting and attractive. Who knew?"

Half an hour later with a giant bowl of ice cream, her hair still wrapped in a towel until she could blow out some of the curls, Jordan tucked herself into the couch and told Siri to call her mother. As usual, the phone went to voicemail, but in typical mom style, hers rang just five minutes later.

"Okay. I got the dogs put out. What went wrong?"

"And what makes you think anything went wrong? I mean, eight-thirty for a date. Most mothers would be thanking the Lord for their daughter's good sense in coming home at a reasonable hour on a work night."

Her mother would have nothing to do with it. "Spill it, girl."

"Well, where do I start?"

"Is he—I mean *was* he cute?"

"Scary cute in that hipster, semi-tall, dark, and handsome with a nice beard sort of way."

"Ouch."

And that's reason #242911194...point 4 why I love you.

"So, what happened? Are you sure it's as bad as you think?"

What else could she do? Jordan took a giant bite of double chocolate crunch and grumbled, "Bladders, Mom," around a mouthful.

"Sorry, you must be drowning your sorrows in frozen chocolate. I didn't quite hear that. It sounded like 'bladders.' Did you ask why it matters?"

"Nope." Jordan took another bite, smaller this time, and let it mostly melt before she repeated herself. "You heard me right. Bladders."

Ever the zoologist, her mother confirmed that indeed, most mammals have them. "Except rats—no wait, that's *gall*bladders. But what does that have to do with your date?"

"Well, I have a little-known fact for you, Mom. Most mammals of over one kilogram take approximately twenty seconds to empty their bladders. Cat or elephant, it doesn't matter. Twenty to forty seconds is the norm."

Her mother protested that it had nothing to do with the problem with her date. Jordan begged to differ. "First the guy spent about twenty minutes explaining why it was the same time for all mammals—"

"Predators. I know. I didn't know about twenty seconds, though."

Good. You're rolling with it. At least it'll give you a laugh now. With that thought prompting a smile—and another huge bite of ice cream, of course—Jordan moved in for the kill. "It's all in the urethra. An elephant's is huge, of course. A cat's, not so big. And never fear, he's got the scientific journal to back up his information. Very thorough."

"Wait. Your *date* read to you out of a scientific journal on the mammalian emptying of bladders?"

"Yep—or tried. He didn't actually read much to me. First, he *told* me all about them, and then before I could get a word in edgewise, he pulled out his phone and started reading the study."

Her mother's groan helped soothe the irritated edges of her emotions. "I am so sorry. I get what you mean. He will be single for a long time if he doesn't figure out how to talk about books and movies or something a bit more benign." A pause hinted at what would come next. "How'd you get out of it?"

"I dug a twenty out of my purse, stood the minute he finished reading, dropped it on the table, apologized, said I didn't think we were compatible, and bolted."

"At least you didn't dine and ditch..."

And in that reply, Jordan heard everything she needed to. "I think he's nice, Mom. I do. I just—I don't know. Maybe he's autistic and I was just a jerk, but I couldn't listen to any more of it."

"You don't have to, Jordan. The right guy is out there somewhere. You'll either find him and be happy, or not and you'll stay single and happy that you didn't settle for someone who makes you miserable."

"And regale me with stories of bladders and urine during dinner. Yeah." Instant pain came with her next bite, and Jordan jumped up, hand to her head. "Thanks, Mom. I'm going to bed. I've got an ice cream headache now."

"I love you, girlie. Just keep up the faith or whatever I'm supposed to tell you religious types. Sending happy vibes."

Happy vibes. "Love you, Mom."

Five minutes later, Jordan sat in bed, iPad in hand, staring at the website she'd seen advertised that afternoon. "I said I wouldn't need it, but..."

Betwixt2hearts.com. Of course, there were options—personal matchmaker or computer generated based on commonalities and interests. It also included a nice long list of questions—including those needed for a background check. *I've got nothing to hide, I'm sick of blind dates,* and *I'm also ready to meet someone. How weird is it to admit that?*

The temptation to "do it later" convinced her. "I never do it later. Never." In the time it took to type in the memorized credit card numbers and hit submit, she'd done it. Step one to a new life. Step two... open the email. When it came in. It would take a while, surely.

I hope.

A momentary twinge of regret struck as Selby's phone alarm chimed the five-minute warning before her favorite class began. "Heath better appreciate that I missed organic chemistry to try to experiment with his."

The dashboard read nine-forty by the time she pulled into the parking lot at The Coventry. A quick text to Reid Keller earned her an even quicker reply.

> **REID:** COME ON IN. BACK DOOR.

That's all it took for her to bolt from the car. He stood there, sleeves rolled up, a curious expression on his face. "Selby Karras?"

A lifetime of introductions on support-raising tours didn't end with three semesters at the University of Rockland. Selby stuck out her hand automatically and thanked Reid for giving her a few minutes of his time. As he shook it, she translated his confused expression. "Sorry... habit. But seriously, I appreciate you talking to me."

"Not sure what I can do," he protested.

"Kelsey said if anyone could help, you can."

"Well, I wasn't shy or awkward, though..."

"But someone helped you get a move on anyway. What did it?"

Reid opened the kitchen door and urged her in out of the cold. "It was taken out of my hands. My landlord decided to deliver the flowers and card I'd ordered for my mom to Kelsey. It said how much I loved her. And I couldn't deny it even when I had to confess that it was meant for someone else." He smiled at her wince. "Yeah, awkward, but it did make me say something sooner than I'd intended."

"Forced... how can I *force* Heath not to talk about weird, random animal facts?"

Reid had picked up a knife and had reached for a zucchini. He had. But that stopped him, knife poised as if ready to throw. "You want to force him *not* to do something? Does he really think girls are interested in animal facts?" His eyes widened, and a smile formed. "Little brother? Maybe... twelve? Thinks—"

"Older brother—almost thirty. Still traumatized by our mother forcing him to ask a girl out every time we were in the States—for cultural literacy."

"Cultur—"

Selby couldn't take it. "Trust me, we had weird classes in our school."

Knife replaced, arms folded over his chest, Reid gave her a, "This I gotta hear," look and asked, "Such as...?"

"Commercial Jingles 101. The History of Sitcoms." At his look of disbelief, she added, "Socialization of American Children."

"Homeschooled?"

She nodded. "On the mission field, no less—Dominican Republic."

"Aaah... I get the literacy then. I guess..." He picked up the knife again. "But it didn't work out for..."

"Heath." Selby shook her head and leaned against the prep table, fascinated at the speed with which he turned the zucchini into perfect slices. "No... what worked in awkward situations while visiting churches to raise support didn't work with girls. But he'd already trained himself to do it. And the more interested he is, the worse it is."

She waited a moment, uncertain if she should risk mortifying her brother further and then threw discretion in the waste bucket beside Reid. "Over a hundred dates since coming to live in the States."

The next question—so obvious she almost answered it before he could ask, but it wasn't nice—not nice at all. So, she waited. After the better part of one of the longest minutes of her life, Selby would have given up, but then he asked.

"How did he get so many girls to go out with him?"

"Girls like him. They give him their number. He sends a text message or tries to email. People also like to set up the MK." Reid's blank look prompted her to translate. "Missionary kid. So, he gets lots of blind dates. Once he thought he'd meet someone at church for a first date. He did great all the way through the sermon. After the final hymn and prayer, he stood, turned to ask her if she'd like to go out for coffee, and said, 'Did you know African civet coffee isn't the only partially digested coffee out there? In India, rhesus monkeys spit out coffee cherries and then they're harvested, cleaned, and roasted.'" Selby shrugged at Reid's incredulous expression. "She chose to take that moment to excuse herself."

Reid reached for more zucchinis. And began chopping again. "I would have, too."

"Anyway, as you can see, I need help. Kelsey said to talk to you. What do I do?"

"I'd say talk to Wayne at The Pettler. I mean, he's the one who came up with getting us together. I didn't do any of it. Maybe he'd know?"

Within ten minutes, she'd said goodbye, driven across town, and burst into a humid florist shop. A woman with dark hair and a wide smile greeted her. "How may I help you today?"

"I'm looking for Wayne? Reid sent me. About Kelsey's flowers."

The woman started to respond, but a voice from behind the curtain called out, "Send her back. Reid just messaged me to say you were coming."

"But, Wayne—"

"Now, love. I'll keep working!"

Despite the exasperated look that crossed the woman's face, the moment she stepped into the back, it softened. She moved to Wayne's side, kissed his cheek, and whispered something that sounded like, "Don't meddle. It won't work every time."

Ignore her. Meddle. Please.

Wayne pointed to a stool and asked to hear her story. So, as if she hadn't already done it that morning, Selby went through the history of their respective childhoods, Heath's disastrous dates, and her desperation to find him something that would work. "Reid thinks you're just the man for the job."

If she'd expected Wayne to snap his fingers and shout, "I've got it," the moment she finished, Selby would have been disappointed. In fact, she didn't expect him to do it at all. But he did. He actually did—just after more of life's excessively long minutes.

"I've got it! There's a new dating service based out of Rockland—Stamped with Love—but it's countrywide. It's a great concept. They do snail mail with service-provided post office boxes and everything. Maybe if he writes to someone and really gets to know her, he can explain his nervous habit and—"

She had to stop him before he convinced her. "No, no. Sorry. But that's not going to help him overcome it. It's just going to prepare some girl for the awkwardness. We need a way to get him *over* it."

For the next twenty minutes, they discussed a dozen ideas, but Wayne's only contribution was the snail-mail dating service. Even as she left, he gave it one last plug. "After all, he doesn't have to try to be anyone but himself. They can progress to phone... and then maybe Skype. You know, get up and walk away if he starts to spout stuff. Come back with duct tape over his mouth or something."

If he hadn't winked right then, Selby would have blasted him for making fun of her brother. *That's my job.* Instead, she thanked him anyway and pretended not to see her speedometer inch closer and closer to the right as she sped back to Rockland.

One idea formed as the snowy landscape whizzed past. *"... he doesn't have to try to be anyone but himself..."*

"Maybe that's the problem. Maybe he needs to quit trying to be himself and practice being someone else—someone who doesn't cope with awkwardness by relating the digestive habits of cattle."

The numbers stared back at him—a nice, round five-thousand dollars in the furnishing category. Hands spread out over the cheap, Formica dining table, he relaxed. "Hey, Selby! It's time!"

Only then did he recall that she hadn't come home from classes yet. A glance at his phone showed a message he'd missed.

SELBY: STOPPING FOR STARBUCKS. TEXT ME IF YOU WANT
ANYTHING.

But before he could respond, keys rattled in the door before she burst through, a carrier with two coffees. "I took a chance that you'd like a peppermint latte before they're gone."

His eyes strayed to the bookcase while her back was to him. *How do I give a clue for that?*

"Heath?"

"Sorry... just thinking about how to give you a hint for your gift." He turned the laptop around and pointed to the furnishings column. "I have enough to buy the table, chairs, and still keep a buffer."

The latte landed before him without spilling *too* much, and she squeezed his shoulders. "Did you order yet?"

"I thought I'd have you do it. You know how to tell them what we want. As long as it's like the reclaimed scaffolding one we saw, I'm good."

"Of course! But the benches you were going to choose—ugh. Ugly *and* uncomfortable."

He still didn't know if he agreed. "But they match... and benches mean we can put more people here."

"Because you always have more than eight people over, right?" Selby plopped down in the chair next to him and dragged his laptop over to face her. "I'm ordering this now before you decide that you need triple what you spend before you spend it."

Well, a lifetime of weighing every dime spent doesn't go away overnight— not for some of us, anyway. It wasn't a fair thought, and he knew it. Still, Selby had adapted to American life much easier than he had.

"There. Read that... and then I figured out half your problem. So, you'll want to hear it."

He glanced around the room again before the idea hit him. "And while you tell me, you might wander through the forest for your gift."

She'd made it three words into her "brilliant idea" before his words registered. Selby whirled in place and gave him *that* look. The one that he never quite knew what to do with. "Did you say to wander through the forest?"

"Well, ignorant pessimists might say the graveyard." As Heath winked, he added, "And that's *all* you're getting out of me."

Watching her process the semi-riddle might have made a braver man snicker, but one didn't mock Selby Karras. Then, as if she hadn't been confused a moment before, she made a beeline for the bookcase, not stopping for breath as she laid out her plan. "It's all in the act. You go into it as someone else. You're not Heath Karras the Miserable. You're cool Heath who isn't nervous around beautiful women—especially not ones with freckles—and who knows how to set *them* at ease by controlling the conversation with questions and insightful observations about everything except animals."

"So, be fake."

Selby jerked a book of fairy tales from the shelf—the one his grandmother had given him when he was four—and flipped through the pages. When it ended up empty, she shoved it back on the shelf and turned to look around the room again. Then his words registered, if the indignant look on her face meant anything.

Before she could object, he continued. "Because all dating advice out there says the same thing, right? To be an interesting date, just pretend you're someone you're not because *that* is what girls really like."

"No..." she whirled to face him, hands on her hips. "I don't mean *that*. I just mean that you know who you are with everyone else. And with practice, you would be with freckle-faced women, too, right? So, you're going into your next date with the mindset that this *is* who you are. It's not something you're *telling* yourself to do. It's who you *already* are. See?"

"I see that you're trying to mortify me even more than I thought."

"I'm trying—" There, Selby cut off her own words. "Wait. Forest. Graveyard..." A smile formed as she rushed back to the bookshelf. "Tree carcasses. Only you...." One finger flipped along the titles until she saw it. A moment later, the wrapped book lay on the soon-to-be-ousted Formica table, and she peeled the wrapper off in one motion.

"Happy Christmas."

"November..." She read the gold imprint on the leather cover of the journal. "Gratitude—thanksgiving." The hug she gave him almost soothed her next words. "You promised, Heath. You said you'd try."

Of course, he had. Refusing Selby? Impossible. So, he'd just agreed, sure she couldn't come up with anything more miserable than what he'd already endured. *Do not ever underestimate her skills again.*

"Heath?"

"I'll do it, of course. Well…" She fired a look at him—one daring him to back out now, but he wouldn't. "I should amend that. I'll *try*. We both know I'm not likely to succeed."

Her fingers flipped through page after blank page as if between those lines of nothingness she'd find the perfect idea. When she stopped turning, unease churned in his gut. She had.

"I've got it. It's kind of silly, but it'll work." At his, "gimme your worst" look she grinned. "It's so simple, too. We don't *expect* you to do great with any of them up front. It's about practicing, not about finding *the one*. Not yet."

Maybe I should have stayed on the mission field. Seems easier than the dating minefield, anyway.

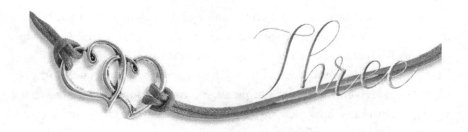

Three

The call came at ten-thirty. Arnie Holtz. Jordan tapped the screen and answered while trying to keep the sigh from coming through in her voice. "What's up with the mail, Arnie?"

"How'd you know it was the mail?"

"It's ten-thirty. Dickie just finished your street."

The grumbles, half-hearted as they were, ranged from her being a smart-aleck to spying on him. But eventually, he got to the point. "Don't like to bug you on a Saturday—day off and all…"

"That's a lie, and you know it. You'd bug me every day and twice on holidays if I'd let you get away with it."

"Fine. Glad for an excuse to bug you," he groused. "Is that better?"

Jordan decided that the cat and mouse routine had gone on long enough, so tossing aside her novel, she sat up, leaned forward, and grabbed her coffee as she asked again, "What's up?"

"Got a letter. From a law office. Don't know what it is, but it's um… will you come? Just for a minute?"

A last longing look at the novel she'd waited months to have time to read almost stopped her from asking the question he knew she would. "Can I bring you anything on my way?"

"Well, I heard The Deli has Rubens again…"

"With extra kraut?" Why she bothered asking, Jordan didn't know.

"And a bottle of that fizzy lemonade?"

"Well..."

Her heart softened at the half-crack she heard in Arnie's voice. "Be there in twenty."

As expected, he stood there on his porch on Dogwood, hands stuffed in the pockets. Waiting. A smile formed as she pulled into the drive. *Lord, help me remember that he's just lonely. I need to remember that.*

Arnie came to "help" her inside, as if he were the overpaid, every-other-weekday caregiver. He carried her purse and bag of food and insisted that she hold onto his elbow as he led her up the treacherous, ice- and snow-free walk. "Nice day, isn't it?"

"It's freezing, you ornery old coot, and you know it."

"You only call me that when you don't think you should tell me you love me."

And of course, you know that. Still...

"Mind if we read the letter first? I don't want to eat if that thing's going to upset my innards."

Unease crept closer to her own heart as she settled everything inside and flipped through the mail. Three letters, she filed in the "to be paid" slot of the 80's reproduction rolltop desk he used. Well, *she* used for him. The last was from Roth, Jothikumar, & Sylmer, in Rockland—family law. "Family law? Do they handle estates?"

He shook his head. "Roth handled adoptions back in the day."

Something in his voice made her send a sharp look his way. "Um..."

"It's not good. I know it. I just don't know how. Do they give you death announcements for adopted kids?"

It didn't sound like anything she'd ever heard of, but Jordan couldn't say. For the millionth time, she gazed around the room—exactly as it had been decorated by his wife, Helen, back in the eighties. The neo-Victorian wallpaper, lace curtains, and Home Interiors wall decor placed exactly as the demonstrator had probably suggested, complete with wall sconces on either side. Their wedding photo flanked by their last couple portrait.

And not a single photo of a child anywhere. They hadn't been able to have any.

"Jordan?"

"Are you sure you want me—?"

"I can't do it, but I didn't think I should throw it away—not that."

I knew you threw away some of your mail. Time to have important stuff sent to a PO box and to get you on some shut-in mail lists so you get real mail.

The once-overstuffed couch swallowed her as she seated herself and peeled back the envelope flap. Creamy letterhead from the firm with Roth's contact information hinted that Arnie had guessed right. "Do you want me to read it aloud or..."

"Read it first. Then tell me."

The letter looked as generic as possible—on page one. Flipping it to the next page, the paper changed to inexpensive computer printer paper and only a hand signature at the bottom. Floyd Brighton. "Do you know a Floyd Brighton?"

Arnie shook his head. Anyone watching him would have assumed he was as calm as could be, but that twitch below his eye gave him away. "Someone from the law office?"

"No..." Jordan held up the first paper. "This is from Roth's legal assistant. She says that a man contacted them about an adoption fifty-one years ago. They believe you are the man that this guy's looking for. This..." She shook the second letter. "It's from the Floyd Brighton. Want me to read it?"

"Is it bad?"

Jordan just smiled and began.

Hello,

My name is Floyd Brighton. When my biological mother was pregnant, she arranged for the offices of Joshua Roth to find adoptive parents for me. I was adopted and never had any interest in finding my biological parents. I had friends over the years who had also been adopted, and I never understood why they wanted contact with the people who had either selfishly or selflessly relinquished their parental rights. The former were people I didn't want to be associated with. The latter deserved the privacy they'd asked for.

Then my parents were killed in an accident a couple of years ago. I was their only child. Most of the rest of my family is on the west coast, so family became a priority in a new way. My letter to my birth mother was returned with a handwritten, "deceased" on it.

Arnie groaned. "Barbara? Dead? Everyone's dying." She'd have gotten up to hug him, but he pressed her to continue. "Please."

> I didn't think the agency knew my father's name, but when I asked if I could send a letter to him, they said they would forward anything I sent. So, I'm sending this letter. If you are the father of a baby boy born May 4, 1967, at Brunswick Community Hospital, and if you would consider meeting me, I'm sending my number.
>
> I don't want anything from you—not anything like money or help. I'm doing well. Have my own drywall business. Have a great wife, three kids, and my first grandchild due any day now.
>
> I don't expect explanations. I just want to know you if you're out there. I was too late for my biological mother. I hope I'm not too late, in any respect, for you.
>
> Floyd Brighton
>
> (930) 555-9035

Arnie sat, elbows on his knees, head in his hands. "I wanted to marry her—Barbara. I wanted to raise that baby together, but she said no. Back then, a father couldn't get custody if he wasn't married. So, I said goodbye and that was it. Met my Helen..." His voice cracked. "We couldn't have children. I even tried to contact Roth and see if they could tell me if the child had been adopted. I never knew if it was a boy or girl. The secretary did tell me that they had placed the child."

"Do you want to call?"

The man's head wagged like a puppy's tail. "No... no. But if you would... Tell him you'll meet him? See if he's okay? Do a search on the Giggle? See if he seems legit?"

"It's *Google*. Not 'The Giggle.'"

"Google, giggle. Same difference. Can you do that?" He reached for his wallet. "I'll pay extra." Her piercing glare worked. With a sheepish expression, Arnie scratched his back and assured her he just had a pinch back there. "But you'll vet him for me?" He frowned. "That's what they call it, right? Vet?"

"I'll cyber-stalk him until I can tell you what size shoes he wears and where he stands on immigration."

That worked—just as she'd known it would. A tirade on the evils of modern immigration practices filled the room as Arnie unfolded the paper wrapping of his Ruben and spread it out on a tray in his lap. If she hadn't been there, he'd have leaned his recliner back, but he'd have paid for it later, too. So, with the corned beef, it's best that she *was* there. The heartburn...

Neither of them spoke until Arnie balled up the paper wrapping and tried to make a basket into the brown paper bag on the coffee table. And missed. As usual. "There goes—"

"Your NBA career." Jordan grinned at him. "I know."

"And you'll look him up... Floyd?" Arnie's nose wrinkled. "Unfortunate name."

"Why's that?"

He grinned at her. "I won Barbara away from Floyd Oberon. He treated her bad. I told her she deserved better. She agreed." A softer quality entered his tone as Arnie continued. "Then she agreed too well—she deserved better than me, too."

That, Jordan couldn't ignore. "Not true, Arnie. She just got a big head."

A call from The Pettler startled Selby right out of her organic chemistry assignment. "Hello?"

Heath looked up from where he prepped food for the week and gave her that, "What's up?" look.

"Wayne here—we talked the other day?"

"Yeah..."

The man plunged onward as if he hadn't noticed her panic. "Got Kelsey to give me your number. Hope that's okay..."

"Sure. Fine. What's up?"

"Well, I was talking to my sister and learned that my nephew is starting up this *online* dating thing—"

"You told me—snail mail and—"

"No, no. That was the one I recommended, yes. But this is new. Online. They have an app for security and everything. There's a lot of people already signed up in the Rockland area—which is what gave me the idea. You could sign up your brother for it. That'd be a good way to meet folks. Maybe get to know them first…"

The temptation to brush off that idea fizzled in the wake of the realization that it wouldn't have to work that way. That's where she could find lots of people for Heath to practice on. "What's the name of the site?"

"Okay, it's betwixt-2—like the numb—uh—*numeral*, hearts-dot-com. I can text it to you. Just send a message and tell Camden that I sent you. I should get good uncle points for this or something."

True to his word, the website, betwixt2hearts.com, showed up in a text message a minute later. Trading textbook organic chemistry for creating a little for Heath, Selby opened a new tab in her browser and typed it in. With one click on a heart labeled, "Join to find your heart-mate," an application process began. But as each screen passed, one after the other—not showing what kinds of questions he'd need to answer, of course—she deleted the profile and started again.

Fifteen minutes into it, Heath came and hovered over her shoulder. "What're you doing?"

"Filling out this online profile for this site—Betwixt. If they aren't too weird, we'll fill one out for you, but you have to give them all kinds of information first."

"Like what?"

"Employment history, residence history—that'll be a fun one for them—and stuff like that. It's like a credit application or something."

He squeezed her shoulder and went back to packaging his weeks' worth of food. "More like a background check. It's probably some kind of safety measure to make sure you don't have a felony or something."

"Probably…" the reply spilled out, and Selby hoped she said what she thought she did. "Didn't read the fine print…"

After twenty minutes, the actual profile questions appeared. One by one, she plowed through them with a lack of thoroughness that would ensure a terrible match if she actually intended to go through with it. But the site offered a fourteen-day money-back guarantee. She'd request it the minute she was done.

At "What is your most bizarre quirk or talent?" she winced. Selby leaned back in her chair and eyed her brother with as much nonchalance as she could muster. "How truthful do we have to be with these things?"

Heath leaned against the counter and returned her gaze. "Like what? Don't say you're thirty if you're fifty. Don't say you love hiking if you are allergic to fresh air. But I can't see you doing those. So... like I asked. Like what?"

"It wants to know your most bizarre quirk or talent."

Her heart constricted at the agony on his face. "Well, I think we just ensured that I don't have an excess of women beating down the door to meet me."

"Do we have to put your *most*? What about the fact you can whistle 'Jesus Loves Me' through your nose?"

"Because that's so much less disgusting than dung beetles."

Selby leaned back in the chair, profile abandoned, and crossed her arms over her chest. "Trust me, my brother, it is." Head cocked, she tried to think of the perfect answer. "I think I'll put down that I first got married when I was nine. It's true..."

"And Dad annulled it within half an hour."

"Still, it was legal."

"To Johanny, anyway." Heath began covering containers again. "I nearly got into a fight over that one. I was so mad at him."

She typed in her marriage answer before protesting. "He proposed, I accepted, we gathered our bridesmaids and groomsmen. I even had my white Easter dress to wear."

"And Mom's sheer curtain to cut up into your veil."

She couldn't help but grin at him as the memory of her mother's ire over that curtain. "If Eimy hadn't told Mom about the curtain, no one would have known until I was fifteen and Johanny's priest blessed it."

"Which is why I gave Eimy candy every week for a year."

"I would have confessed in six years..." Selby winced. "Wouldn't I?"

"Who knows? Just finish that thing and tell me how bad it's going to be."

He had a point. But by the time she got through the first twenty questions, she didn't know if it ever would end. At, "Describe your perfect date," she quoted Miss Rhode Island from *Miss Congeniality* instead of something more original. *Besides. Who else will be quoting movies with their answers?*

And with that, the rest of her answers were just that—movie quotes. Life motto? The one about hairy legs, courtesy of *Return to Me*. For her life's priorities, she said the world would be a better place if everyone valued cannoli over guns—courtesy of *The Godfather*, of course.

"So glad I watched *You've Got Mail*."

"Do I want to know?" Heath started across the room, but she waved him off. "I'll take that as a no."

"I wouldn't know how to answer half of these if Mom hadn't done those cultural literacy classes. This is so much fun now."

Heath settled himself into place next to her and smiled. "So... fake answers?"

"For a fake profile, yes." She hit "next" and a final summary of herself popped up. "Okay... we've got this. I'll request a refund later." After flexing her fingers and tapping a new window, Selby was ready to begin. "Card?"

Though Heath made a show of exaggerated reluctance, Selby thought she caught a hint of excitement in him, too. Still, he asked, "Do you really think this'll work?" as he slid the card across the table."

"Not at first. But with practice. We just have to practice you being who you are inside on the outside. That's all."

And the work began. Employment, health, education. Easy-peasy. Explaining why he didn't see his parents often—not so easy, but at least they saw grandparents on holidays, and he lived with his sibling. "That would be me... score one for closeness without unhealthy dependence!"

Hobbies—not many. Some of the questions, she could answer without thinking. Others captured her attention—and her heart. "So... what is the most important thing you are looking for in another person?"

He didn't even hesitate. "Aside from being sold out to Jesus first, which I already said, then someone totally comfortable in her own skin. If she likes who she is, I probably will, too."

"Why do you have to be my brother? If it didn't gross me out to think about it—no offense—"

"None taken."

"—then I'd be in love with you by now."

"Thanks. Maybe there's hope." Heath pointed to the next screen as the slide zipped past. "Does it really ask if I'm looking for a woman with children? Isn't that just begging for pedophiles to crawl in?"

She hadn't even thought of it. "I'll send them an email voicing our concerns. Meanwhile, are you okay with divorced or single moms?"

Of all the questions he'd hesitate on, that one surprised her. Heath sat there, hands wringing in his lap, eyes closed. Was he—he was! He was praying! Eventually, with an agonized expression on his face, he sighed. "I'm okay with single and widowed mothers. But until I study more, I don't know about divorce. I want to say I don't care, but I was talking with someone at church last month, and I can't get his words out of my head."

"Judgmental, much?"

Heath pleaded with her. "Just put it down. I don't want to start studying this after saying it's no big deal to me and then meet the perfect person just as I find out that Don's right."

As much as it galled, she put it down. "I think I'm glad I switched to Anglican."

At that, he pulled the laptop from her, hit the next button, and told her, "Wise men still seek Him."

With a squeal, Selby hopped up, kissed his cheek and began scanning the room. It took longer than it should have to find a small package covered in burlap and under the manger in her creche. "Oh, how clever! Seek *Him*. I love it."

Unlike all the other gifts, this had nothing related to the month associated with the day of Christmas. And, as predictable as it was, Selby couldn't help but squeal again as she unwrapped the first little bottle— frankincense. The next, of course, would be myrrh—the two essential oils she wanted most and couldn't afford. "Heath, these are so expensive. I—"

"*Feliz Navidad*. Now open the last one." And with that, he went back to typing in answers that she hoped wouldn't send the organizers running.

Of all the things he could have done for gold, a tiny charm with #seekingHim... "Oh, Heath..."

"Like it?"

"Love it. But you know..."

His eyes met hers over the top of the laptop screen. In unison, they said,

"People will ask if I—you—found Jesus yet."

"It's a good opener," Selby mused. "I just realized that. Thanks."

"So happy to have you here. I would never be doing this..." Heath waved at the screen. "—if you hadn't come."

"We've got this, Heath. We do. They'll find someone who thinks you're almost as amazing as you really are. And after you've been married for a few years, she'll figure out just how amazing you really are. Probably after—"

"The birth of our third child, I know, Miss Marple."

Selby only did a curtsy and moved to take over the profile process. He'd agonize over some answers for hours if she didn't. "Okay, so what about your willingness to relocate."

"Only within commuting distance."

"Got it..."

Four

The modern office with its sleek lines, on-trend furnishings, and latest in technological gadgets always seemed out of place to Heath, but he stepped in and waited as Ann Weik's receptionist asked if she could, "Send him through."

The director of Rockland's zoo welcomed him with a smile. "So glad you could give me a few minutes to go over your resume and your goals for the department. We would, of course, prefer to keep this position in-house, but you are young..."

The interview process began. Most of the questions he'd expected, but a few felt very much like the previous evening's profile process. So, when Ms. Weik asked, "And what would you say your greatest personal weakness is," Heath choked.

"Um, probably my propensity spout random facts about the animal kingdom when I'm nervous—usually while on a date." A sickening sinking feeling struck his gut as he realized that she hadn't meant *that* personal. Things became even more horrifying as he found it impossible to keep silent. "I have very few second dates, as you can imagine. No woman wants to know the life cycle of a dung beetle or the mating habits of chimps over salmon and rice pilaf."

Silent orders to shush it failed. Heath would have continued, but Ms. Weik blinked at him. "I've got one for you. What about the time it takes to empty a mammal's bladder?"

"Twenty seconds—up to forty. It's all about—" Dismay poured from his pores in a disgusting display of nervous perspiration. "I know I haven't asked you out, Ms. Weik. How'd you know...?"

"My daughter is Jordan Aylward."

And there goes any chance at this promotion. Unsure what else he could do, Heath murmured something about her having a beautiful and gracious daughter. "She wasn't rude—even after I was. I appreciated it."

The awkward silence began. Heath tried *not* to avoid her piercing gaze, but it wasn't easy. Desperate for some sort of closure, no matter how awkward, he rose. "I suppose you would probably prefer I go. I'll understand—"

"Sit down, Heath."

Heath sat.

Like a CEO in a boardroom of a Fortune 500 company, ready to exact some evil takeover, Ms. Weik sat there, hands tented under her chin, watching him. Just watching. "Are you religious, Heath?"

"I'd say that most people who aren't Christians would call me religious, yes. I prefer faith-filled."

"That'll work. Tell me something."

He winced at what question she could ask. Still, his career might still be salvageable. He had to try. "Yes?"

"Did you enjoy your time with Jordan before...?"

"Before I ruined her appetite and made her think I was some Hannibal Lecter in training?"

"She didn't think that. She did, however, remark that you would be single for the rest of your life."

Ouch.

"I agreed with her... then." Ms. Weik leaned forward. "Now, I'm not so sure."

"I liked her. She was funny, kind, and..." What did he have to lose? Hopefully nothing. "Um... well, she had freckles."

A slow smile appeared on her face. "Oh, really? And you..."

Explaining would probably seal his fate, but he couldn't lie, either. "I grew up in the Dominican Republic. Only sixteen percent of the country is white. I saw very few freckles, so every time I came back to the States on furlough, I liked them more and more—so cute. Almost like the body is saying, 'I want more color, too!'" Of course, he couldn't stop there. No... he had to blurt out the rest of the truth. "They also remind me of this spotted llama I saw in an animal park when I was little. I begged for weeks to be able to buy that llama."

The expressionless mask Ms. Weik wore fell off. Laughter bubbled over. "I've always liked you, Heath, but never more than right now."

"Glad I didn't just ensure I got myself fired for insulting the boss' daughter."

"Did you mean to insult her?" He didn't even have to answer. Heath's face must have given away his horror because she laughed again. "Didn't think so." A second or two passed before she added, "Did Jordan tell you where she lives?" At his nod, she smiled. "Then you should know that my daughter is an understanding and forgiving girl. She doesn't know it, but she's also a romantic. She'd respond favorably to someone who was a secret*ive* admirer."

"Meaning?"

"If you want another chance, you'll have to take the initiative. Make it possible to figure you out but don't advertise it, either."

The perspiration thing ramped up to epic proportions. "You think?"

"Yes. Now get out of here. I'm pretty sure Roger needs input on the new chimp enclosure."

Heath jumped up, considered offering to shake her hand and rethought that at the clammy feeling. "Thanks." At the door, she called him back. "Yes?

"Be sure to request... um... privacy for those chimps, will you?"

With an hour between classes and only a ten-minute walk, Selby decided she'd better call Betwixt and tell them what she was doing with Heath's matches... and why. It would go to voicemail. Everything did it seemed. So, she didn't even bother waiting to get inside. With temperatures hovering at a balmy ten degrees, she hit the call button the moment she stepped out the door and got ready to leave a message.

A man picked up a moment later. "Thank you for calling Betwixt, I'm Camden Hutchins, how can I be of assistance?"

"Oh! A real person. Novel idea. Wayne Farrell from Fairbury gave me this number. Um, I'm calling about my brother's account."

"Sorry, we do not—"

Selby didn't have time to be told all about the privacy policies she'd read thoroughly the previous evening. "Yes, I'm aware of safety issues. We respect that. But my brother has given me permission to have his information. I can even log into his account. I just need to ask you about dates."

"I cannot share that information."

The explanations began. Her brother's social awkwardness, the multitude of failed dates. Her plan. "I'm just asking that you not put him with his *perfect* match right away. I guarantee you. He'll botch it. We need lots of messed up dates, first."

"I can't just give women dates that I know aren't good for them. They're paying for careful consideration of their wishes—not to be guinea pigs. My answer is no."

Impatience, combined with chattering teeth, made her next statement both difficult to spit out and a danger to the two years of very expensive dental work their uncle had sprung for when she arrived in Rockland. "Surely, you have some in the Rockland area who aren't matching well with anyone yet? Be up front. "We have a forty-six percent match for you. The other party is willing to meet if you are. Would you consider it? Blah, blah, blah."

Still, "Camden" refused. "No. We use a carefully researched algorithm. It provides the best possible and most compatible match based on answers given during our—"

"—extensive profile process. Yes, I've read the web copy. Oh, and you have a typo on the privacy policy page. I think it's at the end of paragraph three."

"Umm... Thanks."

"Look, my brother is a great guy. Every word of his profile is true—

strengths, weaknesses, all of it. You can see for yourself that he's a catch. But until you see that random facts thing in action, you can't really understand how debilitating it is. He just needs a chance to learn how to resist that urge, and my plan will make it happen. But not if you give him the perfect match right away. It'll take a few tries to perfect the process."

"Process or no, I cannot give out personal information."

Her huff might have been rude—probably was, if she were honest with herself—but Selby didn't care. "Look, I just want to be able to help him figure out which girls to go out with first. Is that so bad?"

Again, Camden refused.

"Wayne said you have a partner. Why don't you talk to her? Ask her how she'd feel if no one gave *her* a chance to become the best version of herself. I suspect she'll be more understanding. Oh, and take down my number so she can call if she has questions."

"I—"

Selby didn't give him a chance to argue. "On second thought, I'll just text it to this number. That's easier for all of us." *And she probably has access to the texts so she'll actually see it.*

"It isn't necessary. I cannot and will not do this. Thank you for your interest in our service, and if we can be of any further assistance, don't hesitate to shoot us an email or use the chat box for quick answers to questions. I don't know why Uncle Wayne gave you this number, but we do not publicize it and would prefer you not use it."

It had almost been too easy. No, Camden didn't sound all that helpful, but Wayne would do something about him, and his partner... "Any woman involved in matchmaking is going to see finding just the right girl for someone like Heath as a challenge. That's all I need right there."

The lace was starting to get to her. It wasn't that Jordan didn't like lace but rather that she didn't like such a superfluity of it. Yes... a *superfluity. It's the best word for it. Even if it is a bit over the top for a Fairbury bungalow.*

Then again, the lace was over the top for said bungalow. She'd never asked if Arnie kept it around because it reminded him of Helen or because he liked it himself, but the temptation had become almost unbearable. Only her mentor's words, *"Some people cling to the past with everything they have because they know their future is short"* kept her opinions to herself. For now.

Still, maybe just a *little* less? At least on tables where food could stain it? *I could rip it while trying to get out that marinara...*

Guilt struck hard and fast. No. Jordan Aylward would *not* destroy someone's property just because it annoyed her. *Wait'll Mom hears about that.*

"Jordie?"

Only Arnie dared call her "Jordie," and while she'd never admit it, she liked it. "Yes?"

"Did you happen to check out Floyd Brighton?"

After an exaggerated glance at her watch, Jordan winked at him. "You made it a whole hour and a half. I'm impressed."

"Nearly blurted it out when you walked in the door."

"I thought so..." She dumped some peroxide in a bowl, dropped the lace in it, and shoved it under cold water. "Be right there, and I'll show you what I found."

Arnie didn't go, though. He came over and fingered the cheap lace runner with a lost expression in his eyes. "Maybe you should just throw it out."

Though hope welled up, his tone stamped it down again. "I think I can save it."

"I guess. They're good quality, unfortunately."

"Unfortunately?"

He nodded, poking it once more. "They just won't wear out—no matter how many times I wash them."

As she dried her hands, Jordan turned to face him and gave him her best, *"You'd better level with me"* look. "Do you *want* them to wear out?"

"Of course. You don't think I *like* all this fancy stuff, do you?"

"It's in your house..."

"Helen's doing. She saved all her allowance to buy the decorations herself. I spent mine on golf clubs—good ones. Still can't keep a ball out of the sand trap."

A Crossroads Collection

Some people might have asked why he didn't just get rid of them, but Jordan knew. "Well, if you'd like *me* to wash them, I think I can ensure that you don't have to put them back out again."

"I'll give you a raise."

"Don't need one. Not for that. But you're going to owe me a piece of that red velvet cake truffle that Audrey makes when I show you all I've been doing to check out your son."

Arnie clutched his chest, and Jordan's heart kicked it into double time at the sight of the perspiration beading on his upper lip. "It's really him?"

"Well, the lawyer wouldn't have forwarded that letter to the *wrong* person, would they?"

Even Arnie couldn't argue with that.

"Now, come sit down. How's your heart feeling?"

"I've got the healthiest heart in the country. I just haven't ever heard anyone say that before. 'Your son.' Always wanted a son. Wouldn't've known what to do with a girl, but I was a great boy—did all the things a boy does. Fish, hunt, baseball, army—you name it, I did it."

Jordan let him talk as she led him to the couch and pulled out her laptop. Showing him the information on her phone would be sure to set off a tirade against the tiny screens. "Okay, I started with his name and came up with his drywall business, so I went to Yelp."

"What's that?"

She explained the website that rated businesses and showed the yelp rating. "He has mostly five-star ratings. One guy gave one star, but if you look at it, it's just for having a higher estimate than someone else and not being willing to match a low bid. I think it'll get taken down if the company sees it."

"Glad to hear he's not a pushover."

"Then I went to Facebook. I mean, if he's a good business guy, maybe he's a good guy, too."

Arnie leaned close as the window popped up with the large profile picture she'd left open for him. Anyone doubting the veracity of Floyd Brighton's claim to be Arnie's son would just have to look at the picture. Without a word, Arnie stood and went to a drawer in the desk. He flipped through several envelopes and pulled one out.

Back at the couch, he shook the contents into one hand, flipped through, and removed a photo from the stack. "He's my boy. No doubt about that."

"I agree. Or you have a younger doppelganger."

He set the picture down. Side by side, you would have thought it was the same man—right down to the thinning center of the head. Arnie must have been thinking the same thing, because he thumped the picture and said, "He'll have nothing up there in five years or less. All the men in my family are blessed that way."

More pictures showed a wife and him holding a baby. "You're a grandpa and a great grandpa both."

Of all the clients she worked with, Arnie Holtz would have been the *last* she'd ever imagine breaking down, but the man clutched her laptop as if a lifeline and wept.

"I'll contact him, for you. I'll meet and have coffee—see if he's as nice as he seems. It'll be okay. You'll see."

Five

The chances of finding Jordan on the streets of Fairbury at the exact time he rode through town, looking for the ice blue Honda Fit with the JORDANA license plate. Having watched her drive away had that one advantage. Now to find it... and hopefully not waste all the gas he'd burned driving all the way to Fairbury just to begin a silly "semi-secret-admirer" plan.

Worst of all, even if he found the car, Heath hadn't decided what he'd *do*. It was one thing to say, "Show your interest" but an entirely different thing to *do* it in a way that would intrigue rather than creep out the intended target. *Now I sound like a military guy on a mission.*

After two loops, the cop on the corner began to watch without hiding his interest. That wouldn't do at all, so Heath pulled into the drive that led to a parking lot behind The Fox Theater. There it was—her ice blue Fit. Almost as if God had said, "Here you go. Now do something."

Except Heath didn't believe God worked that way—not usually, anyway. The car there meant one of two things. First, that he could just find a way to leave a note on the car and call it good. Second, that he could also do a little reconnaissance. *Maybe I wouldn't like her if I knew her better. Watching makes sense. And maybe then I can figure out how to leave a note or something.*

With that in mind, Heath climbed from the car and started to lock it.

However, the parking lot lights shone on his hoodie in the back seat. With a hood, he might disguise himself better. People often remembered his hair more than anything else... *Yeah. Definitely.*

It was too cold for just the hoodie, so Heath pulled his coat on over it and took off toward the street. A glance left showed a few shops and The Grind. *She might like coffee. Could buy her next cup if they know her here...*

Jordan wasn't in The Grind, however. She wasn't in Bookends, the music store, or a crafty store promising to help create the most beautiful scrapbook layouts for Valentine's Day, either. He pressed onward, checked out The Diner, glanced in the candy store, the little delicatessen, and even around the corner to a mailing center.

However, just as he'd decided to go back and see if the flower shop was still open, Jordan stepped out of the post office. He passed her, but she didn't seem to notice. *I'm probably kind of forgettable in a totally unforgettable way.*

At the corner, he turned to see her talking with someone—an older man. Her arm came around the guy's shoulder, and as they approached, he heard her say, "—emailed me back. I'll meet with him this week, and if he's the man I think he is..."

He couldn't explain why his heart sank, but it did. *She's already met someone else.*

Heath might have turned away, but her next words stopped him. "I don't have to keep being the middleman, Arnie. If you're ready to take over, I can give him your number and—"

"No. I trust you. Did you check out his wife?"

It's not a new date. Relief he couldn't explain washed over him. *Have to think about what that means later.*

"Arnie" told her to enjoy her coffee and promised to call when he got home. "Thank you, Jordie. You take better care of me than any daughter I could have hoped for."

"No offense Arnie, but I'd be your granddaughter—or close to it."

The original coffee idea resurfaced, with a shot of inspiration. He hurried into The Grind just a minute or two before her and at his turn, slid a ten-dollar bill across the counter. Keeping his voice low, he said, "I want to buy Jordan's coffee. Keep the change, but can I get a coffee sleeve and a marker? I'd like to leave a note on it."

Never had he been more thankful for teen baristas with overly-romantic notions fueled by a steady diet of Hollywood and television. The girl nearly sighed as she passed them. "It's totally sweet of you. Guys don't do stuff like that anymore." With each word, the girl's voice grew louder until Heath couldn't hear the door for her not-so-subtle hinting.

He assumed the red-eared guy cleaning tables in the corner was the object of her ire but tried not to show he understood. Instead, he thanked her for it and took it to the edge of the counter where he could write in relative peace. Figuring out *what* to write—not so peaceful.

By the time he'd finished, he expected her to be in line already, but instead, Heath jerked open the door and almost barreled into an astonished Jordan. "I'm sorry. Did—?"

"Aaak. I almost—are you okay?"

Heath grinned and stepped aside. "I'm fine. Sorry about that."

"Have a good night."

A glance back as he let the door close behind him showed Jordan watching him. Was it—? *She blushed!*

His more rational, scientific side argued that stepping inside out of the cold had produced the rosy cheeks. *Then again, she looked back. That counts for something. If she remembered me, she wouldn't—unless she doesn't hate me... yet.*

The dearth of available men in Fairbury. It had been her favorite rant since moving to town, and every woman at church and in her social group said the same thing. There were more single guys than women in town. Jordan was just too picky.

When she nearly plowed over a reasonably handsome guy, with a decided lack of wedding ring—not that she'd *looked*, of course... *Yeah, I totally looked. Single unless he's of the "rings are a sin" or the "just lost five hundred pounds, so it fell off" persuasion.*

That he could be a cheating jerk who kept his ring off whenever away from home did cross her mind. Jordan dismissed it. There'd been no tan line, no indent—nothing to hint of a usual ring. Not that she'd looked for those either. *Ahem.*

Dark hair? Probably—if the beard color meant anything. With the hoodie he'd worn under his coat, she could only guess. Striking blue eyes. No ring. Never had the lack of left-handed jewelry been of such obvious import.

Import. First superfluous and now import. No more nineteenth-century literature for a month—no, two.

Only after she'd given him one last look, and caught him glancing back at him—how embarrassing! Only then did she turn and allow the rich scent of coffee to invade her senses. It might be scientifically unverifiable and possibly even ludicrous, but every time she entered The Grind, Jordan became more convinced that caffeine particles were unleashed in the air with each mocha or latte made. Just sniffing the air could clear the mind.

Aya, her favorite barista, bounced up. "Isn't he cute? What's his name?"

Jordan shrugged. "I don't know."

Eyes wide, Aya reached to her left. "Your usual?"

"Yeah..."

The girl dragged a cup with a wisp of steam exiting the tiny sip hole from behind the counter. "Here."

"That was fast?"

"Cutie got it for you."

Lord, can I just thank You that she didn't call him "Mr. Hottie" like that last man she salivated over? Yeah. Thanks.

Right about then, Aya's words clicked. "Wait, that guy? He bought me this? How'd he know I was coming in? He was going out when I left?"

"I don't know, but he just came in, bought it—great tipper, too—and asked for a sleeve and Sharpie."

Sleeve. Jordan turned the cup until a short message appeared. *Did you know your freckles make me smile?*

"That's not exactly helpful..."

"What is it? Jason wouldn't let me read it—made me promise."

But Jordan didn't answer. In fact, she didn't even reply until the cold air from outside blasted her as she opened the door. "Night, Aya. Thanks. And be nice to Jason. He's one of the good ones—just too young for me, unfortunately."

A glance through the window as she passed showed one of those still vignettes that Norman Rockwell would have captured. Aya leaning over the higher counter side, head in her hands—Jason trying his best not to look her way, a smile on his lips.

The coffee, perfect. The message, cryptic. Officer Joe stood at the corner, hands stuffed in his jacket and looking much too cold. Seeing him gave her an idea.

A wave, a smile, she hurried to his side and pointed at The Grind. "Did you see the guy who just left there?"

"Dark hoodie and work overcoat?"

"Yes!"

Joe just nodded.

"Well... do you know who he is?"

Everything in Joe's demeanor changed. Just as the first snowflakes of a predicted heavy snowfall landed on her sleeve, he stepped toward the street. "Did he bother you? He sure seemed odd. If he's who I think he was, he—" Midsentence, he pointed at a car that pulled out from behind The Fox. "That car. I'd recognize that Flex anywhere. He pulled out his phone and called for another officer, but the car turned up the square a ways and then pulled out toward the highway. "He's going right past the station. Get that license number."

They stood there, shivering while waiting to hear back from whoever Joe had spoken to. "Hey, want a coffee? I could go get—"

He shook his head. "I'm going home in an hour. Unlike Alexa, if I drink coffee when I need to sleep, I won't.

Jordan had nearly finished the coffee before the call came back through. Joe looked ready to blast someone as he listened. He jabbed the phone screen with his thumb and shook his head. "Sorry, Jordan. Judith tried, but the car was too far down the road before she could catch up—too far out of our jurisdiction."

"Well, thanks for trying."

"I'll keep my eye out. We don't need people harassing—"

"Oh, no!" She felt her cheeks heat and shifted out of the light. "He just bought me coffee, and I wanted to thank him. I just don't know who he is."

As sincere as she was, Joe didn't look convinced. "Well, if you see him again, make sure someone's around when you do it. I didn't like the way he hid back there behind The Fox and then showed up in a hoodie and wandered all over the place without buying anything."

She waggled the empty cup and began backing across the street. "But he did. He bought my coffee. Night!"

Instinct nearly prompted her to toss the cup in the garbage as she passed The Fox, but Jordan opted for a photo first. *Mom'll want to see this.*

By the time she turned into her drive, the snow came down thick, heavy, and coating everything with a fresh layer of white stuff. By the time she got settled inside, picture taken and sent to her mother, a fire crackled in the little fireplace that D.C. hadn't had time to remove before leaving for Syria.

When she finally sat curled up on the sofa, phone and novel in hand, her mother's reply came.

> MOM: SECRET ADMIRER? I THOUGHT THOSE WERE OUT OF STYLE.

Jordan shot back a reply.

> JORDAN: I HOPE NOT. THIS GUY WAS CUTE, AND THAT WAS A NICE WAY TO SEMI-INTRODUCE YOURSELF.

Mom shot back one more reply.

> MOM: EXCEPT HE KNOWS YOUR NAME, AND YOU DON'T KNOW HIS.

Something about the words didn't ring true, but Jordan couldn't decide why. Just as she fell asleep, the reason became obvious. *I don't know if he said my name or not. He could have just said the next woman who comes in if he knew I was coming... somehow.*

Six

A phone appeared where her organic chemistry text should be. Heath's voice boomed in her ear. "They matched me. What do I do?"

Almost as disoriented as if she'd been ripped from sleep, Selby blinked at the screen. "What?"

"You're the one with the great plan. Fix this!"

Just a first name. Whitney. A circle beside the name showed a dark-haired woman wearing red, but it didn't tell Selby much. Just as she tapped the photo, her phone buzzed. The woman—she had to be ten years older than Heath. "She's pretty..."

"She's..." closed out of the larger picture and tapped her name. "Forty-one."

"You said ten years either way... And you need practice. So, let's do this."

A fresh round of objections followed—just as she'd expected. For every anticipated protest, Selby shot back a carefully rehearsed rebuttal that he'd never be able to refute. In the end, he sank down beside her on the saggy couch and asked for his first assignment.

"I'm going to give it everything I have so you can't blame me when it fails." He shot her a pained look—one that almost broke Selby's resolve. "And it will fail."

"Oh, ye of little faith. If you just had a mustard seed's worth, you could move mountains of dung beetles from your mind the next time a freckle-faced girl winked at you."

Heath just waited, thumbs paused.

No one can say he doesn't try. That's big, anyway.

The first message they wrote together. Her reply came immediately. She was eager to meet. Shoving her textbook aside, and settling into the corner of the couch, Selby grabbed the phone and reread it. "Sounds desperate."

Heath blanched.

Good. You need to be nervous. Selby typed out a response and passed it to him. "How's that?"

HEATH: HOW WOULD YOU FEEL ABOUT COFFEE WEDNESDAY NIGHT AFTER CHURCH. ESPRESSO YOURSELF IN BRANT'S CORNERS?

Resistance settled over Heath's shoulders. Just as she expected him to wrap it tightly around him and refuse to agree, he nodded. "Okay. I'll go to church in Brunswick."

She tossed aside the phone and flung her arms around him. "Thank you."

"Thank me?"

"You did this, knowing how hard it would be, because you trusted me. That's big. So yeah, thanks."

Her phone blipped before he could answer. She fumbled for it, and as she tapped in her password, Heath said, "Should I at least exchange a few more messages before I agree?"

"Coffee after church isn't a big deal, is it?"

"I guess not."

What else he said, Selby didn't hear. The message: from Betwixt. Subject? Your first match.

"Oh, no..."

"What?"

"That fake account?"

Laughter boomed out across the room. "You forgot to cancel?"

"Yeah."

"Well, maybe they found one of our true loves then, right?"

Fingers flying as she scrambled to read the contract once more. Thinking aloud, she muttered, "Whew. First match is free. They haven't charged my card yet. I'll just send a message to cancel now..."

"Don't." Heath reached for her phone and put it behind his back. "Seriously," he added at her protest. "Just listen. If you do this, too, I'll have an idea of how you as a girl feel about it. Right? And you can give me better pointers."

"I have school! I don't have time for this."

He pushed away her hands as Selby fought to retrieve her phone. "You know how you burned out last semester. You can just agree to occasional chats, and one or two meets a month. Any guy who doesn't respect your need to study isn't the one for you anyway, right?"

Smiling—yep. It disarmed him. Selby dealt a knockout punch to the idea in one simple, irrefutable argument. "That's true. I do need to make that happen. But we both know I can't afford this. I'll just have to imagine things. That won't be too hard."

"You're right. You can't afford it."

Defeat sucker punched her and knocked her smug refutations out cold as she realized what he'd say next.

"But I can."

"That's a low blow, Heath."

His smile disarmed her—the one that made the sides of his mustache dance each time he tried to repress it. "Yeah... but you'll say yes, won't you?"

Without a word, she tapped the message and read it. The guy's profile—something about it felt familiar the more she read. "Hey, Heath. Old movie. Black and white. One of those strong, silent type actors. He plays a hick, I think. I keep seeing him by some old farmhouse."

"That only describes a dozen or two movies we've ever seen."

"He says just one word. 'Hopin'.' Know what movie that is?"

How he'd remember a single word from a movie she couldn't identify any better, she couldn't imagine. It was insanity, but still... Selby read the message again. "The question is, 'Do you believe in the idea of a soul mate?' And the answer he gives is, 'Hopin'.' That's so familiar."

Heath closed his eyes and said it a few times... deeper... higher... with an accent. He jerked bolt upright. "You sure the guy said it? Could it have been a girl? Coonhounds baying?"

That's all she needed. "*Sergeant York*! I should have known. Gracie Williams says it when he says he'll see her around."

"Yep." Heath's gaze fell on her—she could feel it. "Um... why do you think it's that?"

"I think that's how we got matched. Listen to this one. 'What would you hope for most from a connection on Betwixt?' He answers, 'The beginning of a beautiful friendship.' That's from Casablanca."

Heath leaned over and tapped the reply button on the screen. "If they found someone else who answers in movie quotes, he's got to be the guy for you. Is there a picture?"

A lump filled her throat. She hadn't let herself look too closely. That first glimpse had hinted that he looked a little like Johanny. "Yeah."

"And?"

With the chat box open in the app, she couldn't show him the picture so while Selby worked to construct a clever response to, "'Make my day' and respond to this message."

Instead, she just sighed and said, "The tiny thumbnail they gave me hinted that Johanny might have a doppelganger."

"Make that a good reply."

"I was thinking about asking him if he was in a coma."

Heath took the phone and read it. "Why?"

"Then when he says no, I could tell him I was glad, or I'd probably spend the night confusing him."

His laughter prompted her to do it. His, *While You Were Sleeping* guess confirmed it. If he could remember a romantic movie when he'd only been into animals, war, and westerns told her there was a shot. "Okay... here goes."

The reply shot back a moment later. "Oh, dear. Oh, oh, dear. I might be in love already."

"Why?"

"He just wrote back, 'That's it. You're the one for me. I'm here ready to 'eliminate lower back pain.'" Heath didn't remember it, but she did—a two-week Hallmark Masterpiece binge with her mother when she was fifteen. "It's *Follow the Stars Home*. Best proposal ever."

"I'll remember that."

Tuesday morning, before he'd even made a dent in the email pile clogging his inbox, a message came in from Ann Weik's assistant. "Ann wants you in her office in ten. Does that conflict with anything on your calendar?"

Assistant speak for, "You'll be here and on time, right?"

"On my way over."

"Thank you. She's in a weird mood today."

Uh, oh...

With two minutes to spare, he found himself sitting in the chair opposite his boss again, unsure if he should feel like the guy vying for a promotion or the guy asking for a parent's approval before dating her daughter. Both—nerve-racking.

The last few letters of whatever she'd written down ended in a trailing scrawl. Heath couldn't read it, and he could tell no one else could, either. "Sorry. Just finishing a few things. Now, first, about that promotion."

Job mode. Got it.

"The board objected to your age and lack of experience for the head of the mammal department."

"I understand. It was—"

"So, I told them that either they hire you or they find a new director."

How was he supposed to respond to that? A couple of stammers only earned him a *look*—one he suspected that meant more than, "Spit it out, man."

Heath tried again. "That is kind of you, but of course, they didn't accept. I'm content where I am for now."

"They did not accept my resignation. They put you on a two-year probationary period. During that time, they'll look for a candidate that will please *all* of us, and you have the chance to wow them with your efficiency and care of our residents."

Residents—he'd almost blundered the first time he heard her refer to the animals as "residents." It had been his first hint that the seemingly cold woman who had hired him actually loved the creatures in their care.

The meeting he'd dreaded for the eight and a half minutes he'd endured the wait had turned out great! "I can't—wow. Thank you. If I can—"

"You can. Prove me right. Now, the coffee..."

So much for this being a great meeting...

"That was genius. She's so curious about who it could be. That note—perfect. I caught on right away, but I had inside information, of course."

"I second-guessed that choice of words all night. Too personal... too ambiguous? I mean, how could she possibly know I liked the freckles? But I made it possible to find me if she'd wanted to race out of there."

Something in Anne's demeanor shifted. Her snowy blouse draped elegantly over arms that, seated like that, reminded him much of Jordan's. *I must have stared at her arms when I was trying not to stare at those freckles.*

"Well, let's just say it's good that you got around the corner before she could catch up. She stopped to talk to one of the local officers—see if he saw you. He did. He thought you were skulking around town. That almost got me in trouble."

"Why?"

Ms. Weik gave him an enigmatic smile. "I almost laughed. She'd want to know why I thought it was funny. I can't lie to her—not that she's gotten all religious. But I can't tell her the truth... Awkward."

Interesting. Your daughter *gets "religious" so you decide that means you can't lie to her. I wonder what that means in the bigger picture.*

"Heath?"

His vision cleared and he nodded at her. "Yes, ma'am?"

"Don't. Even. Think about calling me that. I'm not a ma'am kind of person. I keep meaning to tell you that. And now that you've been promoted, maybe you'll stick with Ann like I told you to when I took over this position."

To his chagrin, Heath almost echoed, "Yes ma'am." He stopped himself just in time. "Sorry, Ann. My mother's from the south, so..."

"Old habits die hard. So, what do you have planned next?"

Admitting he didn't know—probably not the wisest plan, but especially after her comments about being honest due to her daughter's faith, even evasiveness seemed out of line. "I don't know. I just know it'll be Wednesday night. Late-ish or immediately after work. It depends on if I can find her anywhere."

"She goes to church Wednesday nights—in Fairbury. They have an after-church thing. Coffee, snacks, *et cetera*. She tries to stay for most of them."

He'd stop… either on the way there or back. Hopefully, by then, he'd have some kind of inspired idea. "Thank you for being encouraging, Ms.… Ann. I know I'm throwing out blind long shots, but I keep hoping to get a feel for who she is while I do it, so I'm taking it slow. She was kind to an elderly man the other night."

"Arnie. A son he relinquished for adoption fifty years ago has found him. Jordan's making sure he isn't some kind of scammer."

Heath would have replied… somehow. However, Ann seemed lost in a thought that she'd eventually share with him, and something deep within his spirit prompted him not to distract her from that. And there it was—the shift. Ann looked up at him, leaned back with her hands folded in her lap, and met his gaze. "Can you tell me something?"

"I'll try." What else could he say?

"Why do religious people have to go to so many church things. Jordan's there Sunday mornings and many nights, Saturday nights for some singles group, Wednesday nights for Bible study, a women's study once a month, and I don't know what all."

Sometimes, being a missionary kid had its perks. "We don't *have* to be anywhere, Ann." His eyes scanned the room, and the answer came to him. "You love art, right? Real art?" He pointed to a few pieces around the room—the magnificent painting of a mandrill behind her.

"Obviously…"

"So, when do you go to art museums?"

"Whenever I get the chance—often on my lunch breaks if I'm downtown."

Heath didn't have to explain further. He just needed to wait. And wait…

Again, the tented fingers, her head resting on them. Her eyes piercing him. "So, you're saying that religious people consider church kind of like a hobby?"

He shook his head. "Christians consider ourselves a family. We love each other. We want to spend time together. We love Jesus. We want to spend time with Him—learning more about Him."

"Kind of like you want to learn more about Jordan, so you look for ways to see her?"

"Exactly." The question brought up one of his own—one he'd already talked himself out of asking. Twice. But he couldn't ask Selby without telling her about the secret admirer plan, so he'd waited.

"You have a question for me, don't you?"

"Sort of. It'll probably get me orders to stay far away from your daughter, but it's been bothering me. And if I should stay away, I need to know."

"Let's hear it."

The story emerged in sputters and spurts. Finding her car accidentally, looking all over town, seeing her with the old guy. "At first, I thought she was dating someone already. I was disappointed—a lot more disappointed than reasonable for having only met someone once. It..." He swallowed down several words that flew toward his lips and settled on one a little less intense. "...unnerved me."

"I can see why—if you thought you were already attached to Jordan. Do you *really* think it's that? Or were you just looking forward to trying a different approach to getting to know someone who intrigues you?"

Relief doused him and left him almost nauseated. "That's exactly it."

Something in Ann's features changed. She leaned forward as if to see through him. "You were ready to walk away, weren't you?"

"If I couldn't come up with a reasonable explanation, yes. I'm messed up enough without adding..."

"Premature attachment?"

"That'll do it. That. I'd be trading one problem for another. But you're right. I'm anxious to try this I want to get to know her better if I can. Losing the opportunity... I didn't like that idea."

He thanked her again for the vote of confidence with the board and the semi-promotion and rose to leave when Ann stopped him. "You took a risk telling me. I respect that you did. Thank you, Heath. I'm glad to know I can trust you like I thought I could."

"Yes, ma—Ann."

"Just keep me in the loop. I'm already enjoying seeing two different perspectives on the same thing."

Silently, Heath said, *Yes, ma'am.* Aloud, he just agreed. "Will do. Thanks, Ann."

On his way back to his desk, Heath got the call—the Grevy's zebra was foaling. "On my way."

Seven

Curled up in her favorite hidden away corner of the campus library, Selby copied out citation references as she chatted with her match—Kevin. Between lulls of movie speak, they asked questions—about movies, of course. Actors, favorite lines, genre... so far, so good. *After all, he hates horror, too.*

Heath's text came through.

> **HEATH:** HEADING OUT. PRAY FOR ME.

It might be an unfair test, but Selby couldn't help but zip the message to Kevin.

> **SELBY:** MY BROTHER IS GOING ON A DATE WITH SOMEONE FROM
> BETWIXT TONIGHT. PLEASE PRAY HE IS CALM.

She hesitated, her pen in her mouth, her knee holding open the book to the copyright page, and her fingers hovering over the keys. *Why not. We live once, right? And praying without ceasing is Biblical. Asking for prayers of the church when we're sick. Well, dung beetle conversation almost fits. So here goes.*

> **SELBY:** HE TENDS TO SPOUT BIZARRE, RANDOM ANIMAL FACTS

Little marching dots in a circle told her Kevin had begun to respond, but they stopped. Several seconds passed. Several more followed.

KEVIN: WOW. I THOUGHT MY MOVIE MALADY WAS A PROBLEM. DEFINITELY PRAYING FOR HIM.

A snicker accompanied her fingers as she replied.

SELBY: SPEAKING MOVIE QUOTE-EESE (OR QUOTES WITH EASE, I'M NOT SURE WHICH IT IS) COULD NEVER BE A MALADY. IT'S A QUALITY I WOULDN'T WANT TO HAVE TO GIVE UP FOR ANYONE OR ANY REASON.

The lights flickered, signaling time for the library to close. Not for the first time, Selby almost hid. She knew exactly how she could, and as long as she didn't go downstairs, no motion detector would send off alarms to security. *So relaxing... just me and a world of books...*

Her stomach rumbled, and the bar glowed at the bottom of her screen.

KEVIN: WELL, TUTORING SESSION IS OVER. LIBRARY CLOSING. GOTTA GO. ENJOYED OUR "MOVIE DATE." CHAT SOON? TOMORROW? SCARLETT O'HARA CLAIMS IT'S ANOTHER DAY.

What were the odds that he was at another library closing at ten instead of eight or nine? Slim—that's what. She zipped back a quick, *You'll have me at hello*, courtesy of *Jerry McGuire* and threw everything into her bag. He wouldn't expect her there, but if she could get to the door...

Selby flew. Down the stairs, past several people who protested at her one-woman stampede, and to the door. A small bench near the double entrance gave her a spot to pause, check her phone, and watch. His message popped up the minute she tapped the screen.

KEVIN: GOOD ONE. I CONSIDER IT FLIRTING, THOUGH. THAT MEANS I CAN, TOO. JUST GOTTA FIND A GIN JOINT TO GET YOU TO

WALK INTO.

SELBY: "YOU DO THAT LITTLE THING."

She saw him just as he got the message, walking alongside the most gorgeous girl she'd ever seen. Skin like a sunset reflecting off onyx—dark but warm and welcoming. If anyone epitomized Selby's personification of beauty, this girl did. Kevin didn't even seem to notice. He paused and read the message, before calling after the girl. "Zoe? Does the line, 'do that little thing' sound familiar?"

"Line? Like a movie?" The girl laughed. "No. It's probably one of those old musicals or something. Gotta go. Jax is waiting out front. Night. And thanks. I think I'm slowly getting the hang of this class."

"You're doing great."

He wandered past, repeating the line to himself, and despite the stupidity of it, Selby followed. Within two turns, she knew where he was going—The Hut. It took effort—way too much effort, actually, but Selby managed to pass him on the other side of the street and make it into The Hut first. Barely.

She stood at the counter, mind blank. The bored guy behind the register just glared. "What'll you have?"

"Um... I—"

"I'll just get his order." The guy looked over her shoulder. At Kevin, most likely, but Selby couldn't afford to look. He might recognize her. "Know what you want?"

"I'll have 'whatever she's having.'"

She didn't believe in love at first sight, but Selby did wonder if love at first quote was a thing. Knowing she'd never be able to make a decision now, she turned, looked him square in the face, and said, "*Meet Me in St. Louis.*"

His voice caught up with her just as she reached for the door handle. "No, *When Harry Met Sally*. Wait..."

Again, Selby caught and held his gaze before slipping through the door and into the street. She backed into the first doorway and waited until her phone buzzed. Him.

KEVIN: DIDN'T KNOW THE HUT SOLD GIN. MAYBE YOU'LL STAY
NEXT TIME.

No response seemed adequate. While Selby worked to come up with *something*, another one popped in.

KEVIN: IS IT AGAINST THE TERMS AND CONDITIONS TO TELL YOU
THAT YOUR PHOTO DOESN'T DO YOU JUSTICE?

Movie quoting ability gone, Selby floundered, fizzled, and failed. An attempt at flirtation? Also failed. She tapped out a quick reply, just one word.

SELBY: THANKS.

Espresso Yourself. He'd been there once when someone broke down at the church in Brunswick and needed a ride to Brant's Corners. Being on his way back to Rockland, Heath had volunteered. The town only had half a dozen businesses, but one was a rather trendy and impressive looking coffee shop. The coffee—better than he'd had almost anywhere.

He'd shot out of Bible study at The Assembly in Brunswick and pushed the speedometer a little to the right of legal to get to Brant's Corners before Whitney would arrive. Only two cars were parked in front of the building when he pulled up, and if the people inside sitting at tables on opposite sides of the great window belonged to them, Whitney wasn't there yet.

The rich aroma of roasted coffee beans drew him inside the moment he cracked open the door. A table in the corner beckoned him. Visible to all but with a hint of privacy—optimal, wasn't it?

Heath just hadn't expected the awkwardness of sitting at a table with nothing in front of him. If he got up and requested water, she could come in and think he was ordering without her. *Lose-lose.*

The word reverberated in his mind until it blended into one, long, awkward cry of *loser...*

A car pulled up, and as the side windows passed, Heath knew it would be her even before she stepped out of the car. Whitney's profile had included her passion for essential oils. Large letters stretched across that back-side window. *There's an oil for that.* The motto for a company he'd *wanted* to get his frankincense and myrrh from. Hard-sell sales tactics had sent him elsewhere. *Please don't let her be like that.*

Just in time, he realized he could open the door for her—and should. His mother would expect it. If the expression she gave him meant anything, he'd made either a very wise or terrible decision. Either way, she was pleased. "Hi! I'm Whitney. You're Heath, of course. Thanks so much for agreeing to meet so soon. I'm not good at online stuff."

What else she said, Heath couldn't be sure. Between something about being constantly misunderstood on the internet, and something about her doubts that an internet dating thing could actually work, she ordered a drink he couldn't have replicated if he tried. And when she asked twice if they'd remembered that she needed *soy* milk, Heath decided for the first time, that the dung beetle might be a blessing in disguise

Or I could talk about kopia luwak. I mean, it fits the setting.

Selby would kill him. He'd deserve the long, slow, torturous demise she'd have in store. *Besides, with a voice like hers, it'll probably be how squirrels can't vomit or burp. I think I'm glad I can. I might need it.*

"—do you want? My treat."

That snapped him out of his thoughts. "I've got it, but thanks. I'll just have a plain black coffee." *With a double shot of whatever will keep me awake on the way home.*

"I have some cardamom in my purse if you'd like it. I love it in coffee. So many health benefits, too. It's an antiseptic, aids in digestion, helps with the aftereffects of chemo, and..."

Lord, help me, I know what's coming...

"It's even purported to be an aphrodisiac."

"Well, my digestion is fine, I don't have cancer or an infection, and I like to trust my love life to the Lord."

They stared at each other, and while he suspected she was aghast at his opinions on cardamom, Heath simply celebrated self-control over his nerves. *This probably means there's nothing about her that will interest me and I wouldn't have been weird at all, but I'm taking it.*

Ten minutes later—minutes that didn't include a word about a single essential oil, in fact—Heath relaxed and laughed at a story about her ferret doing its "happy dance."

"They call them a war dance, but my sister says it looks more like the ferret is drunk—or that it is ferret legging, too."

"Legging?"

"English sport where they put two ferrets in a guy's pants, cinch them at the waist and legs and count how long he can endure the bites and scratches—" The girl's horror stopped him—for once.

"Oh! That's awful! I... ew... ugh. You could get horrible infections from bites like that."

"You should go to competitions, then, right? Take your cardamom?"

He saw it—just in time. If she hadn't been as aware of her surroundings, or perhaps the fact that her coffee was still a dangerous temperature, Heath had no doubt that he'd be sporting it in his face. She jumped up, grabbed her purse, and without a word—an unexpected but enormous blessing—stormed to the door and out of the coffee shop.

At least I'm not burned. I'd deserve it, too. I bet she wouldn't have even shared an oil for my injuries...

Before he got up to go, Heath shot a text message to Selby.

> **HEATH:** I DID NOT TELL ANY OF MY USUAL STORIES. IN THAT RESPECT, THE DATE WAS A SUCCESS. I DID, HOWEVER, INSULT HER PASSION FOR ESSENTIAL OILS, I THINK. SHE LEFT IN RECORD TIME. SHE DID NOT THROW HER COFFEE IN MY FACE. I'M CALLING IT A WIN.

Selby's reply left him standing by the door, blocking the way.

> **SELBY:** I MET KEVIN FROM BETWIXT. ACCIDENT, BUT I MET HIM. HE THINKS I'M PRETTY.

There was only one word necessary for a reply.

> **HEATH:** WHAT?!!!

SELBY: TELL YOU ABOUT IT LATER. I'LL BE LATE. NOT WITH HIM.

That held some reassurance. He'd been all for the matching because he'd been confident it would take weeks for her to even consider a meet up—likely not until Spring Break even. A glance at the time said he could make it to Fairbury long before Jordan left the church—if he hurried. And if she didn't decide to leave before the end of fellowship time.

All down the dark, winding road from Brant's Corners to Fairbury, Heath reviewed the "date" and winced at the reminder that dates were reviewed. "Ouch. That'll be a rough one. I deserve it, too. But could she *be* more stereotypical of a direct sales zealot?"

He may have asked himself the question, but sanity insisted that he not answer.

When a Fairbury officer passed him on the other side, Heath slowed again. Getting a ticket wouldn't be worth it. Several glances in the rearview mirror showed the car disappearing in the distance. The cop wouldn't turn around now. "Saved me with that one, Lord. Thanks."

At First Church in Fairbury, Jordan's Fit sat right under a light, making it unnecessary for him to even enter the parking lot. He pulled up front, car idling, and racked his brains for some idea—any. Coffee was his biggest strength. That sleeve could say a million different things, but he needed her to get one, first. And, she wouldn't get one if she didn't know he had one waiting.

Then it hit him. Inside ten minutes, he'd wedged a coffee sleeve into her door, just above the handle. Inside fifteen, he'd settled himself in a corner with promises from Aya not to tell Jordan he was there. If she recognized him, great—maybe. He sat head bowed over his Bible and tried to pay attention to the verses he'd failed to focus on during Bible study.

She entered half an hour later. Micro-gazes—just longer than a glance but not long enough to be an actual gaze—told him she'd hardly looked his way. Even when he heard Aya say Jordan's drink had been paid for again, she looked out the front rather than around the room. Aya's giggle didn't even give him away.

I think that's good. I'll ask her mom if it comes up. Wish I could tell Selby. She'd know.

First Church of Fairbury had many things going for it—an engaged congregation, a loving minister, plenty of activities for the community to engage in, and no guilt over how many of those you did or didn't choose to be a part of. However, as with every church, one glaring flaw occasionally overshadowed all the good. For First Church, it was their inability to serve a palatable or even bearable cup of coffee.

Swill. That's what some old movie or book would call it. It'd be right, too. To The Grind and then home.

Something wedged in above the door handle caught her attention. Without touching it, she tapped the flashlight app on her phone and stared at it. Jordan blinked. "A sleeve? Coffee sleeve? From—" The memory of the guy and the coffee, of his slightly flirty comment about her freckles, rushed at her.

"It might get me blown up, but I've got to look. Find someone to teach Mom about Jesus if I die, okay, Lord?"

A voice nearby called out, "Did you say something, Jordan?"

Liz Whyte has the hearing of... whatever animal hears really well. A snicker followed that thought. *I bet that guy from the restaurant... ugh. Heath. That's his name. Don't know why I always want to call him Keith. Anyway, I bet he knows what animals hear well.*

"Jordan?"

"I'm fine. Just talking to the Lord. Have a good rest of your week, Liz."

With that, Jordan climbed into the car and using the dome light, looked over the sleeve. No writing. "Maybe I'm supposed to go to The Grind? Is that dangerous? While she deliberated, she told her phone to call her mother. "Got another coffee cup sleeve on my car outside the church. This guy has to know me, or else he's stalking me and I'm going to die. I'll miss you."

"Don't die. What'd this one say? Send me a picture."

"That's the thing. It's blank. Think it's a hint to go to the coffee shop?"

"Maybe..."

Even as her mother speculated, Jordan tried to get a picture that didn't have huge shadows or blown-out sections from the flash or lack thereof.

"Hey, Mom?"

"Yeah? Got that picture?"

"I'm trying here. Anyway, think it's stupid to go to The Grind in case it was a hint?"

Her mother didn't even pause to answer. "Why would it be stupid? It's a public place. There's a cop on every corner there."

Jordan started to agree when something inside caught her eye. "Wait..." she unhooked the tab from the slot and laid it open. "Oh! He wrote on the inside this time. It's longer."

"What does it say?"

"Um..." Jordan couldn't help the smile that formed. "I hope this guy isn't a creep, because I like him already. It's from a Bible verse in First Thessalonians. It says, 'Therefore encourage one another and build up one another, just as you also are doing.' And then he added below that, 'Your love of the Lord and His people shows. It encourages me. There's coffee waiting for you at The Grind—tonight, tomorrow, whenever. It's waiting. God bless you.'"

"Wow."

Jordan had to agree. A shiver ran over her, prompting her to start the car, blast the heater, and bless the Lord for the invention of seat warmers. "I'm going."

"Tonight?"

"Why not? Maybe he's lingering around, and I'll see him again."

With promises to call as soon as she knew more, and a snapshot of the inside of that sleeve, Jordan shot out of the parking lot with more recklessness than she'd like to have to admit to any of the local officers. Instead of her usual parking spot behind The Fox, she allowed herself one right up front—just so Officer Joe couldn't complain. And, knowing the guy had known where to find her, *twice*, did awaken caution bells.

A quick scan of the area didn't show a man in a work overcoat or hoodie. "Maybe he's inside." She grabbed the sleeve and her purse, pumped a double shot of courage through her heart via a quick prayer, and strode to the coffee shop door. Half a dozen customers sat and stood around the room—none in work overcoat or hoodie.

It's too cold for just a hoodie. Her reflection in the door gave her pause. *My hair's a tangled mess. I should have taken the time to straighten my hair tonight. Ugh.*

Someone heading her way prompted her to pull open the door and hold it. "Hey, Todd. Did my book come in yet?"

"Should be here on Friday. My shipment got rerouted to Orlando. I guess the books wanted to be beach reads or something." When she only gave him a pained smile, Todd continued. "Sorry. Anyway, yeah. Two-day delay."

"I'll come in Saturday afternoon then. Thanks!"

"I did get a few new audiobooks for the rental shelf."

"Did you get that one everyone's been raving about—with the new Netflix movie? Takes place on Guernsey?"

Todd nodded. "I've had a dozen people asking about it, so I took a risk."

"Put me on the wait list."

He promised. Something in his expression hinted he might ask her out again, and Jordan had a "three strikes, and then I tell you off" policy on date requests. This would be three. "See you then. Thanks. I've got a coffee date, so I'd better go."

Truth stretched? Jordan decided that it depended on your definition of a date. *And I do. I have a coffee date with a secret admirer. How cool is that?*

Aya beamed at her but also seemed unable to look her in the eye. "Your usual?"

Jordan passed the sleeve across. "Do I have to give this to you, or just show it?"

"Just show. Jason's making it. I took a chance that you'd want it."

As promised, the coffee was paid for, but Jordan dropped a couple of dollars in the tip jar. "Who is this guy?"

Aya clamped her mouth shut and shook her head. From the back counter, Jason called, "She promised she wouldn't tell. And it's killing her. Don't tempt her."

Well, if I get desperate, I know I can get her to talk. But this is fun for now.

A group of teens—from the youth group, if she knew her local kids like she thought she did—burst through the door, laughing and talking. Jordan just stood there, reading the sleeve and marveling at something as old-fashioned as a "secret admirer."

But it's not, I guess. Schools still do secret Valentine fundraisers. Same thing...
"Jordan!"

One thing that had always amused her about The Grind was how the owner trained employees to face the cup label and sleeve outward. So, when she reached the counter and saw it turned toward the back of the room, she turned it around and smiled at the message. *Thanks for playing my silly game. Hope you have a nice week.*

"Thanks, Jason."

Two steps from the counter, she turned. "Aya? Did he know my name or..."

"I think he said Jordan Aylward the first time. Maybe. But just Jordan today."

Hmm... so he does know me. Has to be from church, then. Who else? Unless Todd... No. Todd was *not* the guy from last week, and Aya had specifically said it was the guy she'd bumped into on the way in. *That's a relief.*

She'd regret it later, but Jordan couldn't resist standing out front and watching for Mr. Admirer. *Where'd he meet me? It has to be church. How else would he know I'd be there tonight?*

A man stepped from the shop and strode her way. Dress coat, beard, cropped hair—dark. He nodded at her as he passed. "Good evening."

"To you, too."

The response came automatically, but her mind spun. Something about the voice sounded familiar—a minute trace of an accent she couldn't place. Movement in her peripheral vision distracted her. Just down the block, a man in a work overcoat passed under a street light. Beanie. And if shadows didn't create what wasn't there, a beard.

Gotcha.

The man drew closer—similar build... everything. His next pass under a street light also brought his head up. He smiled at her. *Terry, from the farm store. Of course, it is.*

A shiver ran through her, announcing that it was time to give up and go home. *Next time.*

She'd made it halfway to Primrose Lane before the idea struck her. "Call Mom."

Her phone informed her that the call had been made just seconds before her mother answered. "Well? Did you meet him?"

"Don't think so. Well, for a minute, I did. Saw a guy in a beanie and work coat and thought it was him, but it's a guy I've met a time or two—happily married with teenaged daughters. But *he* bought me another coffee. I'll send a picture of this sleeve, too. Oh, and he knew my name—maybe my full name the first time. But he knows it. So, he has to have met me somewhere. I'm thinking church."

Her mother made noncommittal noises that could mean anything from "definitely" to "are you nuts?" The final verdict came as Jordan neared Primrose Lane. "It's possible, I suppose. Makes as much sense as anything."

"What do you think of me stopping in tomorrow and asking Aya to make his next cup on me?"

"What if Maya's not there when—"

"Aya—without the M."

"Right," her mother continued. "What if she's not there when he comes in? He might not get it."

That was true, but someone else might give the guy up. Aya had her wannabe boyfriend to help her keep her word, but the others... "Well, I can try. I'll sleep on it." A yawn escaped. "And speaking of sleep, I'm home and tired. I'll talk to you tomorrow."

"Let me know if you decide to tell him."

"Okay. Love you, Mom. See you Saturday night for dinner."

The expected protest came. "You should reserve Saturday nights for your dates."

"Well, maybe when I have regular ones, I'll consider it. For now, you're my date—best one I've ever had. You never stand me up, you laugh at my jokes, you tell me how amazing I am, and despite being a zoologist, you do not spend all your time chatting about the bodily functions of animals. So, thanks for that."

"High praise..."

Jordan shivered out of the car and to the front door. "Sure is. Trust me. Night, Mom."

Eight

Even without opening her eyes, without looking out a window or checking a weather report, Jordan knew it—a fresh dumping of snow meant a morning of shoveling—away from the foundation, off the sidewalks, out of the driveway. "D.C. needs to spring for a blower. He's never been here in winter."

D.C. was also from Arizona where the wind just swept away the few inches of snow he got in one of those sleepy suburbs outside Phoenix. He didn't know about an overnight dump of a foot... Her phone powered up and blinked at her. Make that a foot and a *half* of snow in ten hours.

"It better be stopped."

She shivered from her covers, dashed to the window, checked out the sky, and dove for the bed again. The clock on her phone rolled over to eight o'clock, and the furnace kicked on. "Should've waited fifteen minutes."

She did wait this time. Facebook greeted her with several memories, a "friendaversary" and twenty notifications of things she couldn't care less about. A cousin posted cute pictures of her daughter on Instagram. Her mom posted pictures of the polar bears actually enjoying themselves. It would mean more visitors on a day when people might have ignored the zoo. There it came. The reminder. *Animals get bored when they don't have visitors. Use those new passes you got for Christmas to keep our residents happy. Be sure to stop and see our polar bears and Siberian tigers. They love the cold!*

If she didn't have house maintenance to do, she might have gone herself. The memory of polar bears rolling and playing in the snow propelled her out of bed and into several layers of clothes. A cup of hot coffee, double stocking hats, and her puffiest coat. Inside thirty minutes, she began the attack on the walkway to her door.

A text came in after she had finished sidewalks, driveway, and front walk. Standing in the kitchen sipping her second cup of hot chocolate, Jordan read the message from Bookends.

> **BOOKENDS:** REMINDER, YOUR BOOK IS HERE. I'VE GOT GUERNSEY
> HERE FOR YOU AS WELL. LIZ WHYTE IS CONCERNED FOR YOUR
> SOUL. READING TRASHY NOVELS, ARE WE?

"If you count something other than *Pilgrim's Progress* and the Bible as trashy like she does..."

The reminder did spur her to dig faster around the foundation. No, she shouldn't *have* to do it, but an older house didn't have the same features to protect the basement that newer homes did. So, gloves on and a scarf added to her "outfit," Jordan braved the snow again and thanked the Lord for small bungalows.

I'm going to get this done, take a hot shower, get ready, and after I go into town, I'll go see Mom. I'll listen to that audiobook on the way. And if I work quickly enough, I'll stop and see the polar bears. The giraffes would be inside, but maybe they'd be in the public enclosure. Something about those tall, graceful creatures pulled at her. *Yes... I'll get Dave to take me back if they aren't. Sandy gets so lonely in winter.*

He'd awakened at five. Laundry done, bathrooms scrubbed, kitchen mopped. Heath also needed groceries, but that could wait until he got back from Fairbury. He did, however, make a shopping list.

A glance at his phone showed nine-fifteen—perfect timing for arriving at ten o'clock in Fairbury if traffic didn't slow him down. A second glance at the phone prompted a double wince. Another Betwixt notification from Camille. It wasn't that she didn't sound interesting. She did. But it didn't hold the appeal that his game with Jordan did. The way she'd responded to him, even when he could see that she was looking for someone else... it fit what he'd guessed of her.

She's truly kind.

Another glance at the phone confirmed the cause of his second wince. *It really is January nineteenth already. How does that happen? I just gave Selby her last gift yesterday. Or the day before, maybe—at most.*

Selby hadn't awakened, even as he scrubbed the bathroom. She'd probably been up until the wee hours chatting with Kevin. It wouldn't be the first time. He'd read their messages—ninety-five percent movie quotes. Four percent filler. One percent emojis—on her part, of course.

And more subtext than any book or movie I've ever read or seen. His sister was smitten—or as much as she could be with someone, she'd never actually conversed with, much less met.

An accident in his apartment building's parking garage dragged out his escape, but despite all temptation, and the fear he'd be too late, Heath managed to keep his speed at two miles over the limit. He didn't even regret it—not when the sign for the Fairbury turnoff appeared.

Fairbury itself bustled with shoppers—tourists out to get a "deal" on this year's after Christmas sales. *Almost four weeks after Christmas, and they're still shopping. It's crazy.*

Bookends—packed. Anyone who said small bookstores were extinct had never visited Fairbury and its thriving establishment of literary offerings. Parents of bookworms tried to stem the tide of dollars dancing gaily from their account to the register at the front of the store. Parents of reluctant readers promised to sell a kidney if their offspring would only choose a book or twenty. When that didn't work, video games added to the bribes with better success.

Calendars—already at half off. He'd forgotten to buy one every time he'd been at the store in the past two months. Selby mocked his "unnecessary" habit of hanging one on the fridge when he had a perfectly good one on his phone, but a lifetime of checking the fridge for the date did not disappear even after almost ten years back in the States. He snagged one of the safari animals and grumbled at the loss of the ease of just buying one from work.

Next year, they'd better go back to paper calendars. Otherwise, I'll just suffer for the first couple weeks of January and get one at half off.

The crowd thinned at the register, leaving Heath a perfect opening. The owner, he assumed, reached for the calendar. "Whew. I hoped marking them down a bit sooner than usual would move more. Seems to be working. I might break even at this rate."

His plan for saving money fizzled at that news. "I usually buy one at work, but this year they went digital. Then I kept forgetting until I saw that display."

"Do you know how many people have told me something similar? I'm considering doing a "Surprise Calendar" next year. You tell me what size and features you like, and I mail one out when they come in."

"Sign me up."

The guy laughed.

Heath leaned one forearm on the counter and shook his head. "It wasn't a joke. As long as you don't send me something that'll call my masculinity into question—I do that enough on my own, thank-you-very-much—then we're set. Can I pay for that now?"

A little girl—she couldn't have been ten—bounced up to the counter clutching a book of poetry. *The Best-Loved Poems of the American People.* She caught Heath trying to read it and beamed as she addressed the guy behind the counter. "Hi, Todd! I found out it was my grandpa's favorite poetry book, so I want it, too. It has 'Annie and Willie's Prayer' and 'Casey at the Bat!'"

The second sounded familiar, but he didn't know the first one. "I'll have to look up Annie and Willie later. Go ahead. Mine will take a bit of time anyway."

"Really? Thanks! Mom says if I hurry, we can get cocoa at The Grind before we go to Great Aunt Doris's house."

Judging by the way the girl's nose wrinkled at 'Great Aunt Doris's name, Heath surmised the woman was not a favorite person to visit. "Can I give you a hint?"

"Sure."

"Ask Great Aunt Doris to look at the index and find one of her favorite poems. Older folks just like to know that people still care about what they think. When they don't, sometimes they seem grumpy, but they're really just hurt."

Without relinquishing the book, the girl passed a twenty across the counter and peeled off the sticker on the back—an obviously seasoned buyer. Todd counted change, passed over a bag that Heath suspected would never be used, and laid a receipt on top. "Let me know which one was your favorite, Dee."

"I will. And get the new Valimar series, okay? I want those next."

"Valimar it is." The moment the girl stepped away, Todd pulled out a notebook marked "Special Orders" and passed it to Heath. "Just put your email and phone number in there. I'll get it set up and invoice you when it's time to send out. And thanks for Dee. She really hates visiting Aunt Doris. The old gal is a bit crusty, but you nailed it. And Dee's a lot more like her than she knows."

He was related to Dee. And if that was the case... "Named for her?"

Todd nodded as he rang up the calendar. "Yep. Second cousin—or cousin removed a time or two. I can't keep that stuff straight. Total is—"

"I actually wanted to ask a favor." Heath glanced around, and once satisfied that no one, especially Jordan, could overhear, explained his mission. "I know Jordan Aylward has a book on order here. I wanted to pay for it and maybe add a note to it for when she comes in?"

"Sure! Your name?"

His beard would only hide some of the redness creeping up his neck and heating his face. "Um, that's the thing. I don't want her to know it's me. Not yet. It's sort of a thing." At the skeptical look that formed on Todd's face, Heath threw out his only "reference." "Her mom's my boss. You could call Ann and get her okay if it made you feel better."

But even before he got out Ann's name, Todd's expression cleared. "You're not asking for personal information. It's fine. I get so paranoid about identity theft over Christmas that I forget not everyone is out to ruin the lives of my customers. Got paper?"

Heath pulled out the small notebook he'd brought and reached for a pen in the cup before him. A smile formed at the words on the mug. *Carpe librum—seize the book!* "Great mug."

"We have them in the gift corner. My favorite is the one with the fox that says, 'Not today. I'm booked.'"

With the paper before him, the pen in hand, and Todd watching while pretending to wrap up the calendar, all the note ideas he'd rehearsed sounded lame. Heath wrote Jordan's name first... and then took much too long to put the comma after it. "What's the book she's buying again?"

"You mean *you're* buying?"

"Right. The one she ordered."

Todd gave him an odd look before answering. "*Black Beauty.* She said it was one her mom bought her the year her dad died, so she never read it. Now she can't find it, so..."

Jordan had lost her father as a girl. He'd always assumed a divorce. In fact, he thought he'd heard Ann refer to her "ex" a few times. "Got it. Thanks."

The note flowed. Easy to do when your paper is small, and you don't want to use more than one sheet. All written, he folded it in half and tucked it into the book. That's when curiosity overrode sense. "What's the Guernsey audiobook?"

Todd passed it across. "It's a huge thing again after the movie came out. We sold a bunch when the book first released, and now we're getting more requests."

"Should I read the book or listen to the audio."

"If you like audio, go with that. They have different narrators for each person writing the letters—it's epistolary. And it's hilarious in places." He dropped his voice and glanced around as if about to share state secrets. "I'd lose my reputation as a spec fic guy, but I finally listened when people couldn't stop talking about it. It was great."

Heath pulled out his wallet and retrieved the three twenties he'd brought—cash didn't give a name. "I've got an audiobook subscription, but if you have it in stock..."

"Well, Jordan's first on the list and then—"

"No," he broke in. "I want to buy it. My sister will like it, too."

Todd shook his head. "Sorry. I just got the one. People tend to rent them from me and then order the ones they want to keep—it's cheaper than a subscription."

"Good to know. Okay, so I need to pay for Jordan's stuff separately so she can have the receipt. Can we do that?"

Todd pulled out tape, wrapped a small piece around the middle of the note and slipped it into the front cover. A moment later, he had the receipt added, and all of it in a bag—book rental included. "Hers is nineteen fifty-three."

By the time his own package was paid for, Heath came to a decision. "Hey, do me a favor."

"Sure..."

"Order another copy of that audio. I'll come in sometime next week?"

"Make it after next Friday, and you're good. The audios sometimes take more than a day or two."

Perfect. Maybe I'll see her again.

"Your name?"

Heath grinned. "That's the clincher. You have to either let me pay for it now without a name or you have to let me pay for it when I pick it up—without a name."

"No name?" Just as Heath thought Todd would refuse, the guy grinned. "I like the sound of this. Can't wait for Jordan to come in now. I've got it. Just stop in any time after two on Friday or call after two on Wednesday if you want it sooner. It'll probably be here."

"Thanks." A last glance up showed Todd eying him closely. "And if you'd be kind enough not to give Jordan *too* much information about me, that'd be great. It's no fun if she guesses too soon."

"So, she knows you, right? I mean, you know her name..."

Heath shrugged and tucked the calendar under one arm. "Define knows. We've spent time together. We have a mutual friend or two." Todd leaned forward as if waiting for more, but Heath refused. "That's all you're getting out of me. Sorry. Have a good one."

In the music store, down the side street to a vintage clothing store, and past a library—the town resonated with him in ways he hadn't expected. *It's nice here. Wonder what the houses are like...*

A drive through residential areas only increased his curiosity. Larger two-storied homes, smaller turn-of-the-century bungalows, and even row houses—he found them all. But when he turned on a street in an area full of flower names like Honeysuckle, Lilac, and Primrose, and saw what he thought was Jordan shoveling snow by a house, he turned around and shot out of there.

At the turnoff for the highway, he told his phone to message his boss. "Just confessing now. I was exploring Fairbury and think I ended up on Jordan's street. Was hard to tell. Turned around and drove out before I could be sure. Just thought you would want me to tell you."

A reply came in just a couple of minutes later, read to him by his phone's British accent. "What street?"

"Reply. Primrose."

When no message followed, Heath took it as verification. *Need to get approval to use the information. I could do so many cool things if it weren't creepy. I wish I could ask Selby...*

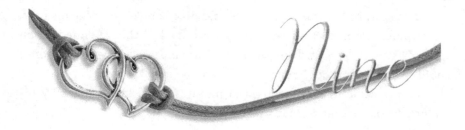

Nine

A reply to her email to Floyd Brighton arrived just before Jordan left for town. Standing at the little butcher block counter, she sipped a cup of hot cider and read it.

> To: jordan.aylward@thelettersbox.com
> From: fandwbrighton@thelettersbox.com
> Subject: Re: Biological search
> Ms. Aylward,
> Thank you for taking the time to contact me. I have little doubt that your employer is the man I've been looking for. I would be happy to meet with you anytime you say. A public place is preferred for me as well. You said Fairbury works best for you. Would you prefer The Diner or The Grind?"
> You have my number. Feel free to call and set up a time. I will say that evenings, very early mornings, or weekends are best for me.
> Thank you for taking care of this for us. I look forward to meeting my biological father if that works out.
> Floyd Brighton

A call to Arnie assured her that finalizing the meet still met with Arnie's approval. So, with a suggestion of six o'clock the next morning at The Diner zipped to the number she'd copied from the original letter, she grabbed her dry coat, wallet, and keys. Inside ten minutes, she'd finally made it to the counter at Bookends.

"Hey, Todd. You're busy!"

"There's that winter concert this afternoon. Folks are just shopping first." He grabbed a small brown shopping bag and slid it across the counter. "There you are."

Jordan pulled out her wallet and reached for her debit card. "How much?"

"All paid for."

She frowned. "I don't get it." The moment she said it, Jordan *did* "get it." Her "secret admirer" was back. "Wait. Did a guy with a beard come in? What's his name?"

"He refused to give it, but yeah. He had a beard. Left a note in the book for you." Todd glanced around before leaning forward. "He also ordered the Guernsey book—on audio. He's picking it up."

A smile formed. "You'll tell me when he's supposed to be coming in?"

"Maybe..."

That was Todd-speak for, "I can be bribed."

With the bag in hand, Jordan tried one more thing. "Did you see him leave? Did he get in a car or walk?"

"Walked—toward The Diner, if that matters."

"How long ago?"

A man cleared his throat behind her, so Jordan stepped aside. "Sorry... Todd?"

"Maybe an hour?"

That's all it took. She bolted from the building, glanced around the square for anyone wearing a work coat, wearing a hoodie, or had a beard. One work coat and three beards—none of them right. Jordan walked toward The Diner, but no one inside looked like Aya's "Mr. Cutie."

He likes the Grind... Only when she'd gotten inside and ordered her usual did Jordan realize that really, all she knew is that he knew *she* liked The Grind. *Wonder how...* At the corner table, where she could watch the whole room, Jordan pulled out the book and the audio disc. The audio looked like any other one—except for its ridiculously long and bizarre title.

Black Beauty. Blue background, scrollwork, block typeface. It looked like a collector's edition. She had requested hardback, and now a twinge of guilt struck. *Must have been pricey.*

The receipt stuck out from the middle of the book, but the note wasn't there. It slipped from between the cover and flyleaves before she could turn back—just a small 4x6" piece of lined paper. Nothing too surprising. Still, it didn't look like the paper scraps with "Bookends" printed on the bottom that Todd handed out when people requested. The paper was too white— too slick. Too thick.

And taped. If she'd brought her purse, she might have had a pair of nail scissors to slice it with. Instead, she got up to grab a tack off the bulletin board that hung nearby. She used it to pierce the tape. As expected, it tore open without any resistance after that, and after returning the tack, she settled in with coffee and her note. In small, half-cursive, half-print, the note showed more of the personality of the writer than she'd been able to see with marker on a coffee sleeve.

Jordan,
Black Beauty. Good choice. Warning. If you're anything like my sister, you'll need to keep tissues handy.
At the age most girls read and fall in love with Black Beauty, I read The Jungle Book and became even more of an animal lover than I already was. If you haven't read it, I recommend that next. After all, I'm listening to your audio. The least you could do is read my suggestion, right?
Your sorta secret admirer

"Sort of secret..."

It just confirmed that someone knew her. How or from where, she didn't yet know, and part of her almost hated to find out. The notes were cute, simple, and not creepy like she would have assumed if someone had warned her it was coming. *I'll let it go for now...*

"Letting it go," however, proved harder than she'd imagined. Despite finding her audiobook completely enchanting, her mind would wander at this word here, that turn of phrase there, and every time the narrator for Juliette said the name "Sidney."

She just didn't know why.

A text message from her mom said that a struggling zebra foal brought all hands on deck at the zoo.

MOM: MEET ME THERE?

The modern miracle known as speech-to-text zipped her reply of, ON
MY WAY across airwaves to her mother's phone without the need for her to
remove her hands from the wheel. "So glad I bought this car."
The car replied. "Should I send, 'So glad I bought this car,' to Mom?"
"Maybe not. No, don't send."
"Sending, 'So glad I bought this car.' Message sent."
Thanks to her rogue car assistant, the first thing her mother said when
she arrived at the equine enclosure and requested admittance was, "Glad
you bought your car, but is there any particular reason?"
"It sent it for me. How's the foal?"
"The vet's with him now. Come over here to the observation window,
and you can see. The mare's caring for him, he seems to be eating, but..."
Jordan leaned against the cold concrete and peered through the
Plexiglas at the foal. "He looks weak. Or is it a she—the brown stripes?"
"All foals are born with brown. They darken later."
A man walked past with arms full of blankets and a phone on speaker.
The voice on the other end said, "Did you get the blankets? We need those
here now."
"Almost there. Sakir is bringing formula."
Jordan shot a look at her mother. "The mare's not producing enough?"
"Sounds like... or they're going to test and see." Mom pulled out her
phone and sent a message. A moment later, the phone rang. "Hey... guy.
What've you got for me?"
Guy? Since when does she call anyone guy?
"Oh... good call. Okay, do you need anything from me? Well, thanks for
coming in. Just let me know. I'm taking my daughter out, so I'll be off-site,
but I can come back if we need anything. Make sure the vet gets that mama
some better supplements. We can't lose either of them."
"Can't lose." It was Ann Weik-speak for, "It'll break my heart of one of
them dies."
A thumb shot up over the head of one of the men and women working
with the foal. Blankets arrived—a bottle. Once the foal attacked that bottle

with the kind of gusto one would expect from a semi-starving animal, her mom decided it was time to go. "They'll be fine. Tilly's just not producing enough, I guess. They'll up her feed and get it taken care of. Meanwhile, that's what bottles are for."

At the gate, Jordan tugged her mother toward the public parking lot. "Come with me. I want to show you something."

"But I thought we—"

"We'll take my car. Trust me."

Only when her mom slid into the seat and held the shopping bag did Jordan realize she'd have to confess to never having read that book. "So... remember when you bought me *Black Beauty*?"

"Yeah..."

"I never read it. Lost it after Dad, and..."

Mom eyed her before pulling the book from the bag. "So, you bought me a copy to replace the one I *gave* you?"

"No... I bought one to replace it so I could read it. Just my way of making it right, you know?"

Her mother's expression hinted that no, she did not know.

"Well, anyway. I ordered one that looked a little like the one you got me, and it came in. Went to get it today. It, and the audiobook I rented, were already in that bag. Paid for." Jordan reached over and opened the cover to reveal the note. "He wrote something."

"Can I read it?"

"Yeah! That's why I'm showing you. I can't figure out how he knew about it. I think I told Alexa Hartfield about it a week or so ago. If that note hadn't been there, I would have been sure she did it. It's the kind of person she is."

"I still think it's weird that you go to church with a thriller-slash-horror mystery writer. And a famous one at that."

And I still wonder if that fact isn't what'll finally get you to listen *about this whole "religious kick" I'm on.*

Mom's voice broke into her thoughts. "This is kind of sweet..."

"Right?"

"I like the 'sorta secret admirer.' Sounds like you should be able to figure him out." She read it again, her voice mumbling below her breath.

"You don't think he's a creep, do you? I mean, did the bookstore guy know what he looked like or anything?"

She got orders to head to Ravenwood Grill, and waited to get onto Dreyfus Way, before answering. "Todd says the guy had a beard, but he didn't get a name. I think it's gotta be the same one, right?"

"Probably. How safe is Fairbury?"

"I—"

Mom broke in. "No, really. Like if he showed up at your door, would you be surprised or scared?"

That wasn't something she'd considered. Still, fear didn't fit the picture of what she'd seen. "No... I'd be surprised—maybe even alarmed for a minute, you know? Just because it'd be so unexpected. But half of Fairbury knows I'm house sitting for D.C. Why shouldn't he?"

"You'll be careful though, right?"

They were the exact words she'd expect her mother to say. The problem was, Mom didn't sound concerned at all. It took most of the way to the restaurant to find the best description of what she'd heard. *It sounded like an afterthought.*

The ride up the elevator gave Heath time to check his phone. Almost midnight. Ann's text messages still showed. From the first, WE'RE BEHIND YOU. DON'T TURN AROUND, to the assurance that Jordan wouldn't have been creeped out about him finding out where she lived, to the most recent, HOW ARE TILLY AND MOSI?

Name's official, then. Mosi—firstborn.

Heath shot back a reply now that he had a moment to do it.

> **HEATH:** WEAKNESS SUBSIDED AFTER A FEW FEEDS. WE'RE
> HAVING HIM NURSE FIRST, THEN SUPPLEMENTING. TRYING TO
> BUILD TILLY'S SUPPLY, TOO. NIGHT. THANKS.

Selby lay asleep on the couch, her phone on the floor beside her, organic chemistry open on her chest. He managed to get her book set aside, her phone picked up, and a blanket over her before he banged his knee into the end table and knocked over a lamp. She jerked upright. "I know martial arts!"

"I know. You spent months practicing on my shins."

"Heath?"

As he righted the lamp and turned it on, he grinned down at her. "That's me."

"How's the baby?"

"Doing better. Why don't you go to bed?" The suggestion—wasted. She pointed to the end of the couch, and the moment he sat, settled herself in beside him just as she had as a little girl who expected him to read her a story. For the 4329th time. "I take it you have to talk?"

A giggle escaped. "You need to train my future husband in all my quirks. It'll save lots of frustration for him."

"Or make him rethink his decision."

"You love it, and you know it, big bro. You always have"

Being an only child for eight years did that to a kid. Heath just wrapped his arm around her, tucked the blanket in better, and waited. She'd tell him everything when she was ready and not a moment before.

The words flowed almost immediately. "I almost went to meet Kevin. I was so tempted, but you couldn't leave if I needed you, and I promised..."

"Thank you."

"They have that monitor on the app. They'll send help to my GPS location if—"

"If you're even *there* after that alert goes out. Remember, he knows it exists, too. And he's probably a great guy, but still. I'd feel better being close the first couple of times."

A sigh—exasperated or resigned. He couldn't tell. Still, it was a sigh instead of a protest. That helped. "Well, he invited me to his church tomorr—or probably *this* morning, huh?"

"This. Yes." His church. That would be an interesting thing after she'd settled herself into the Anglican church scene. Their more casual Dominican services were much more like the average seeker church than the ritualized Anglican. "So, are we going?"

"I love how you just asked instead of sounded put out. No. I'm not ready for that. Coffee tomorrow—I mean, tonight?"

"Sounds good."

"How about as a kind of, sort of double date?"

Camille—the new girl. She'd probably sent messages that he'd ignored all day. "I don't know. If she sent—"

"She did. I responded for you. I told her it was me and that you were dealing with a work emergency."

His stomach rumbled just as Heath thanked her for that much at least. "I probably should get something to eat."

"Did you eat at all today?"

That was the problem. He couldn't remember. His gut told him that he'd been too nervous before he went to the bookstore, but had he afterward? The Diner had been too full, coffee hadn't sounded appetizing, and nothing else came to mind. He'd gotten the call about *Mosi* and shot back to Rockland without a care about speed. A ticket for that would have been a reimbursable item.

"Nope."

"Scrambled eggs or frozen pizza?"

Although his rational, mature self insisted that scrambled eggs was a better choice, Heath opted for pizza. "I'll take a shower."

"Good. You smell like a barn."

"You snuggled up..."

Selby grinned as she stood and offered him a hand up. "I didn't say I didn't like it... I just figured if you smelled like one, you might need a shower to sleep. I'll get the food."

He'd almost turned on the shower nozzle when Selby's previous words registered. With his head sticking out of the bathroom door, he shouted across the apartment. "Do I have a date tomorrow?"

"Coming!" He repeated the question on her arrival, and she grinned. "Same time. Same place. *Opposite* sides of the restaurant."

It could be worse... Heath shut the door. "Okay."

The praying began the moment the first blast of hot water hit his back.

Ten

Eyeshadow—since when did she bother with it? Jordan couldn't remember the last time she'd opened the palette of neutral-ish colors and attempted to swipe one on her right eyelid. "It's not even about meeting *me*. This is ridiculous."

The left eye got a semi-matching swipe. An attempt at a darker crease in the middle... it looked more like a color wash gone wrong. She tried the other side—better, but still a mess. A slow blink sealed the decision. With one motion, Jordan divested each eyelid of its unfortunate color. Eyeliner...

A groan escaped. "Why do I even own this stuff?"

As usual, the mascara wand ended up in one eye before she'd managed to get the job done, but mascara was a must. Without it, she didn't *have* eyelashes. "There." A hint of lip gloss of a pink so natural that it almost didn't count followed and Jordan surveyed the results. "Maybe I should have worn scrubs—to look professional.

That idea tanked when she saw the time. "If I make it by six it'll be a near miracle. Forget changing."

More snow greeted her as she stepped out the door. Just a couple of inches, but it annoyed her just the same. "I need to get that Cox kid to blow it for me. It'd be worth the money."

With promises to herself that she'd stop by The Grind for coffee and one of the kid's business cards, Jordan climbed into her car and did her best to make it to The Diner by six o'clock. Her phone read 6:01 the moment she parked. "Ugh."

At this point, I can only hope he got slowed down by a plow on the way or something.

A nearly empty diner suggested she might get her wish. A text message three minutes later confirmed it.

FLOYD: ACCIDENT ON THE HIGHWAY. JUST ABOUT TO LET MY SIDE THROUGH. I'LL BE TEN MINUTES LATE. SORRY.

Earlene met her at the coveted front corner booth with a menu. "Will this do, sweetie?"

"Sure. Thanks. I'll just have some orange juice right now. I'm waiting for someone."

"Hot date?"

Laughter bubbled out at the idea of a man her mother's age—married with kids and grandkids, no less—being her date. "Not quite. Just on an interview of sorts."

"Hope you get the job! I'll be right back with that cocoa."

A smile formed. "Um, Earlene?"

The woman pivoted and caught her gaze. "Hmm?"

"OJ."

"Right. Want whipped cream on that?"

I should say yes. "You know how I love whipped cream."

Creamer and a bottle of syrup appeared first. Still, Jordan didn't know if she'd get orange juice, coffee, or just a mug of whipped cream. With Earlene, you never knew. The juice appeared just as a man burst through the door looking flustered—and nervous.

Floyd Brighton. You've got to be. This DNA test is a waste of time and anxiety. She stood and smiled. "Floyd?"

"Jordan?" The man stepped forward, offered his hand, and wrapped his other around theirs as they shook. "So glad you're here."

"It's nice to meet you." She decided to get right down to business. "I brought a DNA kit. You and Arnie will just swab your cheeks, I'll send it to the lab, and in three-to-five days, we'll know."

"That fast?" Floyd looked skeptical as she passed the kit across the table. "I thought it took weeks."

"It used to, and for court-ordered things, it has to go through all kinds of paperwork and channels. I asked around and got this lab as the best and the fastest. Arnie insisted on it. They do online lab results, so that's part of the speediness."

For the first time since he'd arrived, Floyd faltered. "What if he's not my father? And does he want to know me? I mean, really?"

"He didn't want to see you adopted, but that's how things worked back then. Your mother wouldn't marry him, and they didn't give babies to single fathers. He and his wife never had children, so yes. He's eager to meet you. Cautious, but eager."

Earlene took their orders and promised to rush back with his coffee. In her absence, Jordan decided to give him a heads-up. "Ever been here before?"

"A few times."

"Ever had Earlene as your server?"

He shook his head. "Why?"

"Well, I'm going to predict a cup of whipped cream for you. And your eggs will be here, but it might take a while for the pancakes. I bet Officer Chad over there gets them instead."

The incredulous look he gave her would have been funny, but the cup of whipped cream and her refill of orange juice—the one she hadn't asked for—stopped it. He managed to stifle his laugh until Earlene made it back behind the counter. "How'd you do that?"

"She got fixated on whipped cream a few minutes ago. I almost guessed that it'd be on a plate or on your pancakes. Glad I didn't."

They discussed the weather, the accident he'd witnessed, and his new grandbaby. Only when their food, and all corrections to those orders, had arrived did she tell him her next concern. "You should know, Arnie's only holding back by a thread. He wants this family connection as much or more as you do. He's alone—so very alone." That reminded her of something he'd asked. "How does *your* family feel about this?"

"Wendy's all about it. Seth and Angela have both bugged me about it for years."

"But you have three children," she countered.

Floyd had the grace to look sheepish. "Our oldest isn't so keen. He'll come around, though."

"That's almost a relief." At his confused expression, she clarified. "It's just that things can be too picture perfect sometimes. Someone not happy hints that it's normal. You know?"

An hour to the minute from the time she walked through the doors of The Diner, Jordan walked out with Floyd. She promised to text him the website information and took off toward The Grind. The chances of her mystery man knowing she was out and about—slim. Still, despite the twinge of guilt that came when she thought of the money expended to play cat and mouse games, she almost hoped he'd have been there when she stepped up to the counter and gave her order.

"Four sixty-three. Do you have a punch card?"

Oh, well... next time, maybe.

Clinks, murmurs, laughter, phones ringing, names called, gurgles and squirts—the symphony of a coffee shop. The scents were nearly as overpowering, but something about them comforted as well. The familiar has a way of doing that.

Why Selby thought them arriving together, *early*, was a good idea, she didn't know. Across the shop, hands twiddling, Heath looked more miserable with every passing second. She slid her phone toward her and after only half a second's thought, tapped out a message.

> **SELBY:** READ AN ARTICLE, PLAY A GAME. DO SOMETHING.
> YOU'RE MAKING ME NERVOUS.

His reply? Predictable.

> **HEATH:** YOU'RE NERVOUS? I'M THE ONE MEETING SOMEONE WE
> BOTH KNOW WON'T LIKE ME.

The worst part of all was that she couldn't argue. A flash in the window amended that. No, the worst part of all, for him anyway, was that *her* match showed up first. Just as he opened the door, panic set in. She zipped a text to Heath.

SELBY: I DON'T KNOW WHAT TO DO? SHAKE HANDS? HUG? JUST STAY SEATED AND SMILE? RUN?

Heath had no time to answer. As she rose to greet Kevin, who offered an awkward hug that suddenly felt adorable rather than miserable, Heath made exaggerated, cartoon-like chuckling motions. *You are so dead*, she mouthed.

"I was right, you know." He inched toward the counter. "What can I get you?"

"I—" Selby frowned. "What were you right about?"

"Your picture doesn't do you justice. Coffee?"

As much as a nice hot cup sounded, she'd have a hard enough time sleeping without adding caffeine to the mix. "I was thinking cocoa, but I can get it."

"Don't get me in trouble with my mama." Kevin scowled at her and winked. "She taught me right. If you don't believe me, ask her."

"It's kind of hard to ask someone you've never met..." A movie line popped into mind and Selby ran with it. "My mom agrees with Forrest Gump's mama."

In her peripheral vision, Selby saw Heath rise just as Kevin said, "We can fix that."

"Sure. I'd like that." A warning bell went off with a not-so-subtle hint, but what about, she didn't know. She only saw Heath.

Camille—gorgeous. Stunning, actually. And by the way her brother looked panic-stricken, she probably had one or two freckles, artfully placed by the hand of a loving God. She'd never seen Heath's process of "miseration" happen with a stranger. Already it was worse than anything she could have imagined.

Desperate, she zipped him a text.

SELBY: ASK HER IF SHE ENJOYED TODAY'S SERMON.

At that moment, he stood and moved to the counter.

Coffee. Well, you got that far, anyway. Now read the text.
He did. A reply shot back.

> **HEATH:** SHE'S GOT FRECKLES. AND SHE CAN TELL I'M NERVOUS.
> SHE THINKS IT'S "CUTE." GET ME OUT OF HERE.

Wasn't going to happen. Nope. Selby gave waiting Kevin a smile before
constructing a new message.

> **SELBY:** REMEMBER. YOU ARE CALM. YOU KNOW HOW TO MAKE
> PEOPLE FEEL COMFORTABLE. YOU'RE GOOD WITH MAMMALS.
> SHE'S A MAMMAL. JUST THINK OF HER AS ONE OF YOUR CHARGES
> AT THE ZOO.

His reply prompted a snicker—just as Kevin returned, no less.

> **HEATH:** DID YOU REALLY JUST CALL MY DATE AN ANIMAL?

"Care to share?
"I hear when you share you get friends, but..."
He passed her a napkin with her cup and seated himself. "Look, the way
to my heart—totally through movie quotes. But the way to move in and
stay forever? Veggie Tales. Don't torment a guy like that on the first date."
Her face had to have turned some shade of red or pink... Selby prayed
for the latter and decided to risk running him off for good. "Warning: That
guy in the corner with the blonde who is too gorgeous to be fair to the rest
of womankind? That's my brother. Heath." She scrolled up the messages to
her first and passed the phone. "Remember, he has... issues with dates."
"Are you saying I'm going to see that in action?"
It happened in horrific, mesmerizing slow-motion before Selby could
hope to explain. Though she couldn't hear Heath, she could see his mouth
moving non-stop. The woman grew stiffer, sat up straighter, and then
planted her palms on the table with enough force to rattle their cups. If
they'd been ceramic, the whole room could have heard them.
"Uh oh."
The stool squeaked as she pushed herself off it. "If you think," Camille

the no-longer-a-viable-option screeched, "that I care about the lifetime relationship habits of *barn owls*, you've got another thing coming."

Don't do it, don't do it, don't do it.

His lips moved, and Selby didn't need to know how to read lips to know what he'd said. *Think. It's think. Another* think *coming.*

"What's wrong?"

Heartsore, Selby turned her attention to Kevin. "If you didn't hear that, it's probably a good thing. Look, can I trust you? Tell me I can trust you."

"Of course—"

"Will you take me home when we're done?"

"Sure, but—"

"Be right back." Selby dashed across the room before Camille had even made it out the door.

"I tried..." Heath groaned and faceplanted into the table. "I just realized something."

This would not be good. "What's that?"

"I talk to the animals that way. Tell them what their fellow critters do when they're nervous or happy."

You just made this a million times harder. A glance back at Kevin showed the guy concerned but uncertain. Selby grabbed Heath's hand and dragged him to their table. "I want you to meet Kevin. Kevin, this is my brother, Heath."

Heath shook hands and winced. "You saw that?"

"Not much of it, but I got the gist. Sorry, man."

"Kevin said he'd take me home if you want to go." The look on Heath's face. She snickered. "And I know how to use public transportation if I feel even the tiniest bit uneasy."

"Not good enough. Text me. I'll get you an Uber."

"I officially like you."

Selby and Heath stared at Kevin. Selby found her voice first. "Why?"

"Doesn't trust the strange guy. I like it. And I'll be happy to get the Uber."

"Rather not, but thanks." Heath just *looked* at Kevin.

Kevin nodded. "I get it. That's fine."

"Okay..." Selby folded her arms over her chest and eyed both guys.

"This testosterone match is now over. The estrogen wins." She turned to Heath. "Go away. I love you, but go. Drown your sorrows in some mint chocolate chip." To Kevin, she added, "If you're going to side with him about these things, it will put a damper on our relationship."

Kevin promptly sat down, leaned back in his chair and thumbed his nose at Heath. "Sorry, man. Gorgeous girl with a killer sense of humor trumps brother. Every time."

And so begins one successful date....

"See you later, kid." And with that, Heath turned away.

She watched him leave with a heavy heart. "He's so amazing, but at this rate, no woman is ever going to get a chance to see it."

Kevin took a swig of hot chocolate as if it had been a frothy glass of beer and wiped his lip with the back of his hand. "Let's do something about it, then. We're 'burnin' daylight.'"

"John Wayne, but I don't remember which one. And there's just one problem with that."

He gave her a half-quirked eyebrow as a question.

"It's nighttime."

Eleven

Dressed and ready for work and oatmeal "cooking" before him, Heath scrolled through emails, messages, text notifications, and just about anything else to avoid opening the Betwixt app. The message had popped up when he awoke. "You have one new message from Camille."

Instead of reading it, he went back to a text message from his best friend, Dan.

> **DAN:** HOME TOMORROW. WHAT'S UP WITH THE DATES? ANY BETTER WITH SELBY'S CRAZY IDEA?

That was an easy response.

> **HEATH:** NO.

He couldn't leave it there, so Heath shot back a bit more.

> **HEATH:** JUST ABOUT TO READ A MESSAGE FROM LAST NIGHT'S DATE. I THINK IT'S GOING TO BE BRUTAL.

Silly as it might be, once he'd said he was going to read, he had to read. Heath clicked open the app and tapped the "View my message" button. One swipe of his thumb showed the whole message. Knowing it would be bad didn't buffer the punch to his gut.

I just thought you should see the review I left. Maybe it'll help you interact better some other woman. Meanwhile, don't contact me again. I am not interested.

The review followed.

Worst date of my life. It lasted about ten minutes maximum. I'm sure Heath is a nice guy, but if he thinks I care that barn owls are more monogamous than humans, he's got another THINK coming. He's got the social skills of a monkey, but don't ask him about them. He could probably bore you with stupid information about them for hours, too.

Then again, it could be worse. She did say he was probably nice. "I'll take that, I guess." He didn't know if Brittney had left a review yet, but since they didn't get to see reviews, he'd never know.

He clicked on the next notification and there it was. A message from his next match. Mary. Before Selby came out and stopped him, Heath zipped Mary a message.

HEATH: PLEASE SEE THE ATTACHED COPY OF A REVIEW POSTED THIS MORNING. IT IS NOT AN UNFAIR REVIEW. I DID GET NERVOUS AND BABBLED ABOUT RANDOM FACTS. IT IS A NERVOUS HABIT AND AN OCCUPATIONAL HAZARD.

That's all he could do. If she agreed, he'd go. He'd promised to try. *I'll keep that promise, and I'll do my best, but I don't have to want to.*

Selby stumbled out with hair floating around her head in a static ball that looked a little too much like an electrical experiment gone wrong. "Hey... can you give me a ride to school if I'm ready when you are? I want to do some studying in my spot before class."

"Does Kevin know your secret place?"

"Nope."

"That is strangely reassuring and just a little heartbreaking at the same time." An absent kiss on his head. She was worried about something. "You okay, kid?"

Not until she'd spread cream cheese on a bagel and popped it in the microwave for seventeen seconds—she'd experimented second by second until she got it right, of course—and settled into her chair beside him did Selby answer. "Saw your message to Mary."

Why did I tell her she could read it all anytime she wanted?

"You said you'd try."

Ouch. "Look, kid. I'm giving it everything I have. I did better with Whitney, remember? I'm just not going to take advantage of someone, either. She needs to know."

"I suppose..." She'd taken a third bite of her bagel before she reached into her robe, pulled out her phone and tapped the screen. "Read that."

The message—from Kevin, of course—had been left in half movie quotes. "Are these *all* quotes and I just missed half or...?"

"About half, I think." She plopped both elbows on the table and rested her chin in her hands. "What do you think? Should I do a real date? What about school? I can't get distracted."

That he laughed at. "You already are. At least this guy is a tutor. If you need help..."

"Very funny. I don't know... I like him..."

Something niggled in his mind, and it took Heath several seconds to pinpoint what. "Do you like him because he knows as many movies as you do or because he looks like Johanny?"

"Both... and more. I mostly like him because I like his humor. That's why his movie quotes are so great. He knows how to use them. You know?"

"Then get to know him better. Humor is a start," Heath admitted. "It's just not enough to put a foundation on."

His phone dinged before she could respond. A heart. He tapped, and a message from Mary appeared.

> **MARY:** I'LL ADMIT THAT REVIEW DOES BOTHER ME A LITTLE. IF
> YOU'D BE WILLING TO MEET IN PERSON IN A PUBLIC PLACE, I
> THINK THAT WOULD BE BEST. TOMORROW NIGHT AT STARBUCKS
> ON LINCOLN?

Two dates—just two on Selby's new plan, and he was done. Only the fact that he'd promised made him send back a simple agreement with an assurance that he looked forward to meeting her. "I have a date with Mary tomorrow."

"She didn't back out? Yay!" The bagel dropped to the plate as Selby jumped up to hug him. "I'm going to go get dressed. I'll buy us Starbucks on the way."

"Thanks, but no. Having that tomorrow night."

"Want Kevin and me to come?"

The words came out so naturally... as if they'd been a couple for years. *How do you* do *that?*

He hadn't spoken aloud. Heath knew it. Still, Selby turned to meet his gaze. She held it for several seconds and sighed. "You put so much of yourself into these things. It's because you care so much that you do this—make it more important than it needs to be. That's why you get so nervous." She hugged him once more, and as she squeezed him tight, she whispered, "That's why the girl who is willing to get to see the guy behind the dung beetles, chimps, bladders, and barn owls... that girl is going to be the most blessed woman on the planet."

The Fairbury radio station gave out prizes every day of the week—some gifts from local businesses, others came from places that were pretty pricey. Things like Rockland Symphony tickets and overnights in New Cheltenham right along with dinners at Marcello's and The Coventry. Usually, you knew before you called in, but that fourth week of January, they had "grab bag" week.

As usual, Jordan tuned in, ready to try to win. Twice she'd succeeded, giving one of her clients a spa treatment at the salon and another a month's worth of yoga classes. Monday's sur-prize had been a dinner theater, which buoyed her hopes for fun Valentine's ideas for her married clients who just didn't get out without inducement."

"Hey, hey, hey! It's time for the daily giveaway. Today's is a great one. We had to work to secure this one. So, get your calls in. Today's lucky number is fourteen."

She'd tapped the call button on "great one."

A voice on the other end asked her to hold. *I won. Yaaassss!*

Sure enough, in seconds, Drew Anderson came on the line. "Hey, welcome to The Morning Brew. Who's our lucky winner?"

"Hey, Drew. It's Jordan Aylward. What've you got for one of my clients today."

He picked up on her attempted deflection. "Wow! We've got a treat today folks. Jordan Aylward has won a few times now. She takes the prizes and gives them to Fairbury's senior citizens. Well, today's a fun one. I don't know who you have in mind, but you've just won two tickets to the Whitgate Valentine's Ball!"

Jordan fumbled with an appropriately grateful response as she scrambled through every name she could think of. Not one of her clients would want to go to that ball. *Oh, great. Now what? Can you scalp ball tickets? Is that a thing?*

"—think we should try to talk Jordan into keeping these herself. After all, she should get something for all the hard work she does. And she calls in *every* day, folks. Every one. Let's get a few people on the line and see what they think. Jordan, you give Marie your contact information again for our records and congratulations."

Marie didn't need her info. By the time the call had been transferred, Marie had it all set up. "Just stop in for your tickets anytime, and Drew's right. Keep these for yourself."

The radio kept humming with callers agreeing with Drew... all the way to Verna McKay's house. Verna had heard, too. "He's right, you know. You should take your young man and go."

"I'd do it, too. If I had a 'young man.' I don't."

"Well, then there's something wrong with the idiots in this town." The woman shuffled back toward her recliner where she'd sit all day if Jordan let her. "I never did see why God made such interesting creatures as men have so little sense."

You and me both. Agreeing aloud would likely start an avalanche of unsavory comments about men in general. *I can't help but wonder why you want me to have a "young man" if you think they're so useless.*

"If we didn't need them, I'd say let them die off and call it an improvement."

Just as Verna reached for the remote, Jordan pounced. "You promised you'd show me how to make that cobbler." She held up the tote bag of ingredients. "I brought everything you said."

"I'll just rest a spell first."

"No way." Jordan moved in to steer Verna toward the kitchen. "I know you. You'll pretend to sleep all afternoon, and I'll never learn how to bake my way into any guy's heart."

No one had told her that manipulation would become one of the top skills she'd need as a caregiver. Second only to it: negotiation. "I'll even make you one of my fried roast beef sandwiches."

"You drive a hard but tasty bargain."

I do at that...

She'd just measured out the two and a half cups of flour Verna demanded when the old gal asked, "So... how's old Arnie, anyway?"

You have got to be kidding me.

The call came in just as Heath had shut down for the day. He had an hour to get something to eat and make it to Starbucks for the date, and now Ann wanted to see him, which unnerved him more than he cared to admit. *There's something wrong with not knowing why your boss wants to see you—personal or work. Especially when the personal isn't... well, personal.*

A new guy sat in the assistant's chair. "Hi... I'm Heath..."

"Karras, of course. Ann is waiting for you."

"And you are?"

"Oh, sorry. Michael. I'll be taking over. Sarah left for a job in Chicago."

"Lincoln Park?"

Michael shook his head. "Candy company. That's all I know." He gestured to the door. "Ann's waiting, and she has a six o'clock appointment downtown, so you might want to hurry."

It was almost six o'clock now. He'd do better than that. Heath stepped into the office to find Ann pulling on her coat. At the sight of him, she dropped into her chair. "Okay, we need to make this fast. First—"

"Why don't you tell me on the way to your car?"

Relief flooded her features. "Promoting you was the best idea ever. Okay, let's go."

Two okays in a row. Interesting...

"First, we need to deal with the Valentine fundraiser. Almost everything is in motion, thank go—oodness, but I need you to have your assistant follow up on everything I send over tonight. We also need more ticket sales. Only sixty percent are sold. With three weeks to go, that's not enough. We need eighty percent by next Friday at the latest. Without eighty percent, we lose money."

He didn't miss the switch to goodness and decided he'd do what he could to show his appreciation. Then the numbers hit him. "Wait, we have to sell eighty percent of tickets at a hundred dollars a ticket just to break even?"

"It's an expensive event."

"So, all that money for what, four thousand dollars?"

Ann dismissed his dismay. "We'll make so much more in donations and the auctions. But we need to meet that budget or the board won't let us do another one. Also, I'd like to get costs down to sixty percent next year. That'll be one of the best ways to show the board that you're the man for us."

They'd made it to the employee parking garage before Ann added, "Oh, and you know that red panda we had a shot at?"

His heart pounded at something he heard in her tone. "Yes..."

"I've got the approval to use this year's fundraising on it. So, let's get this thing rolling."

"Wow. Okay."

She stopped in the middle of the structure and stared at him. "You'll learn this about me, Heath. I fight for my people. I get them what they need and what they want. But I also expect them to give me everything they've got in return."

"I will. Definitely. Can I give a couple of tickets away?"

"Sure. There are a few good Rockland area blogs and radio stations— TV. Hey... radio. Jordan has won tickets a few times from the Fairbury station. Maybe that's a good place to do it." As if she hadn't stopped, Ann began her brisk walk to her car. "Oh, and do you have a date yet?"

"No... but if my sister gets her way, this app might have someone willing to suffer through a night with me. Hey... it's at a zoo. Maybe it wouldn't be so bad if I went off on a factoid tangent."

"App...?"

He hadn't told her? Heath thought he had. "It's this thing my sister set up. Some website to match compatible people. I promised I'd do it if I didn't find someone, and after Jordan left that night, well... I couldn't back out."

"How many dates?"

"My third is tonight."

She reached her car, tossed the laptop case in the back, threw her purse in the passenger seat, and slid in behind the wheel. Her window rolled down, even as she pulled the door shut. "What's the app? I'd hate to find out you've been had."

"It's legitimate. And they're setting me up with not-too-compatibles at first. Something Selby arranged. She's got an in through a friend of a friend."

"App..."

He swallowed hard. "Betwixt-2—like the number two—hearts-dot-com."

"I'll check it out. When are you contacting Jordan again?"

You're nervous! You want *Jordan to like me. Creepy or cool...?*

"I don't have all day, Heath. I'm late. And we need this donor at the gala."

"Sorry. Tomorrow night. They're doing a good series on Romans at Brunswick, so I think I'll go there and then head over to Fairbury to watch and see if she takes the bait again."

"More coffee?"

He swallowed. Did you tell your secret admiree's mom what you had planned? Ann's drumming fingers answered. *You do if she's your boss.* Heath cleared his throat. "Well, I was going to go with pie at The Diner. Do you know her favorite?"

"She loves the cherry pie there." Ann's agitated expression softened. "You're a nice man, Heath. I hope you get past this. For both your sakes."

"You think she'll like me when I'm not in zoology mode?"

"I think. Night, Heath."

To his disgust, Heath stood there, hands in his pockets, shivering for much too long. Despite the cold attacking his body, the rest of him felt just fine... just fine.

Twelve

Perspiration beaded on his forehead, his upper lip, and in places he hoped wouldn't show. Heath mopped his face with a napkin from a dispenser and relaxed again as the woman who looked like a supermodel version of Mary's profile picture stepped into Starbucks and made a beeline for a man who looked like the personification of a Ken doll up near the counter.

A cold blast caught him by surprise. He turned, and there she was—the sweet, wholesome version of Barbie with a chestnut dye job. Much more his speed.

And it only made everything worse.

He rose, stuck out his hand to shake hers, and found himself enveloped in a weak but sweet hug. "So nice to meet you."

"My mother said you'd be a troll, but you're not!"

Not yet.

"I'll just get me a coffee—"

Heath protested, assuring her that he'd been waiting for her order. That gave him an idea. *In the future, get their order before they arrive. It can be waiting for them. Get the misery over with first thing.*

To his relief, she agreed. "Thanks. I'll just step into the restroom..."

Delaying the inevitable, Heath decided. Part of him just wanted to come out, sit down, and say, "Did you know that squirrels can't burp or vomit?" and call it a night. *Great. That'll be on your mind now. Think if nice factoids. Like...* Unfortunately, that had been the problem last time. He tried barn owls and their monogamous tendencies. Nice, romantic, not involving the less polite topics of conversation that exist in the world.

Polar bears. That'll work.

Mary sat at "their" table, looking just as nervous as he felt. *Because I terrify her or because she's naturally nervous, too?*

A soft, "Thank you," preceded a bout of fidgeting. Cup lid off... fingers play with lid. Twirl with a stir stick... actually stir. Lick stick clean... spin it in place on the table. Return lid to cup... adjust lid until the drink hole matches up with the logo. Twice.

Oh, yeah. She's nervous.

"My mother thinks you are autistic."

You've never met me, she *has never met me, all you have are a few profile answers to look at, and she can diagnose me like that? She should go into business or something.*

"I don't know, of course, but Mother is intuitive that way. Have you ever been tested?"

Heath choked on a sip of coffee. "I've never been accu—uh... no one has ever suggested that before."

"I just wondered. You know, because of your message. You seem nice enough..."

"Thank you?" Heath tried to soften his frustration with a grin. After all, it wasn't her fault he'd inadvertently insulted another woman and made this date awkward before it even had a chance to get started. "I just tend to get nervous around people I don't know. Then I start babbling on and on about stupid zoological facts. Started when I was a kid, you know. Older people thought it was cute and it became a habit. But when you go out with someone, they really don't care about the life cycle of a dung beetle or that barn owls are more monogamous than people. That's the one I did last week."

"Barn owls?"

He nodded. "They're fascinating creatures, but I guess Camille didn't think so. I should have stuck to polar bears. They're amazing."

"Really? How?"

Heath's heart dropped to his stomach. No one but Jordan had ever asked a question, and even Jordan hadn't sounded like she wanted to. "Um, well they date—sort of. There's a courtship period where they play. In the snow. They ski and wrestle... slide down the hills. It's all very flirtatious."

"Oh, how cute!"

She hadn't widened her eyes, wrinkled her nose, or bolted. In fact, she leaned forward—a classic mammalian sign of interest. Heath couldn't wait to tell Selby. Success!

Buoyed by her response, he continued. "Of course, that's after the boars duke it out to gain the favor of the sow. They can end up pretty beat up by the time it's all over."

"Boars? I thought we were talking about bears."

"The male polar bear is a boar," Heath explained. "The female is a sow. Did you know she has delayed implantation? The sow's egg can be fertilized for as much as five months before implantation. Gestation is only three months."

Somewhere between him explaining how the sow has to fatten up for implantation to occur and the time of the cubs' weaning, Mary's eyes glazed over. Heath pleaded with himself to stop talking. Self refused. At that point, he launched into discussions of interspecific breeding between grizzly and polar bears. "They call them pizzleys and grolars."

"And the males are boars for them, too?"

"All bear males are boars."

She stood, picked up her coat and purse, and took a step back. "One could say the same for some human males. Goodnight."

As if a scene in a bittersweet movie, the moment the door closed behind her, a few snowflakes fell. Within a minute, those few flakes multiplied into a thick, steady fall. Heath gathered their trash, dumped it, and pulled on his coat to go.

In his car, he pulled up the Betwixt app and archived Mary. That done, he found Camille and Whitney and archived them, too. It took a moment to find his way back to matches, but when he clicked the right spot, seven flooded into his inbox. Seven with messages from each. Waiting.

What have I done?

Betwixt Two Hearts

Three text messages about an assignment change—an email Selby
hadn't received. It also wasn't the first time. She'd almost been an hour late
for midterms thanks to a time scheduling change. A scroll through her
spam folder showed the missing email, and a few flips back over the past
few weeks showed a few more that should never have gone there.

Selby had just selected several to delete when she saw it.
Bailey@betwixt2hearts.com. *Dated January seventh. I thought his name was
Cameron or something like that...*

Ten names appeared. Five under a list labeled as chosen by a
matchmaker and five generated by the computer algorithm that the guy
had been so insistent about. The best part, however, came in a simple note
that explained that Bailey was Camden's—*That's his name! Not Cameron*—
partner and they'd decided to split the ten names he'd requested between
computer-generated algorithms and handpicked matches by a personal
matchmaker. *Please let me know how the matches work out and if one list is a
better fit for him than the other.*

"Well, *she* is helpful anyway. Bet he got an earful and left her to mop up
his mess. That'll teach him."

Eager to show her appreciation, she shared the story of her accidental
subscription, Heath paying for it, and how she met a great guy. She told
about the coffee date with Whitney and how Heath had almost come home
sporting *eau du* caffeine and the barn owl date.

*Last night was polar bears. He went with those because they're playful and
cute. Everyone likes polar bears... unless you talk about them beating each other
up and the gestation of cubs. Heath said that Mary said the only boars out there
weren't just bears. I suspect she hinted that he was a male pig, too. Either that, or
she doesn't know the proper spelling of bore.*

That done, Selby logged into Heath's account and began sorting the
matches. Hannah first. She screamed high maintenance. Heath could
handle that, but he wouldn't enjoy it and why not save her for a guy who
liked trophy girls?

Ziva. Frankly, she sounded like the coolest girl on the planet, but Heath

782

would be too tame for her. And though people often misjudged him, Heath was *definitely* more of an alpha male when dealing with others. Once he got comfortable with a woman, he'd not take orders well. Ziva wouldn't put up with that.

"One last one..."

Amanda. Oh, yes. Amanda might be too perfect—and that meant a solid test after two more tries with someone who was a little *too* compatible in Selby's mind. "You need to stretch each other a little. She's in the same perfect boxes... no. No... She's perfect—for practicing on. We'll start with these three."

All prepared with her argument, Selby strode from her room on a mission. Heath wasn't in the kitchen, the living room, or his bedroom. A couple of text messages told her he'd gone to get milk.

HEATH: FORGOT LAST NIGHT. SORRY. BRINGING LUCKY CHARMS AS PENANCE.

That meant one thing. She'd eat. Cold cereal—gross. Except for those delightfully frosted oat things with gaily-colored, fake marshmallow shapes. At the table, his Bible. Open to Ecclesiastes chapter nine. Verse ten had been highlighted and a note written in his study journal. *Even if that's just using your hand to wave goodbye to someone else you've driven away and insulted.*

"Ouch." Selby read the verse again. "So, like that one old movie... something about doing thy 'doggondest.'"

The longer she sat there, staring at the open Bible, the notes, the *evidence* of her brother's deep, sincere faith, the angrier she got. "Superficial idiots. Who cares if a guy talks about dung beetles when he will do anything for you? Who cares if he knows more about the mating habits of chimps than the chimps do when he loves the Lord more than life itself? Who *cares*? And barn owls? Camille doesn't deserve him if knowing that barn owls are monogamous is somehow offensive. Her loss."

"Glad you think so."

That she didn't blast a hole in the ceiling with her head might be considered proof of a benevolent God. "Don't sneak up on me like that."

"Sneak? I kicked the door shut!"

Selby would have had the grace to blush—if she could have produced one on command. "Sorry." Heath passed her the box of cereal, and she hopped up to kiss his cheek. "My prince *charm*ing."

"You're pathetic." He dug out his disgusting "pillows" of wheat rejects and broke two in a bowl and poured milk over them.

"I'm pathetic? Look who is eating the chaff—that part usually saved for animal feed."

If he hadn't been laughing the whole time, anyone watching might have thought Heath was angry. Between chortles, he gasped out, "Shows what you know. The wheat is cooked, smashed, run through rollers and stripped."

"That's even worse." Selby couldn't prevent a snicker or two of her own. "They take the stuff that yummy bread is made of and give it the texture and flavor of dried out straw. No wonder people are avoiding wheat these days. It's really a protest against the travesty of what people do to the poor stuff."

"Says the woman eating oats that smell and look like cat food."

"At least they had the sense to add pink hearts to mine!"

Heath took a large bite of his cereal, chewed slowly, and swallowed with relish. Selby mimicked him, but as she finished, she added, "No one is going to believe that I'm not happier with my sweet, yummy goodness than you are with that soggy pile of scarecrow leftovers."

A small splash of milk landed on the table as he almost dropped the bowl to the table. "You win."

"We both knew I would."

"I had to try," Heath insisted.

"You did. And as your forfeit, you have to do a rapid-fire on the next three dates. I guess I got an inside scoop because I know all of them at once. Got a letter from Camden's business partner. *She* has sense. So, you're going out with Hannah, then Ziva, then Amanda."

"Amanda seemed nice."

She shot him a look. "You knew about all these girls and didn't tell me?"

After another deliberately chewed bite of shredded wheat, Heath wiped his lips and leaned back in the chair. In a move that imitated their father exactly, he laced his fingers behind his head as if ready to settle in for a discussion. "Found a spot that shows everything last night. I didn't know it was there. And apparently, I signed up for ten matches at some point." He eyed her with suspicion. "Was that you?"

Selby shook her head. "Innocent as far as credit-card-charged, but I'll have to find that spot, too. Do you want to message these girls and set this up or should I just send you when and where when I get it situated?"

His eyes closed, and anyone who didn't know him would assume he'd just nodded off. Selby knew better. Praying. He was praying. "It's against my better judgment," Heath replied at last. "But I kind of feel like I should let you handle these first ones since I'll probably botch them." He leaned forward, eyes piercing her. "Are you sure this is right to do? How would you feel if you found out that you'd been used to help a guy get—never mind. You'd be glad you could help."

"That's right. Don't forget it."

Thirteen

Wednesday evening at five o'clock, Jordan led Arnie to her car and let him open her door for her. Once she'd settled behind the wheel, he shut it and hurried—as fast as he could shuffle—around to his side and climbed in. "You don't have to do this, Arnie."

"I want to. You're going beyond your duties, and I appreciate it." He offered her a wink. "We could even have coffee and cherry pie at The Diner afterward. You could tell me more about your new audiobook."

Dinner at Marcello's followed by The Diner? Possibly overkill for the little she'd done. Still, he was a dapper man, and she hadn't had a date that good since—well, she didn't know since when. For the first time since she'd done it, Jordan remembered the service she'd signed up for. *Better see what's up with that. I don't think I got an email.*

"When did you say the results of that test might be in?"

Jordan backed out of his drive and rolled down the street. "I dropped it off directly at the lab on Monday. If it got to the actual processing part of the lab by Tuesday, it's not unreasonable to have word by Friday. Monday or Tuesday at the latest."

"Velma told me that those fast tests on TV are faked—that it takes weeks."

"It used to, and for court proof, it would have to go through more rigorous testing than they have to do for paternity, but trust me. If this thing comes back and says more than oh... eighty percent chance, I'd say it's a given."

"That much, huh. It's amazing. We thought blood typing was the height of science when I was a boy. Watching blood serum clump together under the microscope—fascinating."

"Kids still find it cool."

They rode in silence almost to the square. But as she turned toward Marcello's, Arnie sighed. "Jordie?"

"Yeah?"

"Am I an old fool for hoping? I had sisters," he rushed to explain. "I was the only boy cousin on Dad's side. I'm the last of our branch of the Holtzes. I know he won't ever carry the Holtz name, but to think that I'll die with a son and grandsons—maybe great-grandsons..."

A lump choked out any hope of a verbal response. But when she'd pulled into the parking lot and put the car in gear, Jordan reached over and gave him a hug. "I think having conflicting feelings would even be normal. Knowing there's more family out there—great news. Not being sure if you're ready to deal with a bunch of unfamiliar relatives... also totally understandable."

"Wish I'd have invited him tonight. I don't think I care if the DNA is a match. I want to be there for the boy."

"He's fifty."

"To me, that's a boy. I feel like I just became a man the other day." Arnie put his hand on her arm. "Just hang on a minute there. I'll get that door. My mother taught me right."

Who could argue with gallantry? Not Jordan Aylward. Not at all.

On the way to Brunswick, Heath stopped in at The Diner and paid for coffee, pie, and tip. He'd planned to use a torn-out sheet of their order pads, but when Vickie the frowzy-headed server with her hair tucked in a net that looked ready to pop at any moment heard that he wanted to leave a note for someone as a surprise, she shook her head. "They use tickets like this all over the place. Let me get you a to-go box. We'll cut the top off. It says 'The Diner' right on top with our logo and everything. Then..." she hesitated.

"She. She'll know," Heath finished.

"Oh, I do love a good romance."

"You can't tell her it was me. You'll ruin it. She's got to figure this out for herself."

Vickie missed the implication in his words. "Now, how could I do that? I don't even know your name."

"All I'm saying is don't give me away if it comes up. Please."

When he walked in at twenty past eight, Vickie's surprise transformed into understanding. "Oh! Gotcha. I'll forget you were even here."

"Can't do that. If she notices you avoid me, she might get suspicious. Just treat me like any other customer. It'll be fine."

Now, if he could only make himself believe it. Between the very likely odds that Vickie would blow it and give him away and the even likelier odds that just seeing him... *again*... would make her suspicious, Heath planned for this to be his last chance at convincing her that there was more to him than a mind full of random and useless facts.

Except they're not useless to me. Well, maybe the dung beetle. They aren't mammals or even birds.

They did, however, fascinate him. When he was six.

He ate pie—cherry in honor of Jordan—and drank coffee. The coffee was in honor of the forty-minute drive home. If she paid attention to everyone in the room, the identical order might give him away.

The longer Heath waited, the more he hoped she wouldn't.

Plates clinked, silverware rattled, and if percussion to the symphony of the diner, a bell dinged at random moments. A phone rang. Vickie's laughter bellowed out over the room as she told someone that he needed more variety in his life.

Between bites of pie and sips of coffee, Heath prayed—of a sort. Most of the words he lobbed heavenward were jumbled, fragmented, weak. Only the comfort that the Holy Spirit would translate them into acceptable offerings to the Father kept him from giving up in defeat.

Then she appeared. A jingle of the door, a call from a booth behind him, a wave... she even met his gaze for a moment before she turned away and carried her note to the register and spoke low to Vickie. That girl—she'd get a double tip for it—sat Jordan where they could see each other without straining, but it wouldn't make for a natural place for the eyes to rest.

She's good.

Jordan's surprise at the pie and coffee—visible. Not to mention, lovely. Heath hadn't noticed it before, but that's when he realized she used little if anything in the way of cosmetics. *Maybe something on her lips? I think that's a bit of shimmer. Or maybe it's just lip balm.*

He pulled out the notes on the gala he'd brought to go over and flipped through them, one by one. After each page, he looked up. Once he caught her gaze and nodded before looking down again. *Why can't I be this casual while I'm actually* on *a date? Maybe I need a lot of interaction with someone online before the date. Maybe Selby has this all wrong.*

Several times, Heath could have sworn her eyes were on him. Nerves tightened themselves until he feared one or more would snap, and the noise of the room bowed over them until they screamed in protest. Still, he read, marked places that needed further follow up, and forced himself to make a list of potential guests to invite to purchase tickets. He'd get on the phone in the morning.

Vickie stopped to fill his coffee and whispered, "I think she's texting someone. I also think she's almost ready to go."

That's all it took. Heath pulled out cash, left it on the table, and reminded himself to pull money from his furnishings account to cover the sudden drain on his entertainment budget. "Thanks. I owe you. I'll be back."

"Hopefully *with* her," she whispered. "Jordan's the nicest girl. I don't know why she's still single."

"Maybe she prefers it," he mused.

As he passed her table again, he nodded. She hardly acknowledged it. *Yes!*

There was no sight of her car on the square. A jog to the parking lot behind The Fox found it empty save the beat-up, green Charger that had been there every time he'd come. Up side streets... down again. Nothing. A last-minute thought sent him racing to the church—and in a circuitous route when he saw her just ahead of him.

With each footfall, he tried to form a coherent thought—something that would strike the kind of cord he meant to without making him sound pathetic and desperate. He found it just as he reached the car. The sounds of clunky heels—probably boots, he imagined—barely reached his ears, but they grew closer and closer.

Heath pulled pen and sticky note from his pocket and scribbled, *I've never met someone so naturally lovely.* A moment later, with footsteps clearly approaching and growing louder with every second, he thought of another one. His hands shook as he scrawled even faster. He'd just capped the pen when her voice called out, "Hey! What are you doing?"

One hand slapped the sticky note to her window beside the first, and the other waved before he took off at a brisk walk. When the sounds of pounding footprints approached, he glanced back, ready to take off at a run. However, she stopped beside her car and peered at the notes.

A moment later, her voice rang out, "Who are you?"

Every bit of him insisted it was a bad idea, but Heath couldn't resist. "Just someone who hopes for a chance to get to know you better... someday."

Only one person in her life had ever dealt with letters on a regular basis. While her "admirer" only left the briefest of notes, it was the closest she could come to anyone knowing what to think of it. So, on her way home, Jordan called. "Hey, Michal. Look, I have a situation to run by you. Do you have a minute?"

Considering how brief each non-encounter had been, it took just about that minute to share it all. "What do you think? Sweet? Creepy? Safe? Should I have chased him? Demanded he stop and let me know who he is?"

"I think it's sweet, definitely. And totally romantic. Safe? I don't know. Of course, if it isn't safe, sweet and romantic go out the window. I'd want someone around just in case he's not, but he seems to be pretty out there and public if he involves other people in it. That's not like black roses on your doorstep or anything."

Michal had a point. In a place like Fairbury, anyone could probably tell him where she lived—or at least the name of one or more of her clients. "So, what do I do? Do I try to find him? Wait for him to be ready to reveal himself? I mean, I think—I'm pretty sure, anyway—that he was in The Diner with me the whole time. He left about ten minutes before me, but he was at my car when I got there. I don't know what took so long."

"Might indicate that he didn't know where your car was."

Jordan hadn't thought of that. How would he know she'd decided to walk off the day's heavy meals and dessert? "Good point."

"Look, don't be stupid, but if you are enjoying this, then so what? Just don't agree to meet in a creepy abandoned barn with chainsaws hanging in the doorway, okay?"

"Well, I'd have to buy a white nightgown first, wouldn't I?"

"True..." Michal's laughter—always so infectious. "And it's too cold for that right now. Do white robes count?"

"Not unless you're racist idiots."

As Jordan pulled into her drive, Michal added one more suggestion. "Talk to your mom. She has years of dealing with all kinds of guys—both in personal relationships and at work. She might see something I'm missing, but I just want to know what happens next. So maybe I'm not the one to ask, you know?"

"I'll call her now. Thanks, Mickey. And let's hang out soon. I miss you."

"Carol agrees—insists we get together after Valentine's Day."

"Deal. Hey, do you want tickets to that Whitgate Valentine's Ball? I won some, but my clients can't go."

"Sorry... already have plans." Michal threw out a few other names and retrieved them just as quickly. "Nope. I can't think of anyone who doesn't already have plans."

Except me. The thought startled her into an abrupt disconnect. "Since when do I even care about Valentine's Day? It's just a guilt-producing..." Nope. For the first time in her life, Jordan couldn't convince herself that she didn't care about being alone on *the* romance holiday of the year.

Shower, teeth, cozy PJs... Jordan waited until she'd snuggled into bed and had the lights out, ready to go to sleep, before ordering Siri to call her mother. For once, Mom picked up on the first ring. "Did he strike again?"

"How'd you know?"

"It's Wednesday. He knows you go to church. He did it last week, so..."

It made sense. Wrapped in a cocoon of blankets, Jordan closed her eyes and related the events of the night. "So, on the first note—I think it was part of a carry-out box from The Diner. It had the logo and everything. Anyway, it said, '*It took some doing, but I found out you enjoy cherry pie from The Diner. There's a piece and coffee waiting for you whenever you feel like it. I hope you'll enjoy it tonight, though.*' I went in case it meant he'd say hi."

"But he didn't."

Something in her mother's tone sent panic waves through her. "How do you know this stuff?"

"Because if he did, you would have led off with, "I met the guy!"

Mom had a point. "Anyway, I am pretty sure I saw him. He looked my way a couple of times. I wasn't suspicious because he didn't look away. Just nodded and went back to work on some papers he had with him. But he had a beard. So did the guy at The Grind. Actually, there's something familiar about him."

"Familiar how?" Her mother answered the question before Jordan could respond. "Oh, well You'd know him. At least a little. I mean, he knows enough about you to know your name and where to find you. Do you think he's a local?"

Jordan admitted that she assumed as much. "He has to know me or someone who does. When I got done and walked back to the church, he was at my car."

"At your *car!*"

"You think that's creepy?"

In the darkness of her room, with only faint moonlight peeking in through the window, her mother's voice sounded extra loud over the speakerphone. "Probably not, no. He's letting you see him. That makes sense. I just didn't think he'd do it this soon. So why was he there if he didn't introduce himself."

"He left two notes. One said I'm, and I quote, 'lovely.' The other said that one of the most wonderful things about freckles is that compared to the general population, it's rare to have them, so that makes them beautiful and valuable. This guy likes freckles."

Her mother recommended keeping her car in a more public place in the future. "I doubt it matters in a place like Fairbury, but you can't be too careful."

"I thought that, too, but I doubt he'd have stood there writing notes if it hadn't been. Since it all turned out, I'm glad I didn't." She swallowed hard and added, "So... would it be crazy to leave him a note next week? 'Dear Freckle Freak—'"

"Don't call him a freak!"

"Joke, Mom. Deep breath... 'Dear Freckle Freak. Thanks for keeping my sweet tooth fed and my veins flowing with caffeine. Can you leave a longer note next time? Tell me a little more about you?'"

Silence. Somewhere, a cat yowled. Jordan threw back the covers and cursed that cat with chasing dogs for getting her out of bed. Still, all the way to the back door to see if she could convince it to come in, her mother still didn't say a word. "Mom?"

"I'm thinking. Do it."

"Really?"

"Yeah. Oh, and do you want to be my plus one at the gala? Ron can't go. Business trip. On Valentines' week. Yay for our marriage."

Her mother might complain, but Jordan heard it. Relief. Ann Weik loved her husband, but Ron was just rough enough around the edges to make important social occasions awkward for her. "You'll survive. Do something special for him when he gets back. And if I don't have a date, I'll go. But I'll have to borrow one of your dresses. I can't afford something appropriate for that thing."

Sleep consumed Jordan almost before she said goodnight. Dreams swept her in the arms of one of the guests at the gala... arms that belonged to a semi-faceless man with a beard... and freckles.

Fourteen

Heath's text message came through minutes before Selby stepped into the library.

> **HEATH:** GOT A MINUTE? YOU'RE GOING TO WANT TO HEAR THIS ONE.

Fifteen minutes later, Selby sat in her cozy nook, laptop resting on crisscrossed knees and fingers dancing across the keys. Guilt plagued her until her sense of humor overrode it. *Might as well make it as funny as it was. Heath was laughing.*

She started with Hannah.

Bailey,

Heath has plowed through three dates in as many days. It all began with Hannah from the second list. They met for lunch yesterday, and he said it started off reasonably well. Hannah is the talkative sort. So, with her tongue flapping a mile a minute, he didn't have a chance to get an offensive word in edgewise. Unfortunately, someone taught her that it isn't nice to dominate the conversation.

She began to ask questions.

According to Heath, it went something like this.

Hannah: So, you're a zoologist? What does a zoologist do?

Heath: Actually, I'm mammologist. I'm in charge of the mammals at the zoo. Did you know mammals aren't the only animals that produce milk? Pigeons, flamingos, and emperor penguins do, too. Actually, it's the *male* penguin that produces the milk.

Hannah: (butting in). Do you have to know all those kinds of things to do your job? Are you like a docent at a museum?

Heath: No—

Hannah: So what else does your job entail?

Heath: Well, right now I have to finalize the park fundraising gala. It's a big deal. Fortunately, my propensity to spout random animal facts works to my advantage at a time like that.

Hannah: Well, at least you have a use for them. What do you do in your spare time?

Heath: (he says at this point he was grateful for someone who would take charge and badger him with questions so that he didn't chatter like a magpie). I hang out with friends and my sister, go hiking when I get the chance, and serve in my church.

At this point, Hannah made the mistake of taking a drink and leaving things quiet for too long.

Heath: Did you know magpies do not like shiny things? They're scared of them. They do, however, recognize themselves in mirrors. And a group of magpies is called a parliament.

Mistake number two commenced. She asked if he knew anything about "koala bears"—being her favorite animal.

Heath: Well, they aren't bears, actually. (Here is where he did the best dating move he's ever done! He added...) But you'd think they should be with all the "Koala-fications" they have. (I giggled. So did she. Alas, he kept talking. Big mistake. Huge.) They also have fingerprints so similar to human ones that they have created problems in criminal investigations. Oh, and up to ninety percent of female koalas have chlamydia. It helps keep the population down when necessary.

Hannah decided that perhaps koalas weren't her favorite animal after all, and she decided for certain that Heath knew just a little too much about creatures for her comfort. She did, however, finish her sandwich to the steady drone of Heath explaining the types of eucalyptus leaves that koalas *do* like versus the ones they don't.

Then came Ziva last night. They met at Crumpets—Ziva's choice and treat since she invited him. Yes, that's how it began. Heath almost didn't go. I told him to practice. He went.

Ziva grilled him with the speed and efficiency of a military interrogator, decided he was not the man for her, and took her order to go inside five minutes of sitting down. Heath didn't spill one single random fact.

We're calling it a win.

This morning was Amanda. I just got Heath's text begging me to let him out of his promise to do this. Amanda asked to meet for breakfast when she got off her shift at an all-night diner. In a familiar place, she felt safe.

And he liked her. Their server commented that if Amanda didn't want him, she'd be happy to step in. Amanda acted a little jealous of her coworker's carefree interaction. Heath noticed, and it reminded him of the coppery titi monkey. They've been documented as exhibiting jealous tendencies and are monogamous animals. This is important.

He managed to convince her that his factoids were proof of his own nerves because he found her interesting and not because she was so socially messed up that he'd chosen to mock her. That got her asking questions. He answered honestly—about every single date he'd messed up with his particular social disability. From dung beetles to monogamous monkeys, he shared them all—right until he looked up and found her asleep.

In the booth.

Her fork in hand.

And every employee in the place staring at him in dumbfounded amazement.

Still, to his credit, he did not give all the individual creatures' details. Just which ones he'd shared and how the woman reacted.

Oh, and when she woke up, she apologized and asked if he would record himself telling her all of it all over again. "I don't sleep well, but I was *out*. I feel better than I have in weeks," I believe were her words.

This takes us through six names. Onto the next four. I hope to knock three out this weekend so he'll pay for the next ten. I think the momentum thing is working.

Next up, and in order, are Selena, Daphne, Kendyll, and Alyssa. I'll keep you posted."

Selby

One glance at the website was all she needed. Jordan ignored the ticking clock that meant Arnie would be calling any minute and zipped Floyd Brighton a text.

JORDAN: WHEN DO YOU WANT TO SET UP A MEETING. TESTS
CAME THROUGH. AN UNSURPRISING 99.937%

Before starting the car, she clicked back to the results page and tossed the phone on the seat. Halfway to Arnie's, the first notification came. "Why'd I ever teach you how to text?"

By the time she reached his street, the third pinged. A fourth hit just after she turned into his driveway. It would say, "Ignore those text messages." A glance at her phone before she pulled her coat back on and opened the door proved her right. Arnie stood in the middle of the living room, his tablet-sized phone in hand. He gave a sheepish wave.

Jordan slipped as she stepped out of the car. If she hadn't grabbed the door, her head would have made contact first with it and then the icy asphalt. Instead, her phone flew from her hand. *Please land in snow. Please land...*

It did. Jordan grabbed her roof rack with one hand and shoved the door shut with the other. By the time she'd navigated to the edge of the drive, Arnie had made it to the bottom of his porch steps.

"You all right, Jordie?"

"Fine... fine. Better salt the drive, though."

"I'll get the Cox boy over right away."

She retrieved her phone, wiped it down with her sleeve, and powered it on. Unscathed. *Thank you, Jesus—no flippancy intended. But wait. You knew that. Whatever. Thanks.*

They'd barely made it indoors before she thrust the phone into his hands. "Take a look at that."

"Results?"

"Yep."

He didn't even look. "I won't know how to read them."

"They read them for you, Arnie. It's very clear."

Arnie must have heard what he needed to in her tone because he didn't wait another second to look. "Ninety-nine-point... that's pretty positive. You said over eighty..."

"That's what I told Floyd, too."

"He's seen this?"

Her phone dinged. "I suspect that's him with a plan for a meeting." One look at her messages confirmed it. "He's eager—wants to knock off early from work and come see you. He'll bring dinner. He wants to know if I'll stay."

"Will you? Can we make something so he doesn't have to bring anything? I could order—"

"We'll make dessert."

Arnie protested. "He's a guest—my *son...*"

Seeing a man weep had never been easy for her. Watching Arnie sob like a little boy whose mother died—heart and gut wrenching. She helped him to the couch, put her arms around him, and held him as sobs wracked his body.

One handed, she pecked out a reply.

JORDAN: YES

After talking to Amanda for an indeterminate length of time without even realizing she'd fallen asleep, Heath had zero confidence in his ability to ever capture a woman's attention, much less keep it. He'd drafted half a dozen text messages to Selby. He deleted all but one requesting to talk.

Two hours later, he had a date with Selena—who wanted to meet him at The Grind. Heath refused. He suggested Espresso Yourself in Brant's Corners or Starbucks. Selena countered with "The Confectionery"—which told him she wasn't a Fairbury resident. Fairbury-ites misspelled the name...just as the owner had.

Despite knowing it would make her assume he lived there, Heath sent back a simple but hopefully not too terse reply.

HEATH: CANNOT MEET IN FAIRBURY FOR PERSONAL REASONS.

Selby would ask about that.

The Pizza Palace in Brant's Corners became the next option. He took it.

And that's just one more to go before I'm done with all these things.

His new assistant, Jadyn, arrived with the latest numbers on tickets for the gala. Eighty-seven percent sold. "I have thirty names to go."

"I'll buy you a ticket personally if you can get the rest of those sold by the end of today."

"Deal. Let's go with eighty-seven and a half percent."

An hour later, she was at ninety. He went to the website and ordered a ticket. With the printed receipt in hand, he carried it out to her desk and laid it atop her list of names. Half had been scratched out. "You're going to win this. Just a bit of incentive to keep you going."

"Guilt, you mean."

"Whatever you want to call it. I want that part of my job done. It's worth it."

When she stuck her head in the door at ten to four and said, "Sold out. And I have three people on a wait list."

"Call the caterer. See if they can accommodate ten more. If so, call them back and sell the tickets. We can't lose that money."

"I'll ask about fifty—not request it, but ask for the possibility. Then I'll see if I can sell them. I think I can send out a newsletter to our donors. So far, only thirty-five percent of regular donors are coming."

Numbers flew at him—numbers he couldn't care less about. The number that *did* matter was the current 100% attendance. "You did it."

"The price is too low. People don't think it'll be a class act. Next year, two-fifty a plate. Trust me. It's been a hundred for twenty years! In five years, you should be up to five hundred a plate. This is a fundraiser. People know that. So let them raise funds with *all* aspects of the event."

Heath stood, stuffed his laptop in his bag and grabbed his coat. "Come with me."

If he didn't know better, he'd say Jadyn was nervous. Okay, maybe he didn't know better. As they stepped into Ann's office and he pointed to the door, proof arrived. "What've I done?"

Heath shot a questioning look at Michael and received the assistant's nod. "Proven you need a raise for one. C'mon."

Ann looked up, and dismay coated her features. "What? If you tell me—"

"That Jadyn has sold out all the tickets and has the potential to sell between three and thirty more if the caterer can adapt? Yes. She also has ideas for the future. I think you should hear her out. I'm going to celebrate by leaving early, checking on Tilly and Mosi, and making a trip to Fairbury for a... *project* I have in mind. I may have to stop by an acquaintance's house there—"

"I think you'd have better luck visiting Arnie Holtz's house. Have fun."

"Flowers?"

"Trees, I think."

Jadyn listened to the back and forth, obviously lost. "Should I be able to follow this?"

A unified, "No" prompted a shrug. "Okay."

"I'll text you the street in a bit."

That's all he needed. "On my way. I have an audiobook to pick up. He's got stationery, too. I need large sticky notes."

She pulled out index card sized ones—hot pink. "Like these?"

Only a moment's hesitation. "Yeah. I'll do it. They'll be easier to see."

"Watch for my text. You might have an errand that'll take you right there, but you want to be... discreet."

Don't let her see me. Got it.

At every stop light, Heath worked on his notes. One for her car, one for the church. One for Bookends... if he could find a book to stick it into that wouldn't sell before she could get in there. The Confectionary, The Fox. The Grind. The Pettler.

Once on the highway, he prayed. Ann's text came just as the turnoff for the rest stop loomed ahead. Impatient, Heath pulled off, read it, zipped back a, "thanks" and shot back out onto the highway. The empty road tempted him to fudge a bit on the speed limit, but conscience stopped him. Mostly.

In Fairbury, he stopped first at The Confectionary and bought the requested half dozen cheesecake stuffed strawberries. While the teenager behind the counter wrapped them in a box that resembled a deviled egg carousel and tied them with a ribbon, he stuck the sticky note with a sketch of a steaming cup of coffee to a flier taped to the door. In minutes, he was back out the door and on his way to Dogwood Lane.

Once there, he zipped Ann the requested text message.

HEATH: HERE

A reply came thirty seconds later.

ANN: GO.

Despite Ann's assurance that she would ensure Jordan was otherwise occupied, Heath didn't relax until a middle-aged man answered. "Can I help you?"

"A gift from Jordan's mother. Congratulations." What for, Heath didn't know, but he jogged back down the steps, nearly slipped on ice by her car door, and paused just long enough to stick the note to her window.

Heath's eyes caught the raised lock and smiled. *It's Fairbury. No one locks their car here.*

A moment later, he'd stuck the note to the *inside* of the window, tucked down into the track in case the cold made it fall off.

Then the fun began. Heath picked up his audiobook at Bookends—and left a note by a James Herriot "Treasury." One note at The Grind and another stuck to the inside of the ticket booth at The Fox. The woman in The Pettler helped him hide one in there, and the last went on the inside of the mini marquee by the door of First Church.

And if it's not too much to ask, Lord... please let her have time tonight. I'd give anything to get to see some of this.

Fifteen

Once he'd choked back whatever emotions lingered, Arnie managed to get the house picked up. He then sat in his chair, hands in his lap like a girl waiting for her first date to show up. Any attempt to joke fizzled as Arnie turned and blinked at her. "Did you say something?"

"Nothing important. Want to watch the news while we wait? He said he'd stop and clean up, so it could be a bit."

"There's nothing wrong with honest labor. Sweat and dirt are byproducts of industry."

Jordan tried a bit of diplomacy. "He wants to make a good impression. He's like the new kid at school just hoping one of the popular kids will notice him."

"That's how I feel. Like when I waited for Barbara to come downstairs on our first date. Her mother grinning at her father. Him glaring at me. My insides almost took off and left me behind. Took halfway through a romantic movie for me to get over it and have nervous innards because I was with a gorgeous girl."

She squeezed his shoulders before moving to take a seat on the couch. *Time to be casual... relaxed. One of us needs to be.* Jordan tried to prop her feet up on the coffee table, but the lace and crystal just wouldn't allow it. They stared at her with disapproval dripping from each thread in the lace and dangling teardrop on the candy dish that should never have made it past the design board.

"He'll want to hear your Barbara stories—Helen, too. But you knew his mother. No one else does."

"Barbara had a little sister. Forgot about Joyce. I wonder if she's still around."

"I'll start a search..."

Five minutes in, Arnie stood and began pacing. Jordan asked a few questions to distract him—several that wouldn't be helpful, even—but it didn't work. Ten minutes after that, he stopped. Froze.

"Is he here?"

"Don't see anyone." His eyes pierced right through her. "Would I be disloyal to Helen if I put away her pretties? I don't see how any son of mine will be comfortable in a house full of lace and things."

Jordan jumped up and began removing every bit of lace from the room—including the valance and side panels of the picture window. Between each thing, she glanced out, and dove for the next. "What about that candy dish."

"Don't suppose you could drop it... on the driveway?" Only when Arnie shook his head and groused that if he did, Floyd might slip and get hurt did she realize he meant it.

"How about I put it away in case it's actually worth something. Some of those older pieces are."

"It was Helen's grandmother's—Victorian."

She'd just replaced the sconces after finding a perfect outline of them where the wallpaper had faded around them when she saw a truck pull up. The man sat out there, watching the house but not moving. Jordan couldn't take it.

"I'm going out. This has to be hard for him, too. Just wait here, okay?"

"Got it. Should I put coffee on? We didn't get dessert made."

"Once you guys are comfortable, I'll start something or dash down to the bakery." Arnie's panicked look amended that thought. "On the other hand, maybe we won't have room for it."

Arnie nodded at that one. "Or the appetite." He glanced around the room. "Looks a sight better in here. I hope she understands."

"She wants you comfortable. I'm sure of it."

"That's true. My Helen was a first-class hostess. Okay..."

That bit of relaxing is all it took for her. Jordan bolted from the house, sans jacket, and shivered down the steps to the street. Floyd took one look at her and jumped from the truck—right on schedule. "What are you doing out here with a coat?"

"I thought you might need help carrying something in."

He eyed her as he came around to the passenger side. "You thought I might need help coming in. You're right. I feel six."

"That's what I told him. Arnie said the same thing—feeling like the new kid and hoping the others like him." She weighed the wisdom of oversharing and went for it. "Look, he broke down when he found out you really are his son. If you're not sure about this..."

A resolute expression overtook the apprehensive one. "I'm sure. Introduce me to my—to..."

"Arnie's fine. He doesn't expect to be anything else."

Two bags from Olive Garden—the guy had smart taste. At the door, Arnie took everything from both of them and scurried to the kitchen. Floyd shot her a look, but she just led him through the house. "He's nervous, too. Remember that. He's so hopeful but doesn't want to show it."

They found Arnie in the kitchen, gripping the counter. "Arnie? Floyd's here."

"I can go..."

"No!" Arnie whipped around, tears in his eyes. Jordan imagined that it was like staring at a face that could have been a slightly-malfunctioning Dorian Gray-like mirror. The words blurted out as he stood there, shaking. "I wanted you. I have to tell you that." The tears rolled down his cheeks in torrents. "I wanted you, but they didn't give me a say."

Jordan stepped back in time for Floyd to move closer. He reached out to touch Arnie's arm—or maybe it was to shake the man's hand. She couldn't tell. One minute they stood suspended, reaching out, inches separating them. The next, they clung to each other.

Whew. That's a relief.

Somewhere in the middle of lasagna and breadsticks Floyd set down his fork and sagged against the back of his chair. "If I'm going to be a part of your life, I need something else to call you. My mom will find a way to convince the Lord to send her back to give me a thrashing if I call you Arnie and I can't do Mr. Holtz. I just can't."

Arnie's silence grew awkward... horrible. Jordan tried to stay out of it, but the longer Arnie took to control his emotions, the less confident Floyd became. She stepped in. "Were you looking for a father-slash-dad alternative, or something more nick-namey—like 'Captain' from *Dead Poets Society*?"

"Well, I'd thought something family like, but not if—"

Arnie broke in. "I called my dad Pops when I got older. Thought I was too old and manly for 'papa.'"

"Pops is nice. Would you be comfortable with that? I'm not sure how comfortable papa would be for me..."

"No need, Floyd. It was a Holtz thing—right up until I got too big for my britches in high school. Then I went fifty years without ever saying papa... until his funeral. By then, pride didn't matter as much as it had a month or even a week before."

Just as she and Floyd got ready to go, Arnie hugged them both. "Thank you for this." To Floyd, he added, "For looking. I've wondered about you so many times. I'm glad to know you had a good life—one that included God."

"I worried about that," Floyd admitted. "—about your faith. So glad to know you have it—faith in Jesus, I mean."

"That's Helen's doing. Not sure I'd ever have seen it without her."

Floyd grinned. "I can't wait to hear about her. I'll need a name for her, too. Think about that, okay?"

The minute the door closed behind Floyd, Jordan stepped closer to Arnie. "Are you okay?"

"I'm good... real good. Thanks, Jordie. If you hadn't met him—checked him out—I'd still be wondering. Then again," he teased, "you got some cherry pie out of it, didn't you?"

"Cherry pie?" Something about that sent off warning bells, but she couldn't figure out what. "I met him for breakfast, remember?"

"That's right. But I know you had cherry recently..." His confused look concerned her, but something else niggled—something she couldn't pinpoint. "Well, I'll go. Just call if you need something."

She hadn't backed out of the drive before two messages pinged back to back. Arnie's came first.

> **ARNIE:** FLOYD WANTS TO BRING OVER PHOTO ALBUMS
> TOMORROW. I'LL SEE HIM AS A LITTLE FELLOW. THANKS AGAIN.

Floyd's was a simple request for her to call when she could. She tapped his name and waited for the connection. "You okay, Floyd?"

"Better than okay. How do I feel like I've known him forever? Have you ever seen him flick his thumb back and forth when he's thinking?"

"All the time." Then she understood. "You do that, too."

"Yep. Saw it tonight and it nearly made me lose it. I never had those things with my parents. Most of their mannerisms were theirs. I had a couple of adopted friends who picked up some, but I never seemed to. Had my own."

Jordan had to admit it would be a good feeling. "He's excited about the pictures. Thanks for doing that for him."

"I want to bring my wife, my boys—Eliana, our granddaughter. Can you see him holding her? He never got to hold me."

She heard the squeal of tires, and her breath caught before she managed to blurt out. "Floyd? Are you okay?"

A second or two that felt like micro-eternities passed before his choked voice reached her. "Yes. I'm sorry. I've tried to be content with a good life with parents so wonderful that I wasn't really curious about my biological parents. Now I can't imagine life without a man I've only seen once. It's a bit..."

"Overwhelming?"

"Yes."

She promised to pray and signed off. *Imagine how Arnie feels...*

Sixteen

Two reschedules of the date with Selena put Daphne ahead with coffee and donuts just three blocks from his apartment. Heath walked. A woman appeared from around the corner just after he did and walked toward him. About the time he reached the donut shop door, he recognized her. Daphne.

Did he wait there? Go in? Walk to meet her? Heath chose the latter. He stuck out his hand and introduced himself. "Daphne? I'm Heath Karras."

"Is that Middle Eastern?"

"No... Greek." *No Minotaur talks. No animals. Tell her you like her coat—or her smile, if she ever does it.*

As if jerked by invisible puppet strings, Daphne's mouth formed a brief smile. "Like my name. Greek for some kind of... something. I can't remember what."

"She was a Naiad—the daughter of Peneus."

"Who's he?"

They'd reached the donut shop door, and before Heath could reach for it, Daphne jerked it open and gestured him inside. Call him old-fashioned, but it rankled. There wasn't anything to do but focus on her question and not let it get to him. "Um... either a river god or it's a she who was a nymph. There are lots of stories." A sag of relief brought only guilt. *I should not be so proud of yammering about Greek gods instead of God's creation. There's something wrong in that.*

"Oh."

They'd ordered before he asked what she meant.

"Just... I don't know. I think that's why I can't remember. I wanted it to be something cooler than a stupid water thing.

"Well, it's a lovely name. Mom wanted to name me Daphne if I was a girl, but then when I was born, she liked Heath, so poor Selby got an English place name, too—from the words willow and farm or settlement." He couldn't repress a grin. *A whole conversation and I haven't mentioned a single animal.*

"Wait... *Sel*by? Not Shelby?"

"No... the first. It's similar. That one means hut and farm."

She reached for the donut they offered her, but her eyes didn't move from his face. "Wow. You really know like... a *lot* of useless information. Is there a degree in trivia? Is that what you studied?"

The words came as a jolt, but Heath couldn't deflect. He just shook his head and blurted out, "No. Zoology. I'm a mammologist." When her eyes lit up, and she turned to grab the donut the employee held suspended in air, Heath shot a plea heavenward as well as a telekinetic attempt to stop her. *Don't ask. Don't... please don't...*

"So, you know all kinds of animal stuff, too, don't you? What's your favorite thing you've learned about animals?"

"I—" He swallowed hard and accepted his little paper bag loaded with a nice maple bar. Their coffees appeared a moment later. "Um..."

"Come on. Just one factoid."

He tried for something sweet... even somewhat romantic but not over the top. *Dragonflies. That'll work.* The moment they sat in the hard, laminate booths, he wrapped his hands around the coffee cup and gave his least offensive animal fact—one he still found interesting. "The tails of dragonflies and damselflies create a heart shape when they mate. Kind of cool, don't you think?"

She gave him a look that could mean anything from ready to run to curious for more. Her next question answered that dilemma. "Hmm... insects. Interesting. Anything else? What about fish?"

"All clown fish are born male?"

"What?" Daphne's features screwed up into irritation. "Not funny,

Heath."

"No, really. They are"

"Then how do we get more clown fish?"

"Some turn into females at mating time. Weird, right?"

It might have been paranoia—truth be told, Heath hoped it was—but he could have sworn she muttered, "You sure are," into her coffee cup.

"What about you? Do you have hobbies?"

What she answered, he didn't know. He'd done it again. Resisted the urge to go on and on, telling about the two jaws of a moray eel or the lack of vocal cords in giraffes. In fact, he was so proud of himself that Heath missed the part where she answered the question.

If she did. It took everything in him not to tell her about manatees and tiger stripes. And by the time he remembered to ask what she did for a living, she'd finished the donut. "Well, it's been... interesting." Daphne stood. "I think I'll be going. I don't think..." She seemed to struggle for words. "We have enough compatible interests, but thanks for the donuts."

Heath tapped out a text message to Selby as he strolled back to his car.

> **HEATH:** DIDN'T GIVE OUT FACTS THAT SHE DIDN'T ASK FOR. KIND OF A WIN. SHE WON'T SAY YES AGAIN, THOUGH. OH, AND EVEN IF SHE WANTED TO, I WOULDN'T HAVE. IT WAS JUST NOT A GOOD FIT. PERIOD.

The time—just after nine o'clock. He didn't have another date until six-thirty... in New Cheltenham. Fairbury wasn't even on the way, but he'd have time to catch Jordan if she planned to do his scavenger hunt. The previous evening she'd just gone home and disappeared into the garage. Now...

It was ten before he pulled up in front of the music store, but he let the car idle to keep him warm as he finished one of the letters in the audiobook he'd bought. Frustration mounted as the writer went on and on about every topic but the one that piqued his interest. It was just a mention of soap in passing, but the respondent didn't ask. Then, in a quick postscript, she asked about the soap, and all was well. Heath tapped his phone screen and turned off the car.

A walk around the square and behind The Fox Theater showed no sign of Jordan anywhere. A pass by the music store caused a double take at the sight of a service dog inside. *That... is a strange-looking service dog.* At that moment, the German shepherd glanced over at him as if to say, *Ya think?*

At ten twenty, her Fit zipped around the square and slowed to a crawl as the local cop pointed at her and shook his finger. *It's like time out in Fairbury instead of law enforcement.*

He made it to the opposite corner by the time Jordan rounded the movie theater building and strode toward him. In her hand—the sticky note, but she didn't even look at it. She plowed toward him as if on a mission.

Braced for impact, Heath waited for her to recognize him and unleash pent-up fury. She didn't. Her gaze locked on something behind him, Jordan scurried past. A glance back showed her making a beeline to The Diner.

Oookay. Maybe she's doing things out of order? Got a call?

Heath followed.

Jordan dodged pedestrians with the skill of an obstacle course runner. A slick patch—frozen coffee it seemed—nearly tripped her up, but she managed to make it to The Diner before the alarm on her phone sounded. Once inside, she silenced the alarm and begged for the back-corner booth before Earlene could sit her up front.

The wait began. Gary Brighton had asked to meet at ten-thirty, but a text message apologized for a delay.

JORDAN: CLOSER TO TEN FORTY-FIVE. TROUBLESOME CLIENT.

That was it. Still, Jordan took the words for an apology and ordered Coke and fries. Earlene eyed her. "No pie?"

"Not today. I just feel like something a little simpler."

"There's nothing simple about fries, honey. I mean, *I* am a french fry."

It was probably the long night of little sleep, but Jordan didn't follow. "Okay, 'splain, Lucy."

"Very funny, Ricky. No, really. My husband says it all the time. I'm a french fry. I'm a hot potato, I bring people happiness, and I'm a little 'salty.'"

"Nothing 'salty' about you, Earlene, unless you used to work a fishing boat on the ocean. You're the nicest person I've ever met."

Earlene winked and said, "Yeah, but you don't live with me. Hank's a good guy, but he's not perfect. I can afford to let loose the snark with him. He doesn't give me tips. I'll get that Dr. Pepper right away."

She'd made it three steps away when the words registered with Jordan. "Hey, Earlene?"

The woman looked back. "Yeah?"

"Let's make that a Coke, okay?"

"Coke..." A shake of the head. "Right. Got it. Coke."

Finally alone, Jordan set her phone aside and looked at the pink sticky note. Just a single Bible verse. *"...not forsaking our own assembling together, as is the habit of some, but encouraging one another; and all the more as you see the day drawing near." Hebrews 10:25*

"What does it even mean?"

A glass appeared before her. "What does *what* mean?"

"Found this in my car this morning. I figure there's some kind of message in it, but I don't know what."

"Well," Earlene said, pulling out a straw as if she always did drink and straw in the same trip. "I've always heard it with church. You know how preachers are. They want to get you in those doors. Maybe it's a hint you need to go to church more."

Jordan didn't notice the woman leave. Her mind swirled with possibilities. *Church...* "Yeah, that could be it..."

"What could be it?"

The deep male voice jerked Jordan out of her musings. She jerked her head up to meet the stony gaze of a man with dark hair... and a beard... a man just like... "Um... and you are?"

"Gary Brighton." He pointed to the bench opposite her. "Mind if I sit?"

A bunch of dots connected. Arnie saying he'd liked a girl in school who had freckles. Arnie asking if she liked her audiobook. Arnie asking about pie... "It was Arnie, wasn't it? You did all that stuff for Arnie. *He's* the sorta secret admirer."

"Arnie Holtz? My dad's so-called father?"

The fuzzies that had begun to warm up chilled instantly. "Excuse me?"

"I want to know just what Arnie Holtz expects to get out of my father."

Indignation flared. She sputtered, fumed, and sputtered some more. A drink of Coke steadied her enough to break into a weird tirade about "that old guy" thinking he could butt into their lives. "Excuse me?"

"I said—"

"I heard you. That was me trying to calm myself before I said something rude."

Gary glared.

"Let me remind you, *Mr. Brighton*. Your father contacted my client. Not the other way around. *Your father* asked to meet. Not Arnie. The DNA tests prove that your father's adoption lawyers found the right man—"

"So *you* say."

"Excuse me?"

He folded his arms over his chest, still glaring at her.

"What?"

"Just waiting for you to calm yourself before you keep saying stuff that's rude."

Jordan fumbled for the cash she'd stuffed in her pocket. Dropping ten dollars on the table, she scooted out of the bench and paused by Gary's side. "Just a hint... accusing someone of having ulterior motives when that person didn't initiate contact—*that* is rude. If you have a problem with this, talk to your dad. This isn't on Arnie, and it certainly isn't on *me*."

She bolted from the restaurant before the temptation to say what she really thought overpowered her. Forget that. It already had. All the way out the door and down the sidewalk toward the church, she blasted him for everything from his bullish attitude to using Arnie's desire to give her a surprise against him. "Despicable."

"That's right. Good word for it."

That voice. It would become the voiceover for her nightmares. She whirled and glared. "Leave me alone. Do you get that? Just go."

"I want to know just what your—"

"He's a *friend*. And you letting him use you with this whole sorta admirer thing and then turning on him? Yeah. Despicable just about covers it."

Gary's eyes held conflicting emotions. Anger? Definitely. But there was something more to it. Confusion. "I don't know what you're talking about with this admirer stuff, but I do know that I want you to tell Arnie Holtz to leave my father alone. It's sick to prey on a man in his grief."

"That's rich! Your *father* is the one who dragged up—"

The man stepped closer—too close. Natural instinct demanded she step back. Anger and a refusal to be intimidated propelled her forward. They stood, puffy coats nearly touching while she stared him down.

Fear grew like cancer, and any second now, she'd capitulate. The angrier his features became, the more self-preservation overrode pride and anger. Just as she would have stepped back, Gary grabbed her shoulders.

"Tell him—"

Someone separated them. One second, she'd been about to knee the guy into a new career in overrated musical theater, and the next, another body stood between hers and Gary Jerk-ton's. "I believe she told you to leave her alone."

"This is none of your business."

"That's what's wrong with this country! We ignore when people like you break the law. Yeah. *Law.* You just manhandled a woman. And in five... four... three..."

She followed intervener's head and saw Officer Brad jogging across the street.

"What? You can count backwards. How great for you. Now butt out."

Brad stepped up before the new guy could respond. "What's the problem?"

Gary had no problem spinning it in his favor. "This guy just pushed into our conversation."

That, Jordan couldn't let go. "Actually, Gary grabbed me. This guy stepped in to help." She eyed the new guy and offered a smile. "Thanks, by the way." Something familiar in his face stopped her. Her eyes darted from him to Gary and back again. "Wait..."

"Jordan?"

Her gaze shot back to Officer Brad. "Yeah?"

"Who do you want to go away?"

"Hey!"

Jordan shot a glare at Gary. "Him, actually. He just insulted Arnie and me and accused us of trying to..." She blinked. "Well, I don't know. What *were* you accusing us of?"

He ignored her. Focusing his attention on Brad, Gary spun a tale of two conniving people out to milk Floyd Brighton for all he was worth. If the guy had any brains, he'd have shut his mouth—fast. But he didn't. The longer he spoke, the more Jordan fumed, and the more rigid Brad became.

That's when the other guy murmured something in her ear. "Maybe call the dad?"

"Duh!" She whipped out her phone and dialed. Gary shot a nasty look at her. "What?"

Jordan ignored him as Gary answered. "Hi. Sorry to bother you. We have a situation here. Can you talk to your son?"

"My son?"

"Gary is here accusing Arnie and me of attempting to—I don't know—swindle you out of your life savings or something. I don't get it. Anyway, there's an officer here, and I'm about to just ask him to have Gary arrested for harassment—if that's a thing."

Officer Brad whipped his handcuffs off his belt with speed that should have indicated much experience with arresting folks. He'd probably only used them half a dozen times in his whole Fairbury career. "Yep. I can do that."

"Hey! It's no crime—"

Floyd's voice jerked her back to the phone conversation. "Can I talk to Gary?"

She passed her phone over. "Your father."

Never had she seen a man cower faster. The one-sided conversation? Enlightening. Gary still had a lot of respect for his father—and love. Her heart softened as she saw the scene through new lenses. *I might have been concerned, too.* More rational thoughts reminded her that it would be reasonable if Arnie had found Floyd rather than the other way around.

With each passing second, the hostility and aggression on Gary's face softened into a subdued shell of its former self. "But Dad—" A moment later, he nodded. "All right. See you in a few." He eyed her. "Unless she presses charges. It seems to be a thing."

Brad piped up just then. "Oh, it's a thing. One I recommend, actually."

Jordan shook her head. "As long as he promises to leave me alone from now on, we're good. You'll have to play with your handcuffs another day."

"If Nichole didn't live here and love her job, I'd be in Rockland by now."

"If you married her…"

Gary broke in. "Can I go? Dad expects to meet me in thirty minutes. I just have time if I leave now."

Brad let him go and returned to his spot at his favorite corner on the square. Gary mumbled a half-hearted apology to her and glared at the other guy as he left. Jordan turned to him as well. "So, are you a sorta secret rescuer as well?"

Seventeen

It wasn't supposed to play out like this. In Heath's version of things, she'd follow the scavenger hunt, maybe she'd notice him at every place. And finally, at The Diner, she'd come sit at his table. They could try again. Maybe. He could mix up that last one if he got there first...

"Maybe I shouldn't have butted in..."

"You probably diffused something awful."

"A jerk like that should have been arrested."

Jordan shoved her hands and phone in her pocket. "No, he's just worried about his Dad. I get that. I do. He just addressed it the wrong way."

Don't be amazing about something like that. You'll give me hope.

The pink sticky note appeared from her pocket—folded, half-crumpled. She shook it at him. "You?"

Heath shrugged and gave a weak smile—one he hoped looked genuine at least.

"So, is this the church?"

"Yes."

"What do I do there?"

She hadn't figured it out yet. Excitement gave life to that smile. "Check it out and see?"

Despite temperatures hovering in the low single digits and wind that occasionally blasted them from the side, she stood staring at him. "You look so familiar—not just because you were at the coffee shop or The Diner. Your voice…"

"Some people think they hear a trace of an accent in it."

"'Trace of an accent…' Where have I heard that?" Jordan stared at the note, back at Heath, and shrugged. "I feel like I should know you."

"Maybe you should go check out the church."

Jordan shot a look at him. "Are you coming?"

"I'll be around. Later…" He turned to go.

"Are you going to tell me where I know you from?"

"You'll figure it out."

An exasperated huff followed that one. "Yeah? Then why not tell me?"

After three steps back toward the diner, Heath called back, "I've got to give me a fighting chance." To himself, he added, *And time to figure out why I can talk to you like this and not on a date. Maybe Selby…*

However, despite his words, he sprinted down one of the side streets and arrived at the church just after her. Jordan stood at the front walk, staring up at the building as if expecting to see some message spray-painted across the front. She strolled out to the parking lot. And walked back again. All it would take was a single text message. That message could also kill any chance he had. *She'd see my name.*

Heath tried the next best thing. Ann.

HEATH: SPOKE TO JORDAN. SHE'S ON A SCAVENGER HUNT. STUMPED AT THE SECOND SPOT. NOT BODING WELL FOR THE SUCCESS. DO I STICK AROUND AND TELL HER IT'S ME OR WAIT FOR ANOTHER TIME?

Three minutes later, just as he'd almost given up and shown himself, her reply came through.

ANN: GOOD IDEA. BE THERE AT EVERY STOP. HELP IF SHE ASKS. MAKE HER HAVE TO WORK TO FIND YOU. I'LL DO WHAT I CAN.

A minute later, another one came through.

ANN: SHE JUST ASKED FOR HELP. WHERE SHOULD SHE LOOK?

HEATH: DOOR MARQUEE.

Sherlock would say the game was afoot.

"Okay, Mom. Where do I find this thing? And am I going to end up some guy's prisoner or something?"

"Stay in public places, and you'll be fine."

Jordan didn't quite know what to do with a response like that. "I can't believe you're not telling me to run. I think that's what a responsible mother would do."

"Since when have I ever been responsible? Now. What about some kind of bulletin board? Do they have something like that inside? For reminders about potlucks and Bible studies?"

"Listen to you gettin' all churchy. Yeah. There's one inside..." She jogged up the step and reached for the door handle, but her peripheral vision caught a blur of pink to her right. "Wait... the marquee. There it is. It's got a drawing of a ticket that says 'admit two,' and then it has a note below it that says, 'Do you talk during movies?' I don't. That's a relief." As Jordan turned to go, she caught sight of a coat disappearing around the tall junipers that served to block the parking lot from the street. "I think he was here."

A dash down the walk and to the sidewalk showed him power-walking down the street. "I think he's keeping an eye on me."

"Well, have fun, but seriously. Don't go into any alleys or anything stupid like that. And call me. I'm going to be going nuts here."

At The Fox, Heath stood, his back to her, staring at a poster of the new time slip Valentine's movie. A hint? Maybe. She could take it as one...

The ticket booth showed her next clue. A pink sticky note with *Jordan* written on it. When she asked for it, the girl in the booth handed her the note and two tickets. To the Valentine's movie, of course.

Jordan moved beside him to check out the poster as well. Without looking his way, she sighed. "I hope it is the sappiest move I've ever seen."

"Oh? You like sappy movies?"

She shrugged. "Sometimes. This time I just want to see if my date likes them or if they make him squirm."

"Who's your date? Maybe I know him."

Not letting you off that easily. Jordan turned to go to Bookends—and hoped she was right about what the picture meant. "I'm not sure yet. I guess you'll have to wait and see."

The doors to Bookends showed nothing. No pink in the window. Nothing outside to interest her. She reached for the door handle and found it pulled open by someone behind her. Without even looking back, she charged inside. "Thanks."

"You're welcome."

Jordan froze. *There's something creepy about this. But it's nice that there's help, too. Maybe.* An idea formed as she looked around the front part of the store. In seconds, she described the scene to her mom without lowering her voice at all. *I've become* that *person—making the whole store listen to my conversation. Extenuating circumstances, right?*

"He's totally following me. I don't think it's creepy—yet. He got me tickets to that new Valentine's movie."

"Tickets plural?"

"Yeah. Maybe I'll let him go with me—if I ever figure out who he is."

Mom began hacking and coughing. "You—" she gasped. "You think you know him?"

"Something about him is really familiar. At first, I thought it was because he'd been where I was, but his voice..."

"Well, if it's not setting off warning bells, it's good, right?"

"Except that I'm walking around Bookends looking for a pink sticky note and no idea where to find it."

Again, the choking. "Um, where is he?"

"Somewhere in here. He opened the door for me."

"Good. I'd have to let him have it if he didn't treat you right. So, why don't you go find him? Maybe he's there to be your hint."

Something in Mom's words felt... off. Before Jordan could think much about it, a tween stopped her. "Hey. Did you say you were looking for a pink sticky note?"

"Yeah. Did you see one?"

"There's one over in the Biographies and Memoirs. I have to do this paper on Hammurabi, and I was over there looking. It's sticking out between two books, but there's the name Jordan written on one edge."

"Thanks!"

The guy stood leaning against a bookshelf, a book open in his hand. Jordan couldn't help herself. "Fancy meeting you here."

"I love a good book." He snapped the one he'd been "reading" shut and pushed it back onto the bookshelf.

Jordan took note. A biography of Jane Goodall. "Wasn't she the woman who studied apes?"

"Chimpanzees, but they aren't a safe subject for me. See you around."

With that, he bolted from the store. One second, he'd been standing there, and the next, she heard the door bells jingle. "Jordan?"

That's when she remembered her mother was still waiting for her. "Sorry. Found the book—and the guy. He was reading about Jane Goodall and then just ran when I mentioned apes."

"At least he didn't go on and on about the mating habits of chimps. Improvement."

"What?"

Silence.

"Mom?"

"I need to go. Call me if you need me."

She wouldn't let it go that easily. "What aren't you telling me? You know something." The wheels turned, and cogs clicked into place, but the only answer made no sense. "Mom?"

"Bye, Jordan. Love you."

Dead air followed. *Whatever. I'll deal with that later. What does this one say?* It showed a half-plucked daisy stem with petals—or what appeared to pass for them—falling down. "The Pettler."

"It's just down the street—catty-corner across the square." A blue-haired lady smiled at her. "Do you need me to show you?"

"I've got it. Thanks."

There was no sign of the guy—none. All the way to The Pettler, she mulled her mother's words. *Why would Mom ask about the mating chimps?*

Why would anyone talk about that with someone they don't even know? It'd be like—

She came to a standstill—right in the middle of the street. Brad shouted at her, but Jordan couldn't move. *That guy. With the bladders. Heath... something. He had a beard, didn't he? Dark. Why am I so bad at faces?*

A car's horn blared, and it ripped her out of her thoughts. She stared at Brad who shouted, "Jordan! Get out of the street!"

A glance back showed a man screaming at her from inside his car. "Right. Move."

At the corner, Brad asked if she was okay, but Jordan just waved her hand at him. "I'm thinking."

"Well, next time think anywhere but in the street."

How would Mom know Heath? Oh... In seconds, she had the zoo's website pulled up. Staff. There he was. Head of the mammalogy department. Heath Karras. As director of the entire zoo, her mother would be his immediate boss.

She shot Mom a text message.

JORDAN: YOU KNEW ALL ALONG?
MOM: YES. WAS IT A LIE NOT TO TELL YOU? I'M SORRY.

As if appearing out of thin air, Heath's back disappeared into the doorway of The Pettler. Jordan dashed across the street in pursuit, but just outside the shop door, she zipped back another text.

JORDAN: NOT A LIE. CONFUSED. TALK LATER. HE'S SAFE, RIGHT?
MOM: WOULD I HAVE ENCOURAGED YOU TO PLAY ALONG IF I DIDN'T KNOW HE WAS?

Mom... words. We will have words. Heath stood by a barrel of daisies and handed her one as she entered. Jordan paused. "Thanks. Talked to Mom."

"How is Ann?"

Despite every attempt to look and sound severe, Jordan snickered. "Panicked that I might be seriously ticked off at her right now."

"Don't be. She took pity on a guy who isn't good at dates and helped him—and by him, I mean me—figure out how to try to show that he... um,

I am not a complete troll."

"Is there a sticky note, or do I just pluck the petals off this daisy?"

The wince on his face—she'd berate herself for thinking it was cute later. Heath shook his head. "I always thought that was a cruel, barbaric thing to do. It's like tearing wings off butterflies."

"You just earned two brownie points." Her gaze swept the cheerful little flower shop. Unlike the semi-dark and dingy places Jordan recalled from her childhood, the store was bright, well decorated, and inviting. The humid air mingled with the scent of carnations. *That* she still remembered and still loved.

A woman stepped forward. "Hello! What can I help you with today?"

"He was here first."

The woman gave Heath a secret smile. "Yes, I know. I have already helped him. Yesterday."

That caught her attention. "You did this yesterday?"

"After I dropped off cheesecake filled strawberries, yes."

"After you—" If she hadn't answered the phone, she would have answered the door at Arnie's. And the car... "Hey, when did you put the note in my window?"

"After I left the strawberries with the guy at the house on Dogwood."

He'd waited for her around town. She knew it. And then he'd come back today. "Um... thanks." To the woman, she added, "I need a pink sticky note. Do you have any of those in stock?"

"*Lo siento,* Jordan, no. I do have something here with your name on it, though."

"How do you know my name?"

"You asked for the pink. You speak to Heath. I know this. Come with me."

From a small floral case behind the counter, the woman pulled a wrapped gardenia still on the stem, and tucked into the ferns and baby's breath behind it, was a small, pink, sticky note daisy. "There are meanings to flowers. My husband has taught me these." She pointed to the gardenia. "One of the meanings of the gardenia is hope."

Jordan shot a look at Heath. "Hope for what?"

"Second chances."

Well, he'd certainly worked hard for one. She had to give him that. Jordan turned back to the florist and asked, "Okay... what about the daisy?"

"Daisies have many meanings. One is that the giver can keep a secret."

"I'll say."

This time, Heath groaned. "I didn't know until yesterday that you have a hard time with faces. I was sure you'd recognized me in The Diner last week."

Embarrassment made her curt... almost rude. "Right. Whatever. So, any other 'meanings' I should know about?"

"Oh, sure. There's purity, innocence, true love, and..."

Jordan saw it. The woman had made Heath squirm on purpose. *Good for you. I'll send my apology flowers to Mom from this place. Just as soon as I let her have it.*

"... new beginnings."

A poke through the pink daisy showed that she'd have to unfold it to read. "Do you remember what this said or showed?"

"Yes. It was a strawberry—sort of. There was something in it. Maybe it was supposed to be a blob of chocolate. Not good drawing."

The woman's Spanish accent grew thicker the more she spoke. From the back, a voice called out, "Lena, she's supposed to work for it."

"You stay out of this, Wayne Farrell. This is my job." The accent—even thicker with Js sounding like "ch." "She knows. I see it in her eyes."

Jordan did know. She called out thanks and nearly ran to The Confectionary. Heath was already there, seated at a table, watching. How'd he get out of the shop so fast? When had he even left?

The candy case—pink-free. The same went for the ice cream case, the shelves, the tables. Everything. Jordan tried to meet Heath's gaze, but he only stared at the door. Exasperated, she turned to the woman behind the counter. "I'm looking for—" A chair scraped against the floor. "—a pink sticky note."

"I'd be looking at posters or fliers..." The woman winked at someone behind her. Heath, of course.

When she turned to the door, there it was, stuck to the back of a flier. A steaming coffee cup. This time, Jordan had a plan.

Heath opened the door. Jordan smiled in an attempt to disarm him. It worked, too. Then she bolted down the street. It took a few seconds, but the sounds of footfalls behind her told her that he'd caught on. Another second or two passed before she heard him ask—right behind her, of course— "Do you want me to beat you or not?"

"If you can."

She should have known he'd be fast. He sprinted ahead and disappeared inside. In her defense, she had to dodge a woman coming out of The Market with a giant rolling handcart. *Like I could have beat him. That dude is fast.*

Heath sat, arms folded, feet propped on an extra chair, and not even panting. Under the bulletin board. Under a pink sticky note that had words this time. *Pie and coffee at The Diner? Lunch at Rositas?*

Eighteen

Jordan sat down beside him and fingered the note. "Rosita's will be busy—so will The Diner."

"True..."

"I'm calling Mom. Hang on." A second later, she grabbed his sleeve. "Come with me."

Heath came.

They passed through a narrow space between The Fox and a small resale shop just down from the square and ended up in the parking lot. Her Fit sat parked there.

"Hey, Mom? How much do you trust Heath?" The silence nearly killed him. "Enough to trust him at my house? Alone? With me?"

An eternity passed in the next fifteen or so seconds. A few "Mmm... hmmms" followed before she shoved her phone at him. "She wants to talk to you."

Ann sounded excited. "She's willing to bring you home. That's big. It means she's not mad at me, still trusts me, and willing to give you another shot. Don't blow it."

"Can't promise that last one, but so far, so good. Ice broken, maybe?"

"Don't know, but if prayers of someone who doesn't really think they do anything but bounce off the walls helps, then I'll throw some out into the cosmos."

Ann... we're going to have to talk Jesus someday. "Prayer is never a bad idea, Ann. I'd be honored to know you were praying for me. Thanks."

Jordan gaped at him. When he passed back the phone, she took a step back. "Maybe I should rethink this. You may be some kind of witch or wizard or whatever they call guys who do evil things to get their way."

"Or, maybe your mom just likes me and hopes that if she throws words at her walls, the 'cosmos' will give her favor and help me keep my bladder, dung beetle, and mating chimps stories to myself."

Astonishment transformed into utter disbelief in one sharp intake of air. "What? Not really. Chimps? And you picked up Jane Goodall?"

"I had to get out of there before I blew it."

She pointed to her Fit. "That's my car. Want to have lunch at my house?"

Indecision struck with the force of ptomaine poisoning and twice as virulent. Throat dry, heart pounding, Heath stood there with clammy palms in his coat pockets and feeling eleven again. Courtney Callen. *"Did you know lemurs are the only primates with blue eyes besides humans—just like yours. Will you go to the dance with me? They also are very intelligent—just like you."*

The sandwich approach. As usual, it had failed. Then his mother had called her mother, and the next thing he knew, he was taking Courtney to the winter dance. "Worst furlough ever."

"What?"

Heath snapped to the present with raw honesty that should have served as warning bells for both of them. "Are you sure you want to risk it? Bladders aren't my worst coping mechanism, unfortunately."

"I'll shut you up."

Something told him she would, too. "Um..."

"Get in."

Heath got.

Books talk about those lovely companionable silences that pour peaceful joyfulness into hearts. *Books lie.*

Misery. The misery that gives birth to every awkward and unwanted fact is the byproduct of silence. Awkward, horrible silence... That was more like it.

Unfortunately.

Then Jordan flashed him that smile. How God managed to contain Himself and wait thousands of years before creating it, Heath couldn't imagine. Her eyes twinkled—in broad daylight! Those freckles beckoned like nature's glitter across her nose and upper cheeks.

And now I've completely lost my mind.

"So... tell me something." Jordan pulled onto Primrose Lane just as she asked. She also didn't wait for him to agree. "Just how did you know I'd find the notes today instead of last night?"

"I didn't."

"But you asked," she reminded him as she pulled into the driveway, "if I'd meet for lunch at The Diner or Rosita's"

Heath pulled the crumpled dinner invitation from his pocket. "I got there in time to switch it out."

Car in park, Jordan out, she peered at him over the top. "That was anticlimactic. You should know that."

"I'll remember."

The house was impressive. He didn't know what caregivers made, but it had to be much more than he'd imagined to afford a house in Fairbury at all. Still, the interior seemed a bit... cold for someone like Jordan. "Nice house."

She glanced around her as she dumped her things on a table in the entry. As she shrugged out of her coat, she half-agreed. "Is it? I guess. I like the structure and some of the bigger pieces of furniture, but D.C. keeps it sterile enough for his military-loving heart."

"D.C.?"

"The owner." Before he could ask, Jordan led him through the living room to the kitchen. "Let's see what's in here. Oh, and I'm just housesitting while he's deployed. Saving to buy my own."

That he could get behind. "It didn't seem to reflect you, but then I realized I don't know you that well."

"Or at all..."

An argument formed before he could stop it. "I disagree there. I know quite a few things about you."

Jordan closed the fridge and held up one finger. "Burritos or sandwiches?"

"Sandwiches?"

"Good choice. After being offered Rosita's, mine would just be a terrible reminder of what I was missing out on. Roast beef?"

After assurances that he'd be happy with anything and offering to help, as well as being relegated to the mini breakfast bar and told to stay put, Heath began his assessment. "First, you are the kind of person who, when she's faced with an insufferable bore, listens politely and leaves without being unkind. Second, you invest in your clients far beyond taking them a meal or driving them to a doctor's appointment."

"Yep, I even help them get over their attachment to ugly tchotchkes. I'm a hero." Jordan winced. "Sorry. Still feeling a little guilty over just how eager I was to help Arnie cut the lace and crystal from his life yesterday. Hoping he's not regretting that."

"Well, you also found something understandable in a guy who attacked you today. You've got a great mom who fought for my promotion at the risk of her own job."

Jordan froze. A moment later, she looked up and locked eyes with him. "Wait... you're *that* guy?"

A shiver rippled through him. *What'd Ann say about me?* Not trusting himself to speak without squeaking, Heath nodded.

"Ron was so mad at her for risking everything like that, but she said, 'If they don't trust my judgment, I'll go somewhere they do. He's the best, and I want him.'"

"Wow. I was sure that it was a non-risk—that they'd never actually accept her resignation so they'd be sure she never had to give it."

Jordan slathered all four slices of bread with mayonnaise before wincing and asking, "Um... do you do mayo?"

"Yep. Mustard, too."

"Gross." But she pulled a squeeze bottle from the fridge and set it in front of him. "Anyway, on a happier note, Mom thought one of the board members wanted someone he knew—probably a nephew—to get it. So, she decided you were worth the stand against nepotism."

He accepted his sandwich, gave it a squirt of mustard, and asked the question that he suspected was a universal one. "Why don't they just call it 'nephewtism' and get it over with?"

"*That* is hilarious." Jordan plopped down next to him and stuck out her hand. "Are you praying, or am I?"

If I have to hold your hand... "It's your house, how about you?" Now that he'd spoken the only words required of him, Heath folded his hand around hers and begged God for the ability to focus on whatever she said.

God either said no, or his powers of ignoring the Almighty had risen to nearly blasphemous heights. *Please? Just one moment of clarity?*

"Um, Heath?"

"Yeah?"

"Look, you seem like a nice guy, but I'm not going to sit here and hold hands all through lunch—especially since mine might turn black and fall off before I can finish up that sandwich."

A look confirmed it. He'd gripped her hand with everything he had, and even still, he had to consciously order himself to unclasp said fingers. "Sorry."

"Is that just the 'effectual, fervent prayer of a righteous man'?"

"Not sure."

Jordan took a couple of bites before she remembered drinks. "Soda, water, or coffee?"

"Any chance you have milk?"

Within seconds, she'd pulled a carton from the fridge and poured a glass. "It's whole..."

"My favorite. Thanks. I got used to drinking milk with sandwiches, and..."

A text message came through on her phone. Jordan didn't even glance at it, but Heath saw the name. "Hey, that's your mom. Mind getting it? I don't want her deciding I've kidnapped you and sending that cop. He's too good with those handcuffs."

Once assured that all was well, Ann disconnected, and Jordan slid from the chair. "Excuse me—need a twenty-second break. Be right back."

Heath watched her go, trying to figure out what she meant. Understanding hit just before a door closed. Laughter commenced. His sandwich bite flew across the room and hit the fridge, leaving a nice mustard and mayo blot on a child sponsorship card. He was still trying to clean it off and chuckling when she returned.

"Good one, huh? I've called it that ever since that night. Makes for discretion in the right circumstances."

"Can't wait to tell Selby."

"I can't wait to meet her." Then, as if their first date hadn't been a classic Heath disaster, she said, "What are you guys doing for dinner?"

He groaned. "I have a date. In New Cheltenham. With 'Kendyll.' That's —'yll,' not 'A.'"

"And you don't want to go now that you've talked to me more and—"

"I never wanted to go in the first place. And when I saw the Betwixt list this morning, I wanted to go even less."

She froze. "Wait. Betwixt. Like the .com? That matchmaking service?"

"Is there more than one?"

Eyes closed, sandwich resting on the plate, Jordan sighed. "Yeah. I signed up after our date. Forgot all about it. I bet I've got matches that I'm supposed to review or something."

"You do."

The eyelids flew open. "How do you know?"

Heath just pulled out his phone, pulled up the matches, and slid it across the counter. "Um... there." Her astonishment should have been insulting.

"When did you sign up?"

"The next day."

A smile formed. "You're telling me that within their twenty-four-hour window, not to mention within twenty-four hours of our date, they matched us up?"

"I don't know. I thought I just signed up for one match, but I must have clicked something for more, because a few weeks later, all of a sudden, there were ten in my box." Heath sighed. "There's something sickly, horribly, cruelly ironic in me sitting here able to talk to you about something when I am stuck with a date with someone I don't want to go out with in just a few hours."

Silence returned with a vengeance. Once more, the knowledge that animals with smaller bodies and faster metabolisms see in slow motion became of paramount importance. Heath stuffed bite after bite into his mouth to stop himself from saying a word.

"Heath?"

"Hmm??" *Thank you, Lord, for a full mouth.*

"Two things." Jordan's sidelong glance made him ready himself for another bite. "First, don't go."

The half-chewed bite forced its way down. "What?"

"The date. Don't go." Jordan winced and stared down at her plate. "Is that awful of me to ask?"

Without waiting for her to change her mind, he zipped a message through the app, canceling the date. "I hope not, because that means I'm doubly awful. Can't wait to see what Selby says when she sees I canceled."

"Is she going to be happy that the sorta secret admirer thing kind of worked?"

Kind of worked? Is that good or bad? Heath opted to stick to facts. "I didn't tell her I was doing it."

"Good."

"What was the other thing?"

She grinned and readied *her* sandwich for a bite. "What animal facts are lurking in you right now? I can see them."

"You should not ask me that question." Perhaps it was the way she cocked her head and looked at him—almost like a puppy. Perhaps. More likely, it was the way her freckles drew him in and held his heart captive—silly as it seemed, even to himself. Regardless, Heath began.

"Well, did you know some animals see in slow motion...?"

Nineteen

Not for the first time, Selby pulled her phone from her pocket and tapped out a scathing message for Heath. She also deleted it—also not for the first time. Instead, she continued pacing. Up one side of the room, across, down the other, sidestepping a large planter and a chair.

"I'm about to rearrange this room!"

A key in the lock told her she might not need to. Sure enough, Heath entered and hung his coat on the hook. "Hey..."

"You're supposed to be on a date. With Kendyll."

"About that..."

"Heath!" Selby stood before him, arms folded over her chest, her best glare fixed on him. "You *promised* to do this."

"So that I'd be able to have a date without going on and on about bladders, right?"

"Don't mock me, oh my brother. I have our father's little finger at my beck and call."

He shoved hands in his pockets, but instead of looking properly fearful and chagrined, Heath just shook his head. "I'm telling Dad that you've become a call girl."

"I'm telling Dad that you called me a woman of loose morals."

Heath only made it through another, "I'm telling Dad" before he broke down laughing. "Joke's on you, little sis. I spent all day with Jordan."

Her tirade began and fizzled from an, "I don't—" to an equally intense, "—what did you say?"

"You heard me."

"She's on your list. You *went out of order?*"

Everything shifted then. An unbelievable story emerged—one of a cool guy who set up a secret admirer plan that actually worked, of coming to the girl's rescue, of creating an elaborate scavenger hunt, and of eating lunch and seeing a movie together. More than all that, though, one thing stood out.

"You flirted with her."

The tiny smile he fought to hide said it all. "Maybe a little."

"And she didn't run screaming?"

"She only ran from me once, but that was just for a twenty-second break."

A knowing nod followed that one. Selby flopped onto the couch and hung her head over the chaise end, looking up at him upside down... ish. "You started in on the chimps, didn't you?"

"Twice, but that's not what caused the *twenty-second* break."

Selby sat up and peered at him. "You emphasized that. Why?"

As he repeated himself, twice, Heath pulled out his phone, flipped through it for a moment, and passed it to her. The screen showed them standing before a movie poster. He might not notice it, being somewhat insecure about women for obvious reasons. However, Selby did.

Jordan, Alyward he said her last name was, *leaned* close to him. And anyone who had ever seen *While You Were Sleeping* knew that leaning meant something. Hollywood would not lie about something so important.

Selby couldn't help herself. "Hey, Heath."

"She's cute, isn't she?"

"She's more than cute. That's the most naturally beautiful I've ever seen. Does she even *wear* makeup?"

He shrugged.

"Should've known you wouldn't know. Anyway, look at that picture." When he stared at it much longer than she'd intended, Selby groaned. "She's *leaning*. She *leaned*, Heath!"

"Yeah, well I'm not the 'Everlasting Arms.'"

"I—" The unsuppressed snicker stopped her. Selby eyed the photo again, and her thumbs hovered over the keyboard. "Is her number in here?"

"Um... why?"

"You owe me." Selby scrolled until she found Jordan Aylward and typed out a message.

> **SELBY:** THIS IS SELBY. DID HEATH REALLY SPEND ALL DAY WITH
> YOU?

When her phone pinged, and Heath reached for his again, Selby knew she'd been had. "You knew I'd do that."

"I know you well, little sister."

The pacing began as she read the text message and zipped one back. Minutes later, she and Jordan switched to phone calls. Between replies to Jordan, Selby shot remarks at Heath, beginning with the need to rearrange the living room. "It is not conducive to angst-riddled pacing."

"Rearrange away. Meanwhile, I've got to call Ann. I promised."

It took three seconds after Selby heard Heath say, "Hello," to fully realize what had happened. "My brother had a date—one that went well enough that his date got my number."

Jordan's snicker sounded much too elegant for such a word. "He's a great guy—so far."

Loyalty and deep love reared equally fearsome fangs and hissed out a threat. "He is. Period."

"And I'm sure he'll prove that to me."

"He could prove it at the gala on the ninth..." Selby shot Heath a gloating look before adding, "He needs a date."

"We're already talking about it."

All hope of rational and mature thought or actions dissolved with those words. She squealed like a cheerleader voted prom queen. Twice.

As much as she'd hoped Arnie wouldn't hear about her encounter with Gary, when she arrived Monday afternoon, the old guy looked ready to spit nails. "Are you okay? Floyd called—so did Gary. He apologized. Well," Arnie amended. "They both did."

"It's okay. He was just looking out for his father. Went about it in all the wrong ways," Jordan admitted, "but it ended well enough."

"Floyd said Gary's worried about all this."

"That's true, but it's good. Don't you think? I mean it shows that he's concerned about his father." Desperate for a change of discussion, Jordan swept her gaze over the room. "No offense to your Helen, but this room is so much cozier and more comfortable now. I really like it."

Arnie blushed. "I was thinking about taking out the wallpaper and the sconces, but if you like it..."

"I'd like it even better without. We can do that if you want."

"I've been taking up a bunch of your time. I thought I'd hire Floyd."

Thinner ice she'd never trod. "Um... Arnie? Let me do it. First, Floyd's not going to take your money, and if you let him do it for you without paying him, it'll convince Gary that all his concerns were valid. And second, I'd like to because I like you."

"Can we take the sconces down now. Like... now, now?"

She'd gotten those and the brass butterflies down before Arnie started in on Gary and Floyd again. If she didn't do *something*, he'd talk himself out of a relationship he needed. "Hey, Arnie?"

"Hmm..."

A glance over her shoulder showed him fingering a silk plant. *Please let it go.* Jordan waited until he looked at her before she nodded. "Yeah, that should probably go. Floyd's family might have allergies."

"It's fake."

"Dust." And that settled it for her. "I wonder what Floyd and his wife do for Valentine's Day."

Arnie started in on a story about it being the day Floyd proposed. "They recreate that date every year. The restaurant they went to has changed a dozen hands over the years. It was Italian back then. Became a family restaurant, a Chinese, sushi, and it's Italian again."

"I suppose they'll go the Saturday before, then..."

"No." The hopes that soared crashed down to earth again when he said, "They've got other plans that night."

That would be it. She'd give him the tickets to the Valentine's Day ball, he could give them to Floyd, and maybe Gary would see that Arnie wasn't out to *get* anything but a nice relationship with his son out of the whole deal. Perfection.

"They invited me over for dinner. Wendy called just before you came. I didn't say yes, but if you think it's okay..."

"Call her right back and say yes, Arnie. You can always change your mind between now and then. But if you don't, you'll always regret not knowing."

Arnie sank into his chair and closed his eyes. "He's a good man, my son." As he had every time he'd said the word, a sigh escaped with "son."

"I agree. I checked him out, remember? Church website—he's always doing something for someone. His wife posts loving things about him on her wall and his. They raised three kids who love him fiercely."

When he reached for the oversized phone that would *never* fit in her back pocket, Jordan relaxed and went back to removing unnecessary bric-a-brac. *And I just have to figure out what to do with those tickets since I can't ask Heath to the thing.* Not for the first time, she wondered if she'd be going to the gala with him or her mother. *Either way, I get to dress up and see him in his element. And maybe that'll loosen him up more. It might be worth the dung beetle to get to see him more relaxed.*

A smile formed just as Arnie set aside the phone again. He demanded to know what it was. Much to her disgust and delight, Jordan couldn't keep it in. "Would you be surprised to learn that I had a sorta secret admirer?"

"I'm more surprised that you don't know of many not-so-secret ones."

"I thought you sent him—at first. But then I saw him standing behind Gary. They really look a lot alike." Arnie looked skeptical. "No, really. They're about the same height, same build, both have dark hair and beards..." She pulled out her phone and found the picture to show him. "See..."

"Nice looking boy. Odd that beards are back after being gone for so long. He keeps his nice and trim. I like his face."

You sound like that angel in It's a Wonderful Life. *But then, I like his face, too.*

"Where'd you meet him?"

With that question, Jordan told it all. From the first flutters of attraction when they met in the lobby of a Rockland restaurant and her walking out, to signing up for a dating service, the secret admirer stuff, him rescuing her from Gary, and the coincidence of Betwixt, and the movie. Most of the movie, anyway.

"And he works for your ma?"

"Isn't that weird? And we signed up for the same matchmaking service."

Arnie eyed her. "You skimmed over that movie awfully fast. What aren't you telling me? What movie?"

She named it.

"Romance, huh? Sounds promising. Helen and I saw Dr. Zhivago on our first date." Arnie eyed her. "So, did he hold your hand?"

Face hotter than a sunburn in August, Jordan shook her head. "No..."

"But?"

"He wanted to."

That red face flamed even hotter as Arnie slapped his leg and bellowed, "Atta girl, Jordie!"

A snowstorm warning had sent him to check on all of the animal departments—just in case. Tilly and Mosi were doing well, the arctic animals had been given access to indoors and outdoors, and the tropical animals had all been settled in for a "long winter's nap."

With nothing else to do but get trapped there or go home, Heath forwarded anything he might be able to work on from home, grabbed his stuff, and hurried out to his car. Once he'd started the engine and the seats began warming, he pulled out his phone and zipped Jordan a text message.

HEATH: HEADING HOME. YOU SAFE?

Her reply came in the form of a call. "Hey, I'm home early. Arnie sent me home. He's getting soft and selfless now that he has family to badger him."

"I'd hoped this one would miss us. I thought we could meet for coffee and I could practice my conversational skills on you, but..."

"Alive is better. Hey, your sister. How much do you like her guy from Betwixt?"

Just as she asked, an alert popped up on his phone. Heath settled his phone in the dash cradle and headed for an exit. "As much as I can with the little time I've spent with him. She likes him, though. Selby wasn't looking for anyone, so it'd have to be someone pretty special to pique her interest. Why?"

"I won tickets to the Valentine's Ball. I would have asked you, but I figured you have to go to the gala, don't you?"

"I was going to ask if you'd decided..."

Jordan didn't give him a chance. "My next thought was that maybe Kevin?"

"You're better with names than faces."

"Yeah... anyway, I thought maybe he'd like to take Selby. I'd give them to him if he wanted them."

Heath grinned. This would be perfect. "I'll give you that number if you give me a promise to go to the gala with me."

"What about my mom?"

What Ann had to do with it, Heath couldn't imagine. "What about her?"

"I'm supposed to be *her* date."

Troublesome, but not unsurpassable. "And if I get her to agree?"

"Fork over the number. That's not even a dare—or a question. It's a done deal. She's positively giddy about us going to the movies. So is Arnie."

A car slid toward him in that slow-motion spin that signaled a loss of control. Heath braced himself for impact, but the car stopped a few feet away. A slow exhale preceded his response. "Add Selby to the ranks of the thrilled. She said I should make the movies *all* my first few dates until I'm comfortable. Wish she'd thought of that four weeks ago. It might have saved a lot of money and mortification."

"For the time being, I'd prefer not to know about other dates."

Heath made it around another sliding vehicle before he let out another relieved exhale and said, "And I'd prefer not to have had them."

"Deal... for now."

Lord, I'd appreciate some compatibility, some chance of romance, and perhaps a nice long fifty or sixty years together because You and she had mercy on me and let that whole falling in love thing happen.

What he couldn't decide was which was worse—that it might not happen or that it might not happen with *her. It's too soon to know, but it's not too soon to hope. I hope...*

Twenty

The zipper stuck just at her bra line. Selby wrestled, wriggled, and wailed until she gave up and did the only logical thing left. "Heath! Help!"

As expected, Heath appeared in seconds. "Don't tell me you ripped it. I'll be dead meat—or fired."

"No... but the zipper's stuck. I can't get it up or down now!"

His hands clung to the sparkling chiffon, and Selby spent the next minute praying he wouldn't snag it badly enough to show. "My fingers aren't made for tiny zipper pulls!"

Nothing would budge it. Not up. Not down. Nowhere. It clung to that spot as if determined to stay put and look ridiculous. Selby thought of every trick she knew, but the risk of getting any lubricant on the dress—not helpful. "Let's try heat. Maybe it'll soften the plastic just enough to let it slide."

In the bathroom mirror, she watched as Heath fought to heat up the zipper without burning her. Instead, he rinsed his hands several times to cool them off and tried again. And again.

The teeth moved up one... two... she could feel the slow crawl up the zipper. Then it shot upward, and the entire back popped open. "Noooo."

Heath just stared. "I better call Jordan."

"Your boss is going to kill both of us. Then Kevin will fall in love with Jordan, and we'll have to watch them for eternity."

"Not sure about your theology there, but okay then."

He put her on speakerphone and Selby began the tale of a destroyed semi-designer dress. "It's ruined. What'll I do?"

Jordan, however, had a perfect solution. "First, you just sew her into the dress. She won't need it off before you get home, anyway. So, just sew her into it. Then we'll take it to the dry cleaner's, and their tailor will replace the zipper."

"Great idea. But I can't sew, and I doubt we have what we need. What do I get and where, and how do I do this well?"

Laughter hinted that he'd owe her... but after two weeks of daily flirting and three dates, Selby suspected that owing Jordan didn't bother him in the least. Jordan promised to be there inside an hour if the roads permitted. "Just get your makeup and hair done and be ready to bolt. I'll sew as fast as I can when I get there."

Selby slipped on a hoodie for modesty's sake, making the ensemble look like gangsta couture. "I like it. Snap a picture, will you?"

"Zip it up."

Her gut twisted into inelegant knots. "Is the dress indecent?"

"No..." At her pointed look, he added, "Kevin'll enjoy a bit of surprise when he gets here. Don't give away the whole thing."

Tears pricked her eyes. "That's what Dad always says about modesty."

"He's right. Some girls never get that, but even guys who aren't in the church usually like something left to discover."

After snapping her picture and sending it to Kevin for her, Heath went back to dressing himself. Dressing and praying—a lot. He'd never taken so long to get ready for anything, but with each new thought, he'd pause, pray, and pray some more. Selby called out for him twice, but he ignored her.

Never thought I'd be praying to fall in love with someone. Always thought it would be asking what to do about the fact that I did. If she's not right for me, can I know it sooner rather than later? Because Jordan's pretty awesome, and stupid as it might be, those freckles make a fool out of me.

"Heath! Come on! I need help with this comb!"

Grabbing his bowtie on the way out, Heath bolted for the bathroom where she stood stabbing the rhinestone encrusted comb into a controlled, curly mess of an upsweep. "How do you make that look good?"

"Does it?"

That moment of vulnerability? Adorable. While he centered the comb just as she wanted it, Heath wondered if Jordan had those moments. Maybe?

"Looks amazing. Kevin's a lucky guy."

"I'm calling it blessed. This was obviously a God thing. How else did two people just goof off with a profile application and end up together like this? It's God." She gave him a sheepish grin in the mirror. "And I might be falling for him. How do I do that and finish school, too? I promised Mom I wouldn't let a guy mess up my studies."

Time for an older brother reality check. "Okay... first. How'd you do in school the past three weeks?"

"Okay, okay. You're right already. I get it. Fine. Deal. I'll go wait for Jordan."

He thrust the strip of fabric at her. "Tie it first? Mine look dreadful."

"Don't I know it."

The doorbell rang as soon as she stepped back and said, "It'll have to do. Let me go get Jordan while you go pray or something. You look green— about the color of a mandrill's coat."

"I accept the metaphoric slap with gloves across my cheek and call you out. Beware, little sister. You'll pay for that."

Her cheeky grin, her laughter at the door when Jordan came in, the sincere apology... the text from Kevin thanking him for sending the picture. It all combined into one truth he really wasn't ready to deal with. *My little sister grew up.*

Wearing denim blue silk the exact shade of her eyes, hair swept up, *makeup* that covered her freckles—unfortunately—Jordan stood on the coffee table, holding the neck of Selby's dress and pulling thread through the layers at the back. "Wow."

"My sewing skills or my mother's ability to just 'happen' to find a dress that isn't at all too big or long for me and, oh... just 'happens' to match my eye color?"

"Both. Not to mention the transformation from most gorgeous girl I've ever seen to an even more amazing girl overnight."

"Stop flirting, Heath." Selby glared at him. "She'll get distracted, poke me, and we'll have blood all over this thing, too."

Heath couldn't stifle a grin when Jordan shrugged and said, "Well, she has a point..."

The doorbell rang before Jordan finished, so Heath slipped out into the hall. "Sorry. Dress malfunction. Repairs in progress."

Kevin just nodded.

"Nervous?"

Another nod.

"She doesn't bite..."

This time, he got a chuckle out of the guy. "This is it... crunch time. Can we spend an entire evening *conversing* instead of playing, 'movie quote madness'?"

Heath didn't remember much of his English lit classes, but one thing he'd hoped to learn and never had. Selby and Kevin had perfected it. "Ever hear of a little thing called subtext?"

Silence answered in the affirmative.

"That's what your flirting is, Kevin. All the movie quotes, the things left unsaid but spoken as well? Subtext. Trust it."

The door opened, and Jordan poked her head out. "Selby wants pictures."

He shrugged. "If Selby wants pictures..."

Kevin agreed. "Selby gets pictures."

The lights, the music, the flowers—the gala couldn't have been more beautiful. If the lack of tightness in her mother's smile meant what she thought it did, it had also been a success. Jordan's gaze swept the room and settled on Heath. *For me, too.*

However, one thing marred the night's perfection. She'd forgotten the worst part of being a date of the folks in charge. *Stuck here for another hour at least.* Heath would have to sign invoices, stow the donations in the safe, say goodbye to every single last guest.

A smile formed at a new thought. *But Mom doesn't have to.*

She wove through the lingerers—those people who used events like this for either business purposes or their rare social gatherings. People like that never wanted to leave. One man stopped to compliment her dress. Another woman asked for directions to the restrooms.

Once she made it to her mother's side, Jordan sagged against a column and smiled. "Did it go as well as I think?"

"We may have an endowment from the Fillmores. A big one. It'll be discussed at their trust meeting next month, and then we'll hear."

Jordan hugged her mother and whispered, "I'm so happy for you. Go home. We've got this."

Mom just smiled and watched Heath. "What do you think the chances are that you guys will work out?"

If she'd asked the day before, Jordan wouldn't have known how to answer. Something had changed, however. Heath hadn't paid much attention to her all evening, but not for want of trying. Twice he'd spouted some odd fact that told her exactly what she needed to know. "He's still interested."

"Duh."

"I am, too. More every day."

After another look his way, and after giving Jordan a once-over, Mom nodded. "So, I didn't blow it—helping him out, I mean?"

She squeezed her mother in a hug that lasted longer than most. "Nope. Even if we don't work out, you did the right thing—for both of us."

"But you want this, right?"

Her gut told her it was too soon to know anything, but her heart sang an operatic, *yes!* Jordan opted for middle ground. "If everything stays about the same or gets even better, definitely. Two weeks and a few sweet attempts to make contact isn't enough. Not for me."

"I've known him for four years, Jordan. He's the real deal. If he'd been older..."

"And you hadn't already found Ron..."

A sweet smile formed—that one Jordan had never seen her use for any other man. "Yeah... I might have chosen him over Ron. And for *me,* that would have been a mistake. But you..."

"Ron's back, isn't he?" At her mother's surprised look, Jordan shook her head. "I know you too well. You keep looking at that clock. Go home. We've got this."

It only took another fifteen minutes, but her mother complied. Then, Jordan went into hostess mode. She moved to Heath's side, gave him a small smile, and turned to the husband of the woman Heath discussed zoo management with. "Do you understand any of this?"

"Not a thing. It's Adele's passion. You?"

"My mother tried to make me understand it, but little of it stuck. I do love to come see the animals, though. Always did."

The man stuck out his hand. "Ben Woitzel."

"Jordan Aylward. My mother is Ann Weik."

"And your boyfriend is Heath Karras. You're set for free passes to the zoo for life."

Heath huffed. A glance at him showed mock indignation frosted with a layer of despair. "I should have known she only liked me for my animals."

"And your factoids." She turned to Ben and grinned. "On our first date, I learned all about the bladders of mammals. Fascinating topic."

"She didn't tell you," Heath added, "that she also walked out the minute she could. It took patience, persistence, and prayer to get us to where we are today."

"I'm lousy with alliteration, so I'll just add that his sorta secret admirer plan didn't hurt."

The wife shifted her attention to Jordan. "Sorta-secret?"

Just enough color filled Heath's face to make her wonder if he was embarrassed or overheated. "I made myself visible and available. She just didn't remember me—even after listening to me drone on and on about bladders that night." He winked at her. "She even missed giveaway hints from guys who were supposed to be helping me."

Jordan eyed him with more than a little suspicion. "What?"

"Jason? With the cup? He made a point of turning the logo around?"

"Yeah..."

"He pointed it at *me*, not you."

She and the woman spoke in unison. "How would anyone catch that?"

Heath shrugged. "Someone determined enough?"

"I'll get *you* for that later."

It worked—her plan to hint to the stragglers that they should go without actually hinting. In less than three minutes, the couple left. Three others followed. In half the time she expected it to take, the room stood empty—except for them.

"I just have to wait—"

"To sign invoices, take donation slips and checks to the safe..."

"You've been through this."

She slipped her arm through his. "A time or twenty. So, what do we do first?"

A representative for the catering company showed up before he could answer. "Looks like invoices." He pointed to a large staircase in one corner of the room. "That leads to a cool balcony overlooking the city. I don't know if you've seen it, but it's amazing. I'll be done here soon."

Climbing stairs, even a stunning curved case that really was overkill for a ballroom balcony, didn't appeal to her after an evening in heels, but nighttime city views happened to be a favorite of hers. *Still doing the Empire State Building at night someday.*

Halfway up, Jordan removed her shoes. Her feet enjoyed instant new life—at least for a few new steps. At the top, a look back showed Heath watching her as he signed something. Appreciation—what for, Jordan didn't know—but she saw it in him. Perhaps he was too far away to be sure, but she chose to believe it.

Her next thought whisked away on distracted wings at the sight of the cityscape. Lights dotted the night sky, and in the distance, between two of the city's tallest skyscrapers, she could see the pink lights of the Steele Building. *Next month, green. Blue in July. Orange in October. Red in December. I wonder who thought of that.*

The cars, even near midnight, kept a steady stream up Waterbrook in an odd display of "running lights" that looked much like the Christmas displays they'd had as a girl. Ambulance lights flashed as cars parted to make room—well, most of them. One idiot stuck to the center line of the four-lane road as if oblivious to the oncoming emergency vehicle. And then, just as the ambulance changed lanes to go around, the car shot over and nearly took off the bumper.

"Idiot!"

"Well, I am..." Heath's voice near her left ear almost sent her through the ceiling. "But you don't have to shout it to the world."

She turned and eyed him. "Did you see that jerk?"

"The one being pulled over by a cop right now?"

A second look showed the guy being escorted to the side of the road. "Good. Serves him right."

Heath didn't respond to that. Instead, he pulled out his phone, tapped the screen, and old music she'd heard somewhere began. He tucked it in his front jacket pocket and offered his hands. "Dance with me? You missed your ball, but one dance?"

"I've never been much of a dancer." Despite the protest, she put her hands in his. "I'm more of a sideline watcher. Especially with dance music. People do some funky moves. It can be pretty funny." This guy, however, could *dance*. "You must dance a lot. You're good."

"Uh... it's more like my mother and her cultural literacy lessons. She made us learn to waltz and to sway in time to the music."

"You *waltz?* Who waltzes anymore?"

"The son of a woman on a mission to ensure her missionary kids don't hate her for not knowing every cultural nuance her kids might have encountered had they been brought up in America."

The music swelled around them—some guy singing about not being able to take his eyes off her. The voice wasn't great, but if the look Heath gave her meant anything, he'd chosen it deliberately. Hope, uncertainty, confidence, *connection* swirled with each note, each step. *I want to fall for this guy. I'm teetering at times already.*

His chuckle brought her back from her reverie. "Um... so your mom did what? Got you dance lessons?"

"Made us watch movies and go to dances. I had to ask a girl every time we were home on furlough." Heath's jaw set. "Other kids came home on furlough and got to travel around the country doing school out of the back of a car. We had to go to school at Grandma's house and immerse ourselves into American culture—with after school and holiday 'enrichment classes.'"

The memory of Selby's many movie-quote riddled texts. "Like movies?"

"From the beginning of the talkies through each year we were there. Third grade, seventh grade, eleventh and twelfth grades... Quizzes—you name it." Heath pulled her close and swayed. "All the times I had to go to some school dance with some girl who went to church with us and whose parents forced their daughter to go with the missionary kid."

The picture of a miserable Heath trying not to talk about bumbling baboons or velociraptors tugged at heartstrings that were already singing along with a song she didn't know. "So, your random facts things... we can thank your mother for that?"

"Blame would be more like it." Heath grinned down at her. "Not that I'm bitter or anything."

"Thank."

He gave her a spin at the end of the song and punctuated it with a questioning look. "Huh?"

Stepping back, she explained her thoughts. "Your mom put you in awkward situations." Jordan ticked off one finger. "That prompted you to formulate a defense mechanism." The next finger wiggled as she tapped it. "Your awkwardness focused on girls." She ticked off a third. "Which only intensified your social awkwardness with them." This time, Jordan wiggled her pinky finger.

For a moment there, Jordan was certain he'd kiss her. Soon or not, she was ready for it—more than ready. Eyes locked, Adam's apple bobbing... the epitome of awkward boyhood in an otherwise confident man. Heath broke their connection with one word. "And..." He tapped the phone again and "Unchained Melody" began. That song she knew.

"And that meant that years later, you'd still be trying to have that second date, which meant some other girl didn't snap you up before I had a chance. Sounds like a great mom. Tell her thanks... from me."

When his eyes darted to her lips and then over her shoulder again, Jordan decided she'd been right. He'd need a little help. That, however, left two options. She could take the initiative... no. No, she couldn't. He felt enough of a failure for even hesitating. It showed in the way his jaw twitched, and his breathing grew forced as if conscious.

"Hey..."

That caught his attention. Heath gazed into her eyes, and Jordan took the chance. "Did you know..." She reached for his hand. "That sea otters like to hold each other's paws while sleeping—"

"So they don't drift apart?"

"Mmm... hmm... guess you knew that. How about Gentoo penguins?"

He pulled her closer. "They propose with a pebble."

"I think that's crazy romantic."

"It's what humans do," Heath said. "We just cut and polish ours."

Jordan slid one arm around his neck. "Well, then. Do you know about the Jesus Christ lizard in the Amazon?"

Heath shook his head before brushing her lips with his. "No..."

"It runs on water."

"Nice one. You almost got me."

She slid her other arm around his neck as she said, "It's true."

"Am I going to scare you away if I kiss you?"

"Nope."

"Don't be so sure about that..." Heath winked and pressed his forehead against hers. "I've never actually done this before..."

Jordan thought she murmured something about practice and perfection, and if she did, it was wasted. As enjoyable as practice might be, perfection... well, as first kisses went, perfection couldn't be more... perfect!

Epilogue

Dear Bailey,

Happy Valentine's Day!

I thought I'd give you a quick update. Jordan Aylward was a winner. Funny thing is, his first date with her, before he signed up with Betwixt, is what prompted us to contact my friend who sent me to Wayne who sent me to you. She signed up, too! You matched her with Heath, and now they've been dating for a couple of weeks. They're so cute. And Heath is totally over his issues.

Okay, that's not quite true. He still does it, but now Jordan just thinks it's cute. Sometimes she does it back, which is strangely adorable. I think they'll last. As in "till death do them part" last.

I think Kevin and I are going to last, too, but don't tell him that. I can't get serious about anyone until I'm done with school. So, we're pretending we don't think each other is *quite* as awesome as we really do.

Pray for me. If you pray, just pray. Because I'm gonna need every bit of self-control I can find.

Well, Kevin is back from parking the car, so I'd better go.

Thanks for all you did. If anything super adorable comes up, I'll be sure to let you know. And, if we have invites coming out in the next year or three, I'll be sure to send you one.

Happy matching,

Selby Karras

The End

Part of this story is true. Granted, it's a small part, but it is. Picture the scene. Denny's on a Wednesday night. My partner in literary crime—literally, we were both writing mysteries—left for the night just after midnight sometime. Another Denny's regular came over to my table and took her place.

That should have been a clue.

Peter often came and sat with me, talking about this thing or that. From him, I learned all about coding computers, typesetting, metal lathes, Grand Lodge and other Masonic fellowships, the evils of Creationism, and all things sci-fi.

That night, I learned about the habits of mammalian bladders. At the top of a very resonant, sonorous voice. While I was eating my dinner.

Forty minutes he droned on about them. At least. It could have been more, but it was a full forty minutes after I started counting (which, I admit was almost immediately). Then he pulled out his phone and read me the scientific study. No joke.

I was so angry and frustrated at the loss of working time (shame on me) that I went home, woke up my husband, and announced that Peter would be single for the rest of his life.

Usually, I enjoyed my conversations with Peter, although sometimes his timing wasn't so good—like that night. Still, he gave me a great idea for my third Madeline Mystery, Fine Print and taught me a lot.

Alas, while I was at a conference this November, he died. I already miss seeing him... sometimes. I just don't miss some of those random fact lectures. However, of all the things Peter taught me, the one that matters and means the most to me is something he never knew he did. He taught me that people really are more important. Period. I'm so glad I set aside the work I had planned for myself to make time for a person that night.

I pray that somehow he changed his mind on Jesus in the week before his death.

CHAUTONA HAVIG
Author of *Random Acts of Shyness*

Questions

1. Do you think Selby's plan for overcoming Heath's issues is kind? Biblical? Does it matter that she wouldn't mind if someone did it to her when she knows others would? How does **Matthew 7:12** apply?

2. Jordan's mother isn't "religious," but she does respect her daughter's faith. Her unwillingness to lie to Jordan because of that faith raises an interesting question. How often do we change our behavior based on who we are with or are trying to impress rather than acting as we do because it's right? See **James 4:17**.

3. One thing you find in many romance novels is the idea of "love at first sight" or what I like to call "insta-love." Selby joked with herself that "love at first quote" might be a thing for her. The question remains, though, with Christians who are called to love one another simply for the fact of their mutual faith in Christ is that kind of "instantaneous" love possible? See I **Timothy 6: 1-2** (while this speaks of slaves to masters, it still speaks predominately about believer to believers despite their "station" in life).

4. Each girl handled Heath's "malady" differently. Anger, directness, kindness, sleep... While anger is understandable, what does the Bible say about reacting in anger? See: **Galatians 5: 19-20**, **Ephesians 4:26**

5. Heath accepted that singleness might be God's plan for him, but he preferred his singleness not be because a personal failing prevented any other option. Do we get to decide how, why, or when we accept God's will for our lives? Then again, had he decided this was God's will simply because it was difficult for him, he would have missed out on what may truly be a gift of God in his life. How do Christians discern the will of God in their lives? See **Romans 12:2** (hint: the word "prove" is defined from the Greek as "to test or by implication, approve" – source Biblehub.com/romans/12-2.htm).

About

Chautona Havig lives in an oxymoron, escapes into imaginary worlds that look startlingly similar to ours and writes the stories that emerge. An irrepressible optimist, Chautona sees everything through a kaleidoscope of *It's a Wonderful Life* sprinkled with fairy tales. Find her on the web and say howdy—if you can remember how to spell her name.

Newsletter:	chautona.com/newsletter
Website:	www.chautona.com
Blog:	www.chautona.com/blog
Goodreads:	www.goodreads.com/Chautona
Facebook:	www.facebook.com/chautonahavig
YouTube:	www.youtube.com/user/chautona/videos
Twitter:	twitter.com/Chautona
Pinterest:	pinterest.com/chautonahavig
Instagram:	instagram.com/ChautonaHavig
BookBub:	www.bookbub.com/authors/chautona-havig

The Rockland Chronicles

Aggie's Inheritance Series   (4 books)
Past Forward: A Serial Novel   (Six Volumes)
HearthLand Series: A Serial Novel   (Six Volumes)
The Vintage Wren   (A serial novel beginning 2016)

The Shopkeepers of New Cheltenham

The Ghosts of New Cheltenham
Something Borrowed, Someone Blue

The Rockland Chronicles

Argosy Junction	Confessions of a De-cluttering Junkie
Discovering Hope	Corner Booth
Not a Word	New Year's Revolutions
Speak Now	Premeditated Serendipity
A Bird Died	Random Acts of Shyness
Thirty Days Hath...	

And many more titles...

Dear Readers,

Thank you for reading our *Betwixt Two Hearts* collection! We hope you enjoyed reading each individual book, as well as seeing how they all wove together in the setup and larger story of the first book. Isn't it amazing to think of how interconnected we are and how even seemingly insignificant actions can be significant when used by God? As the reader, you get the perspective of knowing what the characters don't. In this case, Camden and Bailey will never know how God used their matchmaking website, and specifically their struggles, to instigate his plans in the lives of others, just like you may never know how God is using you. Just imagine!

This is a unique set of books, with each story fitting together like a puzzle piece. Since all of the stories have a point of intersection, we call it a Crossroads Collection. If you are eager for more, please check out the other Crossroads Collections! In each of them, you will find new books tied together at the crossroads one book in the set.

We also have more Crossroads Collections in the works! If you would like to be notified of new and upcoming collections in this series, please sign up with Amanda Tru's email newsletter below. She is excitedly organizing more of these multi-author sets of this type and will notify subscribers as subsequent collections are release.

Finally, if you enjoyed this collection, please help spread the word, write a review, ask your library to stock that hardback, and/or recommend it to your friends! This collection will only be available for a limited time, so be sure to help spread the word and also snag the paperback version that will last long after the eBook collection disappears. Eventually, each set will be disbanded and the books published individually. So, read them as complete sets while you can!

Thank you again for reading. We hope you enjoyed our stories and that they sparked your imagination, touched your heart, and even made you think. We wish you the best and hope that you know the blessing of encountering the one, true God who gets to be the author of your book, putting together all of the chapters to draw you to Him and make beautiful the connection betwixt your heart and His.

Sincerely,

Amanda Tru, Cathe Swanson, Kari Trumbo, Alana Terry, Carol Moncado, & Chautona Havig

The *Betwixt Two Hearts*, Crossroads Collection Authors

Newsletter Sign Up:

www.amandatru.com/newsletter

Out of the Blue Bouquet, a Crossroads Collection
Floral folly fables from Hallee Bridgeman, Alana Terry, Carol Moncado, Chautona Havig, & Amanda Tru
(www.amazon.com/dp/B077MWTWGC)

Yesterday's Mail, a Crossroads Collection
Misdelivered mail tales from Alana Terry, Cynthia Hickey, Hallee Bridgeman, Chautona Havig, & Amanda Tru
(www.amazon.com/dp/B07G81ZGQZ)

Under the Christmas Star, a Crossroads Collection
Ornamental yarns from Lesley Ann McDaniel, April Hayman, Chautona Havig, Alana Terry, & Amanda Tru
(www.amazon.com/dp/B07J9ZF7VY)

Betwixt Two Hearts, a Crossroads Collection
Dating site stories from Amanda Tru, Cathe Swanson, Kari Trumbo, Alana Terry, Carol Moncado, & Chautona Havig
(www.amazon.com/dp/B07MCBFY8N)

The Wedding Dress Yes, a Crossroads Collection
Wedding dress dramas Alexa Verde, Chautona Havig, Hallee Bridgeman, Alana Terry, & Amanda Tru
(www.amazon.com/dp/B07QPL85L9)

When Snowflakes Never Cease, a Crossroads Collection
Heartwarming wintery accounts from Hallee Bridgeman, Alana Terry, Chautona Havig, Jaycee Weaver, & Amanda Tru
(www.amazon.com/dp/B07ZX3PR5T)

Did you miss *Out of the Blue Bouquet, a Crossroads Collection*?

Out of the Blue Bouquet

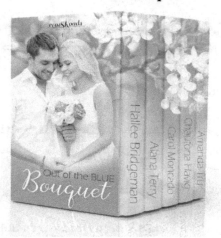

Some of today's Best-selling Christian Authors weave five unique yet connected stories together in this collection where misdirected floral deliveries lead to lives changed.

Courting Calla, by Hallee Bridgeman.

Seoul in Love, by Alana Terry.

A Kærasti for Clari, by Carol Moncado.

Premeditated Serendipity, by Chautona Havig.

Out of the Blue Bouquet, by Amanda Tru.

www.amazon.com/dp/B077MWTWGC

Did you miss *Yesterday's Mail, a Crossroads Collection*?

Yesterday's Mail

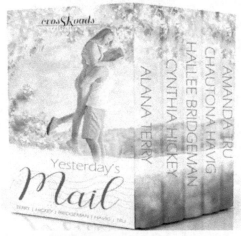

Some of today's Best-selling Christian Authors weave five unique, connected stories together in this collection where lost mail finds unexpected purpose.

Sleepless in Seoul, by Alana Terry

Like Ships Passing, by Cynthia Hickey

Chasing Pearl, by Hallee Bridgeman

Operation Posthaste, by Chautona Havig

Yesterday's Mail, by Amanda Tru

www.amazon.com/dp/B07G81ZGQZ

Did you miss *Under the Christmas Star, a Crossroads Collection*?

Under the Christmas Star

Some of today's Best-selling Christian Authors weave five unique, connected stories together in this collection where handmade Christmas ornaments lead to miraculous answers to prayer.

Comfort and Joy, by Lesley Ann McDaniel

Brushed with Love, by April Hayman

Tangoed in Tinsel, by Chautona Havig

Shattered Pieces, by Alana Terry

Under the Christmas Star, by Amanda Tru

www.amazon.com/dp/B07J9ZF7VY

Did you miss *The Wedding Dress Yes, a Crossroads Collection?*

The Wedding Dress Yes

Some of today's Best-selling Christian Authors weave five brand-new, unique, interconnected stories where the first yes is for the wedding and the second yes is for the dress.

Season of Surprises by Alexa Verde

Something Borrowed, Someone Blue by Chautona Havig

Black Belt, White Dress by Hallee Bridgeman

Sewn Together by Alana Terry

The Wedding Dress Yes by Amanda Tru

www.amazon.com/dp/B07QPL85L9

Did you miss *When Snowflakes Never Cease*, a Crossroads Collection?

When Snowflakes Never Cease

Some of today's Best-selling Christian Authors weave five all-new, unique, interconnected stories where a record-breaking blizzard warms cold hearts and lives change forever.

Blizzard in the Bluegrass, by Hallee Bridgeman

Buried Secrets, by Alana Terry

Wrong About Mr. Wright, by Chautona Havig

More Than Enough, by Jaycee Weaver

When Snowflakes Never Cease, by Amanda Tru

https://www.amazon.com/dp/B07ZX3PR5T

CPSIA information can be obtained
at www.ICGtesting.com
Printed in the USA
BVHW051157301121
622870BV00008B/567/J